COOLER THAN COOL

ALSO BY C. M. KUSHINS

Nothing's Bad Luck: The Lives of Warren Zevon

Beast: John Bonham and the Rise of Led Zeppelin

COOLER THAN COOL

THE LIFE AND WORK OF ELMORE LEONARD

C. M. Kushins

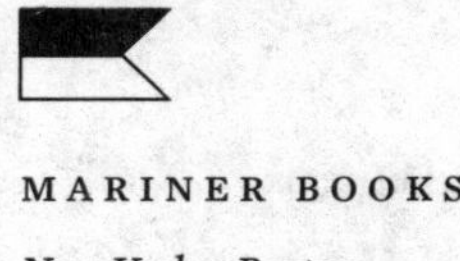

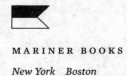

MARINER BOOKS

New York Boston

HarperCollins books may be purchased for educational, business, or sales promotional use. For information, please email the Special Markets Department at SPsales@harpercollins.com.

FIRST EDITION

Designed by Chloe Foster

Library of Congress Cataloging-in-Publication Data has been applied for.

ISBN 978-0-06-330686-8

25 26 27 28 29 LBC 5 4 3 2 1

For Diana—always . . .

and

William Clark—one of the good guys

You got used to it, that was all. You made up your mind you were going to be good at it and not panic. It was something you developed in your mind, a coolness. No, cooler than cool . . . It was a coldness you had to develop. The pro with ice water in his veins.

—Elmore Leonard, *The Big Bounce* (1969)

CONTENTS

AUTHOR'S NOTE

Upon his death in August 2013, Elmore Leonard was still at work on multiple projects.

There was his position as executive producer on the hit series *Justified*, for which he was always attainable by the show's writers for story consultation. There was also the in-progress novel that would remain unfinished at the time of his death—*Blue Dreams*.

Leonard had also sat with his daughter Jane Jones—the oldest of his five children, who for more than three decades had acted as his typist and creative confidante. Together, they had scoured through his personal archive, pulling drafts and notes for the many in-person appearances, lectures, and essays Leonard had prepared over the course of his sixty-year career. They'd worked to assemble a chronological order of the many writings, forming a loose manuscript for the memoir that Leonard wouldn't live to complete. After his death, the archive was soon transferred to the Ernest F. Hollings Special Collections Library at the University of South Carolina. It is a distinct honor for me to be presenting those efforts here.

Although this book wouldn't exist without the aid and advocacy of all the individuals and entities listed in the acknowledgments, I am especially indebted to the generosity, patience, and faith of the Leonard family—his first wife, Beverly, and children Jane, Peter, Christopher, Bill, and Katy, as well as their spouses and children. All readers will benefit from their contributions, especially sharing their father's incomplete memoir—which has been inserted into key passages of importance throughout Leonard's life.

• • •

It is my hope that these sections, when combined with Leonard's journals and personal correspondence, will better convey his creative process and personal ambitions.

More important, it is my hope that all present and future authors who, much like this author, credit Leonard for their love of writing will find a bit of themselves in his words. And find the needed inspiration to write every day—whether they feel like it or not.

—CMK

COOLER THAN COOL

CHAPTER 1

Childhood, 1925–1943

Although Elmore John Leonard Jr. would long be associated with his adopted home of Detroit, Michigan, the themes that would shape his life and work were firmly rooted in the history of his birthplace—New Orleans, Louisiana.

Leonard's family had long ties to the Southern city and its neighboring provinces. It had been to New Orleans that his great-grandparents, Michael Leonard and Bridget Gavin, emigrated from Ireland before marrying in January 1820, choosing the fifth ward in Avoyelles Parish in which to raise their six children.[1] Their fifth, William Martin Leonard, was born in September 1867. At the age of twenty-four, William married Margaret Connelly, affectionately known to her family as "Maggie."[2] Like her husband, Maggie's parents had emigrated from Ireland: her father, John Connelly, just north of Dublin in Meathe; her mother, Mary Ryan, from Tipperary.[3] After their wedding, William and Maggie Leonard settled in Ward 1—locally regarded as one of the parish's "uptown" wards, nearer to culture and the more prosperous businesses. At 924 Terpsichore Street, they eventually had six children of their own: William Jr. in 1892; Elmore John on November 30 the following year; Irma Gertrude in 1898; Emmett Mathew in 1900; Isabelle five years later; and Urban Maurice Leonard two years after that.[4]

During the decade and a half that it had taken to raise their half dozen children, William and Maggie Leonard integrated themselves into many prominent social circles of the city—which William playfully referred to as "the Irish channel." As a practicing Catholic who ensured his family always attended weekly Mass, he joined the local chapter of the Knights of Columbus and St. Vincent de Paul's Society; as an industrial engineer, he qualified for membership in the Association of Stationary Engineers.[5] In the latter capacity, William worked in sugar—specifically in maintaining the expensive machinery used for its production.[6]

In December 1908, William was working as chief engineer for the Palo Alto plantation, located seventy miles west, on a corner along the Bayou Lafourche near Donaldsonville—a Greek Revival homestead originally built in 1852. By 1900, Palo Alto land had changed hands to owner Jacob Lemann's grandsons—Arthur, Monte, and Ferdinand.[7] The three sons would become William Leonard's employers at the plantation, as well as the last to see him alive.[8]

When William Leonard first started his tenure at Palo Alto, the traditional method of producing the sugar crop was known as the "Jamaica Train"—an arduous task of turning cane stalks into granulated grains over barrels and scalding kettles. By 1900, Palo Alto's sugar house had become completely converted to steam power, but no further innovations had shortened the days or disseminated the labor of the plantation's workers. This was especially true as the autumn rolled around; October signaled the beginning of *roulaison*—the "grinding season." William Leonard's job as chief engineer required him to stay in Palo Alto from October through January.[9] In late December 1908, William was notified that the grinding season had been extended due to a particularly abundant cane harvest. Ultimately, he would be needed back on-site at Palo Alto just after the Christmas holiday.[10] Although William Leonard's boardinghouse was large enough to accommodate his entire family, racial tensions among neighboring plantations had escalated, with more than a few murders around the plantation's acreage left unreported and unsolved. Ultimately, William decided to keep his family a safe seventy miles away.

On Monday, January 4, 1909, William was settled in for dinner in his private quarters when he heard an explosion from the direction of the sugar house. Under the massive strain of too much steam pressure, the cylinder head of the centrifuge's main boiler had finally blown. By the time Leonard's assistant burst into the dining room to notify him of the emergency, the centrifuge had jumped its bearings, tearing its way across the factory floor.[11] As soon as William Leonard entered the room, he was struck in the abdomen and nearly disemboweled by the speed and thrust of the heavy machinery; the chief engineer was pronounced dead at ten thirty that night. He was forty-two years old. The *Picayune* noted the family could have consolation that William Leonard "was an exemplary man, devoted husband and loving father, whose first thoughts were of those dear to him and whose actions towards his fellow men were beyond reproach." The funeral was held at the house on Terpsichore Street two days later at three o'clock in the afternoon.[12] Widowed Maggie Connelly Leonard, then thirty-seven years old, would now provide for her six children on her own. After their holiday recess was over, her two oldest sons, William Jr. and sixteen-year-old Elmore—whose own youngest son would later go on to change the face of American crime literature—dropped out of school and joined the adult workforce full-time.

William and Maggie Leonard's second-born child, Elmore John Leonard Sr., born November 30, 1893, had shown an early talent for painting and had aspirations of becoming a professional artist. At eighteen, however, he took a correspondence course and became an accountant, soon finding employment with various fruit companies in Central America, and sent much-needed funds back to his mother at home.[13] Elmore returned to New Orleans in 1917 and was drafted into the Great War, soon assigned to Harris County, Texas, for the full duration of his time in the US Army, eventually earning the rank of second lieutenant, infantry.[14] Before leaving New Orleans for Harris, however, Elmore had fallen in love with Florentine Amelia Rive—"Flora" to her family. Stationed in Harris for just under a year, at the end of 1918, Elmore sent for Flora and the two married in a civil ceremony on December 7—less than a month after the war had ended.[15]

Flora Rive was born on July 14, 1895, like her husband, in New Orleans. She was the oldest child of Adolph Julius Rive and Amelia Madeline "Mamie" Schrenk; although both hailed from the city, Adolph's father, Ernest, had originally emigrated from Prussia, while his mother, Amelia Riedinger, emigrated from Baden, Germany. Following the modest Texas civil ceremony, Elmore and Flora Leonard returned to New Orleans and moved into her family's home above her uncle's shoe repair on Camp Street.[16] It was there that their first child, Flora Margaret, was born on September 29, 1919.

While Adolph Rive's dual employment as an organ technician and dealer provided steady income, the young couple had moved into an already full house: aside from Flora's parents, there were her four younger siblings—Elsa, Adolph Jr., Eugenie, and Emile—all of whom still lived at home.[17] Hoping to earn enough money to attain a single home for his young family, Elmore Leonard got a job with the Ernst and Ernst accounting firm. The hard work paid off and, in 1920, he, Flora, and young Flora Margaret—or "Mickey," as the child was called—settled into one of four family flats at 2029 Carrollton Avenue.[18]

Within a few years, the combined stability of a steady income and a home of their own allowed Elmore and Flora to plan for a second child. When their son was born on October 11, 1925, Flora's parents had already assumed that the child would be named for his father: Elmore John Leonard Jr.[19] He was baptized at the Rives' local parish, the Church of the Incarnate Word on Apricot Street, by its pastor, Rev. Joseph F. Pierre, fourteen days later. The boy's soon-to-be favorite uncle, Adolph Jr., acted as godfather.[20]

By 1927, Elmore Sr. had left Ernst and Ernst to join the growing automobile industry, taking a job with General Motors, aware that the job could necessitate frequent relocation. He found his niche at GM within their Chevrolet Motor Company division, first as an auditor, then as general office manager, assigned to a team of location scouts for the company's dealership outreach across the country.[21] As part of the new position, Leonard was expected to travel extensively to the automaker's many zone offices throughout the country. In 1929, the family moved to a rented home at 5147 Miller Avenue in Dallas. The stay was short-lived, however, as Leonard was almost immediately transferred yet again, this time to Oklahoma City. There, the Leonard family settled into a new home at 1715 North Linn Avenue.[22] Fortunately, the second move came with advancement; the senior Elmore Leonard was placed in an executive position within GM's dealership planning and development division.

Although he was only five years old at the time, Elmore Leonard Jr. later recalled that in 1930, his father suffered an auto accident while on the job: "He was on the road doing something and got into a car accident and came home and was in the hospital . . . he used a cane for just a little while."[23] For an executive whose livelihood depended on consistent mobility, that accident might have contributed to the now thirty-six-year-old Elmore Sr.'s consideration for yet another new position within General Motors.[24] Following the family's next move—this time for only a period of six months in Detroit, Michigan, where the young Elmore Leonard received his First Holy Communion at Visitation Church on Twelfth Street, downtown—Elmore Sr. accepted a job in the company's Buick Motor Company division in Memphis, Tennessee.

At their new home at 2388 Poplar Boulevard, he and Flora hoped for a period of stability. However, Memphis represented many aspects of the Great Depression.[25] With the Wall Street crash of October 1929, the prosperity of F. Scott Fitzgerald's Jazz Age screeched to a halt; only a few years later, the Dust Bowl's own ecological drought redefined the aims of economic survival for American families. Even as a child, this didn't go unnoticed by the younger Elmore Leonard. "When we lived in Memphis, we were several blocks away from a railroad line," he later recalled. "And bums would get off the train and some of them would come by the door and ask for a handout. My mother always made them a big sandwich."[26]

The country's economic straits had also paved the way for new cultural figures representing the country's collective social frustrations. For young Elmore Leonard Jr., the romantic outlaw presented in the daily newspapers proved a great source of fuel for his imagination. "I read somewhere that the most impressionable age for children is between 5 and 10," he later said. "I was between 5 and 10 when all those desperadoes were roaming the Midwest and holding up banks. They were kind of folk heroes . . . Those bank robbers of the '30s truly influenced me. John Dillinger, Bonnie and Clyde, Pretty Boy Floyd . . ."[27]

Young Elmore Leonard's fascination with the modern-day outlaws was best demonstrated in a snapshot taken during his childhood: with his left foot propped on the running board of an Oakland sedan and a toy revolver in hand, he aims the barrel directly at the camera, a mischievous smirk on his cherubic face. "I'm quite sure I was inspired by a shot of Bonnie Parker of Bonnie and Clyde fame," he later remembered, "where she's standing in front of a car with a pistol in her hand and a cigar hanging out of the corner of her mouth . . . I struck that same pose when I was nine years old."[28] That notorious photo of Parker ran only months before she and her lover, Clyde Barrow, were gunned down in a hail of police gunfire near Sailes, Louisiana, in May 1934. Leonard later recalled that it was the gun itself, and its promise of violence, that had fascinated him; at the age of making his first few neighborhood friends, playing cops and robbers—and soon, sports—expanded his youthful social circle. "That fall of [1933] . . . I had a lot of friends in Memphis," he recalled. "I didn't want to leave." Upon learning that his father would have to move the family yet again, this time back to Detroit, Leonard remembered crying.[29]

> In the fall of 1934 I arrived in Detroit with a southern accent, a blend of New Orleans, where I was born, Dallas, Oklahoma City and Memphis. I was nine, and for a while kids kept after me to say things like "honey chile" and "sugah," getting a kick out of the way I spoke. My mother took offense saying, "They should talk—listen to how they roll their *r*'s." My mother believed northern women had big feet.

The family found a flat in their previous residence at the Abington Hotel and Apartments at 700 Seward Avenue.[30] The only difference the second time around was that their new quarters were on the top floor. The apartment house—truly a functioning boarding lodge for larger families—came equipped with its own drugstore on the lobby level, as well as a dining room where nightly dinners were served for a small fee of forty and sixty cents. Elmore Jr. and his older sister, Mickey, rarely took advantage of the available suppers, however, as their mother was a superior cook. The Leonards' rental had only one bedroom, so young Elmore regularly slept on a convertible Murphy bed in the living room he shared with his sister.

While still in Memphis, Elmore Leonard Jr. had maintained solid academic standards; a homework assignment, dated April 4, 1933, boldly displays his perfect score in arithmetic, although he was much more interested in English and grammar.[31] Upon their arrival in Detroit, his parents quickly enrolled him in the nearby Blessed Sacrament School at 82 Belmont Street, behind the adjoining cathedral. As he got a little older, Elmore would take the streetcar with Mickey or walk the length west of Woodward Avenue alone, although by the time she entered high school Elmore had made enough neighborhood friends to walk with them.

The routine remained the same after the family moved into a larger home at 70 Highland, Tract 904, in Highland Park, bringing them even closer to Blessed Sacrament. Elmore's two closest friends, brothers Gerard and Jackie Boisineau, lived in the Leonards' building on the top floor; Maurice Murray—a quiet boy a year older—and Phil Koscinski, whose father was a Detroit judge, lived only a few blocks away from the church. The group also befriended Leo Madison, who, Leonard admitted, was the first African American child he'd ever met, and whose family had come to Detroit during the Great Migration—a time when waves of both Black and white laborers had moved north for employment opportunities within the automobile industry.

> Those years streetcars were rattling up and down Woodward Avenue from the fairgrounds to the river. We'd hop aboard and ride downtown to Hudson's to visit the toy department, or to the Vernor's ginger ale plant, then at the foot of Woodward. You'd get free samples if you took the tour . . .

Elmore and his friends shared after-school adventures around Detroit, making the city their personal playground. On Saturdays, the boys would often catch the matinee at the Fisher movie theater, looked for Ken Maynard and Tom Mix serials, or "ran around if the main attraction was *Camille* or anything like it." After Mass on Sunday, the gang would reconvene and take the Windsor Ferry to Canada "for a nickel."

Although Elmore had taken note of the poverty that was commonplace throughout Memphis, he never noticed the diverse economic standings of his friends' families. "I didn't see that they were any different," he recalled. "My working-class friends, I felt, were the same as I was." He noted, however, that Elmore Sr. and Flora never seemed to socialize with his friends' parents. It was only after his best friend, Gerard Boisineau, reported his own father's promotion at work that Elmore finally realized his family was regarded as being on a different social level, due to Elmore Sr.'s career advancement. "My dad was an executive with General Motors and Boisineau's dad was a construction worker," Leonard recalled. "I remember Gerard saying one time, 'My dad's making $300 a month now,' and couldn't help but understand how much more his own father's job paid."

During the earliest years of his son's life, Elmore Leonard Sr. would often be away for weeks at a time but, since their move to Detroit in 1934, Leonard Sr. had worked his way up to the executive level for General Motors, reporting daily to his office on the fourteenth floor of their West Grand Boulevard office. Although the senior Leonard still traveled frequently, now in charge of scouting the locations for GM's expanding Buick, Oldsmobile, and Pontiac dealerships, he was still home more often than in the past. (The younger Elmore Leonard later recalled his father's routine of dressing in his suit and tie in the mornings, and of getting his dark hair combed straight back and layered down in the same, unchanging style.) When he was home, he would make a point each night to invite his son to sit on his lap, later beside him, for their "telling time"—a chat session to hear about the boy's adventures that day. "My dad was dry, funny," Leonard recalled, adding that he "got along very well" with his father. In turn, both parents were doting and loving toward each other and were "always showing affection to one another."

Yearly family vacations often included treks back to New Orleans to visit Flora's siblings—a practice that had remained consistent throughout their various moves to Dallas, Oklahoma City, and Memphis. Young Elmore always looked forward to those trips with excitement, claiming he enjoyed seeing his uncles in New Orleans. Throughout the rest of the year, the four usually ventured into prospering downtown Detroit, as the city was bustling with all sorts of new entertainment. On one memorable occasion, the four nearly got to see Frank Sinatra perform with the Tommy Dorsey Orchestra. However, Dorsey quickly took to the microphone himself and announced that Sinatra was a no-show; the crooner "simply didn't feel like it." More often than not, however, the family would go to the movies or baseball games at Navin Field or Briggs Stadium, and later, Tiger Stadium. Leonard fondly recalled that at that time, it cost only "$1.10 to sit in the grandstand."

Baseball was a passion for the entire family; Elmore Sr.'s father had even belonged to a neighborhood sandlot league during his youth in New Orleans. Now, the younger Elmore Leonard spent hours playing with his own friends, usually assigned the first-base position. With no organized junior league in Detroit to speak of, he and his buddies used the nearby vacant lot—Sweeney's Field—for their games. Entering the fifth grade, Leonard had slowly begun to develop his pitching arm—a tricky task for a southpaw with no formal training. Leonard's third passion was reading, or, more important, the act of storytelling—which wasn't something shared by his father. "My dad was traveling a lot and he didn't read much," he later admitted. "That is, he read the paper and he read the *Financial Times*, and he read *Forbes* and those magazines, but he didn't read what I was interested in."[32]

What the junior Elmore Leonard *was* interested in were the adventure tales and literary classics that Mickey read to him every night. She had started her little brother at a young age with fairy tales and children's books, such as *Cinderella, Treasure Island, Little Goody Two-Shoes,* and

The Adventures of Huckleberry Finn. Many, if not all, had come from their mother's membership to the Book of the Month Club, which also allowed young Elmore access to more adult-oriented popular novels of the day, like author Rafael Sabatini's *The Sea Hawk* and *Scaramouche*.[33] Flora Leonard had also joined the Delphian Society, an early social club for women. Delphian members would meet regularly to discuss art and culture and were distributed current bestsellers for group discussion.

The combination of Flora's love of reading and Mickey's bedtime stories soon made Elmore a voracious reader.[34] At school, Leonard already excelled in reading and writing, showing a particular affinity for using new vocabulary words in a creative way—much to the amusement of the nuns. "I always wrote a pretty interesting sentence using the word," Leonard remembered. "It'd have something to do with a western or the police or something like that." Over the next few years, Leonard's literary taste both matured and refined well ahead of his preferred adventure stories. Before even entering high school, he'd binged Lin Yutang's *The Importance of Living*, as well as *Out of Africa, The Yearling,* Carl Van Doren's biography of Benjamin Franklin, and some Horatio Hornblower for good measure. During high school, he moved on to Richard Wright's *Native Son*, Arthur Koestler's *Darkness at Noon*, and John Steinbeck's *The Moon Is Down*. But nothing would affect Leonard quite the same way as his discovery of Ernest Hemingway's *For Whom the Bell Tolls*. "[That] was the novel that would eventually get me started as a writer," he'd later recall. However, it was his love of movies that made Elmore a passionate storyteller—a natural skill that included a great reliance on dialogue. A frequent passion for the boy was replaying the plot and details of his latest favorites to his neighborhood buddies—an activity Leonard described as "telling movies." He later explained, "I was, say, ten or eleven years old [and] we lived in an apartment building and three or four of us would sit on the stairs and somebody would say 'tell us *Captain Blood*!'—and I'd 'tell' them *Captain Blood*, all the way through. And I 'told' *Captain Blood* I don't know how many times."[35]

Much later, Leonard would share a childhood memory with Boston University professor Charles Rzepka, perhaps hinting at his earliest predilection for dialogue and oral storytelling: "I remember in Oklahoma City, I had an imagined friend who I called 'Boyee,'" Leonard remembered. "I was always talking to Boyee, and talking about him and all . . . [In later years] my mother would tell me about it."[36]

> By the time I turned ten in 1935, I was fascinated by trench warfare during World War I. My favorite books were Arthur Guy Empy's *Over the Top* and Erich Maria Remarque's *All Quiet on the Western Front.* I had already seen the picture starring Lew Ayres and Slim Summerville, but it was the book that inspired me—for the first time in my life—to write something other than a school assignment.
>
> What I wrote was a play set in No Man's Land, staged it in the fifth grade classroom and used the rows of desk to simulate barbed wire: American doughboys on one side, Krauts on the other. The plot: a coward redeems himself by rescuing the hero hung up on the wire.

The cinematic adaptation of Erich Maria Remarque's bestselling German WWI epic had given the boy his first look at trench warfare and set his imagination reeling—especially the story's antiwar sentiment and the quirky behavior of the soldiers portrayed. "I was very influenced by that [film]," he later recalled. Remarque's novel, first published in Germany in 1928, had been an instant international bestseller, leading to translations in more than thirty languages during its first year of publication. In the United States alone, the book had been serialized in more than eighty newspapers—including the *Detroit Times,* where young Elmore Leonard first encountered it in prose form.

Inspired by the serialization, young Leonard put pen to paper for the first time and made his earliest attempt at writing, condensing the lengthy epic into a briefer scene in the trenches. When it was completed, he showed it to his fifth-grade teacher—the much-feared and disliked nun Sister Estelle. (The strict disciplinarian had also been Elmore's teacher the previous year and, as he recalled, all the children had been relieved to be rid of her—only to find that she'd been promoted to teach the higher grade.) To young Elmore's surprise, the older nun—who memorably pronounced "Arkansas" as "Ar-*kansas*"—was impressed enough with the aspiring writer to allow him to organize a performance of his *All Quiet* adaptation in the classroom. "It had to be put on in the classroom because I used the [rows of] desks as 'no man's land'—the barbed wire," Leonard remembered later.[37] "I cast it and I made all my friends the main parts." He invented an original character for the play's hero—"Captain Hayes"—and gave the lead to his best friend, Gerard Boisineau; classmate Jack Griffin played the story's original protagonist, Paul Baumer. For the role of Himmelstoss—the "coward" who ultimately displays the needed bravery to save his fellow soldier—Elmore cast his slovenly buddy Zenon La Joie. Unsure of what to do with Leo Madison—his only African American friend—Leonard gave him a part as a German soldier. For the trenches themselves, Leonard and his pals overturned all the desks in the room, which they then proceeded to crawl underneath. As Blessed Sacrament's principal, Mother Generosa, watched from the teacher's desk in the front row, Leonard announced the title of the play and fired an unloaded air rifle at the ceiling. Then he "got out of the way."

As he approached puberty, Elmore's athletic abilities had also continued to mature. During eighth grade, he and his neighborhood friends learned that an organized youth baseball team had finally been introduced to Detroit and immediately joined the local Detroit Sandlot League.

Thirteen-year-old Leonard entered ninth grade in the fall of 1938. Having left Blessed Sacrament, he began his freshman year of high school with a one-year stint in Catholic Central—a small preparatory school on Harper Avenue operated by the Congregation of St. Basil, priests of the Basilian order. Although he later recalled that his family wasn't particularly "devout," the Leonards continued to attend Mass every Sunday, as well as holy days of obligation throughout the year. "On Good Friday we would go to the Stations [of the Cross] and things like that," he remembered, "but there wasn't any aspect of the religion that my mother was [stuck on]—and certainly not my dad." He later claimed to have had a significantly more devout approach to his Catholicism than his parents; during the fifth grade, he had even been a member of the church choir, for which Flora insisted her son have "the nicest looking cassock." Even during his high school years, Leonard left a half hour early every morning in order to attend a short Mass before that day's classes. For a brief time just before entering Catholic Central, he even considered a spiritual calling. "It seems that when I was in about the eighth grade, I thought of becoming a brother," he recalled. "Once, I mean a very short time, because I saw pictures of their seminary, and they were playing baseball and I thought, Oh, you know this could be fun . . . But then about the same year or the next year, I discovered girls."

Later that year, the family moved to 18900 Northlawn Street, near Seven Mile Road, only a block away from the Jesuit-run University of Detroit High School. After only one year attending Catholic Central, Leonard switched to the closer school, later claiming it "was the best move" he ever made during his early teenage years. Likewise, Mickey Leonard had opted to continue with a Catholic education as well, enrolling in Marygrove University for girls, a college run entirely by nuns.

Leonard had no problem with the Jesuits' strict approach toward both catechism and general studies. In fact, he later admitted that the Jesuits had taught him "how to think," and held lifelong gratitude for the work ethic the Society of Jesus embraced. "And there was quite a difference in the feeling of the school, the fact that they were a little more serious about [education]," he claimed, offering up the Jesuits' use of the Socratic Method as a method of critical thinking.[38] (Incidentally, the Socratic Method—largely built upon rhetoric and dialogue for its tenets of problem-solving, also gave the Jesuit order a unique appreciation for storytelling—much like young Leonard himself. He later remembered one Jesuit instructor spontaneously presenting to the class a copy of Jules Verne's *Michael Strogoff* and proceeding to read it aloud as part of that day's seemingly unrelated lesson.)

Leonard excelled almost immediately upon his transfer to the University of Detroit—thanks in no small part to the discovery that he had long needed glasses to correct his vision. As he remembered, the first time he tried a pair, he immediately thought, "Oh my God, I can read the blackboard." Of perhaps equal importance for a pitcher, Leonard's vision now led to a marked improvement on the mound. At University of Detroit High School, he played first string in Class A for their team, the Cubs, later claiming that he was just "good enough" to make the cut—especially on a team that lost most games.

It was during this time that he was given a nickname that would stick for the rest of his life. He later told journalist Paul Challen: "It was my second year of high school and a guy in the class—just a guy that I happened to know in the classroom—said, 'I'm going to start calling you Dutch—you need a nickname'—and boy, he was right—because I did. 'Elmore' was a lot to handle back then." His new namesake was Emil "Dutch" Leonard—a journeyman pitcher whose career started in 1933 with the Brooklyn Dodgers, then included stints with the Chicago Cubs and Washington Senators, ultimately holding a career record of 191 wins and 181 losses. For teenage Leonard, however, the nickname would extend well past the baseball diamond, soon becoming the preferred term of endearment from those closest to him. Ultimately, Emil Leonard's younger namesake would go on to become the better-known "Dutch" Leonard.[39]

At University of Detroit High School, it wasn't long for Leonard to be recognized for more than merely his baseball skills. Entering his junior year, he had also successfully tried out for the school's football team, playing number 66 for the identically named Cubs. "I played center my first year," Leonard later recalled. "I played on the reserves—what they called 'the Bantams'—[and] we played other reserve teams from other schools." Leonard's football coach, Bob Tiernan, had originally played for his alma mater, the University of Montana, as a lineman, and took seriously his duties training the young athletes of University of Detroit. Tiernan had ensured that the team would get new red uniforms during Leonard's junior year, and he made sure that every player's laces were sparkling white. The young coach had spotted Leonard's natural abilities on the field and, although the junior weighed only 130 pounds, had an eye to move him from center to quarterback. That summer, the coach invited Leonard and a few other serious prospects to his summer home at Flathead Lake in Missoula, Montana, for a few extra months of intensive practice. Leonard later recalled excitedly climbing into Tiernan's station wagon with five other players, including classmate Jerry Finneran, whose younger sister, Ruthann, was a close friend. "We'd go out there for about a month," Leonard recalled. "The center always backed up the line and I made a lot of tackles."

Over the course of the summer, Tiernan, whom Leonard remembered as a gruff, no-nonsense, "all business" type, instilled in the young men the basics of blocking and tackling—the latter of which was already among Leonard's specialties. However, the additional training paid off. When Leonard began his senior year that fall, he was confident enough to try out for the varsity team. "I remember one practice before the first game in the afternoon," he recalled. "I made three tackles in a row, and [Tiernan] said, 'You're going to start [on] Saturday.'" Leonard was then switched to play quarterback-wing quarterback, primarily responsible for taking the ball from the center sometimes for the "hand off." Although he also played for the school's baseball team, Leonard was particularly proud to thrive on the football field as, admittedly, the football team was significantly better than their counterparts on the baseball team.

> When I was a kid in high school in the early '40s, I used to go to the Paradise Theater in downtown Detroit to hear [Count] Basie,

> Earl (Fatha) Hines, Jimmy Lunceford, [and] Andy Kirk and His Clouds of Joy with Mary Lou Williams on piano . . .
>
> I rode the Jefferson car to the Atles Lager Brewery ("The Beer in the Green Bottle") where I worked after finishing at U of D High before going into the Navy. There was a reefer [a modified refrigerator car] you could talk in and grab a cold one any time you were thirsty. I worked at Atles not much more than a week before my mother made me quit, wanting to know if I was coming home happy from work or a party.[40]

Playing two separate sports for the school only boosted Leonard's popularity among his peers; although his personal interests also included hours of reading and discovering new authors, he was far from bookish. He had been elected class president and, more important within his social circle, enjoyed frequent jazz concerts and underage drinking. ("Dutch" wasn't the only new name Leonard had recently acquired; he'd also gotten his hands on a fake driver's license in the name of "James Harry Landino" and quickly put it to use.[41]) Leonard and his friends would often take their dates to the amusement park and music hall at Eastwood Gardens, located just outside of Detroit's city limits on the north side of Eight Mile Road. Still under eighteen years old, Leonard and his friends had no trouble procuring alcohol, "rye and ginger ale" to start, then switching to bourbon. "Early Times," he recalled.

In just under one year, Leonard had been issued a new name (as well as a fake ID) and his first set of glasses—both of which would become signature elements of his identity. But it wasn't until he revisited his interest in writing that the third defining characteristic began to take shape. At the time, Leonard's reading shelf continued to be on an advanced level, and now included Jesse Stuart's *Taps for Private Tussie*, Ted Lawson's *Thirty Seconds over Tokyo*, and Richard Tregaskis's *Guadalcanal Diary*—the first major wave of new fiction inspired by the ongoing Second World War.[42]

Ultimately, it was Hemingway's *For Whom the Bell Tolls*, published in October of 1940, that held the greatest impact on Elmore Leonard's young development as a writer.[43] As he later claimed, up until that point, nothing had affected his perspective on literature and storytelling more than that epic tale of the Spanish Civil War, and it would begin his lifelong love and appreciation for Hemingway's work. He also recognized many of the same tropes his favorite Western writers used for adventurous tales of the Old West. "That's how I learned to write, studying Hemingway," he later said. "I studied very, very carefully how he approached a scene, used points of view, what he described and what he didn't, how he told so much just in the way a character talked."[44]

In 1943, Leonard penned his first short story, "Dicky"—a tale of woe told from the perspective of an incarcerated narrator; in its twist ending, the reader discovers that Dicky is a bird in a cage. Attributed to "Dutch Leonard," the piece ran in the school's literary publication, *The Cub*, marking his first publication. (In a unique creative twist, Leonard would again adopt an animal's perspective only once more—an alligator—fifty years later; at that time, the *Houston Post*'s James Hall would write: "It's a very strange interlude, going into the gator's mind like that, an odd and risky moment, even for Leonard, who is used to dipping into some pretty exotic minds . . . Yet, I, for one, come away totally convinced that this is how an alligator thinks, the very words it uses. And if it doesn't think this way, then by god, it should. Such is Leonard's magic."[45]) Leonard's talent didn't go unnoticed by the Jesuit faculty. He later recalled one Father Skiffington offering his pupil the needed encouragement. "You could have a future in writing," he had told Leonard, based solely on the quality of his student's submitted assignments.

It was also during Leonard's senior year that his father was relocated yet again. Under fifty years old, Elmore Leonard Sr. was still eligible for the selective service.[46] However, he was able to attain assignments through his job that kept him from a second military tenure. As the younger Leonard later recalled, "My dad had something to do with the government then, through General Motors, [as] the war was on." However, the GM position mandated a move to Washington, DC. At the time, Elmore Jr. was just starting his senior year and sister Mickey had just graduated from college—now doing her own part for the war effort preparing invoices for tank parts at the Chrysler plant downtown.[47] It only made sense that Elmore Sr. and Flora make the move without their grown children, although living arrangements would have to be made. Luckily, coach Bob Tiernan understood his star quarterback's plight and didn't want to see the youth lose his new scholastic and athletic opportunities. With Elmore in a bind, the coach graciously opened his own home to him. Leonard later remembered, "My mother and dad moved to Washington, and [Tiernan] said, 'Well, come live with us' . . . I lived with Tiernan for almost a year." The coach had two children, a boy and a girl, and Leonard shared a room with Tiernan's son for the remainder of the school year.

Aware that his pending graduation would also call for self-sufficiency, Leonard was soon brainstorming various possible long-term plans.[48] He considered Georgetown and its School of Foreign Service, vaguely envisioning himself as a diplomat in some exotic corner of the world, an ambition largely inspired by his love of the movies.[49] However, Elmore Leonard Sr. initially had other plans for his only son. "Dad wanted me to go to Princeton and become an engineer," Leonard later said. "I don't even know if engineering is taught at Princeton . . . , because he was in automotive, in General Motors, and that seemed like a good background to him." Aside from his disinterest in engineering and a lack of suitable skills in advanced mathematics, Princeton was also decidedly secular in its approach to higher education. For Leonard, one of Georgetown's greatest appeals was its status as a Jesuit university in the Ignatian tradition. In an effort to put off making a final decision, first Leonard attempted enlistment in the Marine Corps just after his high school graduation. Due to his poor eyesight, however, he was promptly rejected.

As he weighed his options, Leonard and a few buddies opted to spend their postgraduation summer by taking a road trip. In June, a close neighborhood friend of Flora's won a sweepstakes hosted by a local supermarket; as a graduation present, Leonard was bestowed with just enough money for an adventure with his friends. They instantly chose Los Angeles.

It was also a practical time for the young men to get out of Detroit for a few weeks, as June 1943 heralded the breaking point of long-gestating racial tensions within the city. While Elmore Leonard Sr. had benefited from the outgrowth of the auto industry, he had been only one of hundreds to migrate to Detroit for work during that time. During the previous decade, the Great Migration of Black workers to the north had caused a nasty stir of vocal dissension among the more racist factions of the blue-collar community. During the same month that Elmore Leonard Jr. graduated from the University of Detroit, the Packard Motor Car Company finally allowed Black employees to work beside whites on their assembly lines. In response, twenty-five thousand white employees walked off the job in what was known as a "hate," or "wildcat," strike, effectively slowing down the critical war production.[50] The tensions boiled over on the warm Sunday evening of June 20 on Belle Isle, an island in the Detroit

River, when a brawl started between a group of Black and white residents on the Belle Isle Bridge. From there, a three-day riot spilled over into the city proper. Thirty-four people were killed and more than four hundred wounded—twenty-five of whom were Black, and most at the hands of the white police force.[51] Later, renowned crime novelist Ross Macdonald, writing under his birth name of Ken Millar, used the Detroit riots as the backdrop of his 1946 novel, *Trouble Follows Me*.

For the better part of that summer, Elmore Leonard and his friends hung around Hollywood and Vine, scouting for celebrities and talking their way into at least one red carpet premiere. There, they got a close-up look at leading man Tyrone Power in his Marine uniform; the matinee idol didn't suffer from poor eyesight. "My first trip to Hollywood was in 1943, before going into the Navy," Leonard later recalled. "We visited 20th Century-Fox and watched Betty Grable loop a number for *Pin-Up Girl*; rode the Santa Monica bus past Ciro's and the Mocambo on our way to the beach—past the Swanson Building, too, on the Sunset Strip, but failed to notice it."

Upon his return from LA, Leonard discovered that with the Selective Service Act in full force, there were still other areas of the US military that would accept his own physical limitation.[52] Two years earlier, and less than one month after the Japanese attack on Pearl Harbor, Rear Adm. Ben Moreell of the US Navy had expressed the need for a naval construction force to build advance bases in the many war zones throughout the world. The green light granted by the US military sowed the seeds for the earliest incarnation of the Navy's construction battalion—nicknamed the "Seabees" for the regiment's initials. To obtain men with the necessary qualifications, physical standards and age requirements were made less rigid than in other military branches. After December 1942, however, President Franklin Roosevelt's Selective Service mandates proactively sought younger men, although their physical acumen remained flexible. Soon, younger men with only rudimentary skills were deemed acceptable for the construction battalion. The flexibility of enlistment also included a recruit's height, weight—and eyesight.[53]

Elmore Leonard turned eighteen on October 11, 1943. He was drafted into the "Fighting" Seabees the same day.

CHAPTER 2

Seabees and the Pacific Theater, 1944–1946

"THIS IS TO CERTIFY THAT E.J. LEONARD, JR. S1C USNR WAS DULY INITIATED INTO THE SOLEMN MYSTERIES OF THE ANCIENT ORDER OF THE DEEP, HAVING CROSSED THE EQUATOR ON BOARD THE S.S. AZALEA CITY, BOUND FOR [SECRET DESTINATION] ON THE 9TH DAY OF OCTOBER 1944, LONGITUDE [SECRET]."

—"ANCIENT ORDER OF THE DEEP," US NAVY MEMBERSHIP CARD[1]

Officially, Leonard's job was to maintain an airstrip used by Allied fighter planes and both US Navy and Commonwealth pilots. He would claim, however, that his chief duty as an unassigned seaman had been to hand out beer.

Weeks earlier, Leonard had sailed from Treasure Island, in San Francisco Bay in California, where he'd been stationed at the Shoemaker Navy Training and Distribution Center following six months in Newport, Rhode Island. Now inducted into the Navy's unofficial brotherhood of southern hemisphere veterans, he had reached New Guinea, a brief stop toward his final destination—Los Negros in the Admiralty Islands, Philippines.[2] "I have been in New Guinea two weeks and already I am in love with the place," he wrote to Ruthann Finneran, the younger sister of friend and former classmate Jerry Finneran. "It is indeed a preview of paradise. A warm, friendly sun, a balmy breeze, refreshing cloud bursts, and cool evenings—what more could one ask for . . . ?"[3]

Later that month, Leonard would be shipped to the spot where he would spend the bulk of his military tenure, the Admiralty Islands. His very first stop, however, had been the furthest cry imaginable from the military's promised adventures: Newport, Rhode Island—location of the US Naval Training Center in Middleton—where it had taken all of twenty-hour hours for Leonard to write Finneran out of boredom. "This morning, I take my pen in hand with a rather heavy head," Leonard wrote on April 2. "Too many milkshakes. But no regrets whatsoever."

In later years, Leonard would later reveal the preliminary cause of his alcoholism had not been one of depression, but of boredom. He and his high school buddies had included beer and hard liquor in nearly every social activity once the option had been made available to them; Leonard, at least, had a fake ID prior to his eighteenth birthday. Now in the Navy, *every* social activity Leonard attended featured free or discounted booze—not including the overseas use of important beer as an alternative to polluted local water sources. With that routine, Leonard's extracurricular activities became ever more adventurous and his dispatches home often bawdier and more candid. "I met the most fascinating girl last evening," he boasted to Ruthann Finneran not long after arriving in Newport. "There I was, standing in the middle of the stag line at the 'YMCA Saturday Nite Frolic,' when all of a sudden, this beautiful white sweater walks by. Immediately, I said to myself, 'God, what a personality she must have to wear a sweater like that!' To my amazement, I found that she talked exactly like Katharine Hepburn and wore Harlequin lenses to boot."

He added, "I just finished reading *A Tree Grows in Brooklyn* [and] I'm heading for Brooklyn on my next leave. It sounds like a lovely spot."[4]

Despite Leonard's humorous insistence that his military service had accounted for little more than distributing beer and taking out the trash, his time in the Seabees would be crucial in shaping the man and author he would later become—expanding his worldview and providing enough experiences for years of creativity, new personal philosophies, and reassessed faith. First love and the loss of his virginity; lasting friendships with diverse peoples from other countries and the strong camaraderie of his fellow officers; and evolving enthusiasms for literature, movies, and alcohol would all deepen before Elmore Leonard returned to Detroit. Ultimately, those combined passions would dictate the rest of Leonard's life and career—and, perhaps most important to the future author, his voice.

Leonard had made the most of the six months spent stateside in Rhode Island and then Northern California. During his second week stationed in Newport, Elmore Sr. and Flora met him in Boston for a few hours of sightseeing; likewise, they met him at the midway point the following week, and the three of them enjoyed Providence together.

(Much later, he would admit to his grandson Alex that one particular rowdy night too many brought about the end of his fake ID "alias," James Harry Landino—still with a twinkle in his eye over some long-ago improvisation. Alex Leonard recalled, "He went to Baker's Keyboard Lounge, which is like one of the oldest jazz clubs in Detroit. It's still there, and everybody plays there—it's famous for their whiskey sours. Well, Elmore got carded . . . They noticed that it was a fake, so he had to appear in court. And so did Baker, the guy who owned the Keyboard Lounge." Not one to admit defeat so easily, Leonard had the ultimate ace in the hole. Alex recalled, "Elmore showed up in his Navy dress uniform. He walked into the courtroom and the judge just threw it out."[5])

From the very beginning of his first few travels with the military, Leonard revealed the bulk of his observations to Ruthann Finneran, who would prove to be his chief confidante, although their relationship would never progress beyond platonic. As two middle-class young adults from nearly identical backgrounds, both seemed to find it easy to ask each other candid questions about life and career advice. As Leonard's boredom and alienation abroad deepened, Finneran would also, although unknowingly, become privy to her pen pal's growing dependence on alcohol and habitual carousing. Before leaving Rhode Island, Leonard wrote Finneran:

> Tuesday, May 9, 1944
>
> *I wish I were home right now and we were discussing intimate secrets . . . At this stage (of my life), I'm leading a very liquid existence . . . As long as there is a bar in either Boston, Providence, or Newport, you know I'll have fun. You would really be surprised (I know you wouldn't be shocked) at little Dutchy and the amount of beer and liquor he can consume now . . . Good God, Leonard! What are you saying? Last Sunday in Providence, I drank an ensign under the table. The very first time I go out and associate with an officer and I out-drink him . . . There's no flies on me.*

> Monday, June 5, 1944
>
> *I stopped having my "after supper beer" (5) last week, and since then, I put on five more pounds . . . But I don't want to get too fat,*

so I'd still better have my little beer every once in a while. I know as soon as I get home, my little old mother will start pouring it down my throat with all the gusto she can muster.

Only a few weeks earlier, Ruthann had confided in Leonard her own trepidations about which college she should attend: the Catholic Marygrove College—the alma mater of Leonard's older sister, Margaret—or a co-ed public institution. He responded, "As I said before, at Marygrove, you will learn to be a sweet, virtuous little girl—but that's all. This is all that the nuns know, so naturally this is all that they can impart to you . . . Nuns are so narrow-minded, but priests are so straightforward."

The lifestyle of military service came into direct contact with Leonard's devout Catholicism. At eighteen years old and still sowing his wild oats, he began to preach the opposite, hinting at a larger internal conflict with his own beliefs. He wrote Finneran:

I, myself, plan to attend Georgetown [University] at the conclusion of hostilities. I can see now how people may lose faith by attending a non-Catholic college. Even around here, one could lose faith by associating with very "loose" companions and finally believing the warped philosophies of these people; just think how easy it would be to lose faith at a huge institution where a great brain like Bertrand Russell is preaching "Free Love" and making it sound very emphatic. Soon you start saying, "Maybe this guy's got the right idea . . . it sounds pretty good to me . . ."

The fellow I go around with all the time is an atheist, through and through, and sometimes, I have to admit, he starts me wondering—but this is because I live with him, eat with him, and continually listen to his ideas. That's why I want to hurry and get back to a Catholic school where I can have the truth pounded into me so deep, I'll never forget it or doubt it for one split second.[6]

By way of a naval base in Norfolk, Virginia, Leonard was ultimately shipped to the Treasure Island's Distribution Center in Northern California. With San Francisco not far to the southwest and Oakland to the southeast, it wasn't difficult for Leonard to find nightlife during the weekends. Although this first sojourn in Treasure Island would be the shorter of Leonard's two assignments there, he quickly found a number of favorite jazz clubs and after-hours bars.[7] On August 3, Leonard passed his physical exam—"the darkest day" of his life, he recalled. "We were told in a lecture that from here you only go one direction—southwest—any day now. It's all for the best, though. When I come home dripping with medals, you can gather the girls together and 'hail the conquering hero.'" With only one weekend before setting off for California, Leonard and a few other officers headed to Washington, DC, where they did a fair amount of "sightseeing through the window of every saloon in town." They also took a few girls to the movies—the group grabbing balcony seats as an excuse to drain a quart of rye—and ran around the Washington Memorial until four in the morning. The girls hung out with the young officers through two picnics the following day before parting ways. Then, in a particularly candid moment to Finneran, Leonard reported: "Once again, we go to the lighter side—I have never been to so damn many 'girlie shows' in my life. Every time there's a lull in our life, we hop over to Ocean View and sit in on a red-hot sizzling Burlesque. I've seen so many, I can do the bumps and the grinds with the best of them."[8]

Leonard arrived at Treasure Island on September 18, 1944. Two weeks later, he sailed aboard the SS *Azalea City* to New Guinea.

> *I am with a Construction Battalion Maintenance Unit, which automatically makes me a "Seabee" . . . Being with the CB's, especially a small unit like this one, has a lot of advantages. This is about the friendliest bunch I've ever run into. We live in Quonset huts (tin igloos)—sixteen to a hut, not counting the pin-up girls. The chow is good, beer three nights a week (7 bottles total), swimming in the ocean, and [a] show every night . . . although it does rain a little practically every day. One rain in New Guinea and you're up to your ankles in mud. (E.J. Leonard CBMU 585, Admiralty Islands, November 23, 1944)*[9]

Following their journey, the SS *Azalea City*, carrying Leonard and his unit, CBMU 585, briefly docked in New Guinea. The men then joined up with an Australian troop carrier headed to Los Negros in the Admiralty Islands—their final destination. There, the Seabees had been assigned the ongoing maintenance of an airstrip used by Allied fighter planes as a Pacific Theater checkpoint.[10] By November 1944, the dual capture of

Manus and Los Negros islands had made the Admiralties a stronghold in cutting off supplies from Axis forces throughout the Pacific.[11] The assignment of Leonard's regiment was, more or less, one of maintenance and strategic gatekeeping.

CBMU 585 reached the Admiralties on November 8. By choice, he was quickly granted his first assignment. Along with a half dozen other men, Leonard would shove off for the open sea singing, he claimed, "Fifteen Men on a Dead Man's Chest." When they reached the two-mile mark, they would shove bags of garbage over the side of the ship. "It's a pretty simple job," Leonard reported home, "so when I saw it, I immediately said, 'That's for me.'"[12]

By January, however, Leonard's detail had changed and, with it, his demeanor. He'd been assigned as an engineer, although he admitted bluntly to having thrown "math out the window" by the second year of high school and now did "not [have] the faintest idea what the hell [was] going on" during the majority of his daily shift. It was, to Leonard, eight and a half hours a day, six days a week, and half a Sunday's worth of confusion. He admitted to sneaking out and watching the movements of the other engineers, "taking all sorts of mysterious measurements," in a bid to mimic their knowing behavior. Ultimately, however, Leonard threw up his hands, writing, "The Navy does not think I'm a storekeeper; I do not think I'm an engineer. I'm sure God did not have me in mind when He created the universe." As the holidays approached, a combination of boredom and loneliness sunk in. "I am definitely either a square peg in a round hole or a round peg in a square hole," he added. "I've decided that my best bet is to hand in my resignation and come home on the next barge."

Leonard's new position, frustrating as it was, did come with a certain amount of respect and prestige. Holding fast to the feeling, Leonard soon decided to take advantage of some of the courses offered aboard the ship. At the time, Leonard was still adamant that Georgetown's academic and moral standards were the best fit for him—even if a major or career focus still eluded him. "Starting next week, I am a night school pupil," he told Finneran. "School is the damnedest thing to try and escape—it even follows you into the jungle. An outfit near here is giving classes in Algebra, Spanish, English, Trig, Slide Rule, Physics, History, and a couple of more. Two nights a week and an hour a night. I've decided on Trig and Spanish."

He signed off, "Ambition sneaked in somehow and smacked me right in the face."[13]

When Ruthann Finneran reported that she had made it a point to occasionally drop in on Leonard's aging parents—now back in Detroit, once again, from Washington, DC—he revealed his guilt for having left home at the young age he had. "I started thinking that perhaps I did run around too much and didn't spend enough time at home," he wrote. "Naturally, I love them as much as anyone could, but, like anything else, I didn't appreciate them fully, which is probably quite natural, until I had left home and it was too late."[14]

Leonard's loneliness subsided somewhat upon learning that Ruthann's younger brother, Jerry, was bound for New Guinea with his own division. He was hopeful the two might cross paths, he wrote Finneran, "but naturally the chances are slim." He went on, "Jerry and I have had some good times together—especially in Montana. I can still see him sitting in the front seat of that convertible in Missoula with a brunette on one knee and a phonograph on the other. He didn't know which one to start playing with first. At the time, I was in the backseat with a blond discussing the panorama of a Montana night."[15] His spirits were further lifted when his Christmas presents from Elmore Sr. and Flora arrived—on February 7.[16] However, Finneran expressed her apparent concerns for Leonard's well-being and the frequency with which alcohol seemed to appear in his stories. In his next letter, Leonard was apt to reassure her about his habits, although abstinence didn't appear to be on his list of New Year's resolutions. "Driving with a glow is the least of my worries, for the simple reason—I'd never get so drunk I wouldn't be able to drive," he wrote. "I've come to the point where I know how much I can drink and still be happy. When I go too far, I disgust myself. But anyway, what transportation we use is beside the point; we could bat around on a pogo stick and still have a howling good time."

Have you heard Lord Leonard's "Ode to Spring" . . .

"Ode to Spring (In the Admiraltys)"

I. O to be in the Admiraltys
Now that spring is there

And whoever wakes in the Admiraltys
Will find some morning unaware
That coconut bugs are in your hair
And roaches come pouring from their lair.

II. O to be in the Admiraltys
With a fighting CBMU
We use a knife to eat our peas
And the cooks we'd like to sue.
You can get used to anything almost,
Except the Spam they call a roast.

III. I'd better end my ode, Ruth,
Before my talk becomes uncouth
Far from me to abuse your ears
With vile talk about the hostile years.
I only look forward to "our night to howl"
Which will be a success, fair weather or foul.
Finis.

(E. J. Leonard, CBMU 585, March 19, 1945)[17]

Leonard's chief responsibility of beer distributor continued, or so he continued to report home—exhausted after handing out fifty cases' worth in a single day. With the water being notoriously laden with pollution and bacteria, naval officers were implored to drink anything bottled that could be provided—and beer often came cheap.

Leonard had since stopped mentioning the college courses provided in the Admiralties, although his letters to Finneran took a decidedly more literary tone during the spring of 1945—his passion for reading not only as strong as ever, but his interest in writing reinvigorated for the first time since grade school. "I am now reading Somerset Maugham's *Christmas Holiday*," he wrote on May 11. "This is a dirty book to end all dirty books. If you only saw the picture, don't let it fool you. In the picture, Deanna Durbin is a beat-out songstress, whereas in the book she's a 'hostess' in a Parisian house of ill-fame . . . I've read most of Maugham's works and this is about the lowest he gets . . . he doesn't leave much to the imagination."[18] Weeks later, he reportedly finished reading *The Feather Merchants* by Max Shulman—the "funniest damn piece of literature" he'd ever read. He also shared with Finneran a poem he'd just completed, although he prefaced the lyric with "You know I always write better when

I'm doped up . . . [so] you'll know that this little miscarriage of literature was conceived on the night of May twenty-seventh," adding, "The poem of the week is now included through the courtesy of 'Leonard's Literary Guild.'"

"Great American Tragedy"

He grabbed me by my slender neck
I could not call or scream,
And dragged me to his dingy room
Where we could not be seen.

[He] tore away my flimsy wrap
And looked on my form.
I was so cold and damp and scared
While he was hot and warm.

His feverish lip pressed to mine
I gave him every drop
He drained me of my very self
I could not make him stop.

He made me what I am today
That's why you find me here.
A broken bottle thrown away
That was once full of beer.

Finis

Whether Leonard's apparent interest in poetry was fleeting or merely for Finneran's benefit, he was significantly more interested in devouring novels and movies. Following the death of FDR, Leonard claimed Truman would do just fine as incoming US president, as "anyone who can play a piano with Lauren Bacall"—Leonard's new favorite cinematic femme fatale—deserved the position. "Speaking of Lauren," Leonard added, "that's one babe who can pack her shoes under Leonard's sack any night—and she's only one year older than I am—hard to believe, isn't it?"[19] When Leonard's bawdy language would sometimes take Finneran aback, he would soon funnel the more outlandish humor into the dialogue and names of characters he'd begun creating. In a particularly playful moment, he wrote:

But now all you Literary Guilders, here's an added feature. If you're dissatisfied with your monthly book, return it and get your money back. Remember, Leonard fans, his monthly selection is guaranteed to be spicy, hip, and sexy—just the way you like it. After all, you literary fiends, each and every book is written by a woman—it's bound to be pretty raw, huh?

Now we hear from Ophelia Gluch, the Guild's noted reviewer, who will give you an inkling of what this month's book, Strumpet At Dawn, *deals with:*

Miss Gluch: (in a rasping voice) "Hiya, kids! Strumpets At Dawn *is just what youse kids have been waiting for. To make it short and sweet—Genevieve Claptrap thought a red light meant only STOP, until one morning she woke up and found one hanging over the front door. She learned the hard way. It seems that her boyfriend, Gregory Shmirtz, was hard up for cash and, since he held rather communistic ideals—share what you have with your comrade—why not also share Genevieve with the boys and make some moola to boot. Everything went along smoothly (for Gregory) until Hyman, the village idiot, accidentally kills Gregory with a welding torch. Thus Genevieve is left without a—let's just say 'manager,' a veritable waif of destiny. Finally, Genevieve falls into the hands of Sash Crum of the Weehawken Vice Squad.*

"To make a long story short, Sash feels sorry for the little bitch and, at the same time, falls in love with her, so he takes the overdeveloped youngster into his home and makes her Mrs. Crum. Being a housewife is monotonous to an ex——, so, longing for the red lights once again, she walks down to the Bowery and is swallowed up in the hurly-burly. Finally, she dies at the age of seventeen from too much cocaine. Sash Crum, in grief, jumps off the Tri-Borough Bridge.

"Ain't that what youse been waiting for, kids? Real down to earth stuff."

Leonard ended his letter, "How I got on that, I don't know, but once I started, I had to finish. I hope you don't mind my little stories . . . Someday, I'm going to get good and drunk and write a book."[20]

At 9:02 a.m. on the morning of September 2, a ceremony was held on the deck of the battleship USS *Missouri*, welcoming the global dignitaries needed to sign a prepared "surrender document" that had been drawn up, vetted, and approved by all invited. Six pens were shared by the nine men to sign the respective dotted lines and, by 9:25 a.m., the ceremony was finished. The Second World War, which had lasted a staggering 2,194 consecutive days, was declared over in just under twenty-three minutes.

It was apparent that the men of 585 would be shipping out to new assignments for the following year. Leonard had set sail for the Philippines aboard the HMAS *Kanimbla* at the end of August, where the men docked in Sangley Pointe in Cavite, Luzon—"just a stone's throw from Manila"—for nearly two months. With the announcement of the war's end, and little to do, the men were granted a generous "liberty" day to bum around Cavite's bars and clubs, or the actual twenty-seven miles to Manila, every four days. "The towns are blown to hell and, naturally, that doesn't stop a good time," Leonard wrote after his first month there. "This is the only place in the world where you can walk into a bomb crater and walk out drunk with half your money gone."[21] The new liberty privileges couldn't come at a stranger time, as the war's end had resulted in all sorts of shortages and shipment delays; with American beer out of the question, the men were told, in the interim, to indulge in the harder liquor. "They said you only drink whiskey and only certain kinds, only certain makes—and that's what we did," Leonard later recalled. "We would go to walk out of the base and go around the bay from Manila, go in there and sit down and get a bottle and drink it." According to Leonard, his routine in the Philippines was even more lax, although he was granted numerous different jobs to make the time pass. "I worked in the store and I sold them shaving cream and stuff, and a native would come in and he'd want some *'lap lap,'* which is just a mattress cover. I'd give him a mattress cover and he'd give me a couple of—what were they called?—'cat eyes'—which they got out of the ocean. I don't know what a cat eye is. It's like a half a marble."[22]

While in the Philippines, Leonard made one decision that would leave an indelible, and later infamous, mark on him. One afternoon, he had decided to further join his naval brethren by getting his first tattoo, envisioning an elaborate depiction of the Seabees emblem, proudly displayed in multiple colors. While in the shower, however, Leonard's wallet was stolen, forcing him to borrow a bill from a fellow Seabee. At the tattoo parlor, Leonard discovered that his friend had accidentally shortchanged him, leaving Leonard nine dollars short of his intended ink. With the meager choice of a three-letter Seabees abbreviation or his own nickname, Leonard chose the latter—forever having "Dutch" emblazoned in red and black on his left shoulder.

Borrowed time didn't stop Leonard from falling in love with a local girl just before the month's end. "Her name is Estella," he wrote to Finneran. "[She's] seventeen-years-old and she's a hostess at the Sunset Bar." Of Filipino and Spanish descent, the young woman was the chief front-house coordinator of the dubious watering hole, "run by a rum-dumb Yank who drank his way through the Jap occupation," the love-struck Leonard reported. Only a few nights earlier, he had been sitting at a table with a few of his compatriots and spotted Estella at the bar in the company of a sailor. As he attested, the two made eye contact across the room, "and that was all there was to it." She abruptly left her companion and sidled next to Leonard where, as he put it, they "stared at each other for the rest of the night." To Leonard, the young woman had eyes unlike anyone else in the world—even his beloved Lauren Bacall. "One look into those deep, limpid black pools and I was through," he wrote. "The last time I saw her, she asked me to come back after my discharge and we'd live together—just like that, without batting an eye. I'm not one to commit adultery, but it's not a half-bad idea. Once she dragged me over to her shack and let her mother give me the once over. Those two gals are cooking up something and I think I know what it is. (Correction: I'm afraid I know what it is.)"[23]

Unluckily for a young man celebrating his nineteenth birthday, the romance came "to an abrupt halt" only weeks later when the Sunset Bar closed up shop and Estella was forced to fall back on another career—one that "I rather frown upon," he wrote. "She now lives with a bunch of MPs and does their washing for forty pesos a month. I think Estella missed her calling." He added, "It's just as well that Stell and I broke up—I discovered (quite by accident, mind you) that she has lice—hordes of them."[24]

Following his brief experience with both first love and heartbreak, Leonard resigned himself to more seclusion and more reading. Inspired by Finneran's excitement over his previous recommendations, Leonard quickly went out to the PX and purchased for her a recent favorite among his shelf—Max Shulman's episodic slice-of-life soldier tale *The Feather*

Merchants. With that care package, he noted, "Whether you've read it or not, please save this precious manuscript so I can read it for the fifth time when I get home . . . How Maxie can keep himself in such a peculiar mood long enough to write a whole book, I don't know. He must spike his coffee with adrenaline every morning . . . When you finish it, get a hold of *Barefoot Boy With Cheek*."[25]

On December 17, Leonard boarded the USS *Tazewell*, bound for home. There were numerous stops along the way, and his return journey lasted nearly half a year. It would take Leonard up to Seattle, then back through the Panama Canal aboard yet another ship, the USS *Towner*. He would reach Norfolk, Virginia, and, finally, home by early spring.

Much to Leonard's delight, however, their very first stop was a return to Treasure Island, in San Francisco Bay. Before embarking on his grand tour of the Pacific in 1944, Leonard had spent a few memorable nights around Northern California and immediately set out to find the best jazz music in the Bay Area. He later recalled, "We got back from the Pacific in January 1946, tied up at Treasure Island in San Francisco Bay, and I headed straight for Oakland, where Stan Kenton was playing that night . . . I remember standing in front of the stage, looking up at June Christy singing 'Buzz Me Baby.'" (Leonard had picked a great time to stop in on Kenton's band, which was then going through a creative evolution of its own; Kenton's new staff arranger, Peter Rugolo, had only recently joined the orchestra, bringing with him a love of classical masters, such as Bartok and Stravinsky—leading to oodles of experimentation while playing on the road. It was this ultra-hip, modern incarnation of the new Stan Kenton band that electrified Leonard. At the time, Kenton had only recently recovered after a five-month hiatus from the road, refueled with an ambition to break out of the traditional venues that usually hosted his orchestra—rented movie theaters on a dark night, or ballrooms booked in advance—to larger rooms, like concert halls—and playing a new form of modern compositions recently labeled "Progressive Jazz."[26]) Leonard was already a jazz fan, having used his fake ID in the name of James Harry Landino—for access to after-hours clubs back in Detroit. However, he would soon admit to finding inspiration in the improvisation and evolving creativity that jazz music seemed to embody.

The USS *Towner* arrived just outside of Seattle on the second day of March, already in disrepair and headed for its own decommissioning six weeks later. Leonard, however, had his own plans: "Two hours from now, I'm going to hit the beach with sixty cents in my pocket and really raise hell."[27] Following their arrival in Seattle on January 25, they headed toward the Panama Canal on March 19 and reached Norfolk, Virginia, on April 10. The ship was decommissioned exactly one month later.

Leonard was formally discharged the same week.

CHAPTER 3

Aspirations and Traffic, 1946–1950

> I entered [the University of Detroit] in 1946 following 30 months in the Navy . . . I decided to stay in Detroit and take advantage of a Jesuit education . . .
>
> I signed up at U of D to major in English; I've always loved to read and did have the hope of writing fiction someday. I graduated in 1950 with a PhB degree in English, a minor in Philosophy, and the next year I sold my first story to a magazine.

Things were quite different when Leonard returned home from the war. Parents Elmore Sr. and Flora had returned from their brief move to Washington, DC, although his sister, Mickey, opted to remain there, having found lucrative clerical work at the Senate office; she soon met and married a young attorney named Joseph Madey, himself a Georgetown graduate.[1]

Ultimately, Leonard decided to put his GI Bill toward enrollment for the University of Detroit's fall semester.[2] He'd already attended its affiliate prep high school and even enjoyed the curriculum and atmosphere. "I got to really like U of D [High School] a lot," he later recalled. "In fact, I felt on graduating that I pretty much had my education, and was wondering, 'What am I going to do when I come back from the service?' Then I went to U of D [University] and took English and minored in Philosophy, just for something to do."

Like Georgetown, the University of Detroit was regarded as one of the country's most prestigious Jesuit-run institutions. Initially named Detroit College and located on the corner of Jefferson Avenue, it soon expanded; upon its fiftieth anniversary in 1927, then–acting president

Fr. John P. McNichols oversaw the college's move to a sprawling campus in northwest Detroit at Livernois and Six Mile Road.[3] Leonard's freshman year not only welcomed the university's first alumni president, Rev. William J. Miller, but more than seven thousand new students—many of whom were servicemen returning on the GI Bill. There would be an additional 1,500 the following year. (By the end of the war, 137 drafted students would have been killed in action.) In order to meet U of D's expansion, Miller approved forty-one new faculty members and, on June 30, 1948—during Leonard's junior year—the college and its affiliate high school were split into separate entities.[4]

Leonard easily picked English as a major; when not with his friends, he was usually reading, anyway. But for his minor, he was initially unsure. After four years of studying Latin and two years of Greek, Leonard was adamant he not retake those dead languages, ruling out majors that would include them as prerequisites—including his preferred choice, History. Finally, he settled on Philosophy, as, when compared to other Catholic institutions, U of D's curriculum was decidedly contemporary.[5] During Leonard's first year, he benefited by studying under the current department heads: Rev. Burke O'Neill—a jovial man in glasses, with short, slicked hair graying at the temples—and Rev. Peter Nolan, fair and younger, but with the serious eyes befitting his place as head of the Philosophy department. U of D required 128 hours of class time, and Leonard's specific degree program required a full twenty-four hours for English and eighteen for Philosophy. His first-semester grades were consistent and unsurprising: he'd gotten a C in History, Bs in Spanish and Religion, and As in both his academic wheelhouses, English and Philosophy. The following semester, he'd maintained his B in Religion, yet dropped a grade in nearly everything else, including English.[6] He did, however, pledge his first fraternity—Alpha Chi.[7]

Leonard's grades steadily improved during the first semester of his sophomore year, with straight As in Philosophy, Religion, and Speech; his reading level and comprehension should have given him an easy A rather than the B earned in English but, as he explained later, his interest in writing was only beginning to return.[8] "When I was at U of D, I did pretty well on tests and the instructor said, 'Why don't you just come to my office instead of coming to class and we'll discuss different works?'" he later elaborated. Rather than in the classroom, Leonard and Professor Eugene Grewe discussed such varied works as Byron and Shelley and poets of the

Early Romantic era; likewise, they discussed the Philosophy curriculum, from Plato's *Republic* to existentialist Jean-Paul Sartre, whom Leonard learned to appreciate, although his favorite was Aristotle, as "the Jesuits liked [him] so much."[9]

Regardless of his classroom performance, Leonard's personal literary tastes continued to mature. During his military service, he'd passed the time by reading; once home, his shelf was newly stacked with Richard Wright's *Black Boy*, Evelyn Waugh's *Brideshead Revisited*, Agnes Newton Keith's *Three Came Home*, some George Orwell, and more Steinbeck. But the manner in which Leonard earned his passing English grade would later prove more important to his eventual career path than he had anticipated. When he required extra credit after his paper on Thackeray's *Vanity Fair* earned him a D, Grewe encouraged him to enter the annual short story competition sponsored by the on-campus creative writing club "the Manuscribblers," promising that any of his students who entered would get an automatic B in his course. Leonard recalled that he "entered twice," once for each consecutive year.[10] For their annual competition, the club had been able to recruit a local agent to help select the winner. "I entered and came in among the top ten," he later recalled. "The first one was called 'The Kitchen Inquisition.' It was about a chef who was very short and always needed help. And I don't recall what the outcome was . . . But that particular story was pretty much in the second person. It's all 'you' all the way through. I don't know why. I probably didn't know any better."[11] But what Leonard *did* know, he threw into the story. Told almost exclusively through dialogue, the short tale follows the disgruntled head chef taking orders from a cluster of upper-crust bourgeois women during a regular meeting of their book club. The action then follows Wallace, the chef, as he returns to the kitchen and indulges in employee back talk with the rest of the staff:

> "Honestly, Ethel," Mrs. Willoughby declares assuringly, "Wallace reminds me more of Reginald Gardner every time I see him. He's so suave and efficient, too."
>
> Whenever Wallace or any other member of her household staff is complimented, Mrs. Beauchamp invariably lets slip her aren't-I-the-lucky-thing sigh, secretly prides herself for being an employer par excellence, and simply replies, "Oh, yes," but with a casualness that implies more than anything else, "It was nothing, really."

Leonard also managed to spoof both his mother's ladies' club and Ruthann Finneran's defense of *The Canterbury Tales* in one fell swoop:

> "Wally, you stupid jerk," replies Max, impatiently, "you think only ball players get famous? Chaucer was a writer . . . I think. Wasn't he the guy that used to write vulgar stories a long time ago?"

As Leonard would learn later, authors of vulgar stories could, indeed, become as famous as ballplayers—and that effective dialogue didn't necessarily require adjectives and adverbs. In his later fiction, he would also make similar use of dialogue over extraneous exposition, as well as a recurring trend of displaying the background activities of the elite class's servants.

Leonard's wordplay, character names, and his satirical titling of fictitious books came directly from his often bawdy improvised tales to Ruthann Finneran (especially his ongoing "Leonard's Literary Guild" installments), relying perhaps on as much dialogue as a radio play or film script than a work of short fiction. For the finale that an older Leonard claimed not to remember, it is revealed that an unseen character—variously referred to as "F.B.," "F.B., Jr.," and "Junior"—is actually Mrs. Beauchamp's former butler, who'd had the fortitude to acquire stock market tips on the job and parlayed them into a fortune of his own. (It was a plot device that beat playwright Samuel Taylor's 1953 stage production *Sabrina Fair* by six years, and its blockbuster film adaptation, starring Humphrey Bogart and Audrey Hepburn, by seven. Leonard would also revisit those themes and scenario in a novel of his own nearly four decades later.)[12]

Indeed, Leonard's story placed in the top ten for the competition, and ran in the November 19 issue of the student-run *Varsity News*. It was Leonard's first published work. In what amounted to just over a quarter page's worth of prose, Leonard had tapped into a number of themes and narrative devices that would permeate his work for years.

He ended the semester with As in both Philosophy *and* English.

What had been most unique was the young author's dependence on dialogue, and his grasp on street parlance and dialects not often found in the work of his immediate peers. While his biting critique on high-middle-class living was not unlike the writings then found in the work of John

O'Hara and Ring Lardner—both regulars in such mainstream "slick" magazines as *Collier's* and *The New Yorker* and both soon to be favorites of Leonard's—his apparent comfort with a vernacular "sound" came from a more likely source: the street itself. Even amid the nation's racial strife (Jim Crow was in full swing) a combination of his Catholic ideals and a childhood among ethnically diverse friends had infused Leonard with both a curiosity for and acceptance of marginalized and foreign communities—a trait that was atypical of his peers. Having felt his very first pangs of romantic love for Estella, a barmaid of Filipino and Spanish heritage, Leonard had an apparent indifference to companions' ethnicities or ideologies; unless, of course, he found them fascinating enough to pump with questions. In the case of his musical tastes, seeking out his favorite jazz performers often led Leonard to Detroit's more segregated Black neighborhoods—a hard sell to the young women he often courted on campus.

But companionship wouldn't be an issue for much longer. Of new friend William C. Marshall, Leonard would later joke that their dynamic was him primarily writing Marshall's book reports—a fact that would come in handy years later when Marshall went on to become a licensed private investigator in South Florida, thus becoming a major resource for Leonard's fiction. (Both men would joke that Marshall merely owed him for the decades-old favor of helping him pass English classes, save for one specific assignment that brought an end to the new friends' schemes. For that, Marshall would later joke, he'd received two grades—"an 'A' for writing and an 'F' for plagiarism."[13])

The following year, however, Leonard's wild nights with Marshall and the other guys would become numbered. He soon met Beverly Clare Cline (later, Decker), a petite blonde two years his junior, then pursuing her two-year degree in Secretarial Science.[14] The daughter of Myron and Lillian Conway, Beverly was born January 9, 1927, and had an upbringing similar to Leonard's. They had attended the same high school and run in similar social circles, leaving them both wondering why they hadn't met before; Beverly had even sat behind Ruthann Finneran in a number of classes. "[We met] somewhere at a party when he was a senior at college," Beverly later recalled. "On our first date, we went to a fraternity party in Port Huron. We sat on a hill and I don't know how, but we were talking about music. I started to sing 'Good Morning, Heartache,' and he was just like, 'I've never known a girl who knew Billie Holiday before.'

And I asked him, 'What, does that impress you?' Elmore dropped me off that night and my parents were waiting up in their pajamas. My father looked outside and said, 'Who is this guy?' And Elmore just said, 'Good night!' But when I got inside, I got drilled with questions: 'Who is he? Where do you know him from? What does his father do? Is he Catholic?' But, eventually, they loved Elmore."

According to Beverly, her love of music and quick wit impressed Leonard plenty, and they were going steady in a matter of weeks. "He bought us kazoos right after we started dating and we'd go sit on that hill every day and play those kazoos. We would mostly do two parts, like, 'La-da-da-da,' and then the other would go, '*Da*-da-da-da . . .'" She added, "But he always wanted to be a writer when we were together, and just read and read and read all the time."

They announced their engagement six months later.[15]

While Leonard's academic record would remain largely unexceptional for the duration of his time at U of D (his grades continued to fluctuate between As and Cs, even in advanced English coursework[16]), he had begun spending more of his free time trying his hand at fiction writing.

Although never a full-fledged member of the group, Leonard attended more Manuscribblers meetings. For their 1948 short story competition, he attempted a more straightforward tale, later telling Boston University professor Charles Rzepka, "The second one was kind of a love story. A guy was in love with this girl—they're both very young—and he comes to her house for a party and he finds out it's her engagement party. She's engaged to somebody else. They end up in the closet necking, and upstairs, they just fall on her bed and they're kissing and having a good time. And that's a true story . . . I was the guy."[17]

He came in second place and was approached by the same literary agent who'd judged the competition the previous year. This time, she recommended Leonard join a Detroit-based writers' group with which she was affiliated; he agreed to consider it. For the time being, however, he had yet to even choose a clear career path.

An English major, Leonard nonetheless showed no interest in becoming an educator nor an academic—and although he dreamed of the life of a writer, unlike many of his heroes, he made no attempts to write or submit commercial fiction until the very end of college. While not entirely aimless—he acknowledged that writing would play a role in his future, somehow—his indecisiveness and mediocre grades had left him vulnerable to parental nudging. In September 1948, Elmore Sr. decided he'd finally had enough of being moved all over the country for the better part of his adulthood and accepted GM's offer to buy half of a Chevrolet-Buick-Oldsmobile dealership, Rio Grande Motors, in Las Cruces, New Mexico.[18] To alleviate the mounting pressures of running it alone, he now hoped his son would join him in the business. Leonard later recalled, "I think the comfort of the surroundings of working in General Motors with all those people around you, how can you screw up? There's always somebody that's going to pick up the ball, and I think then [for my father] to be on his own [for what] this was really the first time in his life."

At first, Leonard was tempted to take his father up on the offer; his wedding to Beverly was planned for July, and the stability of a family-run auto franchise could provide the young couple a solid financial start. There was, however, a potential move to New Mexico for the two to consider. Regardless, Leonard looked into enrollment in the General Motors Dealers' Son School—the corporation's official finishing school for family-run dealership locations. "He wanted me to come out and work for him once he had this dealership going," he later remembered. "And the idea was first I would go to the Chevrolet dealer's son's school, which was in Detroit—part of the 'Chevrolet vision.'"[19] He also said, "The idea was that when I graduated, I would go out and join him and become a car dealer. I wanted to get married and do all that, so I thought, 'Well, okay, let's do that.'" There was only one catch, however. As Leonard later admitted, "I don't like cars."[20]

But just as the University of Detroit had simply made more financial and practical sense over Georgetown University, so the logic of following his father out west now seemed the most prudent—regardless of Leonard's personal feelings on the matter. After all, it had been Elmore Sr. himself who had shelved his own artistic ambitions in the name of family so many years ago. With only his senior year left to go, Leonard tentatively agreed to his father's suggestion and planned for dealers' son school following U of D graduation. Nearing the end of his junior year, however, an unforeseen turn of events mirroring his father's own youthful crossroads presented itself when, on March 24, Elmore Leonard Sr. died suddenly of a brain hemorrhage at his office in Las Cruces. He was forty-six years old.

Beverly later recalled, "Elmore's dad was the greatest guy—so friendly. He was from New Orleans and called everybody 'chief.' Everyone loved him . . . He moved to New Mexico to open his own car dealership and, one day, got to work, put his head on the desk and just died right there."[21]

"We only got to know each other after I came out of the service," Leonard later remembered, "then we would play golf together and go to the bar after and have some beers, and it was fun. We got along very well."[22]

Leonard assisted his mother with sorting out Elmore Sr.'s insurance and military pension, but was then tasked with figuring out what to do with his father's portion of the New Mexico dealership. "I was finishing at U of D and living with a friend, and my brother-in-law said that we should go and see the regional manager in Dallas and try and retain the dealership," Leonard recalled.[23] "[We] tried to hold on to the dealership, because my dad only owned half of it. He was paying, I think [General Motors financial affiliate] 'Motors Holding,' so much a month, for the rest. And then, of course, at that time they were selling cars as fast as they got them. I thought, yeah, I guess I'll go to work for them in a dealership [but] it did not appeal to me at all." He added, "I was doing it to please—well, finally, when [Elmore, Sr.] died—to please my brother-in-law . . . It would give [him] something to do."[24] However, when he and Joseph Madey visited the GM regional manager—a close friend of Elmore Sr.—about acquiring the late Elmore Leonard's half of the business, they were instructed to take it up with the mortgage lender, Motors Holding. "They said no—thank God!" Leonard later recalled. "It would have been the worst business I could ever have been in, selling cars." The Las Cruces deal squashed, Joseph Madey instead opened his own law practice in Little Rock, Arkansas, where he and Mickey would remain settled, raising five children; Mickey herself had been able to secure clerical work at the secretary of state's Commercial Code division—a position she would hold for fifty-five years.[25]

Leonard's ambition and maturity left an indelible mark on the regional manager, however, and—perhaps out of respect for the late Elmore Sr.—he inquired about the younger man's future plans. "He said, 'I understand you're interested in writing,'" Leonard later recalled, "but I don't know how he could have known that, because I hadn't written anything. My mother must have told him I wanted to write someday, but I wasn't writing because I was reading, and I was reading very closely—and deciding most people use way, way too many words." Noting Leonard's talent and passion for reading and language, it was suggested that Leonard parlay his newly minted college degree into an advertising career—especially as Detroit represented the nation's entire automotive industry, all of which employed the most prestigious marketing firms. Before sending Leonard on his way, the manager handed him his business card, scrawling on it the number for Colin Campbell, an account representative for one of Detroit's largest advertising firms, Campbell-Ewald. Leonard leapt right on it. "[Campbell] had come up through production, and he didn't know anything about what was good [writing] or not," Leonard recalled, adding that one of the seasoned rep's chief responsibilities was finding "widows" (a single word left dangling alone on a line of copy) within the proposed advertisements. "He said, 'Well, have you thought about media?' I had never heard that word before—it wasn't a popular word back then—but I said, 'Oh, yeah, media!' And that's how I broke in."[26]

Juggling his studies, pending nuptials, and assisting his mother in finalizing her late husband's affairs, Leonard decided he'd complete his last semester at night school. Although he had received a C+ in English Drama—his lowest grade for the year—Leonard's reinvigorated interest in writing had greatly assisted in bringing up his overall grade point average: a B+ in Shakespeare I, and dual Bs in Shakespeare II and the Age of Milton.[27] Fortunately, the majority of the coursework Leonard required for graduation could be electives—flush with the reading and creative writing assignments he knew he could handle while working a nine-to-five day job.

Leonard and Beverly were married on July 30, 1949, with classmates John "Jack" Huber and Elaine Watts acting as witnesses.

For the first six months, the young couple stayed with Beverly's aunt in nearby Dearborn. As Leonard prepared for his new job running "office services" for Campbell-Ewald, Beverly began her search for an apartment, preferably closer to the firm's downtown headquarters. By the first month of 1950, they had found a small place of their own near Blessed Sacrament Cathedral.[28]

"The first place we lived, near Blessed Sacrament, was just awful," Beverly later recalled. "I remember I was pregnant with Jane and would sit in the bath and look out the window and the next building was just so far away—and this place was dirty. He'd go to work and I'd have to go back to bed. Then, Elmore's mother came when we lived in Lathrup Village, and she stayed for years. I'm not really a good cook, but she'd criticize everything. I almost cried."[29]

Beverly was pregnant during Leonard's graduation ceremony, and her young husband was already preparing to join the workforce that October.[30] He then began his tenure as Campbell-Ewald's "youngest married office boy," running a daily routine that he would later describe to biographer James Devlin: "You would deliver messages around, go buy plane tickets for people, things like that, and I did that about nine or ten months." His efficiency as an office factotum soon earned a slight advancement working "traffic" for the next two years—"taking the ads from the production department to the proofreader, from the proofreader to the account guy, to get all the signatures." Leonard admitted it wasn't long before he told himself, "I gotta get out of here."[31]

Rather than bemoan the menial assignments that he'd usually be given, Leonard worked diligently during the day and began attending his night classes the following semester. This practice of having a full-time day job, while supplementing either education or income, would be Leonard's common routine for the next fifty years. For now, however, his incentive for career advancement was more immediate: At the end of the summer, Beverly discovered she was pregnant. The happy couple soon realized they would again need a larger home. Out of both ambition and practicality, Leonard wondered what steps would have to be taken to become a professional author. He started by following up with the writers' group referred to him by the Manuscribblers' judge the previous year, attending weekly meetings while also working for Campbell-Ewald during the day and attending school at night.

There was one other addition to his routine that wouldn't waver during much of the next decade: Leonard, still a devout Catholic, rarely missed visiting daily Mass at nearby Blessed Sacrament Cathedral. "I was going to Mass—not mass—but to receive Communion almost every morning through the '50s and '60s before going to work," Leonard later told Charles Rzepka. "It was me and a half-dozen old ladies . . . I'd just take five minutes to receive Communion and come out. While I was working at Campbell-Ewald, I'd go have Communion first and then go to work." According to Leonard, he wasn't quite sure where the seriousness of his beliefs stemmed from, as he was, admittedly, "more devout" than either of his parents, and his social circle included friends of various ethnicities and faiths.[32] As a testament to the similarities of their respective upbringings, Beverly took part in the majority of Leonard's religious practices, though not with her husband's apparent severity. She later recalled, "Three or four days a week, Dutch would get up at four o'clock in the morning because, at our church, they had the Holy Eucharist exposed, so somebody had to be there to guard it before the priest arrived. And different people would volunteer, including Dutch. He would do that and just sit in the church for an hour before Mass."[33]

Leonard later recalled, "In the early part of my first marriage, we would say the Rosary Novenas all the time for things—and I believed it—and often it worked."

In later years, Leonard would always defend his commercial approach to literature, citing "mainstream" fiction as the most assured outlet for a writer to be *read*. As his father, Elmore Leonard Sr., had been forced to abandon his own youthful artistic ambitions for the good of his family, Leonard now sought a way to strike a balance—to perhaps either supplement a stable income with fiction writing, or truly make a mark as a full-time professional author, the odds of which were decidedly slim for the father-to-be. Later, he would credit his mother for his own burgeoning literary ambitions, although he was never convinced she was as serious about it as he would eventually become. "My mother always wanted to write, but she didn't write enough," he would later tell Charles Rzepka. "Her stories were so old fashioned they had no chance. Maybe in the '20s they might've [sold], but not in the '40s or '50s . . . She didn't have any guidance and she couldn't find any guidance."[34]

For pragmatic reasons, Leonard considered short story magazines—especially the pulps—to be the ideal finishing school for woodshedding his technique; in essence, be paid to learn on the job. "I decided, if you're going to write, let's study a particular genre, concentrate, research, and learn how to work within the framework of this genre," he later told *The New Black Mask Quarterly*. "A genre has a form [and] that's great when you're starting."[35]

Leonard's plan was to write and revise a marketable story while attending the writers' group. Just prior to joining—the period when Leonard claimed to be "reading very closely [and] deciding most people use way, way too many words"—he had studied crime masters Fredric Brown and Erle Stanley Gardner, particularly enjoying Gardner's Bertha Cool–

Donald Lam stories written under the "A. A. Fair" pseudonym. He also became enamored with the early thrillers of future Travis McGhee creator John D. MacDonald. "I read [MacDonald] like a textbook in the '50s," Leonard later recalled. "He was writing about real people who came over a lot more real than ordinary characters you would find . . . [MacDonald] was breaking a lot of rules and getting away with it in the stories he did for *Saturday Evening Post, Collier's,* and other slick magazines. Although he was well-known, it took MacDonald a long time to hit the best-seller list."[36] He later added, "I read John D. MacDonald in the early 1950s and said, 'This is what I should be doing.'"[37]

With those authors in mind, Leonard opted to try his hand at hard-boiled crime fiction. By the time Leonard stopped attending the group's regular meetings, he had completed his first professional short story, "Seven Letter Word for Corpse"—later revised as "One Horizontal."[38]

In this, Leonard's first "true" short story, he hadn't included many of the tropes or devices recognizable in his later work. He did, however, draw on his intimate knowledge of downtown Detroit's nightlife, primarily the Black jazz clubs he'd frequented in his single years; his use of "black and tan, more black than tan"—watering holes unofficially immune to racial segregation, but preferential to the Black patrons who weren't afforded the option to drink elsewhere—not only marked his continued application of vernacular and slang terms, but also gave him an excuse to use observations from real life. (Indeed, the "Jade's" depicted in the opening scene was a real club located below the luxurious Hotel Imperial, located just north of downtown and west of Woodward.)

For the first time since his high school effort, "Dicky," Leonard also opted to use first-person narration—a common trope of the modern crime market, especially the authors he was reading and studying at the time; having completed Fredric Brown and John D. MacDonald, Leonard moved on to dark moralist James M. Cain and, to a far lesser extent, the gritty detective fiction of Mickey Spillane. The short tale is told by the protagonist, Stan Ellis—a young Detroit man hell-bent on revenge after the shooting of his older brother, Cliff, a bottom-rung henchman himself. While holed up at a nearby cottage and nursing an embittered and wheelchair-bound Cliff back to health, Ellis stalks "the pool room crowd" seeking his prey—a gruff hoodlum named Marty Carrito. After a few doses of liquid courage, Ellis finds and threatens Carrito, his "man at the bar," igniting the more seasoned gangster's fury.

The darkly humorous tale stood mature in its pacing and language; Leonard had crafted a story economic in its language and not less sellable than many of the pulp stories authors pumped out for pennies per word. For unknown reasons—whether mixed-to-negative feedback within the writers' group or the author's own misgivings—Leonard chose not to publish "One Horizontal." He instead reconsidered which literary genre would suit him best. Although he'd set his first mature story in his own home city and populated the tale with locations and characters with which he was familiar, writing in a contemporary setting immediately placed Leonard in the same arena of his hyperbole-driven, plot-obsessed contemporaries—admittedly, his weakest suit. Rather than face discouragement, Leonard, instead, looked to another massively popular genre—one not only literary but common on American airwaves, in movie theaters, and now, on television sets: the Western.

But before Leonard could focus his energies on attempting a follow-up short story with publication potential, he had more pressing matters with which to attend to: just in time for their second wedding anniversary, he and Beverly had found a new, larger home at 17460 Redwood Avenue in Lathrup Village—and only two months shy of Beverly's due date.

Although Leonard tried not to let his crushing schedule get to him, years later he would admit to having one particular nightmare that plagued him as he approached his twenty-fifth birthday. "When I was starting out writing, I had a dream," he told Charles Rzepka. "I was always falling down these stairs . . . They were steep and narrow, and I'd fall down, and you wait for yourself to hit the bottom and that never came. But it was that tightening up on the way down."

Leonard added, "Then I started to sell and I never had that dream again."[39]

CHAPTER 4

Ad Men and the Arizona Territory, 1950–1952

> To find the time to write fiction (I was working for an advertising agency at the time) I began getting up at 5 A.M. and would hope to write two pages before seven, when I'd have to get ready to go to work. I'd make myself write at least a paragraph before putting the coffee on the stove. If I didn't begin working, I got no coffee. I did this for most of the first ten years . . .
>
> Why I chose the Western genre in the beginning, I'm not sure. For I know now I was influenced more than I realized at the time by film noir (though I'm still not able to define it accurately or completely) . . .
>
> I sold my first story to a magazine that I wrote in longhand and then typed on a Royal portable . . . I was twenty-five, in 1951.

Leonard and Beverly's first child, Jane Clare Leonard, was born on August 11, 1950.

Having earned his U of D diploma midyear thanks to his night school classes, he was able to narrow his routine down to daily Mass and work. Like his hero, Ernest Hemingway, Leonard began rising at dawn, often starting his day by removing his Book of the Month Club edition of *For Whom the Bell Tolls* from the shelf and thumbing through its pages "just to get the feel of it, just to get the mood of it."[1]

For the six months that he and Beverly had their small apartment near Blessed Sacrament, he would write either at the kitchen table or on the living room sofa—a habit that spilled over to their new Lathrup Village home. He'd also made a habit of helping himself to unlined yellow pads used as scratch paper by Campbell-Ewald's copywriting department, as well as a few of their twenty-nine-cent Scripto pencils. After he was satisfied with where the scene was heading, he would type the story—a few pages at a time—on the Royal portable typewriter Flora had recently gotten him as a gift. Finally, he would study how the typed words looked on the page, making an onion-skin carbon copy only for his perfect, final revisions.[2]

As the family would continue to grow in size, Leonard continued the tradition set forth by sister Mickey, telling his children nightly bedtime stories. Unlike Mickey, however, Leonard would make up his own funny, adventurous tales, coming up with silly characters with humorous names. During the next few years, Leonard would often tuck little Jane and, the following year, her younger brother, Peter, into bed before beginning his own nightly writing routine—lulling them to sleep with made-up stories about a little boy "Bobby" and his daily adventures.[3] (Over time, he varied the lead characters, but kept up the playful mischief that continued to amuse his children: "The best one was called 'Audrey McDonald Got Locked in the School,'" Leonard's youngest daughter, Katy Dudley, later remembered. "Each night, he would tell me about a different adventure she had . . . I always wished I had written them down—it would have made a great book."[4])

But now, as he sat feeding and rocking Jane on the couch, Leonard kept a pad and pencil beside him. With her nestled on his shoulder, he could carefully reach down and write with his free hand.

> In 1951 when I began writing and made my first sale to *Argosy*, the market for westerns was wide open. Book publishers, Hollywood studios and magazines, the *Saturday Evening Post* and *Collier's* and at least a dozen or so pulp titles like *Dime Western*—the better pulps paying two cents a word—were all looking for Westerns.

Although Leonard knew his talents would have been better suited elsewhere, he continued to work Campbell-Ewald's "traffic" for the following few years. He had begun vying for advancement early in his agency tenure, although it would take a while to work those ranks: Campbell-Ewald's clientele included some of the biggest automakers in the country. Leonard, however, was a veteran and college graduate and knew he could do better, even supplementally—and a solution couldn't come soon enough: that spring, Beverly discovered they were expecting their second child.

Unbowed with the presumably false start that "One Horizontal" represented, Leonard considered the next popular genre to crack. "I looked for a genre where I could learn how to write and be selling at the same time," Leonard later recalled. "I chose Westerns because I liked Western movies. From the time I was a kid I liked . . . *The Plainsman* with Gary Cooper in 1936, up through *My Darling Clementine* and *Red River* in the late forties."[5] Cooper, in particular, would become one of Leonard's favorite leading men, forming a loose archetype for many of the author's later protagonists. And in the 1950s, nowhere could Leonard spin better morality yarns with heroic lawmen and fiendish outlaws than in the Western pulps. He later admitted, "I felt that there was a good possibility to sell them—to sell to Hollywood."[6]

For a young author looking to improve their technique in the hopes of breaking into a more serious literary genre later on, the pulps were also ideal for "practicing" in public, learning what styles and devices worked and what didn't, with just the right size audience. There was also the likelihood of that audience expanding; aside from the genuine pulps that specialized solely in Western tales—*Adventure, Argosy, Blue Book, Dime Western, Zane Grey's Western Magazine*, among many others—there were the mainstream "slicks," printed on the glossy paper suitable for such prestigious authors as Ernest Hemingway, F. Scott Fitzgerald, and John O'Hara—*Collier's*, *The New Yorker*, and the *Saturday Evening Post*—that would also, occasionally, run a Western story deemed worthy of its audience. Those high-tier magazines were often scouted for potential film and television adaptations, making them calling cards for those authors published within their pages. He later recalled, "I hadn't read many Westerns, [but] I began to notice the Westerns in the *Saturday Evening Post* and *Argosy*. I liked the fact that in this market you could aim at magazines that were paying $850 or $1,000 for a short story and work your way down through *Argosy*, which was paying $500 or $1,000, to *Bluebook* [*sic*], and then down to all the pulp magazines."[7] The slicks might have doled out advances for an entire work or serialized novel, but the pulps coughing up two cents per word also inadvertently encouraged many of their regular authors to load their prose with the extraneous verbiage Leonard despised (although he later admitted to enjoying a few Western authors, such as Luke Short, Ernest Haycox, and James Warner Bellah[8]).

Leonard looked to give his take on the "adventure story" tradition but remove as many of the unnecessary words that usually bogged down plot and energy. As his personal point of reference, Leonard looked to what was still, at that time, his favorite book, later elaborating: "When I was writing Westerns, it struck me—*For Whom the Bell Tolls* was a 1940 Spanish Western . . . I thought of it as a western—out in the mountains with guns and horses, you know?"[9]

He began with what he already knew of the Western genre, pruning details and tropes from the books, films, and television shows with which he was well familiar. In what would become a normal practice, Leonard started with a single character—here, an aging sheriff named for his friend Bill Martz. The archetype of the morally just lawman surrounded by an indifferent or corrupt atmosphere was tipped from Leonard's own favorite Western movies, the sheriff's characterization intentionally reminiscent of both *The Gunfighter*'s Jimmy Ringo (including stoic leading man Gregory Peck's signature mustache) and the star of the *For Whom the Bell Tolls* cinematic adaptation, Gary Cooper—both of whom Leonard viewed as templates for an ideal hero. Leonard had realized early on, however, that the names of his characters were crucial in bringing them to life, and Bill Martz's had to go. Peter Leonard recalled, "Elmore got the name from his best friend, Bill Martz. 'Bill' didn't work well, so he changed the name to Charlie."[10]

Although enough differences exist between the versions to separate them as wholly different stories within Leonard's canon, he wrote "Charlie Martz" and "Siesta in Paloverde" consecutively. Both versions introduce Charlie Martz—a former gunslinger turned overly mellow lawman in an already sleepy New Mexican town; and both stories build to the same nail-biting conclusion: a showdown between Martz and a former nemesis he'd long ago sent to prison, now back, and hell-bent on revenge. Leonard himself later remembered, "I wrote about a gunsmith that made a certain kind of gun. I sent it to a pulp magazine and it was rejected, [and] I decided I'd better do some research." (The gunsmith in question was the German armorer responsible for repairing Martz's Colt, and was named "Adolph Schmidt" for Flora Leonard's younger brother, Adolph Rive Jr.; Leonard peppered both versions of the story with the names of friends and family.)

Leonard's first attempt at research had been cursory, at best. He had collected pamphlets on antique firearms, such as *Heike's Hobby Catalogue* and *Collectors' Rim Fire Cartridge List*, and used their antiquated technical descriptions to give more accuracy to the story's details. However, he had hoped that his abundance of gritty dialogue would be enough to carry the story, removing unnecessary detail that "other authors were better at" in order to utilize his own strongest suit; years later, upon his return to contemporary crime fiction, Leonard would again use this technique, and to great success. This time out, unfortunately, editors were unimpressed, leaving Leonard to devour as many books on the time period and the geography of the Old West as he could handle. For accurate character names, he even dug out an old phone book that his late father had once sent to him from Las Cruces, New Mexico.[11] Leonard later recalled, "I read *On the Border with Crook*, *The Truth About Geronimo*, *The Look of the West*, and *Western Worlds*, and I subscribed to *Arizona Highways*." Founded the same year as Leonard's birth, *Arizona Highways* magazine was an official monthly published by the Arizona Department of Transportation, and it was known for its exclusive coverage of the Native American populations of the Southwest and neighboring regions. "It had stories about guns," Leonard added. "I insisted on authentic guns in my stories—stagecoach lines, specific looks at different little facets of the West, plus all the four-color shots that I could use for my descriptions, things I could put in and sound like I knew what I was talking about."[12] He added later, "If I needed a canyon, I'd go through the magazine, find one, and describe it."[13] Leonard would keep his subscription to the magazine for the next decade, using its articles and lush pictorial details as primary sources on daily life in the Arizona Territory. "I liked Arizona and New Mexico," Leonard later said. "I didn't care much for the High Plains Indians. I liked the Apaches because of their reputation as raiders and the way they dressed, with a headband and high moccasins [running] up their knees. I also liked their involvement with things Mexican and their use of Spanish names and words."[14]

Leonard ran to Woolworth's and bought himself an oversized pea-green accounting ledger—the word "Record" boldly inscribed across its cover—and began carefully organizing each new detail of his research into corresponding sections. On the inside flap of the ledger's cover, Leonard began by listing the books he'd be using for reference. Now that he'd selected the Apache nation as his focal point, he began with William Foster-Harris's *The Look of the Old West*, *Life Among the Apaches* by John C. Cremony, Frank C. Lockwood's *The Apache Indians*, and Morris Edward Opler's two-volume *An Apache Life-Way*, along with *Myths and Tales of the Chiricahua Apache Indians*, noting indigenous fables for references he could make within his own work. For a better look at the daily life among the white townsfolk, Leonard consulted William Howard Russell's *My Diary, North and South,* Paul Wellman's *Death in the Desert: The Fifty Years' War for the Great Southwest,* and the following year, Bruce Siberts's *Nothing But Prairie and Sky.*

Leonard combed through his new books and magazine clippings, jotting down bits of information and random facts for future use. He also looked back on the philosophy texts he'd read and discussed in college, writing down a few favorites that would, perhaps, guide the themes of the stories he would write: "Neither the sun nor death can be looked at with a steady eye," he noted from La Rochefoucauld; from ancient Greek biographer Diogenes Laertius—apparently a favorite—he wrote, "Those who want the fewest things are nearest to the gods," "Even the gods cannot strive against necessity," and finally, "The descent to Hades is the same from every place."

In parentheses, Leonard offered his own interpretation: "*It's the same distance to hell no matter where you die.*"

Leonard's recent reading into the Arizona Territory began to pay off, slowly at first. With his second serious endeavor—tentatively titled "Tizwin"—he ambitiously broke the story into three distinct chapters of decreasing length, making it his longest story to date. He largely introduced the characters through dialogue, veering away from the lawman archetype, instead using his newfound knowledge of the US Cavalry and independent, freelance Indian scouts to shape the plot. In this instance, Leonard brought the themes of age, mentorship, and experience to the story's two leads: Gordon Towner—a young lieutenant, still wet behind the ears, on his first patrol—and Matt Cline (a wink to Beverly's maiden name)—a seasoned tracker not only familiar with the terrain surrounding Canyon Diablo, but with the experience to travel among the Apache nations that populated the territory.[15] The dynamic between the men and the protocols used to find Apaches were all products of Leonard's study, while the story's memorable climax—which he would repurpose for an early novel only a few years later—was an outshoot of his growing interest in Apache culture. Much as he had done in "Siesta in Paloverde," Leonard looked to circumvent Western clichés by penning a climax that deliberately lacked the traditional "shootout" associated with the genre (Charlie Martz had used his gun to *hit* someone, not shoot them, after all). Similarly, he now considered ending the story with its own unique twist, concocting a showdown of bravery and virility displayed not with guns drawn, but rather willpower and endurance. Having long since been indoctrinated into social circles that viewed competitive drinking as a test of masculinity (both high school baseball and football teams, the military, and an advertising job where many coworkers were of the "three-martini lunch" generation), Leonard used the idea of a drinking game for the story's finale. He had gotten the idea from an Apache spirit called "tizwin"—mashed and fermented maze kernels, blended with mesquite or saguaro, and served hot. While one aboriginal nation from the region, the Tohono O'odham, considered the strong drink as sacred, the Apache people served it at social gatherings; the more rambunctious and youthful among the tribes particularly enjoyed the drink's fast-acting ultimate effect: hallucinations and blackout drunkenness. Leonard not only based the climax of the story around a "tizwin" gathering (in this instance a "throw down" of tizwin between Towner and Lacaveo, the Apache warrior who'd ambushed his men), he scratched out his working title, "First Patrol," and replaced it with the name of the drink.

Rather than his full name, Leonard opted to use a professional byline, which had been the preference of both his high school and college newspapers; he signed both stories "Dutch Leonard." He knew enough not to immediately shoot for the slicks; instead he researched the highest-paying pulp magazines and settled on *Argosy*. Because "Tizwin" was novelette length, Leonard would be, presumably, in line for their highest-pay offerings. On April 23, however, he heard back from John Bender, the magazine's associate editor. Bender declined the story but signed off with an offer of hope: "The first half of the story creates some good tension and offers a promise of interesting characterizations, but the latter half of the story fails to deliver on this promise . . . I should rather not suggest a revision on this particular piece, but if you have other stories of this period of American history, I should be very happy to give them a look."[16]

Leonard took Bender's request for more work seriously and immediately began a follow-up submission. As for "Tizwin," Leonard later recalled, "The editor at *Argosy* passed [the story] on to one of their pulp magazines at Popular Publications, and they bought it."[17] Before that future sale to *10 Story Western Magazine* occurred, however, Leonard also quickly sent "Tizwin" off to Fanny Ellsworth, the managing editor for the Thrilling Fiction Group—also known as Thrilling Publications—

responsible for numerous pulp titles of various genres, including a number of Westerns: *Exciting Western, Masked Rider Western, Popular Western, Range Riders Western, Rio Kid Western, Rodeo Romances*, and, of course, their seminal *Thrilling Western*. Strangely, however, Ellsworth wrote, "We read your contribution, 'Tizwin,' with interest, but I regret to say it would not fit into any of our publications at this time."[18]

> The story appeared in the December 1951 issue under the title "Trail of the Apache" and began: "Under the thatched roof ramada that ran the length of the agency office, Travisin slouched in a canvas-backed chair, his boots propped against one of the support posts. His gaze took in the sun-beaten, gray adobe buildings, all one-story structures, that rimmed the vacant quadrangle. It was a glaring, depressing scene of sun on rock, without a single shade tree or graceful feature to redeem the squat ugliness."
>
> You hear all that writing in there? I don't do that anymore.

Using more of his expanding knowledge of the Apache people that his research was affording him, Leonard immediately began what would become his first professionally published story, the seven-chapter novelette "Apache Agent." Set in 1880, the story focused on Captain Eric Travisin and his search for sixteen Apache braves who had recently escaped his custody at the Arizona-based Camp Gila scouting and relocation agency. He's aided in his search by interpreter Barney Fry (married to a "Tonto woman"—a rescued former hostage of the Apaches) and an inexperienced would-be agent, William de Both. While the story was an original scenario and displayed Leonard's evolving practice of breaking his stories down into "scenes," he opted to flex his literary muscles and veer from his usual ample dialogue. What he retained, however, were similar elements and characterizations from his previous attempts; like the Charlie Martz tales and "Tizwin," Leonard's preoccupation with mentorship and technical mastery shone through in his depictions of Travisin and de Both. As future Leonard scholar Charles Rzepka would observe later, it is in "Trail of the Apache" that Leonard's personal views on discipline are first displayed.[19]

On August 17, Leonard finally received the validation he had been working so hard for when *Argosy*'s John Bender accepted "Apache Agent" for publication and, in a very rare instance of overt generosity on behalf of a pulp magazine's budget, the editor paid Leonard one thousand dollars for first and second North American serial rights. While the young author was then completely unfamiliar with copyright law or how residuals worked, he quickly agreed to the terms. Bender had asked Leonard some biographical details for their "upcoming issue" column, and offered another promising send-off: "By all means," he wrote, "send more fiction."[20]

Leonard received payment for his first story two weeks later. In the accompanying letter, however, Bender did make a stipulation. He wrote, "We should like to use the byline 'E. J. Leonard, Jr.' or 'E. J. Leonard' in preference to the 'Dutch' byline which you have affixed." As the story's upcoming publication approached, Leonard was further notified that the editors were changing its title. Finally, "Trail of the Apache" by *E. J. Leonard* was set for publication in the December issue.[21]

The editors at *Argosy* weren't unique in planning their upcoming issues nearly a third of a year in advance. As only one of forty-two monthly titles owned and distributed by Popular Publications, *Argosy* was also only one of a dozen Westerns in Popular's line alone. Fortunately, *Argosy* paid upon acceptance rather than publication, leaving Leonard free to pump out and submit as many new stories as he could before "Trail of the Apache" even saw the light of day. Whether or not there would be a demand for more stories by "E. J. Leonard" was yet to be seen. For now, *Elmore* Leonard set to work writing more stories—first for John Bender's unspoken "first look," then others. Unfortunately, between Bender's acceptance of then–"Apache Agent" in August and its eventual publication, he would reject every submission Leonard sent his way.

There would, however, be other silver linings before Leonard's year was out. While Bender didn't see fit to run Leonard's "Medicine" in his own magazine, he acknowledged the new story's quality and potential and referred it to an affiliate publication: "I've taken the liberty of showing this one to [*Dime Western Magazine* editor] Mike Tilden, who tells me he has taken some material from you. Mike is quite pleased with 'Medicine' and will take it as it stands if you do not have another market waiting for it. So, if you like, shoot it right back to him for a quick sale." Leonard quickly responded in agreement and, under the new title "Apache Medicine," the story ran in the May issue of *Dime Western* the following year.[22] And while Bender had sent a rejection for Leonard's "Cavalry Boots" only two days after Christmas, in the spirit of the holidays, he nonetheless forwarded Leonard's first fan letter.[23] It had been addressed to *Argosy*'s senior fiction editor, James O'Connell: "I wish to congratulate you upon publishing a story not only vividly written, but with such an excellent background of facts," S. S. Garber wrote. "It is very seldom the fiction writer knows the details of the various Indian tribes as they used to exist. Mr. Leonard, in my opinion, is an outstanding fiction writer. I shall hereafter purchase your magazine in hopes that you will have more stories by him."

For his part, senior editor O'Connell was quick to respond, thanking Garber for his feedback and concurring with his own opinion of Leonard. "In fact," he wrote, "['Trail of the Apache'] is one of my favorites in the December issue. Mr. Leonard is a fairly new writer, but we're expecting fine things from him."[24] (What wouldn't have been noticed by either the senior editor or his associate editor, John Bender, was the name copied on Garber's letter: Leonard's brother-in-law and would-be auto dealership partner, Joe Madey, who was, in actuality, Garber's former coworker at the Washington, DC, law office. Madey photocopied the "S. S. Garber letter" and soon popped it in the mail to Leonard. Madey playfully signed along the bottom: *"Merry Christmas, Dutch!"*[25])

> More than 30 years ago I suggested to my first agent, Marguerite Harper, that she critique my stories; then I'd fix them up before she showed them to editors and we'd get fewer rejections. Marguerite, who looked like somebody's maiden aunt and probably was, said, "You learn how to write and I'll sell it." And she did.

Leonard might have been frustrated with the early rejections his follow-up stories had received, but the acceptance of his first story in April had heralded a number of new blessings in the author's life. In July, he and Beverly celebrated their second wedding anniversary; they were now settled into their first real home; Jane had turned one year old in August; and on October 7—only four days shy of Leonard's own twenty-fifth birthday—his first son, Peter Anthony Leonard, was born. As he approached a quarter of a century, Leonard found himself a husband, two times a father, and—upon *Argosy*'s December issue—a published author.

Rather than veer too far from a track that seemed to be working, Leonard kept at his digging into the Apaches, turning out two drafts before revisiting his dual affection for lawmen and outlaws. But while Leonard had had early success with one sale and the promise of a second, he was still viewed by editors as just another young author sending out unsolicited manuscripts. His talent was evident, but he was, nonetheless, still fighting for the full attention of any editor digging through their slush pile. That changed with a single letter forwarded to Leonard by Popular Publications editor Mike Tilden, dated November 20, 1951:

"A day or so ago," the letter began, "I happened to see an advance copy of the December *Argosy* magazine and, thumbing pages, before I knew it, I was deep into your Apache story. You seem to have a real knowledge of these Indians' habits. The story intrigued me mainly because it is almost without dialogue and must be close to fifteen-thousand words, and yet it's compelling."

The surprise letter had come from Marguerite Harper—a self-employed New York literary agent in her mid-fifties. "I don't normally write authors just because I see a story in a magazine that interests me," she continued, explaining that nearly all of her clients had come through referrals of other, trusted authors. Among others, she represented Luke Short, Peter Dawson, and T. T. Flynn—yet Harper found herself in an unforeseen bind, as numerous writers from her roster had been drafted into military service in Korea. Having come across "Trail of the Apache" and been impressed with Leonard's writing, she'd contacted Mike Tilden on the chance he knew Leonard. "Do you think you could be benefited by an agent?" she now asked Leonard. "Or have you given any thought to it? And if not, will you do so?"[26]

Leonard knew he had enough raw talent to be selling more work than he was, yet for weeks he'd had more strikes than hits. Aware that having an experienced, professional agent in his corner could make a world of difference, he dashed off a lengthy letter to Harper, loaded with questions about the publishing industry and fiction markets. Using his thousand-dollar sale of "Trail of the Apache" as his point of reference, he first inquired about the feasibility of leaving Campbell-Ewald for the life of a professional author. Harper—who functioned without the aid of a full-time assistant and always typed her own correspondence—responded within the week.

She opened her letter with the first of many pieces of advice to the young author—one that he would not only take, but would use as a creed for the next forty years:

"DON'T GIVE UP YOUR JOB TO WRITE."

It was a sobering mantra to be hit with so early in a budding career, but one which Harper emphasized to all her clients. She elaborated, "I say this very seriously. You ought to know right at the beginning that writing for a living is a most hazardous occupation. Of course, it can still be done—and is—but the word 'security' can hardly be attached to it as a means of livelihood; though a very good one can sometimes be made by it."

For Leonard's guaranteed success, Harper wrote, he would have to set his sights on two realistic goals—working his way out of the pulps and into the more prestigious slicks, and to complete and publish a first novel. She promised to help Leonard achieve both: "The way to make any real money is to aim at the slick . . . If you can hit the [*Saturday Evening Post*] with a western serial, that is the thing to do. They are repeat buyers." According to Harper, Leonard would then be able to parlay that serial into a published novel, making "some real cash" on both sales. She also suggested a deadline-oriented schedule for specific types of writing would keep the author's goals on track: "If you can't get a slick sale, the thing to aim at is short stories and one or two book lengths a year and, of course, while television cannot expand now, there is still the money to be paid for movie sales if they can be made and other sales to come like radio and television." She closed with a final word of immediate advice: "I think you are going to make your job difficult if you narrow your effort down to doing just Apache stories . . . There were so many of the movies that were pillage and death and fire and ruin—and done with so much emphasis on brutality, that the public got sick to death of tales about Indians and their warfare."

Harper's knowledge had been hard-earned through years of experience climbing the ranks of the highly competitive, largely male-centric publishing industry. As a freelance literary representative, she didn't have a larger agency with which to function, leaving all client outreach and industry research to her alone. Making things trickier, she was a middle-aged woman specializing in a men's action genre read and written almost exclusively by men—and for more than twenty years, she had thrived in it. By all accounts, her clients loved her—both for the obvious work ethic that regularly produced results in their favor, and also for the personal investment Harper made in each one of them. She was born Marguerite Ethel Harper on January 12, 1895, in New York City; her parents, Philip and Lydia Harper, were Canadian transplants who had come to the United States in 1894 after the birth of their first child—Marguerite's older brother, William. After a brief stay in New Jersey and the birth of a third child, Phyllis, the family was settled in Brooklyn by 1910.[27] William was the first to move out, and Phyllis was married and gone by 1925.[28] In 1928, Philip Harper died, leaving Marguerite to spend the next few years helping her mother.[29] However, she had already started her career as a literary agent the previous year, establishing a single office on Madison Avenue and, in 1931, an apartment at 2 Horatio Street, on the sixteenth floor overlooking the Hudson River. When the Depression hit, however, Harper was forced to relinquish the office space for a "desk up in Radio City [Music Hall]" used only for messages, and now she conducted almost all daily business from home. She even admitted to Leonard she was ready to leave the city and move to the more affordable Westchester, keeping only an office in the city somewhere near Grand Central Station.[30]

When Harper had been coming up through the ranks of the publishing industry during the 1930s and 1940s, women were often relegated to women's magazines or children's literature, while men were often granted more prestigious projects or "serious" literature, all of which made for additional roadblocks in building client lists and securing lucrative deals. More often than not, women were paid less than men for the same work, and they often lacked access to the financial resources necessary to establish themselves as literary agents or editors—including staff support and basic expenses. Like Harper, many women of the publishing and literary agency fields were forced to rely on their own resources—such as typing their own business correspondence and working from home. "I would add that I work hard," she advised Leonard in her second letter. "I have no other income other than what we can earn in commissions and no immediate family to help in any way. In 20 years, I haven't yet had a two week vacation, so I take weekends as often as I can get them and days here and there in the summer. So, if you think we can benefit each other, send some stories along."[31]

Deeply encouraged by Harper's words, Leonard was more motivated than ever once the December issue of *Argosy* finally hit newsstands. As he and Beverly prepared for the holidays with young Jane and newborn Peter, Leonard also quickly rewrote "Tizwin" for Mike Tilden, who had requested a number of last-minute revisions. Planning to send Harper a few of his previously rejected stories in the hopes of future placement, he sent "Tizwin" along first—both the original and revised version. "I like the original best by far," she quickly wrote back. "I don't see Mike's criticism of the other version. It seems to me that if everything has to be spelled out for simple readers, it could have been done by a simple sentence . . . But the first version is too long for slick consumption. And the second version strikes me as a hurry-up job. No short story today should be over 5,000 [words]."

Harper signed off with an important warning to Leonard that she would repeat consistently over the course of their relationship: "At the risk of seeming to repeat myself, I want definitely to impress upon you the fact that you will run into real difficulties with editors, no matter how well you conceive and write your stories, if you do story after story based on this theme of the soldier or scout, or the homesteader or the rancher or the miner stalking the Indian . . . But straight western writing, unless you can hit [the *Saturday Evening Post*], hasn't much to offer these days . . . The western movies that have been the greatest successes have nothing to do with Indians at all."[32]

Leonard accepted Harper's mentorship and quickly put her advice to use, alternating the subjects of his new stories and, eventually, incorporating civilian characters and shades of domestic life into the plots. Much to Harper's chagrin, however, he proved stubborn when it came to eliminating Apaches, the cavalry, or local lawmen and outlaws from his narrative palette. Later correspondence would indicate a mix of frustration on Harper's part and reluctance on Leonard's. But while Leonard would soon yield and make frequent attempts at contemporary fiction, those stories wouldn't have the same success as his Westerns; his developing style was largely dependent on the lush detail and historical accuracy that his readings of the Arizona Territory had provided. For now, however, both Harper and Leonard were happy to see where their collaborative efforts led them; they had their answer in only another few weeks:

"Well, it hasn't taken me too long to get my first sale for you," Harper playfully boasted via telegram on December 24—her successful submission of Leonard's "Road to Inspiration" being a perfect last-minute Christmas gift. "Have sold First North American Serial rights . . . to *Zane Grey's Western Magazine* for $110.00."

Harper continued, "Where is that rejected story you were going to send me? And how about something new also? Happy New Year and I hope we can benefit each other greatly in it."

Leonard sent Harper "Cavalry Boots"—fresh off John Bender's rejected pile. Within days, she had sold it to *Zane Grey's Western* for one hundred dollars. A few weeks later, she also sold his "Eight Days from Willcox" to *Dime Western*—its title changed to "You Never See Apaches"—for publication at the end of the year.

By the start of 1952, Leonard had literary representation and had seen his first story on the magazine racks. Rather than a New Year's resolution, he began the diligent morning writing routine that would form the bedrock of his creative life for years. "I decided that I was going to have to get up in the mornings to do it with a growing family," he later told biographer Paul Challen. "I was tired when I got home, and I had the children to think about, to spend time with . . . I realized that I was going to have to get up at five in the morning if I wanted to write fiction."[33]

To keep the momentum going, Leonard would then continue once he got to work. "I'd put my arm in the drawer and have the tablet in there and I'd just start writing and if somebody came in, I'd stop writing and close the drawer."[34] He later admitted, however, "It was a chore . . . but I know that's what I had to do. Thank God—you know, I wouldn't be sitting here if I hadn't have gotten up at five."

For the precious few hours that Leonard was afforded by waking up before dawn, he soon moved out of the living room and set up a small home office in the basement. Years later, son Peter Leonard could still recall his father's first home office well: "When I was about eight or nine, I'd wake up every morning and see my father writing," he said. "In the early days, he would be in the basement and I would come down the stairs and stand there and just watch him. He was so caught up in what he was doing, so immersed in his work that he didn't even notice me . . . And eventually he would look up and see me and say, 'Come over here.' And I would go over and he would show me what he was doing, writing in longhand—his unlined yellow paper. He had a Royal typewriter on a stand next to this red desk that he sat at and, five feet away, was a waste-basket with all these yellow balls of paper around it. They were scenes that didn't work, shots that missed. That's a pretty vivid recollection of him."[35]

Peter's younger brother, Bill Leonard, shared similar memories of their father's earliest writing routine. "I often got up quite early, also, so I was up when he was up, but I left him alone with respect to what he was doing . . . I didn't start reading his stuff until *Forty Lashes, Less One* in

1972 and went forward from there, reading everything of his—and almost always the original manuscripts as he would complete them. Before that, my mom had told me his stuff was 'too adult' for me."[36]

Now with a modest sanctuary in which to focus, Leonard began what would be one of the most prolific periods of his career. Nearly half of his complete Western short story output would be penned in his new basement office over the next two years—as well as his first novel, which he would begin the following spring. In later years, Leonard would always credit his work ethic and early morning hours for his eventual success. "You have to write well enough to get someone's attention," he claimed. "The writer has to have patience, the perseverance to just sit there alone and grind it out. And if it's not worth doing that, then he doesn't want to write. Hemingway said, 'Anyone who says he wants to be a writer and isn't writing, doesn't.'"[37]

CHAPTER 5

Advances and Advancement, 1952–1955

> I think the mistake most beginners make, they're more concerned with creating something that sounds like writing, with clever images, descriptive passages, than they are with discovering their own basic attitude about putting words on paper. They want to *have written* before they know why they want to write or realize it's going to take at least ten years to begin to learn how to realize that style comes out of attitude, not the clever arrangement of words.
>
> Some, of course, learn faster than others.

Leonard kept up steadily for the first half of 1952, publishing six stories by year's end. Aside from Harper's placements of "Cavalry Boots" and "Road to Inspiration" to *Zane Grey's Western*—the latter's title changed to "The Colonel's Lady" for publication—as well as the similarly retitled "You Never See Apaches" and "Under the Friar's Ledge" to *Dime Western*, she had also successfully sold two of Leonard's stories that he had both completed on May 14: "Outlaw Pass"—published as "Law of the Hunted Ones" in *Western Story Magazine*—and the Western morality tale, "Along the Pecos," which *Zane Grey* ran as "The Rustlers" the following year.

Still, she attempted to steer Leonard away from solely writing Westerns, insisting he diversify his subject matter. "I think what you need most to put your sights on is the reason for fiction," she wrote in February. "Its primary aim is ENTERTAINMENT. It's to write characters who can be made believable . . . The editors at [the *Saturday Evening Post*] have a way of putting it—could you take this character home to dinner with you, or for a weekend, and would you enjoy his company, or at least be interested in his behaviour?"[1] Leonard took the advice to heart. With each story, he leaned a little heavier into characterization and plotting, continuing with his recurring themes of mentorship and mastery. And although Harper was able to place everything, she remained adamant regarding Leonard's subject matter and, occasionally, his aversion to criticism.[2] When Leonard had initially sent her "Under the Friar's Ledge," she was blunt with her criticism. "I read the new story this morning and I can't whip up much satisfaction about it," she had written.[3] Leonard had actually been dipping, ever so slightly, into the realm of the supernatural. For the first time, he took her to task, insinuating her preoccupation with other clients, and suggested a formal agreement between them. Harper took neither suggestion lightly. "Frankly I don't know whether you are asking me to argue with you about the Juan story or not. But I am not going to do so . . . I am not a teacher of short story writing. My job is to sell stories . . . I don't know what book you read that told you how to conduct yourself as a writer, but I'd say as a quick rejoinder, that it sounds like hog-wash . . . I have never had a signed agreement with any author, which most agents do have [and] do require . . . At the same time, I very definitely do not wish to work as hard as I do work for my authors and [then] have you walk out on me after I have opened markets and tried to improve your sales and rates."

Leonard chose not to explain to Harper why "Under the Friar's Ledge" had been of such particular importance to him: the story had been the product of Leonard's recent research into a specific region of Mexico, which he had selected as the location of his first novel, tentatively entitled *The Crosses of Soyopa*. His research ledger had since ballooned with new knowledge on the region's tribal nations and culture—so much so, the young author had taken to checking off bits of information that already made their way into his fiction. "Apache [will] arrange rocks in such a way in a wide circle around him, so that anyone approaching will dislodge the rocks and give himself away," he'd noted from the January issue of *Arizona Highways*, continuing, "[It is] generally, asserted that boys captured from a civilized race and brought up by Indians became more dangerous and greater enemies than the Indians"—the latter a theme Leonard would use in multiple story arcs.[4] Regardless, the two quickly reconciled, with Harper inquiring at the month's end, "Have you stopped writing or are you on vacation again?"—unaware of the longer hours Leonard had been pulling in order to work on his larger manuscript.

Leonard completed "Under the Friar's Ledge" on July 1 and sent it to Harper along with another story, "Long Night," that featured no Apaches, sheriffs, scouts, or outlaws; *Zane Grey*'s editor asked Leonard to cut two pages, then bought it for May the following year. However, on September 1, *Life* magazine published a story that would immediately pivot Leonard's themes and the economy of his prose—Ernest Hemingway's comeback novella, *The Old Man and the Sea*. In it, Hemingway had used his "iceberg theory" style of minimalism to the max, stripping his narrative nearly to the bone to tell the seemingly simple story of an old Cuban fisherman and his existential battle with a large, prized marlin. The fifty-three-year-old author had pumped out his first draft of just over twenty thousand words in only six weeks and, upon its publication in *Life* magazine, the novella had restored his reputation as a master of American literature. In May the following year, it was awarded the Pulitzer Prize for Fiction.

Heavily inspired by Hemingway's latest, Leonard studied it closely and immediately began his own experiment in minimalism. He crafted his own simple Western tale wherein the characters' true motives of honor and personal sacrifice would be displayed through dialogue and actions, described in even fewer adjectives and adverbs than his previous works. In only a few days, he had outlined the tale of one man's duty to escort a captured fugitive to the scheduled train to Yuma prison. At dawn, lawman Paul Scallen and outlaw Jim Kidd bunker down in a hotel room and watch the clock tick toward the time of the train's arrival—ten after three in the afternoon. Having already resisted every one of Kidd's attempts at bribery and intimidation, Scallen watches from the hotel window as the members of Kidd's gang gather outside, ready to make their move.

"I got your new short yesterday and will get it read today," Harper wrote on August 28, apparently more interested in Leonard's novel. "How about going ahead with something else until I write you about this?" According to Harper, although the book seemed to be on a wobbly start, she had had the confidence in Leonard to offer the book, sight unseen, to Dell editor Don Ward, in the hopes of its acceptance as a serialized magazine tale, leading into a Dell paperback publication.[5] The third week of September, Ward finally offered his feedback on Leonard's sample pages. "There is some good stuff in it but it moves awfully slowly," he had written to Harper. "My feeling is that Leonard might be well advised to try more novelettes before tackling a full-length novel. He certainly has a lot of promise."

By this point, Harper appeared pleased that Leonard had put a substantial dent in a novel at all; she considered showing it to Mike Tilden, who had been more than happy to accept more offbeat work from Leonard in the past.[6] Within the week, Tilden had agreed to read the book's progress, but insisted that, first, Leonard complete his outstanding revisions to "Three-Ten to Yuma." Harper reported, "Mike will buy [it] if you will do a new ending that is more clear and plausible." She offered, "Inject a motive. Establish for the reader did the outlaw turn soft? Was the deputy on the up and up? Pin it down—what happens to Charlie? Spell it out, Mike says, pin it so the reader understands what is happening here." Under Hemingway's spell, Leonard had been deliberately trying not to "spell it out" with the story's climax. However, it was the first time he'd received aggravated feedback from an editor. "Dutch, how can you do this to you and to me?" Tilden had scrawled on the rejected first draft.[7] (Leonard later recalled, "The story was in *Dime Western* . . . I got ninety dollars for it. The editor insisted I rewrite one of the scenes and do two revisions on my description of the train. He said, 'You can do it better. You're not using all your senses. It's not just a walk by the locomotive. What's the train doing? How does it smell? Is there steam?'"[8])

Leonard completed his revisions the following day.[9] Looking back on it later, he admitted the value in the lesson he'd learned. "[Tilden] made me work for my ninety bucks—which was good. It was in the magazine and then, within a year, a producer saw it and bought it."[10]

Harper continued to work with Leonard on his drafts of the newly retitled *The Crosses of Las Olivas* as she juggled her own hectic schedule. In April, she had forfeited her Manhattan apartment after twenty-one years, opting for a more affordable place in New Rochelle, while also maintaining a small space at 50 East Forty-Second Street for her daily mail and messages. "Best of all," she wrote, "it's across the street from the Grand Central, to which I must commute and close to all the publishers—or most of them."[11] Indeed, Harper was situated directly next door to Little, Brown—which was currently looking for a new Western author to add to their own roster. Seizing the opportunity to hype her clients, Harper quickly met with their editor, John Woodburn, who was already familiar with Leonard's short story work. However, the publisher was interested only if Leonard would be willing to shelve his in-progress novel for a pumped-up version of "Trail of the Apache."[12] It was a tempting offer, yet Leonard opted to complete his nearly completed *The Crosses of Las Olivas*. He instead took Harper's earlier advice on subplots and character conflict, and soon brought those elements to the novel's third act.

Aside from her first choice, Little, Brown, Harper also gave paperback competitor Gold Medal until the end of the month for a response before walking to their offices and personally demanding one.[13] On November 5, associate editor Richard E. Roberts notified her that head editor William Lengel had, indeed, read the book and, like Little, Brown, required revisions. "Mr. Lengel tells me . . . if it is as successful as we think it will be, he will be glad to issue a contract with an advance," Roberts wrote. ". . . [Leonard's] writing shows a great deal of promise and we think he can produce a very good Gold Medal book."[14]

Before a decision could be made, however, Harper wrote Leonard with a startling update: Little, Brown's John Woodburn had suddenly died of a heart attack. With Gold Medal now their most viable option, she explained their offer of two thousand dollars based on paperback royalties: "I think these paper cover deals are wise ones for authors . . . If you would wish it, though, we can still go after a hardcover publisher. That decision is up to you. There is prestige still in hardcover books. The difference is that then you must split all paper cover money 50–50 with the hardcover publisher."[15]

Leonard ultimately agreed to make the revisions that so many editors had suggested to him. "I wasn't sure I wanted to go on [with it]," he later recalled. "I rewrote the first chapter four times."[16] But from then until the end of the year, he worked on little else, meticulously writing and rewriting portions—taking a particularly long amount of time perfecting the third act, which Harper was champing at the bit to receive. Just after the first of the year, she hammered the point home: "Whatever happened to the 100 pages you were going to send me??????" Harper had since gotten back the manuscript from Gold Medal and, apparently, William Lengel was enthusiastic about the material. In the interim, yet another publisher had shown interest—Western Publishing, which hoped to serialize it in their monthly, *Western Magazine*, then collaborate with Dell for a paperback release. However, Leonard used the rest of 1953 to make good on his promise of keeping a current byline, juggling new stories with the ongoing rewrites of *The Crosses of Las Olivas*. That April, he finished "A

Matter of Duty," run as "The Last Shot" by *Fifteen Western Tales*, and the following month, "Rich Miller's Hand" was sold to *Western Story Magazine* and run as "Blood Money." The month after that, Leonard completed "Rindo's Station," which finally brought him back to *Argosy*. After using much of the summer months to work on his novel, he nonetheless completed another story, "The Woman from Tascosa," in September.

Midway through the process, Leonard learned what would be, perhaps, the most important lesson in his lifelong productivity when he expanded his morning routine to a full-time 5 a.m. schedule. He later remembered: "Most of the writing was done at night, but with the TV and kids, it took eight months to do the first half of the book. Then I did some early-morning writing and the second half only took eight weeks."[17]

He and Beverly also learned something else: they were going to be parents again.

Leonard wrapped up his revisions by the first week of May. In total, he'd rewritten more than thirty thousand words, delighting Harper, who called it "a great improvement." She added, "I am very keen on it. After talking about you and about the novel, before it came, to Houghton Mifflin and Ballantine, I submitted it to them for their joint venture."

In a similar fashion to Western Publishing's initial plan to partner with Dell for a serialization-to-paperback business strategy, Harper's new leads had partnered for a simultaneous hardcover *and* paperback release of specific genre titles.[18] While Leonard cranked out the final pages of the manuscript, Harper met with Houghton Mifflin to discuss the pages he had already completed; however, they, too, had revision requests of their own. "Now I could go elsewhere with this story," she wrote, "but I think it would be advantageous for you to tie-up with this [Houghton Mifflin–Ballantine] set-up," Harper wrote. "How about finishing it as quickly as you can and letting [Houghton Mifflin] see it as a finished product? You could write some shorts in between for dough."[19] At that, Leonard continued to revise the book while averaging a new short story per month.

On September 10, Harper was finally able to secure Leonard's formal contract with Houghton Mifflin, getting the first-time novelist a three-thousand-dollar advance—a thousand more than Gold Medal's offer and nearly his full annual pay at Campbell-Ewald. In an arrangement that would become boilerplate to Leonard, it would be split three ways:

a third upon signing, another upon completion, and the last upon publication; since Leonard was near completing the book anyway, Harper assured him that he would be able to collect the second installment relatively quickly and, as a "rush job," he could collect the full amount within three or four months. However, she added that Gold Medal had also circled back an offer—a flat three thousand for everything up front. "But if you don't need money fast," she countered, "it becomes a case of whether you would like the combination publication. [Houghton Mifflin] is one of the top publishers, and if this paper thing ever blows up, you would still have a publisher."[20]

> About a month after finishing the book, a letter came from my agent. Bev picked up the mail, called me at work, and read the letter over the telephone. Houghton Mifflin had agreed to publish. That was a big day . . .
>
> The contract came shortly after. I read it—all four pages and even the small print—as soon as I got home that day. In fact, I think I signed it before taking off my hat and coat.[21]

For all of Leonard's growing pains with the book, he had benefited tremendously by the rapid turnaround. His latest draft was not only accepted, but he also heard from his new publisher within days[22] and had the galley proofs by the end of the month. Finally, he was formally introduced to the first book editor with whom he'd be working, Austin Olney. "We are all very enthusiastic about the book here and are pleased to have it on our spring list," Olney wrote on October 30. "I hope that you will like the looks of the type and will find proofreading a pleasant task." Hoping for a January release, Olney also returned to Leonard his original manuscript and a set of instructions to read it and have it returned to him as soon as possible.[23] He was also told that a new title would be needed. Leonard chose *The Bounty Hunters*.

Only three days later, Olney wrote to Elmore again, sending along the description of *The Bounty Hunters* for use in the publisher's spring bulletin and advising him it "will probably be used on the jacket flaps of the hardbound edition." He added, "If you'd like any revisions in it, now is the time."[24] The editor wasn't exaggerating: Houghton Mifflin publicist Constance Decker Rogers had mock-ups for the book's dust jacket copy the same day, imploring Leonard to proofread it just as quickly. "We go to press on the jacket very soon," she wrote.[25] By the end of that week, Leonard heard the words from Harper that he'd dreamed of since being a child "telling movies" on the street corner to his friends: "Have some movie interest here in NY," she wrote—cautiously adding, "though usually one can discount any NY interest as 99% of it is done in California."[26]

In her last letter of 1953, Harper made a resolution for both of them, writing, "Have a Happy New Year and let's resolve to make some real money from writing."[27]

While still working on more stories to submit to Harper, Leonard had already begun outlining a follow-up novel—tentatively entitled *The Devil at Randado*—and hinted at its existence to Olney. In return, the editor had asked for first-look rights twice before *The Bounty Hunters* had even been published.[28] On January 8—a day Leonard later admitted he'd never forget—he finally held the contributor copies of his first novel in his hands. "Dear Mr. Leonard," Olney wrote in the accompanying letter, "I am very glad to send you, hot off the press, copies of the hard and paperbound editions of *The Bounty Hunters*."[29]

Both editions featured different, yet similar cover art—colorful illustrations of the titular heroes on horseback against the Western skyline. There would be no more "E. J. Leonard" or "Dutch" on any professional bylines; on the back of the hardcover's dust jacket was *Elmore Leonard*'s publicity photo for the first time, boldly grayscaled to a cool bluish tinge.

The following Tuesday, Leonard's first novel met the public. "Our publicity department tells me that review copies have been sent to papers all over the country, especially to the *Detroit Free Press* and the *Detroit News*," Olney notified Leonard on January 15. "Reviews are often a long time coming out, but I think you can hope for a pretty fair sampling across the country . . . Happy Publication Day!"[30]

His first-ever review was positive, although somewhat mixed: "A better than average Western, and a bit more complicated," ran Boston's *Sunday Globe*, "this is a story of the last days of the Apache, and the last days of many a white when ruthless hunters collected whites' scalps also for the Mexican bounty . . . The story moves, but the heroics are not overdone."[31] Only days later, the first glowing words came out of an Alabama daily—seemingly praising Leonard's own brand of lean prose and minimalist leanings, a Hemingway takeaway: "There is something new under the sun," the review began. "For here is a book that, in one reviewer's opinion, is better entertainment than the 'blurb' on the jacket would lead one to believe. It is a first novel that holds the reader's interest unwaveringly, freed completely of over-writing."[32]

From the beginning, it appeared as though even the most discerning of reviewers saw the potential in Leonard's writing, with the *News-Herald* in Hutchinson, Kansas, declaring, "Lovers of Western fiction will find a bright new champion in Elmore Leonard, who has finished his first novel, *The Bounty Hunters* . . . This book will turn up on film before too long, probably with tough-guy Alan Ladd cast as the scout."[33] But perhaps the most memorable review Leonard received for his first novel—the one he continued to quote for the rest of his career—came from Hoffman Birney at the *New York Times*: "A first novel and a good one," the critic had written.[34]

With those types of strong reviews forming a consensus among the critics who read Westerns—and with another baby on the way—one thing became apparent to Leonard: he had, indeed, been underpaid working "traffic" at Campbell-Ewald. After two and a half years, he left the agency for a smaller one "to learn the advertising business," as he would later tell biographer Paul Challen.[35] No more booking travel plans and itineraries for executives, or filing the expense accounts and invoices of high-level copywriters; in his new position, Leonard was finally allowed to write copy of his own. He'd only had to become a published author for the opportunity. But along with the prestige of advancement, Leonard also gained a substantial pay raise with his new employer—as well as a master class in small business operation, which he would later use as a high-paid freelancer. "I was impressed with the whole operation for a while," he later claimed. "It paid the bills while I was learning how to write fiction."[36]

With the publication of *The Bounty Hunters* came another exciting "first" for the Leonard family, when Elmore, Beverly, and even little Jane and Peter were visited by Bill Rabe from the *Detroit Free Press* for a full two-page spread. The feature story, "A Detroiter Tells: How to Be an Author," included staged re-creations of important moments from the novel's journey from conception to print—Elmore, Beverly, and the kids playfully posing in the living room, in the kitchen, and even at the mailbox to dramatize the "big day" when Beverly retrieved the Houghton Mifflin contract. For the photo op, Beverly curled her hair and Elmore—for the one and only time—donned his fedora to look far more mature than his twenty-nine years. "A novelette sold to *Argosy* over two years ago started all this," Leonard told the *Free Press*. "Since then, about sixteen other stories of mine have been accepted by various Western magazines." He walked the reporter through the process of typesetting and proofreading of the finished novel, although he later told biographer Paul Challen, "I found myself X-ing out more than I was writing and I thought, 'This is ridiculous—I should just write it out in longhand and *then* type it.' And that is what I'm still doing."[37]

In conjunction with Leonard's debut, the *Detroit Times* even booked an interview at the family's home—sans the author himself, instead focusing on Beverly and the two children. "Though she's frank to admit that Western movies are not exactly her favorite entertainment, Beverly Leonard probably has seen more of them than most women," wrote Jean Whitehead. "She is the wife of Elmore 'Dutch' Leonard, whose first book, *The Bounty Hunters*, was published last month." Posing with little Peter in a cowboy outfit—shotgun included—while clutching Janie beside her, Beverly detailed her courtship with Leonard, as well as the process of living with a working professional novelist: "Going to the movies or watching Western films on TV comes under the classification of 'research,'" she told the *Detroit Times*. "You know, when Dutch and I were married in 1949, I'm afraid I didn't take his writing very seriously. Then came the day two years later when I found the letter from *Argosy* magazine in our mailbox saying they were going to print Dutch's first story." Beverly told the reporter that living with Leonard was, usually, "easy as pie," continuing, "I usually have dinner ready when he comes home—he's a copywriter for an ad agency—[and] after he tucks Janie and Peter in bed, he sets up his typewriter on the dining room table, and nothing seems to bother him, unless he's working out something particularly tricky . . . I do help him choose the names for his characters sometimes. We often use those of our friends, or else resort to the phone book his parents once sent from New Mexico, for ideas." She added, "Occasionally, Dutch will hand me a page or two for my opinion of something he's uncertain about. But most of the time, I wait until they're in print to read his stories."

The *Times* concluded, "The Leonards are now taking conversational Spanish in preparation for a visit to Mexico and the country that has been Dutch's inspiration."[38] With the book completed and in stores, Leonard was fast to look at the experience retrospectively. Staged in the living room in a look of repose—feet up, a hardcover of *The Bounty Hunters* open in his lap—Leonard offered his final thoughts: "Looking at the book now, bound and dust-jacketed, I wonder why it took so long to write. That's what I'm doing, wondering."[39]

Elmore and Beverly Leonard welcomed their third child, and second son, Christopher Conway Leonard on May 12, 1954. At the time, Leonard was already putting the finishing touches on his first draft of *The Devil at Randado*. Only two days before Beverly went into labor, editor Austin Olney had written that he had conferred with Houghton Mifflin's New York editor, Julien McKee, about the material, and both were excited to see the manuscript.[40] By the end of the summer, the novel was complete, fully copyedited, and sent off to Houghton Mifflin's production department. Olney wrote on August 5, "As you know, I had a few reservations, but in spite of them, I think it's an even better book than *The Bounty Hunters* and I have great faith in your future as a novelist . . . Julien tells me that you're hatching a new title."[41]

Following the good reviews and consistent sales of *The Bounty Hunters*, Marguerite Harper had been able to negotiate for Leonard a second contract for the same money—three thousand dollars—but, with Leonard's track record for meeting deadlines, only two installments: half upon signing, half on publication day.[42] By the end of September, Leonard had the galley proofs for the newly retitled *The Law at Randado* completed and returned. "I wish all our authors were so prompt," Olney wrote. But he added some suggestions for the next book—especially when it came to Leonard's predominant dependency on realistic dialogue to carry his scenes. "Certainly, in writing a story the author should not intrude himself too much and let the action develop naturally and the characters explain themselves," the editor wrote, "but dialogue can be as artificial a device as asides to the reader . . . I think anything you do too self-consciously is liable to be less convincing and I have the feeling that you are a natural writer."[43]

For his second novel, Leonard had built upon many of the more progressive themes and scenarios that had populated his early short stories. The first book had shown a unique empathy toward both the indigenous and Mexican communities portrayed within the story, and Leonard set his next one among the same landscape—including the bias and racial tensions that often ran rampant in small Old West towns. And much like what was then considered the gold standard of Western literature—Walter Van Tilburg Clark's 1940 bestselling morality tale, *The Ox-Bow Incident*—Leonard centered the story's drama around a racially motivated lynching. (Leonard had seen William Wellman's cinematic adaptation while serving in the Seabees and considered it one of his favorites.[44]) In this instance, the idealistic young deputy Kirby Frye is mocked and prevented from serving justice against a murderous, bigoted battle baron, Phil Sundeen, and his posse of bloodthirsty civic leaders for an illegal lynching. Leonard's novel opens with a pair of cattle rustlers captured while both Randado's sheriff, John Danaher, and deputy Frye are away on respective trips. In their absence, a self-appointed "committee" of wealthy townsfolk, led by Sundeen, take it upon themselves to craft a kangaroo court and sentence the town's two prisoners to death. Impatient to execute the suspected rustlers, the mob doesn't wait for the local lawmen to return. The lynching itself—from the mob's decision to enact their personal justice to the final moment the two prisoners hang—is presented long and meticulously, Leonard using otherwise common details such as types of rope and knots, to chilling, realistic effect. When Frye returns and learns what has happened, he is understandably furious. It is then that Sundeen himself instigates the public shaming of Kirby Frye, bringing both his authority and very manhood into question. "Now if it was me," says Sundeen, "I wouldn't pick a deputy that whined like a woman."[45] Against the advice of the townspeople, Frye attempts to arrest the wealthy Sundeen for his role as ringleader—but instead is beaten to a pulp and, in a last act of humiliation, stripped of his pants. (Leonard would revisit this scenario, as well as its moral implications, numerous times over the course of his Western career.) The novel's second half chronicles the young man's revenge against Sundeen and his men.

Leonard had not so much recycled his favorite themes from previous stories but, as future work would demonstrate, had begun to refine what he deemed most important. Young Kirby Frye, while not necessarily Christ-like in his choice of profession and willingness to kill in the line of duty, is nonetheless the first of numerous heroic martyrs the author would create. When reflecting on the attributes that Frye had demonstrated and contributed to his position as deputy, Sheriff John Danaher admires that the young man is "sensitive without being emotional, that he was respectful without being servile, and that he was a man who would follow what his conscience told him ninety-nine percent of the time"—all qualities Leonard would later bestow on his ideal protagonists, heroes and criminals alike.

By the end of 1954, Leonard's status as a novelist had taken noticeable precedence over his short story output. Houghton Mifflin's rapid turnaround had led directly into a second book, and those two advances had paid far better than the magazines. To Leonard, focusing on novels just seemed to make more financial sense.

However, Marguerite Harper remained adamant on two points: that Leonard maintain a current byline and—of greater importance—that his portfolio desperately needed non-Western work. It was a genre, she insisted, that would soon be on a greater decline. For his part, Leonard did attempt non-Western stories on occasion, largely inspired by the popular authors he enjoyed—Hemingway and John O'Hara among them—but almost always to a disappointing response. As a back-up strategy, Harper submitted those of his Western stories she deemed particularly worthy to the higher-tiered slicks—also almost always to a negative response from their editors. "I was disappointed by rejections from the better-paying magazines—the *Saturday Evening Post* and *Colliers*," Leonard later remembered. "They felt my stories were too relentless and lacked lighter moments or comic relief. But I continued to write what pleased me while trying to improve my style."[46] Retrospectively, however, he admitted the literary expectations that the Western dictated. "I wasn't writing *Range Romance*. I was writing action stories, six-guns going off, violence a natural part of it, the reason for reading a Western," he added. "Later, I developed ways of having the violence happen more unexpectedly and low-key—'*And he shot him*.'"[47]

Although Leonard was discouraged, Harper's strategy would eventually pay off in equal measure. His style and assurance as a storyteller had steadily improved with each short story and revision; his novels, however, had benefited from the experimentation more so than his stream of salable stories. He had branched out with characterizations and downplayed the Western tropes that Harper and his editors had long warned of overusing; regardless, many of his most recent stories had been initially rejected before finding success with one or another pulp: "The Gift of Regalo" had finally been accepted by *Western Short Stories* and changed to "The Kid," and one of Harper's least favorites among Leonard's stories, the semisupernatural tale "The Nagual," had finally sold to *Two-Gun Western* after other attempts elsewhere. (Leonard had been saving the concept of a "nagual"—a "*person in the form of an animal*" out of Apache folklore—as a potential story idea within his ledger for years.[48])

Leonard was specifically keen that Harper place "The Hanging of Bobby Valdez," another morality tale, for two reasons: although its protagonist would later be de-aged, "Bobby Valdez" was a character with whom Leonard was still experimenting for future use, and the story's "hanging" scene was a literary point of pride, which had been a product of his initial research for the still in-progress *The Law at Randado*. "After so long, [I] have finally sold 'The Hanging of Bobby Valdez' to *Argosy* for five hundred," Harper wrote at the end of January, suggesting that Leonard do a "quick cut" of his new novel in the hopes of pitching it as a serial to one of the slicks. She wrote, "One of the good [magazines] is looking for a thirty thousand worder—Western acceptable . . . Maybe you could let me see what you have so far?"[49] Unfortunately, *The Law at Randado* was still far from the stage of completion that the unnamed *Saturday Evening Post* required. However, Harper's faith in his abilities and her belief that he could, in fact, make the cut for the *Post* motivated Leonard to reconsider writing a few *literary* Western stories, should such an opportunity arise again.

In between completed Western stories or larger projects, and almost always under the influence of a newly discovered author to appreciate, Leonard continued to take additional stabs at the type of satirical domestic vignettes associated with John O'Hara, Roald Dahl, and John Cheever. Once the galley proofs for *The Law at Randado* were completed, Leonard had quickly penned "Arma Virumque Cano"—the satire of an unsuspecting husband robbed by the pretty, teenage hitchhiker he'd offered a ride home from school. Somewhat cryptically, Leonard had cribbed the story's title from Virgil's epic poem, the *Aeneid*—the translation meaning "Of arms and the man I sing"—one of his mandatory readings while at the University of Detroit.

Another contemporary non-Western, "The Italian Cut," followed soon after, a story built almost entirely on the dialogue between a young married couple in the throes of a heated, alcohol-infused argument. Both stories—as well as a later tale of a would-be adulterer on a business trip,

"Evenings Away from Home"—contained those touches of the contemporary scribes Leonard followed.

The year 1954 continued to be one of experimentation for Leonard, as he also made his first attempts to break into different mediums. In April, he wrote a fifteen-page outline for a proposed television movie-of-the-week—an espionage thriller, rather than a Western. Using memories of his time in the Pacific Theater, Leonard set the action of *Malaya* among the political goings-on at a resettlement camp in the Malay Peninsula. Although Leonard was inexperienced in writing or formatting a Hollywood treatment, it was a skill set he would master in the years to come. His research had revealed the requirement of approximately one page per minute of screen time, and his writing technique was already dependent enough upon setting and dialogue to carry the fifty-eight-scene outline as if by an experienced screenwriter.

Most importantly, Leonard's use of a present-tense narrative style would later become a signature of his contemporary crime "sound": "*Peter Flood, slouched in a chair with his feet on the desk in Bong Haw's library, a drink in one hand, the telephone in the other. He is talking to Singapore, trying to arrange a flight home to England in a shorter time than is ordinarily required.*"[50]

Even at this early stage, Leonard had sound reason to be eyeing Hollywood. His first book had already raised eyebrows among film executives in New York, and most importantly, Harper had recently mentioned her association with Los Angeles–based agent Harold Norling "H. N." Swanson—legendary around Hollywood for his elite roster of clients. "Swanie," as he was affectionately known, had had a career in the movie business almost as long as the industry existed, and, in 1924, he had even recommended to one famous client that he reconsider the name of his most recent manuscript. Leonard, always amused at the anecdote, later recalled, "He told a writer he represented named Fitzgerald he didn't like the title *East Egg*. 'Change it to *The Great Gatsby*.'" Over the ensuing years, Swanson had gone on to close the film deals for James M. Cain's *The Postman Always Rings Twice,* Raymond Chandler's *The Big Sleep,* and John O'Hara's *Butterfield 8*—all box office hits that had been unceremoniously respectful of their source material. Having collaborated with Swanson to sell a few stories by client Luke Short to television, Harper hoped the high-powered agent could help Leonard achieve the same type of success. Unfortunately, neither *Malaya* nor *The Bounty Hunters* proved salable. "I haven't been intentionally avoiding your query about the movie interest," Harper wrote on November 5. "Swanie reported from Hollywood that he followed it up and that it amounted to nothing worthwhile. There are a number of people in Hollywood, usually they are lawyers who try to acquire movie rights for clients on a straight percentage basis. They are usually considered too questionable to pay any attention to at all."[51] Undaunted, however, Harper kept at her diligence. Only a few months later, she reported, "Kirk Douglas['s] studio was very much interested in *Law at Randado* but decided on some other story."[52]

Leonard shelved the unsold *Malaya* outline for short story fodder, later rewriting it as the politically charged "Time of Terror" and adding an action-packed climax featuring a former race car driver turned officer using his skills behind the wheel to prevent the rebel coup. Most surprising, it was around that same time that Leonard made his one and only attempt at writing for the daily comics, writing thirty-six installments of a proposed comic strip. At one page per daily episode, *Bowie Kidd*, as it was called, chronicled the adventures of its titular protagonist—"Twenty-one years old, sandy-haired, slim-hipped, a little above average height." Kidd is a heroic scout, born and raised in the Arizona Territory. "He has been a cowboy, dispatch rider and a guide for the army (civilian contract scout), and is the latter when the story opens," Leonard wrote in his pitch. "He knows all about the Apache, even some of their dialects, and can read sign like an Indian." Kidd's chief personality traits, however, seemed accurately in-line with his creator: "Speaks Spanish, too, which is not really unusual. He's an all-around cool customer, but not a show-off type. Boyish smile, easy to like, soft spoken. People, especially those who oppose him, tend to underestimate him."

The Law at Randado was released in hardcover by Houghton Mifflin in January, with Dell's paperback edition slated for a summer release. The early reviews for his second endeavor set the stage for another productive year: "Elmore Leonard's second novel keeps to the high standard set by his first," wrote Nolan Sanford in the *Houston Chronicle*. "This sort of novel is true to life as it was in the Old West . . . For every rootin' tootin' officer-killer like Wild Bill, there were a hundred like Kirby Frye. And it was the Kirby Frye-type who really settled down the lawless element . . . Leonard's Westerns are to be classed as historical fiction. His manner of presenting a story leaves nothing to be desired in suspense, action, and authentic atmosphere."[53] A brief review that ran in the *Oakland Tribune* also noted the deliberate slow build with which Leonard had constructed the story's climax, stating: "A hard, grim story is told in a tight, quiet manner and builds like a snowball rolling downhill."[54]

Although not as elaborate or space-consuming as the two-page spread dedicated to *The Bounty Hunters*, the *Detroit Free Press* again turned its gaze upon the local boy made good with a quarter-page article on Leonard's sophomore release. "Writing novels at twenty-nine years old, a Lathrup Village author takes the West as his setting and sells the books on the East coast, although he has been neither East nor West," the feature read, printed below a large portrait of Leonard, in tie and shirtsleeves, at his Royal portable. "But the subject matter and good characterization seem to carry the stories for Elmore Leonard." The *Free Press* had interviewed both the Leonards for the piece, with Beverly playfully recounting how she had taken only one stab at typing one of her husband's manuscripts. "It took about a week to do one page," she told the reporter, "so I gave up. I have enough to do taking care of the three children."

The article went on, "[Leonard's] writing is done with considerable research, making up for lack of on-the-spot observations . . . [And] just written is a quarter of a book, which he sent last week to his agent with an outline of the rest of the book. If publishers are interested, he will complete it this winter."[55]

Houghton Mifflin was, indeed, interested in the next book—and as soon as possible. Rising to the challenge, Leonard had *Escape from Five Shadows* nearly completed by the time the paperback of *The Law at Randado* was released in June.

Leonard had found another reason to use plenty of his Spanish.

In August, Harper sold to *Argosy* what would prove to be one of the most important stories of Leonard's early career: a seven-chapter novelette entitled "The Hostages." Its title changed to "The Captives" for the magazine's February 1955 issue, the story was almost immediately scouted for serious film consideration.

For the story, Leonard built heavily on the theme that seemed to most resonate with him since childhood: cowardice versus heroism. He wrote of an everyman, Pat Brennan, who manages to grab a lift to Bisbee aboard a chartered Hatch & Hodges stagecoach—only for it to be hijacked by outlaw Frank Usher and his murderous goons, Billy-Jack and Chink. In an effort to save his own life, fellow passenger Williard Mims covertly suggests to the gang that they, instead, hold his wealthy wife, Doretta, for ransom. They do, yet kill the man out of disgust, leaving Brennan to save his fellow hostages. In true Western fashion, Brennan overcomes the gang and makes off with Mims's widow.

By the following summer, however, Leonard's novels had taken priority; he was already deep into his third book before *The Law at Randado* had even been released. "Dear Dutch—Julien and I have both read the first 112 pages of *Escape from Five Shadows* and so far we like it a lot," Austin Olney wrote on April 27. "So far, I think the story has more unity and consequently more intensity than in your previous books and I am looking forward very much to seeing the rest."[56] In June, however, Harper also sold Leonard's first Western short story in six months, "The Boy from Dos Cabezas" to *Western Magazine*, which ran it as "Jugged" another six months later. In the accompanying check, Harper enclosed the sum from two anthologies that had both selected different stories of Leonard's for inclusion in upcoming titles: "Trouble at Rindo's Station" and "Saint with a Six-Gun" for Bantam's *The Old West*, and "You Never See Apaches" for the same publisher's aptly titled *Cattle, Guns and Men*.[57]

But even with two novels down and a third on the way—as well as a full portfolio of short stories, some of which were already being reprinted—it wasn't one of Leonard's bylines that proved an accurate prediction of things to come: "*Here are twenty-six men and women*," the full-page advertisement read in *The New Yorker* that June, the text printed over a group shot reminiscent of a class picture—all the subjects clean-cut in office attire. "*They are the copy department at Campbell-Ewald's Detroit headquarters office. Their average age is 34 (not counting the head man, back row center!). Examine them carefully one by one, or give them the once over treatment of a professional sizer-upper . . . Without such leadership, talent withers. With it, talent bursts and blooms . . . and form . . . naturally . . . believably . . . and become a credit to the profession of advertising and to the job of selling.*"[58]

The advertisement's headline: "*Most Likely to Succeed.*"

Bottom row, fourth from the left: Elmore "Dutch" Leonard.

CHAPTER 6

Chevys and Hollywood, 1955–1961

I found out what kind of coffee cowboys liked and the guns they favored, wrote only Westerns through the '50s, sold thirty short stories, five novels, and made a couple of sales to Hollywood—*3:10 to Yuma* and *The Tall T*—while I was writing Chevrolet ads to make a living . . .

People at signings ask if I'll ever write another one. I say probably not.

Marguerite Harper's June report that earlier attempts to sell *Five Shadows* as a serial to the *Saturday Evening Post* had reached a dead end was easily overshadowed by her significantly better update regarding the movie rights to the novelette "The Captives." She wrote, "My Hollywood representative, [H. N.] Swanson, has sold the picture rights to a new, small producing group consisting of, I think, a brother of John Wayne's."[1] By August, she circled back with the contract.[2]

Harper had included a warning to the excited author, however: "I do hope you aren't going to make the mistake that so many authors make when they get a movie sale . . . It is very easy to lose the driving force that I think an author must keep alive—must exercise—in order to have a fertile mind for ideas. You are young—and you have a family—and it would be nice to be able to increase your income from writing so that you might get some trust funds or annuities going."[3] She also warned him that payment could take months, which it did, arriving in October.

Harper kept the momentum going that same month by fulfilling her second promise to Leonard, landing one of his recent stories in the ever-elusive *Saturday Evening Post*. "The price is $850.00 and they will pay a thousand for the next one they accept—the next short," she wrote. "This pleases me a lot. It means much to get in the *Post*."[4]

Although Leonard had assigned most of his focus throughout the second half of 1955 to finishing *Escape from Five Shadows*, his own promise to submit more literary Westerns—especially those with less action and more female characters—had come to fruition with "The Waiting Man," completed earlier that same month. With the story, he had kept his eye on an upper-echelon publication, where a flat fee was paid for quality of any length; likewise, Leonard geared the story toward Harper's ongoing pleas for more romantic subplots and diverse character types—here using only the threat of violence and a stoic female lead to retooling a "Romeo and Juliet"-like forbidden romance as the starting point of a revenge tale. The story's eponymous "waiting man" is Phil Treat, a former soldier and hunter who—much like Jimmy Ringo in Leonard's beloved *The Gunfighter*—has an unfortunate reputation as a retired quick-draw artist. Having run away and married the daughter of his cattle-baron employer, Treat has come under the ire of the old man, now finding his modest homestead with wife Ellis under constant harassment by his wealthy father-in-law and his men.

Harper sold the story just in time for Leonard's thirtieth birthday.

Along with Hemingway (with whom he'd begun to find "limitations," including an apparent "lack of humor") Leonard soon discovered another lifelong influence in obscure American author Richard Bissell—stylistically similar to Leonard's ideal authorial voice. He later explained, "There's a line from Mark Twain, through Stephen Crane to Hemingway, and I learnt from Hemingway—but the man I studied, too, was Richard Bissell, who was the only American writer since Mark Twain to have a pilot's license on the Mississippi."

Much of Bissell's use of dialogue and easygoing sense of humor resonated with Leonard. Born in Dubuque, Iowa, in 1913 and ultimately attaining a degree in anthropology from Harvard University, Bissell had used his experiences working in his father's garment factory to write a humorous 1953 novel about a workers' strike, *7½ Cents*. It sold to Hollywood as the musical *The Pajama Game* and won the young author a Tony Award. Earlier in his youth, however, Bissell had worked his way up from deckhand to captain of riverboats, which fueled his follow-up novel—and Leonard's personal favorite—*High Water: A Novel of Adventure on a Mississippi River Towboat*.[5] But much like his youthful discovery of Ernest Hemingway and recent appreciation of Richard Bissell, a new book by old favorite John Steinbeck would further enhance Leonard's development. "It was one book in particular, *Sweet Thursday*, published in 1954, that did the job," he later wrote, enamored with how Steinbeck's marine scientist Doc performs every conceivable excuse *not* to sit and write, such as sharpening every pencil in his mug and feeding the building's rats. "It amazed me that a writer as renowned as Steinbeck knew the tricks of putting off writing," Leonard elaborated. "It encouraged me that it was part of writing and not a disease." But a different passage in the novel's prologue would stay with Leonard indefinitely: Steinbeck, playfully breaking the fourth wall, offered his own term for the pretentious tendencies to show off through exposition—"*Hooptedoodle.*"[6]

That summer, Leonard also saved an article sent by Harper from the July issue of *Author & Journalist*—a monthly trade magazine aimed at the pulp industry and its freelancers. He kept in his ledger "From Idea to Plot," by Wilfred McCormick—a motivational essay for novice writers on how to make time for writing. McCormick went on to enumerate twenty-two rhetorical questions, each one designed to enhance a prospective author's focus on moving the story forward.

From McCormick's list, Leonard circled only one: "*From what different viewpoints might this story be told?*"[7]

By the end of 1955, Leonard had his weekday morning regimen down to a science: up at five o'clock sharp for two hours of uninterrupted writing (still two pages completed before putting the water on for his morning coffee), then showered and suited up for the office—ready to wolf down breakfast and help Beverly feed Jane, Peter, and infant Christopher—then receive the Eucharist during eight o'clock Mass. Finally, he arrived at Campbell-Ewald by nine.

With his third novel—the in-progress *Escape from Five Shadows*—Leonard was taking his first stab at the brutal dynamic between prisoners and their oppressive jailers. In this instance, Corey Bowen—falsely accused of horse theft—is sentenced to eight years' hard time on Frank Renda's nearby Five Shadows labor camp. With only the help of love interest Karla Demery—who is working to attain for Bowen a new trial—and Lizann Falvey—the warden's frustrated wife who secretly hopes Bowen will assist in her husband's murder—the hero spends the majority of the novel plotting numerous suspenseful escape attempts from Renda's clutches, all with varied degrees of success.

With *Five Shadows*, Leonard had the confidence to break away from the perspective of his chief protagonist for more extended periods of the story, fleshing out the motivations and behaviors of even his most diabolical antagonists.[8] His chapters now alternated among the various perspectives of his supporting characters, giving his fiction, for the first time, the feel of an interconnecting plot containing an ensemble of characters. In the end, Bowen indeed makes his escape from the hellish Five Shadows camp, and the climactic showdown sees Renda's hired gang from the Mimbres Valley lower their Springfield rifles to Bowen, having changed sides and leaving the villain both unarmed and unmanned. In the end, an exhausted Bowen returns to Karla Demery, presumably to settle down, his life as an escaped convict happily behind him. Leonard's denouement especially pleased Harper and, by September 14, Austin Olney—equally pleased—wrote that the manuscript was already being put into galleys, with an aim on a spring release.[9]

With Leonard's reputation as a Western author growing, Campbell-Ewald saw fit to match Leonard with their truck division, writing copy geared toward the same rough-and-tumble demographic that, essentially, would read like a Western paperback. "Truck ads I had an easier time with," he later admitted. "You could be straightforward with a truck . . . I've never been any good at similes and metaphors."[10] Much like his father before him, Leonard was soon sent traveling around the country for company "field work," gathering customer testimonials from satisfied truckers. "I would call on the Chevrolet dealer, who would then introduce me to a truck owner who had some fantastic story to tell about his trucks," he would later claim, prompting the owner to "say something colloquial," in the hopes of shaking loose some down-home phrases to tinker with. However, Leonard's favorite—"You don't wear that sonofabitch out, you just get tired of looking at it and buy a new one"—proved too gritty for Chevy.

An earlier trip to Colorado during the winter of 1957 gave Leonard a heavier issue in his personal life to address. "I always took pride in my capacity to drink," he later wrote. "One time, I think it was in Alamosa, I was out for the evening with a trucker." According to Leonard, the evening started as planned, with the two men getting along and plenty of usable material for the truck testimonials adding up nicely. "We were drinking whiskey and we had dinner. We were drinking brandy and beer and he said, 'I haven't met a lowlander yet I didn't have to put to bed.'

Elmore John Leonard Jr., circa 1927, age two.

The future creator of Deputy US Marshal Raylan Givens—seen here in 1929, age four.

During his career-long tenure as a manager and location scout for General Motors, Elmore John Leonard Sr. was forced to transplant his young family repeatedly to match the expansion of the growing automotive industry. For the first few years of his life, young Elmore lived in his birthplace, New Orleans, Louisiana; Dallas, Texas; Oklahoma City, Oklahoma; and Memphis, Tennessee, before settling down in Detroit, Michigan. Seen here, circa 1929: Elmore Sr.; Margaret (or "Mickey"), age nine; and Elmore Jr., age four.

All photographs courtesy of the University of South Carolina Special Collections unless otherwise noted.

University of Detroit High School sophomore portrait, circa 1941, age sixteen.

At only eighteen years old, Leonard became a member of the US Navy "Fighting" Seabees and headed for his tour of duty in the Pacific Theater, circa 1944.

Stationed in Los Negros, Philippines, circa 1944.

First wedding to Beverly Clare Cline, July 30, 1949, with Beverly's aunt Clare Croley (*center*) and witnesses Elaine Watts and John "Jack" Huber.

The day following their wedding, "Dutch" Leonard and his young bride prepare for their honeymoon.

subscription collectors, spies, recruiters, propagandists, couriers and supporters generally.

Inmates stay in Taiping from 2 to 6 months or even longer. Resettlement is considered to be the most important phase of his rehabilitation and it is here that the Malayan Chinese Association gives considerable assistance by finding him work and keeping in close touch with him later.

REFERENCE:

LIFE MAGAZINE	March 12, 1951
SAT EVE POST	May 12, 1951
NATIONAL GEO.	JAN. 1953

An experienced rubber estate manager may make \$1400.00 Straits dollars. With small side jobs in addition, he can make about \$500 per month in American money.

His house may be white stucco with water tanks on the roof to supply running water inside (Remember, it rains just about every afternoon).

He has his own generator for inside house lights as well as searchlights about periphery of his living area, around barbed wire enclosure.

COLISEUM — place to drink in K-L.

Beginning with his very first Western short story, "Trail of the Apache," Leonard began heavy research into the Arizona Territory, aiming for an authentic realism that would set him apart from other pulp writers. For a full decade, he kept his story notes and lush details about various Native American tribes and territory scouts in a hardcover Woolworth's ledger, which he used as a creative bible during the entirety of his Western fiction years.

15/Three-ten To Yuma
Leonard

~~see~~ the train ~~... less than a block away now.~~ He prodded Kidd to move faster. By the time they reached the end of the street he could feel them close behind.

"Tell him again!"

"DON'T SHOOT, CHARLIE!" Kidd screamed ~~it into the air~~.

The whistle blew ~~again~~ as they mounted the plank steps to the shade of the platform ~~and somewhere a~~ conductor called, " ... Gila Bend, Sentinel ... Yuma!"

~~The end of the train was farther up the platform.~~ Scallen said, "The second to last car," and pushed Kidd, angling across the platform toward the car. It was painted red and next to the wide sliding door was stenciled:

U.S. MAIL
BAGGAGE
168

~~There were~~ hurried footsteps on the platform and ~~someone~~ shouted, "Stand where you are!"

~~He heard them run up and stop close behind ... perhaps twenty feet away.~~ The whistle blew again and there was a hissing from the engine as the wheels strained, turned slowly then stopped. ~~The~~ couplings clanged together.

"Throw the gun away, brother!"

Charlie Prince stood off to the side with a pistol in each ~~xx~~ hand. Then he moved around between the two men and the train. "Throw it far away and unhitch your belt."

Scallen felt ~~the~~ sudden panic, but he held the shotgun tight against Kidd. He ~~mumbled~~, ~~"I swear~~ I'll cut you in half!" Kidd's body was stiff, with his shoulders drawn up to his neck. ~~He heard~~ the outlaw ~~say~~, "Wait a minute...." but wasn't sure if he was talking to him or Charlie Prince. ~~Past~~ Kidd's shoulder he ~~could see~~ the gunman holding the two pistols.

And suddenly Prince shouted, "Go down!"

There was a dead silence ... a fraction of a minute that seemed longer, then Kidd dove, rolling on the wooden platform. Scallen saw the two pistols come up, one ahead of the other, and he squeezed both triggers without moving the ~~shotgun~~. ~~He heard~~ a scream and ~~caught a~~ glimpse ~~of~~ Charlie Prince grabbing

16/Three-ten To Yuma
Leonard

his chest ~~as he~~ dropped the shotgun and swung around drawing his Colt's. He fired in the motion without waiting for a target. Six men were moving in different directions ... he fired again, then again and saw a man go down.

Then he was spinning back toward the train. Charlie Prince lay face down. Kidd was crawling, crawling frantically and coming to his feet when Scallen reached him and shoved him from behind.

"Come on!...." He yanked Kidd's collar savagely and dug the pistol barrel into his back. The train was beginning to roll, the whistle screaming shrilly, as he ran Kidd across the platform toward the ~~open doorway~~. "Run, dammit! Run!"

The whistle shrieked again as they neared the mail car and as it died off gun fire errupted in the station shed. A bullet smashed the window of the door as he pushed Kidd into the opening. He fell off balance as Kidd disappeared, then struggled to his feet and ran for the door that was moving away again. He was almost at the end of the platform ~~k~~ when he came abreast of the doorway and dove in.

The train picked up speed and crossed the San Pedro River bridge out of Contention.

Kidd was on the floor, stretched out along a row of mail sacks. He rubbed his shoulder awkwardly with his manacled hands and watched Scallen who stood against the wall next to the open door.

"You really earn your money," Kidd said with a frown.

The clatter of the train wheels and his own breathing ~~was~~ loud in his head. He felt as if all of his strenght was gone, but he couldn't help smiling at Jim Kidd. He was thinking the same thing."

EJL

Following the September 1952 publication of Ernest Hemingway's *The Old Man and the Sea* in *Life* magazine, Leonard immediately used the same form of minimalism in the first draft of his latest story, "Three-Ten to Yuma," much to the chagrin of *Dime Western* editor Mike Tilden.

By 1957, two of Leonard's Western stories—the novelette "The Captives" and the short story "Three-Ten to Yuma"—had been put into production for major cinematic adaptations. Seen here, the young author with his sights on Hollywood.

In 1961, Leonard took an apparent "hiatus" from fiction in order to focus on his advertising career and life as a family man; in reality, he continued to hone a "modern" literary voice while also taking on jobs as a screenwriter of short-subject documentary films. Seen here, the Leonard family prior to the birth of youngest daughter Katy (*left to right*): Peter, Beverly, Bill, Elmore, Christopher, and Jane, circa 1963.

The Leonard family had long frequented Pompano Beach, Florida, as a vacation spot prior to Elmore's purchase of the Coconut Palms motel for his aging mother to operate. Seen here are Christopher, Bill, Peter, Elmore, Beverly, and Jane in 1963 after a long day of group clam digging. (Note young Chris, on the left, and Bill in their rope belts, and the enormous blue marlin—an homage to *The Old Man and the Sea*—that, unlike Santiago, Elmore didn't actually catch.)

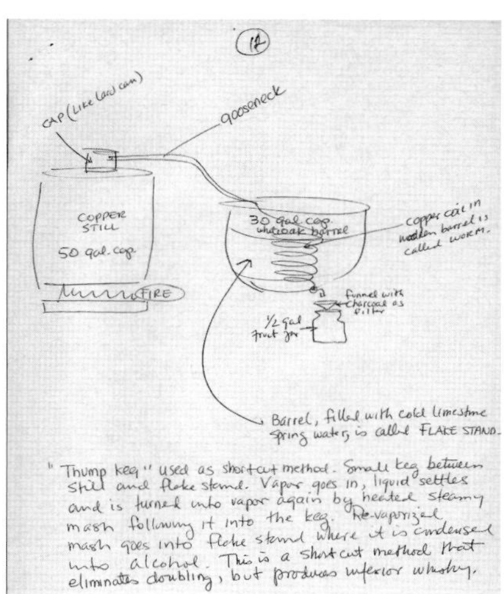

For nearly three decades, Leonard conducted his own in-depth research into the subjects that would inspire his detail-oriented fiction. For his 1969 novel *The Moonshine War*, Leonard not only made multiple trips to the near-destitute areas of rural Kentucky, which would become a recurring setting in his work, but created numerous sketches of the clandestine machinery used to produce the black market booze.

Following what Leonard deemed a disastrous adaptation of his first contemporary crime novel, *The Big Bounce*, he made a proactive initiative to pen the screenplays for his own adaptations—beginning with the Prohibition-era thriller *The Moonshine War*. Dressed more like a tax auditor than the popular author of the film's source material, Leonard visits the movie set in 1970.

In 1970, Leonard and Beverly were finally able to take the grand tour of Europe that had eluded them for the first decade and a half of their marriage. While visiting London, Greece, Rome, and Paris, a now chicly dressed Leonard continued to noodle with three separate screenplay projects while also brainstorming for his next contemporary crime novel.

During the early 1970s, Leonard's schedule was almost predominantly full of ongoing screenplay assignments—all of which would prove crucial to the development of his evolving literary voice. Seen here, a now counterculturally in-tune Dutch Leonard poses for a photographer in his first office in downtown Birmingham, Michigan, the theatrical poster for *Joe Kidd* proudly displayed behind him.

We were probably at five thousand feet. I thought, 'What is this? I know skinny guys back in Detroit who drink four or five martinis for lunch. They could kill this guy sitting at a table. He wouldn't last an hour with these guys in little three-piece suits.' Before the evening was over, he was chasing a waitress down the alley." To fight his own hangover the following morning, Leonard drank a few beers, then headed to the trucker's office to check on him. Leonard recalled, "He looked up, red-eyed, and said, 'Oh my God, I never want to see you again.'"

Leonard had never stopped to address his growing dependency on alcohol. Since his teenage years, he'd viewed drinking as a common social norm and a demonstration of masculinity: the former while at work, and the latter reinforced through years of athletic comradeship followed by military service. "When I think back to my twenties, social events always had to involve drinking," he later wrote. "If someone came by, I'd always offer him a drink. I would be happy to see people drop in because then I could have a drink. I didn't realize, until later, that I welcomed this excuse."

Leonard later acknowledged the drinking hadn't come, as often assumed, from a place of depression or stress; rather, nearly every daily routine he'd held since high school seemed to, at least, reinforce that single habit. "Drinking was always fun," he recalled. "We'd never go anyplace that didn't serve liquor. I always felt conversation was more stimulating and the evening was more exciting when we drank. I got to the point, though, where I believed that I was bored when I wasn't drinking. Talking to men in business was kind of boring for me, anyway, not being business oriented. Advertising was different because there were a bunch of swinging guys in it. But with the client, the straights, the manufacturers, I felt that I would have to drink in order to sit and listen to them." Although Leonard claimed to have never indulged before noon, even his strict morning routine involved a mandatory stop at church, which included sacramental wine (a problem averted during his semi-agnostic later years). However, "Noon was always that magic time when it became all right," he later wrote. "If you could just hold out until noon. Sunday morning I used to hold out and then come back from Mass and have a big bowl of chili and a couple of ice-cold beers . . . Hangovers never bothered me because all I had to do was drink a few ice-cold beers or a real hot, spicy Bloody Mary and I was back."[11]

Neither his family, friends, nor coworkers (including literary associates) would suspect an addiction below the surface; conversely, he was not only recognized for his extracurricular achievements outside of Campbell-Ewald, but was championed—his literary success viewed as a point of pride for the entire agency—and the only addiction of Leonard's that mattered, according to their October 1957 advertisement in *The New Yorker*, was the one "for hard-fleshed words."

Marguerite Harper had initially brought Swanson into the fold to assist in selling Leonard's *Malaya* television outline, but had then retained his services during the Batjac/John Wayne negotiations, which had fallen through. On December 12, however, Harper wrote with good news: For "Three-Ten to Yuma," Columbia Pictures was offering four thousand dollars, of which approximately two thousand five hundred would be Leonard's, he later recalled, adding that, at the time, "no-one else was offering anything." He added, however, it then "took them about three years to get it into production."[12]

Producer David Heilweil had been successful in his pitch of "Three-Ten to Yuma" to The Associates and Aldrich—the production company owned by Robert Aldrich, director of the gritty war film *Vera Cruz* and the recently released noir adaptation of Mickey Spillane's *Kiss Me Deadly*. Although the director opted to pass the reins to another filmmaker, he hired seasoned screenwriter Halsted Welles to pen a proper adaptation—changing the names of Leonard's lead protagonists and padding the material up to a full-length feature film script—then sold it to Columbia Pictures for one hundred thousand dollars.

By the time shooting began in Tucson, Arizona, the following year, however, another Leonard adaptation had already beaten it to the screens. During the summer of 1956, director Budd Boetticher had shot his own adaptation of Leonard's "The Captives" in Lone Pine, California, for the Producers-Actors Corporation. Originally, producer Robert Morrison was to handle the project for John Wayne's Batjac Productions with longtime Wayne collaborator Andrew McLaglen making his directorial debut. But when the film itself exchanged hands to another company—Randolph Scott's Producers-Actors Corporation—Scott himself selected Boetticher to direct.[13] The tight shoot had taken less than twenty days, with screenwriter Burt Kennedy writing an extended prologue to stretch the action an additional twenty minutes of screen time, and dependable leads Randolph Scott and Maureen O'Sullivan had been cast as protagonists Pat Brennan and Doretta Mims. However, due to another, unrelated film having already registered the title *The Captives*, Boetticher and screenwriter Burt Kennedy considered *The Tall Rider*, before finally settling on *The Tall T*.

Leonard was particularly pleased with lead actor Scott who, coincidentally, bore an uncanny resemblance to his former football coach and father figure, Bob Tiernan. Over the following few years, Leonard made it a point to stay in touch with the charismatic actor, sending him issues of pulps with his newly published stories, always in the hopes that they would collaborate again.

In an effort to make up for the Mexico trip they'd long ago postponed, Leonard and Beverly instead flew to New York City during the middle of January 1956. There, they finally met Marguerite Harper in person for the very first time, as well as Houghton Mifflin editor Julien McKee.[14] The couple also attended Sunday Mass at St. Patrick's Cathedral and visited a number of the city's most famous jazz clubs. (Leonard's interest in jazz music had never wavered, and he'd recently discovered musicians Chico Hamilton and Ahmad Jamal before catching Marian McPartland during her residency at the famed Hickory House. Following a show in New York, Leonard hung around afterward and met cornet player "Wild Bill" Davison, who convinced him to pick up a horn of his own. Frustrated, Leonard quickly dropped the instrument, joking that it had been more difficult than the kazoo.[15]) In April, Leonard's debut in the *Saturday Evening Post* ran as "Moment of Vengeance." As predicted by both Harper and Swanson, the exposure in the slick magazine had been just the thing to bring Leonard's name into the wider lens of the mainstream public. She wrote, "There have now been three separate interests in the TV rights to ['Moment of Vengeance']. We have temporarily said 'no' to all of them while we try to get something concrete in a movie interest. Assume you agree?"[16] He did and, only one week later, Harper reported that Meridian Productions had offered the best deal—eight hundred dollars, less her and Swanson's commissions; the money was right and the exposure was priceless.

Escape from Five Shadows was released by Houghton Mifflin in hardcover in June.

Advance copies had been sent to media outlets a few months prior to the publication date and the early reviews had been consistently strong.

"Corey Bowen successfully escaped from Five Shadows, but it wasn't easy," wrote Hal Buerge in the *Birmingham Eccentric*. "Lathrup author Elmore Leonard didn't intend it to be when he created Bowen, a high-principled, rough-hewn and steel-nerved gentleman of the Old West who was convicted of a crime he didn't commit and ended up in Five Shadows . . . The popular young copywriter for Campbell-Ewald Advertising Agency in Detroit also has had twenty-five of his short stories published in various Western magazines since he started writing in 1951 . . . launching him on his career which seems to be gaining momentum with each passing year."[17]

Later that week, the *New Center News* ran a profile on Leonard, featuring his first publicity photo (taken by Beverly in their kitchen): cross-legged and casual, arm resting on the back of his chair, clad in checkered sports coat and a sheer button-up sweater. "Elmore Leonard, New Center District's most prolific writer of Westerns, reached another goal in his career when one of his fictions was accepted by *The Saturday Evening Post* and reached the public in the April 21 issue," read the article. "Mr. Leonard, who is employed with Campbell-Ewald's Chevrolet Accounts Group as a copywriter, spends about eight hours a week writing in the basement 'studio' of his Birmingham home—set up as a last sanctuary from the distractions of a lively brood of youngsters."[18]

Leonard revealed plans for his fourth novel to be the most ambitious to date, setting the action during the final days of the Civil War. He added new complexities to both his new characters and the structure of the novel itself. Protagonist Paul Cable is clearly the hero—returning home from two and a half years of service in the war—yet his background is that of a Confederate soldier, and one who admittedly fought not for ideologies, but as a societal expectation. Joined by his wife, Martha, and their three children, Cable finds their homestead commandeered by corrupt Union soldiers turned horse traders. Outnumbered and unarmed, Cable's hopes for a peaceful retirement are dashed as he fights to regain his home by any means possible. Tensions are amplified by corrupt storeowner turned gunrunner Edward Janroe—a former Confederate officer who once psychopathically executed a line of 120 captured Union soldiers.[19]

The story itself—tentatively entitled *Saber River*—had gone through numerous structural revisions and title changes. Additionally, Leonard had remembered Harper's insistence that women had also been an integral part of the Western landscape and, in response, worked to strengthen the character of Martha. Aware of his intentions for *Saber River*'s eventual publication, Harper provided him with numerous sets of notes: "I like it a lot . . . it has suspense—though I could do without the brutal attack on Cable." She also stressed concern that the first three installments were already reaching one hundred pages—a length more akin to a full-length novel than a salable serial.[20] Leonard agreed and revised the story appropriately.

When Leonard quit Campbell-Ewald the first time, he'd been making three thousand dollars a year—an annual income on par with a single book advance. He'd left for approximately a year and a half, using that time to establish himself as an author of popular fiction and prove his moneymaking potential. When he returned to the firm, this time as a copywriter, he was offered seven thousand dollars annually—"Big dough in those days,"[21] and more than double his value before. With Beverly pregnant with their fourth child, Leonard was content to be back at the office—now located on the executive floor.

Following Campbell-Ewald's full-page ad in *The New Yorker* the previous year, the agency now took out another—this time with only a single employee profiled. *"Meanwhile, back at the agency . . ."* the ad read, *"Elmore Leonard was sighting along his trusty Remington, drawing a bead on a particularly nasty word. For 'Dutch' Leonard is a connoisseur of words. He likes to make one do the work of two."*

Leonard had been staged at his actual desk, redecorated to truly fit the motif of a Western author: a cow's skull nailed to the wall behind his head, arranged beside dual six-shooters and the same Remington held by then-three-year-old Peter Leonard for the *Detroit Times*' 1954 family profile. With Leonard posed pensively with pencil and cigarette, the copy continued, "As a rising young star of Western novels this gives his prose a spare and muscular quality; his gunsights never become entangled in fancy verbal foliage; he builds character for his characters out of what they do, not out of 1,000 words of steam-heated description." The ad even included a brief snippet from *The Bounty Hunters* as a sample of Leonard's style.[22]

Marguerite Harper found the advertisement amusing and quickly saw a pragmatic use for the additional exposure. "I had seen the nice publicity from your firm in *The New Yorker* and sent Swanie that copy of it for his use," she wrote. "It doesn't hurt in negotiations to have that info at hand."[23]

Leonard would later look back on his years in advertising with mixed feelings, admitting that it had provided a more-than-comfortable lifestyle for him and his family, while also being the greatest adversary to his writing routine. "I'm glad to be out of it," he later told Paul Challen. "You had to write *cute* . . . [and] you could get away with an incomplete sentence, but so what? I was doing that anyway."[24]

> FADE IN:
> 1. EXT. RANCHO SAN SEBASTIAN—NIGHT—EST. SHOT
> We're on a CLOSE SHOT of the heraldic skullplate and long curving horns of a steer mounted on the estancia's entrance archway above block letters reading: "RANCHO SAN SEBASTIAN."[25]

Leonard had no contractual approval rights to the half-hour teleplay adaptation of "Moment of Vengeance" by television scribe Lowell Barrington. It was, however, relatively faithful as directed by Alvin Ganzer for the *Schlitz Playhouse of the Stars* anthology series. The episode aired on September 28 and featured Ward Bond as cattle baron Ivan Kerogsen and newcomers Lane Bradford as the stoic Phil Treat and a young Angie Dickinson as Ellis. As hoped, the program provided the traction Marguerite Harper needed; the second week of November, she reported the film version of "Three-Ten to Yuma" was underway at Columbia Pictures—although they'd been lowballed on the property's value. "Did you see this annoying bit?" she wrote the second week of November. "Here is the proof that it just does not pay to make a sale of this kind. I got Heilweil up only three to four thousand . . . and he goes and sells the property to Columbia and it is to be a feature film with Glenn Ford and Van Heflin! It gets pretty exasperating."[26] (It would take Leonard a few more decades to reach the same level of exasperation with Hollywood—but he'd get there.)

When the first few media announcements for *The Tall T* ran in the trades, even Marguerite Harper admitted she'd forgotten completely about the production. It opened on April 2 to positive reviews.[27] Leonard and Beverly were invited to the film's premiere at the Broadway Capitol Theater in downtown Detroit. He later recalled, "I saw that one in a screening room with Detroit newspaper critics . . . I remember the film coming to the part where Randolph Scott has Maureen O'Sullivan lure Skip Homeier into the cave. One of the critics said, 'here comes the obligatory fistfight.' But Randolph Scott grabs the shotgun, sticks it under Skip Homeier's chin, pulls the trigger, and the screen goes red. They didn't say anything after that."[28] Beverly remembered, "At the screening at the Fox Theater, Randolph Scott came out to greet the crowd—all from Detroit—and he said, 'Well, it's wonderful to be back in Chicago!'"[29]

Despite Scott's blunder, his appearance garnered widespread local news coverage and boosted Leonard's local celebrity status. Yet, if indeed Leonard was going to become as famous as some critics were predicting, Marguerite Harper had determined it would have to be with a publisher other than Houghton Mifflin. Marguerite Harper had long been pestering both Austin Olney and Julien McKee for a straight answer regarding *Saber River*; when the publisher had stalled, then offered less money than Harper believed the property deserved, she and Leonard had opted to go to Dell for a more lucrative paperback exclusive.

Leonard sent McKee at Houghton Mifflin a personal note on June 13. "I've enjoyed working with you, with Austin Olney, too," he wrote. "I want to thank both of you for the encouragement and assistance you've provided during the last few years."[30] McKee responded: "It is a shame that the market for [Westerns] in cloth editions has dried up so completely because of the extraordinary number of Western stories being offered the public in paper, in the movies, and on TV."

McKee added, "However, that's the way the ball bounces."[31]

Earlier that month, Leonard had already invited his new editor at Dell, Donald Fine, to his Birmingham home to meet the family. Admittedly a fan of Leonard's earlier novels, Fine was optimistic about their pending collaboration on the newly titled *Stand on the Saber*, and had expedited the author's four-thousand-dollar advance. And, although he'd only begun a brief character sketch, he revealed the idea for his next novel—an intimate, character-driven twist on "The Captives," now featuring a hero raised by Apaches and his fight to save a stagecoach of white travelers from a band of thieves. Fine soon wrote Leonard, "If [the book] comes out as well as you hope, it should be something we can show Macmillan or some other trade house."[32]

Leonard and Beverly welcomed their fourth child, William Rive Leonard, on July 20, 1957.

"Congratulations to you and Beverly and best wishes for a happy life to the young man," Harper wrote on July 23, mustering her best wishes through an otherwise trying week. "I have lost Peter Dawson," she revealed of her longtime client and friend. "He passed away yesterday. I am very unhappy about it . . . I think it would be a good idea if Congress would leave the Frank Costello's alone and look into the 'grab' that some publishers practice on authors and agents."[33] The nearly unanimous raves that accompanied the August 7 release of Columbia Pictures' *3:10 to Yuma* did appear to cheer the agent, however, as well as keep the already excited Leonard focused. Overall, Leonard was pleased with the film, and both critics and moviegoers seemed to agree. Leonard's personal favorite review, however, came via the airwaves from famed gossip columnist Walter Winchell. He later recalled that the legendary broadcaster called it "three hours and ten minutes past *High Noon*."[34]

In October, rather than a card for Leonard's thirty-second birthday, Marguerite Harper sent a rather mixed update: the *Saturday Evening Post* had passed on *Stand on the Saber*. Having exhausted nearly all the existing Western magazines and noted book publishers in her seven years representing Leonard, Harper was not alone in her frustrations; her old friend Mike Tilden had recently been laid off when numerous Western pulps folded throughout the previous year. Regretfully, Harper cut to the real point of her letter: "The *Post* editors had decided that Westerns have lost their terrific popularity—claim their readers don't want many of them."

Every character archetype and scenario apparently banned from mainstream publications were the very ones that had led to Leonard's earliest success. "How about switching from straight Westerns to adventure—maybe tied in with business—possibly laid right in Michigan?" Harper wrote.[35]

In response, Leonard considered stories that could, indeed, feature the more rural areas around Michigan's thumb region where he'd grown up. For his subject, he picked a topic widely covered in the local news—the plight of foreign migrant workers and their fight for a decent wage, revealing shades of Steinbeck; for good measure, and as an homage to Hemingway, he made his protagonist a retired bullfighter.[36] Harper was pleased with the piece, "The Bull Ring at Blisston," but had difficulty placing it for a year and a half, finally selling it to *Short Stories for Men Magazine* for their August 1959 issue. The week before Thanksgiving, she wrote, "In the meanwhile, Marlon Brando's outfit is looking for a

Western and [Dell editor] Knox Burger told his man about your book . . . He called me and we had quite a talk . . . he knows Swanie well and I wrote Swanie to hold [the manuscript] I had sent him for this man to show Brando."[37] Enthralled at the suggestion that Brando might be the next major leading star attracted to his work, Leonard instructed Harper to ask Swanson to make fifteen professional-grade mimeographs of the manuscript and begin a campaign to push it upon major studios, and not to bother about the out-of-pocket cost of the efforts.[38] However, despite Swanson's seemingly endless connections around Hollywood, neither of the proposed projects went forward.

On the second of January 1958, Leonard's optimism perked with the arrival of the *Stand on the Saber* galley proofs. "How are future projects going?" Donald Fine asked. "Keep in touch if you have any hot or warmish ideas—or, for that matter, just keep in touch in any case. Marguerite has probably been singing the blues to you about the state of the Western market, and with some reason, but I suspect you're one of the good ones that can survive comfortably." Fine added, "It does occur, though, that sometime you might want to try a suspense novel . . . Meanwhile, Happy New Year, best to Beverly."[39]

But, for the first New Year's in half a decade, Leonard started 1958 admitting disappointment at missed Hollywood opportunities and, more so, in the growing difficulties in selling new work. He had Fine's galleys completed and returned within two weeks, although the editor immediately sensed an attitude change in his author. "I got the feeling that writing was getting to be a big, damned chore to you when I talked to you, and that you'd tightened up considerably," Fine wrote. "It shouldn't be; you've got a house, a job (which is more than most writers can say) and you've got talent. What the hell more do you need? End of lecture."[40]

At that point it had become apparent that *Saber River* wouldn't make a hardcover release in the United States. Harper offered advice, writing, "All you need is to get away from the Western field . . . And I am sure you now see the wisdom of my long ago telling you that, since you were married, you ought to stay on with the salaried job . . . You made an acceptable income additionally last year and I don't assume you want to throw it overboard."[41] Leonard later recalled, "My editors and agents . . . said, 'Don't *have* to write. You'll become a hack, writing under a bunch of different names. Do it at your leisure, and do it right.'"[42]

Between 1958 and 1959, only "Fury at Four Turnings" and "The Bull

Ring at Blisston" would sell—the former retitled as "The Treasure of Mungo's Landing" for *True Adventure*'s June 1958 issue, and the latter over a year later. In March, Harper asked, "Are you doing any thinking of a book?"[43]

In fact, Leonard was already working on a new book—developing the tale of an Apache-raised white man he'd first mentioned to Donald Fine months earlier. Later, Leonard would recall that the seeds of the story had started with a single image, a setup for a great scene: A lone figure waving a white flag to signal their surrender, then safely approaching the enemy. "That never happens in real life," Leonard later said, "the guy with the flag just walking away." Instead, he imagined a scenario where the bad guy would admit defeat, only to come face-to-face with his adversary and realize he's made himself vulnerable to a greater loss—his own life, as he is shot at point-blank range.[44]

Even from the beginning, Leonard only had one title in mind, a product of his language classes with Beverly: the Spanish word for "man"—*Hombre*. And although it would go on to become one of his most famous Western stories, he remained quick to remind all later interviewers that, while the book was completed by 1959, it was "rejected by publishers for nearly two years" before Ballantine finally bought it for $1,250.[45]

He'd begun the grunt work on *Hombre* in the spring of 1957, sporadically updating Harper about its progress.[46] At that point, he hadn't even settled on the distinctive first-person narrative style that would distinguish it among all his later work; his first draft—nearly eighty pages in polished prose—was from the more familiar third-person narration. Dissatisfied with the draft, Leonard started from scratch that June, opting to retry from a more experimental perspective. Harper sent a note of encouragement, writing, "Am sorry to learn you got stopped on the novel just when you were moving along nicely. Hope you can get along on it soon."[47]

Leonard now started the story from the point of view of character Carl Everett Allen, whose relationship to the titular "hombre," John Russell, was more akin to that of *The Great Gatsby*'s narrator, Nick Carraway, and that novel's eponymous protagonist. In that same vein, Allen is used almost more as a narrative device than the other, more colorful, characters that populate Leonard's story—beginning with John Russell himself. Leonard's initial notes and correspondence began with the very concept of a white man—or half Apache—raised along fellow Apaches, and the existential crossroads he would reach if confronted with a return to white society. In Leonard's eventual story, John Russell's return is provoked by the notification that his longtime benefactor has died, leaving him valuable property in the town of Bisbee. Only reluctantly does Russell accept the inheritance, silently ruminating on the inevitable troubles he'll face in adjusting to an unfamiliar culture. Although Russell spends the duration of the story as an object of ridicule and bias from the very same stagecoach passengers he's fighting to protect, he ends up taking a bullet in the back (again, à la Jay Gatsby) in a bid to save their lives.[48]

With not a single word out of place, *Hombre* was as compact as Leonard's early novelettes—a format that seemed to fit him perfectly. "It seems to me very well done and I found it compelling," Harper wrote on September 22. "How about trying to condense this for a chance shot at [the *Saturday Evening Post*] and doing it in three or four parts? Then going on with it, as is now, for the book deal????"[49] At that time, however, Leonard was still woodshedding the varied perspectives of his characters. That same month, Leonard finally heard from Donald Fine, somewhat optimistically for the coming year. "*Stand on the Saber* has been retitled *This Land Is Mine* and will be released sometime next April," Fine wrote. "I hope you like the new title."[50] But Leonard didn't—and *Last Stand at Saber River*, as it was ultimately retitled, was finally released as a paperback original in April 1959.

But unlike Leonard's preceding novels, this one garnered little fanfare. Harper had been able to negotiate for hardcover release in the UK with Robert Hale, Ltd., where it was retitled *Lawless River* for an August release. The irony didn't pass by Leonard, who, like editor Donald Fine, considered the finished novel to be among the author's best and most mature works. The two had worked closely throughout the summer of 1957 on intricate revisions and structural changes, ultimately crafting a novel that Fine himself believed transcended the Western genre.[51] Yet it was only getting a hardcover release in another country, and under a different title at that.

Throughout the next year, Leonard worked on *Hombre*, although the numerous warnings regarding non-Westerns continued to plague him. In an effort for supplemental income, he combed through his older published short stories, considering if any might be worthy of adapting for current television shows—perhaps the plots repurposed to fit the characters of a standing series. He dashed off the suggestion to H. N. Swanson and included a copy of "Trouble at Rindo's Station"—one of Harper's most recent sales. "Last night, watching the first *Laramie* show over [on NBC],

I thought of a story of mine that would fit their format pretty well," Leonard wrote the agent. "Then I thought, why not send some more stories that might be suitable for other programs?"[52] Swanson responded within the week. "The *Laramie* show has currently filled their quota story-wise, and until they know whether or not they will be renewed, they are not in the market," he wrote. "However, just on the chance that they will be picked up, we are showing this to their story editor."[53] Harper responded a few weeks later: "Swanie sent me a copy of his letter and I wonder if you understand how these series get done on TV," she wrote on October 20. "I am sure you have noticed, as I have, that one seldom sees a recognizable Western writer's name on the TV screen. I certainly have never heard of the names of the majority of writers getting the credits."[54]

Soon, a new correspondence Leonard initiated proved to be just the thing to help him through the doldrums of an unforgiving literary market. He had taken the time to write what he later insisted was his "one and only fan letter" to a fellow author whom he'd recently discovered: an obscure sportswriter turned novelist named Wilfred Charles "W. C." Heinz. In 1949, Heinz had developed a small, dedicated readership after famously penning a critically acclaimed piece for the *New York Sun*, "Death of a Racehorse." Clocking in at less than one thousand words and written in real-time as the aforementioned horse was injured and air-lifted off the track in front of the crowd, the article had earned the columnist favorable comparisons to Ernest Hemingway and a shift toward fiction. His 1958 novel about a fighter's personal journey to the middleweight championship, *The Professional*, had even gotten the attention of Hemingway himself, who called it "the only good novel I've ever read about a fighter, and an excellent novel in its own right."[55] Ironically, Heinz replied to Leonard's fan letter on Leonard's thirty-third birthday. "You are only the second person, outside my circle of friends and acquaintances, who has felt compelled to comment to me or my publisher about *The Professional*," Heinz wrote. "The first was Ernest Hemingway, who cabled his compliments to Harper & Row about six days after the book came out. You are a writer, however, and understand, as does, of course, Papa, and that is what gives your letter added importance to me . . . Characters, to live, must be permitted to speak for themselves, each with his own manner of speech and level of thought. The writer should keep out of there. He should not tell, but show." Heinz added, "Also, I'm happy that you admired the restraint. The best fighters I have known have all had that—the ability to keep the fight moving at their distance and always directly in front of them, pursuing their aim with a quiet purpose with all kinds of hell breaking loose on all sides from the throats of the amateurs."[56]

Leonard's correspondence with Heinz proved to be the encouragement and creative feedback needed to get *Hombre* to the finish line—something that seemed strangely elusive as Leonard's star at Campbell-Ewald continued to rise and the market for his Western fiction didn't much improve. At the beginning of that year, Marguerite Harper had begun working exclusively from her home in New Rochelle—and her reasoning wasn't particularly encouraging. "With business this bad these past few months and not much improvement hoped for before the fall, I am going to work from home [and] come into town when necessary," she wrote.[57] Leonard had suffered his own discouragement during this period, on yet another business trip to collect Chevrolet customer testimonials. This time he had been sent on a whirlwind trip to North Dakota, Montana, and St. Louis, and an incidental pass through Arizona helped solve at least one issue he'd been having with his writing. As Leonard later wrote to his then-grown son Christopher, "I was halfway through [*Hombre*] in '59 when I happened to go to Tucson, saw the mountains for true and had to rewrite them when I got back home."[58]

On October 26, Don Fine responded with another disheartening update: "I'm sorry to say I have sent this back, with regrets," he wrote. "As I mentioned, our Western inventory is just too chockful to take on any writer, even one of Dutch's stature."[59] On December 8, Harper wrote to Leonard that current Fawcett Publications editor Knox Burger had passed on the book as well.[60] As the months passed, she continued to wait on Avon as a backup publisher as the holiday season came and went. "Very glad to hear from you," Harper wrote on May 27, elated to finally hear from Leonard after five months of silence. "Yes, I have had a rough time with *Hombre*—it's just been considered too short for a book after all and too long for *Argosy* and the others who sometimes condense these." Leonard had also asked if rewriting *Hombre* from the ground up might better its chances for a sale; Harper pulled no punches in telling him not to waste his time. However, Harper added, "You write fiction too well to quit."[61]

> Even when I was being rejected by some of the major houses for writing what they considered downners, or passed on by as many as a hundred

> film producers at one time, I still believed I was doing okay, knew how I wanted to write, so I stayed with it.

Despite his apparent aversion to countless pleas for contemporary fiction, Leonard admitted later that it was more the daunting and intimidating prospect of going head-to-head with literary peers already well-established in writing the exposition and dialogue required to represent the contemporary world. He had just mastered the Western, and now it was all but gone.

By 1961, he was ready to face facts and accept the challenge of developing a new sound—one that would fit into a salable genre. But that would require two things Leonard couldn't manufacture while working full-time and co-running a household that seemed to get ever tighter as the four children got up in age: time and energy. Finally, by mid-March, Harper wrote to Leonard with the first real glimmer of financial hope in nearly two years: she had sold *Hombre*, first to Robert Hale, Ltd., for a hardcover release in the UK, then to Ballantine as a paperback original—seven hundred fifty dollars upon signing, five hundred on publication. "Now I feel as though I performed a miracle," she wrote.[62]

But netting just over the same amount that he'd earned for his very first novelette, "Trail of the Apache," a decade earlier didn't sound like much of a miracle to Leonard. With the new year, Leonard had been notified that there was potential for a second miracle—his profit-sharing agreement had reached fruition at Campbell-Ewald, giving him the option of $11,500 if he were to leave. However, to run the house with Beverly and the kids, even that amount wouldn't last for very long. Aware that if he didn't devote himself full-time to developing a new, contemporary sound, he would never be able to write the salable crime novel his agents eagerly expected of him. Leonard calculated a timeline and estimated it would take him approximately six months to produce a quality manuscript, then get back to advertising—if necessary. Eleven thousand five hundred dollars sounded like just enough to carry that amount of time.

Future interviewers would humorously note that Leonard never seemed to forget the date he quit Campbell-Ewald for good. Journalist Malcolm Jones later commented, "[Leonard] recited the last day of his last day job with so little hesitation that the date might be branded on his tongue."

March 16, 1961.[63]

CHAPTER 7

Bouncing, 1961–1970

> I wouldn't care to relive any of those years along the way . . . And I wouldn't care to revise any of my past work. If nothing else, it indicates that I'm making progress, still learning, still trying to make it better . . .

Only a few months into 1961, Leonard found himself fired up at the prospect of waking up and worrying about nothing other than writing fiction—the very strategy his agents and editors had warned him *not* to do. The original intention had been to spend half a year focusing on a contemporary novel—something mainstream that the *Saturday Evening Post*, *Collier's*, *Harper's*, and their lot couldn't ignore. Only that wasn't what happened.

Later critics would often romanticize Leonard's apparent "hiatus" from fiction—the approximate five-year interval when he begrudgingly pulled himself away from his writing.

However, the thirty-two-year-old advertising executive would also defend his decision; as the Western market continued to dry up, Leonard's executive-level advertising career prospered, causing a reassessment of his priorities. Temporarily putting his writing on hold, when a larger home became available in the more-upscale Birmingham, both Leonard and Beverly chose to put the money toward a down payment on a two-story, four bedroom at 420 Suffield.

"When we moved, the new house was built for $13,000," Peter Leonard recalled. "It was in a subdivision—the land behind the house was just dirt. Elmore would set up empty cans and bottles on a wall back there and bring out BB guns and we'd shoot the cans and bottles off." He continued, "Not long after, a bird flew in our house and Elmore ran and got one of the BB guns and started shooting at it. He missed and blew out a windowpane."

However, the new house also allowed Leonard to set up a proper home office on the first floor.[1] He soon buckled down to two tasks—preparing *Hombre* for print and getting his freelance copywriting off the ground. Quite by luck, he'd recently reconnected with William "Bill" Deneen, a former high school classmate one year younger who had since gone on as a successful independent documentarian of educational and industrial films. Deneen had been impressed with his former classmate's literary success and quickly doled out Leonard's very first screenwriting job: penning *The Man Who Had Everything*—a half-hour recruitment film on behalf of the Franciscan Order. The project also led Leonard to a lifelong friendship with the film's subject, a thirty-year-old priest named John "Juvenal" Carlson—"Juvie" to his close friends and family—recently ordained and preparing for missionary work in the Amazon. Intrigued by the young man's quiet and pensive demeanor, "[Deneen] brought him here to Detroit," Leonard later recalled. "And he was really a great guy. [Juvenal] always smiled and never acted anything like a priest." Christopher Leonard later recalled, "Father Juvenal came to town one time and we all got to know him . . . One day, Elmore was going to Michael's—the place in downtown Birmingham where he'd buy all his beer and wine—and he and Juvenal traded clothes. So Juvenal stayed with me in the car wearing Elmore's dress shirt and tie and Elmore went into the store to buy alcohol dressed as a Franciscan."[2]

Since their first collaboration had gone well, Deneen hired Leonard as a freelance screenwriter on a project-by-project basis, one thousand dollars per script. For a page approximately twenty minutes in length, Leonard earned about fifty dollars—the most he'd ever been paid, outside of his novels. He sent an update on his recent undertaking to Marguerite Harper, who was less than enthusiastic: "When can you try something for [the *Saturday Evening Post*]?" she wrote on April 1. "You write well enough to get back in there."[3]

In total, Leonard would write at least ten scripts for Deneen, although he would also occasionally rewrite other material, earning a crash course in script doctoring. Leonard's originals, however, included the completed *The Man Who Had Everything* and 1961's *Frontier Boy of the Early Midwest* in 1961; between 1962 and 1965, he would go on to also write

Deneen's *French and Indian War*; *Western Movement: The Settlement of the Western Valley*; *The Settlement of the Northwest Territories and the Mississippi Valley*; *Puerto Rico: Its Past, Present, and Promise*; *The Danube Valley and Its People*, and a profile of Detroit's oldest confectionery, the Awrey Bakery.[4] "I was very confident in [Deneen's] ability," Leonard later said. "He was very good. He was cool [while] shooting."

Another perk to working with Deneen was the periodic international travel. In 1964 while in Spain shooting two films about the Iberian Peninsula with his crew, he had been able to haggle for use of the big-budget sets left over from director Anthony Mann's recently wrapped epic, *The Fall of the Roman Empire*. For the soundstage, Deneen had an ambitious three-picture shoot in mind and invited the entire Leonard family for the marathon schedule. At that point, Leonard was already mostly finished with the two scripts that Deneen had assigned—one for each emperor, Julius Caesar and Claudius—and was only awaiting Deneen's payment. "Finally, he paid me and I took my family to Europe," Leonard later remembered. "I think we landed in Paris, and then we went to Spain and met him and went to the set . . . It was quite a set for that time."[5] Peter Leonard later recalled, "I remember we went to Paris, then flew to Madrid and Elmore rented a car . . . We stopped in a little town, Toledo, which is famous for its silver. I asked my father if I could buy some switchblade knives for me and my friends and he said, 'Sure.' So, I ended up buying seven switchblades. My mother had a fit. She said, 'You can't do that, Dutch.' But it worked."[6] Peter's younger brother, Bill, had an even more vivid memory—his father taking the entire family to a real-life bullfight at the historic Las Ventas Bullring. "I was only about six at the time," Bill Leonard recalled. "All I remember was blood!"[7]

Their sister Jane Jones recalled, "When we got back from Spain, we were in the car and I heard Dad say they only had something like sixty dollars in the bank—and my mother said, 'Do we even have *that* much?' "[8]

For Deneen, at least, the high quality and production value of the recent films got his own client's attention; in November 1965, Encyclopedia Britannica bought out his company and persuaded him to accept a role as their vice president of production in Chicago; two years later, Deneen left to start his own rival short educational film division at Columbia Pictures.

By that point, however, Leonard had earned his own contract with 20th Century Fox.

He was soon a one-man writing factory, officially registered as "Elmore Leonard, Inc."

While his former contract with Campbell-Ewald did not forbid Leonard from pursuing his former clients, he was able to specialize in the niche companies that provided Chevy owners with the necessary accoutrements the vehicles required for optimal performance. Thanks to a referral from a former coworker, he soon had the ear of George Hurst—the young founder and chief designer of Hurst Shifters. (In the meager four years since the company's founding, Hurst had made his unique line of transmission shifters a standard among drag racers and serious speed enthusiasts. In only a few more years, having rebranded as the expansive Hurst Performance company, Hurst would gain personal prominence as the designer of the "Jaws of Life" emergency system.) Leonard later recalled not even knowing what a "Hurst Shifter was" when he received the call from a friend "completely saturated with martinis," claiming the entrepreneur was in the market for an independent like Leonard. "I said, 'I don't have an office.' And he said, 'Well, have him come to your house,'" Leonard added. "I did call up a guy in New York who knew cars inside and out, and he told me about shifters and about Hurst and so on."[9]

The following day, Leonard convinced Hurst that a larger advertising agency would already have numerous high-profile clients, thus relegating his needs to less experienced writers. He proved it by producing a full sample campaign only two days later: a photo displaying an elephant's foot about to crush one of Hurst's prominently displayed shifters. Leonard's slogan read, *"Guaranteed for life—Unless."* (Christopher Leonard recalled, "We had a fake elephant's foot by the front door where we would keep all the umbrellas. Elmore took it and used it for the ad."[10])

Leonard followed up his home run with similar, equally humorous full-page ads for Hurst, which ran in *Hot Rod*, *Super Stock*, and *Car and Driver* magazines.[11] Now an independent contractor, Leonard also signed Eaton Chemicals, a manufacturer of dry cleaning products, and single-handedly wrote all their public relations literature: advertisements, brochures, and pamphlets, using the opportunity to print up some elaborate brochures for himself. Hard-backed sepia-toned envelopes displaying a flower unfolded with the centered message, "*Freelance Writer with fresh ideas.*" Leonard, of course, wrote the internal copy himself:

Advertising. Sales Promotion. Motion Pictures.

10 years with Campbell-Ewald. Documentaries for Encyclopedia Films.

5 Novels, 31 short stories published; 2 made into movies. Freelancing for the past full year.

Elmore Leonard.

Hombre was released by Ballantine in paperback in September 1961. Leonard immediately had trouble finding copies on store shelves.[12]

The following month, Marguerite Harper wrote to Leonard that she'd had to move abruptly to a new place in Eastchester, across from New Rochelle. She urged, "Aren't you going to write anything anymore? Couldn't you try a short for the *Post* in November?"[13] Three months later she prodded again, "What happened to all those grandiose promises of some fiction writing? Or some saleable articles? I worked awfully hard for the authors I represented. And now I need income and some stories to sell it . . . Aren't you even going to follow up the book with another one? After all *I did* sell them all."[14] (Despite Harper's frustrations, Leonard later admitted that he'd had to repeatedly borrow money from friends during that time, then pay it back once royalty checks would come in. "We were living month to month on Hurst money," he told Mike Lupica. "The years 1961 to 1966 were the low point, definitely . . . I had probably resigned myself to writing again sometime, but never fulltime."[15] He later elaborated, "The sale of *Hombre* to [20th Century Fox] for a movie gave me that chance."[16])

Unbeknownst to Harper, Leonard was, indeed, attempting a return to fiction. The time in Spain had kick-started a few ideas for contemporary stories, and Leonard had returned home with notes for two new shorts. With "A Happy, Light-Hearted People," he wrote one of his only "slice of life" vignettes, in full Hemingway mode, parodying the uncultured behavior of American and British tourists at an upscale Spanish hotel—all from the perspective of Paco, a young, overworked concierge. Harper was unenthusiastic. "There are so few magazines that have any space, except for staff writers, for episodic things of this kind," she wrote. "Write something . . . with some guts to it."[17]

Leonard's time on the set of *The Fall of the Roman Empire* also inspired the satirical "The Only Good Syrian Foot Soldier Is a Dead One," his very first potshot at the Hollywood studio system. His protagonist is Allen Garfield, a wannabe star originally from Royal Oak, Michigan, who has been typecast as an extra for his ability to "die" realistically on screen. Now clad in a toga on the set of a big-budget historical epic, Garfield is privy to the impatience and near lunacy of both the film's stars and its megalomaniacal director. Leonard had also used the story to pour out a few other observations he'd made while dealing with Hollywood the past few years: "*Write a script about all the waiting and standing around smoking cigarettes and the absolute disregard for anybody else. Write about the director who doesn't know what to do next and covers up practicing his golf swing with a sword.*"[18]

The story ends on a comically tragic note as Garfield is finally given his big moment of screen time with the film's leading man—only to be accidentally impaled by the incompetent star's prop spear.

Although Harper was unsuccessful in selling either story, both indicated that Leonard—with whatever writing time he was able to muster—was working, almost exclusively, on developing a non-Western, contemporary literary voice.

During the first week of 1965, what could only be described as a small miracle occurred. Harper reported that "interested parties" represented by the new Ziegler Agency in Beverly Hills had contacted H. N. Swanson regarding the film rights to *Hombre*. Indeed, producer-screenwriter Irving Ravetch and wife, Harriet Frank Jr., only a few years removed from their critically acclaimed Faulkner adaptation, *The Long, Hot Summer*, had loved Leonard's novel and were seeking to adapt it themselves. Directed by Martin Ritt and featuring A-list leading man Paul Newman and his wife, Joanne Woodward, that film's success now had the team again looking for another potential collaboration, and *Hombre* fit the bill. Leonard recalled, "I remember them writing to me saying to me, 'We're interested in reading more of your material, that maybe lightning would strike twice.' Well, I didn't think of it as lightning at all. I just thought of it as work—hard work, and aiming for the screen."

Over the next few months, the couple worked out the script and made a successful pitch to 20th Century Fox, greenlighting the project with Martin Ritt back at the helm. Ravetch wrote to Leonard on July 12, "Congratulations! We've just been notified that Twentieth Century Fox has decided to go ahead with our film version of *Hombre* . . . you'll be getting a check for the rest of the money pretty soon."

Leonard later recalled, "They only gave me ten-thousand dollars for *Hombre* . . . It wasn't much, but it freed me."[19] (He would, however, enjoy pointing out that he'd been paid the same figure as Ian Fleming for the television sale of *Casino Royale* to CBS.[20])

After the first check cleared in May, Leonard made an announcement to his family. As Beverly and the kids sat around the table eating breakfast, he joined them from his basement office. "I'm going to make my run," he said.

Leonard and Beverly soon learned that they were going to be parents for the fifth time. The happy news motivated him to pick up his daily writing routine for the first time in nearly five years.

Within months, he wrote Harper with the news for which she'd been begging—he was halfway finished with his first contemporary crime novel: "It's taking longer than I thought," he wrote, "but at least when I'm through, I'm not going to have any doubts. I'm still having title trouble . . . My working title is *Mother, This Is Jack Ryan*. What do you think?"

He added, "From Swanie's letter, I take it you were ill. Hope it wasn't anything serious and you're feeling okay now."[21] Harper wrote back, "I am not too wise about titles, but this one of yours seems a little cumbersome."[22] She ignored the inquiry about her health.

By the end of 1967, it was apparent that Leonard needed an office space outside the home. He set up camp at a three-room suite above Whaling's Men's Wear at 199 Pierce Street in downtown Birmingham. He also took on a personal assistant, Janet Smart, who would usually end up juggling the average three projects Leonard would have at any given time. "I loved his downtown Birmingham office," his youngest son, Bill Leonard, later recalled. "It was minutes from my grade school so I often popped in on him unannounced after school, often with a friend. His desk faced a black leather couch with an abstract oil painting above it—it was mostly black and olive green with a bit of white in the center—it looked just like headlights emerging from a dark place. I believe my dad said [the artist] was 'just cleaning his brushes.'"[23]

Leonard continued to work on *Mother, This Is Jack Ryan* exclusively—no more short stories. In December, he wrote to publisher Betty Ballantine, "Don't know if you heard or not that *Hombre* sold to Fox to be made into a picture. I'm told Paul Newman has been announced for the lead. Enclosed are five copies of the Publisher's Release, which I would appreciate your dating, signing and returning to me as soon as you can. Marguerite Harper is having eye trouble and is severely handicapped, or else she would be handling this. Sincerely, Elmore Leonard, Elmore Leonard, Inc."[24]

Leonard hadn't corresponded with Donald Fine at Dell in years, but he knew the editor would jump at the chance for a contemporary crime novel. "I'm on the last chapter of a new book that's going to go about [one hundred thousand] words," he wrote to Fine. "It takes place in Michigan, this year, and right now I feel good about it. I think it's fresh and somewhat offbeat."[25] The world in which Leonard would now be placing his stories was a far more complicated place than the Arizona Territory of a previous century: the Civil Rights movement, student protests, women's liberation, and the Vietnam War would all be the external stimuli for Leonard's new heroes and villains alike. In fact, Leonard realized, it wasn't always easy in the modern world to tell them apart. The archetypical "strong, silent type" that had represented the stoic all-American hero—personified by the likes of Leonard favorites Gary Cooper, Gregory Peck, and Randolph Scott—was being slowly replaced by a more pensive, introverted type of protagonist: one more existential and in tune to the changing social norms of the modern era. Leonard's chosen title, *Mother, This Is Jack Ryan,* was meant to be an introduction to the character in more ways than one. Although unintentional at the time, the novel's protagonist would set a new standard for the author's ideal hero: a regular everyman who could be courageous when needed, decent in both his ethics and morals, though flexible in his personal perception of either—and with an internal moral code that circumvented the law of the land, although he could suffer periodic bouts of self-doubt along the way. And like many of his characters' names, this one, too, was inspired by a close buddy. Leonard later recalled, "This is an old friend, Jack Ryan . . . He would go up to Joe Buffa's Bayside Villa [with us] as part of the group, after I was married. And it seems to me he lived in Highland Park and his dad was a bus driver."[26]

There were many autobiographical elements to the novel, Jack Ryan's own Detroit upbringing and love of baseball only a few. A flashback reveals that Ryan had once dangled from the rooftop of a friend's home—an event that had occurred in Leonard's own life as a child, watching schoolmate Maurice Murray perform an identical feat off the Boisineau brothers' roof. Likewise, the solitary Ryan spends many nights joining his older sister's family for dinner—and a healthy dose of familial guilt—in a relationship not unlike Leonard's own with his sister, Mickey; the mentorship offered to Ryan by unofficial father figure Walter Majestyk also resembled elements of Leonard's relationship with high school coach Robert Tiernan; Majestyk himself loves to share stories of his time as a Seabee in World War II, stationed outside the island of Los Negros.[27]

This was his first novel since *Hombre*. Leonard envisioned a now more complex structure with ample room for interesting secondary characters who could help shape the story's plot. The middle-aged owner and proprietor of Ritchie Foods, Ray Ritchie, is wealthy, married, and arrogant—traits that all disgust his younger mistress, debutante and former "Cucumber Queen" Nancy Hayes, who also happens to be having another affair with Ritchie's foreman, Bob Rogers. Also under Ritchie's nose, Nancy is planning to knock over the cucumber business payroll kept in his lodge; upon meeting Jack Ryan, she instantly assumes he'd make a perfect partner in crime. (One element of Nancy's background that didn't require research, however, was her not-so-innocent hobby of seducing the fathers of children for whom she babysat, then financially extorting them with threats of misconduct accusations. It was a direct usage of his earlier, unpublished short story "Arma Virumque Cano.") At the novel's conclusion, Ryan is saved from Nancy's scheme to murder him at the lodge thanks only to Walter Majestyk's last-minute invitation to watch the Detroit Tigers game on television with him. (In a humorous play of self-reference, Leonard had Majestyk previously in front of the television watching a broadcast of *The Tall T*.)[28]

Leonard and Beverly welcomed their youngest child, Katherine Mary Leonard, on February 19, 1966. Throughout that year, Leonard wrote and *rewrote* nearly all of *Mother, This Is Jack Ryan*—all through individual scenes and piecemeal chapters—rearranging portions and making substantial edits along the way.

During the process, he continued taking sporadic editorial advice from Marguerite Harper—to a lesser extent now, however, due to her undisclosed illness. She had advised H. N. Swanson that Leonard had a contemporary novel in the works, and, in the condition she was in, appreciated any assistance he could offer Leonard in making the sale. Halfway through reading Leonard's completed revision, she was hospitalized and had the manuscript sent to Swanson.[29] In turn, Swanson quickly wrote to Leonard with updates and his own curiosity about the new book. "I checked with Fox, who tell me *Hombre* will not likely be released for another four or five months," the agent wrote on May 31. "Then of course will come weeks of cutting, dubbing, etc. . . . As you can see, it will be some time." Swanson saved his true intent until the end of the letter, signing off: "Marguerite Harper tells me you have a new book which is not a Western which I look forward to seeing."[30]

> The morning of September 14, 1966, the phone rang and I spoke to Mr. H. N. Swanson for the first time. He asked if I had actually written this off-beat novel about a guy named Jack Ryan—surprised, I suppose, because it wasn't a Western. I convinced him I was the author and Swanie's next line was one I'll remember as long as I live. He said, "Well, kiddo, I'm going to make you rich."
>
> I know for a fact I believed him, because it gave my confidence a shot I can still feel today . . .
>
> What I didn't do, sailing now on Swanie-inspired confidence, was take the advice of editors and turn the book into a formula story. "Don't lose your nerve now," Swanie said in a letter he wrote in July, 1967, "we have the tiger by the tail. I would suggest you do what you're going to do to it, but do it fast."

Following an inspiring telephone call with Swanson, Leonard quickly followed up with Harper. Although she'd been pushing Leonard to write a contemporary novel, by the time his life and finances had allowed for its completion, she was too ill to handle most of his business affairs. Over the phone, she confirmed Leonard's suspicion that Swanson would be taking over the reins of his representation—at least when it came to *Mother, This Is Jack Ryan*; with Harper's blessing, Leonard followed up with Swanson the same day: "I just spoke with Marguerite on the phone. She said she would like you to handle the book, as well as possible motion picture sales." Swanson submitted the *Jack Ryan* manuscript to Houghton Mifflin first, with the intention of sending it next to Dell and New

American Library. He even met up with publisher Ian Ballantine himself, advising, "We want hardcover and a big advance."[31]

Within the first month, however, each of his selected publishers declined the book, all citing the same objections. "*Mother, This Is Jack Ryan* by Elmore Leonard needs a lot more than ten-thousand words taken out of the front of the book," wrote Dell's new senior editor—formerly of Gold Medal Books—Richard E. Roberts. "If you actually get a picture sale, our interest would rise sharply, but always with the above in mind."[32]

But while Swanson remained adamant that the book did not require a major rewrite, by the first week of November, directors Don Siegel, Otto Preminger, and Martin Ritt—recently finished with the final cut of *Hombre*—had also passed on the property. Three days before Christmas, New American Library also declined. By the first week of 1967, Swanson and Leonard both agreed that, perhaps, another rewrite might be in order. In an attempt to reassure Leonard about the quality of the work itself, Swanie again emphasized the timeliness of the story and its youthful roster of characters. "I think your boy is a Steve McQueen–rolling stone kind of fellow who thinks people who work at steady and prosaic jobs are from Squaresville," he wrote, "[who] ends up deciding [Nancy's] way is wrong and sees that she is going to go on to her own destruction."[33] And in a move that would, ultimately, lead to Leonard's final version of the novel, on January 23, Swanson added, "I just laid down the current issue of *Esquire*, having read the lead article called 'The New American Woman' . . . It brings to mind that these are the ingredients of which Nancy is made. Get the magazine and read it tonight."[34] Leonard took Swanson's advice and devoured the feature story, of which the sub-headline read, "*And what rough beast, its hour come at last, slouches towards Los Angeles to be born?*"—taking copious notes on all the latest fashion trends and cultural shifts that would shape an empowered and sexually self-aware modern debutante like he envisioned Nancy Hayes. Although he was regretful of the title change later, Nancy's obsessive quest for the "biggest bounce"—evidently the new, hip terminology for cheap thrills—came from the *Esquire* profile.

However, as Leonard kept up with his new revisions, the rejections continued to pile up. He would later recall the final tally clocking in at eighty-four—coincidentally, the same as the number of days since Hemingway's Santiago had caught a fish before landing his prized marlin.

• • •

Hombre was released by 20th Century Fox on March 21.

A private screening of the film was booked by the studio in downtown Detroit, with Leonard and Beverly allowed to invite forty of their friends and family members to attend. The *Detroit News* sent a reporter-photographer team to the event, running a full-page feature—"The Suburbanite Who Writes Westerns"—the following week. Playfully labeling Leonard as "the Birmingham adman who pens cowboy stories before breakfast," Dale Stevens wrote, "Watching *Hombre* unfold on the screen was not a new experience for Leonard . . . Elmore said he wasn't nervous. But he watched *Hombre* proceed with grave concentration. Now and then he would laugh at a clever line inserted by the scenarist who had adapted his book. Once, when I asked him if a particularly funny adult line were his, he said, 'No, but I wish it was.'" Leonard added, "Newman's Indian wig cost four-hundred dollars. If there were enough Indians in the picture, the wigmaker would have made more than I did."[35]

While Leonard had written the story as far back as 1959, by the late 1960s, social norms had dictated a new subgenre that readily accepted the author's long-standing approach to historical realism. Soon, Leonard found himself and the *Hombre* adaptation at the forefront of the evolving "Revisionist Western" movement—a perfect fit for the author's overtly cinematic style and empathetic approach to characterization. When Leonard had written to Swanson that previous July, the agent had estimated that both studios and audiences alike were, indeed, still willing to accept the Western as a form of entertainment, although a certain amount of social relevance had become a prerequisite. "However, the old conventional Western will not go with today's producers," Swanson wrote. "It either must have a parallel with some modern theme, such as race equality, and it must have a girl worked importantly into the plot . . . A great number of fine books would have been bought for the screen if a girl had had something to do with the plots."[36]

It was clear from the first month that *Hombre* was a blockbuster hit in cinemas, providing more leverage to H. N. Swanson in his bid to unload the now-retitled *The Big Bounce* once and for all. The one person, however, who wouldn't be able to share in Leonard's recent—and upcoming—success was the woman who had discovered him. At two thirty in the afternoon on April 20, Leonard received a Western Union telegram from

Marguerite Harper's sister, Phyllis Hatch, notifying him that his first agent and mentor had passed away.[37]

On August 5 of the previous year, while traveling with friends, Harper had handwritten her final letter to Leonard, instructing him not to send any further mail to her New Rochelle home. "Would advise not sending it until the revision is satisfactory to you," she wrote. "Top editors are apt to be on vacations now." According to Harper, she was "motoring with friends" and was unsure when she would be home.[38] It was only later that Leonard learned she had been hospitalized. In nearly her half a century representing authors, Harper had successfully navigated the often harsh world of the literary industry, going toe-to-toe with powerful and influential editors of some of the most popular men's magazines and publishers. Among her many clients, Harper had pushed Peter Dawson, Luke Short, T. T. Flynn, and Elmore Leonard into the spotlight of Western fiction fame, landing each one coveted placings in both pulps and slicks, on television and in movie theaters.

At the time of her death, she had been the exclusive representative of all of Leonard's Western canon, save his 1951 debut. She was seventy-two years old.

Although Leonard had not planned on writing further Westerns after completing *The Big Bounce*, Swanson's tip that the Western was on its way back, and in a more progressive form, got Leonard reconsidering an earlier plan to expand an earlier short story he counted among his favorites. In "Only Good Ones," he had told the simple story of a young Mexican sheriff named Bob Valdez who, not unlike *The Law at Randado*'s Kirby Frye, is treated with harsh indifference and disrespect by the white townsfolk he serves. At the beginning of the tale, Valdez is summoned to a standoff between a posse of townspeople, led by wealthy rancher Frank Tanner, and a Black man named Orlando Rincon, falsely accused of actually being a murderous fugitive named Johnson. Rincon is held up with his pregnant Apache wife in their meager shack as Valdez arrives on the scene. Despite a face-to-face negotiation wherein Valdez learns of the man's innocence, Tanner and his men trick the young sheriff into killing their prey for them.

Upon its first appearance in Macmillan's 1961 *Western Writers of America Anthology*, "Only Good Ones" was also Leonard's final short story for twenty years.

Leonard's plan to expand the original story's plot set its protagonist on a mission of vengeance on the deceased's behalf. "I think [it] is one of the best Western short stories ever written," Swanson wrote. "I like your idea of expanding it into a book, but I feel your proposed enlargement is not large enough to sustain book-length . . . Does this mean that you want to put aside the changes on [*The Big Bounce*] to do this? . . . I'd like to have both done and in my hands yesterday."[39]

However, there were numerous reasons that Leonard had been pushing to expand the story. In Bob Valdez, Leonard had found a perfect vessel for themes he'd been aiming to tackle, all wrapped up in a lean, action-driven revenge tale: Sympathetic views of both the Apache natives and Mexican transplants depicted within the story were a perfect mirror to the ongoing Civil Rights struggles and Vietnam War coverage depicted every day in the *Detroit Free Press*. Also, an expanded version of Valdez's story could further shape the martyr figure he'd been developing since *The Law at Randado*. In Leonard's own way, he was writing for the times—and the Hollywood sale of *Hombre* proved that both dramatic *and* thematic envelopes could be pushed. And, as *The Big Bounce* continued to collect rejections, Leonard had a third reason—Swanson needed a new property to shop. Although Swanson was signed only to represent Leonard's film interests, there was the possibility of selling "Only Good Ones" to a studio first—a strategy that could inspire a potential publisher to quickly purchase an expanded literary version. He began expanding the short story right away and, for the sake of clarity, renamed it once again—something tough that better resonated with the story's straightforward revenge theme. He picked, simply, *Valdez Is Coming*.

> By the time I was into the next book I felt I should have an agent in New York, besides Swanie in Hollywood, someone to replace Marguerite Harper and deal with publishers directly. All Swanie said was, "Why? I have a phone." He didn't press it.
>
> It wasn't long before I learned that Swanie's phone was more effective than the interim agent's presence in the book-buying marketplace—and that was that.

In May, Leonard signed with Max Wilkinson of the Littauer and Wilkinson firm at 500 Fifth Avenue to replace Marguerite Harper in his literary interests. Swanson needn't have said another word, aside from reminding Leonard that Dell had shown interest in publishing *The Big*

Bounce pending a movie deal. This meant Swanson would still be in Leonard's corner for at least that one book and, potentially, the film deal for *Valdez Is Coming* once Leonard completed it.[40] Ultimately, Swanson would be doing most of the grunt work on Leonard's two most promising current projects over Wilkinson, anyway: in August, he performed the apparently impossible, selling a six-month option on the film rights to *The Big Bounce* to Greenway Productions for $2,500. If Greenway could make the film happen with a major studio, they'd agree to Swanson's purchasing price of twenty-five thousand dollars. In the hopes of putting a fire under Wilkinson, Swanson stressed to Leonard a specific clause in his contract: Greenway would double their purchase price if *The Big Bounce* were to be released by a major publisher in hardcover within the year.[41]

Much to Leonard's surprise, his novel had been optioned by an unlikely admirer. Producer William Dozier had started his career decades earlier as a studio screenwriter before parlaying his own small production company's string of noir hits into an even more lucrative television career. At the same time he was optioning *The Big Bounce*, Dozier was most recognizable to American audiences not so much as the producer of his two campy hits—*Batman* and *The Green Hornet*—but as their uncredited announcer; each week, it was Dozier's baritone that reminded viewers to again tune in at the same bat-time on the same bat-channel for the next installment. Swanson closed the deal on August 29, further motivating Leonard to see the original novel placed with a good publisher, as doubling his payment would be coming at the best financial time. As he later recalled, "Fifty thousand bucks was about what I was going to have to borrow, quick."[42]

He also rushed to finish *Valdez Is Coming*. Having wanted to expand the original short story for as long as he had, the novel seemed to write itself. He'd even been able to tune out the latest Jimi Hendrix album that Peter and his buddies were spinning on the turntable. Later that afternoon, Leonard had proudly announced to his son, "I wrote eight pages today."[43] As son Christopher Leonard also recalled, his father even brought the work in progress to the family's annual summer vacation in upper Michigan. "Every summer we would go up north with about six or seven other families," Chris Leonard said.

According to the younger Leonard, his father hit a snag in the story during a beach outing, and asked the children for help in solving Valdez's escape scene. "One day Elmore—he'd always be on the beach with his writing pad in his lap—says to all of us, 'Kids, here's the scene. I just wrote this. Tell me if this is going to work. The guy—the star, Valdez—he gets caught by some bad guys and they tie him up to a long pole that's about ten feet long up his back. And then they take another one that might even be ten feet long or short or whatever. And they tie his arms out so he's crucified in the scene. What does he do? How does he get out of it?'" His father turned the scenario into a game, sending the kids into the woods to find an appropriately sized tree branch to use to re-create the scene. "We tied Elmore up to a crucifix, [and] he couldn't stand up because a ten-foot pole has him. He's still got arms out and he's just roped tight around . . . and he can't stand up, and he's going, 'Oh, this might not work' . . . So he himself comes up with the answer, which is he runs bent over and he runs between two trees hoping he can break this one that has his arms. And so he does, he runs between two trees and of course you hear the crack—like cracking in the middle of his back."[44] (Most readers of Leonard's Westerns and recent novels would have likely been surprised to learn at least one inspiration for Valdez's crucifixion and symbolic resurrection: at the time, Leonard had been volunteering as a Sunday school teacher of Catholic catechism. "When Dad was teaching catechism, the students were all teenagers," Chris recalled. "I remember he'd say that there was this one student, 'He's such a smartass.' So, one night he came home and I asked him, 'How was the class?' And Dad goes, 'That kid was mouthing off again. I told him to shut up and he wouldn't shut up—so I took an eraser and he said something back to me and I threw it at the top of his head, chalk-side down, and he looked like a skunk.'"[45])

Although deliberately muted, *Valdez Is Coming* would represent the most overt references to Leonard's own Christian ideals. During this period, his devotion to the Catholic Church remained at its strongest, as he continued to not only attend daily Mass but had insisted on sending all his children through the parochial school system. "I wrote the book in three weeks—or five weeks," Leonard later recalled. "I remember I called H. N. Swanson . . . and I said, 'I got something that I know is going to be a movie. If you get a producer in your office, I'll come out and pitch it, and I'll bet you anything he'll buy it.' And he said, 'Send me the story,' which I did—and he sold it immediately."[46]

Leonard had taken Swanson's advice and applied a subplot to the original story, expanding both the roles of Frank Tanner and his mistress, the young debutante known as "Gay Erin," as well as Tanner's chief lieutenant, El Segundo—a deadly doppelgänger of Valdez who, as a former tracker himself, keeps a secret respect for the underdog sheriff's spirit and skill.

On September 12, Swanson wrote to Leonard that he'd recently entertained a representative from the author's UK publisher, Peter Hale of Robert Hale, Ltd., in his office, and that *The Big Bounce* had piqued his interest. "I suggest you pass this along to Max Wilkinson," he wrote. "An early hardcover English edition might speed up the placing of it in America."[47] Before long, however, producer William Dozier hired first-time director Alex March, and assigned his son, Robert Dozier, the job of adapting Leonard's novel—much to the author's chagrin. With the film adaptation gaining traction, the necessity of a book sale only grew steadily. By November, Swanson had already sold *Valdez Is Coming* to producer Ira Steiner, with the intention that Burt Lancaster and his company co-produce and star. He even had the contract already in hand. "They feel they'll probably get Marlon Brando for the picture, also," Swanson wrote. "It will be a blockbuster, that's for sure."[48] (Unfortunately, the enigmatic leading man soon shot down their offer. Leonard recalled, "Brando wouldn't do it because . . . his background in the story was that he had been a scout and he had shot a lot of Apache Indians. So he wouldn't go for that and so they said well, we don't need you."[49])

But while Swanson's chief concern remained a book sale for *The Big Bounce*, Leonard's first instinct had been to lobby for both screenwriting jobs. "Right from the beginning, I wanted to get a job adapting one of the books or stories,"[50] he later claimed. "I wanted to write [*Valdez Is Coming*] because it was a one line story. It just shot ahead. I knew I could write it and I didn't get a chance to."[51]

Leonard strategized writing an original screenplay that could be written concurrently with its companion novel, allowing for a simultaneous sale. Right before the holiday season, a serendipitous visit to the local library provided Leonard with all the inspiration he'd need for the story. He had quickly devoured *Night Comes to the Cumberlands: A Biography of a Depressed Area* by noted journalist Harry M. Caudill, and became fascinated with impoverished areas within Appalachia and the American South. "I've got a good story," he wrote Swanson that week, "one that comes out of the characters and that I can tell effectively. I feel that I'm in my element, so I'm not worried about over-writing or over-doing the hillbilly sound of it."[52]

For his setting, Leonard had chosen Prohibition-era rural Kentucky, prior to the founding of the Tennessee Valley Authority and when electricity was still home-generated.[53] Within days, he'd completed a ten-page detailed outline for *The Broke-Leg War*—a contemporary novel with the atmosphere of a Western:

> The story takes place within a short period in the spring of 1930, during the high point of the great moonshine wars of Eastern Kentucky. This is an area of worn-out farms and worked-out coal mines and small towns where the good old boys meet on Saturday night to get drunk and raise hell. The people are farmers, ex-miners, moonshiners, county lawmen, Prohibition agents and Louisville-type gangsters . . . The people are real and the dialect will be served in moderation.[54]

Leonard had more or less made composites of the types of people Caudill had profiled so richly in his book and from that created characters that could easily have come from his earlier Westerns—although with a down-home sophistication. Of protagonist Son Martin, Leonard wrote: "He's a likable enough guy . . . He's an individualist, a loner at heart with a mind of his own. He's something of an *Hombre* or a *Cool Hand Luke* or the Machinist Mate in *The Sand Pebbles*. He makes the best corn whiskey in or around Broke-Leg County, Kentucky, and as long as he's passing out his whiskey and life is peaceful, everybody's happy and agrees Son Martin is about the best good old boy around. But as soon as Son Martin's single-minded attitude brings about a problem—screw Son Martin. Get him."[55] The "problem" is the unwanted attention from federal law enforcement that a specific rumor about Martin has generated; according to the townsfolk, Martin's deceased father had buried 150 barrels of top-tier illegal moonshine on the family's property, and with rumors that Prohibition laws may soon be repealed, everyone is eyeing the potential fortune that the perfectly aged moonshine could yield. "If it sounds complicated," Leonard wrote Swanson, "please don't worry about it. Most of what you read here is atmosphere and background information. The story itself will be tight. The plot and theme will be clean and simple."[56]

By the final day of January, Swanson had sold the outline to MGM—which saw potential in another *Bonnie and Clyde* blockbuster—for fifty thousand dollars; the first installment granted Leonard the coveted role as screenwriter. Producer Martin Ransohoff, owner of Filmways Productions, and responsible for such rural sitcoms as *The Beverly Hillbillies*, *Mr. Ed*, and *Green Acres*, was willing to take a chance on Leonard's ability to expand the outline into a filmable script, but insisted on meeting him first.[57] In preparation, Leonard mapped out the entire story in enumerated scenes, making both a script and matching novel easier to pace. Aside from the copious notes he'd pruned from *Night Comes to the Cumberlands*, Leonard had typed up methods on moonshine production and studied a dictionary of the colloquial dialect common throughout the American South. In an effort to soak up local color firsthand, he booked a trip to Kentucky, stopping in the town of Somerset. While there, he interviewed a few locals and made notes on their way of life and ideologies:

> Warning to moonshiner—"If you hear three shots, you know there's hell in the air."
> Nice home, clean, well-kept—"Right smart little house."
> Mortally wounded—"Shot him too dead to skin."

Keeping his head buried in his notebook, Leonard also noted some residents' views on the overtly alcoholic lifestyle and rampant racism. He'd spent time interviewing one local man in his early sixties named Buck Beshear, a hard drinker and manufacturer of moonshine. "I'd go out to milk the cows about 4 a.m. and have me three or four good pulls of moonshine in the barn," Beshear told Leonard. "Boy, it'd make breakfast taste good . . . I drank moonshine 'stead of water out plowin'." Leonard had noted his skepticism that Beshear claimed to drink two to three gallons of "corn" per week, annotating the quote: "Doubt it."

One major issue that Leonard had initially also doubted until he saw it face-to-face was the vitriolic bigotry that was, apparently, a sort of hive mentality around Beshear's neck of the woods—the older man throwing out filter-less racist lingo, fully aware that Leonard was capturing every word. Asked how African Americans are treated in the community, Beshear had no problem sharing his views: "Niggers? Why, we treat them as equals in Somerset. Election time, we even go out and get them, pay them something for their time coming in to vote." As Leonard kept writing, Beshear went on: "We used to have a sign, 'No niggers allowed in town after sundown.'" He had then asked his young granddaughter what she thought of the African American locals, again using the same racial slur, to which the schoolgirl had responded, "Why they're even cleaner and better dressed than some of the whites."

Leonard noted to himself, "I don't believe it." He labeled the section in his notes: "*Local Intelligence*."[58]

The finished product, once delivered to Swanson, earned Leonard the response he was looking for: "I can tell you right now this script is as excellent a job as any of our screenwriters could turn out . . . At any time you want a career as a screenwriter, I'm ready to run with you." Swanson's sign-off Leonard would never forget: "*Whenever I am asked what kind of writing is the most lucrative, I have to say ransom notes.*"

Leonard highlighted the line and filed it away.[59]

Following a family trip to Florida and the Bahamas in February, Leonard agreed to fly to Los Angeles, first class and all expenses paid. Swanson had been able to negotiate thirty-five hundred a week for Leonard to remain in Hollywood and work on the script.[60]

Swanson's efforts also earned Leonard his Writers Guild of America membership—a clear path toward financial stability.[61] It was a needed blessing as he was ready to give up on trying to sell *The Big Bounce* as a US hardcover edition. During the time that Max Wilkinson had been attempting to make the sale, Leonard had already completed *another* novel and was in the early stages of converting *The Broke-Leg War*—recently retitled *The Moonshine War*—into a proper novel. With Wilkinson already behind on two properties, Leonard began considering Swanson's offer to represent all his work, both literary *and* film. First, however, were his responsibilities to producer Martin Ransohoff and newly appointed director Richard Quine, who expected Leonard to be present for both preproduction meetings and occasional visits to the set in Stockton, California—far from accurate to his original Kentucky setting. To Leonard's bewilderment, actor Alan Alda, known primarily for his television success, had been paired with British theater actor Patrick McGoohan, as Son Martin and antagonist Frank Long, respectively. (Apparently, the star of hits *Secret Agent* and *The Prisoner* was less than enthusiastic about the upcoming shoot, telling the *Los Angeles Times*, "You have to do something from time to time to pay the rent."[62]) As Leonard later recalled, "I'd go out to Hollywood, stay all week, and go home weekends. I'd go to [Richard Quine]'s house every day and we would sit around and talk about what we were going to do . . . broad, general terms, never specific, about what should be in the picture. I thought we just wasted an awful lot of time, until finally, I wrote the script and then I was fired . . . They had another writer for maybe a week and then I was hired back on—Quine liked me and got me back." He added, "The picture was also miscast . . . After a number of takes of one scene, Patrick McGoohan came off the set, walked up to me, and said, 'What's it like to stand there and hear your lines all fucked up?'"[63]

To Leonard, it wasn't nearly as bad as *reading* them equally fucked up. In February, he had returned from the Bahamas to find a copy of Robert Dozier's adaptation of *The Big Bounce* waiting for him at home. To Leonard, the day would live in infamy. "Sorry you didn't like Dozier's screenplay," Swanson wrote. "Be sure that Max gets a copy of [*The Big Bounce*] to Robert Hale in London as fast as possible. Your contract does not specify that the hardcover must be from an American publisher, actually, and can be on any side of the water. I think this could be the solution to your problem."[64]

Leonard had his own solution to the problem: with only the finishing touches to go on the novel of *The Moonshine War*, there was nothing preventing him from beginning another screenplay for a similarly rapid turnaround. He soon began notes for a tale of two inmates contained behind those walls, ostracized for being the only minorities within the prison's population. Gradually, Leonard's Westerns had taken on more socially progressive lenses, making his chief protagonists either half Apache, raised by Apaches, or Mexican. For what would soon be titled *Forty Lashes Less One*, Leonard created two new characters—one African American and one Mexican but of Apache descent, intent on making their plight in Yuma and journey toward freedom his most unorthodox and toughest yet. He shared the concept with Swanson, but held off on starting a first draft. Having told the former head of Columbia Pictures, producer Mike Frankovich, the bare bones of the story, Swanson reported back, "[Frankovich] was most interested, but said, 'Why does he have to be an Indian—why couldn't he be a white man?' Don't let this throw you because I said, 'After you buy the property, you can write the part for Lee Marvin if you want to.'"[65] Regardless, Swanson was able to sell Leonard's concept to Bantam by the end of August—as a novel.[66] Only weeks later, he had the ear of Harry Caplan of National General Productions who was "already taking an interest" in the new property and encouraged Leonard to follow up with the producer.

While in Eastern Kentucky earlier in the year, Leonard had also taken a side trip to Florida for a real estate sale. Once his work had really begun to sell to Hollywood, he'd had it in mind to set his mother, Flora, up somewhere she could safely enjoy her twilight years and have something to do. He found it in the form of a one-story multi-unit motel called the Coconut Palms—just under two thousand square feet in Pompano Beach, Florida, and already owned by Beverly's family. She recalled, "I had given Dutch an ultimatum twice: 'She goes or I go.' The first time, I came home and he said, 'She won't leave.' The second time, I was pregnant with Bill, and I told Dutch, 'I really can't deal with her any longer. I'm going to visit my parents in Florida and you tell Noni—which is what we called her after Jane was born . . . The day I was leaving, Dutch's back went out and he couldn't get out of bed. My uncle had to come to take me to the airport. But when I got back home, she was gone." Beverly added, "She went to Florida and lived with her sister until Dutch got her the hotel."[67] Once both the checks for *The Moonshine War* and *Valdez Is Coming* had cleared, Leonard had been able to begin negotiations for the motel, finally purchasing it outright for Flora in November.

Bill Leonard later remembered, "We always drove to Florida on Easter break, straight down I-75, and my dad was very anal about it. We would be in the car at five a.m. and just keep moving. He always wanted to make good time and never stopped to eat, so we'd just have crappy sandwiches that we'd packed. We barely stopped to *pee*—my brother Chris and I had to pee in a mayonnaise jar—because my dad insisted we had to make good time." He added, "I always wondered, 'How can my grandmother—this cute, small, frail woman—run a hotel? Isn't it scary when people knock on the door in the middle of the night?'"[68]

Leonard himself noted there wasn't a single palm tree on the grounds.

Although the timing was unintentional, Leonard got an additional financial boost just before Christmas, as Max Wilkinson finally solidified a deal with Gold Medal to release a paperback of *The Big Bounce*. (The UK hardcover release hadn't qualified for the doubled purchasing price; however, Wilkinson's paperback earned them half that amount.) Unfortunately, there wasn't enough time left for the book to hit the stands before the film's March opening—another day in Leonard's life that would forever live in infamy. "In the case of *The Big Bounce*—served to the customers yesterday at the Trans-Lux East and West Theaters—art is still something to be found in museums," wrote A. H. Weiler in the *New York Times*. "This hothouse item about swinging sex and crime, junior division, filmed in color in the picturesque Monterey area of California, is composed largely of ersatz thrills, explicit and often amateurish dialogue, and a hedonistic attitude toward practically everything . . . 'Have you ever thought of doing something else' [Van Heflin] asks our hero at one point. It's a question that could have been put to almost everyone concerned with *The Big Bounce*."[69] Swanson was quick to check on Leonard following *The Big Bounce*'s reviews. "Both [*Hollywood Reporter*] and *Variety* reviews on *Bounce* were dreadful," he wrote. "'It didn't hurt Elmore Leonard, though,'" Swanson quoted, "'because the screenplay was the whole problem here.'"[70]

Over the years, Leonard would have fun refining the story of his first experience watching *The Big Bounce*—or at least part of it. He and Beverly hadn't attended the New York premiere on March 5, but they caught a weekday matinee with friends later that same month. "After it opened in New York, several friends and I went to see it," he later recalled. "A lady in front of us said to her husband, 'This is the worst picture I've ever seen.' They walked out and we walked out about fifteen minutes later."[71] (For decades, he would humorously cite *The Big Bounce* was "the second worst movie ever made," claiming that the sheer laws of statistics dictated that *something* had to be worse. Following the release of the 2004 remake, Leonard announced he'd finally found it.[72])

Leonard retained his hopes that *The Moonshine War*'s hardcover release could still establish success in the non-Western market, and Swanson's early negotiations with Doubleday—a first-time publisher for Leonard—indicated such a deluxe release.[73] On the first day of June, Leonard followed up with Swanson's contact at Doubleday, Harold Kuebler, offering updates and his own timeline for the foreseeable future. "I've been commuting to Hollywood for the past four weeks, going there Monday morning and coming home at the end of the week to sit at the table and be the Father. I've been staying this week for [Jane's] high school graduation and to finish the revision of [*The Moonshine War*], then going back June 9 to hand in the final pages."[74]

At the beginning of July, Leonard buckled down to dive into the *Forty Lashes Less One* script. Over the past few months, he'd already penned an expanded sixty-page version, broken into a three-act structure. He'd placed the action in 1909 when government officials were preparing to close the eight-foot walled Yuma dungeon indefinitely. He had two protagonists in mind: Raymond San Carlos, a Mexican inmate with partial Apache heritage, and an African American inmate named Harold Jackson. Hating each other at first, Jackson—a deserter of the Spanish-American War later convicted of murder—and San Carlos—doing time for killing a white cowboy—soon become reluctant friends and allies due to a vicious common enemy: a psychotic purveyor of jailhouse contraband, Frank Shelby, who acts as a collaborator within the Yuma walls. The brutal treatment of Jackson and San Carlos from both the guards and their fellow inmates quickly draws the attention of Yuma's interim director, Everett Manly, a Holy Word Pentecostal preacher who naively believes empowering the two men will boost their morale and feelings of self-worth. Handing them historical books on the Zulu warriors and Apache nation, respectively, Manly allows the two men the bonus privilege of jogging together every day—unwittingly inspiring the men to summon their inner courage and draw upon the strength of their ancestors. And as the clock ticks toward Yuma's final days of operation, their newfound endurance and confidence becomes tested as Shelby plots his own escape at their expense.

It was far more brutal than his previous stories. But Leonard also amped up the humor, as the exchanges between the two men and their shared plight among the bigoted guards and fellow inmates contained much of the irony and sarcasm that would define his later crime novels. For characterization, Leonard had thrown himself into the types of literature Manly would assign his captive pupils. Raymond San Carlos proved to be the easiest, as Leonard was well-versed in both the histories of the Apache nations and Mexican territories. For Jackson, however, Leonard took notes on Shaka Zulu and other historical African tribal leaders, emphasizing the Zulus' "great black and white shields made out of cowhides," as well as their discipline and mandatory service as a warrior. However, he wrote, "similar to forced marches in a European army . . . [Zulus] would be told to run 20 miles in one direction . . ." for building endurance, providing an advantage over their white oppressors. For Yuma's interim director, the misguided man of God Mr. Manly, Leonard combed through Biblical proverbs for the most relevant citable quotes, typing them as "Verses from the Bible about punishment for sins."

Leonard had the first draft completed by the final day of August and got the revisions to Swanson just over two weeks later. And while Ira Steiner shopped *Valdez Is Coming* elsewhere, Swanson sold *Forty Lashes*

Less One to his former copyright rival for fifty thousand dollars. In January 1970—after "studio deductions and agency commissions"—Leonard cleared just over half.[75]

That month also saw the Doubleday hardcover release of *The Moonshine War*, the reviews of which were enough to give Leonard a sigh of relief. "Whether the success of the *Bonnie and Clyde* movie is responsible for the trend, there is today, nonetheless, a very real, and significant flow of black, rustic comedies mixed with violence and set in an earlier era, preferably Prohibition days," wrote Carl May in the *Nashville Tennessean*. "Elmore Leonard's new comedy (soon to be a movie) is an admirable example." May added, "And the Eastern Kentucky locale is reasonably authentic, so let us hope the movie will be filmed there,"[76] unaware that the production had recently wrapped in California. In West Virginia's *Dominion Post*, critic Andrew G. Fusco wrote, "In a way, the book is a social criticism, but in another way it doesn't seem to have the 'hidden message' which has become the keynote in modern literature. Leonard has a story to tell and he tells it well . . . If you read nothing else all year, do read this. It's pure Americana and it's great."[77]

Leonard was also profiled in the *Birmingham Eccentric*—the first major feature interview he'd held in his new office. A photographer had come along, posing the newly bearded author in shirtsleeves and tie, lost in the pages of a brand-new hardcover edition of *The Moonshine War*. For the shoot, Leonard had blown up his old family photo—"Dutch" at age nine, aiming his gun to the camera in a Bonnie Parker pose—and hung it above his desk.[78]

While revising *Forty Lashes Less One* for National General, Leonard was already eyeing another, lobbying hard to adapt *Valdez Is Coming* himself. Assigned director Sydney Pollack, however, had insisted on his own screenwriter, David Rayfiel, whose track record with the director already included 1965's *The Slender Thread*, as well as critical darlings *This Property Is Condemned* and *Castle Keep*—the latter starring Burt Lancaster. During preproduction, however, Pollack walked, taking with him screenwriter Rayfiel. Experienced stage director Edwin Sherin, making his film debut, was brought in as his replacement. Rather than enlist Leonard, Lancaster had instead plugged in his own screenwriter—producer Roland Kibbee—and they moved the production to southern Spain.

This time, Leonard was allowed to stay home.

CHAPTER 8

On the Line in Hollywood, 1970–1971

I've heard of writers who claim they don't read their reviews—and find that almost impossible to believe. You write to please yourself first, if you're serious and if you're honest. But you're also communicating. Otherwise, why have the work published?[1]

Dear Swanie—Don't delay on $50 thousand National General check," Leonard wrote on January 15. "I'm about to be overdrawn."

The last Leonard had heard from the company had been before the holiday season, assured they were still proactively pursuing Richard Brooks to replace Sydney Pollack on *Forty Lashes Less One*.[2] Within days, Swanson had National General's check in hand—just under thirty thousand dollars after studio deductions and Swanson's commission. With that financial reprieve in place, Leonard continued the *Forty Lashes Less One* revisions—a task he'd been juggling since September. "How are you doing with the changes?" Swanson wrote on February 19. "Do you think you'll be old and gray before this thing is wrapped up?"

However, Swanson also wrote bearing gifts: a two-man production team at Columbia Pictures was seeking a screenwriter for their new film, a drama inspired by the famed union organizer Cesar Chavez and his crusade for fruit pickers' rights. Leonard had researched similar terrain for *The Big Bounce*, so his name had been thrown into the ring. "Are you interested?"[3]

Indeed, Leonard was; he viewed *The Big Bounce* and the soon-to-be-wrapped *Valdez Is Coming* as missed financial opportunities, and more screenwriting work meant more exposure. Yet, juggling all the screenplay rewrites was already causing significant gaps of time in his fiction writing. With *Moonshine*, Leonard had not only picked the topic himself but had complete control over both the novel and the screenplay. In effect, he'd answered to no one, at least until the sale. Now, Leonard would be the hired gun, working at the whims of two executives. Fortunately for Leonard, the executives themselves were experienced and seemed passionate about the project. At fifty years old, former screenwriter Edward Lewis was the more established of the production team, having parlayed a standalone deal with Kirk Douglas in 1956 into a ten-year partnership with the star. Lewis then made a name for himself producing hits *The Last Sunset*, *Lonely Are the Brave*, and Stanley Kubrick's *Spartacus*—for the latter two, successfully bringing long-blacklisted screenwriter Dalton Trumbo home to a welcoming Hollywood. Unlike Lewis, the younger Howard Jaffe had only one credit under his belt as the associate producer for *The Happening*, an ill-fated counterculture caper that had starred Anthony Quinn as a mob boss abducted by a band of antiestablishment hippies. But unlike Lewis, Jaffe was considered Hollywood royalty through pedigree: his father, Leo, was the president of Columbia Pictures. It also helped that they would be working alongside Gabriel Katzka, coproducer of the James Garner thriller *Marlowe*.

When Leonard didn't make an immediate decision, Swanson circled back the first week of March and informed him that Jaffe was in New York and hoped to visit the writer in Detroit on his way back to Los Angeles. Swanson had also stipulated to Jaffe that other producers, such as Ira Steiner, had been seeking their own audience with Leonard, the writer having made it clear he'd rather work on projects than "talk them to death." Leonard agreed and met with Jaffe the following Friday.[4]

Following a March meeting at Leonard's Pierce Street office, Leonard went running to skim current magazines and newspapers for more fodder on migrant fruit pickers and their union woes. He started by reexamining his older research for *The Big Bounce*, pulling the same July 1965 *Detroit News* pictorial profile of Michigan-bound Mexican braceros—the migrant workers who slaved over fields of beets, cherries, strawberries, and cucumbers—that had inspired Jack Ryan's introduction. For his part, Jaffe sent copious notes on Cesar Chavez and the famed 1965 "grape strike" led by the union leader in Delano, California, to Leonard's home. But the producer's dictums soon followed; he had already typed up his own ideas and loose character sketches—primarily composites of characters and archetypes he'd liked in the films *Lonely Are the Brave*, *The*

Defiant Ones, *Cool Hand Luke*, and *Viva Zapata!* Of course, all were familiar to film buff Leonard.[5]

With the *Forty Lashes Less One* revisions completed the first week of March, Leonard was able to throw himself into Jaffe's full cache of notes, including sketches of an earlier, aborted project entitled *See How They Run*. From those dozens of pages, he cherry-picked the elements from which he was granted carte blanche. One particular figure Jaffe described as "like the Joseph Wiseman character in *Zapata*" seemed worthy of expanding: a "Christ figure who couldn't make it in his own country [and thus] went to the U.S. to reform and help and preach there."[6] It was the producer's original historical inspiration, however, that soon gave Leonard his title—*Picket Line*.

Jaffe had based the lead character on Reies Tijerina, a real-life activist within the Chicano Movement and militant spokesperson for Hispanic and Mexican Americans' rights. Jaffe had named his own character "Teorina"—which Leonard quickly corrected to the proper spelling, and began envisioning the part as an aggressive doppelgänger to the Cesar Chavez character. However, Jaffe also insisted that Leonard add a love interest—"preferably a woman of Mexican heritage [in order to] utilize one of the unique Mexican courting customs." And despite whatever well-meaning progressive intentions Jaffe's passion project was meant to convey, his directives to Leonard were rife with a whitewashed misunderstanding of cultures and experiences. Regarding the Mexican people portrayed in the film, he dubiously advised the author, "Despite the fact that they seem organized in the daytime, their actual organization is haphazard—free time is chaos, undisciplined, rowdy, drinking—they are unable to manage—to govern themselves." On April 14, Jaffe sent Leonard a copy of Peter Matthiessen's social biography, *Sal Si Puedes (Escape If You Can): Cesar Chavez and the New American Revolution*, as well as journalist Eugene Nelson's *Huelga: The First Hundred Days of the Great Delano Grape Strike*. "Unlike California," he wrote Leonard, "many of Texas' problems have been involved with the incredible conflicts and contradictions within the structure of the [Catholic Church]. Although we would have to handle any matters of the church very delicately, we may be able to give our picture a *Man for All Seasons* dimension that we never before considered."[7]

Although another sheaf of notes on the topic followed at the end of May, Jaffe had needn't worry about the writer's knowledge regarding the current frustrations of the Catholic Church. A devout Catholic for nearly all his life, Leonard had been intently watching modernizations within the Church, and had already begun collecting articles on the topic from Beverly's *Life* magazines and his own subscription to the *National Review*. Profile after profile described fractured congregations throughout the United States, each citing the next generation of American youths as harder to retain. It was, after all, the same generation that sought the next, bigger bounce that had inquired if God was dead.

Throughout April, Leonard and Jaffe held numerous brainstorming sessions over the phone. The last week of the month, Jaffe revealed he'd been having issues with Columbia Pictures with *Picket Line* as it stood, ending any hope to start principal photography in June. With no other option but to work with his current revisions, Leonard agreed to circle back once he and Beverly returned from their upcoming trip to Europe. "Hopefully we can make a quick deal with this one; I'm having money problems with the IRS," Leonard wrote to Swanson the following day. He also shared with Swanson the latest concept that had grabbed hold of his imagination. "Have got a new story idea half-outlined," he wrote. "*Jesus Saves*—which could turn out to be the best one I've gotten my hands on . . . I'll work on it while we're away and finish as soon as we get back."[8]

In order to deliver the promised progress on *Jesus Saves*, Leonard had quickly hammered out a rough thirteen-page outline for himself and brought it along on the trip—primarily character notes and plotting through the first act.

For *Jesus Saves*, Leonard returned his focus to the American South. In June 1968, he had torn an article out of *Esquire*, "Power in Their Blood," Robert Sherrill's profile of four modern preachers struggling to modernize with the urban communities of the "New South." It had been the rise of conservative evangelical preachers that had piqued his interest the most. He'd even initiated a brief correspondence with controversial televangelist Oral Roberts, who claimed he had founded his eponymous university in Tulsa, Oklahoma, under direct orders from God. (On Saturday mornings, Leonard would frequently watch the "fire and brimstone" preacher on television with his son Bill, apparently amused by the televangelist's behavior.[9]) Via letter, he had asked Roberts for more information on his massive congregation, making a five-dollar donation to his church, but leaving out his true research incentive. Roberts followed up two days later, explaining to Leonard his three-part strategy for deliverance:

> *First, you make God your SOURCE of supply (see Phil. 4:19) . . . Second, you must start GIVING—giving of yourself to help others—giving of your love, time, talent, money, etc. Then God will multiply back what you give (Luke 6:38). Third, START EXPECTING MIRACLES. God will surely send miracles to you, therefore, you must expect these and be ready to receive them.*

Roberts added, "I just can't help but feel that SOMETHING GOOD IS GOING TO HAPPEN TO YOU, Brother Leonard."[10] Still clutching to the tenets of his own faith, Leonard had channeled the conflict between the spirit and the flesh into *Picket Line*'s flawed protagonist—but there, he'd pulled his punches a bit, toeing the line with Jaffe's character notes. With *Jesus Saves*, however, Leonard was following his own instincts on an original story. "What I want to dramatize," Leonard noted, "is that after the emotionalism and razzle-dazzle of religion have been spent, there remains only one real test and that is the giving of self." True to form, however, he later added to the finished treatment, "At the same time, I want to dress up the story with long white Cadillacs and modern, gaudy merchandising to present the commercial side of selling God and saving souls."[11]

As Leonard scholar Charles Rzepka later observed, "[Leonard] was part of that left-leaning progressive wing of Catholicism that really got a terrific boost in the [1970s] with the ecumenical movement and liberation theology. I think that affected him tremendously and was eventually responsible for his lapsing to the extent that he didn't attend Mass anymore, he didn't believe in the rituals. But that left-leaning progressive attitude that does appear, like in *Bandits*, you find it all in a lot of places in his writing and sometimes more prominently than elsewhere. He had said of Dorothy Day that you live the life of Jesus, you don't just give it lip service or go through the rituals involved . . . I think he really was rooted in his little brush with existentialism back in college."[12]

Leonard had been comfortable enough to give *Jesus Saves* a contemporary setting, painting the story's landscape with observations from hours on the road to Pompano Beach and back. And although he would again be delving into the American South, this time, the action would take place in

Dalton, Georgia, not far from Chickamauga National Military Park. There, Leonard introduced Reverend Bill Hill—a charismatic fortysomething dime-store Oral Roberts and former rock and roll manager whose claim to fame is his role as leader of the Church of the True Faith, "home of the World's Tallest Illuminated Crucifix." Hill's brainchild, the True Faith church, also included a garden pavilion, Meditation Chapel, cafeteria, and a gift shop where visitors could purchase, among other things, True Faith kneeling cushions and a seven-inch scale-model battery-operated replica of the blue neon crucifix. The sprawling congregation also included a choir of young girls, whose star attraction—a nineteen-year-old baton-twirler Leonard ultimately named Louly Falkner—happened to be Hill's barely legal dirty little secret. Pulling a thousand dollars a week during True Faith's first year had afforded Bill Hill's building of the massive crucifix, "Jesus Saves" blaring in blue neon across its arm's width.[13] But as Leonard's story begins, hard times have since fallen on Hill, the novelty of his beloved landmark long since worn thin. While desperate for a new attraction, Hill learns of a local man purported to have miraculously healed a surgery-bound cancer patient. Hill immediately sees dollar signs. Throughout the story, Hill acts as Pygmalion, watching as faith healer Lindell Reason's real-life miracles overshadow the phony con jobs he'd usually install for religious spectacle—legitimized in Hill's own mind as "staged cures." But as Reason's sweet-natured innocence begins to deteriorate with fame—his naivete soon replaced by egoism and promiscuity—Bill Hill begins to look inward, questioning his own moral fiber. (Leonard added that Hill liked to "play games with his conscience," a sentiment cribbed from French psychotherapist Claude M. Steiner's recent study, *Games Alcoholics Play*, which he'd read earlier in the year.)

By the film's climax, Hill is inspired to confess all his sins to the full crowd at the foot of the enormous crucifix. He pleads to the angry crowd, many wearing shirts with Lindell Reason's image. Leonard wrote, "Hill has now gone all the way, sacrificed himself in trying to save others from a life of idolatry. And they turn him down cold, boo him off the stage." In the end, a downtrodden Bill Hill walks away from True Faith, the words of Lindell Reason—ever in character—blaring from the stage's loudspeakers all the way to the road: "You know something, friends? The natural-born goodness of people never ceases to amaze me . . ." Hill recites those same words to himself as he walks the road alone—not quite healed, but almost certainly saved.[14]

• • •

Leonard soon took a much-needed reprieve and traveled with Beverly on their long-postponed vacation, joined by two other couples for a nineteen-day tour of European cities: Allan and Nancy Hayes, and Bill and Lou Martz. Their itinerary landed them in Heathrow Airport, working counterclockwise to Rome, a rented yacht along the Greek islands, and finally, the group's departure from Paris.

Leonard brought along a travel journal, his push to write every day whether he felt like it or not, as well as for venting his sarcastic indifference to most of the touristy sites. Following a visit to Bodiam Castle in East Sussex on their second day, he'd had to take his Early Times straight at a pub across the street; there was, apparently, "no word in England for ice." After dinner at Overton's back in London, an altercation with a local cab driver resulted in new inspiration for *Jesus Saves*. "[The driver] was called on his gross overcharge, of course," Leonard wrote in his journal that night, "but when he told us about his wife in the hospital undergoing a tumor operation, our hearts went out to him and we gave him a generous tip." Leonard quickly added that detail to faith healer Lindell Reason's first miracle.

Before leaving London, Leonard met his longtime British publisher in person for the first time. "Innes Rose of Farquharson, whom Beverly and I had lunch with, has never been through the Tower [of London]," he recalled later. "We told him that was alright, we had never been through the Ford plant." On Friday, Leonard and the group flew to Rome and checked into the Hotel Valadier on the Via della Fontanella and headed for the Spanish Steps. Of St. Peter's Basilica, he wrote, "Inside, there is one spot on the wall where they could have put in another angel, cherub, saint or something, but I guess they wanted to keep it low-key and not overdo it. Restraint is a good number if you have it and can appreciate it."

On May 11, the group flew to Athens, then Hydra, allowing Leonard to continue his personal observations:

Wednesday, May 13

We left Hydra this morning at five o'clock . . . Milos is known for Venus, the statue without the arms that was discovered here in 1825. The statue isn't here anymore, as you probably know, and there isn't anything else either.

Thursday, May 14

Women are always being carried off in this part of the world. Usually by Turks—the Turks brought a bunch of Greek slave girls here in 1603 who inter-married and that's why Crete today is known for its beautiful women. The place to see them is at five o'clock in the afternoon in the barber shop getting their shaves.

Tuesday, May 19

We all like Athens very much and understand what Humphrey Bogart meant when he said, "Athens, you're like a dame. With a mustache."

Leonard was still quoting Bogie as the group made its way to Paris—this time *High Sierra*—Bogart comparing Paris to "a big, beautiful dame." "God, you talk crazy," Ida Lupino had replied. "Oh no, Ida," Leonard wrote in his journal, "we will testify to the fact that Humphrey was right . . . [Paris] is a happy, friendly city and that its reputation for being cold and heartless—and the people rude—is not true."

He was soon aware that the group's warm reception was likely due to the presence of his French connection within the city: Georges Fronval, a former actor turned journalist and—under a multitude of pseudonyms—author of numerous studies on the American West. Born Jacques Garnier, Fronval had gotten his career start as a film critic at the age of eighteen, even making a brief on-screen appearance in Jean Renoir's *The Grand Illusion*. He had then pivoted toward his love of American Western films and literature, going on to pen biographies of Geronimo and Buffalo Bill Cody, as well as studies of Native American language—all virgin territory in the French language. Now at sixty-six years old, Fronval was the only European member of the Western Writers of America—and he knew Leonard's early work very well. Of his new friend, Leonard later wrote, "[Georges] is low and wide, with close-cropped gray hair, a craggy face and an awful-smelling French cigarette in the corner of his mouth that dribbles ashes all over the wide expanse of his French double-breasted suit." He added, "George *is* Inspector Maigret. If he doesn't look like a cop, nobody does." With that image in place, Leonard was happy to have Fronval act as their group's unofficial tour guide through Paris.[15]

• • •

Upon their return, Leonard completed the *Jesus Saves* treatment the first week of June.

"*Jesus Saves* has all the earmarks of a successful screen story and book," H. N. Swanson wrote on June 8, relieved the material had commercial appeal. "Some weeks ago, when you first told me about it, I had a few reservations, the main one thinking that it would be compared with *Elmer Gantry*. However, you have ducked that very neatly and the injection of religious rock music makes it very palatable."[16]

Much like the white Cadillacs and gaudy religious merchandise, the hip country rock and roll soundtrack had been clearly stipulated from Leonard's earliest notes and was meant to be more than simple background ambiance. "The religion I want to describe is emotional, delivered with a back-country beat that works itself up and takes off in a shouting, church-shaking frenzy," he wrote, citing modern blues-rock duo Delaney and Bonnie as a comparable representation. "This is beginning to sound like a musical, which it's not in any way. But there are definite sounds I hear that emphasize the mood of the story." Leonard explained an appropriate choice of music would set mood and atmosphere without dialogue, making up for the exposition that a screenplay wouldn't allow. With *Jesus Saves*, Leonard claimed he wanted to "demonstrate a theme expressed" in Bob Dylan's music, particularly his philosophical hit, "Like a Rolling Stone."[17] Swanson vowed to get copies out to producers before the following week's WGA strike deadline, urging his young client to "get down on your 'prayer bones!'" Leonard, who had initially pushed for WGA membership for its consistent benefits, had been a member of the Guild less than a year.

Upon his return from Europe, Leonard also found yet another sheaf of notes from *Picket Line* producer Howard Jaffe waiting for him. He moved fast, tackling as much of Jaffe's work he could squeeze in before a potential strike killed the project. Hoping to replicate *The Moonshine War*'s successful bids for both print and screen, Leonard labeled his *Picket Line* progress as a "treatment of a proposed novel and motion picture." Just as he had used *Night Comes to the Cumberlands* two years earlier, Leonard supplemented Jaffe's care packages with his own trips to the library. He combed through Frank A. Kostyu's recent study on the geographical impacts of harvesting, *Shadows in the Valley*, and studied similar reports by C. Seldon Morley, the agricultural commissioner in Kern County, California. He also reached out to fellow Western author and Arizona native Robert MacLeod, another exception among the writers with whom Leonard kept in touch. According to MacLeod, the first order of business was in choosing the perfect crop at the center of the narrative—something geographically correct, but also somewhat egalitarian in symbolizing the strikers' cause. After all, Chavez had had his grapes. "Dear Dutch," he wrote on May 20, "To my mind, onions lack the charisma of cantaloupe or honeydew melons, so by all means, go ahead and use the latter!"[18]

It wasn't long before Leonard's storytelling instincts began to clash with producer Howard Jaffe's expectations. He wrote to the producer on July 12, reporting his progress on reading the copious amount of material sent to him; he'd even garnered more than thirty pages of his own notes. Leonard claimed the very image of a picket line held symbolic weight, as every book on Cesar Chavez and similar social movements had all dictated the necessity of a line drawn between opposing forces.[19] Chavez's own words to biographer Peter Matthiessen had resonated with Leonard, and had worked their way into both his notes and in-progress film treatment: "*If a man comes out of the field and goes on the picket line, even for one day, he'll never be the same . . . The picket line is where a man makes his commitment, and it's irrevocable; and the longer he's on the picket line, the stronger the commitment.*"

Leonard had admittedly latched on to Chavez's words, explaining his own perception of the picket line's significance from the writer's standpoint: "Now consider for a moment that individual commitment is the key idea: a man standing up to be counted in spite of his fear of the overwhelming odds against him," he wrote, acknowledging the strongest theme to permeate his work since "Three-Ten to Yuma" seventeen years earlier—and the essence of Hemingway's *For Whom the Bell Tolls*. He proposed an everyman character who could act as the audience's lens into that world—not unlike playwright Robert Bolt's original stage production of *A Man for All Seasons*, one of Howard Jaffe's original templates for *Picket Line*'s structure.[20] Although not in the cinematic adaptation, Bolt's common-man character existed solely to explain the more labyrinthine elements of sixteenth-century British monarchy, often breaking the fourth wall to provide commentary. For Fred Zinnemann's 1966 Oscar-winning film version, Bolt himself had dissolved the character into various new ones, allowing minor characters like the Thames ferryman, the local jailer, and, memorably, the executioner to relate needed exposition through more-natural dialogue. A fan of Zinnemann's *High Noon*, Leonard had seen the *Seasons* film, but not Bolt's original play—and he had no intention of allowing a character to speak directly to the audience. However, an inserted everyman could display much of the empathy missing from the story.

In his lengthy letter to Jaffe, Leonard described his own everyman—someone with whom the targeted US audience could relate: a particular field worker who could be introduced to the audience by walking off the picket line amid the growing chaos, even as accusations of betrayal are hurled at him. He elaborated on the character as a C student in college—not an athlete—who enjoys an occasional beer but "conserves his energy," perhaps because he "isn't much of a lothario." The picker would also have longish hair—though he wasn't a hippie—and appear both self-conscious and introspective. Although Leonard had named the new protagonist Bud Davis, his literary Jack Ryan loomed large. He summed up his own philosophy, asking somewhat rhetorically, "Do you stand up and do what your conscience dictated, or do you duck and make excuses and rationalize your way through life? . . . I believe he adds a dimension that we missed completely in our discussions." (Aside from creating young Davis, Leonard had also given proper names and backstories to the two key protagonists inherited from Jaffe's notes: Tijerina was now "a tough, thin-lipped Chicano" ex-con out of East Los Angeles named Chito Cruz, soon to be renamed Chino Rojas, and, for the Christlike union leader, Leonard wrote Jaffe, "Let's stop right now calling him the Chavez character and name him, if you will, *Vincent Mora*.")[21]

Unbeknownst to Jaffe, however, Leonard had not only already completed his first draft of the *Picket Line* treatment—citing full chunks to the producer within the letter itself—but had also gone ahead and started what would become a 112-page typescript in prose form. With *The Moonshine War*, Leonard viewed the 1920s American South as an extension of the more familiar Arizona Territory—a canvas upon which Old West morality could be set against the changing zeitgeist of an evolving America. Now with *Picket Line*, Leonard attempted it again. As *Picket Line* opens, the strike has been going on for a week. Bud Davis, melon satchel around his neck, watches from afar as the enigmatic organizer for the Valley Agricultural Workers Association (VAWA), Vincent Mora, exchanges fiery words with the Wade County Rangers—Leonard's stand-in for the real-life Texas Rangers. Inspired by Mora's nerve, Davis joins up with the strikers, making enemies of both his employers and other white citizens who now view the young man as a traitor to his race. However, Davis's bravery doesn't go unnoticed by onlooker Chito Cruz, a sympathizer to *La Causa*, reluctant to use Mora's peaceful means, and *Picket Line*'s second act was meant to focus on Cruz's own evolution from bystander to proactive soldier.[22]

Leonard walked a fine line within the typescript, adding as many of Howard Jaffe's initial notes and elements from his recommended readings that could carry a narrative plot. But aside from various vignettes centered around the eponymous picket line itself, the film's primary drama came from the causes and effects of organized acts of civil disobedience: Vincent Mora's successful "peace march" and, much to Howard Jaffe's chagrin, Mora's public self-starvation, à la Gandhi. However, when Chito Cruz soon discovers Mora secretly succumbing to dual temptations—lust for a local woman and breaking his fast—it proves too much for both men: Mora steals Cruz's car and shamefully escapes into the night, while Cruz assumes the mantle as union leader—and chief revolutionary. Disillusioned by a false savior, Bud Davis leaves the picket line and returns home.[23] Vincent Mora's unceremonious display of cowardice must have come as a shock to Howard Jaffe, who had already nixed Leonard's intentions to sacrifice the character at the hands of the Wade County Rangers.

None of these elements jelled with Jaffe's original vision. A crucial detail the young producer had failed to emphasize to Leonard was his passion for Haskell Wexler's cinema verité docudrama *Medium Cool*—a unique blend of fictional story set against real footage of the 1968 Chicago student protests. Leonard, however, had put as much research into *Picket Line* as he would any of his literary fiction—including a layered plot with structural time beats and character arcs—and anticipated an enthusiastic response from Jaffe.

The release of MGM's *The Moonshine War* didn't help Leonard's growing agitation. While the novel had received positive if dismissive reviews, many had mentioned the upcoming film optimistically. (The *San Francisco Examiner* had previously described the book as "light summer reading," advising readers that they may "wait for the movie they're bound to make of it."[24]) Once the film opened, however, those expectations were hardly met. "A great deal of care was obviously put into the film—the attention to detail and the evocation of time and place rival for accuracy with last year's *They Shoot Horses, Don't They?*" wrote Richard Cuskelly in the *Los Angeles Herald-Express*. "All the more disappointing then that the movie does not really work."[25] Much of the critics' ire was directed at attempts to capture the characters' regional dialects and culture. "Performances are misguided and given to extremes," wrote the *Hollywood Reporter*. "Alan Alda gives the most convincing portrayal perhaps because it is under-portrayal . . . The screenplay by Elmore Leonard is based on his novel of the same name and is one of those specimens which should have remained a novel for better enjoyment." The review accurately predicted, "*The Moonshine War* will be rejected at the box office."[26]

Swanson quickly saw the writing on the wall. "Well, we got killed, as per the enclosed reviews," the agent wrote on June 25. "I think people around Metro blame [Richard] Quine more than [Martin] Ransohoff for what apparently went wrong here." He added, "Don't kill yourself!"[27]

Leonard later told critic Patrick McGilligan, "Let's face it—Dick Quine was not the guy to direct a picture about people who live in 'hollers' and talk funny. He had done mainly comedies that were hip at that time—*The Moonshine War* didn't stand a chance."[28]

Following weeks of silence from Howard Jaffe, Leonard prodded Swanson to contact the producer regarding the final *Picket Line* treatment. On August 11, the agent reported back the inevitable: upon reading Leonard's typescript in July, Jaffe had nixed the project, but hadn't bothered to notify the screenwriter himself. "I spent quite a bit of time this afternoon with Howard Jaffe," Swanson wrote. "He feels that he wouldn't be able to turn [*Picket Line*] into the kind of story he wants and therefore suggests we offer it elsewhere."[29]

While he had been well compensated for his work, Leonard's emphasis on *Picket Line*'s deadlines had pushed other projects to the sidelines. He sent off his own letter to Jaffe, insisting that some form of response earlier would have, at least, been courteous. And while he did get an apology from Jaffe in mid-September, the producer didn't sugarcoat his feelings on the submitted material. "Dutch," Jaffe wrote, "I am terribly disappointed in the material. I have not lost interest, but truthfully I cannot get involved with the project as it stands now. Had it been what I feel we discussed, I might have been able to move it. However, now all the intimacies and relationships, and particularly the story line, are not at all what we talked about . . . I'll write in the near future, as everything is hectic now. Hal Ashby is directing my Paramount pic and William Fraker my suspense piece."[30]

Leonard spent months on *Picket Line*. He had been advised by friend and producer Max Youngstein that, although *Jesus Saves* had a solid plot, it would be difficult to sell on the basis of a brief treatment alone. Leonard quickly mailed Swanson twenty-two additional pages to pump up the bundle, inquiring in the same letter, "What happened to [Gabriel] Katzka and *Picket Line*?"[31] To this, Swanson's response was mixed. "Katzka has been in the Roosevelt Hospital in New York City for tests for over a week and doesn't know when he's getting out."[32]

On the same day Howard Jaffe's apology-cum-explanation arrived, Leonard again heard from Swanson with another project runaround: "I've talked today with [producer] Sidney Glazier . . . he says he's got to get two projects on the floor first, but in about six weeks he'll come back to me and discuss *Jesus Saves*." He added, "The whole town is frozen over, as you must have guessed. However, we're in there punching for you."[33]

Leonard gathered his eight months' worth of *Picket Line* material and shelved it for scrap.

CHAPTER 9

A Nifty Guy at Loose Ends, 1971–1972

> If you're communicating, or trying to, it would seem natural to want to know whether or not you're succeeding, critically as well as commercially. You might just as well face it, when you present your work in the marketplace you're going to get a response, applause or boos, because that's the way it is.[1]

Leonard considered *Valdez Is Coming* his finest Western to date and remained convinced its upcoming film adaptation would lead to more Western sales. In hopeful anticipation, he began writing his first original Western screenplay.

Bypassing the usual months of peripheral research, Leonard instead dipped into his collection of scrap and fastened together a new scenario with familiar, yet original, character tropes. He started with the type of protagonist he knew well: a former Indian scout turned bounty hunter—cut from the same literary cloth that had carried his earliest stories, but now he added contemporary shades of social justice and a decidedly bureaucratic villain that had been meant for *Picket Line*.

H. N. Swanson, however, was reluctant to see Leonard cherry-pick elements from *Picket Line* that could potentially damage future sales; hoping for a quick turnaround to network television, he instead urged the author to keep the full story intact as a sellable novel. Leonard assured Swanson that he had enough excess material for multiple projects and soon proved it with four consecutive original scripts, all assembled from the patchwork of *Picket Line*. The first original screenplay to benefit from Leonard's *Picket Line* archive would be the new Western. Aiming to retain *Valdez Is Coming*'s Burt Lancaster as the lead, Leonard ended the year by pumping out the treatment, wavering between the titles *Sangre de Cristo* and *Two Days in Sinola,* before finally settling on *The Sinola Courthouse Raids.* Leonard then paired the completed outline with a "concept sheet" for the second screenplay he was considering: a turn-of-the-century drama about one coal miner's fight against a large mining syndicate. Entitled *American Flag,* Leonard envisioned Steve McQueen as its hero, a riff on *Picket Line*'s "one man for a cause." He sent both projects to Swanson who, by November 13, was already swaying Leonard to adapt the horror drama *The Bloody Benders* for producer Robert Anglund. In an effort to end 1970 on a high note, Leonard unceremoniously agreed, and met not only with Anglund but with a number of other Hollywood executives who had been asking for face-to-face appointments with him.

While grateful for the work, Leonard would also remember that year's end in a different way: the first sign that excessive drinking was affecting his health. "One day, I came back from California throwing up blood," he later wrote. "I was in the emergency room and they couldn't stop the bleeding. They said they had to look in and see what the trouble was." At first, Leonard's physician had suspected an ulcer, claiming the only other probable cause would be acute gastritis—an affliction, he noted, usually found only "in skid-row bums." Surprising them both, it was, indeed, acute gastritis. In an unusually candid moment toward the end of the year, Swanson offered a few choice words of wisdom to his client: "Hope you are feeling okay and are on the wagon a reasonable part of the time. Last night Groucho Marx said, 'I'm getting to the age where I really chase young girls, but only if it's downhill.'"[2]

Unfortunately, Leonard's health scare didn't immediately lead to sobriety. "I did ease off [drinking] for a little bit after my surgery," he wrote, "but within a month, I was gradually drinking again, until finally I was right back where I had been . . . It was still seven years before I had that last drink."[3]

Swanson wrote to Leonard on January 18, enthusiastic that, despite *The Bloody Benders* being stuck in development hell, Robert Anglund was keen to discuss both *Jesus Saves*—now undergoing such suggested title changes as *Let's Hear It for Jesus, Noble Love,* and *Illumination*—and *The Sinola Courthouse Raids.* "I told him we didn't like to sell you just to do a treatment but I quoted him $50,000 for the complete job," Swanson wrote.[4]

As he recuperated from intestinal surgery, Leonard much preferred to work on *Sinola*—even as Swanson continued to push *Picket Line*'s television potential. To this, Leonard wrote, "I've already blown six months researching and writing what you have, and it would take two to three more months to finish it, which could turn out to be a wasted effort . . . I would rather write *Sinola* than finish *Picket Line*, anyway." He added, "But if that one doesn't sell and if we don't hear back from [Robert] Anglund, I'm going to be back in adland next week."[5] Unknown to most outside his family and friends, Leonard had, in fact, already been forced to fall upon his old advertising and copywriting skills—writing an industrial film for Chevrolet, no less. This time around, however, the assignment couldn't have been more prestigious. Through his old contacts at General Motors, Leonard had been offered work on the massive public relations campaign for the new Chevy Vega, working alongside John DeLorean on a car the famed engineer himself despised. At forty-five years old, DeLorean—the superstar engineer with Hollywood charm—had spent his entire adult life climbing the ranks from the GM assembly line to his place at the top of the company. By 1970, Chevrolet's sales were in excess of three million cars—a new record for the division, and second only to the entire Ford Motor Company catalogue. But to DeLorean, image was everything. He enjoyed the unprecedented level of mainstream fame his success had afforded, and spent just as much time in Hollywood as he did in Detroit. His tailored suits (shirts tieless and opened at the collar), and preferences for foreign sports cars and movie starlets had made him a household name. He'd recently begun courting his soon-to-be third wife, model Cristina Ferrare—twenty years his junior—and, as he sat across from Leonard, was preparing for surreptitious cosmetic plastic surgery overseas: a more-prominent jaw line, à la Kirk Douglas. DeLorean's behavior irked the majority of his GM executive superiors, however, and only begrudgingly had they ever appointed any levels of advancement. In that vein, DeLorean viewed his assignment on the new Chevrolet Vega to be one of spite. Now hoping to attract the same youth market he'd reached with the GTO, he determined they needed a big-budget "announcement film" to attract dealers and potential buyers—one with a good script written by, if possible, a professional Hollywood screenwriter.

Slipping back into his old advertising suit, Leonard conducted rounds of interviews with DeLorean, gathering data on both the subcompact vehicle and the enfant terrible engineer in equal measures, observing the eccentric designer's routine and style.[6] And while the experience might not have done much for the sales of the Chevy Vega, it did inspire its two unlikely collaborators in other areas: Leonard's reinvigorated interest in the Detroit auto industry would help shape his contemporary fiction only a few books later, and DeLorean would cite the Vega assignment as his signal to finally put a long-gestating passion project into effect: "I [then] decided to go off and try to do something more ethical from the standpoint of something that would last," he later admitted, "and that's where the stainless steel car concept came from."[7]

Although the previous year's WGA strike had been avoided, Swanson used the experience to teach Leonard an ongoing strategy to always keep him working: attract a major star early, then allow *them* to make headway on a project even during a strike—something completely within union guidelines, as long as the written material isn't tinkered with. Actors with their own independent production companies—such as Burt Lancaster and Steve McQueen—were perfect for such an approach. With that in mind, Leonard urged Swanson to send *The Sinola Courthouse Raids* to Lancaster right away. Both were surprised when the star's producing partner, Roland Kibbee, returned the treatment on February 3, citing woes for the production company; apparently, *Valdez* had been the final project under their commitment with United Artists.[8]

Unbowed, Swanson already had a laundry list of backup producers. In a matter of days, he reeled in producer Sidney Beckerman, who saw *Sinola* as a perfect star vehicle for Clint Eastwood and his company, Malpaso Productions. Beckerman had already worked behind the scenes on another Eastwood hit, *Kelly's Heroes*, and had a multipicture deal with Universal in place. Taking his cue from Beckerman, Eastwood's production partner, Jennings Lang, purchased Leonard's *Sinola* treatment for the star's approval.

"OUR RESIDENT WRITER OF VIOLENT FILMS IS A QUIET GUY WHO LIKES TO HEAR GUNS GO OFF . . . ON THE SCREEN."

The February 7 headline was a mouthful, and for his first two-page feature story spread in half a decade, Leonard was prepared to give the *Detroit Free Press*'s Sunday magazine an even bigger earful. "I'll never live in Hollywood," he told journalist Bettie Cannon. "I'll work in Detroit or I won't work at all."

Leonard had invited Cannon to his Pierce Street office after her interview request the previous year. "Once I'd sold *Hombre* in 1966," he continued, "producers told me, 'Now, Elmore. You'd better move out to the coast now.' That's because producers like to peek over your shoulder every 15 or 16 pages. Well, I can't work that way and be independent and productive." Leonard emphasized his disdain by grabbing that week's issue of *Variety* magazine—the Hollywood bible—and using it to swat a fly on the windowsill. Cannon was struck by the modesty of both the office and its inhabitant, writing, "Birmingham's Elmore Leonard isn't your regular *reel-life* Hollywood writer. No Silk Ascot. No blonde receptionist. He greets you himself in his shirt sleeves, button down collar and tie . . . You are reminded of the local headquarters of your Republican congressman." Amused by Cannon's expectations for meeting a Hollywood screenwriter, Leonard was at ease sharing updates on his home life with Beverly and the kids: "Our children are Jane, [twenty], Peter, nineteen, and a student at EMU; Chris is sixteen and a junior at Brother Rice; Bill attends Holy Name and he's thirteen; Katy is five . . . They are not much interested in reading. They love movies. They see everything."

He also used the opportunity to share his latest creative processes working as both a functioning novelist and a professional screenwriter, admitting, "I would rather write the novel first and then the screenplay . . . In the screenplay, I seem to be trussed up in the format. You certainly can't use any descriptions. The camera does that. The novel is easier and freer for me. The first thing in adapting a novel to the movies is to cut it in half." He added, "If I can stick to this schedule I write one-hundred and twenty-five pages a month if I'm lucky. At one page a minute of screen time—loosely, very loosely—my schedule calls for one book every eight weeks, not counting research time."

Leonard's candid observations surprised Cannon. Before leaving, she made a final observation of Leonard's office decor—the many posters that lined the rear wall: wounded soldiers on the western front, circa 1917; the Spanish matador Manolete, his sword held to a charging bull; police officers surrounding the body of outlaw Clyde Barrow. The final picture, Cannon wrote, was the most recognizable of all. "Ernest Hemingway—bigger than life and looking amazingly like . . . *Elmore Leonard*."[9]

At the time of the interview, Leonard was multitasking three projects—*Jesus Saves*, *American Flag*, and *The Sinola Courthouse Raids*. Although

Sinola took place in turn-of-the-century New Mexico, he had recycled much of his background research into real-life Mexican-American activist Reies Tijerina for *Picket Line*, specifically Tijerina's infamous June 1967 raid of the Tierra Courthouse in the name of stolen ancestral lands.

For *Sinola*, Leonard retained much of Tijerina's character traits for new antagonist Luis Chama, who leads his own unsuccessful courthouse raid at the story's start. Chama is thereafter pursued by a ruthless, white landowner, P. J. Cable, and his posse. For an added edge, Cable hires a former bounty hunter named Joe Kidd to capture Chama. However, Kidd disapproves of the cutthroat and violent methods used by Cable's right-hand man Frank Harlan, and soon begins to understand the justice behind Chama's cause—the return of his people's stolen ancestral land. Kidd flips sides and, in doing so, makes himself an enemy of Harlan and his men.

For the protagonist Joe Kidd, Leonard combined elements from his earliest Western heroes, throwing in characteristics of *Picket Line*'s Vincent Mora and its ur-Tijerina prototype, Chito Cruz. Although a tough-as-nails, jaded frontiersman, it is with his eyes and ears open to the community struggles and racism around him that the Anglo cowboy changes his allegiance, taking a stand for what's right—even if it alienates both sides of the conflict. (For the character's name, however, Leonard reached much further back in his notes, cribbing the last name from his proposed 1956 comic strip, *Bowie Kidd*.[10]) Leonard set to work on the full screenplay while Swanson continued negotiations with producer Sidney Beckerman. Clint Eastwood, however, was already interested; while filming the Civil War drama *The Beguiled*, the star had been handed a copy of Leonard's treatment by Jennings Lang and, apparently, saw the property as exactly the type of project he'd been seeking for Malpaso Productions. In only three years since its inception, Malpaso's box office track record was seven for seven, including that year's action blockbuster, *Dirty Harry*. Now, *Sinola* had been chosen as Eastwood's follow-up, and the film itself would be responsible for continuing the star's winning streak.[11]

On March 8, Swanson secured Sidney Beckerman's purchase agreement for *Sinola*—a joint collaboration with Eastwood's Malpaso Productions, officially putting the film's wheels in motion.[12] *Variety* ran the announcement on April 7.[13]

With his name on the dotted line, Leonard had three months to complete the script. *Jesus Saves* and *American Flag* would have to be put on hold.

After nearly four years of studio red tape, a change of directors and lead actor, and five months of actual shooting in two countries, *Valdez Is Coming* finally opened on April 9. It drew a mixed response from critics and moviegoers. "*Valdez Is Coming* takes about 30 minutes to set up the major thrust of the story, but from then on, it is as taut a Western as a follower of this genre could demand," wrote Ken Barnard of the *Detroit News*. "The ending of the film may stretch credibility for some viewers, though you arrive there with a sense of having had your taste for adventure well served."[14] Although Burt Lancaster's performance garnered praise, his turn as the "Christ-like" lawman was largely overshadowed by claims of whitewashing and misguided antiracist themes. *Time* magazine's Stefan Kanfer wrote that the film's "continual editorials about racism give the film contrived relevance," a sentiment echoed in *New York*'s description of Lancaster as an "Uncle Tom–type Mexican American."[15] Stanley Eichelbaum of the *San Francisco Examiner* was largely unimpressed with the film as a whole; he was among the few critics who picked up on Leonard's initial allegorical intentions. He described Lancaster's protagonist as "a Mexican messiah whose mission is to assure us that the Biblical warning about the wages of sin will not go unheeded . . . He's actually tied to a cross and forced to crawl through the wilderness in a hamstrung position by a band of racist villains who are going to be taught a lesson in Christian ethics." Of course, Eichelbaum was unaware that Leonard had, in fact, taught Sunday school catechism during the time he wrote the novel—although he'd saved his mock crucifixion experiment for vacationing with his own children. Eichelbaum added, "The movie is nonetheless better than the simplistic parable that lies behind it."[16]

A modest hit, *Valdez Is Coming*'s theatrical run nonetheless helped to boost Leonard's bankability and solidified his reputation for penning socially progressive action in the *Hombre* vein. Leonard himself was pleased with the film, singling out the joint efforts of screenwriters Roland Kibbee and David Rayfiel in retaining his subtle climax in lieu of a traditional shootout. He later recalled, "It amazed me that the film version ended exactly the way the book did, with the bad guy choosing to back down rather than go for the gun." Over the coming years, Leonard would rarely walk away as satisfied with his adaptations. He added, however, "I didn't like the way [Burt Lancaster] was made up. He had a lot of Max Factor all over his face . . . They could have done a lot better with a character actor, you know?"[17]

Most of June in LA was spent attending meetings with the *Sinola* team: producer Sidney Beckerman, Clint Eastwood, and newly hired director John Sturges, whose previous Western endeavors, *Gunfight at the OK Corral* and *The Magnificent Seven,* were considered classics. Leonard flew to Detroit for a long respite at home on June 17, but was back at Universal Pictures first thing the following Monday. The studio had set Leonard up in his own office, making him more accessible for last-minute meetings and mandated revisions—both of which were common, although Leonard found the experience unusually bearable. "Eastwood was the easiest guy in the world to get along with," he later recalled, adding that the star would make suggestions directly to director Sturges. "The only time I can recall him saying anything was for the scene where Joe Kidd is confronted by an armed faction near the end of the second act." As Leonard remembered, Eastwood had insisted that his gun be drawn—something Leonard was adamant a true lawman would only do if truly necessary. "Eastwood said, 'But my character has not [yet] been presented as a gunfighter.' He turned to Sturges, 'Don't you think I need my gun out?'" But the director had sided with Leonard, reminding the star, "The audience knows who you are—they've seen all your pictures." When Leonard eventually saw the finished film, Eastwood had his gun drawn. Sturges, however, soon proved to be less than dependable: a longtime alcoholic, the director would sometimes drool during meetings; later, while filming important scenes, he would exclaim, "That's movies!" to no one in particular, making his directions and motivations unclear. Leonard later recalled, "[Sturges] was so in love with *The Magnificent Seven,* he was using outtakes from that picture."[18]

Of greater concern to Leonard, however, was producer Sidney Beckerman's unsolicited habit of rewriting his dialogue, forcing Leonard to quickly redact Beckerman's changes before the Columbia secretary could type and distribute it. As Leonard had expected, many snappy lines had been removed to match Eastwood's stoic leading-man persona. Also, for both time constraints and actor mandates, characters had been merged: Luis Chama was portrayed as less sympathetic and more villainous (an effort to make Eastwood's Joe Kidd seem more heroic), and the chief antagonist, ruthless land baron P. J. Cable, had been dramatically downsized in order to hand the dialogue to henchman Frank Harlan (the casting of Robert Duvall, whose turn in the soon-to-be-released *The Godfather* was already generating Hollywood buzz, called for producers to pump up the Harlan character as the major heavy; he was now the land baron *and* leader of the cutthroat posse). Unlike with *Valdez Is Coming*, however, Leonard was told *Sinola* needed a new action-packed finale.

In August, Leonard received a telegram from *Sinola* producer Sidney Beckerman, relaying Eastwood's enthusiasm for the changes, thus approving the shooting script; they were set to begin principal photography in Old Tucson, Arizona, that spring. "We will start casting next week and I'll keep you informed regarding same so that you can visualize your characters as they relate to the actors who are playing them."[19] An announcement of Beckerman's *Sinola* acquisition soon ran in the *Hollywood Reporter*, also mentioning the producer's other project for Universal—the disaster epic *Earthquake*—then being penned by *The Godfather* novelist Mario Puzo. According to the announcement, *Sinola* had been budgeted at $3 million, while *Earthquake* was granted another million for additional special effects. John Sturges was slated to direct both films, and would hop from one project immediately to the next.[20]

Two weeks after the announcement, *Sinola* was renamed to emphasize Eastwood's lead character. Leonard finished his final revisions for *Joe Kidd* on September 15, just in time for principal photography to begin in November.[21] Leonard later told the British Film Institute, "That wasn't my title."[22]

Leonard soon returned his attention to *American Flag*. In an effort to drum up early interest, he had already shared with Sidney Beckerman the bare bones of its plot. He wrote Swanson at the end of August, "I told [Beckerman] he could have it for $100,000 and he said send it to him; wants first look, the way we gave Ira [Steiner] first look at *Sinola* . . . Sturges also likes the basic idea. But I have a lot of filling in to do before it's a story."[23]

American Flag was Leonard's latest take on the "one man standing up for a cause" theme that had permeated much of his fiction and, thus far, all of his film work. Like *Sinola*, the basic premise came from his *Picket Line* research. There, Reis Tijerina/Chito Cruz had evolved into antihero Luis Chama; with *American Flag*, Leonard took shades of both Cesar Chavez/Vincent Mora (minus the social justice crusading) and Bud Davis characters in order to create Bob Miller—an everyman ore miner whose discovery of gold upon his land sparks the film's one-man war against an adjacent corrupt mining company. Leonard set the story in the same Mojave, Arizona, region of his earliest pulp stories, and retained the post–Old West timeframe of *Forty Lashes Less One*.

In lush detail, he described the workings of a single camp owned by a mining syndicate—the eponymous "American Flag"—and the daily lives of the small community members dependent upon its presence. Earning three dollars a day, minus a dollar for room and board, a legion of eighty men alternates grueling shifts mining the Cerbat Mountains and occupying the "scattering of board structures, adobes and tents" of the small makeshift town. With a population that's 90 percent male run by a ruthless corporation, animosity runs deep and tempers run high. In the opening scene, former "American Flag" ore miner Bob Miller returns to camp after an eight-month prospecting venture, proudly announcing that his own staked claim had just come in, forty ounces of gold to the ton. Jealousy runs high and there's no sympathy when, only days later, a demolition blast orchestrated by the American Flag company buries Miller's fortune beneath tons of raw earth—and refuses to take any responsibility. After a fruitless confrontation with the company's soulless representative, Frank McCall, Miller vows to take the matter into his own hands, igniting a crescendo of escalating cat and mouse vignettes. It's only a matter of time before the obligatory showdown takes place right in the middle of the mining camp.[24]

Like all of Leonard's Hollywood output, *American Flag* was an action-oriented Western with allegorical shadings. And much like his previous heroes, Leonard's own perspective on Miller came from his own persona. He wrote, "The focus of the story is on Miller, because the story comes out of him, his attitude, the way he stands up and refuses to be pushed around . . . His manner is quiet, easy going; he seems almost naïve in the apparent simplicity of his attitude. But beneath his reserve is a rock base. Once he makes a stand, his antagonists will wear themselves out trying to budge him." Writing to H. N. Swanson soon after, Leonard had noted his recurring allegories: "Any theme similarity between it and *Hombre*, *Valdez*, and *Sinola* is purely intentional. The loner stands up against heavy odds and won't budge. In this instance, it's a Western version of the little guy vs. the big corporation."[25]

As intended, Steve McQueen had been handed the treatment and was quickly hooked on Leonard's story. His first inclination was to have it produced by First Artists—the vanguard production company he co-owned with fellow actors Paul Newman, Sidney Poitier, Barbra Streisand, and soon, Dustin Hoffman. (The stars had joined forces for the new company in 1969, agreeing to lower pay in exchange for greater creative control of more personal projects. Their distribution partner, National General Pictures, agreed to pay two-thirds of production costs, but would also have a say in all approved projects.) Much was riding on the company's upcoming debut releases: Streisand's *Up the Sandbox*; Newman's *Pocket Money* and *The Life and Times of Judge Roy Bean*; and McQueen's *The Getaway*.

At the time, McQueen had been looking for a replacement vehicle for the film adaptation of the novel *The Presbyterian Church Wager*—a property for which he'd been scooped by Robert Altman and Warren Beatty when the duo filmed it as *McCabe and Mrs. Miller* earlier that same year. Still burned by the financial losses of his failed passion project, the racing epic *Le Mans*—and his recent estrangement from his wife of sixteen years, Neile Adams—McQueen needed a win. He refused to make sequels to previous hits and, following the 1968 success of *Bullitt*, turned down any films where he'd play a cop. And unlike contemporary rival Clint Eastwood, McQueen had grown weary of traditional Westerns.[26] Seeing box office potential in *American Flag*, he contacted Swanson and asked if Leonard was available to meet to discuss the project in North Hollywood, home of the star's personal company, Solar Productions. It was rare that a major star would request a face-to-face meeting without studio "suits" present. Steve McQueen, however, likened his position as founder of Solar Productions to that of millionaire Thomas Crown—his favorite among his roles—and on *American Flag*, the notoriously picky McQueen would act as both star and producer.

Leonard met with McQueen at the Solar Productions office in LA the second week of October, agreeing to McQueen's minor revisions and leaving with a sense that the project was set in motion. "I thought the meeting Friday went very well," he wrote to First Artists' Patrick Kelly on October 26, "and was especially glad to learn McQueen is high on the story and sees the characters essentially the same way I do."[27] In later years, however, Leonard would also remember the meeting for different reasons: "When I first met [McQueen], he'd had an accident riding his dirt bike out in the desert the day before and he slipped his pants down to show me this huge scrape on his hip that we bandaged while we were talking about the movie. He was going with Ali MacGraw then, and he wanted her in the picture." He elaborated, "[McQueen and I] were going to sit down and discuss the screenplay, and I was so hungover that I was absolutely dying for a beer . . . We had lunch in his office and he said, 'What do you want, pop or beer?' I said, 'Oh, I guess I'll have a beer.' I couldn't wait to get it down."[28]

Accordingly, he revamped the *American Flag* outline as soon as he returned to Birmingham. Most of McQueen's suggestions were minor, and to be expected: more action and a greater emphasis on the dramatic side of McQueen's Miller character. However, Leonard had also promised McQueen he'd add more screen time for the intended female lead, Ali MacGraw. Leonard revised the story so characters Bob Miller and newly renamed Leila connect earlier, with her saving Miller in the desert following an attack by lead antagonist E. J. Hicks and his men. From there, the two become romantically entwined, fighting the corporate operation as partners. He also made mandated changes to the story's antagonists. As he had previously done with *Joe Kidd* villains Frank Harlan and E. J. Cable, he combined *American Flag*'s smarmy office manager Frank McCall with lead henchman E. J. Hicks (not stretching too far for their names), making them one ruthless villain. However, he created a new villain to flesh out the risk factor and dynamics—the mining company's equally ruthless owner, Mr. Hanley.

McQueen had particularly loved the story's title and insisted that "American Flag" be repurposed not as the villainous entity but, rather, as the symbolic name of his character's camp, thus forcing Leonard to rename the adversarial corporation "Barranca Mining." In order to get going on the screenplay's revised drafts, Leonard requested a nonfiction tome, *Ghost Towns of Arizona*, be sent to his home for additional research; it was at least, he claimed to First Artists' Pat Kelly, "a place to start."[29]

Leonard wrote to Swanson on October 6, "I need the money from Universal as soon as possible. If the beginning of photography is November 1, then I hope the check is dated that day. I'm hanging on by my fingernails," asking that the fifty thousand dollars due him for *Joe Kidd* be split in half, as a second installment made the following year would greatly ease the coming tax burden.[30]

Principal photography on *Joe Kidd* continued throughout November in Old Tucson, Arizona. With the outdoor scenes and B-roll already shot at

June Lake, east of Yosemite National Park, director John Sturges's team—led by Eastwood and producer Sidney Beckerman—had moved into town just as Paul Newman's collaboration with director John Huston, *The Life and Times of Judge Roy Bean*, was closing up shop. They wrapped in the middle of December, having to continue revising action sequences along the way.

One of the last scenes to be filmed—primarily due to logistics and cost—was the larger-than-life climax that Eastwood insisted be tacked on to Leonard's original, dialogue-heavy finale. It was soon suggested that a steam locomotive crash through the saloon, allowing Joe Kidd to shoot his way to the courthouse—although there was debate regarding the finale's source: as director Sturges insisted the climax was his brainchild, having observed that the narrow gauge of the standing Old Tucson railroad tracks already stopped at the saloon wall; other crew members recalled stumped producer Bob Daley offering the barroom spectacle as a joke, only to find everyone had taken him seriously. Regardless, Eastwood loved it—even if Leonard, ever resistant to cartoonish tropes, didn't. The ending was shot with the train crash, leading to a proper courthouse showdown between Kidd and Frank Harlan: having turned the tables on the posse, Kidd gets his kill shot of the villainous land baron by hiding in the judge's chair—a symbolic stance as judge, jury, and now, Harlan's executioner.

Joe Kidd wrapped by the end of the month, and was tentatively planned for a release the following summer. And even with their first collaboration still in postproduction, Clint Eastwood was already prepared to work with Leonard again, surprising the author by calling him at home at the end of January.[31] Peter Leonard later recalled, "I remember my brother saying, 'Dad, it's Clint Eastwood,' and then everybody ran for a phone. And by the time I got to the phone, I could hear them fighting over the extensions." (He later added, "[Sometimes] the phone would ring and it might be Clint Eastwood or Steve McQueen calling to discuss script revisions. Elmore would take the call, and my sister Jane would run upstairs, unscrew the mouthpiece on another phone and listen to the conversation."[32]) The star was looking to commission more work, inquiring if Leonard had any existing story ideas that could be adapted into a starring vehicle for Malpaso Productions. "Do you have anything like *Dirty Harry*, only different?" he asked. The problem, Eastwood explained, was that while *Dirty Harry* had made a fortune for Warner Bros., the star himself didn't own a piece of the character or its copyright. Now, he needed something similar—another "guy with a big gun"—that he could control for higher profits. Only months earlier, independent filmmaker and actor Tom Laughlin had defied the odds by self-producing his action-drama *Billy Jack*, playing a half-breed Navajo and former Green Beret who enacts vigilante justice against enemies of his fellow indigenous peoples. Laughlin made the film out-of-pocket for $800,000 and had been impassioned regarding the film's message; when he couldn't find a distributor, he released it himself—ultimately recouping his money and netting more than $50 million once Warner Bros. lent a hand. Eastwood wanted that type of success for his Malpaso Productions and gave Leonard free rein to toy with a more progressive action character—a hero for the people.

It didn't take long for Leonard to assemble the needed scrap for a wholly original story. With *Picket Line* all but dead in the water, the characters of Vincent Mora and Chito Cruz were left in the wind; Leonard quickly combined elements of both into a new protagonist. Likewise, he added a small dose of both *American Flag*'s Bob Miller and bounty hunter *Joe Kidd*'s shared philosophy as the "one man standing up for a cause," but now considered a secular, common threat that could be relatable as a villain to movie audiences—making the "cause" the very act of survival itself. "That night, I got the idea," Leonard later recalled, "and [Eastwood] called the next day . . . He said, 'Good, work it up.'"[33]

Leonard created an amalgam of his most-recent antiheroes and put them into a modern setting: an independent cantaloupe farmer who goes up against a larger enemy—in this case, a local mafia hit man subbing for *American Flag*'s corporate entity—who just wants to protect his business and the migrant workers in his employ. To appease Eastwood, Leonard made it a point that the protagonist—named Joe Doran—had no law enforcement background; rather, he was a former military officer who, following his discharge, had served a small prison sentence, giving him a slightly rebellious edge. In fact, Leonard made it a point of stating that Doran's job was a flexible element to the story. In the opening scene, Doran would display a compassionate act of masculine nonconformity by taking part in a vicious brawl set in a bowling alley, with Eastwood's hero defending his friends against a gang of loudmouthed bullies. Carted off to the local jail, Doran rubs his cellmate the wrong way—an infamous mafia gun-for-hire named Frank Renda. When Renda's preplanned escape goes awry, Doran apprehends the killer himself, hoping to use the killer as a bargaining chip to have his assault charges dropped. Instead, Renda escapes; when he then beats his own charges on a technicality, it isn't long before he sets his goons on the farmer who tried to trade him back to the cops. As Renda's harassment escalates (Doran knows he's being followed and soon finds his cantaloupe crops destroyed), a spray-painted billboard outside the melon field declares his ultimate intention: "JOE DORAN IS A DEAD MAN!" Taking this as a declaration of war—and with no help from a passive local police force—the former Green Beret breaks out his hunting gear and begins to take out Renda's gang one by one, leading to an old-fashioned shootout outside Renda's luxurious hideout.

In an effort to further attract Clint Eastwood to the property, Leonard made a few additional tweaks to his old *Picket Line* source material: as Eastwood was known to love his home in California's seaside town of Carmel, Leonard set the new story in nearby Castroville—making a potential film shoot cheaper and easier for Malpaso Productions to organize. At Eastwood's request, Leonard even changed farmer Doran's business from picking cantaloupes to artichokes—a crop more native to Eastwood's Monterey County.

Leonard completed the initial twenty-five-page treatment for *Joe Doran Is a Dead Man*, on February 4, 1972.[34] He later recalled, "So, I worked it up and went out to Hollywood on something else and I went to see [Eastwood], and I felt sure he was going to buy it and do it. But by then he had acquired *High Plains Drifter*, which he really liked a lot." Leonard, however, remained adamant that *Joe Doran* become something tangible. In an appeal to Eastwood on March 7, Leonard admitted that something elusive had been bothering him about the film treatment, concluding that the protagonist's profession needed a place in the story itself—at least at the story's start. "As it is, he's an artichoke farmer," Leonard wrote. "He could be an onion grower for that matter, or even a druggist. We've discussed the fact that his occupation doesn't seem important; but now I don't feel that's necessarily a valid assumption . . . The story is essentially a life or death situation that the main character brings on himself. However, I believe the story would be stronger and more interesting if what he does becomes important to the plot." He continued, "It might be ideal if what he does gets him involved in the plot to begin with . . . I have some time now so I'll get on it."[35]

But it was to no avail; Eastwood remained adamant that *High Plains Drifter* would be Malpaso Productions' next project. Looking back, Leonard would later pin the failed deal on the film's setting, his deliberately placing the action in Eastwood's Carmel backyard. "What I thought," Leonard recalled, "is that Clint'll love this because he can go home from work, not knowing he didn't *want* to go home."[36]

Leonard still believed that his action-packed hybrid of *Picket Line, American Flag,* and *Joe Kidd* could be solid commercial fare. He'd even left in the revisions Eastwood had demanded, starting with the protagonist's name. A year earlier, when Eastwood had retitled *The Sinola Courthouse Raids* to the more palatable *Joe Kidd,* Leonard had been in agreement. Now, with that in mind, Leonard went back into his new treatment and crossed out all mentions of Joe Doran, opting instead to repurpose a last name he'd previously enjoyed using in *The Big Bounce.*

He scribbled over each in corrective blue ink: "*Mr. Majestyk.*"

CHAPTER 10

Birth of the Cool, 1972–1974

> Publishers have always liked my work, but were unable to sell it because it didn't fit neatly into a category. At least, that's what they told me. That my work was a sort of a hybrid. Not literary, but not pure thriller either . . . The publishers kept insisting that if they couldn't label my books, or if I didn't have a continuing character, they couldn't sell them.

Leonard wrote to H. N. Swanson on February 25, "[John] Foreman, when he was here Sunday, kept expressing surprise at my office and home and the way we live. I think he expected to see Ma and Pa Kettle at the Trailer Camp. He commented with some amazement on my older daughter's boyfriend wearing a tie. I said to him, 'It's Sunday, isn't it?'"

It was unprecedented that Leonard would take a meeting at his home on a Sunday morning, but John Foreman wasn't necessarily like others who often made similar requests. Foreman was the other half of Newman-Foreman Company—the production entity Paul Newman had founded just after the 1967 release of *Hombre*. Together, he and Newman had produced *Butch Cassidy and the Sundance Kid*, as well as both of Newman's obligatory projects for First Artists, *The Life and Times of Judge Roy Bean* and *Pocket Money*. As Steve McQueen still hoped to sway First Artists into cofunding *American Flag* as his next project for the company (he'd ultimately committed to Sam Peckinpah's *The Getaway* as the first), both Newman and Foreman were curious to hear more about Leonard's treatment.

Hollywood assignments had already kept him from new fiction for nearly a year and a half. Since then, Leonard had devoted himself exclusively to screenwriting, considering penning a film's companion novel—or "novelization"—only if the money was right. As a result, Leonard had little time to experiment with his fiction, to apply the lessons learned from his year and a half toiling with *The Big Bounce*. He expressed his growing concerns on the matter to Swanson. Leonard later recalled, "[Swanson] called to ask if I'd read a recently published novel called *The Friends of Eddie Coyle*. I told him I hadn't heard of it and he said, 'This is your kind of stuff, kiddo, run out and get it before you write another word.'"

Leonard took Swanson's recommendation and breezed through George V. Higgins's critically acclaimed 1970 debut in one sitting, later claiming "[I] felt as if I'd been set free, [thinking] 'so this was how you do it.'" Like Leonard, Higgins was an anomaly in the publishing world. At only thirty-three, the Boston native already had a full legal career behind him, having served as deputy assistant attorney general for the Commonwealth of Massachusetts and had fought organized crime in a multitude of other, higher government positions. Higgins had also honed his writing skills through both his education and his day job: he too had learned the Socratic Method from Jesuit priests at his own alma mater, Boston College, as well as careful study of the wiretap recordings used in his criminal cases; the latter had proven that an emphasis on realistic dialogue could create gritty urban characters.

Composed of nearly 90 percent dialogue, *The Friends of Eddie Coyle* was directly inspired by the ruthless traffickers and killers Higgins saw (and heard) in Boston courtrooms every day—their murmured conversations obscuring true, violent intentions and cruel street politics, all under a veil of slang and vague insinuations. One could listen closely and become horrified by the hidden world of pathetic, jaded henchmen lurking beneath—a world populated by men whose survival instincts supersede morality and loyalty. In this world, there are no "friends"—a lesson brutally learned by Higgins's unwitting protagonist, Eddie Coyle, a longtime hood so low on the mob totem pole, conspiratorial gang members and law enforcement agents alike don't remember he exists. In Higgins's hands, the deceptively simple, dialogue-driven story played like Greek tragedy among thieves, the tone reminiscent of Jim Thompson and dialogue inspired by Higgins's own champion, John O'Hara. Most important, there were no good guys or bad guys in Higgins's world, only real people who were a product of their environment and their decisions—and they could *talk*. Leonard took careful note. However, he was more impressed with Higgins's technique beginning each scene with action already occurring, forcing the reader to catch up with the characters mid-conversation. Likewise, Higgins would often alternate character perspectives from scene to scene, allowing readers to decipher each one's attitude and agenda. With those innovations in place, the author could eliminate extraneous descriptions of people and places. "What I learned from George Higgins was to relax, not be so rigid in trying to make the prose sound like writing," Leonard later recalled, "to be more aware of the rhythms of coarse speech and the use of obscenities . . . Most of all, [to] hook the reader right away."[1]

Leonard was now determined to adapt some of Higgins's devices within his own work. He just needed a new book with which to experiment.

During their February call, Swanson also presented Leonard with another tangible project to consider, an assignment from famed producer Walter Mirisch, whose decade-long string of box office hits already included three Academy Award Best Picture winners: *The Apartment*, *West Side Story*, and *In the Heat of the Night*. Mirisch, the youngest of three sons to a Polish immigrant father and younger mother, had initially worked his way to head of production for Allied Artists Studio—a small division of the Monogram Pictures Corporation; in 1957, he founded The Mirisch Company, then went on to bigger and better things, primarily for United Artists. He had recently purchased the film rights to Arthur Hailey's *Wheels*—a history of the Detroit automobile industry presented as a decade-spanning, sweeping epic, à la James Michener's *Hawaii* (another film adaptation Mirisch had already produced)—and he sought a suitable screenwriter. Aware that Leonard was a proud resident of Detroit, he had turned to Swanson, inquiring if his client would have any interest in writing the script.[2] Leonard later recalled, "Walter thought I was right for [*Wheels*] since I lived in Detroit and had spent several years writing car ads. I remember asking my agent . . . 'Do I have to read the book?' and Swanie saying, 'It won't hurt you.'" Swanson urged Leonard to accept the gig, especially as his other properties remained in production limbo. Leonard responded the following day, "I've been thinking about *Wheels* . . . And when I think about it, I realize that I know more about the automobile business than anything I've ever written about."[3] Although he quickly digested Hailey's bestseller, he later admitted, "Hailey was so wrapped up in endless character development and background that he failed to capture the essence of what the automobile industry is. It's not about making cars; it's about selling them."[4]

The first week of March, Swanson sent the full pitch for *Mr. Majestyk* to Mirisch, who immediately saw it as a star vehicle for Steve McQueen and convinced United Artists to pay Leonard to write the screenplay. Unbeknownst to Mirisch—or to Leonard and Swanson, for that matter—McQueen was ready to throw his hands up with *American Flag*. The star had just wrapped on Sam Peckinpah's rodeo drama *Junior Bonner*, and he was already in Texas with Ali MacGraw to begin principal photography on *The Getaway*—again for Peckinpah. "Over a period of time, I tried to get Steve McQueen interested in [*Mr. Majestyk*], but I couldn't get him to commit," Mirisch recalled. Nevertheless, Leonard finished the rewrites to *American Flag* and prepared for a week in Grand Bahama with Beverly, bookended with visits to his mother in Pompano Beach until the first week of April. "As I mentioned on the phone, I'll have paper and pencil with me, so no time will be lost," he wrote Swanson. "The pages might have sand stuck to them, but that can always be brushed off. Right?"[5]

What Leonard yet hadn't mentioned was that he'd finally found the perfect novel with which to apply his new, post-Higgins writing technique—a novel of *Mr. Majestyk*.

On the surface, he hadn't tinkered too much with the initial plot points of *Joe Doran Is a Dead Man*, essentially plucking its lead protagonist and cat and mouse storyline, and setting them into the world of *Picket Line*. A few characters made it past the transition, including Larry Mendoza, now reimagined as Majestyk's field manager and closest friend, and Frank Renda's moll, Wylie—although now downgraded as Majestyk's love interest in order to make room for tough and pretty union leader Nancy Chavez. Like *Picket Line*, the story opened with a panorama of picking fields—now the melon crops of southern Colorado—and dozens of migrant workers lining the road, each hoping to be selected for Vincent Majestyk's team. (Leonard reused *Picket Line*'s "gas station restroom" scene to introduce the enigmatic farmer, with Majestyk replacing Chito Cruz in defending a group of workers against a bigoted attendant.) Upon returning to his farm, Majestyk is soon harassed by local thug Bobby Kopas, who attempts to bully Majestyk into using his unqualified field workers to pick his crops. When the situation turns violent, Majestyk's act of self-defense lands him in county jail. (Leonard replaced Joe Doran's bowling alley brawl with Majestyk's shoving Kopas down in self-defense, seamlessly overlaying his revisions nearly beat for beat on top of the original *Joe Doran* treatment. From there, however, the stories were nearly identical.)

"I'm happy with the story now, confident it will work, and see all kinds of possibilities for the development of nice, tight scenes," he wrote to Swanson on April 14. "You may recognize a couple of scenes I pulled out of *Picket Line* (the opening and the scene in the gas station) which fit in as though they were designed for this story. I've always liked these scenes and was determined to use them somehow or other. Also, I think it's time for a Polish hero. As long as he doesn't screw up too much."

Indeed, studying *The Friends of Eddie Coyle* had paid off. Leonard had successfully written new scenes told from other characters' points of view, as well as revised a few older ones in the new style. Admittedly cautious, he offered Swanson a disclaimer: "I hope the reader realizes there will be scenes told from the point of view of Renda and Tommy Kopas. And it stands, in simplifying the story line, it's all told from Majestyk's point of view."[6] He rushed copies of the new treatment and sample chapters to Swanson that same afternoon. However, Leonard was at a slight disadvantage regarding the novel's eventual publication. Previously, *The Moonshine War* had been published before the film's release, meaning changes to the shooting script couldn't possibly affect the hardcover novel. But Walter Mirisch had already fully committed to producing *Mr. Majestyk*—sharing his intention to begin principal photography the following year after completing *The Spikes Gang*, starring Lee Marvin. While the closed deal was excellent news, it also meant that, much like *The Big Bounce* before it, the film would hit theaters before the novel's publication—rendering *Mr. Majestyk* the book to a mere paperback novelization.

Leonard flew to LA to meet with Mirisch on May 24, the same day the *Mr. Majestyk* acquisition made the front page of the *Hollywood Reporter*. During the afternoon meeting, Leonard took notes while Mirisch suggested revisions: Leonard lengthened the first act's climactic capture of Frank Renda, fleshing out the killer's desperate attempts at bribery, pleas now made reminiscent of biblical temptations and—of lasting importance to Leonard's future portrayal of female characters—requests from the actress cast as Wylie, Frank Renda's moll and accomplice, Lee Purcell. While in both Leonard's shooting script and ensuing novelization, Wylie is a traditional femme fatale—even clad in a bikini while somewhat passively listening to Renda's revenge schemes—Purcell had insisted that the character be sufficiently modernized to the social norms of the times. "[Originally] I had turned it down," she later recalled. "I had trouble with the character . . . I got to the location and studied the script, I immediately thought, 'Well, this is a very one-dimensional girl. She's just '*the girl*'—and I had already played a lot of '*the* girls' . . . So, when it came time to come up with a look for Wylie, I didn't want to do the typical cleavage-pushed-up, skirt-hiked-up cliché. I told them, 'I want to look like my aunt, very sophisticated—hair in an elegant bun, with big hoop earrings.' And they went for it, making the character more of a *consiglieri*—something more like an attorney having an affair with her client, as opposed to a damsel in it for kicks."[7]

The following month, Columbia Pictures officially passed on *American Flag*. "This is a competent commercial script by an experienced screenwriter, and therefore deserves serious consideration," Columbia Pictures' hired consultant wrote on July 26. "Upon serious consideration, I recommend that it be rejected." According to the memo's author, the screenplay contained more "liabilities than assets," including its revenge motif and a lack of sincerity in the protagonist's motivations, finally assessing it as "a lukewarm piece of material." He added, "As for the notion that the two old buddies join hands to reject their old girlfriend (the only girl in their lives), we leave that to the Freudians."[8] (The twenty-six-year-old freelancer who had advised Columbia Pictures against Leonard's *American Flag* was only two years away from selling his own first script, *The Yakuza*, to Sydney Pollack—and four away from writing *Taxi Driver* for Martin Scorsese. But future auteur Paul Schrader was also a quarter of a century away from the day he'd ask Leonard if anything among his dozens of properties was available for him to direct—and be curtly told only a single one was left.)

For now, however, Columbia Pictures' hard pass on *American Flag* presented producer-star Steve McQueen with two options: abandon the film, or convince First Artists to let him shop it for another cofinancier. With *Mr. Majestyk* in full swing in Colorado and *Joe Kidd* about to hit theaters, Leonard and Swanson allowed McQueen to let it ride.

• • •

Universal Pictures released *Joe Kidd* on July 19.

Reviews were lukewarm, most citing the revenge-themed film as familiar terrain. The film's climax—which Leonard hadn't written—drew much of the critics' ire. "It's pretty much as usual in *Joe Kidd*," wrote *Time* magazine. "[Eastwood] rights matters soon enough, even going so far as to drive a locomotive smack through some of Sinola's newest buildings. The set seems to have been constructed solely with this event in mind, looking as it does like something plucked from the window of F.A.O. Schwarz." Again, however, Leonard himself remained relatively unscathed. The *Los Angeles Times'* Kevin Thomas wrote, "[The film] forthrightly depicts injustices to Mexican-Americans, which strikes a note of contemporary awareness without seeming to strain for relevance. At the same time, *Joe Kidd*, well written by Elmore Leonard, manages to be a satisfying, traditional-style adventure entertainment, set against the rugged natural beauty of New Mexico."

Regardless of its mixed reviews, *Joe Kidd* was a box office hit for Warner Bros. and Clint Eastwood's Malpaso Productions, grossing over $6 million worldwide.

Bantam officially rolled out *Forty Lashes Less One* in mid-October—more than two years since Leonard finished writing it. Although the publisher would surely get first-look rights toward Leonard's new book, he knew presenting them with a movie tie-in could be problematic; movie novelizations rarely received the same critical attention as a proper novel—meaning Leonard's follow-up to *Mr. Majestyk* had to be particularly strong. With that in mind, he had high hopes for his latest proper novel, tentatively entitled *Backfire*. Leonard packed his notes and wrote to Swanson on November 25, "In case anybody wants to give us money and you have to get in touch with me next week, I'll be in Pompano Beach, Florida . . . we'll be home Monday night, Dec. 4." He added, "This, you understand, is a business trip."[9]

To Leonard, the final lesson learned from reading George V. Higgins's *The Friends of Eddie Coyle* had been the author's intimate use of his native Boston, adding new levels of realism and grittiness to the prose. As a proud resident of Detroit for more than thirty years, Leonard decided to use the same strategy for the new book. In that regard, the aborted assignment adapting *Wheels* for Walter Mirisch couldn't have come at a better time; Detroit was already a hot topic in the national headlines due to the automobile industry and the city's economic decline. While the previous decade had seen the nation's crime rate double—the social breakdown associated with anti–Vietnam War student protests, the Civil Rights movement, and rampant drug use all cited as contributing factors—Detroit had been hit especially hard. Within only a few years, theft, violent assault, and ghastly gang murders had become commonplace within the urban areas of the city limits—as was the rise of heavily armed street gangs. In 1967, the city reported 281 homicides; by 1972, the number had ballooned to 672—nearly triple those of New York or Chicago. The once-thriving metropolis once known as "Motor City, USA" had become "*Murder* City" in the media, touting the highest crime rate in the nation, emphasized by an era of unemployment and social turbulence. Just as the Great Migration had drawn so many Americans to the city a half century earlier, the mass exodus of major automakers had led to some of the country's worst waves of unemployment; by 1970, one out of every three adults in Detroit was unemployed or on welfare. (Asked later his opinion on the causes of Detroit's decline, Leonard was candid in his views: "The fact that 700,000 left town and moved out to the suburbs," he told journalist Anthony May. "Oh, we still produce more cars than anybody but not to the point where we can be cocky about it."[10])

Having reimmersed himself in the Detroit automobile industry while adapting *Wheels* for Walter Mirisch, Leonard decided to incorporate his expertise into the new novel. Even his time with John DeLorean had paid off, as the iconoclast's demeanor and world of suburban affluence on the outskirts of Detroit would work their way into the new protagonist—the owner of a moderately sized automotive parts plant. The only research required on Leonard's behalf was some knowledge of the specific car parts themselves, some of which he was already familiar with thanks to his freelancing days. To stay up on current trends, Leonard studied the Stilson company's full line of machine tool and material-handling factory accessories, noting the industrial jargon associated with conveyor rolls, urethane bumpers, vacuum lifters, lock clamps, and production adapters.

For the book's climax, however, Leonard researched the practical applications of dynamite and bomb defusal.

• • •

Leonard's opening words rang like a starter's pistol—"*He could not get used to going to the girl's apartment*"—throwing the reader into Harry Mitchell's world mid-scene and evoking the shadowy uneasiness to come. Entering the condominium he'd rented for his much-younger mistress for one of their regular trysts, middle-aged auto-parts executive Mitchell is, instead, ambushed by three gun-wielding masked assailants who force him to watch home movies of his extramarital activities. What's worse, the trio appear to know everything about Mitchell—including intricate details of his financial holdings and investments—and propose an exchange of $105,000 for the telltale film. But rather than yield to the extortionists' demands, Mitchell comes clean to his wife, Barbara, and initiates a manipulative counterscheme to turn the tables on his aggressors. A brutal game of cat and mouse begins, with Mitchell discovering the identities of his blackmailers and planting seeds of deceit among their organization, ultimately weakening their resolve and trust.

Leonard approached the novel with a newly liberated sense of the contemporary, featuring an all-too-human antihero in Mitchell, and three particularly psychopathic blackmailers: Leo Frank, the owner of a strip club where Mitchell's young girlfriend, Cini, had worked; armed robber and killer-for-hire Bobby Shy; and the mastermind, accountant turned pornographer and rapist Alan Raimy. When Mitchell is slow paying up, the trio brutally retaliates by killing Cini with Mitchell's own gun, then forcing him to watch a snuff film of the killing. Although he could now be framed for the girl's murder, Mitchell continues to ignore pleas from Barbara and his attorney to notify the police. Rather, he negotiates the extortion amount down to fifty-two thousand dollars, buying more time to plan his brutal counterattack.

In an effort to separate the novel from any potential adaptation, Leonard considered giving each version its own title. For the book version, he'd tentatively chosen *Backfire*—a reference to the would-be blackmailers' unsuccessful plan; for the film treatment, he chose the extorted prize of $52,000 itself, coolly abbreviated as *Fifty-Two Pickup*. "At the time, I didn't realize it," Leonard later recalled, "but now I see that was the beginning of the voice that I've developed . . . I realized how much fun I could have with those people, that I don't have to make them entirely despicable. I can have fun with the guys who are into crime—*into the life*."[11]

On February 12, 1973, he wrote to Swanson, "I'll have to do some more thinking about a title. The latest idea, *Backfire*, has lost what little appeal it had last week. The book should go another two-hundred pages, or about seventy-thousand words."[12] Leonard put his outline aside and launched into the first draft, nearly completing in just under two months.[13]

In June, Swanson closed a deal with Delacorte for the newly retitled *Fifty-Two Pickup*: ten thousand dollars—half upon signing, then the following installments upon delivery and publication. Leonard was soon introduced to Jackie Farber, the new senior editor at Dell with whom he would be collaborating on his unofficial contemporary *re-debut*. Farber later recalled that editing Leonard was particularly easy, and that the author would always take her editorial suggestions "very well." If there had been any trepidations on his part regarding a further leap into the contemporary crime genre, she claimed, "it never showed."[14] Farber had already discussed the manuscript with publisher Ross Claiborne—then working with Leonard on the *Mr. Majestyk* novel—who agreed that story worked well up until the final act. "After that it races forward, each step falling too neatly into place," she wrote Leonard. "You said you had worked hard on the economy of the prose style, [but] I think you can still fill in with information and keep the style pretty spare." Farber also insisted that Leonard leave Harry "in the dark" for a longer duration of the narrative, claiming, "Even Sam Spade went up a few wrong alleys."[15]

Leonard received the galley proofs for *Fifty-Two Pickup* on September 2, quickly scanning Farber's final continuity questions and signing off on the completed manuscript. Farber wrote back four days later. Swanson had moved on the property just as quickly. The second week of September, Philip Barry, a producer for Tomorrow Entertainment, contacted Leonard directly, expressing his interest to adapt *Fifty-Two Pickup* once the ongoing writers' strike came to an end and assuring him, "Your man Mitchell is exactly the kind of hero the movie audience is looking for today."[16]

Leonard had used the time allotted by the strike to complete the novel of *Mr. Majestyk*—a smart loophole for which Swanson, well-versed in the finer print of union protocols, was able to keep his author clients' hands busy. Now, at Barry's request, Leonard agreed to fly out to Los Angeles on September 22 to meet with the young producer and his project partner, Roger Gimbel. All three were left satisfied with the shared vision of a *Fifty-Two Pickup* film. However, in making the leap from page to screen, both Barry and Gimbel insisted that certain scenes would need to be tweaked for the screen, noting that the source material had been "loaded with dialogue." More directly, Barry insisted Leonard "look for every opportunity to play out scenes in a filmic sense with a minimum of dialogue," unaware that an emphasis on dialogue was the key tenet of Leonard's new literary voice. He was now tasked with pruning through his most mature novel to date for scenes that could be tossed into the fire, many of which leaned on gritty dialogue for the book's rich characterization. Leonard soon admitted to the producer, "It's funny how you can think you have planned a book to develop in film sequences, making the adaptation easy, or at least easier. But it isn't there until you actually think of it as a picture." Running with their agreed-upon changes, Leonard delivered his first draft to Barry the second week of November.

While on the Spanish set of *The Spikes Gang* with director Richard Fleischer, Walter Mirisch continued to brainstorm the perfect replacement for Steve McQueen in *Mr. Majestyk*. It soon dawned on him that on-screen tough guy Charles Bronson was on a career upswing, having recently followed Clint Eastwood's example of starring in a number of European action films, elevating him from supporting player to leading man. "It had been many years since I had worked with Charlie Bronson," Mirisch later wrote, recalling their previous collaborations on *The Magnificent Seven*, *The Great Escape*, and *Kid Galahad*. "I called Paul Kohner, who represented [Bronson], and I told him that I thought *Mr. Majestyk* would be an excellent vehicle for his client, hoping that he and Charlie would agree." The producer even hopped a flight to Los Angeles to solidify funding and further sweeten Charles Bronson's deal, closing on a $2 million budget—$400,000 of which would go to Bronson against 10 percent of the gross. Unfortunately, the actor had already committed to star in an adaptation of Brian Garfield's vigilante thriller, *Death Wish*, the following year. In order to star as Vincent Majestyk, as Mirisch recalled, "[Bronson] needed to start shooting in September, which gave us only a short time for preparation." Although it took some convincing, Mirisch was able to retain most of *The Spikes Gang*'s principal players for the next project, including director Richard Fleischer. "[Fleischer] was coming to the end of a long, difficult shoot, and he wasn't very enthusiastic about undertaking a second film immediately after the first," Mirisch later recalled. "Despite his misgivings, Dick agreed to go along with this plan and segue immediately from one film to the next." Mirisch then dispatched production manager Jim Henderling to scout locations for *Mr.*

Majestyk's melon fields and action sequences. "The watermelons worked out well for us," Mirisch recalled, "because they were more photogenic and certainly a lot more dramatic when bullets were fired into them."[17]

Leonard had all the needed corrections for the *Mr. Majestyk* novel completed by the first week of October and had his secretary, Janet Smart, send off the final proofs to William Grose at Dell. Less than a week later, Grose replied, "You're right, you've got much more in the novel than there is in the screenplay. It's very good. Tight, compelling, and the characters are wonderful. Money is on its way to Swanson . . . Let me know what else is coming out of your typewriter." And after months of back-and-forth regarding *American Flag*, Swanson finally heard from Pat Kelly at First Artists the first week of December. According to the producer, Steve McQueen's Solar Productions had run into "an unavoidable snag in making a deal with [another] screenwriter"—an issue that could have been avoided by retaining Leonard from the beginning. As far as Leonard and Swanson's end of the deal, Solar–First Artists still had eight months to make good on acquiring any leftover rights from their original 1971 agreement. However, this removed Swanson's option to keep hold of Leonard's rights to the property during that time—a potentially minor inconvenience, as all signs pointed to the start of the film's production earlier the following year. If anything, the very fact that McQueen had circled back to the property after two years indicated he still wanted the film made—although the standstill of production hell would continue well into the new year.

Fifty-Two Pickup was released by Delacorte in April 1974.

Although Leonard's hopes had been high in 1970 for Doubleday's hardcover release of *The Moonshine War*, and those reviews had been strong, the lukewarm reception that the ensuing film version received had seemed to have an adverse effect on the original novel. But this would not be the case with *Fifty-Two Pickup*—already regarded by its author, its editors, and, apparently, many critics as Leonard's true entry into the world of contemporary crime fiction.

"For a tough American piece of writing, *Fifty-Two Pickup* by Elmore Leonard is recommended," wrote the *New York Times* critic Harold Schonberg under his frequent nom de plume "Newgate Callendar." "Leonard . . . manages to get into his characters and build a believable situation. The dialogue reads in a natural manner, and is certainly tough enough, yet there is an agreeable avoidance of four-letter words, proving that profanity and toughness do not necessarily have to go together."[18] (Leonard himself later remarked, "The main thing I set out to do is tell the point of view of the antagonist as much as the good guy. And that's the big difference between the way I write and the way most mysteries are written. The problem with most mysteries is the most interesting part of the stories [the crimes] are off-stage. It's done before or while you're not looking."[19])

Leonard was delighted by Swanson's response, especially as it had been the agent who'd intentionally recommended *The Friends of Eddie Coyle* in order to provoke such creative inspiration. Swanson himself later told *Rolling Stone*, "I can't mold a writer. I didn't tell Faulkner what to write, or Hemingway, or James M. Cain what to write. A writer is like a cook. He puts some ingredients on the stove, lets it simmer, takes it off. I think it took Dutch a while to figure out the proper mix of ingredients."[20]

> In the summer of 1974 a friend advised me to stop drinking and start going to AA meetings . . .
>
> I thought I had to drink to relax and have a good time. Or I was self-conscious with people I didn't know well or who didn't drink. At my first AA meeting, I asked one of the regulars, "Aren't parties boring if you're not drinking?" He said, "If you think you're gonna be bored, why go?" Straight talk. If you have a drinking problem, quit. The program will help you develop a new attitude about it.

With numerous deadlines met, Leonard unceremoniously planned a road trip to California and back—alone. It was the first and only time he had taken such a trip by himself, and not under the guise of vacation or to meet with Swanson or other film executives. With *Mr. Majestyk* ready to hit theaters in only a few weeks and *Fifty-Two Pickup* selling well amid glowing reviews, Leonard was finally taking the time to address much more pressing issues that had been building at home—his alcoholism and the effects it had played in the slow erosion of his marriage to Beverly.

Rather than a straight shot to Los Angeles, Leonard planned a longer, meandering itinerary, heading southwest first, then north up through Southern California counterclockwise back to Detroit. He left on July 2 at six fifteen in the morning, bringing along two weeks' worth of casual attire and a small forty-sheet spiral travel journal, scrawling "L.A. Trip by Car" across its cover. By way of Indianapolis, he reached St. Louis, Missouri, by midafternoon, jotting down the colors of various police cars and selections from regional radio stations along the ride. He noted guitarist Jerry Reed's apparent nickname, "the Alabama Wildman," adding the first leg of the drive had already cost "eighty bucks," then made it to Amarillo, Texas, by late the following night.

On the road, Leonard continued his random thoughts:

> *I love New Mexico. Clean and stark and hard. Think of movies, writing, paintings. That principle. The Midwest has a Protestant look. It closes you in. The west makes you want to go . . . New Mexico is scrub, but it's good—the sky is better . . . In New Mexico the sky doesn't go down, like it does in Oklahoma. It goes up . . . Hank Williams—"I'll Think of Something."*

For the first time, Leonard spent July 4 on his own—no barbeque or "Elmore burgers" for the family and their children's friends. He stayed at the Whiting Brothers Motor Lodge in Holbrook, Arizona, noting that the one good thing he could say about the motel's accommodation was the strong water pressure: "It takes the plastic glass right out of your hand."

Leonard soon sparked a lively conversation about music with a hitchhiker he'd picked up just outside Needles named Joe Bravo. At a roadside diner together, Leonard was amused by a brief exchange between Bravo and the waitress: "What do you do in Barstow for fun?" Bravo had asked, to which she'd quickly offered, "You get out of town." Taking his cue, Leonard did just that, and arrived at the Sunset Marquis on July 6. He drove to Las Vegas, finally noting, "I'm getting out of here," but added later, "I lied. Cruised the strip for one more look. But it hadn't changed." Leonard continued to Los Angeles the following morning, stopping roadside in Cedar City, Utah, at five o'clock to write, "Sky beginning to lighten. Looked forward to a big sunrise coming up over the Rockies, but it's been raining. One thing, the lightning was a lot more impressive than the lights of Las Vegas."[21]

Ultimately, Leonard stayed in Los Angeles for a week and a half before heading home, not in a particular rush this time. He knew the inevitability that awaited him when he returned: a promise he had made to himself to attend his first Alcoholics Anonymous meeting.

"I was beginning to disguise my drinks," Leonard later wrote. "I would drink a big Whiskey Collins instead of my favorite, which was Early Times over shaved ice. Twice I was arrested for drunk driving. That was toward the very, very end. Once in Malibu, when I was driving too slow at 2:30 a.m., then a year later in Michigan. I drank for thirty years and nothing ever happened and suddenly, two driving-while-under-the-influence arrests in a year. That's got to tell you something."

When Leonard was released the following morning of his second arrest, he had something to tell the officers at the Birmingham jail, as well. Of the eggs he'd been fed at breakfast, he'd advised them, "You know, it's just as easy to cook it right."[22] After a profile ran in the *Detroit Free Press* wherein reporter Ellen Goodman had alluded to Leonard's apparent intoxication (the one and only such incident), he was inspired to do two things: write a letter to Goodman asking for an apology (which he got), and then to calm himself and reassess his own behavior.[23] "I tried to hide my drinking from myself," he later admitted. "I would sit in my office—actually I had three offices. I had a refrigerator in the front office and in the middle office there was a kind of lounge. I had a bottle of sherry and little glasses there on the table. I would go in there and have a little glass of sherry from the decanter, then I'd have another one. After that, I'd get out the bottle and fill up the decanter where it had been in case anyone noticed." Leonard continued, "Then I'd get a cold bottle of white wine out of the refrigerator and put it in my desk drawer. I'd open the drawer very, very quietly, though no one was in the office, and take the wine out and drink a big, big swig of it and put it back in. Not a soul was near enough to hear anything. I didn't want to hear it."

Before the summer, a number of close friends had recommended he attend an AA meeting just to get the feel of it and, perhaps, to see if he could relate to some of the other attendees' personal stories. "All I had to do was sit at one meeting and listen to the stories to know that I was an alcoholic," he later recalled. "I admitted it at my first meeting. I opened my mouth and it came to me, 'I'm Dutch, and I'm an alcoholic.'"[24]

> I was forty-nine and had been a fairly serious drinker since high school. In the 1950s, martinis and Manhattans were served at cocktail parties and I was happy to go either way . . . Jack Daniels was okay, Wild Turkey was a special treat. There was always a full bottle of wine with dinner, Gallo Hearty Burgundy, ninety-seven cents. After coming home

> smashed from a party, my wife at the time was likely to say, "Your problem is you don't count your drinks." And my smartass reply would be, "Yes, I do, I had fifteen."
>
> I began going to meetings in '74, would maintain my sobriety for a few months, fly off to some foreign land and fall off the wagon. No, jump off: once in Morocco, twice in Israel, several times on the West Coast, undetected.

That same month, after nearly a quarter century of marriage, Leonard and Beverly separated. He found an apartment in downtown Birmingham at 609 Merrillwood Apartments, 225 East Merrill Street. "We always drank," he later recalled. "We always drank together . . . Every single night, we would get into arguments, with me drunk and her part of the way, with me saying vicious things, which I couldn't believe the next day. I was filled with remorse." He added, "I wonder if the booze gave me the courage to leave home, to leave the situation I was in, having been married for twenty-six years. Now that I know what I know, I'm sure I would have done it in the right way with a clear head. But I did it drinking and got away with it."[25]

At his very first AA meeting, Leonard was also given a number of reference materials for the long road to sobriety that lay ahead. He collected a brochure of important meeting locations and contact information, a book of the "12 Steps," another book of more Michigan locations, and emergency contacts. Most important, Leonard received a miniature book of affirmations—much like the small leather Catholic prayer book he'd received as a child for his First Holy Communion—providing a daily reading for each day of the year. It was entitled *Twenty-Four Hours a Day* and was intended to help members in "living one day at a time" through proactive mindfulness, meditation, and prayer. The book's foreword reminded readers, "If we don't take that first drink today, we'll never take it, because it's always today."

A Sanskrit proverb followed:

> For yesterday is but a dream
> And tomorrow is only a vision.
> But today, well lived, makes every yesterday a dream of happiness.
> And every tomorrow a vision of hope.
> Look well, therefore, to this day.

Although Leonard didn't begin using the book until his return from his extended July road trip, had he looked through those dates during his excursion, he might have found comfort in those missed affirmations. As he had crisscrossed the American West contemplating the next stage of his life—jotting down notes about the colors of interstate police cars, discussing jazz with hitchhikers with unusual names, and attending rodeo shows while venting about broken ice machines in roadside hotels—many of the answers he sought could have been found within the pages of his newly acquired little AA book.

His daily prayer for July 7 said it all:

> *Painful as the present time may be, you will one day see the reason for it. You will see that it was not only testing, but also a preparation for the life-work you are to do.*[26]

Mr. Majestyk held its LA premiere on July 17—the final day of Leonard's solo road trip.

The film received mixed reviews from critics, but was a hit during its opening weekend. Vincent Canby of the *New York Times* called the film "mindlessly violent" and criticized Bronson's acting, saying that "he goes through the motions of being an action hero without actually conveying any emotion or depth." Canby also criticized the film's script, saying that it "has no center, no originality, and no reason for being except to exploit the increasingly profitable genre of the action film." *Variety*'s review was more positive, calling the film "a hard, fast action flick that never pauses for breath." Ultimately, the film was a modest success, overshadowed by Bronson's next feature film, which opened only a few weeks later—*Death Wish*. Leonard later admitted he would continue to get residuals for *Mr. Majestyk* for decades: "Walter [Mirisch] gave me a big bonus the moment the picture was in the black." He added that anytime the movie would air on Japanese television, he could look forward to a check for a few hundred dollars. And although he never got the opportunity to thank Charles Bronson in person for his contribution to the project's success, in later years, Leonard liked to recount a brush he had with the star not long after *Mr. Majestyk*'s production. While riding in the same elevator as Bronson at the Ritz-Carlton in Boston, he overheard the excitement the lift operator had at seeing the actor in person. "Charles Bronson! What are you doing here?" To Leonard's amusement, the actor had replied, "I'm checking up on elevator operators."[27]

As hard as Leonard had been working equally on his fiction and screenwriting credits, as the decade built toward its midpoint, he slowly began to see more success on the literary front than the Hollywood scene—although the latter continued to pay handsomely, regardless of the likelihood many projects wouldn't be filmed. Producer Walter Mirisch had taken Leonard's draft of *Wheels* and passed it on to another screenwriter.[28]

Likewise, Leonard's hopes of seeing *American Flag* produced with Steve McQueen in the lead were dashed in the coming year. Although half a decade had passed, Steve McQueen had retained his interest in Leonard's script—although the later revisions bore little resemblance to the initial treatment that had piqued the actor's interest in spring 1970. Soon, while compiling notes for the next novel, Leonard saw the latest revisions by McQueen's own writing team. The final treatment did away with character names entirely, calling McQueen and wife/costar Ali MacGraw by their proper names. With the mandated action scenes and final standoff in place, Leonard made no additions to the last draft owned by McQueen's company. When McQueen's partners at First Artists decided against the film, he opted to shoot *Junior Bonner* for director Sam Peckinpah instead.[29] Following a few more films, Steve McQueen would take a nearly five-year hiatus, returning for only two more films before his untimely death in 1980 at the age of fifty.

Around the same time, Leonard also received one of the most promising pieces of fan mail he'd ever received: "While in Detroit, I had a talk with [producer] Ken Barnard," actor Kirk Douglas wrote from his Beverly Hills home. "We have one thing in common—we are both fans of Dutch Leonard." The actor enthusiastically inquired if Leonard would consider doing a revision—which he felt Leonard "could do beautifully"—on the actor-producer's upcoming Western.[30] Leonard responded with interest immediately, initiating a correspondence between the two. He quickly set to work typing up a few ideas for Douglas's script for *Posse* when it soon arrived in the mail. "My main objection to the storyline is that the five possemen to be the focal point of the story, the main characters in the third act, without a great deal of character development before that," Leonard wrote to Douglas, then filming in London. "But the story, in its development, does not point to this conclusion. It points to a clash between the two pros, two strong-willed individuals who know their business. But this doesn't take place. Instead, 120 minutes of action and character development lead us only to a trick ending."[31] In total, Leonard had sent off over a dozen pages of suggestions and intricate structural changes he felt would make the film more cohesive—and all for free. He soon followed up with Swanson, writing, "I'm not worried about him stealing it, giving the ideas to the original writer. At least it never occurred to me that he might do such a thing. I spent maybe three days on it when I wasn't doing anything else, anyway."[32] (Although Leonard hadn't planned on writing another Western in the foreseeable future, he saved the unused elements from his *Posse* suggestions for future use.)

When early deals with Tomorrow Entertainment for an adaptation of *Fifty-Two Pickup* fell through that November, Swanson immediately set to work negotiating with Israeli producer Menahem Golan to purchase the property; Golan was interested in the story, but insisted that the script be rewritten with Tel Aviv as the setting. Before the year was out, Leonard agreed to fly to Tel Aviv and tackle the "Israeli *Fifty-Two Pickup*"—but first, he had to put the finishing touches on *Bud and Stick, Inc.*—soon to be retitled *Swag*.

CHAPTER 11

Nourishing the Lord of Life, 1975–1977

Am I in my novels? Yes. I play all the parts.

Living alone for the first time in his entire life, Leonard had a schedule that soon became the closest it would ever be to that of a workaholic. Without the familiar comforts of the household he'd helped to establish with Beverly and his children around him, Leonard had opted to take H. N. Swanson's advice: "If I never told you before, I will tell you now—nothing in this world can take the place of work. It's the best companion you will ever have. It will never upset your lifestyle, and there is always the chance it will make you rich, as well as famous."

But if Swanson's pragmatic take on Leonard's situation had the ring of a partner in crime (the agent himself was known to playfully describe his Hollywood wheeling and dealing as "larceny"), the author's latest book only seemed more apropos. At that point, *Swag* had gone through nearly a half dozen title changes, all variants of its dual protagonists' names, Frank Ryan and Ernest "Stick" Stickley; however, at the eleventh hour, the publisher had insisted on using the title of one of Leonard's unsold movie properties—*Swag*—as the proper replacement for the then-entitled *The Frank and Ernest Method*.

During that time, Leonard also struck up a lively correspondence with his son Christopher, now twenty-one and having recently moved to Arizona. "I'm on page eighteen of my new book," he wrote Chris on January 28. "It's now *Cal and Stick, Inc.* Or *Stick and Cal, Inc.* . . . I couldn't make Bud talk the way I wanted him to. But Cal knows exactly how to do it."[1]

Halfway through the book, Leonard received word that his editor,

Jackie Farber, had left Delacorte following the release of *Fifty-Two Pickup*. For *Swag*, he would instead be working with Betty Kelly—later Betty Sargent—who, coincidentally, also hailed from Birmingham. "What a pleasant surprise to find that Delacorte has an author from my very own hometown," Sargent wrote in her introductory letter.[2] By her follow-up letter, she was comfortable enough to call him Dutch; by March, she was confident enough to launch into the grunt work on *Swag*. "Originally, [Leonard] was Jackie Farber's author," she later recalled. "Eventually, we worked on *Swag* and *Unknown Man No. 89* together . . . We had lunch together once in Birmingham when I was there visiting my family. At the time, he was staying in this hotel there and I thought that was really quite sweet. Most of our relationships with authors were on the phone, usually with the authors who didn't live in New York. But we had a very warm, friendly relationship."[3]

For the novel, Leonard had started with a very basic premise: what if two men partnered up for a *professional*, dogmatic approach to armed robbery? No flash, no violence—just a concrete set of "rules" that could be used as a form of style guide for maximum illegal profit. He had sent an early, detailed outline to Swanson, emphasizing the characters' conflicting personalities: "Bud and Stick should be giving each other side-long glances almost from the beginning," he wrote. "Both are funny, easy-going and low-key. But there's a difference. Stick is a natural. Bud puts it on; he's a showman."[4]

Perhaps the most fun that Leonard had while constructing the novel, however, was coming up with the aforementioned rules that guide his characters through their criminal career, entitled "Some Rules for Successful Armed Robbery" (later worked down to ten definitive rules):

1. Always be polite. Say please and thank you.
2. Always look good—neat and lean—but not too sharp.
3. Never call your partner by name, unless it is a fake name to throw off a witness.
4. Use as few words as possible, unless faking some kind of accent: again, to throw off the witness.
5. Always use a stolen car on a job. Don't worry about the witness seeing the license plate. That's what it's there for.
6. Never use force if it can be avoided. If you are going to hit

somebody on the head with a gun butt, you might as well shoot them. But shoot first if there's a hero in the house.

7. Do not count the take in the car. Wait till you get home.
8. Never tell anyone your business. Never. Make something up and stick to it. Especially with broads.
9. Never frequent places where underworld types, even gamblers, are known to hang out.
10. Never tell a junkie even your name.
11. If a cop has a gun on you and says come out with your hands up, say yes sir, and do what he says.
12. Don't flash money. If you're going to be a big spender, do it with class. Don't be an obvious spender.
13. Never go back to an old hangout once you've made it and have money to spend. Move to a higher-class neighborhood.

Leonard kept tinkering, omitting a few rules and merging others. He noted at the end, "But in this principle lies the paradox. They are consorting with criminals. They're consorting with each other. And when the pressure is applied to one of them, he turns on the other one—or attempts to—to save his own skin."[5] For research, Leonard combed through library archives and microfilms for similar Detroit-based crimes; the January 1963 armed robbery of the credit office at Hudson's Department Store in downtown Detroit, coupled with an almost identical robbery in 1966—as well as its ensuing investigation—provided him entirely with the novel's third act.[6] Leonard's original treatment had been entitled *Bobby & Stick, Inc.* At first, he'd envisioned both characters to be about thirty years old, with Stick originally hailing from "Ft. Wayne or Indianapolis or Bedford . . . more midwestern sounding than *Bobby*." Stick's birthday also fell on October 11—Leonard's own birthday—and he had a seven-year-old daughter living with her mother in Pompano Beach, Florida. Yet, when it came to the characters' names, he seemed to have the most difficulty; he had first tried out "Robert Stickley" and "Franklin" Schreitmueller, then "Bob Stickley" and "Frank Miller," before apparently settling on "Bud" and "Stick." As Leonard had mentioned to Christopher, he'd had trouble getting Bud to talk.

Ultimately, "Ernest Stickley" and "Frank Ryan" found each other and, as "Frank and Stick," their behavior soon evolved to such authenticity that the novel's darkly humorous denouement and their downfall seemed more than merely logical, but inevitable. Following their first meeting, during which Stick was attempting to hot-wire a car from the dealership where Frank Ryan works, the two join forces and adopt Ryan's list for their new business venture on the wrong side of the law. For four months, their plan works, affording the men a bachelor pad in a hip complex in nearby Troy, populated with young, unmarried professional women—much to Ryan's delight and, soon enough, Stick's malaise. The younger criminal had been on his way to visit his estranged daughter in Florida when he was nabbed for the opening scene's act of grand theft auto; despite having all the money and success he could ask for, he wishes only to be reunited with her:

> Now what? Sitting in a marina bar, watching gulls diving at the waves and seeing the charter boats out by the horizon, it didn't make the beer taste better . . . He'd say to himself, What do you want to do more than anything?
>
> Go see his little girl.[7]

At the time of the writing, Leonard's youngest, Katy, was the exact age as Stick's daughter; he had also dedicated the book to his oldest, Jane, who was only a few years away from replacing Janet Smart as his full-time typist.

Although Leonard had put the most energy into the dynamic between Ryan and Stick, two of his secondary characters would prove equally important as future archetypes for his novels to come: young assistant prosecutor Emory Parks and Detroit Police detective Cal Brown, who combine their own efforts in bringing down Ryan and Stick. In the end, however, it is Stick's amour, pin-up model Arlene Downey, who unwittingly leads Parks and Brown to the "smoking gun"—the airport locker containing the swag from Frank and Stick's last job: the stolen payroll from Hudson's Department Store. "What do you think I went to the trouble to think up all those rules for?" Frank indignantly asks his partner as they're carted away in cuffs. "You remember the ten rules? We act like businessmen and nobody knows our business. You remember that?" For a novel deliberately built upon the psychology behind dialogue, Leonard chose Stick's parting words very carefully: "Frank, why don't you shut the fuck up?"

Before Delacorte had agreed to publish the novel, Swanson had some misgivings concerning its protagonists. "My main comment can be summed up by saying I think the reader and the audience must like one of the two men, and be rooting for him to get out of the armed robbery, even at the cost of strong measures against his partner," Swanson wrote.[8] Still, Leonard remained adamant that the dynamic between Frank and Stick would work. He completed the first draft a month and a half before his Delacorte deadline. Editor Betty Sargent had it copyedited within two weeks,[9] later recalling, "[Leonard] didn't even require much editing because he was such a good author—so precise. That was one of the things that I loved about his work—no extra adverbs—and I admired that. If there were ever any suggestions that I made, he was very accepting of them and, in my experience as an editor of many, many years, the best authors do that."[10]

Indeed, Leonard had no issues with Sargent's suggestions and changes, but he did remove one scene—later admitting to its truly autobiographical nature. During their very first meeting, wherein Frank Ryan sells Stick on his scheme to launch an armed robbery "business," the criminally ambitious car salesman takes a moment to tell a story to illustrate his point:

> I'll tell you about a time, I was coming back from L.A. I stopped in a place called Mineral Springs, Colorado, have a beer or something to eat. I got to talking to a guy wearing a big cowboy hat and boots. Turned out he was a Chevrolet dealer. I told him I sold cars in the Motor Capital of the world and was going back to do it some more. We're shooting the shit, getting along pretty well, and meanwhile he started drinking brandy with beer chasers. Finally he asked me if I'd like to stay on, be his sales manager . . . Understand we're still doing the brandy and beers. I begin to see what's happening. I buy a round, he buys one. He starts throwing them down faster and I'm thinking, Dumb cowboy asshole, I know a dozen sickly guys who can't pick up anything heavier than a martini who'd kill you before sundown. Finally he says, he looks at me and says, "I ain't ever drunk with a lowlander yet I didn't have to put to bed."[11]

When *Swag* was released March 8, 1976, Sargent followed up with a full bundle of glowing reviews: "I felt you would like to have a look at our entire review file on *Swag*. The reviews have been excellent in all the places that really count, and I'm delighted."[12] In the *Detroit Free Press*, columnist Bob Talbert singled out the book for recommendation, writing, "I've just finished a fascinating view of Detroit from the prolific Birmingham writer Elmore Leonard—It's *Swag* . . . and it probably captures a slice of urban life better than anything else I've read."[13] Likewise, the novel was warmly received in *The New Yorker*. "Despite its old-time title, this is a brutally up-to-date crime novel, and a good one," the review read. "Mr. Leonard is more than convincing with his people and their operations, and he also injects a quality of helplessness and feeling that most agreeably recalls Edward Anderson's masterly *Thieves Like Us*, of the thirties."[14]

There was an additional satisfaction from the recognition of Leonard's peers. For the past few years, the *Miami Herald* had employed contemporary crime novelist, and another Leonard favorite, Charles Willeford as their critic of mystery and thriller releases; as his review of *Swag* would attest, the appreciation was mutual. "This is a crime novel told mostly in dialogue—and very good dialogue it is," Willeford wrote. "*Swag* is an immensely entertaining novel, and the dialogue is every bit as slick as one finds in the novels of George V. Higgins."[15]

He could not get used to putting the old issue of *Arizona Highways* in the office window. It had become a ritual between the two of them: if the coast was clear, he'd put the magazine on display, which was easily seen from her street-level view.[16] On those occasions, Leonard would finally be a little less alone both at his Pierce Street office and, more important, his Merrillwood apartment. And, in years to come, Leonard would credit his relationship and second marriage to Joan Shepard as a major catalyst in maintaining his long-term sobriety. But at the beginning of their relationship, an affair—the first and only for both—had been more like a second life that had to remain hidden from both their families.

Joan Leanne Lancaster Shepard was born February 9, 1928. She and husband, H. Clare Shepard, had known Leonard and Beverly socially for years, both as neighbors and then as mutual members of the Pine Lake Country Club—a well-to-do atmosphere Leonard himself would later parody in multiple novels. Shepard had two daughters of her own, Beth and Bobi, and was a regular tennis partner with Beverly—making her relationship and, ultimately, marriage to Leonard an unexpected and chaotic shift in the lives of both their families. As Leonard and Beverly's marriage had begun to slowly dissolve, so had Shepard's, and they had opted to keep their relationship secret, apparently biding time until a formal announcement could be made to their spouses and children. "She was my tennis partner," Beverly later recalled. "We weren't bosom buddies, but we were friends [at] the country club. I remember on Saturday mornings, Bill and Elmore would want to play tennis, and he'd say, 'I'll call Joan Shepard. She'll come and meet us.'" Although there was nothing suspicious at the time, Beverly remembered one brief incident that gave her pause. "One time, [Joan] dropped me off and 'Rikki Don't You Lose That Number' was just coming on [the radio] and she said, 'I can't get out yet—I have to hear this song, I love it.' And I thought, why would she even know that song? That's Elmore's song."[17] And while Leonard and Shepard's relationship held little resemblance to any character dynamic within his fiction, protagonist Harry Mitchell's own affair in *Fifty-Two Pickup* and its resulting chaos was an easy mirror to Leonard's own personal life; he had even dedicated the book, covertly, "*For J.S.*"

According to Leonard's children, it took time for them to come to grips with the situation. As Peter Leonard later recalled, "When Elmore got with Joan, I was still in the house. I had a room in the basement—I had been banished to the lower level for being a troublemaker and probably deserved it. But that was when Elmore had begun seeing Joan and he came and told me about it . . . it was tough—tough for everybody to try to make sense of. Later, I liked Joan, but our relationship never really passed being sort of superficial."[18] Bill Leonard also recalled, "I felt very defensive for my mother, very protective of her. Katie and I were still living at home when my dad's marriage broke up, so we have a far different perspective than the older three . . . I definitely resented [Joan], whether she was a nice person or a bad person—I just didn't like her on principle. She would say things to me like, 'We never meant to hurt your mother,' and, at that age, that just incensed me. 'You never meant to hurt my mother?—What did you think would happen?' . . . I got over it, I mellowed over time—but it took time."[19]

Although they waited to break the news, Leonard and Shepard were already determined to marry once the dust settled on her own divorce. Peter Leonard added, "[Joan] was very interested in Elmore's work, and I think that was one of the reasons that they hit it off. She would read his pages every day and would comment, particularly on what Elmore was writing as far as his female characters—main character or otherwise—she would comment on what the woman said, how she talked. And he liked that."[20]

Indeed, one of the most noticeable effects that Leonard's new relationship had on his work was his approach to female characters—an issue of ire for many critics. Joan herself would later elaborate, "[Leonard's female characters] in general I felt should have been updated. They were kind of pristine and wore white gloves. Now I think they're more real. At least [Leonard] seems to be identifying with the personalities of women more. They're not all cut out of the same paper doll. They have minds of their own."

Leonard would soon make a daily habit of writing at his desk while periodically looking out to watch Joan tend the garden; both enjoyed the domestic contentment of her immersed in soil and he in his work. (According to Bill Leonard, his father's guilt would playfully subside even more over the years. Upon one memorable visit in the late 1980s, Bill was sitting by the pool with his father when he looked up, only to find Joan cleaning the gutters. "Dad," Bill had asked, "why is Joan climbing on the roof?" The elder Leonard grinned at his son. "Because she can't write books."[21])

Joan's positive influence would also go a long way toward Leonard's sobriety. "I think my present wife, Joan, had a lot to do with my quitting," he later wrote. "She was so supportive, without any pushing or nagging, but with sympathy—the right kind of sympathy. She'd say, 'You are absolutely out of your mind.' Maybe it was the way she said it. 'Why are you doing this to yourself?' she'd say."[22]

A decade later, Leonard would put Joan's literary contributions succinctly into the dedication of what he considered—up to that point—his favorite among his novels: "*To my wife Joan, for giving me the title and a certain look when I write too many words.*"

In December 1975, Leonard took up Menahem Golan's offer to visit Tel Aviv for discussions regarding his "Israeli version" of *Fifty-Two Pickup*. It was sold to the producer's AmeriEuro Pictures Corporation, and Leonard was instructed that the new screenplay should not only move the novel's action from Detroit to Israel, but would require new elements of espionage and foreign intrigue in order to make the story more cinematic. Apprehensive from the very moment Swanson had sold the property to

Golan, Leonard, nonetheless, set up camp at the Tel Aviv Sheraton for two weeks. He was quickly introduced to Golan's production associate Zohar Bar Am—who volunteered to give Leonard a personal tour of Israel while they scouted locations for the new script. (Unbeknownst to Bar Am, however, Leonard was also covertly gathering more ideas for his next novel.)

As had been Leonard's practice anytime traveling without an in-progress manuscript in front of him, he started a small spiral travel journal for his notes and observations:

> *It's cold in Jerusalem in the winter unlike it's cold anywhere else. But Jerusalem is unlike any other city in the world to begin with. I don't know what it is. A feeling that everybody feels . . . There is the King David Hotel and the Hertz Rent-a-Car and the Wailing Wall and the Mosque of Omar and the Via Dolorosa and Arab and Israeli soldiers with M-16s and Uzis and tour buses all over and a little five-foot-three Armenian deacon teaching seven boys English . . .*
>
> *Zohar showed me where he, in one tank, and his friend, Rafi, in another, were cut off by the Jordanians on a bridge overlooking the old city during The 6-Day War . . . Zohar is low-key. He's low-key without, I think, he knows how cool he is. He packs a Czech .765 automatic with two extra clips in his briefcase. Do you know why? Because "maybe one kilogram can keep you alive."*[23]

As exciting as Bar Am's personal tour of Israel was, Leonard was consistently reminded that their daily excursions were work, not play: each location on the itinerary was meant not only to inspire his screenplay adaptation of *Fifty-Two Pickup*, but also to pragmatically see firsthand where Golan had *already* decided they would be filming. Leonard jotted down notes nightly back at the Sheraton—making Harry Mitchell not an auto-parts manufacturer but rather a high-profile US ambassador to Israel, and psychotic extortionist Alan Raimy his conniving personal valet. Once back home, Leonard completed two drafts of the "Israeli" *Fifty-Two Pickup*. He kept the skeleton of his original novel but added Golan's new scenes and plot changes, including a car chase through foreign checkpoints and the labyrinthine tunnels inside King Solomon's copper mines.[24] He later recalled, "Golan wanted me to add more intrigue, more secret papers. I told him, 'You don't want me—get another writer.'"[25] (Golan eventually released his "Israeli *Fifty-Two Pickup*" as *The Ambassador* in 1984—starring Robert Mitchum, Ellen Burstyn, and, in his last film role, Rock Hudson. The final version bore such little resemblance to the original novel, Leonard successfully lobbied the WGA to have his name removed from the film.)

Unfortunately, Leonard's association with the producer would later become an ongoing source of strife on numerous occasions. Leonard and Swanson immediately had to go to near-Olympian feats to attain the money owed. "I wrote Golan a nice letter telling him what a wonderful story I have that takes place in Israel and would be right down his alley and how much fun it would be to work with him again if only I had money to live on while I finish writing the story, the son of a bitch," Leonard wrote to Swanson.[26] A year later, with Golan already telling trade magazines about his upcoming production of *Fifty-Two Pickup*, Leonard was still waiting on payment.[27] In response to Swanson's threat of court action, Golan took on a condescending tone, writing to Leonard: "I really like your sense of humor. You should have been a caricaturist. The fact that we publish ads in the newspapers does not mean that we already have money to pay out. You have already received over $60,000 from us on a script and a picture that never got off the ground. It is not your fault, or maybe it is, since the script you supplied was not good enough to attract actors or investors." While Leonard eventually collected on the money owed from his drafts of *Fifty-Two Pickup*, Golan's admittance to prematurely publishing ads prior to actual production was another matter. It was a practice of Golan's that would greatly—and negatively—affect Leonard yet again nearly a decade later.

Back home, Leonard juggled the notes and first draft of his next novel, as well as another potential screenwriting assignment that could make up for the lost time working on Golan's "reimagined" *Fifty-Two Pickup*. As his future researcher, Gregg Sutter, later recalled, "In 1975, John Foreman, Paul Newman's partner, was producing *The Man Who Would Be King*, directed by John Huston, starring Sean Connery and Michael Caine. Foreman was familiar with and liked Elmore's dialogue and 'wanted to put it to work' in a film." According to Sutter, Foreman was soon leaving for Morocco, so Leonard sent him six pages in care of the airline in New York. Foreman was enthusiastic with the new material and asked Leonard to expand it—which he did, as a fifty-page treatment.

Again, the producer loved it and extended an invitation to Leonard to Morocco for a meeting with him—as well as stars Sean Connery and Michael Caine—who were looking for another joint project. "Elmore went and ended up hanging around the set and hotel until Connery and Caine were available," Sutter added. "After several days, he sat down with them and they expressed their serious interest. Elmore went home thinking it was a done deal and he was going to write the screenplay."[28] Leonard had planned an expansive historical caper perfect for the potential leading men. Initially entitling it *Swag*, then *The Hawkbill Gang*, he had finally found the perfect opportunity to use the setting from *For Whom the Bell Tolls*—the Spanish Civil War. Set in 1938, the action takes place in England, Spain, and North Africa, and tells the story of the eponymous gang of gentleman thieves. Ultimately, producer John Foreman found the pitch too expensive to shoot in England and nixed the project.

Having returned from Morocco, Leonard had one further potential film assignment awaiting him. On July 28, producer Charles Fries wrote to Leonard, picking his brain regarding a new project. "We would like to do a contemporary Boom Town story. Two great Gable and Tracy male characters—Newman and Redford . . . If you have some idea, let's talk." Leonard quickly took his latest unused *American Flag* notes, switched locations and scenarios, and sent Fries an outline entitled *Granduke*. "Another look at the boom town situation," Leonard wrote. "There is a copper mine in British Columbia called *Granduke* that employs about 600 men on three shifts . . . (The town is self-sufficient, much like in *American Flag*, and has room and board, bars, and a movie theater.)" Here, Leonard introduced his most James M. Cain concept yet—having an adulterous wife of one of the miners plot to kill her husband with the help of a young stud. He'd even compared the characters to Lana Turner and John Garfield. Ultimately, however, Fries passed. (Leonard's ongoing international travel may not have led to the film projects he had planned, but that time period did inspire him in other important ways—both personal and professional: "I sat around the lobby drinking for a week, waiting for the meeting," he later wrote. "I stopped off in Paris on the way home and drank some more and came home. The same year, a few months later, I went to Israel to adapt one of my books for a film set in Israel, which didn't make any sense at all to me. But the producer was paying and it was an opportunity to see Israel. I drank as soon as I got on the plane. I drank in Tel Aviv, where there are only two honest-to-God saloons in the whole town . . . I picked a country where nobody drinks to do my drinking."[29])

Beginning with the very first of his visits to Israel, Leonard had used the time to reconsider suggestions from previous editors to bring an older character back for a potential sequel or series. In this instance, Leonard chose *The Big Bounce*'s Jack Ryan—yet immediately set to maturing the character and contemplating where a listless young man like Ryan would have ended up. Deliberately avoiding a police procedural, he made the unlikely, yet playful, decision to make Ryan a legal process server. But more important, the new Jack Ryan would also be a recovering alcoholic, and his backstory and inner monologues would be among the most autobiographical of Leonard's career. He began writing his preliminary notes on court proceedings and the protocols of process servings. He also noted the tactics a process server would use to remain undetected while on the job.[30] As for Ryan himself—now in his thirties and on the wagon—Leonard wrote the character older and wiser, and nearly unrecognizable as a well-adjusted, content, *sober* adult. For the only time in his career, Leonard also dedicated pages to Ryan's characterization. Along with some ideas for clever scenarios wherein Ryan would have to serve papers during strange circumstances (issuing a subpoena to the lead singer of a rock band mid-concert), Leonard also began the earliest outline for the story's three-act structure, taking his yellow note papers and stapling them into a wafer-thin, makeshift notebook. Working within his traditional three-act structure, Leonard chose as his "McGuffin" a missing persons case—in this instance, the elusive recipient of valuable stock holdings. Ryan is hired by the mysterious New Orleans native F. X. Perez, whose specialty is combing through unclaimed assets, then bullying the rightful owner for a lucrative finder's fee, often with the help of a violent Cajun henchman named Raymond Gidre. In the novel, Perez is looking for Bobby Lear, a Black youth whose father had worked for a wealthy white family, parlaying stock market tips on Denver Pacific into an inheritance for his son. Now a small-time hood with a lengthy criminal record, Lear appears to not want to be found. Using a close friend in the Detroit Police Department as his primary resource, Ryan soon finds Lear's estranged wife, Denise (initially called "Rita")—now an alcoholic herself and on the verge of the same self-destruction Ryan once faced. Eventually, the two fall in love and turn the tables on Perez, as Bobby Lear's apparent murder has made Denise the true beneficiary of the Denver Pacific stock. Further upsetting their plans, however, is one of Leonard's most memorable characters from his period—the charismatic and murderous Virgil Royal, a former criminal associate of Lear's looking to collect the stock as an outstanding debt. Royal's vicious killing of Lear—in his one and only scene—leads Ryan to the county morgue, where the body is anonymously tagged as the eponymous "unknown man, number 89."

Leonard had purposely allocated a large section within the manuscript for one of the most gut-wrenching scenes in the book; at approximately the halfway point—and prior to their romance's beginning—Ryan loses track of Denise's whereabouts, leading to Ryan's own fall off the wagon. Leonard had opted to skip over the scene in his first draft, only going back to fill in the large gap, laced with his own experiences in battling alcoholism, once the rest of the book was complete. "To describe why Ryan starts drinking again—to make it natural and believable—will take a little doing," Leonard noted within the manuscript, "but it's important to the story that he does."[31]

In his final draft, Leonard revisited the scene:

> What was he doing sitting here? He could go home right now, take a nap, have dinner, feel a little shitty this evening, get a good night's sleep, and feel about 75 percent okay in the morning. But if he kept going until the bars closed at two, he'd be on his way. Open his eyes in the morning and hope there was still some vodka in the cupboard . . .
>
> Because he was depressed.
>
> Because he deserved a drink . . .
>
> He had had one drink on Monday afternoon. No trouble . . . He had had eight drinks Monday evening . . . two Bloody Marys at lunch Tuesday in Clarkston. He had had four vodkas and tonic during the afternoon. Eight, maybe ten bourbons that evening . . .
>
> His wife or somebody had told him once, his problem was he didn't count his drinks. Okay, he was counting them.[32]

It's only when Ryan decides to cut his losses, sober up, and attend an AA meeting that he finally finds Denise—who is already there.

Like many members of his family, Leonard's oldest grandson, Tim Leonard, would cite *Unknown Man No. 89* as his favorite among his works for very specific reasons. As a next-generation Leonard, Tim hadn't been around for Elmore Leonard's struggle with alcohol, yet he claimed that reading the book during his own young adulthood had taught him much about his famous grandfather's earlier life. "When I read [*Unknown Man No. 89*], it just really hit me in a personal way because I knew it was the first book he wrote after getting sober," Tim recalled. "I guess because it had so much material based on his time in AA. I grew up seeing my grandfather as this larger-than-life character, but now I could see that he was human and that he had also struggled heavily. So, that book lifted me up in a certain way."[33]

Leonard, who was still at the cusp of finally conquering his own dependency, was on an upswing as he put the finishing touches on *Unknown Man No. 89*. He easily met Delacorte's June 30 deadline and was well into revisions on his follow-up novel, tentatively entitled *Hat Trick*, when he took a moment to share his elation with his son Chris:

> *Dear Christopher,*
>
> *It's a quarter to eleven Sunday morning and the sun is shining and I'm listening to a symphony on the classical FM station and it's good. I'm just beginning to appreciate this kind of music . . .*
>
> *Now the DJ says Hayden is coming up, No. 97 in C Major. Well, I guess you do tend to look at it mathematically if they're going to call them by numbers. It's their fault.*
>
> *Boy, it's good listening and looking out over the Sunday morning rooftops in the sunlight. Isn't it funny that it's taken me so long?*
>
> *Still, it's better than if not taken at all.*[34]

Leonard's evolving style of economic prose mixed with realistic dialogue and morally ambiguous antiheroes slowly began to win over consistent admirers—among them, the *New York Times*' Newgate Callendar. The critic had praised Leonard's previous two novels, but in the review of *Unknown Man No. 89*, Callendar would give Leonard's solidified protagonist archetype a lasting descriptor—"the decent man in trouble"—which would meet with high approval by its creator: "Like [George V. Higgins], Leonard's characters, all middle-class or criminal types, speak in a way that cannot be reproduced in a family newspaper. Leonard often cannot resist a set-piece—a lowbrow aria with a crazy kind of scatological poetry of its own—in the Higgins manner. But that is where the similarity ends. Where Higgins wrote only about criminals, Leonard writes about basically decent, ordinary men who get into trouble and have to work their way out of it . . . Leonard is a moralist in his way . . . *Unknown Man No. 89* follows the pattern. It is the story of a not very admirable man who, under stress, discovers himself and becomes a whole man."[35]

While Leonard had grown accustomed to big-name directors being, at least, attracted to his work, *Unknown Man No. 89* had landed him the biggest of all—"master of suspense" Alfred Hitchcock. On July 21, 1977, Universal Pictures entered into a purchase agreement with Leonard, with the intention that the book was to be adapted by Hitchcock. (Upon Hitchcock's death on April 29, 1980, however, Leonard was contracted by Universal to pen a new adaptation. By then, his status as an author had grown; Swanson successfully earned Leonard one hundred thousand dollars, although it would be divided into eight separate installments and never reach production.)[36]

Prior to completing *Unknown Man No. 89*, Leonard had already planned out his next project—a dual novel and screenplay, the story taking place in Tel Aviv. It was during his first visit to Israel, while he had been preoccupied with both Menahem Golan's *Fifty-Two Pickup* script and his own notes for what would soon become *Unknown Man No. 89*, that he hatched the idea for an Israel-set thriller. With the basic concept of an American hiding out within the city, then being pursued by his original aggressors, he slowly began his notes for *Hat Trick*—later, *The Hunted*.

Despite the ongoing issues with his contractual payment, Leonard remained friends with his Israeli valet, Zohar Bar Am, and planned to visit again for further research. "I'm leaving . . . for Israel," Leonard wrote to Swanson. "Once I make contact with an embassy Marine and talk to a couple of friends about Israeli gangsters (one is with Tel Aviv's largest Hebrew daily [newspaper], the other a news service stringer), I'll drive up to Galilee and visit a kibbutz near the Lebanon border and then down into the West Bank area (north of Jerusalem) where I think half the story will take place. Then back to Tel Aviv . . . I'll be home toward the end of May."[37]

Throughout that month, Zohar drove Leonard around, telling stories and giving him an even deeper dive into the local customs. He showed Leonard some of the more interesting spots that could be ideal for new car chases and realistic machine-gun standoffs, and welcomed him into his home to spend time with his wife, Nomi, and their three children.

Leonard stayed at the Tel Aviv Sheraton again, writing notes on everything in the room, including his laundry ticket. To beat the Middle Eastern heat, he'd taken to wearing various handkerchiefs around his neck—a style he'd adopted in the late 1960s—one for every day of the week. ("Lest you think him uncool, know that [Elmore] was cool," his son Peter Leonard later recalled. "He wore Italian boots with zippers on the sides and would take a bandana and wear it as a modified ascot. Even in Detroit, where canoe-sized sedans were the norm, [he] drove a Fiat convertible."[38])

Leonard also compiled updated maps and brochures of Jerusalem and Tel Aviv, and a cultural map of the Middle East; he also devoured the latest issues of *This Week in Israel*. He sought out local watering holes, such as Chez Simon on Shamai Street—home of "the Best Martini" in Jerusalem. A nod to his own love of America's pastime, Leonard had given his latest protagonist the name of a little-known third baseman from the Cleveland Indians during the 1940s and '50s named Al Rosen—nicknamed "the Hebrew Hammer." In reality, Leonard's Rosen is "Jimmy Rose"—of Irish descent and originally hailing from Detroit. Years earlier, Rosen made the near-fatal error of assisting the local government in incriminating a trio of violent gangsters—Gene Valenzuela, Clarence Rashad, and demolition expert Teddy Cass. When the case fell apart, Rose had no choice but to join the Witness Relocation Program; he has since been living in Jerusalem like a seemingly carefree playboy, all on his old law firm's dime. His main contact, attorney Mel Bandy, keeps the now Al Rosen's bank account flush with periodic shipments of cash, carefully sent through customs and hand-delivered by local US Marines. (Leonard had noted to himself, "Ask Menahem [Golan] how someone might take dollars out of Israel and deposit them in a Swiss bank.")[39] Rosen's hedonistic lifestyle as a professional tourist comes to a screeching halt when a newspaper photographer captures him saving his fellow guests from a fire at the King David Hotel. The accompanying article makes international headlines, leading his old Detroit enemies back onto his trail. The only hope in Rosen's corner is the serendipitous assigning of Sgt. David Davis—a US Marine filling in for the normal courier of his cash endowment. Davis himself is at a crossroads in his life, as his tenure in the service is coming to an end. With no plans once he returns to the States, Davis takes it as his personal crusade to protect Rosen and his assistant, Tali Rose, once the murderous Valenzuela and his gang reveal themselves in Israel.

Once home in Birmingham, Leonard spent weeks delving into the psychology of the David Davis character. Leonard envisioned the character, originally named David Day, as tough, but in the middle of an existential crisis; he jotted down pages of notes on Vietnam veterans and the implications of posttraumatic stress disorder—sadly common to many returned vets. In his biographical sketch for the character, Leonard wrote: "Consider—Everyone in it could be the main character if it were from his POV. But—everyone thinks he's good except Day. And Day wins . . . Everyone in the story thinks he's a pro except Day—and Day is the only genuine pro of the bunch. [He] has the intelligence and the natural ability—But he doesn't have self-esteem . . . Day discovers he's a winner."[40] Although the character of Al Rosen had been the starting-off point for Leonard's story, the young, stoic Marine soon took over much of the narrative, and certainly the action.

For Rosen, however, Leonard looked into real-life incidents of civilians entering into the Witness Relocation Program. An article in the January 19 issue of *New York* magazine, entitled "The Alias Program: The Incredible Rise and Downfall of a Mafia Witness," provided Leonard with the true story of criminal Gerald Zelmanowitz, who, after testifying before the Senate Investigations Subcommittee in 1973, was provided with the alias "Paul Maris" by the Department of Justice and relocated to a new, unspecified home.[41] For the first time, Leonard offered a sincere approach to death—no guns or explosives, but the private thoughts of "a decent man" in the *ultimate* trouble:

> It had taken him fifty years to learn that being was the important thing. Not being something. Just *being* . . . He should have known about it when he was seven, but nobody had told him. The only thing they'd told him was that he had to be *some*thing. See, if he'd known it then, he'd have had all that time to enjoy being.
>
> *Except it doesn't have anything to do with time*, he thought. Being is an hour or a minute or even a moment. Being is being, no matter where you are . . .
>
> He wondered if it would do any good if he called out for his mother. Shit, Rosen thought. Just when he was getting there.[42]

Although Leonard was confident in the story—so much so that he soon began a screenplay adaptation for a self-produced venture—he later admitted that the character of Rosen should have been at the forefront of the story, rather than Davis.[43] However, he was still content with the novel when he sent the final revision off to Swanson, although Delacorte had passed on it, citing possible oversaturation by the same author in one year; likewise, Putnam president Walter J. Minton rejected it, as well, doubting he'd be able to sell the number of copies needed to make a profit.[44]

However, Leonard remained optimistic about the book's potential when he soon sat with journalist Michael Ogorek of the *Birmingham Patriot* and revealed, "I have to sell at least one book a year to the movies." More so, however, he spoke about his latest workflow habits, adding, "I try not to write those passages people skip over. Why try to be poetic? I'm not a poet . . . I'm a storyteller, not a preacher. I write in scenes. I like the movie format. It's faster." Referencing his own approach to 1970's unproduced *Picket Line*, he added, "It's easier for a producer to visualize a book as a movie that way." Leonard also admitted that he'd recently done away with a long-standing practice of his creative process—writing a full outline ahead of time. "You can't force a character to do anything," he claimed. "You might know whether a character is a winner or a loser, but the characters do things on their own . . . When I mailed [*The Hunted*] off, I had the sad feeling that the people were gone. It's kind of kooky. I don't know, but I guess I was close to them. I hope it's a good sign; maybe the characters were more lifelike."[45]

And with that mindset, when he was approached during the early part of 1976 by local Birmingham-based independent filmmaker Tom Brank with a proposal to partner up on a project, it only appeared logical to get into film production himself.

In his youth, Brank had tried his hand at acting and moved out west; after only a few minor roles, however, he returned to Michigan and became a stockbroker for Armstrong & Jones—only to soon parlay his business interests into two separate film companies: September Cinema, for commercially minded documentaries, and Cinema 1976, a small advertising firm specializing in commercials. Both were located on East Maple, not far from Leonard's own office. "Originally, Tom Brank was my landlord when I went on my own," recalled Peter Leonard, who, at the time, had just opened his own advertising agency—Leonard & Meyer. "I was only about six months into it and ended up getting a little building in Birmingham, and Brank was leasing it. I finally found out what we were paying for the whole place and I challenged him and he said, 'Well, you know, this is for insurance for my film library.' I said, 'Your film library, is that a joke?' I mean, he had a few films upstairs, you know, but no film *library* . . . He was a con man and I think Elmore realized that fairly early on . . . [The project] never really went anywhere."[46]

However, Leonard had had so much difficulty getting his creative perspective across to so many Hollywood producers, working with Brank initially seemed a good way to take the reins and craft a film the way he imagined it. For their first project, Leonard offered the still-in-progress story of Al Rosen and his exploits in Jerusalem, while still under its original title. "We have a commitment so far of $200,000 for our independent production of *Hat Trick*, and meetings with investors next week," Leonard wrote to Swanson. "I'm not involved with that, though. I'm working on the new book idea and it's developing very well."[47] Earlier that summer, Leonard had sent pages from *The Hunted* to Zohar Bar Am, hoping that his friend could not only provide feedback on the realism depicted within its pages, but also, perhaps, offer some advice on getting a film production off the ground in Israel. "I poured myself a good whisky and sent you 'cheers' which I hope reached you telepathically," Bar Am wrote from his office at the Ministry of Commerce and Industry. "Oddly enough, it seems [there] is a new wave of interest among filmmakers . . . more and more films are set to be made here." Bar Am added, "A personal remark that might serve your next book. You asked me once why the pistol was put in a green plastic bag. The reason is very logical, so it can be used in an emergency, through the plastic bag."[48]

As part of his arrangement with Brank, Leonard handled all the written creative content and conducted outreach to all of the film producers, directors, and actors he knew. Within a few months, they had the interest of directors Joseph Sargent, of *The Taking of Pelham One Two Three* fame, and Peter Hunt, a renowned editor who had started his directing career with the James Bond entry *On Her Majesty's Secret Service*—although both refused to work for scale. Leonard also spoke with director James Fargo, director of the most recent Dirty Harry sequel, *The Enforcer*—but he proved unavailable once Clint Eastwood contracted him to direct the action comedy *Every Which Way But Loose*. After catching a late-night broadcast of an old favorite, John Sturges's *Bad Day at Black Rock*, Leonard picked up the phone and called the director directly; he hadn't seen Sturges since *Joe Kidd* wrapped years before. He soon reported back to Swanson: "We talked, he asked what I was doing and I told him my plan to produce *Hat Trick*, which after next month, when the book comes out, it'll be *The Hunted*. He said he's always wanted to see Israel and offered to direct the picture for scale and points." (At the time, Brank had presented an available budget of just under two million dollars with the prospectus submitted to the SEC for approval—to an attorney who'd aided in the budgets for *The Odessa File* and *The Last Ten Days of Hitler*, no less. Pending the approval, Leonard was in line to collect $150,000 up front and an equal share in the profits—leaving the attainment of a US distributor as the only remaining task.[49])

After representing Leonard's film interests for more than twenty years, H. N. Swanson was *very* comfortable articulating exactly what he thought of the deal: "Everybody in the office . . . strongly advise you not to sign anything until the money is raised." Swanson had crossed out "horrified" in his initial draft before continuing, "You cannot dignify him as a producer of feature films since he has done none. This show is not for a novice to play with . . . We are not dealing with equals on this arrangement and Brank ought to be made aware of this . . . When I sent you the Hitchcock money, I urged you not to put one solitary dime into *The Hunted*. [The] only advantage to the deal is to be able to use the other guy's money. Even at best, there is a big disadvantage in that it distracts you from doing your next book or writing assignment." Swanson concluded, "As your longtime friend and agent, Dutch, I strongly advise you not to get involved with this situation."[50]

Ultimately, however, Leonard stuck it out and continued to work with Brank—first in attempting to get *The Hunted* off the ground, then his later novel *Gold Coast*. But even with fleeting interest from producer Sidney Beckerman, a reestablished RKO Studios, and even an apparently interested Frank Sinatra for the role of Al Rosen, the project fell through. Leonard later recalled, "I wasted some time doing it, and I had no business, really, getting involved to the degree that I did. What I do is write, and that's what I should stick to."[51]

He did walk away with a few lessons learned and fodder for yet another book, however: Tom Brank's initial plan to create a tax shelter out of investors' funds would form the subplot in the upcoming second adventure of Ernest "Stick" Stickley—leaving only Stick's love interest, the sexy and savvy financial adviser Kyla McClaren, to echo H. N. Swanson's words of warning. For good measure, Leonard even named Stick's unassuming employer "Barry Stam" after his and Brank's attorney in Ann Arbor.[52]

• • •

While playing tennis with Joan right before the 1976 holiday season, Leonard fractured a bone and tore the ligaments in his ankle. Adding insult to injury, the space bar of his typewriter broke for the fourth time, forcing him to send it out (again) for repairs. "Otherwise," he wrote to Swanson, "everything's fine. No skiing or tennis for two months. I'll have to work."[53] Swanson wrote back, "Painful though it is, I think the accident to your leg is probably the best thing that has happened to your career in a long time. It means you can't be out chasing women or those dangerous tennis balls and will have to sit and write all the time."[54]

Leonard did just that. During those months, he began a new novel. Taking more than a little inspiration from Joan Shepard, Leonard had decided to make his next protagonist a woman—and an empowered, contemporary one at that. He imagined heroine Mickey Dawson—a doppelgänger for Joan—dealing with a disintegrating marriage and a crushing need for self-worth and self-discovery. Under the guise of a pseudo-sequel to *Unknown Man No. 89*, he'd brought back Jack Ryan, although frustrated housewife Mickey remained the story's hero. But whereas Jack Ryan had helped Denise Leary attain sobriety in his previous adventure, he'd now be on the case in helping Mickey discover her own inner strength.

But first, at nine thirty in the morning on January 24, 1977, Leonard found his own.

Hobbling around in a cast had only made it harder to juggle multiple projects *and* remain a functioning alcoholic; he decided one of those would have to go—once and for all. He poured himself a deliberately atrocious cocktail—Vernor's ginger ale and Scotch, which he later claimed was "awful"—vowing it would be his last. "I think I kind of liked the idea of the tragic figure," he later recalled. "I think that must enter into alcoholism, playing the role of the tragic figure. But within the same moment, I could look at it as bullshit, knowing I was playing roles, playing games. It was inevitable that if I had any intelligence at all, I had to stop. I realized that I had to quit or go all the way and forget about it, the hell with it. Good-bye brains."[55] He later added, "I like my characters more, probably because I like myself more."[56]

Years later, friend and journalist Mike Lupica asked Leonard where he thought he'd be if he hadn't conquered his alcoholism.

"I'd probably be dead," he said.[57]

CHAPTER 12

Dutch Free, 1977–1979

I'm into my work now, all the way, and I'm not straining. I stop at six o'clock, but I'm giving it a full shot every day. I see that I can continue to get better at it. That's an amazing thing, after thirty-two years, to know I can get better . . .

From that, and from experience, I've concluded that you write most effectively when trying *not* to write.[1]

Leonard and Beverly's divorce was finalized in May 1977.

One month later, *Unknown Man No. 89* was released by Delacorte, earning Leonard his best reviews to date. Delacorte's promotion of the book, however, quickly led to Leonard's first doubts about the publisher's understanding of his new contemporary sound. He was mortified by Delacorte's apparent hook—citing protagonist Jack Ryan as a modern-day equivalent to Raymond Chandler's Philip Marlowe, and referring to his Detroit stomping ground as "Motown" (a term Leonard had deliberately avoided using)—only widening the chasm between the author and his marketers. Worst of all, the advertisement had erroneously claimed that Ryan had been the star of Leonard's previous novels. He wrote Swanson: "I saw the ad for *Unknown Man* yesterday and couldn't believe it . . . I can understand now why the sales department has trouble selling my books. Maybe they ought to take their head out of their ass and read one . . . If you can speed up the Bantam contract, I'd really appreciate it."[2]

When Betty Sargent called Leonard soon after, Leonard advised her that *Mickey Free* had already been sold to Bantam; both eyeing its Hollywood potential, Sargent and Leonard had even discussed approaching Ellen Burstyn for the role of Mickey Dawson.[3] She wrote soon after, "I miss you already—and I'm keeping my fingers crossed that we'll be working together again, soon."[4] Unfortunately, *Unknown Man No. 89* proved the final collaboration between the two. (Sargent, however, would go on to a highly successful career in the literary world, first as the executive editor of the Delacorte Trust, then as the fiction and book editor for *Cosmopolitan* magazine. She became William Morrow's editor in chief before, ultimately, returning to her career roots as an editor, working exclusively with bestseller Danielle Steel.[5])

In what was ironically retitled *The Switch* just prior to the galley-proof stage, Leonard had come up with a completely different narrative than the one meticulously laid out in his original notes. He now introduced lead protagonist Mickey Dawson as a kidnapped housewife whose wealthy husband, Frank, doesn't want her back, leaving her dim-witted captor haggling for ways to deal with her. However, Leonard's original plot had been more of a sequel to *Unknown Man No. 89*, with that novel's Jack Ryan serving Mickey her divorce papers in the opening scene. Sensing her hurt and confusion, Ryan takes Mickey under his wing as a process server (in much the same manner he'd led Denise Leary out of the woods of her alcoholism), encouraging her to get out of her comfort zone and bring her inner moxie to the forefront. Once she discovers that her now-estranged husband, Frank, has been secretly building up an illegal real estate fortune under her nose, she enlists Ryan's help in hitting Frank where it hurts—his wallet.

As had become Leonard's regular practice, he'd begun by writing in-depth character biographies for the principal players, taking insight and personal notes from Joan Shepard for his portrayal of Mickey Dawson. Her husband, Frank Dawson, however, inherited his belligerent behavior and macho posturing from real-life members around the country club where Leonard and Joan had first met.

Leonard spent a great deal of time researching the nature of Frank's actual scheme, and how he could use Detroit's destitute economics and slum real estate practices to walk away with a secret fortune. For this, he imagined Frank Dawson as a building contractor specializing in low-cost housing, such as the condominiums popping up in the semi-industrial Detroit suburbs like Sterling Heights and Roseville. As was the trend at the time, those "modern" homes would, presumably, come fully equipped with home appliances—which Frank deliberately overbuys in bulk, using the surplus building materials and home goods for improving inner-city

Detroit ghettos. Using his committee memberships and status as a consultant for Detroit's Community and Economic Development Department, Frank works as a "booster" of fenced goods and large-scale white-collar crime that is successfully hidden from the eyes of the public—and his own wife, Mickey. Through labyrinthine means that Leonard noted in detailed fashion, Frank Dawson's plan sees him use his bank appraisals and insurance coverage to boost his worth, allowing him to ultimately write off depreciation values that he squirrels away. For the stolen goods themselves, Frank works with a gang of experienced, hip young thieves led by Ordell Lewis, who was always "cool" and "in control." Not to be outdone, Frank also has a twenty-eight-year-old mistress—public relations specialist Carolyn, whose style and professionalism already has her pegged in Frank's mind as the next Mrs. Dawson.

Leonard remained adamant that the dynamic between Mickey and Frank Dawson was not representative of Joan's marriage, nor of Leonard's own marriage. Rather, the fears and frustrations that Mickey felt as a modernized "kept woman" were built upon long hours of conversations with his soon-to-be wife. In an unprecedented fashion, Leonard started a separate character file for his new protagonist, entitled "Mickey Free, the Person":

> *We will come to see her as a sensitive person with a great deal of energy, drive, potential that's never been tapped. To some degree, she's been playing a role for 15 years, keeping herself in check . . . be good to your husband and grateful for all that he provides . . . Drink Bloody Marys with the girls at the club and kid their husbands along when they sneak feels on the dance floor and ask you out to lunch . . . She's caught somewhere between [her] mom's counsel and* Cosmopolitan *and can't accept much of either one . . . To Mickey, with her background, divorce is an admission of failure.*

In Leonard's original plot, it's Jack Ryan who serves Mickey her papers, but not before he spots Ordell Lewis's gang sneak into the country club's locker room with sawed-off shotguns in order to catch the well-to-do members with their pants down—and rob them blind (a scene Leonard later repurposed in his next crime novel, tentatively entitled *Seascape* and, later, *Gold Coast*). From there, Mickey and Ryan would form a connection, leading to his offering her a job as a process server.

But with all the time and energy that Leonard had spent on crafting the character of Mickey into a real flesh-and-blood, relatable character, the process of self-discovery took nearly the entire story. And what was more, Frank's secret life as a high-stakes real estate hustler didn't provide the needed stakes for such a revelation.

With folders of notes and nearly fifty pages of the manuscript written, Leonard abandoned the story and started from scratch. Gone now was the resolution of Ryan's saga, which readers of both *The Big Bounce* and *Unknown Man No. 89* would never learn—or what became of Denise Leary, whom Ryan had saved and loved. Leonard noted:

> *He's been living with a girl named Denise who's 26 and a talented fine artist: she loves to paint whales. She also loves wine, which was about to kill her at the time she and Ryan met. Denise had been sober a year, painting and working at Saks Fifth Avenue in Detroit. But she's begun to complain more and more about the restricted life of a salesperson, caught in the middle and taking crap from both sides . . . Finally, Denise has told the department manager what he can do with the job and quits. She's going to California and paint gray whales during their annual trip to Baja. Ryan says bullshit, she's going out there to drink. Denise says she can drink in Detroit, but there don't happen to be any whales here. Ryan knows it's an excuse. Denise isn't comfortable in her sobriety; she feels trapped.*
>
> *This is where we pick up Ryan again.*

But with the removal of Ryan, there was a void in the dynamic. Leonard solved this problem by taking, arguably, his most interesting character—Ordell Lewis—and splitting him into two people, then condensing a few of the characteristics of his ancillary gang members into a second composite character. Leonard then took the dialogue and motivations from the Lewis gang and put them into the thoughts and words of *Ordell* Robbie and *Louis* Gara, two ex-con buddies plotting a sure-fire way to scam Frank Dawson out of his plundered gains. He retained Ordell's place as Frank's main criminal liaison, which also solved a second narrative problem: the stakes that ultimately lead to Mickey's empowerment and "freedom." In Leonard's earliest notes, Jack Ryan had feared for Mickey's safety during the locker room robbery, anxious that Lewis's gang was planning to take hostages. For the new version of *Mickey Free*, Leonard simply took that scenario to the next level, with criminal duo Louis and Ordell kidnapping Mickey in exchange for Frank's fortune. Although Leonard's *The Switch* is primarily regarded for its seminal plot twist, the author himself concocted it out of sheer logic. If Frank Dawson already wanted to divorce his wife in order to marry his younger mistress, why would he even want her back? Leonard's answer: he doesn't. Ordell plans the kidnapping, completely unaware that Frank Dawson had already filed the paperwork to divorce Mickey, hoping to marry his younger girlfriend—renamed Melanie. Aggravated and confused, Ordell leaves the captive Mickey in the hands of Louis and a third partner they'd enlisted out of necessity, a neo-Nazi gun nut named Richard Edgar Monk, and flies to the Bahamas himself. There, he first intimidates Melanie, then decides to work with her. In Ordell's absence—and completely unaware of the new deal with Melanie—Louis and Mickey form an unspoken bond, confiding in each other their confusion over the situation. After Richard Monk—in a crazed delirium of anti-Semitism and frustration—attempts to rape Mickey, Louis saves her and keeps her safe in his own apartment. Louis encourages her to stand on her own two feet for the first time (a lengthy scene based largely on Leonard's long discussions with Joan). When both Ordell and, later, Frank return, they find a very different Mickey Dawson in her place. In the memorable finale, Louis, Ordell, *and* Mickey don their signature Richard Nixon kidnapper masks, preparing to hold Melanie for Frank's ransom instead.

Leonard injected the novel with items inspired by local news. On August 29, the *Detroit Free Press Sunday Edition*'s "for and about women" supplement ran a front-page story entitled "Tennis Mom"—a lengthy profile about Grosse Pointe homemaker Elaine Knight, who had devoted her entire life to her thirteen-year-old son's tennis competitions. "I adore being a mother, a wife, a girl, a lady," Knight was quoted as saying—representing the very essence of the life Mickey Dawson was fleeing.[6] Likewise coverage of the ongoing spike in auto theft throughout Detroit, as well as white-collar real estate scammers, all made their way into shaping characters Frank, Louis, and Ordell. For Richard Edgar Monk, the dim-witted and dangerously racist suburban arms dealer, Leonard drew heavily from a *Time* magazine profile on young bodybuilder and collector of Nazi memorabilia Fred Cowan. The article detailed the neo-Nazi's vast collection of Afrika Korps caps, helmets, military uniforms,

Adolf Hitler posters and Nazi flags, and swastika-stamped knives—all of which made their way into Richard's home.[7]

Swanson had taken a shot at getting Leonard back into hardcover by submitting the manuscript to Doubleday, only to be told that they "would have difficulty marketing it successfully because Louis and Ordell are such likeable and good-natured villains."[8] Only a few months later, *Cosmopolitan* fiction editor Harris Dienstfrey passed on the opportunity to serialize *Mickey Free*, claiming, "It's a good story, but I'm afraid it's too gritty and unpleasant for us. We need a bit more sweetness and light."[9] Still, Leonard had high hopes for the new Bantam deal. However, even as Swanson worked on another deal for Leonard with the publisher—a two-book deal that stipulated a new crime novel and Leonard's first Western in more than a decade—an early issue with Bantam's promotion on *The Switch* gave the author the same apprehension he'd felt with Dell: in February 1978, Bantam's Stuart Applebaum sent Leonard an enthusiastic letter detailing the publisher's new strategy for promoting the book's May 20 release. "It will be part of an innovative promotional display concept we've created called (somewhat inelegantly) a 'Triple Feature Dump,'" the editor wrote. "This retail floor display unit houses three novels under an attention-getting riser and insures additional off-the-racks exposure for your book."[10] But then Leonard finally saw the cover: an artist rendering of, presumably, Mickey Dawson, Louis Gara, and Ordell Robbie—created, perhaps, by an ill-informed illustrator. "It looks like the result of an art director who hasn't read the book, having given a few facts to an illustrator who hasn't read it either," Leonard later wrote. "The two guys are slobs and the woman is an over-age groupie."[11] Following the book's release, Leonard wrote a separate letter to Bantam editor Marc Jaffe. "I really didn't like the cover which, I have a feeling, turns people off," he wrote. "For 15 minutes, I watched people at the Detroit airport pick titles from all around it; and it was prominently displayed. At B. Dalton, I get no display . . ." He added, "I forgot to mention, I haven't seen any triple dumps either."[12]

The first book that Leonard approached with his new sobriety and clarity would prove to be his most experimental—and misunderstood. He wrote to Swanson, "The next one is called *Juvenal* and is spooky. No ghosts, or devils, though strange, supernatural things happen."[13] He had begun dedicating his books to the most important people in his inner circle—*Fifty-Two Pickup* for Joan Shepard, *Swag* for daughter Jane, *Unknown Man No. 89* for son Peter, and he would soon dedicate his first Western in nearly a decade to son Christopher and its follow-up to Bill. But another novel would be inspired by the individual who'd supplied Leonard with years of spiritual guidance for nearly *two* decades: missionary priest Juvenal Carlson, who had been the subject of his and Bill Deneen's 1961 short feature for the Franciscan Order, *The Man Who Had Everything*.

Leonard and Carlson had remained friends, even as the now middle-aged priest's assignments had brought him from the Amazon to the rural foothills in Brazil. In his earliest correspondence with both Leonard and Beverly, Carlson's letters often touched upon their religious devotion to the Catholic Church; by 1977, however, Carlson had accepted, and even embraced, his now-divorced friend's latter-day agnosticism—even assuring him that spiritual divinity needn't necessarily be exclusive to any one religion. Leonard himself admitted that his own devout Catholic practices took a turn following his regular participation in AA. In a self-assessment Leonard recently penned, he'd admitted that, although it had taken a number of years "to get the hang of" attending AA, he'd been able—with Joan Shepard's help—to quit "cold turkey," and without the assistance of a clinic or the church. He had, however, looked into those clinics—not necessarily for his own sobriety, but as research for *Juvenal*.

Leonard's basic premise was relatively simple—at least to him: taking the bulk of the shelved material from 1971's unproduced *Jesus Saves*, and combining it with a new protagonist based on Juvenal Carlson (with a dose of Leonard's own personality thrown in). But unlike earlier protagonist Lindell Reason who, corrupted by fame, used his abilities for self-aggrandizement and celebrity, *Juvenal*'s Juvie solely fueled his own inexplicable stigmata and healing powers in humble servitude to those afflicted with alcohol dependency.

Although he'd already conducted copious amounts of research into many of *Juvenal*'s returning characters from *Jesus Saves* (original protagonist Bill Hill and, in a completely reworked fashion, his assistant, now named Lynn Faulkner, were back), new elements required yet another deep dive into unfamiliar terrain. He quickly filled an entire light-green four-theme notebook with notes, carefully organized for each of the obscure plot points that would make up the experimental novel. Leonard compiled articles on the history of stigmata, as well as the Vatican's stance, taken on a case-by-case basis. He also put together a list of saints with whom the stigmata had been attributed (not by the Church, however), as well as detailed biographical sketches of famous Catholic martyrs—all of whom would later be rattled off verbally by the new antagonist, the modern-day zealot August Murray. He'd paid particular attention to the life stories of St. Francis of Assisi and Padre Pio; in the latter case, the author was equally fascinated by the cult of personality that the modern man of God had attracted, including enough followers and fan letters to satisfy even the most jaded rock star. Biblical passages Leonard highlighted paralleled subjects discussed within the novel, such as idol worship, sacrifice, and the paths of salvation and damnation. "*Ye shall not make with me gods of silver; neither shall ye make unto you gods of gold*," he jotted from Exodus.

For young Juvenal's day job as a healer of Detroit's alcoholics, Leonard visited the Sacred Heart Rehabilitation Center in nearby East Elizabeth, Michigan. As he observed while there, the Stroh Brewing Company was visible from the facility, located just across the footbridge over the freeway, and at night, its large, red neon sign blinking Stroh's acted as a "constant reminder to the residents" not to drink. "The brewery looks like a prison," Leonard wrote, "big, red-brick, formidable-looking building . . . cold." Leonard was also given a private tour of the grounds. (Leonard was already well familiar with AA meeting protocols: he rarely drove himself to his AA meetings, usually escorted by Joan, who took to baking fresh pastries for the rest of the group; they soon nicknamed her "Cookie Lady" as a term of endearment.[14])

Leonard filled the rest of the notebook with the usual assortment of character biographies and details of their ancillary interests. Lynn Faulkner was reinvented as a self-assured career woman—formerly in the employ of huckster Bill Hill—and she was now somewhat happily employed as a record promoter. (Playfully, Leonard added a reference to his own unproduced film treatment for Sean Connery and Michael Caine, naming the current band under Faulkner's promotional care, "HAWKBILL.") Already a music buff, Leonard dove into the current Top 40 hits and researched new trends in rock and roll; he'd entered the era of punk, yet noted that slick pop stars like the Bay City Rollers and Hall & Oates dominated the charts.

Studying reggae music, he added, "A *splif* is a joint/herb is pot—or ganja . . . [Bob Marley] smokes a pound of herb a week, continually stoned." Although it was only briefly mentioned in the novel, Leonard took great interest in the media coverage surrounding the recent death of Elvis Presley. "Died Tuesday, Aug. 16, 1977 . . . WDEE played non-stop music, interspersed with listener calls and bulletins from Memphis . . . RCA has ordered between 3 and 4 million records and tapes—they'll be working 7 days a week in 3 shifts to meet the demand . . ." Ultimately, Leonard was most fascinated with the subculture that promoted the music—especially the lingo. "In the grooves is where it's at—that's the bottom line," he jotted down as an example of industry parlance. In permanent marker, Leonard noted "Promoting Juvenal" and beneath it, "shuck and jive"—a phrase he'd cribbed from an article, but would save for a later book.[15]

The closest to an antagonist *Juvenal* contained came in the form of middle-aged Christian fanatic August Murray—the owner of a local print and copy shop whose real passion lies in organizing like-minded zealots for dramatic "happenings" aimed to emphasize anger over the Catholic Church's modernization. For the character's background, Leonard had saved old newspaper clippings and UPI photos of a real-life Christian zealot, controversial for his political and religious views, primarily around the Michigan Christian communities. Then only on page fifty-five, Leonard wrote to Swanson on July 7, "I'm going down to the *Detroit Free Press* this afternoon to research the antagonist, based on a local militant arch-conservative by the name of Donald Lobsinger, who is always picketing or punching liberals. He's a beauty."[16] Leonard wasn't kidding; acknowledged as a right-wing extremist, Lobsinger was known for his aggressive rally appearances—once assaulting a priest over shifts in Vatican II, and chanting "Kill abortionists" at others. A professional agitator, Lobsinger was a household name across Detroit and once received nearly 74,000 votes as a Republican congressional candidate. For *Juvenal*, Leonard's take on Lobsinger morphed into August Murray—whose grassroots organization Floodgate was based on Lobsinger's Breakthrough alliance—and openly put Donald Lobsinger quotes into Murray's mouth.

For the enigmatic lead protagonist, Leonard used his old stigmata research. He saved a *Free Press* article by syndicated *Chicago Tribune* contributor Charles Leroux on the biological processes that produce tears, taking note of historical hucksters who'd found ways to make statues "weep" as false miracles. He also collected a few issues of *Mission News*—a bimonthly newsletter for members of the Franciscan missionary order. (A mirror to his own intentions of portraying the real-life Juvie Carlson in fictional form, Leonard noted that Padre Pio had been visited by, and then inspired, British author Graham Greene—one of his favorites.) Finally, Leonard reached out to the Catholic Church itself—the Archdiocese of Detroit. "The Church has never during the lifetime of a person, confirmed that they have 'the stigmata' or that God has worked miracles of healing through them," the ensuing response read. The letter—attributed to "an official of the local Catholic Chancery office," who, apparently "would not answer any more questions or elaborate on his statement"[17]—left Leonard to construct his own, more forensic approach to stigmata: a woman's monthly menstrual cycle (a factor that could have, potentially, baffled his regular, predominantly male crime-loving readers). Leonard wrote: "*His stigmata occurs once a month—sometimes, or in the beginning, on the first Friday. There is a day or two warning at which time he begins to feel the invisible stigmata, pains in his hands, feet and side. Then, small wounds appear that heal within two days. The first day a band-aid will be enough to cater* [sic] *the wound. Only bleeds during the day, or for a few hours. But he knows at least 24 hours before that it's coming.*"

Due to the multiple projects Leonard was tackling at the same time—he'd also begun his next proper crime novel, as well as a new Western—potential publisher Bantam assigned yet a third editor to handle the book, tentatively retitled *The Juvenal Touch*. Unlike previous editors, however, Tony Koltz was an aspiring author and devoted Leonard fan already, admitting he usually found Leonard's prose "so seamless that I'm a bit fearful even venturing into questioning small parts of them here and there." However, Koltz continued to itemize the points that had "bothered" him with the manuscript. Chief among them was Juvenal's passivity—particularly his willingness to go along with Bill Hill's schemes for so long.[18] The following day, Leonard received a letter from his British publisher, the message of which he would continue to quote for years. "I hate to have to say this but five of us in this office who are all devout Elmore Leonard fans find ourselves baffled by this book," editor T. G. Rosenthal wrote. "It is simply that the subject matter of this book, no matter how well written it is, seems to me altogether mystifying for our public and we think it would damage Leonard's reputation in British bookshops and libraries, so please forgive us."[19] Leonard reported to his son Christopher, "My Bantam editor is suggesting changes to *Juvenal,* along with the title... My British publisher turned it down, saying it mystified the five people there who read it. Oh well."[20]

By October, H. N. Swanson reported to Leonard that he'd received "an alarming number of rejections" by different publishers, adding, "[The] consensus of opinion; probably the best writing that you have done to date, but unfortunate choice of subject."[21] In the end, Bantam accepted it as part of Leonard's two-book deal. However, after the novel was completed, put into galleys, and had early cover art designed and selected, the publisher still cited trepidations. Leonard remained merely confused by everyone's confusion. "What's to understand?" Leonard later wrote. "It's about a guy who gets the stigmata every once in a while, bleeds from his hands, his feet and his side—replicating Christ's wounds when he was crucified. And if the guy touches anyone who's ill or infirmed when he has the stigmata, he's able to heal them. He goes to work in an alcohol treatment center, bleeds, lays his hands on people going out of their minds with [detox treatments], and the rats crawling up their beds vanish. Religion promoters would kill to have this guy. He meets a young lady who's a punk-rock record promoter. She thinks he's a little weird, but they fall in love and he moves in with her."

The one person who had no problem understanding Leonard's intention was the novel's namesake, Fr. Juvenal Carlson, who quickly wrote his gratitude to the author from his post in Brazil:

> *Dearest D,*
>
> *I really don't know what to say. I guess it's something like when we are silent, we are one. When we speak, we are two. But I do have to speak, even though it might make us two—for a very short while... I read* Juvenal. *And it's you—from beginning to end. You're right there in all your facets and threads.*
>
> *You are one more St. Francis that the Lord has put in my path. And that's much to my joy and growth. It's simplicity. It's tenderness. It's Gospel. It's God. It's Jesus. It's joy. It's got it all. Just like you've got it all. Remember* The Man Who Had Everything?
>
> *You did it...*
>
> *With all love—possible and impossible,*
>
> *Juvie*[22]

Rather than argue with Bantam, Leonard took his cue from Swanson and bought back the copyright. He stuck *The Juvenal Touch*—now simply abbreviated as *Touch*—into his desk drawer.[23]

Leonard now needed to quickly replace the first of his two contracted manuscripts for Bantam; he opted to safely return to the crime genre and his Detroit setting. However, since purchasing his mother the Coconut Palms motel, Florida had become a regular stop for the author and his family. He'd recently reconnected with an old high school friend, William C. "Bill" Marshall, and learned that the fellow University of Detroit alumnus had moved to Florida himself and set up shop as a private investigator. "Elmore showed up here in 1977 with a colossal case of writers' block," Marshall later told the *South Florida Sun-Sentinel*. "His recovery—no, his renaissance—came together in Florida because he was desperate for fresh ideas." Himself the son-in-law of Detroit mobster Joe "Scarface" Bommarito, Marshall took the opportunity to introduce Leonard to a part-time member of his investigations team, specializing in collecting outstanding invoices: Ernest "Chili" Palmer, a former loan shark for mob kingpin Joseph Colombo.[24]

"I didn't start paying attention to the contrast between the beauty on the surface and the corruption underneath [until] I started hanging out with Bill Marshall again," Leonard later told the *Sun-Sentinel*. "In Miami Beach, you've got retired car dealers dressed in bright yellow shirts and paisley pants walking down the street—and right next to them are guys who just got out of a Cuban prison, pachucos with tattoos on their hands for killing people . . . I thought, 'What could happen in a tense setting like that? What characters would emerge?'"

October 21, 1977

Dear Swanie,

Do you know why the guy in Florida, Maguire, who puts on the porpoise show and has rationalized falling in love with the rich 40-year old widow can't get it on with her, even though she likes him a lot? Because she was married to a Detroit syndicate boss who has stipulated she is not to remarry or get serious with anyone else after he's gone. No one sleeps with her after him. If any guy gets too close to her, he's warned, or his legs are broken. If the guy persists, he's dropped in the ocean. And no matter where the lady goes, there's a syndicate group to keep an eye on her.

> *Maguire could be very happy with this lady. But if they run away and she changes her identity, she'll be cut off from her half million dollar a year income. Maguire isn't sure he'd be that happy with her. How does he carry on an affair with her without the Miami Beach mob and their Cuban shooters getting wise? How does Maguire outsmart the bad guys, get the girl and the money without losing his ass?*
>
> *I don't know, but I'm sure there's a way.*[25]

Although Leonard had long shunned the idea of a recurring character or ongoing series, having dealt with early rejections for *The Hunted*, *Juvenal* (now *Touch*), and *Mickey Free*, for the novel initially entitled *Seascape*, he revisited the idea. Initially, he'd considered bringing back Jack Ryan, but Alfred Hitchcock's ongoing preproduction on *Unknown Man No. 89* for Universal Pictures had granted the studio ownership of the character. Instead, Leonard molded a reworked variation on Ryan's personality and background, naming the new protagonist "Cal Maguire"—a small-time Detroit hood, lucky enough to walk free following his doomed robbery at an affluent Birmingham country club. But while he'd gotten the longer end of the stick, his two partners in the humorous robbery—arranged by embittered Detroit mobster Frank DiCilia, who'd recently failed to attain membership to the club—were handed twenty-year sentences. (As playful reference to his previous novel, Leonard even made mention that Louis Gara and Ordell Robbie had been considered for the country club job, but proved unavailable, as they were already in prison.) On behalf of his incarcerated team, Maguire makes his way to Florida to collect the outstanding debt from the recently deceased mobster's widow—forty-four-year-old femme fatale Karen DiCilia. There is an instant attraction between the two, and Maguire is soon enlisted to aid DiCilia with a unique problem of her own: late husband Frank had left explicit instructions that she be cut off from her inheritance of four million dollars should she ever become romantically involved with another man. To Maguire, of course, there must be *some* way to get the girl and the money. Drifting to Florida with no major life goals, Maguire, with the help of his mob-appointed attorney, lands a job assisting as a dolphin trainer at the "World-Famous Seascape Porpoise and Sea Lion Show," an abysmal routine that only makes the sexy Karen DiCilia *and* her dangling fortune all the more appealing. But while Maguire fancies himself a chivalrous knight looking to spring his princess from her ivory tower, he isn't the only suitor eyeing the former trophy wife or her fortune: Frank's former business partner Ed Grossi installs redneck enforcer Roland Crowe, whom Leonard describes somewhat accurately as "*a prehistoric creature from the swamp—man, from some black lagoon—who wore cowboy hats and chulo suits and squinted at life to see only what he wanted.*" Through his backwoods squinting, Crowe sees only a damsel in distress who won't admit she needs a six-foot hick in a leisure suit to make her feel like a woman.

For *Seascape*, Leonard again created a three-way dynamic with Maguire, Crowe, and Karen—yet Karen's form of morally dubious empowerment gave the new story a film noir edge. (Leonard later admitted that, aside from *The Hunted*'s Al Rosen, Karen DiCilia was the only other secondary protagonist whom he should have given the predominant perspective.[26])

The specific research that led Leonard to place such emphasis on Karen and her motivations could perhaps be traced to his earliest interest in true crime: it had been Bonnie Parker, not Clyde Barrow, that nine-year-old Elmore Leonard had mimicked in the framed childhood photo hung behind his desk on Pierce Street. Karen DiCilia, however, had been inspired by a specific historical figure: mobster Bugsy Siegel's longtime girlfriend and accomplice, Virginia Hill. Leonard had found the June 1951 issue of *American Mercury* magazine that featured the very first biographical portrait of Hill. She had been made single only recently following Siegel's Las Vegas assassination and, for a time, was popular fodder in the gossip columns. "In a way, to a great many Americans, the gangster is the last figure to keep the Horatio Alger spirit alive—with a perverse twist—from the gutter to the penthouse stages," the profile read. "All you have to do is dodge bullets, income-tax inspections, and crime committees. Virginia is a Horatio Alger character herself, and one of the most spectacular."[27] For the novel, Karen was not only inspired by the real-life Hill but—in a strange twist of her own—keeps a secret powder room in her Fort Lauderdale home decorated with photos of herself and Hill, her apparent hero.

As *Seascape* was meant to fill the contractual gap left by Bantam's rejection of *Touch*, Leonard went to work fast on his first draft, beginning on January 20, 1978, and wrapping it up by March 27—his second fastest turnaround behind 1967's *Valdez Is Coming*. (He'd celebrated a full year of sobriety on January 24, receiving a medallion at AA.) Before putting pen to paper, he'd called Bill Marshall, asking the seasoned investigator to tackle the needed "local color" details of Fort Lauderdale and some of the more niche topics for the book. Only three days into writing, Leonard heard back from Marshall, who sent him video footage of the dolphin trainers at nearby Ocean World and, later, full contact sheets of photos of the show and its inner workings, plus brochures and a map of the theme park's grounds. Marshall wrote, "*Spanish idioms and slang slogans I will give to you over the phone long before you receive this package.*"[28] (The professional bundle of multimedia tools assembled by Marshall and his investigative team would also form a preferential template for Leonard's later requests of personal researcher Gregg Sutter.) Halfway through the manuscript, however, Leonard had to hop a flight to Los Angeles, as Swanie had sparked television interest in Leonard's older property, *Jesus Saves*—again retitled, now *The Evangelist*—now that its place as the source material for *Touch* meant little to any potential rights conflicts; *Touch* was still shelved indefinitely. During the trip, he wrote his son Christopher and shared both his progress and frustrations:

> March 8, 1978
>
> *I'm on page 167 of* Seascape, *or* Make Him Go Away . . . *What am I going to dedicate to Katy? . . . She requested for her birthday some Judy Blume books. I picked up three of them, read the opening of* Forever, *which begins, "Sybil Davison had a genius IQ and had been laid by at least six different guys." So I only gave her one of them, about a little girl getting the curse for the first time. Something isn't it? Nancy Drew is about 40 now and still hasn't gotten it.*[29]
>
> April 1, 1978
>
> Seascape *is done and gone, 321 pages mailed out Tuesday and I heard from Swanson yesterday. He likes it, "wouldn't change a word" and thinks it has my best heavy in Roland Crowe.*[30]

Leonard had added, "My next project, I'm going to write the first chapter of a Western—*Legends*—and see if Bantam will raise their advance offer from 15 to 25, which they made after reading the outline . . . The story is made up of outtakes from all my other Westerns (find L.A. trip quotes). And, I'll be writing under my Western pseudonym, ISHAM STRUNK. Do you like it? I have to use a pseudonym if I write a Western because they're pushing my real name as a crime-suspense writer."[31]

Bantam was decidedly more enthusiastic about the Western. In fact, it had even been written as a form of assignment, as by 1978, Leonard had no intention of writing any further Westerns. He later admitted to *The New Black Mask Quarterly*, "[*Gunsights*] was [written] in 1979 for Bantam because Mark [*sic*] Jaffe, who was the editorial director at Bantam then, likes Westerns."[32] Running with Jaffe's enthusiasm for a new Western, Leonard had taken only a few hours while in Los Angeles for meetings with NBC to pen a rough outline. Although his earlier Westerns had been relatively short narratives with plots taking place over a mere matter of days, for the Western novel originally entitled *Legends*, he, instead, took his first swing at writing a sprawling epic. Like *Forty Lashes Less One*, which had demonstrated the ending of the Old West era symbolically through the closure of Yuma prison, *Legends* would be set amid the copper mountain ranges of Arizona during the late 1880s, just as industrialization is about to forever change the face and soul of the country's landscape. Uncharacteristically using flashbacks and time jumps to tell the story of longtime friends Brendan Early and Dana Moon—literary stand-ins for *The Bounty Hunters*' Dave Flynn and Duane Bowers—Leonard envisioned his story as a swan song to the Wild West, infusing the story with multimedia references to the passing of time and changing social trends. Local reporters, photographers, gossip-hungry citizens, and even a Buffalo Bill Cody–inspired celebrity stuntman all appear to remind the heroes and readers alike that men like Early and Moon would soon become "legends" of their time—a soon-to-be bygone era of American history. Over the course of half a decade, Early and Moon find themselves on opposite sides of the ongoing "Rincon Mountain War"—being played against each other for control of coveted copper mines by the returning villain from *The Law at Randado*, Phil Sundeen—and finding themselves headline fodder throughout the country.

"The idea of using a pseudonym holds some appeal the more I think about it," he wrote to editor Marc Jaffe, "though I still don't see that it's necessary . . . still I wouldn't mind using 'Emmett Long' for the new one . . . There's another area where we might consider a pseudonym. For my next book, I would like to take Cal Maguire from [*Seascape*] and make him a private investigator. I've never written a private eye before because there are so many of them; but now I'm anxious to do one . . . What if we used the pseudonym 'Bryan Hurd' for the Cal Maguire books, beginning with [*Seascape*]? Use 'Emmett Long' for the Westerns—if there's a market—and Elmore Leonard for anything in between, or out in left field? Maybe a pseudonym is just what I need."[33]

As it had been some years since Leonard had taken on the Western genre, his own style of both writing and of research had evolved considerably. Having recently completed *Seascape*—now retitled *Gold Coast*—Leonard sought the similar deep dive into the Arizona copper country that friend and private investigator Bill Marshall had done for the previous book. He immediately reached out to Chris:

April 6, 1978

> . . . *I was wondering if you would like to do some pictorial research for me and write off what you've charged on the credit card? . . . I need a mountain with scrub growth, timber, rocks, and high pastures. Progressive shots, approaching the mountains and up into the high country and reverse shots looking back. Plus shots of the flora identified by name. Whether it's brittlebush, cliffrose, ocotillo, and so on . . . (If you notice I'm getting ungrammatical and sloppy, it's because I'm getting ready to do the Western. Yahoooooo, buckaroooos!)*[34]

Leonard had reached the midpoint of the novel when he, somewhat playfully, followed up with his son—being sure to casually sprinkle family updates throughout:

May 22, 1978

> *How is your hand?*
> *Did you have an operation?*
> *When are you coming home?*
> *WHERE ARE MY PICTURES? . . .*
> *Your mom is getting married.*
> *Katy and I went to the Fair.*
> *WHERE ARE MY PICTURES? . . .*
> *Am making up descriptions in a book.*
> The Switch *is out.*
> *The wife of the Real Al Rosen called . . .*

Am going to be on 3 talk shows.
Sinatra is interested in The Hunted.
Hard to make up descriptions without pix.
Boy, is it hard.
Mom and hubby-to-be bought a new house.
Katy will have her own phone.
Come home soon. WITH PICTURES.

Love, Dad[35]

By the last prompting, Leonard had received his photographs. Having researched the devastation caused by private mining companies on small towns for the unproduced *American Flag*, Leonard added lush detail from that previous project, demonstrating the daily perils of the relocated natives of Rincon Mountain and their never-ending battles against the mining companies laying claim to valuable land—using thugs-for-hire and corrupt railroad police for intimidation tactics. Future critical biographer James Devlin would note that, even more so than *Hombre*, *Valdez Is Coming*, or *Forty Lashes Less One*, the epic saga of Dana Moon and Brendan Early had a modern "revisionist" tone—including its realistic depictions of the Native Americans' responses to bloody warfare conducted on their rightful land. "The struggle between ragtag Indians, Mexicans, and mixed-blood elements against Sundeen's mercenary force is covered by a large group of cynical reporters who make their headquarters in hotels and bars," Devlin wrote. "The presence of photographers and of Colonel Billy Washington (a Buffalo Bill clone), eager to sign up Early and Moon to tour with his Wild West Show, proves so disconcerting to Sundeen's army of thugs that they desert."[36]

The final day of 1978, Leonard wrote to Swanson that Bantam publisher Irwyn Applebaum had decided against his using a pen name for the novel, adding, "He'd also like to use my original title, *Legends*, and will try to talk Marc [Jaffe] into it. If not, they'll probably go with *High Reaches*, also on my list."[37] (Only six months earlier, Leonard had advised Jaffe, "I like *Legends* because that's what the book is about, the making of a couple of legends . . . I like *High Reaches*, too, which suggests a double meaning and, I think, goes with the tone of the book. But 'Action At' or 'Trouble At' or 'Last Stand At' I think would cheapen the book and make it sound like an Ace double-value edition."[38])

Ultimately, Applebaum, Jaffe, and Leonard settled on *Gunsights* in time for its release in August 1979. Leonard had completed it in time for his second anniversary sober. Christopher Leonard sent to his father what the author would later term "his favorite" fan letter of all—a single sentence: "I'm so proud of you."

Leonard dedicated that one to Chris.

As early as the final revision on *Gold Coast* in March 1978, Leonard had suggested to Bantam editor Marc Jaffe that that novel's lead, Cal Maguire, could be repurposed into a private eye for a standalone series.[39] Had he continued with those initial plans, old friend Bill Marshall would, more than likely, have provided much of the details and context for the protagonist's lifestyle. But an offer from the *Detroit News* had come along—one that promised Leonard a front-row seat to the murder and mayhem covered daily throughout Detroit's mean streets. The editors had reached out to Leonard directly, inquiring if he would be willing to pen an in-depth feature article on the Detroit Police Department's Felony Homicide Division—Squad Seven. Although the extent of Leonard's nonfiction output had been relegated to a few book reviews—which he jokingly referred to as his "book report" assignments—the *Detroit News* was looking for a significantly more literary piece, something along the lines of famed "New Journalists" Joan Didion or Gay Talese. As Leonard later recalled, "I spent weeks with the cops before I wrote a word. This was all new to me and I saw no end to the possibilities. As a result, I spent most of the next three months with the homicide cops."[40] Following a trip to Toronto with Joan, Leonard wrote to son Chris, "They want me to go out with a detective named Dixie Davies, but he's been busy lately. 'Six Killed in 8 Hours in Detroit' was a recent headline."[41] (Davies himself later recalled to researcher Gregg Sutter: "We'd give Dutch a call—even in the middle of the night—and he'd meet us at the scene of a murder. He'd sit in on interrogations and follow cases through to the courtroom."[42])

> For most of three months in a row I listened to conversations in a homicide squad room at 1300 Beaubien, Detroit Police headquarters; a Kojak set with 243 mugshots on the wall. I listened to true-crime tales delivered deadpan, tones of voice that were professionally dry, casual, often cynical.
>
> All but one . . .

> I heard a homicide cop, talking to a witness on the phone, begging the person to come forward and testify, say:
>
> "I give you my word as a man."
>
> That's the one I recall most clearly among all the voices in the squad room and will always remember. A man giving his word to protect someone's life, not as an official of the law or on a bible or in any other context than simply "as a man."

The resulting article, "Impressions of Murder," ran in the *Detroit News Sunday Magazine* on November 12, 1978.

It wasn't long before Leonard's initial plans for a private eye novel evolved into a police story—not a procedural, but rather, a realistic drama told from the squad's perspective. Only a few years earlier, he had introduced two prototypical law enforcement figures, *Swag*'s Cal Brown and his doppelgänger, *Unknown Man No. 89*'s Dick Speed—overt stand-ins for the familiar Old West lawmen that infused so much of his earliest work. He later told *The New Black Mask Quarterly*, "I don't know if there is a similarity other than the Western kind of a hero, that stand-up kind of a guy who manifests his attitude in *Destry Rides Again* . . . [But] my guy is, usually, misjudged . . . He's a stand-up kind of guy, like the Western hero. And by the time the antagonists realize that they've misjudged this guy, he has the situation turned around and he's coming at them."[43]

Leonard had gotten close with the members of Detroit's Squad Seven and continued to visit them and both their headquarters at 1300 Beaubien and, occasionally, in court at the Frank Murphy Hall of Justice. Each of the real-life officers whom he'd witnessed in action would play a part in his shaping of new characters, including their personal quirks, habits, and even mannerisms—making up the ensemble team of Leonard's novel.[44] When he sent updates to Swanson regarding a recent call from Bantam editor Tony Koltz the last week of 1978, Leonard had, by then, narrowed the title down to a chosen few: *The View from 1300, A Cloud of Witnesses*, and even his original working title for *Fifty-Two Pickup, Backfire*. "I told him I wanted to lay another story over *Backfire* and give it a strong female lead—a ladylike, but gutty defense attorney named Carolyn Wilder—who finds herself in danger," he wrote. "The main character, of course, is Dick Speed, the Homicide lieutenant."

Slowly, and by integrating much of the gritty realism he'd soaked up at police headquarters, Leonard began infusing his returning *Unknown Man No. 89* character with background details and personality traits of friends Bill Marshall and Dixie Davies. "Tony wants me to stay away from the strictly police procedural story," Leonard wrote. "I suppose because they have Ed McBain doing those . . . I suggested that Dick Speed be established in *Backfire* as a seasoned homicide pro—seventeen years with the Detroit Police—who is forced to resign from the force after they find out he left Clement Mansell in the basement tomb. Clement is free for the third act and Speed is out of a job. But Carolyn Wilder, in some kind of danger, hires Speed as a private investigator and he finally nails Clement in the nick of time for good." He added, "Dick Speed is now established as the private eye and can go anywhere on assignment—down to Miami for the *Foxhunt* story—and, from time to time, can continue to work for Carolyn Wilder. *Backfire* could even be called *Speed*."[45]

By the time Leonard reached into his old copywriting skills to pen his own press release demo, he'd already changed the book's title once again—*No More Mr. Nice*:

> A double homicide—at first look, two unrelated murders—puts Dick Speed on the trail of Clement Mansell: hit man, stickup artist and extortionist, a modern-day version of a 1930's badman out of the back country of Oklahoma . . .
>
> *No More Mr. Nice* is Number One in a new series of Dick Speed detective thrillers that promises to be fast-moving, "street funny" and frighteningly authentic: the result of Elmore Leonard's months of intensive research with the highly regarded Detroit Police Homicide Section. Here's a fresh new look and sound in detective fiction![46]

Ultimately, Leonard swapped protagonist Dick Speed for a new creation, "Raymond Cruz"—a nearly identical archetype with one small difference: Cruz sported the same signature mustache as Gregory Peck in *The Gunfighter*.

Although Swanson continued to successfully pique the interests of numerous Hollywood producers with all of Leonard's latest work, following the release of *Mr. Majestyk* in 1974, the author himself had largely refocused most of his scriptwriting abilities toward fiction.[47] What was of greater interest to Leonard, however, was that he had been put in the running to pen a dream project—CBS's planned television sequel to Fred Zinnemann's 1952 Western classic, *High Noon*. During his first round of Los Angeles meetings with various television executives, he had used the opportunity to work on the then in-progress *Gold Coast*, and even conceived of what would become *Gunsights*—first as a network pitch.

November 23, 1978

Monday, at lunch, I met with the Charles Fries people (the producers) and Peter Frankovitch, one of the CBS guys in charge of movies, and we discussed High Noon. *(I saw the picture Monday morning at exactly the same time the film was playing on the screen. Amazing? It was high noon by my watch when Frank Miller got off the train. At ten after, he was dead.) . . . I put together a storyline—using bits and pieces from less memorable Elmore Leonard Westerns—and presented it to Fries and Frankovitch Tuesday morning. They said fine, go ahead.*

I took Joan to see Swanson in his Old Hollywood 1937 office and the atmosphere was perfect for the rain coming down outside. I gave him an outline of my next one, called Backfire, *which is based on the Homicide article, and he likes it. (I gave Jerry Bick one, too, and he thinks it could be another* Bullitt*: but we have to wait and see if he likes it enough to pay for it.)*[48]

February 22, 1979

Also I had to finish High Noon II, *which Jane typed in record time and I mailed off to the producer this morning: 96-action-packed-pages . . .*

I hope to be off to Florida tomorrow for a week while the Charles Fries people read High Noon II *and think of ways to mess it up.*[49]

March 23, 1979

*. . . Next month, I'm going to New York to attend the Mystery Writers of America Annual Edgar Allan Poe Awards Banquet as—you guessed it—a nominee for an "Edgar" in the category of Best Paperback Mystery of 1978 for—you guessed it again—*The Switch.

The Switch? *What's mysterious about* The Switch?

Don't ask. Maybe the judges didn't read it but were influenced by the intriguing cover. I know I won't win. Heck, who would vote for that book? It doesn't have a chance . . .

I finished the first revision of the High Noon *sequel, which is now* Valdez Is Coming *(squared), with both the good and the bad guy shooting at each other with big rifles at 400 yards. Better close. Have to go work on my acceptance speech.*[50]

Leonard and Joan married on September 15, 1979. His oldest son, Peter, and Joan's oldest daughter, Beth, acted as witnesses. The couple moved into a new two-story, three-bedroom corner house at 476 Fairfax in Birmingham. Peter Leonard later recalled, "It was a block away from our original house. I was running a lot in those days and I used to run through the neighborhoods. One day, I passed the house that Elmore ended up buying. It looked cool, Georgian manor style, and had a For Sale sign, so I called him up and said, 'You should take a look at this.' He did, liked it, and bought it." Peter added, "And I certainly remember his office there—it was in the living room, which is the biggest room in the house. And he sat at his desk—the desk that I now have and use in my home office. But Elmore would be there all day writing, taking breaks to go out on the patio to smoke and feed the squirrels."[51]

To the left of the foyer, Leonard had set up his two-hundred-year-old oak writing desk in the middle of the den. He set a small table next to the wall for his secondhand Olympia typewriter; above it, he hung two photos: an autographed photo of Ernest Hemingway, dated December 1937, and a framed picture of H. N. Swanson.[52]

After five years at the Merrillwood Apartments, Leonard wasn't living alone anymore.

Joan immediately set to work planting a garden where the ceremony had been held, picking a section of the backyard where her husband could watch from his writing desk.

CHAPTER 13

High Noon in Detroit, 1980–1982

[A reporter] asks what it's like to achieve success "finally, at your age," wondering if I resent the fact that it's taken so long in coming. What I resented was the question. I told the young but balding interviewer I've never considered myself unsuccessful, or that being on a bestseller list had anything to do with it.

My job is not to sell books, it's to write them.

Leonard and Joan settled into their new home on Fairfax, beginning a form of domestic routine neither had experienced in years.

By that time, his children had each gone on to careers of their own. Christopher Leonard was just preparing to return home from Arizona, and younger brother Bill had already returned to Birmingham to work at the J. Walter Thompson advertising agency, beginning his own career writing copy for the automotive industry. Married from 1971 to 1973, Jane was divorced from her first husband and father of her daughters—Shannon and Megan—and had been working full-time for brother Peter. She later remarried, and when her husband found himself out of work, Leonard offered his daughter a gig as his official typist. "I was already in my twenties and married when I started actually working for Dad," Jane later recalled. "I had taken a typing class in high school and one of his secretaries had just left him, so he didn't have anyone to do the typing. I used a typewriter just like him—an IBM Selectric—where you had to put those little 'magic strips' for corrections as he went along and made changes. If he made it different or wanted to change a paragraph or something, I would have to go back through the entire book—that was just the worst part of the job, until I finally got a computer later on. I had to do the screenplays too. He'd say, 'Don't worry about making a mistake, just take your time.' But then the next day, he'd ask, 'Are you finished yet?' I'd get the pages from him and I could smell the smoke on it. Not every page, but when I thumbed through it, I could tell where he was when he had been lighting a cigarette."[1]

According to Jane's oldest daughter, Shannon Belmont, her mother had initially started working for Leonard while still employed with Peter—a hectic juggling act for a young mother of two. "She had stayed home with us when we were really little, then started working part-time for my uncle Peter when I was maybe five," Belmont recalled. "When Elmore had pages for her, she had to drop everything and do the pages. She would sit at the typewriter—later, a Mac—in order to pump out his pages—she would just drop everything."[2] Back at his own home office, Leonard kept up his daily habit of writing a few pages by hand before typing them up into reasonably sized stacks; those he would drive to Jane's—and always with a rare sense of urgency. Jane Jones later recalled, "I found out soon that Dad was pretty paranoid about his manuscripts. I used to drop off the finished manuscripts at his house when I was done and, one time, I put them in the backseat of my car and covered them up in a box, but I had to make a stop first. When I got to his house, he was so annoyed that I'd stopped anywhere with them still in the car—but that's how I learned his routine." She added, "I also worked as Peter's office manager in advertising. But I think he picked me because nobody else had a typewriter. In thirty years, we only had one fight ever. He said, 'You're fired' and I picked up my typewriter and I stormed out. Then Peter came over that night and said, 'Oh, come on, you know I was kidding'—because I had the typewriter!"[3] Leonard's youngest, Katy, was still in school and was on her way toward a career in teaching, during which time she often invited her famous author father to speak to the young students about his career in writing. However, her father playfully had offered her an alternative suggestion. She recalled, "Dad told me to be a cabdriver. He said, 'I think when you graduate from college, you should drive a taxi.' I said to him, 'Are you being serious?' And he said, 'Yes—think of all the people you'll meet and the interesting stories you'll be able to tell.'"[4]

Peter Leonard was now on his way in a long and prosperous career in advertising—and admittedly had had his fill of excitement toward the end of his education in Italy. Just before the disintegration of his parents' marriage, he'd had a brush with the Italian law that would later provide nearly unbelievable fodder for his own fiction writing. "When I was attending Loyola University in Rome, I went out with a group of friends and we were drinking a bit and a good buddy of mine and I decided to grab a cab and check out Harry's Bar—an old Hemingway haunt," he later recalled. As Peter would later reimagine as the opening of his own third novel three decades later, *All He Saw Was the Girl*, an innocent drink turned into a drunken joyride with Peter's friend getting behind the wheel of an unoccupied taxi—which led them both into an unoccupied jail cell. "I ended up spending three days in solitary confinement in Rebibbia Prison," he later recalled. "That was an experience. Me, my friend, and two other guys—a twenty-one-year-old South American pickpocket and a seventy-six-year-old who'd been in prison since the Mussolini era . . . When I got home, there are my parents in the airport to greet me. And Elmore looked at me and he said, 'Son, hard time makes the boy a man.' And I said, 'Did one of your characters say that?' He said, 'Probably.' But he never used my experiences in any of his stories—later, he said it was my experience, so was mine to use. And he was right—thirty years later, I used it in an opening scene."[5] Peter's younger brother, Christopher, recalled his own brushes with the law—as well as their father's always-genteel way of dealing with it. "When I was in grade school, a couple of friends and I figured out how easy it would be to steal a 'hypospray'—this mechanical medical syringe that you could use as a squirt gun," he remembered. "So I shoplifted it from a grocery store pharmacy and as soon as we got on the street, a security guard appeared . . . I was brought to the police station and the cop said, 'Your punishment is that your dad is picking you up. That should be punishment enough.' And I'm thinking, 'Okay, they don't know my dad, do they?'" However, when Chris drove the family station wagon through the garage wall and into their neighbor's property, the elder Leonard was forced to be more creative with his punishment. Chris recalled waiting in dread all day for his father to return from his Pierce Street office. "Dad drove a Mustang at the time and he walks into my room and tosses me the keys and says, 'We're going for a drive and you're driving.' I got real quiet and said, 'Okay' and followed him down to the Mustang. He said, 'You're driving,' and I pulled out. We get to the street and he said, 'Just drive.' And I'm really confused, but he said, 'You need to know how to really drive or every time you drive, you're going to have some kind of problem. You have to get right back on the horse.' And I'm so surprised and relieved. We drove round the block twice, we get home, and he said, 'Oh, and your punishment—you're paying for the garage.' Then he thought about it and smiled to himself like he had just come up with a better punishment just then and said, 'And you're not getting your driver's license until you're seventeen.' Which was much, much worse to a fifteen-year-old."[6]

Not long after Leonard's marriage to Joan, Beverly herself remarried. Peter Leonard recalled, "She married a guy named Bill Decker. I liked him, I thought he was a good guy—a successful businessman, the complete opposite of my father . . . He was an avid golfer who wore white belts and white shoes, drank scotch—that kind of summed him up. Very conservative. But he wasn't really funny or interesting or entertaining—not like Elmore."[7]

Now at fifty-five years old, Leonard himself hadn't touched alcohol in three years. On the third anniversary of sobriety, he penned a letter to H. N. Swanson offering the usual project updates, but stressed his growing concern over publisher Bantam's handling of his work. "I wrote [*Touch*] almost two and a half years ago, [*Gold Coast*] two years ago, and Irwyn [Applebaum] says, '[I hope to] finally get the book out in 1980,'" Leonard wrote. "Well, I'm going to have a new one done in about a week (in your hands), but I'm sure anxious to send it to Bantam and see it die there on some shelf." He added, "I write to be read."[8]

In Leonard's view, his writing had only improved over time, yet his publisher was doing little to get that word out. A letter from editor Irwyn Applebaum six months earlier had already gotten Leonard thinking that a "switch" of his own might be the best course of action. His next message from Applebaum did little to ease his concerns. "Having hurriedly investigated, I find that Bantam will be publishing [*Gold Coast*] in December and that it has been retitled, *The Big Choice*," the editor wrote. "I realize it's close to your *The Big Bounce*, but I don't think it really matters."[9] But it mattered to Leonard; although Bantam had nearly rushed the alternate title past his approval, there was just enough time in the galley stage to veto it in exchange for the more palatable *Gold Coast*. But the damage had been done, and Leonard and Swanson immediately began the search for a new publisher. To both, Leonard's new Detroit police epic, *City Primeval: High Noon in Detroit*—still in its earliest form as *View from 1300*—was too promising to languish on a shelf.

One of Leonard's greatest champions had long been his original editor at Delacorte—its cofounder, Donald Fine. Years earlier, Leonard's departure had been bittersweet, as Fine's encouragement and belief in the young author had poured through every editorial suggestion, always stressing his belief that Leonard was meant for bigger and better things. Ironically, it was just as Leonard had reentered the literary arena in the late 1960s that Fine himself had parted ways with Delacorte/Dell in order to follow a dream of his own: in 1969, he borrowed five thousand dollars from a fellow Harvard alumnus and founded Arbor House, a boutique publisher with emphasis on creating brands of their authors. Their 1978 sleeper hit, Ken Follett's suspense debut, *The Eye of the Needle*, had quickly made Arbor House a force to be reckoned with—and almost instantly made the company a worthwhile asset to the Hearst Corporation. Upon signing over the company to the media conglomerate, Fine—known for his brisk attitude and limited patience for tasks unassociated with the creative aspects of promoting his stable of writers—had told the Hearst representatives, "Okay, now get out of my office." However, Fine was kept on as Arbor House's president, giving him free rein to sign the authors he wished, and to continue his hands-on, nurturing editorial style.[10] He later recalled: "I called Dutch and said, 'Listen, you can afford to go straight. I'll pay you less than you've been getting, but I'll get you across to readers and reviewers how good you are. We'll create a whole new Elmore Leonard reputation.'"

Leonard liked what he heard and signed with his old friend, marking their first collaboration since 1959's *Last Stand at Saber River*. He later told *The New Black Mask Quarterly*, "I expected the publisher to do something. If they really liked my work, they should sell it . . . Don Fine at Arbor House said, 'I'll sell you.' He proceeded to get my material into the hands of, I think, reviewers who were more prestigious as far as having an effect on other reviewers."[11]

For the occasion, Leonard brought something special to the table; on January 28, 1980, he had completed his Detroit police novel.[12]

Lines of dialogue can come from unexpected places.

A few months before marrying Joan and moving out of the Merrillwood Apartments, Leonard had one final visitor there who would prove to be a crucial friend and creative ally in all his future work—Gregg Sutter, a young freelance writer and film noir enthusiast, soon to become Leonard's personal researcher for more than thirty years. Initially, Sutter had visited Leonard with friend and fellow crime fiction expert Russell Rein;

the duo had been working together on a profile of Leonard for their own self-published magazine, *Noir*. At the time, Leonard was already deep into his follow-up to *City Primeval*—a sequel again featuring Raymond Cruz, tentatively entitled *Hang Tough*. Impressed with Sutter's knowledge and research skills, Leonard soon inquired if the young man would be willing to do some digging on his behalf at the local library.

Sutter was born in Detroit in 1951, later noting to *The New Yorker* that the hospital was torn down to make room for a Cadillac plant. Like Leonard, he also attended Catholic school, and ultimately graduated from Oakland University. "My first major was behavioral science, which I still don't know what it is," he recalled. "Then I fell into film history. I thought of myself as a cine-Marxist—sit around the apartment and talk about the Revolution and watch movies. I wrote about Cuban revolutionary posters and Nazi cinema, and got a degree in history, never thinking about what I would do the day I graduated." Upon his graduation in 1969, Sutter began a string of odd jobs, mixing blue-collar labor with his impassioned extracurricular literary interests. He worked publicity for the Women's Symphony of Detroit, and soon became editor of the Detroit Metropolitan Bar Owners Association's newsletter, the *Grapevine Gazette*. Inspired by the experience, Sutter and a group of like-minded friends founded a cultural magazine entitled *Artbeat*, but it folded after only four issues. By the end of 1975, Sutter had taken a job with industrial liquidator Norman Levy Associates. Then, two years later, he began working the line for Oldsmobile. Sutter later admitted that poring over Elmore Leonard novels while on the job proved to be the best form of escapism. "I'd get several air cleaners ahead and try to read two pages before a car was in front of me again," he recalled. "I read *Fifty-Two Pickup* when it came out in paperback, and because it was about Detroit, it deeply addressed a feeling I had of being stuck in a permanent backwater . . . In the summer of 1979, I looked Elmore Leonard up in the phone book and called him."[13]

Although ambitions for *Noir* magazine didn't come to fruition, Sutter was able to parlay the material into a lengthy profile for *Monthly Detroit* magazine. He later recalled, "I interviewed Elmore many more times before my piece appeared . . . [and] the progression from [Leonard's *Detroit News* article] to the publication of *City Primeval* had given me a model for how an author works and the importance of good research." He added, "In January 1981, Elmore called me at the *Monthly Detroit* office, asking if I wanted to do some research on the cops from his new book, *Split Im-*

ages. He had realized that doing extensive research would mean spending too much of his time away from writing."[14]

Early rumblings regarding Leonard's lucrative Arbor House contract, combined with Fine's public relations push, already had the author in higher demand than in previous years. Fine had already had some success with Leonard's latest. "*The Detroit News Sunday Magazine*, reaching some half million subscribers, is going to excerpt the book—a chapter in it—in October to tie-in with the book's publication," Leonard wrote Chris. "Don Fine is all for it and is making the arrangements with [the *Detroit News*]."[15]

H. N. Swanson, however, had had his own success selling *City Primeval*; a sale to United Artists was announced even before the novel's Arbor House debut. "If Steve McQueen has twinges of nostalgia for his *Bullitt* detective romp, he can satisfy that feeling by accepting a firm offer from producers Herb Jaffe and Jerry Bick to topline as a tough Detroit detective hot after 'redneck killers' in their movie version for UA of Elmore Leonard's *Hang Tough* thriller, which they bought off the Arbor House galleys," the *Hollywood Reporter* said in its May 22 issue.[16] They followed up nearly two weeks later: "Hot off the galleys, United Artists has shelled [out] 350Gs, plus a percentage of the profits for film rights, to the forthcoming *Hang Tough* novel by Elmore Leonard . . . Arbor House will publish it in hardcover and Avon subsequently in paperback."[17] In March the following year, producers Jaffe and Bick were able to sign director Sam Peckinpah to helm the project; he insisted on keeping the story's original title even after Arbor House made the switch to *City Primeval*.

Leonard had already completed the screenplay, but a pending WGA strike loomed as the producers set to their location scouting. "Things are looking good, except now it looks like we're walking out April 11 at midnight," Leonard wrote to Chris. "I met with Peckinpah twice; he doesn't say much but gives hand signals to indicate approval . . . I'm becoming familiar with them."[18]

NOTES ON MEETING, WEDNESDAY, MARCH 11, 1981 BETWEEN JERRY BICK, HERB JAFFE, DUTCH LEONARD, AND SAM PECKINPAH REGARDING "HANG TOUGH"

PECKINPAH: More involvement of Karen. Main criticism is that leading man is dumb—character does not come through in playing against the heavy—there is no "simmering" quality—two contemporaries somewhat anachronistic—out of step with the times . . . Add scene to include more V.O. of judge—use trials to help tell story (titles w/vignettes & montages as exposition—tell story—this would involve no greater cost and be worthwhile).

LEONARD: Why more of judge?

PECKINPAH: The judge and Clement in the first part of picture could be a montage played against shooting—confrontation between the judge and [Cruz] (tying into titles)—puts it all in 4½ minutes and you know all the people.

LEONARD: Do you see [Cruz] in the courtroom?

PECKINPAH: Don't know . . .

LEONARD: You know, the judge is based on an actual judge, though it is changed somewhat—James Del Rio—He was suspended for five years and just applied for a private investigator's license—L.A. County. He carried a gun.

PECKINPAH: My father always carried a gun under his robe.[19]

"I think [Peckinpah] has to be [liquored up] and he's on the wagon, which must be a slow, creaking trip for him," Leonard added.[20] "Peckinpah is coming to town around May 1 to scout locations, bringing his 'secretary' and needs a suite with two bedrooms . . . I wonder if there is a place in Detroit like that."[21] For Peckinpah's in-depth location scouting, Leonard's new researcher, Gregg Sutter, drove with the director to the real-life spots depicted in the novel, including both "1300"'s—Beaubien and Lafayette—as well as the Frank Murphy Hall of Justice. "Later, we learned Peckinpah would receive a substantial payment if he rewrote the script," Sutter later wrote. "He hired a ghostwriter who set the story in El Paso. Once MGM acquired United Artists, the film project was doomed."[22]

But while the film version was on track for indefinite production hell, Leonard's original novel was garnering him some of the best reviews of his career. "[*City Primeval*] is a candid, untouched picture of life in the city today, as viewed mostly through the jaundiced eye of a homicide detective. As such, it is a genre novel . . . but it is such a piece of artful simplicity that it manages to suggest the entire microcosm of the city within the microcosm of its gritty plot," Bruce Cook wrote in the *Detroit News*.

"It all hangs together so well, and is worked out so logically, that when the final confrontation between Cruz and Clement comes, it seems almost to have been preordained by fate—and not merely by the author."[23]

For their promised media blitz, Arbor House had taken out a carefully designed quarter-page advertisement announcing both the release of *City Primeval* and its then-in-preproduction film adaptation; the publisher had saved the most praiseworthy reviews for the ad, headlining with the *New York Times'* glowing description of Leonard: "an entertainer of enormous finesse who can write circles around almost anyone active in the crime novel [genre] today."[24]

Leonard was experienced enough to know that the 1981 Writers Guild strike could last an indefinite amount of time—and was readily prepared. At the suggestion of Don Fine, he'd finally made a solid attempt at an ongoing crime series, planning to bring back *City Primeval*'s Raymond Cruz for a second case. However, even in its structure, the novel that would become *Split Images* was a darker, more psychological work than its predecessor. True to form, Leonard had divided the story's focus on Cruz and his latest adversary, a millionaire who kills for sport, his psychopathology cleverly concealed beneath the façade of a lily-white well-to-do yuppie. Still heavily inspired by his own time divided between Birmingham and Pompano Beach, he also divided much of the story's action between the streets of Detroit and killer Robbie Daniel's posh home in Palm Beach. "This being on strike isn't too bad," Leonard wrote to Chris on April 20—only one week into a strike that would last three months. "I'm on page 46 of my new book, *Split Images*, while Swanie and Arbor House decide what it's worth, if anything."[25]

Split Images also marked the first major project for which Gregg Sutter acted as Leonard's researcher. Sutter helped add lush detail to the portrayals of Detroit and Florida, as well as background ideas for antagonist Robbie Daniels and his valet-cum-unwitting accomplice, retired Detroit cop Walter Kouza ("Couza" in the earliest drafts). As a particularly chilling characteristic, Daniels prefers his cold-blooded hunting of human prey videotaped for future self-study, believing he can always refine his techniques; Sutter also helped Leonard scout the latest technologies in home-video equipment, security systems, and heavy artillery; Sutter also produced pages of photocopied reports on similar crimes over the past decades. On April 10, Leonard wrote to Swanson, "I feel pretty confident about this one, with situations and backgrounds I like to write about and,

I think, will appeal to readers—the glitter of Palm Beach life."[26] Although he completed the first draft in just under three months, by the first week of July he wrote to Chris, "[I'm] having misgivings, knowing they won't like it. (Except the part where the killer is stewing because he doesn't know what to wear to an assassination.) [I] Am still on strike, but now with the book finished, I don't want to be."[27]

Leonard wouldn't have to worry about either for very long: after ninety-two days, the WGA strike ended on July 12, allowing him to get back to all film-related projects he'd set on the backburner. He was also elated at the response that *Split Images* received from both H. N. Swanson and Don Fine—although there was a caveat attached to his protagonist. "Did I tell you Swanie thinks the new one is the best yet but can't offer it for sale in Hollywood because of my *City Primeval* contract with United Artists?" he wrote to Chris. "It's considered a sequel with Raymond Cruz, the main character, and featuring the gang from Squad Seven. We could offer it to UA, but if they don't want it, we'd have to wait three years from the release of *City Primeval* as a film or, if it isn't produced, five years from the signing of the contract. Swanie said, 'Change Raymond's name.' . . . So Raymond Cruz is now Bryan Hurd . . . but I'll tell you, he sounds an awful lot like Raymond."[28]

Soon after, Leonard sat with the *Detroit News*' Bill Dunn for a special profile in *Writer's Digest*. "I don't spend a lot of time [in Hollywood]," he told Dunn while chain-smoking Kents. "I just as soon get in and get out." He demonstrated his point by waving the latest revision of Sam Peckinpah's *Hang Tough* in the air. "This is what they want—they want the story. They don't want to socialize with me. It would be a great disadvantage to me to go out there and sit around and socialize and talk about stories all the time, talk about movies and the business, and wonder what the other writers are doing."[29]

It had been easy for Leonard to throw himself into *Split Images* while the WGA strike had been in full swing. However, those weeks left a number of film projects in flux. He had forgone almost all warnings from H. N. Swanson to steer clear of self-production; the agent had even goaded him, "Are you in debtor's prison yet?" By the end of 1979, Leonard had all but lost his patience with RKO Pictures, which had, initially, agreed to produce his and Tom Brank's version of *The Hunted* (again retitled as *Dead Run*). Uncharacteristically, Leonard then penned an aggravated letter to RKO cofounder Shane O'Neil, confounded by the lack of communication between them: "You hear tales in the picture business, people have been getting fucked since before *Birth of a Nation*. It's sometimes part of the deal. In taking money, you assume the position. The striking difference in our situation, it appears that we're assuming the position—or at least asking for it—with only the vague promise of compensation." Leonard went on, "I'm baffled; because in the fifteen or so film contracts I've entered into I've never come up against this situation before. Neither has Swanson in some 40 years."[30]

Leonard followed up with O'Neil's partner, Bob Manby, discouraged with both the failures of *The Hunted*, then of a revamped post-Hitchcock adaptation of *Unknown Man No. 89* to make it to the big screen. "You should hear the reasons why some fifty producers turned down *Unknown Man No. 89* before Hitchcock bought it," Leonard told Manby. "In the past, I have accepted the opinions of others in adapting my novels to the screen and have seen fresh ideas turned into mediocre films . . . My whole purpose in getting involved in co-production is to see my material appear the way I see it and hear it when I write it."[31]

In May 1981, the law offices of Hertz and Schram of Birmingham secured the reassignment of rights from RKO to Leonard and Brank's Hat Trick Productions for *The Hunted*, paving the way for Leonard to reattain the film rights to his book. He would later chalk it up as a three-year learning experience. He wrote to Chris:

November 8, 1980

. . . Did I tell you I got the Unknown Man *screenplay to write after Jennings Lang at Universal gave it to a guy named Adam Kennedy and he turned it into a George Peppard private-eye movie with a lot of finger-snapping dialogue? I told Jennings I would go by the book, simplify it (I've never seen so many phone conversations in one [script]) and emphasize the love story . . . He would like to use "someone like" Dustin Hoffman as Ryan and "someone like" Bill Cosby to play Dick Speed, the cop, making it a bigger part. I told him that it was okay by me.*[32]

January 29, 1981

The script for Unknown Man No. 89 *has been revised as* Happy Hour *(get the drinking connection?) and is about one step away from being a musical . . . Warner Brothers is looking for an action vehicle for Eastwood and I sent them a treatment called* Death Before Dishonor, *based on the tattoo of the same name. I'm waiting to hear. Also waiting to hear about* Happy Hour, *which Universal received yesterday . . .*

Brank is now shooting the battered-wives script I did for the State of Michigan, Appearances, *and we're going to watch him this afternoon.*[33]

For what would prove to be their only fully realized collaboration, Leonard had volunteered to write a half-hour teleplay for Tom Brank to direct: a short-subject public television special on domestic abuse. Completed on March 10, Leonard's *Appearances: A Proposal on Domestic Violence* would feature two elements of note—his only time writing from the perspective of a child, as well as the inclusion of a repurposed opening scene from *Touch*:

FADE IN:
INTL BOY'S BEDROOM—DAY
An ANGLE on KEVIN, nine years old, asleep. Laid out on a chair next to the bed is his Little League football uniform. In the moments before his eyes open we HEAR, faintly, the sound of VOICE OFF STAGE: his father, JACK, and his mother, BARBARA, in the kitchen arguing.

JACK (O.S.)

You don't have enough to do, that what you're saying?

BARBARA (O.S.)

Jack, they meet once a week, that's all. And I saved up for the brushes and paints . . .

JACK (O.S.)

Who in the hell told you you had any talent? You can't even paint a wall, for Christ sake.

BARBARA (O.S.)

I want to learn. That's what the class is for . . .

JACK (O.S.)

I said no!

With the SOUND of a fist striking a table, dishes clattering, a dish breaking on the floor, Kevin's eyes come wide open. In the silence that follows he lies still, listening . . .

BARBARA

How do you feel this morning?

JACK

What's that supposed to mean?

BARBARA

Nothing, I'm only asking . . .

JACK

You count my beers last night? How many'd I have? Come on, I want to know . . . Come on how many beers did I have?[34]

Arbor House released *Split Images* on January 1, 1981. Coming hot on the heels of *City Primeval*, the follow-up novel quickly garnered stronger reviews—particularly for the author himself. "Though he's named George Higgins as a crucial exemplar, it's clear that Leonard also understands Higgins's flaw," wrote Ken Tucker in the *Village Voice*. "Leonard resists mannerism instinctively; it's one reason he ditches his heroes from book to book, always inventing new crooks and detectives who weight the balance between good and bad in quirky disproportion."[35]

As part of his promised strategy, Don Fine had reached out to a few of Leonard's peers for an additional boost. To the author's delight, one of his longtime inspirations came through, initiating a spirited correspondence that would last for years. He first shared with Chris, "Arbor House sent *Split Images* to John D. MacDonald, hoping to get a jacket quote from him and he said (are you ready?): '*Elmore Leonard's* Split Images *is strong and true and persuasive. Leonard can really write. He's astonishingly good. He doesn't cheat the reader. He gives full value. The images stay in the mind a long time. Walter is one of the most dimensional people I have come across in fiction in a long time.*'" He added, "Can you believe it?"[36]

Leonard had studied MacDonald's bestselling pulp mysteries long before MacDonald had even struck gold with his ongoing protagonist, Travis McGee. "I read him like a textbook in the '50s," Leonard had admitted to journalist Peter Rose. "He was writing about real people who came over a lot more real than ordinary characters you would find; I think he was breaking a lot of rules and getting away with it in the stories he did for *Saturday Evening Post*, *Collier's*, and other slick magazines."[37] As part of their mutual appreciation society, MacDonald himself soon responded to Leonard's personal note of gratitude—offering the slightly younger author his own two cents regarding the frustrations of the literary and film industries. "I would never have sold [Travis McGee] down the river had it not been for some wretched tax decisions which clobbered the families of deceased writer friends," MacDonald wrote. "So I sold [Travis McGee] on a reversion basis, and only much later did I find a better answer—putting all the rights, contracts, copyrights and everything into a personal holding company corporation, where there are rules they have to follow for the valuation of the stock."[38]

Although it was becoming increasingly unlikely that *City Primeval* would make its way to production, the success of the sale had worked wonders for Leonard's reputation among filmmakers and studio heads, and both he and Swanson had anticipated the same rapid success for *Split Images*. But after four rejections in just under a month, he admitted to Swanson that, perhaps, his expectations had been too high: "I've been getting by, making film sales on the strength of style and characterization in lieu of a good story. I thought *Split Images* would sell right away because *City Primeval* did. But now I think we were lucky to have made that sale . . . My former editor at Bantam once said my work falls somewhere in between pure genre and literature, sort of a no man's land, and that's why they had trouble marketing it." He added, "So what I'm going to do now is plot better stories. I'll show 'em."[39]

As far back as the previous summer, Leonard had been tinkering with his new protagonist, drawing early inspiration from two of his sons: taking the name of one of Peter's close friends, George Moran, while using the Arizona landscapes surrounding Chris's home. During the summer of 1980, he had even written a twenty-page outline, *Dope: George Moran*, although he continued to think of a proper title. The new story featured a Vietnam veteran turned highly paid fine-art photographer who prefers taking candid action shots of various quirky residents around Florida's South Beach—the "old people, sign-painters, dishwashers, winos, low-riders, and sharp young Latinos who were 'in the life' dealing cocaine and marijuana" on SW 8th Street in Little Havana. As Leonard noted, George Moran considers his work as "recording history." At thirty-nine years old and divorced, Moran is content to use discretion in the contract jobs he accepts; he has a particular disdain for the advertising executives who try to woo him toward more commercial fare, and absolutely refuses to take portraits for hire—no exceptions. When Moran's ex-wife—a fashion model—jabs him for turning down the high-paying photography in magazines like *Vogue* and *Bazaar* that could earn him even greater fame and fortune, Leonard, perhaps, turned the most autobiographical:

> He could also have been shooting machinery and corporate glass buildings for annual reports; but he had never read an annual report so why, he reasoned, would he want to illustrate one? He would turn down a $10,000 commercial assignment in order to hang his own shots at a street fair . . . He smiled easily enough, but not for profit. He lived his own life, carried his independence with him at all times—casually enough, he felt—and was amazed when his motives were questioned. "What are you trying to prove, George?" "I'm not trying to prove anything." "You're trying to be *different*?" George wasn't trying—he *was* different, in a pure sense, in a way that antagonized people who would also like to be different, unencumbered, natural, but didn't have the nerve to pull it off . . .

Moran is more than happy at the top-floor studio of a warehouse off the MacArthur Causeway with a view of the Miami docks that the thirty thousand dollars he makes per year affords him—doubled by the profits he makes secretly running marijuana from Colombia. It's out of sheer professional curiosity that he accepts a surveillance assignment from his buddy, private investigator Marshall Brinks (an homage to Leonard's close friend, Bill Marshall), to tail the adulterous wife of corporate tycoon Bob Robinet. However, when Moran—largely unimpressed with the uncouth millionaire—refuses to shoot Robinet's portrait, it sets off a fierce antagonism that propels the duration of the espionage-laden story.

Although Leonard ultimately abandoned the story, he would retain elements of its plot and various characters for at least a half dozen other novels: its original title had been *Split Images*, although the title would be repurposed for another, later novel; George Moran would still remain the central protagonist for the following book, *Cat Chaser*; Moran's Vietnam buddy, Norris "Cat" Catlin, would provide both Moran's own later nickname, "the Cat," in that novel, as well as *Get Shorty*'s Bo Catlett; Moran's career and style of urban candid photography would later inspire a novel featuring Ernest "Stick" Stickley before Stickley himself morphed into a new original character, Joe LaBrava; love interest Millie Darwin—whose former life as a free-spirited flower child unceremoniously took a turn into an embrace of 1980s "Reaganomics"—would become the prototype for both *Stick*'s Kyle McClaren and *Freaky Deaky*'s Robin Abbott; and, in the latter case, so would Millie's penchant for drugging antagonists to bend to her will.[40]

Aside from maintaining his own growing reputation among fans and critics, Leonard was under the gun to deliver the next book quickly after *Split Images*—the product of his new, lucrative contract with Arbor House. Signed on November 6, 1981, the contract stipulated that Leonard deliver the first of two suspense novels by February 1 of the following year and its follow-up exactly twelve months later. He would be given a combined $51,500 for both, doled out in the usual installments. Never one to run out the clock on a deadline, Leonard was already deep into the George Moran character upon re-signing with Don Fine, and was soon toying with the idea of saving the book's photography subplot for the second contractual offering. He wrote to Chris, "The next book takes place in the Dominican Republic, in the city of Santo Domingo. And it's called . . ."—comically including an ellipsis where he'd come up short a title.[41] He had one, however, by the time a surprise announcement from Arbor House ran only two days following the release of *Split Images*. "I see by the Arbor House 1982 Spring-Summer catalogue that *Cat Chaser* will be published in July," he wrote. "The description of the plot says, 'In a climax as unpredictable as it is exemplary of Elmore Leonard's remarkable talents . . .' The key word is 'unpredictable,' because I'm on page 244 with about 80–100 pages to go and I wish someone would tell me how this thing is going to end."[42]

While less candid, he later elaborated to *The New Yorker*, "One time, I was interested in getting some background on Porfirio Rubirosa, a Dominican playboy, because I had a character like that in *Split Images*, in 1982, so Gregg [Sutter] got me a magazine that had a piece about Trujillo's daughter, who was married to Porfirio. I was reading that, and here a picture of a squad of Marines walking down a street in Santo Domingo, and I thought, 'That's my next book—one of these guys goes back fifteen or sixteen years later to walk his perimeter and meets this girl sniper who shot him.' That became *Cat Chaser*."[43]

Leonard and Joan returned from a vacation and research trip to the Dominican Republic the first day of November. (Leonard and Joan had been in the Dominican Republic for two weeks. Through private investigator friend Bill Marshall, the couple had two contacts awaiting them upon arrival: a Dominican-born attorney named Jose Martinez, and his cousin, Clement Alba, whose husband, Andres, was known to his friends as "Papito." According to Alba, during the 1950s he had been best friends with Ramfis Trujillo, the eldest son of former dictator Rafael "El Jefe" Trujillo. Leonard and Joan took the group out to dinner at a French restaurant in the old quarter the following evening enraptured by the tales they heard about Trujillo's three-decade reign, as well as his ghastly demise: he had been shot twenty-seven times on the way to visit one of his many mistresses, leaving Papito and Clement to fly the body to Paris for burial.)

Awaiting them were two pieces of news: United Artists had officially put *City Primeval* into turnaround, making its chances of seeing actual production close to none; on a significantly brighter note, Leonard wrote to Chris, "Peter is going to be a dad, Julie a mom, in May."[44]

As he had done numerous times in the past, Leonard took copious notes during his excursions with Joan, later stapling them together into a makeshift travel journal—"Dominican Diary." He began with a full day-by-day breakdown of the 1965 invasion, citing the original field movements of the US Marines and Naval task forces assigned to the ground. On an index card, he'd scrawled, "Cocaine: Retail cost, about 75.00 to 100.00 a gram . . . 28 grams in an ounce, making an ounce worth $2,000.00 to $3,000.00. A kilo to 2.2 lbs. worth $60 to $100,000.00."[45] Back in Miami, Bill Marshall had introduced Leonard to a Cuban-born insurance agent named Mike Carrecarte, who had been in the Eighty-Second Airborne Division and had been stationed in Santo Domingo in 1965. Together, he and Leonard had driven where much of the conflict's fighting had taken place, including "the grain elevators on the Ozama River where the 82nd mounted its 106-mm recoilless rifles and shot George Moran by mistake." He wrote to Chris, "I'm spending more time on this one, trying to write better and make the story more intriguing than anything I've done before," adding, "I'm going to AA meetings once in a while, but really feel no need; certainly no compulsion to drink. I took a sip of Joan's Asti the other night by mistake—it was darker than usual and looked like my Vernor's [one calorie]—gagged, spit it in the sink and asked her how a person could drink awful stuff like that."[46]

Leonard began his first detailed treatment for *Cat Chaser* in September

1981. Once he had settled on George Moran being the chief protagonist and all the ancillary characters and basic plot were in place, he penned a twenty-five-page outline of the story, crafting a drastically different plot than his initial use for the George Moran character. He began by digging into the 1965 Dominican Republic conflict, starting with a full play-by-play of the politics behind the invasion Sutter had found in an old *Life* magazine: "U.S. Steps into the Dominican Crossfire."[47] Sutter had also unearthed the *South Florida Sun-Sentinel*'s coverage of the thirty-three Haitian refugees who had drowned on their way to Hillsboro Beach in October 1981, as well as various other articles on the socioeconomic repercussions of the conflict.[48]

Leonard had also made his own hand-drawn sketch of Santo Domingo, as well as a blueprint of his mother's Pompano Beach motel, the Coconut Palms, using the familiar outlay to plot key scenes within the book. Leonard noted on his sketch a near-identical business strategy he'd helped his mother learn over a decade earlier, repurposing it for George Moran's own business woes. And just as he had done writing to real-life televangelist Oral Roberts for researching *Jesus Saves!* in 1970, Leonard reached out to an actual competitor in the Florida motel business, Ed Potter, innocently inquiring about their own property values and interest in selling—not mentioning that it would be the fictional George Moran doing the business mulling. He saved the information on a postcard from "Ed Potter's Ocean Pearl Resort Apartments" on Ocean Boulevard—the card itself prominently featuring a landscape of the complex grounds, piercing blue sky, and palm trees. On the flip side, he wrote, "Moran paid $350,000 for Coconuts in 1974. Now worth 3.5 million, but he won't sell."[49]

Just after the holidays, Leonard wrote to Chris, "I wake up around five A.M. and lie in bed trying to think of what's going to happen after I get to about page 310, to end it, and I can't think of anything. Having the cover already done helps some, but not much."[50]

He completed the first draft January 21, 1982, and had his revisions submitted one week later, on February 1.[51] In a rare move, Leonard was also confident enough to send his progress to fellow author John D. MacDonald, who, unprompted, wrote to Don Fine on his behalf: "With dialogue that sounds exactly right and true, and with people you wouldn't, for the most part, want to meet on the street, Elmore Leonard's *Cat Chaser* maintains the high standards of *Split Images*."[52] MacDonald shared his personalized encouragement for Leonard himself, writing, "The college age people look at me with incredulity when I tell them I am still trying to make the stuff better. If there was such a thing as total objectivity there would be no bad books written or published, and no plays produced. I tell them I am trying to make the author ever more invisible, and keep the words shorter without triteness."[53]

For his part, Fine followed through with the first major public relations push aimed at establishing Leonard as a name synonymous with quality suspense literature. On June 13, the *New York Times* ran a quarter-page ad with Leonard's smiling face—sunglasses, beard, and now signature newsboy cap—the headline penned by Fine himself: "*Who is this guy?*" The cheeky advertisement displayed words of praise from John D. MacDonald and *Publishers Weekly*, and added, "Dutch Leonard belongs in the same company of Chandler, Hammett, John D. MacDonald, George V. Higgins. That's what we, his publishers, say. But damn it, what counts is what you say . . . To encourage you to read Elmore 'Dutch' Leonard."

Not only had Leonard agreed to the ad (his experiences as an adman knew it could work) but, additionally, he welcomed the new public persona deliberately tied to his nickname—"Dutch"—now forever in the public consciousness. Soon, his high school nickname would become a moniker for the initiated: "*Do you read Elmore Leonard? I love Dutch!*"[54]

When Arbor House released *Cat Chaser* in June, critics seemed to agree. "Mr. Leonard, in his 16th thriller, is better at dialogue than anybody else on the block I can think of except Philip Roth," wrote John Leonard in the *New York Times*. "He also manages to put the fun back in adultery and, in the person of Nolan Tyner, he has created a character—the loser we love too much for our own good—just as compelling as the one Raymond Chandler devised in *The Long Goodbye*. *Cat Chaser* isn't as prodigal in its gifts of language as *Split Images*, but Mr. Leonard is incapable of cheating the reader."[55] Two particular points of pride for Leonard came from *The New Yorker*, which had announced the author as "a really first-rate writer,"[56] and the *Miami Herald*, whose mystery critic, fellow crime author Charles Willeford, was a favorite of Leonard's. "If you can't afford to buy [*Cat Chaser*], get your name on the waiting list at the public library as quickly as you can," Willeford wrote.[57]

Leonard had also taken the opportunity of speaking with the *Arizona Republic*'s Peter Rose to comment on his own recent critical success and evolving style. "Only lately, with Arbor House, have I been getting the push a book needs to sell," he told Rose. "I've been writing for thirty years, but I feel like I just started. Part of it is the recognition I'm beginning to get, and part of it is that only in the last five or six years have I developed my style to a point where I know exactly how I want to tell a story . . . I know what sound, and what I want to avoid. I know what characters are effective for me and characters to stay away from. I think I've learned what to leave out."[58] Leonard continued on that theme to the *Detroit Free Press*'s Tom Cybulski, telling the reporter, "I have a very straightforward, economic style. The writing is lean, with no unnecessary words. I'm concerned with characterization. I take ordinary people and put them in unordinary situations and see how they work themselves out. I introduce characters as I go along: the story comes out of how they act and interact . . . My people usually belong to a subculture; they are involved in crime. I like to have characters in that area. They are more interesting . . . I like to be able to keep myself out of it . . . I feel my style is more an absence of style, to let the characters make the story."

He ended with a word of advice for aspiring writers: "I would tell them to leave out the adverbs."[59]

Early plans for a film of *Cat Chaser* fell through, although producers Bill Panzer and Peter Davis did initially find interest with Silver Screen Partners. On their slate for the 1984 season, *Cat Chaser* would have been paired with *Catholic Boys*, later retitled *Heaven Help Us*—the directorial debut of Michael Dinner, who would become a major collaborator in making one of Leonard's future characters one of television's most memorable heroes.

> The best time to begin writing a book is when you least expect to, always at some time before you think you're ready to begin.

In early 1982, Leonard finished his breakfast and poured another cup of coffee. He looked at the wall calendar in the kitchen and a playful thought occurred to him: having served his seven years for taking part in the doomed Hudson's Department Store robbery, *Swag*'s Ernest "Stick" Stickley would soon be up for parole.

Leonard wondered what a guy like Stick would be up to after all these years.

CHAPTER 14

Dickens Rising, 1982–1985

> All of a sudden, I'm asked by journalists and television interviewers, "What's it like to be an overnight success after more than thirty years of writing?" . . . What they really want to know is what you've bought with all that money.
>
> Pete Hamill said I'm too old to go crazy over this sudden success . . . because my satisfaction is in doing the work, performing, not taking bows.

At the beginning of 1982, Leonard awoke to find that he couldn't see out of one eye—later diagnosed as a detached retina—forcing him to cut back on travel for the duration of two routine surgeries and a recuperation period. Ultimately, it would lead to one of the most prolific—and important—stretches of his literary career, producing two consecutive novels that would catapult his status as a major American author, and an unplanned third that would make him a superstar.

With character Jack Ryan "retired" from future sequels due to United Artists' retention of the character, the author turned, instead, to Ryan's literary successor, Ernest "Stick" Stickley—last seen being dragged off in handcuffs beside his loudmouthed partner, Frank Ryan, at the end of *Swag*. Thankfully, Leonard still had full rights to Stick, and considered a number of potential storylines for the Oklahoma-born car thief. As Leonard told journalist Peter Rose, "I feel my main characters are essentially the same guy. I'm a lot more interested in the antagonist. I think the murderer, and what happens offstage, is a lot more interesting than the cop or private eye."[1] He later elaborated to the *New York Times*' Ben Yagoda: "I put myself in [the character's] place . . . He doesn't think he's doing an evil thing. I try to see the antagonist at another time—when he sneezes, say. I see convicts sitting around talking about a baseball game. I see them as kids . . . All villains have mothers."[2]

The world had changed since Stick had been sent to Jackson State Prison. Now middle-aged, he would have to adjust to a world of yuppies and white-collar Reaganites pulling even bigger scams than he and Frank had. Much like Jack Ryan's reappearance following his own seven-year absence in *Unknown Man No. 89*, Stick would reemerge both a little older and wiser, his street smarts honed from doing hard time and having suffered personal losses: he never got to reconnect with his daughter, and his former partner, Frank Ryan, never made it out of prison. (Rather shockingly, Leonard opted to kill off Ryan offstage with an overindulgence of jailhouse potato moonshine—a topic *not* covered in the character's beloved rules for armed robbery and a clear indication that, as far as plotting, the author had more tricks up his sleeve.)

But Ernest "Stick" Stickley wasn't the only one who had evolved over the years; Leonard himself had come a long way in harnessing his style and sound. Although not a direct sequel to *Swag*, for *Stick*, Leonard concocted a multileveled plot with more ancillary characters. Much of the storyline was infused with jabs at the Hollywood establishment and the obliviousness of the "me generation"—all inspired by the author's own experiences in the film industry. With the exception of 1979's *Gunsights*, Leonard had stuck to his post–George V. Higgins dictum that his novels should take place only over the quick duration of a few days, or weeks at the most; *Stick* was no different, following the charismatic ex-con's arrival in Florida and the unforeseen obstacles that further keep him from being reunited with his daughter. While in prison, Stick had been under the protection of fellow inmate DeJohn Holmes—a towering 240-pound gang enforcer grateful for Stick's murder of bar owner Sportree during the events of *Swag*—and he had also befriended a Puerto Rican gangster, Rene Moya. Setting up camp at a cheap art deco hotel in South Beach (complete with secondhand Hawaiian shirts and beachwear, somehow perfectly catered to Stick's own style), Stick finds himself instantly on the wrong side of local drug dealers when a simple cocaine deal ends with Rene Moya double-crossed and killed before his very eyes. Determined to avenge his friend's murder, Stick hides out in upscale Bal Harbour, soon impressing local stock market millionaire Barry Stam with his knowledge of hot-wiring a Rolls-Royce. Amused, the bewildered yuppie appoints Stick as his new chauffeur, providing Stick a front-row seat for Stam's dealings with a crooked independent film producer looking to scam both his fellow investors and the IRS. With the help of sexy investment analyst Kyle McClaren—Stam's financial guru and the latest in Leonard's string of strong female characters—Stick turns the tables on drug-runner Chucky Gorman, scamming him out of $72,500 on behalf of the slain Rene Moya. Leonard wrote to Chris toward the end of March, "The armed robber, driving for Barry, pokes around in the world of high finance, million-dollar investments, looking for a score. I'm going to have to start reading *The Wall Street Journal*. Or else Peter can tell me about it."[3]

With the help of Gregg Sutter, Leonard began researching the various sorts of white-collar schemes then blowing up the national news. He began individual files for different aspects of the characters' backgrounds. A thick manila folder labeled "Cons and Frauds" held dozens of newspaper clippings and library microfilm prints on corporate fraud, money laundering, and SEC protocols for forensic accounting; a long article regarding US-based mobsters working with crooked Mexican officials to use that nation's lottery to launder dirty American currency into "clean" pesos went unused.[4] For accurately replicating the snobbish and condescending social circles in which Barry Stam and his investor buddies would travel, Leonard jotted down ideas for their demographic's trendy lingo ("*He has all the charm of a stopped-up sink*" and "*He couldn't lead a group in silent prayer*").[5]

For Stam's in-depth conversations regarding his finances, however, Leonard put even more effort into the educational background and career of Kyle McClaren, with her strategic knowledge of wealth management far superior to any other character's in the book, and labeled the section, "Stuff Stick Hears." Dual articles from the time, *Newsweek*'s "Women and the Executive Suite," and *Business Week*'s "Women: The New Venture Capitalists," provided the author with real-life examples of the type of woman with whom Stick would choose for his partner in both crime and romance.[6] When prompted to explain her first name, Kyle reveals it to actually be "Emma"—a playful reference to Leonard and Joan's dog.

Leonard soon spoke about his long road to writing *Stick* with Lloyd Sachs of the *Chicago Sun-Times*, whose column, Writers At Work, emphasized the literary creative process. "Early on with *Stick*, Arbor House wanted to know what it was about. And I said, 'I don't know yet, it hasn't gotten going' . . . And I agree that some of my women [characters] have been lacking. But I'm getting better with them; I've been reading pages to my wife and I can tell from her expression whether they're [accurate]. So far, so good."[7]

As the spring rolled on, Leonard gathered momentum on multiple projects—including another long-gestating assignment that had finally gained traction. He wrote to Chris at the end of May: "Monday, I have to put *Stick* aside and write, finally, the *Rosary Murders* script." After years of production hell, Leonard had finally gotten the greenlight to put pen to paper on his film adaptation of William X. Kienzle's 1979 crime thriller, and he had begun his own location scouting for the script. At the time, however, Leonard was exactly "mid-stride" on *Stick* and, begrudgingly, wouldn't return to it for another two months.[8] Upon its completion, however, he immediately sent it over to H. N. Swanson and publisher Don Fine. The latter instantly circled back with his excitement over the material. "I'm at home dictating this and I have a little over a hundred pages to go of Dutch's *Stick*," Fine wrote to Swanson on August 25. "So far, it's not only far and away the best thing that I've ever read of Dutch's—certainly of the books we've published and the ones I can remember—it is one of the handful of best novels ever written in the last twenty-five years . . . [Leonard is] rooted in the reality of living and his craft and his talent, and anybody who can write like these 220-odd pages that I've gone through so far this morning ain't got no problems about getting out of touch with where it's at." He added, "Swanie, this one has got to be a movie, I'm sure you agree with me . . . But in any case, if I may be so bold, the ideal guy to play Stick—even though he is slicked up too much and would need somebody beside himself to direct him and knock off the overly glitzy edges—is Burt Reynolds."[9]

Once *Stick* was put into galleys, Fine sent copies to numerous high-caliber authors he suspected would share his enthusiasm: James Dickey, Arthur Miller, Irwin Shaw, William Styron, Gay Talese, and John Updike among them—although Leonard admittedly hadn't read much of their works. At the time, he had actually been enjoying authors more associated with "Dirty Realism," including Raymond Carver, Jim Harrison, Bobbie Ann Mason, and Jayne Anne Phillips.[10] Fine also apprehensively sent a copy to Norman Mailer, unsure how the notoriously hot-headed author would respond to Stick's personal kinship with real-life killer—and Mailer's literary protégé—John Henry Abbott.[11]

Fine's and Swanson's combined initiatives paid off quickly, making a sale to Universal Pictures months before the hardcover was due to hit store shelves. Despite reports that both Paul Newman and Clint Eastwood had dispatched representatives to place their own bids for the property, the *Hollywood Reporter*'s Hank Grant announced on February 8, "Hot off the galleys, Universal's laid out 350Gs for Elmore Leonard's new thriller novel, *Stick*. Arbor House publishes it Feb. 28."[12] Under the new agreement, Leonard was paid a cool $100,000 for the screenplay as an option—giving the studio a full year to decide whether or not to launch production; if they opted not to, Leonard would keep the initial payment and retain character rights. If *Stick* were to actually become a major motion picture, however, Leonard would get an additional $200,000 for the screen rights, plus 5 percent of the film's net profits (and an additional $50,000 if no additional screenwriter was needed). There was a sole caveat to the deal, however: the studio would retain the rights to the character of Stick until mid-1986.[13]

As anticipated by Fine and Swanson, *Stick* was released to solid reviews and sales; the majority of mainstream critics continued their shared self-revelation regarding Leonard's long career and current success. "Leonard is the real thing," wrote the *Washington Post*'s Jonathan Yardley.[14] However, nearly half of the reviewers made it clear that Leonard's literary achievements were matched only by the apparent success he'd been having with the Hollywood establishment. In a review that was equal parts praise for the source material and enthusiasm for the already announced feature film adaptation, the *Daytona Beach-News Journal* reported, "[Leonard's] kind of writing required intelligence and concentration. It's the way Ernest Hemingway wrote when he was at his best—and it's probably why he was unable to turn out more than five-hundred words of good writing on an average day."

The review ran under the not-so-subtle headline, "*A Plot Just Right for a Burt Reynolds Romp.*"[15]

March 25, 1983

Dear Chris,

Well, Roy Scheider was a real guy, fun to have lunch with and talk about movies. He had a plate full of lox, while I had the half a roast chicken with bacon, and Jennings [Lang] had a dozen oysters

> *and a steak. Roy sat with his back to the room, an expensive place called Laurent. (When Alfred Hitchcock was asked his opinion as to the best restaurant, Hitch replied, "Where they know you.")*
>
> *We had fun casting the picture, suggesting actors for the different roles; but mostly we talked about who should direct. We want a straightforward guy who loves the story and does not spend a lot of time in his head. So if Universal doesn't elect to go with someone like Tom Selleck, the male Farrah Fawcett, or tight-jawed Clint Eastwood, Scheider will be our guy.*[16]

From their very first readings of the material, both Swanson and publisher Don Fine had agreed that an A-list star like Burt Reynolds was precisely what was needed to solidify Leonard's status as a consummate literary success story: an author with a hit novel and an even bigger hit film based upon it. And a major star attached to a potential movie *series* was even better. Swanson and Fine remained more optimistic than the author himself.

By the beginning of 1983, Leonard and Michigan-based filmmaker Tom Brank had dissolved their partnership, Hat Trick Productions, and all of Leonard's time spent writing and rewriting drafts of screenplays of *The Hunted* (as *Hat Trick*), *Gold Coast* (as *Seascape*), *Unknown Man No. 89* (as *Happy Hour*), *City Primeval* (as *Hang Tough*), and endless revisions of *Jesus Saves!* and *American Flag* had amounted to little more than fodder for his novels. Early plans for a *Cat Chaser* adaptation had floundered, and numerous studio executives had indicated that the very action and thriller elements that had made the novel *Split Images* a literary hit were no longer what movie audiences were looking for. After half a decade of negotiations, Leonard had finally been able to begin his adaptation of William X. Kienzle's *The Rosary Murders* while finishing up *Stick*, although no updates indicated when that film would go into production.

But just as Swanson began urging Leonard to pivot his screenwriting abilities more toward the widening vanguard of network and cable television (HBO had recently launched, inspiring scores of writers and producers to pitch original content otherwise cast aside in favor of big-budget blockbusters), a more lucrative strategy to get Leonard paid for both his novel and screenplay became advantageous—largely thanks to the author's newfound fame. Universal Pictures' acquisition of *Stick* was no different, although the experience would prove to be the first in a trifecta of well-publicized incidents that would, ultimately, lead Leonard to finally pen his long-promised "Hollywood" novel. And Don Fine would soon get an unpleasant surprise, taking him out of his ringside seat for the *Stick* film production. "Donald I. Fine has been dismissed as publisher of Arbor House, the company he founded in 1969 and sold to the Hearst Corporation in 1978," the *New York Times* reported on October 26, 1983. "Mr. Fine said that he was dismissed Monday at a meeting that he thought had been called to discuss his effort to buy Arbor House back . . . 'I had no inkling,' Mr. Fine said of his dismissal. 'I was absolutely amazed.'"[17]

However, Fine and Swanson got their wish regarding *Stick*: in July, Burt Reynolds and his entourage flew to South Florida to scout locations for his planned adaptation. His representative, David Gershenson, soon told the *South Florida Sun-Sentinel* the film was expected to begin principal photography the first week of October. (At the time, Reynolds had directed three of his own studio films—1976's *Gator*, *The End* two years later, and *Sharkey's Machine* in 1981. While all three had been critical disappointments, Reynolds's own star power made his contractual projects—such as the *Smokey and the Bandit* action comedies and 1978's *Hooper*—major box office hits.) Reached for comment, Leonard told reporter Bill Kelley, "I've met with Reynolds twice, in Jupiter and Los Angeles, and spoken to him on the phone whenever he's called with an idea for the script. Fortunately, he's got good ideas . . . I don't expect the film to be much different from the novel, especially since Reynolds told me he really liked the book."[18]

Leonard and his entire family had been invited to the set by Reynolds himself—the first time the kids had been able to rub shoulders with some of the celebrities who revered their father's work. Christopher Leonard later recalled, "When we all arrived in Florida, before we even visited the set, Reynolds's 'man'—his assistant or something—came up to our room and said, 'Okay, so when you meet Mr. Reynolds, whatever you do, do not mention his hair. Do not mention his wigs'—like that would be the first thing on our minds."[19] The family was also on hand the night Reynolds filmed a scene depicting Stick as a bartender at an upscale soiree, resulting in his threatening one man with a bucket of water believed to be gasoline. After the shoot, the Leonard kids met the rest of the cast, which Bill Leonard remembered well. "We met Reynolds, George Segal, and Candice Bergen. My brother Chris and I thought it would be funny to mess with Candice Bergen a little bit, since everyone was fawning all over her. So, Chris took my camera and went up to her and said, 'Hey, can we get a picture?' and she obviously thought we meant a photo *with* her. But, instead, Chris handed her the camera so she could just snap a photo of just him and I—and she looked shocked that we weren't just falling over to meet her like everyone else. The look on her face was hysterical. Later, she told my dad, 'You have some *very* interesting children.'"[20]

Reynolds's production faced numerous challenges, including inclement weather around South Florida and constant demands for rewrites to Leonard's script. Reynolds reportedly clashed with additional screenwriter Joseph Stinson after Leonard himself walked away from the production. After completing principal photography, studio executives were dissatisfied with director Reynolds's take on the material, demanding more action and an entirely new ending. Ultimately, the film's release was delayed for extensive—and expensive—reshoots, much to Reynolds's own aggravation. According to reports at the time, the reshoots inflated the budget to nearly double its initial $15 million price tag. Before the reshoots, however, Leonard was already shaken by the cut of the film to which he'd been privy. In the summer of 1984, he and Joan had visited Los Angeles for meetings with his old friend, producer Walter Mirisch, and actor Sidney Poitier for a proposed sequel to *In the Heat of the Night*, which Leonard had been touted to write. While on the Universal Pictures lot, they were invited to a screening of Reynolds's first cut of *Stick*—an experience the author would never forget. He later told *Rolling Stone*'s Diane Shah, "I saw the picture on June 11 at Universal [and] the next day I was up at six a.m., writing a letter to Reynolds, who directed it. Maybe my material is not adaptable to the screen." According to Leonard, he was still stumped on what to write to Reynolds three hours later while having breakfast with Joan at the studio's coffee shop. When Sidney Poitier stopped by to greet them, Leonard asked the seasoned actor his advice. "He told me to be honest," Leonard later recalled. "I was honest for four and a half pages. Double-spaced."[21]

June 12, 1984

Dear Burt,

The one thing I'm certain of and have been from the beginning: you are Stick. You sound exactly like the Stick I heard writing it. You carry the picture . . .

> *But when I view the picture I see, too often, actors acting, actors hitting the wrong word, mugging, overstain or elaborating on a punchline, ad-libbing cliches, setting a record for the frequent use of "asshole" . . . I'm not in a position to question the director's intention or presume to know what might appeal to an audience, so I didn't say anything . . .*
>
> *Maybe the problem lies in interpreting the kind of material I write . . . Producers read my work and ask if it's a drama or comedy and I say it's real life; ideally, you do it with a straight face and hope the audience gets it . . .*
>
> *I'm glad you're a pro and I can say these things to you. I'm not going to lie.*[22]

Leonard forwarded a duplicate copy to H. N. Swanson ten days later. "This is the letter I sent to Reynolds giving him my reactions to *Stick*," he wrote. "So far, I haven't heard a word from him, and maybe I never will. He might be so used to getting praise from people he works with, he may not know how to handle something like this."[23] He got his answer soon enough: Reynolds took to the media to air his own grievances. As Leonard never forgot, once the doomed second version of *Stick* hit theaters in 1985 to rancid reviews, the actor-director appeared on CBS television, infamously telling host Phyllis George, "I thought [Leonard] was a beautiful guy—then he turned on me."[24] In reality, Leonard had kept most of his greatest frustrations within his inner circle, only later divulging the numerous problems that had plagued the film's production. Sean Mitchell of the *Los Angeles Herald Examiner* later commented, "For an author like Leonard, on the cusp of commanding a whole new audience, it might seem that the timing of *Stick*'s release couldn't be better. Except that, from the looks of the result up on the screen, it couldn't be worse. The budding legend of Elmore Leonard, Crime Writer No. 1, now must weather the exposure of a movie that can be compared unfavorably to *Smokey and the Bandit*."[25]

"[My father] was so vocal about it," Bill Leonard later remembered. "I think he had been pretty happy with the early Western adaptations, but nothing contemporary had turned out right. He hated almost every adaptation—and he especially hated *Stick*. He'd say, 'No one understands my characters. They're not *trying* to be funny, they don't *know* they're funny. They just are. You can't cut to a reaction of people laughing!' And no one seemed to understand that."[26]

Critics tended to side with much of Leonard's early observations. "Elmore Leonard's *Stick* could have made a terrific movie, possibly even a terrific movie starring Burt Reynolds, although Mr. Reynolds is more than a little off-base for the title role," wrote the *New York Times*' Janet Maslin. "Nonetheless, he has been cast as Stick by a director who should have known better, that director being Mr. Reynolds himself." She continued, "Mr. Reynolds hangs onto the upper hand at any cost. He stars in showy exercise sequences that have little to do with the story. He directs Candice Bergen, as a glamorous fiscal advisor to George Segal's cigar-chomping, filthy-rich financier, to melt at the very sight of him. When he is hired as the financier's chauffeur, he allots himself a nattier wardrobe than that of his boss. And the dialogue is unfailingly flattering to Stick . . . Through all of this, Mr. Reynolds displays little understanding of the very good reasons why audiences usually like him."[27] The same day, Duane Byrge of the *Hollywood Reporter* offered, "The biggest fall in this film belongs to co-screenwriter Elmore Leonard, whose lean, gritty page-turning novel has been transposed into this bloated, synthetic uninvolving film . . . In Leonard's brilliant novel, the difficulty of Reynolds's readjustment to civilian life is both vivid and poignant."[28] Leonard, however, told *American Film* magazine, "I read somewhere that Bernard Malamud didn't leave his apartment for three weeks after *The Natural* opened—so I'm thinking maybe I should enter a Trappist monastery." He added, "It's all an experience. I don't make a career out of one book or one screenplay. I'm going to do others."[29] Burt Reynolds, however, didn't direct another film for nearly fifteen years.

Not long after the film's release, Leonard hung a copy of its theatrical promotional poster in his office. "*The only thing he couldn't do is stick to the rules*," read the tagline. Soon, his family noticed that someone had crossed out "*rules*" and playfully substituted the more appropriate word "*script*."

Neither Leonard nor Joan would admit which one of them had come up with the cathartic joke.

With the two-book contract with Arbor House now fulfilled, Leonard was again a free agent.

Swanson soon organized a high-profile auction among publishers *and* film producers alike for Leonard's next property. "As noted here August 19, Elmore Leonard's next novel, *LaBrava*, was put on the block, with a floor of $600,000 set by the H. N. Swanson agency," reported Paul S. Nathan in *Publishers Weekly* on September 2, 1983. "Well and good, but because the floor had not been established by a bid by a would-be buyer and no one was prepared to go that high, let alone higher, the book was knocked down for $400,000. 'Swanie' sounded pleased nonetheless when he disclosed the amount over the phone. 'It's still a good price,' he said, and one had to agree, especially since it's $50,000 more than Universal paid for Leonard's latest, *Stick*. Also five-percent of *LaBrava*'s profits as a film, or from any spinoff thereof, will be due Leonard under the new contract." Nathan added, "Again, Universal is the buyer, and Walter Mirisch, who made a movie of Leonard's *Mr. Majestyk* in 1974, will be the producer."[30]

Although Arbor House had paid nearly three hundred thousand dollars *less* for two books only a few years ago, the publishing house had acquiesced and retained their new celebrity author. And while Leonard's contract was a lucrative one, it also came with the same assignment that had caused so much grief with *Stick*'s director, Burt Reynolds—the screenplay. Of the full amount, $150,000 was for the adaptation of *LaBrava*, which once again opened the kitchen door to too many cooks. However, Leonard could breathe a sigh of relief that he'd be working again with producer and friend Walter Mirisch. With *LaBrava*, both hoped to rekindle the easy chemistry that had made *Mr. Majestyk* a positive experience for them both.[31] Mirisch later wrote, "Upon my return to Universal, I presented [producer] Ned Tanen with . . . a book, *LaBrava*, that had been sent to me by Elmore Leonard. It was a most unusual novel with a strong central character. It had the values of a 1940s film noir, and yet was modern. Bob Rehme, who had by then replaced Ned Tanen as head of production at Universal, agreed to acquire it, and we made a deal with Leonard to write the screenplay."[32] (Tanen would soon become the namesake for the antagonist for another Universal blockbuster, 1985's *Back to the Future*—a dubious homage from director Robert Zemeckis and screenwriter Bob Gale after their particularly disastrous meeting with the aggressive executive; Tanen would also "coincidentally" go on to produce the 1994 comedy *Guarding Tess*—an uncredited repurposing of Leonard's still-unproduced *LaBrava*'s key Secret Service subplot.)

Leonard told journalist Lloyd Sachs, "I'm interested in black-and-white photos of the seamy side, like the ones that Danny Lyon did in 1962 of convicts, bikers, and prostitutes . . . When I started, I had my antagonist as the photographer, going back West to shoot cowboys—a role I could almost put myself in, going back to the Westerns. My problem was that I had more fun doing him than Stick, who became more passive. I thought,

'Why not take Stick, who has done all sorts of things, and project him into the situation?'"[33] He elaborated to *USA Today*'s Bruce Cook, "It's another one like *Stick* . . . The trick in writing is to remain calm, try not to choke, avoid adverbs and use not more than five exclamation points, if that, in three-hundred pages."[34]

> If I were to fade back to a safe place, say, just this side of obscurity, at least I'd have more time to write.

While Leonard handled the brunt of his Hollywood ills, his researcher, Gregg Sutter, continued to work on the data-gathering aspects of the new novel. "[Stick] was to be working for a private detective keeping tabs on a female rock singer, who in turn would hire Stick as her bodyguard," Sutter later recalled, adding that Leonard had used feminist punk rocker Patti Smith as inspiration for the object of Stick's protection, tentatively named "Moon"—although the story quickly evolved into a new one in which Stick would, instead, become a professional photographer.

Indeed, Leonard's earliest concepts for what would eventually become *LaBrava* went as far back as the previous year, with initial plans to focus on a photographer as the main protagonist.

> September 16, 1982
>
> *I think I want to write about a photographer, a professional who shoots ordinary people like lo-riders, cotton-pickers, drunken Apache Indians, and whores in Galveston. He's also [known] for shooting celebrities, stars, but he's an independent guy and won't do it unless he likes them. I don't know what happens, if he sees something in a [photo], as in* Blowup, *and it draws him into a search for something . . . I also want to explore the difference between commercial work (craft) and art.*
>
> *Joe Brava.*
>
> *That's the first time I've written his name.*
>
> *I was thinking he might be from Tucson. Or he might be from New Orleans.*[35]

After a few weeks of toying with Joe Brava's background as a renowned nature photographer based in Tucson, Arizona, however, Leonard scrapped the entire lot and attempted to place Stick back into the mix:

November 15, 1982

In Miami, Stick does a surveillance job for Marshall Sisco the private eye, takes a picture of a couple slipping furtively into a motel and wins first prize with it in the Miami Herald's *annual photo contest. Stick has a gallery showing (with his shots of Cubans and old Jewish people on South Beach), a coffee-table book of his photos published, and becomes somewhat famous. He goes to Tucson to shoot town and reservation Apaches and gets another assignment from Sisco, to keep an eye on a girl rock star who has a home up in the mountains and whose life has been threatened, or something . . .*[36]

January 22, 1983

. . . [United Artists has] exclusive rights to Stick, the character, until sometime in 1986. So I'm going to have to take Stick out of the photography book (I'm 60 pages into it) and send in Joe Brava as a substitute. Which is okay, now that I'm resigned myself to it.

Joe Brava could turn out to be a strange but likeable guy.[37]

It had taken Leonard a full month's work to decide to discontinue the adventures of Ernest "Stick" Stickley. Instead, Leonard worked up a fun and unlikely juxtaposition for Joe LaBrava as a nationally recognized photographer of artistic renown against his background as a former IRS investigator–cum–Secret Service agent. He soon elaborated on the character's background: having retired from his government post at the Miami field office, LaBrava eventually indulged a growing interest in photography that began during his long nights conducting stakeouts of suspected counterfeiters. Spending his free time taking black-and-white portraits and candid shots of the various residents along SW Eighth Street in Little Havana, LaBrava had the serendipitous fortune to have his camera handy when two men threw an innocent man over a freeway bridge—and the photo landed on the cover of *Newsweek*.

Before dispatching Gregg Sutter to Florida for the in-depth research needed to bring LaBrava's South Beach stomping ground to life, Leonard reached out to his private investigator friend Bill Marshall. At Leonard's behest, Marshall had taken just over two dozen street scenes of the urban landscape, including the Cardoza and Alamac hotels (often frequented by elderly retirees beneath the structures' respective canopies), the Club

Deuce Bar (a known hangout for the LGBTQ+ community, and a perfect location for quirky antagonist Cundo Rey's moonlight gig as a go-go dancer), and various bars and notable nontouristy spots.[38]

As had been his regular practice, Leonard kept an in-depth notebook-journal as he worked on the book, then still entitled *Shooter*. In his earliest incarnation, the protagonist seemed to reflect Leonard's own inner feelings regarding his recent mainstream success—and the inevitable critical scrutiny that followed. Before settling on the Secret Service background, Leonard had written, "Brava was doing a Chevy truck story in Alamosa, Colorado, when he met the Centennial Chevy dealer who said, 'I never met a lowlander yet I didn't have to put to bed.' Brava murders him with beer and cognac; wipes him out." He added rhetorically, "Is photography like tracing? But you don't set out to create art. You let someone else judge it, make that judgement." A second section, headlined, "The Idea of the Fear of Success," included Leonard's note: "Brava has reached a point where he takes himself too seriously and realizes it; takes everything personally." As mentioned to Chris, Leonard studied the work of photojournalist Danny Lyon, cribbing from the "artist's statement" within Lyon's coffee-table portfolio, and putting them into Joe LaBrava's creative aims.[39] (When brainstorming the possible art books that would have pushed protagonist Joe LaBrava to critical acclaim, Leonard playfully assembled an autobiographical list directly inspired by his own career: *On the Line*, a series of action shots of assembly-line workers in a Detroit automobile plant; *Jews—The Chosen Ones*, a collection of portraits of the many locals and refugees around Israel; *Let's Hear It for Jesus*, a late-1970s photographic study of born-again Christians, "Jesus Freaks," and faith healers; *Cowboys and Indians*, which would include portraits of the same lo-riders and professional rodeo competitors who had grabbed Leonard's imagination during his "lost weekend" of July 1974; and *The Americanos*, for which he noted, "Looks like Cowboys and Indians, but isn't the same thing. It's tongue-in-cheek and Joe's publisher doesn't think it works."[40])

Leonard introduced readers to the character of LaBrava himself through the praise of his friend, the much older Maurice Zola, who, much like his young protégé, made a name for himself as a photojournalist snapping away at a catastrophe—in his case, the worst railroad collision in Florida's history, during the same 1935 hurricane in the Florida Keys that had sent famous resident Ernest Hemingway packing for

Ketchum, Idaho. From that, Zola had been scouted by Roosevelt's Farm Administration, collecting photographs of Americans impoverished by the Great Depression, ultimately retiring to a prosperous life as the owner of valuable South Beach real estate properties. Gregg Sutter recalled, "As a dialogue began to open up between Maurice and LaBrava, the woman in the middle changed from a rock singer named Moon to a retired actress named Jean Shaw, star of imaginary film noirs as *Deadfall, Nightshade,* and *Obituary* . . . I had volumes of material on film noir to give Elmore and, one afternoon in 1984, I brought my VCR over to his house so that Elmore, his wife Joan, and I could watch Jacques Tourneur's *Out of the Past*, featuring an all-time great spidery performance by Jane Greer." Although Leonard didn't cite her directly, he had been quoting his lifelong crush, Lauren Bacall, since his time in the Navy, and her demure femme fatale persona also worked its way into the enigmatic Jean Shaw. As an homage to the film noir genre, Leonard gave the novel's true twist to Shaw herself: having seduced the younger, star-struck LaBrava early on, it's revealed that Shaw plans to dupe Maurice Zola out of $600,000 with her willing accomplice, another of Leonard's signature redneck goons, Richard Nobles, and his own (somewhat willing) partner, Cundo Rey. Ironically, her elaborate scheme turns out to be based on a screenplay idea she'd once unsuccessfully pitched to Columbia Pictures cofounder and film producer Harry Cohn—as legendary for his blockbuster productions as he was for sexually harassing and exploiting his leading ladies.[41]

With the novel set in place and the story itself sold before he'd even put pen to paper, Leonard had only one challenge in front of him—the ending. The story's climax—which saw the (apparent) end of Cundo Rey—had come from a suggestion Israeli producer Zohar Bar Am made to Leonard in August 1976: "*A personal remark that might serve your next book. You asked me once why the pistol was put in a green plastic bag. The reason is very logical, so it can be used in an emergency, through the plastic bag.*"[42] Leonard later revealed to *The New Black Mask Quarterly*, however, "In *LaBrava*, when I was about thirty pages from the end, I said to my wife, Joan, 'Okay, here are the three ways this book can end. These are the three things that could happen to Jean Shaw. She could be arrested; she could die; she could get away with it.' My wife said, 'What if . . .' and gave me a fourth option. I thought, 'Oh, my God. That's perfect.' And it was the one I used."[43]

LaBrava was released by Arbor House toward the end of 1983, allowing ample time for *Stick* to run the full hardcover gamut before its Avon paperback edition. Like its near-immediate predecessor, Leonard's follow-up novel proved a hit among critics and the ever-growing legion of devotees. In *USA Today*, critic Robert Wilson zeroed in on Leonard's strengths as a social commentator, making the first of numerous comparisons to famous Classicists that the author would receive in the coming year: "*LaBrava* is such pure pleasure that I found myself almost dangerously grateful to its author. In weak moments, I even wanted to compare Leonard to Balzac."[44] *Newsweek*'s Peter S. Prescott continued on that theme, yet emphasized a more contemporary comparison. "If a paternity case can turn upon a blood sample," Prescott wrote, "the blood shed in Elmore Leonard's new novel suggests that he's the legitimate heir of James M. Cain."[45]

In the *Houston Post*, critic Richard Fuller added to the novel's ambition, commenting, "Call it vernacular or the American slanguage, Elmore 'Dutch' Leonard does it as well as any American writer these days. My only fear is that he's gotten so good that a half-dozen doctoral candidates are 'working' on him, the way they've Ph.D.'d film noir."[46]

Leonard soon spoke with the *West Palm Beach Post*'s Randy Schultz about his critical winning streak. "Seven years short of his sixty-fifth birthday, Leonard is a hot item," Schultz wrote. To this, Leonard responded, "I think it's ideal, now that I'm here. But if you told me thirty years ago that it would take this long, I don't know if I would have stuck around."[47]

> Quite unexpectedly, in January, 1984, my wife Joan and I were invited to Swanie's home, actually to walk inside for the first time . . . they talked about movie stars who'd been invited here to parties, Swanie showing the patio where Scott and Zelda had danced.
>
> Finally, I happened to mention that in the thirty years Swanie had been representing me, he had driven me past the house twice, but this was the first time I had ever been inside. Swanie said, "Well, you weren't making any real money until lately."

While Leonard was putting the finishing touches on *LaBrava*, producer Walter Mirisch was still working with the legendary star of his

1967 smash hit, *In the Heat of the Night*, Sidney Poitier, in developing the film's latest sequel. (Although the two had already made a successful trilogy about Poitier's tough-as-nails cop Virgil Tibbs, Poitier was coming out of a seven-year acting hiatus and sought a guaranteed comeback vehicle.) However, neither were satisfied with screenwriter Ernest Tidyman's early drafts and quickly considered enlisting Leonard's help.

Unfortunately, they hit a snag with copyright holder United Artists. "Walter Mirisch went to [United Artists] with his idea of making a sequel to *In the Heat of the Night*," Leonard reported to Swanson on October 17, 1983. "They were not interested and would not let him take the rights to it somewhere else. So he has suggested we work up a new story with Sidney Poitier as a big-city cop and asked me to write him a letter covering this proposal . . . If Walter's unable to make a development deal somewhere, I still see a book now with an Atlantic City setting, though the main character would probably not be a cop."[48]

Leonard had already had a promising meeting with the lead actor and had written Mirisch, "We talked about Sidney as a homicide detective drawn into conflict with people in high places who are extremely wealthy . . . They will misjudge his easy manner, dismiss him as a 'polite boy' who's certainly not a threat. And by the time they realize their mistake, someone is going to be looking down the impersonal barrel of Sidney's .38 special. With variations, that's been the basic structure of nearly all my novels." He continued, "At this point, I would lean toward planning most of the action to take place in the Atlantic City area. It looks like a movie set and isn't much bigger . . . I asked my researcher to take a quick look at the Philadelphia-Atlantic City crime scene and he came up with extraordinary material without digging much past the surface. There are wild things going on over there."[49]

The combined efforts of Leonard's own reading and Sutter's research had yielded an embarrassment of riches when it came to Atlantic City's criminal underworld. (As Sutter later recalled, "Elmore thought that maybe some wealthy Philadelphian, who partied with Atlantic City girls, could become involved in a Chappaquiddick-like incident that would result in murder."[50]) At the beginning of January, Sutter was dispatched to Atlantic City for five days, armed with a list of questions for local law enforcement: their preferred firearms, stakeout procedures, morgue protocols for viewing a discovered body, and the likelihood that an officer from another jurisdiction could work alongside them on a case such as in Leonard's evolving narrative. (He'd also brought copies of *City Primeval* and *Split Images* for the officers, as both books demonstrated the level of accuracy Leonard was seeking.) Sutter set up camp at the Holmhurst Hotel on Pennsylvania Avenue and met with officers from the Major Crimes Unit, then scoured "casino row" for more local color and details. He visited all nine casinos, then took photographs of the spacious, modern high-rise buildings along Absecon Island and the affluent homes in Longport Borough. When he returned to Michigan five days later, he had assembled a comprehensive briefing book on par with Bill Marshall's usual Florida investigative packages—nearly two hundred color photographs of possible sites for the novel.[51]

The following week, Leonard had his first joint meeting with Mirisch and Poitier in Los Angeles. He presented them with story ideas that he had hatched from Sutter's trip, impressing both the producer and star enough for further brainstorming. Toward the end of March, Leonard flew to Atlantic City with Sutter, and met up with journalist Anthony J. Lukas from *GQ* magazine. Based on Sutter's recommendation, both Leonard and Lukas were booked at the Resorts International Hotel and Casino. The trio sat and discussed the project with two of the officers from the Atlantic County Major Crimes Unit, James Barber and William McIntyre.

"Let's say that Iris takes a header out of a condominium up on Ventnor," Leonard mused at lunch, "but maybe the cause of death wasn't the fall. Maybe she was dead already. How soon would you find that out?"

"We'd send pieces of organs and blood to the state medical examiner in Newark," Captain Barber told him. "He'd make the final determination."

"Where would Teddy take her?"

"Well, there's a place down under the boardwalk where the bums go to drink," Barber said. "We found a body under there a few months ago."

In the Resorts' Rendezvous Lounge, Leonard and Lukas caught the performance of a pop act calling themselves Michaelina, then Lukas hung back the next morning while Leonard met with William Weinberger, the president of Bally's Park Place Casino-Hotel. Leonard later recalled, "I was introduced to the president of one of the casinos; then he handed me over to a woman who was in charge of surveillance. She took me into the monitoring room where they look at the monitors of every foot of the casino floor. Then she took me to the eye-in-the-sky, where you're standing right over the tables, where you look directly down on the play."[52]

Leonard returned from Atlantic City on March 23 with all he needed for his story. Although by all accounts, he and Sidney Poitier got along well, their collaboration ended not long after. As Sutter later recalled, "Once Elmore became locked into his kind of story, the sequel idea fell apart and Poitier told Elmore, 'Go write a book.'"[53]

It was exactly what Leonard wanted to hear.

> *Dear Swanie,*
>
> *I don't understand what appears your increasing desire to get me into TV writing . . .*
>
> *They want plot. But I don't sit down and plot, I concentrate on people and let the plot happen. They want formula, and formula turns me off . . . If there's nothing on network television I feel is worth watching, how can I write for it?*
>
> *I have to please me first and make money second, and I know how to do that.*
>
> *I WANT TO WRITE A BOOK.*
>
> *—Best, Dutch*[54]

Leonard began his process with two separate notebooks—the "field journal" he had taken to Atlantic City, and a larger, master notebook for the itemized details pruned from both his and Sutter's collaborative research. Although Leonard had set aside *In the Heat of the Night*'s Virgil Tibbs as his protagonist, he retained the character's deep moral code and outsider status. Reaching as far back as his original notes and drafts for 1970's abandoned *Picket Line* project, Leonard repurposed his union leader turned political activist "Vincent Mora," and used the name for his Tibbs replacement. For the novel's title, Leonard had initially narrowed it down to four—*Under the Gun, Rough Trade, Spades,* and *Boardwalk*—before an unrelated film with the same name as the latter left Leonard scrambling for an alternate. "The *Boardwalk* film made in 1979 with Lee Strasberg and Ruth Gordon keeps appearing on television and I'm getting worried about it," he wrote to Swanson.[55]

Leonard had prepared for the Atlantic City trip by combing through nearly a hundred articles clipped and photocopied by Gregg Sutter.

Countless instances of casino malfeasance inspired the inner workings of newly named fictional casino manager Jackie Garbo's world, while additional reports of the mafia's presence within Atlantic City shaped the underground politics through which protagonist Vincent Mora would have to navigate.[56] Among the most useful of those articles to Leonard ran in the October 31 issue of *New York* magazine, "Money Laundering: How Crooks Recycle $80 Billion a Year in Dirty Money," by investigative journalist Nicholas Pileggi—only a year away from his groundbreaking collaboration with real-life mob enforcer Henry Hill, *Wiseguy*, which would be adapted into Martin Scorsese's gangster epic, *Goodfellas*.[57]

When Leonard first began to convert his notes for the Sidney Poitier film into a standalone novel, one of his first acts was to construct an antagonist who would take the place of the high-ranking political and casino officials originally intended. In his earliest form, the psychopathic killer-rapist was closer in personality and background to a real-life counterpart, convicted killer Daniel Lee, even in the character's having served in the National Guard: "No, my conscience doesn't bother me," Lee had told Glen Macnow of the *Detroit Free Press*. "I'm not guilt-ridden. To say I felt bad about something I did would suggest I had power over my actions. But it was not in my power to prevent the rapes or the violence. So I'm not sorry . . . When I look back, I think my sexual deviation was aimed at hurting my parents . . . When I realized I could hurt [my mother] by doing bad things, well, I went all out and used it as a form of vengeance." In and out of jail, Lee committed his first rape while his wife was in the hospital recuperating from the birth of their first child.[58] Leonard saved all the background information and infused elements into the twisted psychology of the then-named Teddy Kozerek, even writing to attorney Bradley Schram for information on the judicial process for the types of "heavy sexual offenses" that would pepper Kozerek's fictional rap sheet.[59] With the details in place, Leonard began his biography of Kozerek, emphasizing his connection to Vincent Mora and the seeds of their longstanding feud:

> On July 25th, 1967, the second day of the Detroit riots (in which 43 people were killed, 700 known injured): Sgt. Vincent Mora, Detroit Police Homicide, comes up against Teddy Kozerek and several other National Guardsmen from Flint, Mich. who are

> bent on "killing some niggers" while on patrol duty and ripping off anything of value . . . Vincent Mora confronts Kozerek and three other guardsmen. They put their guns on Vincent to kill him and Vincent shoots all four of them, severely wounding Teddy Kozerek . . . In July of 1982, Teddy Kozerek is released from prison having served a minimum 14 years. All this time, he's had one thing on his mind—revenge—get Vincent Mora.

Leonard only had one major change to the character—his name. As *GQ* journalist Anthony Lukas later noted, "He often takes his names from people he encounters. Teddy Magyk, the antagonist in *Glitz*, takes his from Eddie Mogck, a sailor with whom Dutch served in World War II."[60] Where once he had created one of his most memorable villains in Clement Mansell—"The Oklahoma Wildman"—Leonard now presented to readers his embodiment of a realistic, perfect evil: "*the Magyk Man*."

For Mora's love interest, Leonard shelved the female rock star angle and revamped the character—known then only as "Moon"—into a sultry casino lounge singer.[61] Having noted the band's repertoire, Leonard renamed the fictional songstress Linda Moon for country-rocker Linda Ronstadt.[62] Leonard had also elaborated to *The New Black Mask Quarterly* his new approach to creating scenes from multiple character perspectives—a tactic inspired by the multi-security camera setup used in casinos' surveillance rooms. To Leonard, the security team appeared to be watching one ongoing narrative from different perspectives: "In *Glitz*, for example, it was in experimenting with different points of view in writing the same scene," he later recalled. "I would write it from one character's point of view and again from another character's point of view—and find that it had a lot more life in it, that it was a little more colorful, more interesting . . . I'm going to continue to do that."[63]

He had also chosen a finalized title for the novel: *Glitz*.

As had been his schedule since signing with Arbor House, Leonard had it completed by the middle of the summer, with the galleys proofed and sent to the publisher on August 27. He began a screenplay adaptation only three days later, completing the first draft by September 22 and quickly sending it to both Swanson and Mirisch.

Over a week before the galleys were even completed, *Publishers Weekly* reported, "Elmore Leonard's next, *Glitz*, has been named a dual main selection of Book-of-the-Month Club following a three-day auction between BOMC and the Literary Guild. The six-figure advance obtained by Arbor House's George Coleman is the largest from a club in Arbor's history."[64]

Internally, Arbor House referred to their outreach strategy as the "*Glitz*-blitz." Aside from Anthony Lukas's *GQ* profile, similar feature articles devoted to Leonard and his latest novel were set for *Esquire*, *Rolling Stone*, the *New York Times Sunday Magazine*, *USA Today*, and the *Washington Post Book World*, as well as priority reviews in the *Houston Post* and the *Los Angeles Times*. Leonard himself was booked for a profile on *CBS Sunday Morning* and committed to various radio interviews.[65] The highlight, however, came with *Newsweek*'s unexpected decision not only to run their profile on Leonard's rise to literary prominence but to feature him on the magazine's cover. A particularly rare acknowledgment for a popular author, the news outlet had made Leonard *the* face of contemporary crime and mystery fiction.

In a profile that ran soon after, *Time* magazine's J. D. Reed even gave him a new name.

The Dickens from Detroit.

In February, the *New York Times*' guest critic wrote what Leonard would later describe as a career-changing mainstream review. Bestselling horror master Stephen King penned one of Leonard's strongest reviews ever. "How good is this novel?" King began. "Probably the most convincing thing I can say on the subject is that it cost me money. After finishing *Glitz*, I went out to the bookstore at my local mall and bought everything by Elmore Leonard I could find—the stuff I didn't already, that is." King continued, "How does this bear on my Elmore Leonard block? Simple. I figured if so many critics liked him, he was boring. Mr. Leonard is far from boring, critical kudos or no. You can put *Glitz* on the same shelf with your John D. MacDonalds, your Raymond Chandlers, your Dashiell Hammetts. In it, Mr. Leonard moves from low comedy to high action to a couple of surprisingly tender love scenes with a pro's unobtrusive ease and the impeccable rhythms of a born entertainer."

King added, "*Time* magazine has called Mr. Leonard a 'Dickens from Detroit.' I haven't read enough of him yet (give me a month or so) to agree, but his wit, his range of effective character portrayal and his almost eerily exact ear for the tones and nuances of dialogue suggest Dickens to me. Although it's only February, I'll venture a guess—*Glitz* may be the best crime novel of the year.

"Even if it's not, I'm sorry it took me so long to catch up to Mr. Leonard."[66]

CHAPTER 15

Hot, Part One, 1985–1989

> Now that I've developed a style that feels natural, one that I can swing with, I want to keep the writing fresh and continue to experiment. I don't want to begin to imitate myself and sound like a piece in *National Lampoon*, where my style was parodied once, broadly caricatured in a way that you could catch glimpses of Ernest Hemingway in the construction.

I'm going to keep writing a book a year," Leonard told the *New York Times*' Ben Yagoda, stubbing out a True green cigarette. "But I'm not going to lock myself up for that many books. I've been busting my butt all these years to be independent."

It was the first time since 1970 that Leonard began a new year with more film work ahead than straight fiction—a situation he later admitted broke the rhythm of his creative routine. However, Leonard wasn't one to complain, especially in the face of the financial success he'd finally achieved. Yagoda was quick to note Leonard's most recent tale-of-the-tape: *LaBrava* had sold 425,000 copies in paperback and beat out Umberto Eco and John le Carré for 1984's "best novel" Edgar award; *Glitz* had been selected for the Book of the Month Club; and all of the author's earlier, out-of-print titles had been reissued to meet demand—all on top of movie sales ($350,000 for the rights to and screenplay for *Stick*, $400,000 for *LaBrava*, and $450,000 for *Glitz*).[1]

Leonard had met the reporter at the Midtown Café in downtown Birmingham where his son Christopher, having recently returned from Arizona, was now working as the chic bistro's manager. Yagoda spied Leonard's preference for driving a Saab Turbo, despite being a longtime resident of the nation's automotive capital ("People tell me I can afford a Mercedes, but I don't want one"[2]), and casual cool: ". . . a navy blue cotton shirt, a tan Shetland sweater, a tweed sportcoat, blue jeans, cowboy boots, and his trademark Kangol cap [and] lighting one of his neverending True cigarettes," Yagoda noted. "Take his eyeglasses. They're the same kind he's worn for 30 years—plain, round tortoise-shell frames, à la Clark Kent. When they went out of style, Leonard didn't switch to wire rims. Now, for what it's worth, they're back in," he added. "With his slight frame, his full beard and glasses, he could be pegged—but for the boots—as a professor at Wayne State University." Yagoda wasn't far off; over the previous year, Leonard had accepted numerous invitations for public appearances, often "in conversation" about the craft of writing or as a guest lecturer.

Leonard's lifestyle had also become incrementally more structured and domesticated. He admitted to Yagoda that he and Joan often stayed home to read or watch television, venturing out occasionally to the movies or a nice dinner. However, he was also quick to map out his busy, upcoming year: he had creatively parlayed an unrelated meeting in Los Angeles into a potential television show with the same setting, yet convinced television producer David Gerber to change the setting to New Orleans.[3] He had also recently told interviewers that in the case of *Stick*, bringing a major star into the fold had come with anticipated compromises; with that in mind, both he and producer Walter Mirisch had no idea of the crusade that they were about to endure in their attempts to bring *LaBrava* to the screen.

Mirisch had continued to work with Sidney Poitier after their own project with Leonard had fallen through, leading to an aborted second project, as well. Mirisch now put those additional eggs into the *LaBrava* basket. He had sent a copy of Leonard's screenplay adaptation to Dustin Hoffman, who claimed to have loved the book yet immediately asked for revisions. In response, Leonard and Mirisch flew to New York on November 16, 1984, for their first of many meetings with the actor. "We made many script changes," Mirisch later wrote. "Hoffman was busy in other films during this period, and we endured many delays in getting access to him. We discussed possible directors with him for the project. Finally, at his suggestion, I submitted *LaBrava* to Martin Scorsese, who agreed to direct. Now we began a new series of meetings with Scorsese and Leonard, sometimes with Hoffman present, and we made further script changes."[4]

According to later reports, Leonard and Mirisch held numerous meetings in Hoffman's New York hotel suite, always attempting to get the actor to actually commit to the project. Once Hoffman began ducking out of meetings on "personal business," Leonard grew weary. He and Mirisch apparently "gritted their teeth" following one such meeting after Hoffman arrived the next morning asking them, "Wasn't it great yesterday, the sun out all day? What did you guys do, go to [Central Park]?" Leonard had then announced to both Hoffman and Scorsese, "Look, it's okay for you guys, but I'm not getting paid for this." Hoffman assured Leonard that he would, indeed, be paid retroactively for the work—although H. N. Swanson laughed at the very suggestion. "They'll never make this picture," he advised Leonard. By the summer of 1985, Leonard was publicly referring to the ongoing process as "laborious."[5] From his earliest interest in the material, Hoffman had demanded a revised outline to restructure the novel's original pacing; Leonard had it completed on May 18, 1985. With the actor's approval, Leonard went off and rewrote the script to those specifications, however, Hoffman then asked for additional changes and rewrites throughout the summer, with Leonard completing four more versions by the end of July.[6] As Mirisch himself navigated a new regime at Universal, he told Hoffman that he'd need to officially commit to the film before Leonard would make any more revisions. Hoffman agreed, asking that the studio contact his agents and attorney to negotiate the final deal. Finally, at the end of 1985, Hoffman agreed in exchange for an estimated $6.3 million, plus 22.5 percent of the gross (although later reports indicated that he'd been trying for double that amount). Universal immediately balked at the request. "This process went on for some time," the producer later wrote, "until the Universal negotiators told me that they found it impossible to make a deal with Hoffman . . . When it was explained to me, I agreed that the requests were unreasonable." He reported as much to Hoffman, who quickly put his attorney, Bert Fields, on the case. "You know the deal you said that Universal wouldn't give Dustin?" Fields reportedly asked Mirisch. "Well, I can get that deal from a new company, Cannon Pictures."[7] At the time, the project had already been rejected by three major studios—20th Century Fox, Walt Disney Productions, and Geffen Films.[8]

But Cannon Films and its owners weren't all that new to Leonard; it was the new movie-making incarnation of Israeli producer-director Menahem Golan, who had notoriously wasted Leonard's time in 1975 for the Tel Aviv–based adaptation of *Fifty-Two Pickup*. Over the previous decade, Golan had done well for himself, breaking into the American market by producing glossy exploitation films on shoestring budgets with major US stars in the autumnal phase of their careers. In an effort for international critical acceptance, Golan had ambitiously varied his production output with Oscar bait, enlisting legitimate art house auteurs like Jean-Luc Godard and John Cassavetes to make their passion projects under the same banner as borderline schlock, such as the Charles Bronson slasher flick *10 to Midnight* and John Derek's softcore drama *Bolero*. Although Leonard had had initial apprehensions about working with Golan again, the producer had, in his own way, made amends for their previous creative disagreements: in 1984, he'd finally produced a version of his "Israeli *Fifty-Two Pickup*," newly titled *The Ambassador*; only a few months later, Golan also began production on a proper adaptation of the novel. Although Leonard had never actually written a script for John Frankenheimer's newly titled *52 Pickup*, both the director and producer insisted that the author get screen credit for the amount of dialogue retained from his original novel. "All I did was add commas where proper names are used in the dialogue, and spell 'all right' with two words," Leonard later said of his participation.[9]

Mirisch had been assured by attorney Fields that if he were to reattain property from Universal in order to work with Cannon "an unprecedented producer's deal would be on the table." Fields had added, "You'll never see [Cannon executives]. They will have nothing to do with the making of the picture. All they do is pay the bills, and you will make the picture without interference." With that handshake agreement in place, Mirisch convinced Universal to allow him to take the property elsewhere.[10] Unfamiliar with the company, Martin Scorsese soon left the project, opting instead to direct Touchstone Pictures' *The Color of Money* with Paul Newman. While Mirisch sensed trouble with the project, Hoffman remained cool, assuring the producer they wouldn't "have any trouble with Cannon." In Scorsese's place, the actor offered up two directors he claimed he could attain: Francis Ford Coppola and Hal Ashby. Coppola was interested, but wouldn't be available for eighteen months. Still digging himself out of the financial hole left from 1982's *One from the Heart*—the film that had bankrupted his American Zoetrope Studios—he'd taken a last-minute offer to direct *The Cotton Club* for producer Robert Evans.[11] Hal Ashby, on the other hand, badly needed a win and was soon wooed on board. Once touted as a leading member of the New Hollywood film movement, the famed director of such 1970s hits as *Harold and Maude*, *The Last Detail*, *Shampoo*, and *Coming Home* hadn't scored a critical or financial hit since 1980's *Being There*.[12]

Considering their history, Ashby was surprised by Hoffman's recommendation. In 1980, Ashby had been tapped to direct *Tootsie* (another film for which Hoffman had wrestled for complete creative control from producers Dick Richards and Robert Evans's brother, Charles), but was forced to quit due to postproduction work on Columbia Pictures' *Lookin' to Get Out*. Ashby had been replaced by Sydney Pollack. Two years later, Hoffman asked Ashby to direct a sequel to *Kramer vs. Kramer*, yet dropped the project while Ashby was still writing the screenplay. In February 1986, Hoffman called Ashby again, asking if he'd want to direct *LaBrava*. The film was slated to begin principal photography in Miami that August, yet Hoffman remained dissatisfied with every version of the screenplay that Leonard had written. The actor had even hired his own screenwriter, Murray Schisgal, to do a new version; Ashby, for his part, began one of his own. According to biographer Nick Dawson, Ashby was particularly excited about dramatizing the love story between Joe LaBrava and Jean Shaw, and hoped to lure a legendary actress from Hollywood's past to the role, such as Debbie Reynolds, June Allyson, or Kathryn Grayson.[13] Unfortunately, it was that exact plot point that continued to nag Hoffman, who was insecure at having to play opposite a love interest older than himself (a rather large irony missed by the star, whose own career had been launched with 1967's *The Graduate*—the very film that had brought the term "Mrs. Robinson" and its fantasies of seductive older women into pop culture idiom). Unfortunately, as Leonard pointed out, that was the very *basis* of the story. Mirisch later wrote, "Elmore Leonard had been a tower of strength through the whole convoluted process . . . He and I went to New York to meet Dustin again, and soon he was making so-called final changes with Hal Ashby."

Hoffman then insisted he get to work as *codirector* with Ashby, a demand that was quickly vetoed by the Director's Guild of America. However, the final hammer fell on *LaBrava* in March, only two weeks after Ashby was publicly announced as the film's director. To everyone's collective chagrin, Golan's Cannon Films had run a deluxe, full-page ad in *Variety* on March 16, 1986, declaring, "*Welcome to The Cannon Family, Dustin Hoffman—We take great pride in announcing Dustin Hoffman star-*

ring in LaBrava. *Begins shooting this summer in Florida.*" For Hoffman's image, Cannon had used a picture that the actor particularly hated—an unrelated still left over from a recent BBC film, *The Last Moguls*. He immediately threw a fit and rang up Mirisch. "Did you see the picture in the trade papers yesterday?" the actor had asked. "They had no right to have a full-page picture of me, advertising that picture, because my contract's not signed." He demanded that Mirisch attain the property back from Cannon so they could, once again, shop it elsewhere. At that point, however, such a move was contractually impossible: Mirisch had already done as instructed by Hoffman's attorney, Bert Fields, and signed with Cannon. As tempers slowly began to rise, Hoffman insisted that Mirisch had made the Cannon deal "without telling anybody. I didn't back out—I flew out. I was frightened of Cannon. They can do anything, and would."[14]

On April 1, *Variety*'s Richard Gold reported Hoffman's departure.[15] Taking a cue from Hoffman, Hal Ashby pulled out on April 22.[16]

According to Mirisch, the aftershocks of the abandoned project tied up *LaBrava*'s movie rights for an additional two years, during which time Golan and his cousin and production partner, Yoram Globus, tried desperately to get Hoffman back on board. They were unsuccessful in their attempts, and the rights reverted back to Universal Pictures. By then, Burt Reynolds's *Stick* had flopped, costing the same studio dearly for its reshoots and advertising—and giving them second thoughts about future Elmore Leonard properties.

Leonard, however, was determined *not* to let the double-punch of *Stick* and *LaBrava* damage the career he'd spent three decades building. He later recalled the frustration that the *LaBrava* affair had kept him "away from fiction for sixteen months," and he vowed never to let such a debacle ever happen again. He'd already been filing away notes and scenarios for his long-promised "Hollywood novel," and the combined egos of Burt Reynolds and, now, Dustin Hoffman finally got his mind turning back toward that project. It would be a little while longer, however, as he'd already blissfully begun his next novel. Seeking consolation from his peers, Leonard soon heard from two fellow authors who both had similar Hollywood experiences under their respective belts. "Dutch, why do you keep hoping to make a good movie?" wrote novelist Donald Westlake—who had had the foresight years earlier to prevent studios from owning his signature character, the professional thief Parker. "The books are ours; everything else is virgins thrown in the volcano. Be happy if the check is good." Likewise, John D. MacDonald wrote to Leonard, "I don't see how you endure those people, and endure group effort, and endure conferences and stupid revision requests and kindred bullshit." MacDonald added, "Please write the Hollywood book and kill them off in ugly ways."[17] It would be MacDonald's final wish for Leonard before his passing at the age of seventy on December 28, 1986.

It wasn't far from what Leonard already had in mind. But as he began his next novel—the New Orleans crime epic he'd been planning since the previous year—he, along with Mirisch, took solace in the film Dustin Hoffman had opted to make instead of *LaBrava*.

Behind closed doors, they were among the only ones who found *Ishtar* very funny, indeed.

Once Dustin Hoffman had washed his hands of the project, Walter Mirisch briefly had the interest of Al Pacino. During an in-depth interview with Mike Lupica to run in *Esquire* the following month, Leonard had received a call from Mirisch with the news.

"Any word on *LaBrava*?" Joan had asked, poking her head out of the kitchen.

"Now Pacino wants to talk to me," Leonard called to her.

"Cold feet?"

"I don't know."

"Can he read?" Joan asked and returned to the kitchen.[18]

FROM JOAN SHEPARD-LEONARD'S JOURNAL—1986:

[January 18]

Elm still concerned about Bandits. *He's afraid it is too "thin"—doesn't know where the plot is going. He works so hard—7 days a week, but harder on this one. Seems to have more doubts about the storyline. He writes—rewrites . . .*

[January 22]

F.F. Coppola and Dustin Hoffman to talk next week. F.F. thinks LaBrava *should be grittier. Dustin wants no violence. It will probably end up more like the book. Poor Elm—probably more rewrites.*

Walter asked how he'd like to have a conversation with Sylvester Stallone and write something for him. No—no—no!

[January 25–February 10]

Things going great for E and words are coming fast! It reads great—best yet, I think . . . E changed Jack Matisse's name to Jack Delaney. He can "talk better"—tough kid . . .

Julie and Peter had a baby boy tonight—Alex . . .

B-day—big 58. E put a candle on our coffee cake and had 3 cards for me. He makes life a joy.

[March 7]

Off to L.A. and back again. . . . E finished the outline of LaBrava *and had it copied and sent to "the Guys" today. He's so tired, working too hard.*

[April 4]

Sunday the book was finished! . . . Mon. Dutch copied it and sent it off to "the gang."

Leonard had been considering his birthplace of New Orleans as a potential story setting for a number of years. A particular interest to him, he enjoyed the challenge of capturing local lingo within his dialogue as closely as his economic style would allow. After all, a detour to Puerto Rico and Atlantic City had resulted in Leonard's biggest hit yet, reassuring him to trust his own instincts. Following the massive success of *Glitz*, New Orleans's native patois seemed an excellent place to branch out.

In the midst of his *LaBrava* dealings with Dustin Hoffman, the *Hollywood Reporter* ran an update on the Arbor House deal, citing Leonard's payment of $1.1 million for *Bandits*—"one of the largest advance royalty payments" in publishing history, and deadline of July 1, 1986.[19]

For years, it had been Leonard's practice to heavily draw inspiration from the daily news, yet *Bandits* would prove a marked difference from any of his novels that had come before. Still leading the titular band of assorted thieves was "a new decent man in trouble"—cut from a similar cloth as Jack Ryan and Ernest Stickley—the "trouble" in which he finds himself would take on an international scope. And just as Leonard had offered light, yet pointed, social commentary on yuppie Reaganite culture throughout *Stick*, so *Bandits* would be immersed in the controversial foreign policies of Ronald Reagan. To the author, however, it was merely an innocent attempt at penning a classic "heist" story. But drawing national headlines had quickly added a political edge to the otherwise traditional caper—although there was little else traditional about the characters themselves. Starting with lead protagonist Jack Delaney, an ex-con now working rather passionlessly at his brother-in-law's New Orleans funeral home. Unable to avoid his assignment to retrieve a dead body from a nearby leper colony, Delaney is quickly swept into a politically charged mission to hide the very-much-alive Nicaraguan mistress of a psychopathic Contra military leader. Protecting her from the clutches of Dagoberto Godoy—who believes the young woman has given him leprosy during one of their trysts—is a beautiful ex-nun named Lucy Nichols, out on her own revenge mission against Godoy for the masses of Nicaraguan civilians he had killed. While dodging the colonel's loyal Contra bodyguards, the tough-as-nails Nichols has been following Godoy's US visit as a Ronald Reagan–endorsed diplomat, collecting donations from various right-wing American industrialists (he carries his personal letter of recommendation from Reagan in his jacket pocket at all times) for his self-serving military coup. Smitten with Lucy and her military idealism, Delaney agrees to help assemble a team to pull off a heist of Godoy's ill-gotten gains: a retired cop named Roy and Cullen, a reformed bank robber—both of whom are old enough to apply for Social Security checks and a subscription to *AARP*.

Whereas *Glitz* had been in the darker vein of earlier Leonard crime fare, *Fifty-Two Pickup* and *City Primeval*, for *Bandits*, the author returned to a slightly lighter tone, which only worked to emphasize the absurdity he saw in the leadership of the real-life Sandinista-Contra conflict. (Publicly apolitical, Leonard nonetheless was a registered Democrat and made generous donations to his favorite candidates every election season. And although he'd long since abandoned regular Catholic practices, his previous time in AA and ensuing secular spirituality kept him instinctively aligned with social underdogs. "A Jesuit-educated Catholic, I'm not as firm in my religious beliefs as I used to be, though I do believe in God and meditate every day," he wrote in an unpublished questionnaire in 1979. "Politically I'm a liberal and usually vote Democrat. I believe in equality of race and sex and have nothing against homosexuals. I feel I'm a tolerant person and have no enemies that I know of.")

Leonard still had extended family members in New Orleans and booked a two-week trip with Joan for the summer of 1986. There, he walked and took notes and photographs of the areas that his new band of misfits would inhabit, the French Quarter among them. Both he and Gregg Sutter had collected folders of articles and op-eds on US foreign policy and the history of the Sandinistas, with Leonard highlighting the most pertinent elements for wannabe dictator Godoy. From various 1984 issues of *Harper's*, Leonard pruned the personal opinions of foreign policy power players, such as CIA director William Colby, as well as an in-depth profile on the children of Sandinista freedom fighters who took up arms while still prepubescent.

Among his annotated scans, "What to Do About Nicaragua" by *New York* magazine's Michael Kramer and Richard Cohen's "If the Facts Fail You, Just Tell a 'Nicaragua'" from the *Washington Post* received the most of Leonard's red ink: he circled the latter's quote attributed to Ronald Reagan, defaming the Sandinistas' cause, while favorably comparing the Contras to America's founding fathers.[20] (Privately a critic of Reagan, Leonard had asked friend George F. Will to make a playful "cameo" appearance with the novel by writing the letter of recommendation from Reagan on Dagoberto Godoy's behalf, but the conservative columnist declined—although he did continue to write favorable critical reviews of Leonard's future work.)

Leonard began his first draft with a concentration on his primary protagonist. He had spent time at the Lynch & Sons Funeral Home in Clawson, Michigan, in order to learn the protocols and procedures for mortuary workers, such as embalming and proper body transportation.[21] Likewise, he'd studied methods for "breaking and entering" into hotel rooms—his new antihero's criminal specialty. Yet the character's name continued to elude him. Only after a few false starts, however, did Leonard discover that in his earliest incarnation as "Frank Matisse" would Jack Delaney have trouble "talking."

He finished his first draft nearly three months ahead of his July deadline, and received the galley proofs from Arbor House two months later. This time, he'd playfully dedicated the work to Joan three times and all his children, as well as the grandchildren who had come along during the busy past few years: *"For Joan, Jane, Peter and Julie, Christopher, Bill and Katy, Joan, Beth and Bobi, Shannon, Megan, Tim, Alex and Joan."*

Bandits was released in January 1986 to a decidedly mixed response—the first time since Leonard had achieved his major mainstream success. However, in the *Washington Post*, critic Heywood Hale Broun claimed the novel elevated the author *past* both Raymond Chandler and Dashiell

Hammett: "Leonard makes a big step towards equality with his distinguished forebears and does something neither of them ever tried: he takes a strong political stand . . . The only thing he has lost is a chance to receive, as other writers have, one of those photo-opportunity medals on the White House lawn."[22] (Ronald Reagan had recently proclaimed Tom Clancy's recent debut *The Hunt for Red October* to be "[his] kind of yarn" and invited the espionage author to the White House to discuss the book; when the film version was released in 1990, its producers gifted Reagan the prop teddy bear used at the end of the film for his advocacy of the source material.[23])

In the case of *Bandits*, at least one rising star saw himself perfectly as the novel's heist-man-with-a-cause: Bruce Willis, a television star who at that point had only a single major motion picture under his belt. Then the breakout star of the ABC network's kitschy prime-time detective series *Moonlighting*, Willis had made it publicly known that he was looking to make the jump to the big screen full-time. Leonard, not much of a personal fan, had actually poked fun at the star's hit TV series within *Bandits*, although it was unknown if Willis himself had picked up on the cheeky reference. "According to the source, Willis will pay $500,000 for a twelve-month option on the thriller," wrote the *Intelligencer*'s Peg Tyre. "Willis's agent denied that the television star was optioning the movie, and Leonard's agent refused to comment."[24]

However, Willis's interest wasn't only accurate, but—at least during the early part of 1987—an understatement. In a joint venture between Willis's Hudson Hawk Films and Tri-Star Pictures, an option was put through just prior to the actor's first day of shooting a new adventure film for which few industry insiders had much hope: on November 2, 1987, Willis left the set of *Moonlighting* and drove directly to Fox Plaza to film his first scene; soon he wrapped a fire hose around his waist and leapt from the exploding rooftop of a Los Angeles skyscraper. By the time *Die Hard* opened in July 1988, Willis's advance payment on the film afforded an extension of his *Bandits* option the previous month. But by then, early estimates predicted *Die Hard* to be an unanticipated sleeper hit—and the actor was being offered nearly every major script in town, leaving *Bandits* to languish.[25]

By then, Leonard was already hard at work on yet another book. With faith that it would not only satisfy his readers but also silence the naysayers who'd taken him to task over *Bandits*, Leonard, uncharacteristically, kept most details regarding the work in progress to himself, only revealing hints of storyline and, ultimately, its title to interviewers—*Freaky Deaky*. Arbor House, however, was already clamoring for the next novel. Fortunately, the keen eye of H. N. Swanson soon caught the fact that Leonard already had an entire novel hibernating in a desk drawer—1977's unpublished "stigmata novel" *Touch*. And best of all, Leonard had retained the rights to it. As Mike Lupica later wrote, "It might be Leonard's best book. Bantam owned it for eight years. Didn't publish it. Didn't know what to do with it. Cut to 1985. *Glitz* hits the list. Leonard is the literary Lana Turner. Bantam calls and says, 'We must publish [*Touch*].' Leonard thinks *ha-ha-ha* and tells Bantam that the rights have reverted to him, which they have . . . [H. N. Swanson] says to Bantam, 'You didn't do your homework.' Offers them the book back for a ridiculously high figure. Bantam demurs. Arbor House, which is where he wanted to go anyway, buys the ten-year-old book for more than $300,000."[26]

Although largely against introductions and epilogues, for the long-awaited release of *Touch*, however, Leonard penned an explanation for the novel's long-delayed release: "The point is that now . . . with even George Will reading my work, [the publisher] suddenly understands the stigmata story and sees a market for it," he wrote. "I just wanted to explain that it's been sitting around for ten years because publishers didn't know how to sell it—not because I didn't know how to write it." Leonard further explained that he'd made no major alterations to the original 1977 galley proofs, aside from a few cosmetic edits and updates to more modern pop cultural references (as a guest on the Morton Downey Jr.–esque *Howard Hart* talk show, Frank Sinatra became Frank Sinatra *Jr.*; Paul Schrader's eventual 1997 film adaptation would modernize it again, featuring LL Cool J).

For a novel that had been initially difficult to categorize and market, Leonard's first major nonthriller was largely well received by critics, if not his regular readership. The consensus among his peers was largely positive, although he'd often receive jabs from William Robertson, who had taken over review duties from Charles Willeford at the *Miami Herald*. In continuing to compare Leonard to George V. Higgins, Robertson wrote, "Elmore Leonard, on the other hand, has no trouble with commerce . . . Perhaps the closest you can come to comparing the two writers is to say that Higgins is a thinking reader's Leonard. Where Leonard is direct, entertaining and, finally, simplistic, Higgins is subtle, entertaining and, ultimately, complex . . . Want to bet whose book is going to sell?"[27] (Swanson had even forwarded it to Leonard, scrawling across the bottom, "*Had to have the last shot!!*")

In the *Los Angeles Times*, critic Philip C. Rule wrote favorably of Leonard's seeming exploration into spirituality, or at least his realistic, gritty approach to the unknown. "While the Church normally takes a standoffish approach in attributing divine causality to such phenomena, it doesn't hereby deny the fact that they happened," Rule wrote. "So what if they did happen to an ordinary person? Someone who lives down the street from you in the same building? . . . By the end of the novel, readers may not believe that Juvenal has the touch, but they will certainly be convinced that Elmore Leonard has it."[28] Likewise, the *Washington Post* enlisted bestselling author and Catholic priest Andrew Greeley to write their review. Greeley found kindred themes in Leonard's handling of the divine lost among the trappings of the material world. "Leonard knows that there is only one area of human behavior more open to scams than religion, and that is sanctity," Greeley wrote. (His review coincidentally ran on the same page as a review for Higgins's latest, *Outlaws*.) "The New York bestseller world is ill-equipped to deal with saints and miracles, much less religion. I suspect the so-called book-reviewing fraternity will be similarly put-off. They will be as wrong as the decision-makers at Bantam. With a modest shrug, Leonard ends his introduction by saying that 'friends of mine who read a lot think it's my best book.' They're right." Greeley added, "The author's personal religious life is his own business and no one else's. It suffices to say that it would be difficult, though not impossible, for a man who lacked faith to turn out as delicate and as subtle a work as *Touch*—skeptical, yet accepting of an open universe in which wonderous events may occur, even if they usually don't."[29]

Before Arbor House's hardcover had even made its street date, H. N. Swanson had sent galleys of the book to his usual checklist of producers and executives. Leonard, however, was apprehensive about pitching *Touch* for the big screen before the novel's release. "I feel very uneasy about your offering it to film people at this time," Leonard wrote to Swanson at the beginning of September. "Especially considering all the stuff of mine that's out there now, I think we should wait." He added, "[Producer] David Brown said he 'worked hard reading the novel,' which to me is an indication he was not the right one to read it in the first place.

Let's keep it out of the studios and wait for some off-beat producer to come along. I see it as the kind of thing John Sayles might do."[30]

Despite his aversion toward writing for network television, Leonard had also completed his two-hour pilot for producer David Gerber, which had come along nearly by accident during an LA trip for a potential film of *Glitz*. After negotiating with Gerber regarding where to set the series—Leonard preferring New Orleans to the producer's Seattle Police Department—they settled on the title *Wilder*. As for Leonard's adaptation of *Glitz*, early interest from Sidney Lumet soon fell apart. "I was all set to make a movie of *Glitz*," the legendary director soon told Bart Mills from the *Los Angeles Times*. "The script was wonderful, but then I asked myself, is this a movie anymore? Will a small detective story work anymore? Has that area been usurped by TV?"[31] Ultimately, Mills was proven half-correct: *Glitz* was sold as a movie of the week to NBC, while the networks passed on *Wilder*. Leonard later told journalist Jean W. Ross, "*Glitz* is being produced right now as an NBC movie. I did three drafts of a script for it as a feature, the last one with Sidney Lumet, but Lorimar then decided it would cost too much money to make it that way . . . So it was rewritten for television."[32]

Following their arduous *LaBrava* saga, producer Walter Mirisch had also approached Leonard about collaborating on yet another project, stipulating it would not be a police procedural or contemporary action film. For the first time in over a decade, there was an apparent demand for Westerns—thanks in no small part to director Lawrence Kasdan's *Silverado*, which had reignited an interest in the genre among baby boomers; that same year, Clint Eastwood had returned to the genre after a decade of contemporary action films with the box office hit *Pale Rider*. According to Mirisch, Leonard had presented him with a scenario not unlike *The Fugitive*, although with the appropriate Western spin: protagonist "Duell McCall"—from whom the story would also take its name—stands accused of a crime he didn't commit, and would spend the bulk of the film both evading the long arm of the law and attempting to prove his innocence. However, Mirisch was unable to find a studio interested in the Western and soon considered aiming the property toward primetime television. Leonard agreed and repurposed his outline into a two-hour series pilot, having the final revision completed on August 8, 1985.[33] He'd also agreed with Mirisch's suggestion to have his television-savvy son, producer Drew Mirisch, helm the project once it was off the ground. Leonard and

Mirisch soon met with NBC network president Brandon Tartikoff, who greenlit the television film as a "backdoor pilot" for a potential series, although he did stipulate a change in the show's title. The executive would foot the bill in acquiring the Eagles' classic rock anthem, "Desperado," if the two would agree to alter the show's name to reflect the song; they agreed, and production was set for Tucson, Arizona.

Desperado aired on April 27, 1987, to strong ratings and reviews. Ultimately, however, NBC opted not to turn the pilot into a weekly series but, rather, a few full-length made-for-TV movies; *The Return of the Desperado* aired the following year, with three more to follow in 1988 and 1989—all without Leonard's participation.

"My lead and my antagonist in all my books are still boys playing guns," Leonard told Michael E. Hill of the *Washington Post*. "The lead is child-like, and the antagonist is childish. I see that in life. I see people as children. What was the bad guy like when he was in high school?"[34]

It had been that exact form of creative empathy that had stilted Leonard on the only produced adaptation he ever wrote of another author's work, *The Rosary Murders*. Based on the first novel of an ongoing mystery series by fellow Detroit native and former Catholic priest turned crime writer William X. Kienzle, Leonard had been approached to write the screenplay right after the novel's 1979 publication. However, there had been immediate friction between Kienzle and producer Robert G. Laurel (despite the fact that the author had officiated Laurel's wedding and personally baptized his children), largely due to the author's insistence that the main protagonist, Father Robert Koesler, remain chaste during the action of the film. Although Leonard hadn't strayed from the character's morality, Kienzle had, nonetheless, filed a lawsuit demanding script approval.[35] Ultimately, Leonard couldn't even begin work on the screenplay for three years. "I think you should call up Laurel and tell him we are through fooling around," Swanson wrote to Leonard on January 5, 1981. "I'm going to bring you other assignments."[36] Once the project gained traction in May 1982, Leonard had had to put *Stick* aside to begin writing the treatment, and finished it on June 17. By September 7, he had the first-draft screenplay completed.[37] It would be five years before production moved forward.

In July 1987, Leonard reread Kienzle's source novel and took apart the storyline and characters, drafting two sets of annotated journals and a finalized script.

The Rosary Murders began its principal photography on April 14, 1986, and concluded eight weeks later, making the production the largest feature film ever shot on location in Detroit up to that point. On August 27 of the following year, the film held its gala premiere at the Fisher Theater and the new Center One atrium turned ballroom. Although Leonard hadn't been involved in the production, he and Joan were invited to join the cast and crew for the event. Over a thousand people attended the event, including numerous stars from the film (Charles Durning grabbed a seat next to Leonard; *The Rosary Murders* would be the second of their eventual three collaborations). Despite the rarity of a major Hollywood-style red-carpet event held in his own hometown, original author William Kienzle declined attendance, perhaps due to his own misgivings over the film adaptation. Local columnist Mona Grigg wrote, "Elmore Leonard was there, having been listed in the credits as co-screenwriter . . . With his newest book, *Freaky Deaky*, already put to bed and waiting for spring publication, Leonard is hitting the promotion trail." Grigg wasn't exaggerating; while Leonard claimed his contributions to *The Rosary Murders*' final cut were minimal, the film's premiere proved an unofficial kickoff to his own *Bandits* publicity tour. The following week, he was scheduled for numerous stops around New York, including a spot on NBC's *Today* and as the headliner for an author luncheon; once back in Birmingham, he was scheduled for a number of book signings, then finally, a stop on Larry King's radio program.[38]

While on the *Bandits* book tour, he spoke with Virginia Greiner of the *Washington Times*. "His next book, *Freaky Deaky*, set in his hometown of Detroit, will be published by Arbor House in April of 1988," Greiner wrote. "It concerns a man and woman who made bombs in the '60s for a cause. Now they make them for profit . . . He wanted to know how to make a bomb, and somebody on the bomb squad came back with a book called *The Anarchist's Cookbook*. He recalls it had 'drawings and everything.'"[39]

At sixty-two years old, Leonard wasn't a baby boomer—although all five of his now-grown children fell safely into that generational description; likewise, Joan's two daughters, Beth and Bobi, were the same approximate age, as was Leonard's researcher, Gregg Sutter. For his next book, Leonard drew on much of that age bracket's collective experiences: student protests for civil rights and against the Vietnam War, Watergate, psychedelic drugs, and the acid-laden experimentation that had led to FM-championed progressive rock and roll. It would be, in effect, a "boomer" thriller—infused with much of the leftover angst of the Me Generation. But as a member of what would later be termed the Greatest Generation, Leonard had already hinted that this succeeding demographic had ushered in the "Reagan 80's," and had joyfully cashed in to pivot from hippie to yuppie—*Stick*'s Barry Stam being a prime example. Somewhere in all that confusion was a solid band of new fictional misfits.

At first, Leonard had toyed with the possible titles *Pressure* and *Fireworks*—the former a reference to his heroic protagonist's stressful position on the Detroit Police Department's Bomb Squad (or, as he noted, "a love affair that develops under pressure"), the latter an allusion to the job itself. Researcher Gregg Sutter later wrote, "[Leonard] turned to cops, with whom he still had many contacts, for character ideas. Instead of Homicide, this time he chose to focus on the Detroit Police Bomb Squad . . . His homicide buddies put him in touch with Sergeant Dale Johnson, who gave Elmore a complete tutorial in bomb making."[40]

Leonard did much of the bomb making and defusal research himself, starting a separate notebook for the information pruned from sessions with Johnson—mainly jotting down key concepts and terms that would make his characters' professional lingo all the more accurate. He'd noted: *"For blowing up a car—3 or 4 gallons of gasoline in plastic bottles wrapped in a primer cord . . . Sometimes a little black powder is used . . . Get dynamite in Yale, Michigan to buy it. Better to steal it."*

In order to realistically describe his antagonists' methods for making bombs at home, Leonard consulted two of the most notorious pieces of underground literature of that time period: *The Anarchist's Cookbook* and *The Poor Man's James Bond*—both favorites of urban terrorists and militia groups (ironically, he had been recommended both books for references by actual Bomb Squad officers). He used *Lenz's Explosives and Bombs Disposal Guide* to study the schematics for "shatter bombs" and "concussion bombs," as well as photographs of the hands of injured bomb disposal technicians. Finally, Leonard dove into different kinds of prescription amphetamines and barbiturates and studied the hallucinogens most commonly used within hippie culture. (He perused through mescaline, Peyote cactus, and LSD butter before ultimately deciding that a

In the years to come, Leonard would credit his second marriage to Joan Shepard and their dynamic to being the leading force in conquering his alcoholism—as well as in shaping his female characters into more modern, empowered, and realistic protagonists. Seen here in New York City, circa 1985.

Although the consecutive debacles behind the film versions of both *Stick* and the ultimately unproduced *LaBrava* caused a temporary standstill in further Leonard adaptations, their real-time book sales greatly boosted the author's readership and international popularity. Seen here in October 1983 on the set of *Stick* with his director and star, Burt Reynolds.

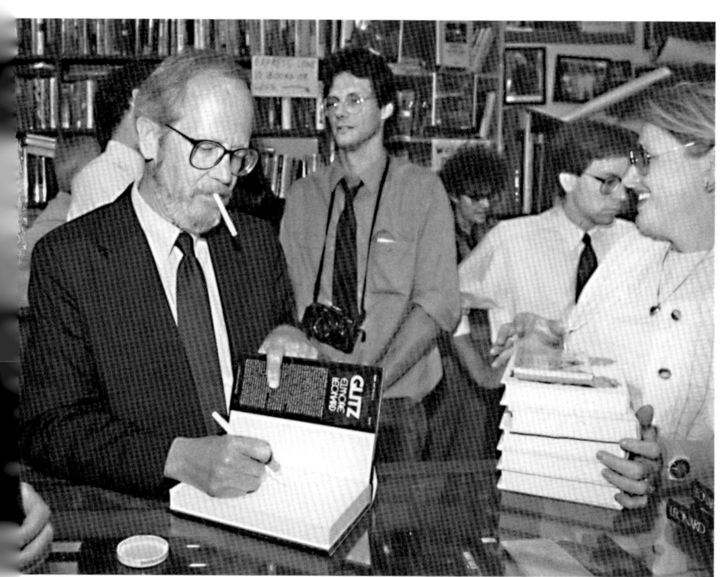

By the mid-1980s, Leonard's in-store book-signing appearances had gone from four or five people approaching him at a card table to packed houses and attendance numbers usually allotted for rock stars. Seen here on the 1988 *Freaky Deaky* book tour, surrounded by fans.

All photographs courtesy of the University of South Carolina Special Collections unless otherwise noted.

While Leonard often joked that he started his fiction career by secretly writing Western stories that he hid within his office desk drawer, those formative years cemented his lifelong process: all stories, novels, and screenplays were written first by hand, a few pages at a time, and in later years, using only his custom unlined yellow paper and Pilot Precise blue-ink pens. Seen here while still using a Montblanc, circa 1989. *Courtesy of the Peter Leonard Collection*

For decades, Leonard hung a framed portrait of his second agent—the legendary H. N. Swanson—above his desk as a reminder that if writing "isn't fun, it isn't worth doing."

With Annie Leibovitz on the set of her photograph for American Express, later entitled *Elmore Leonard, Miami*, circa 1987.

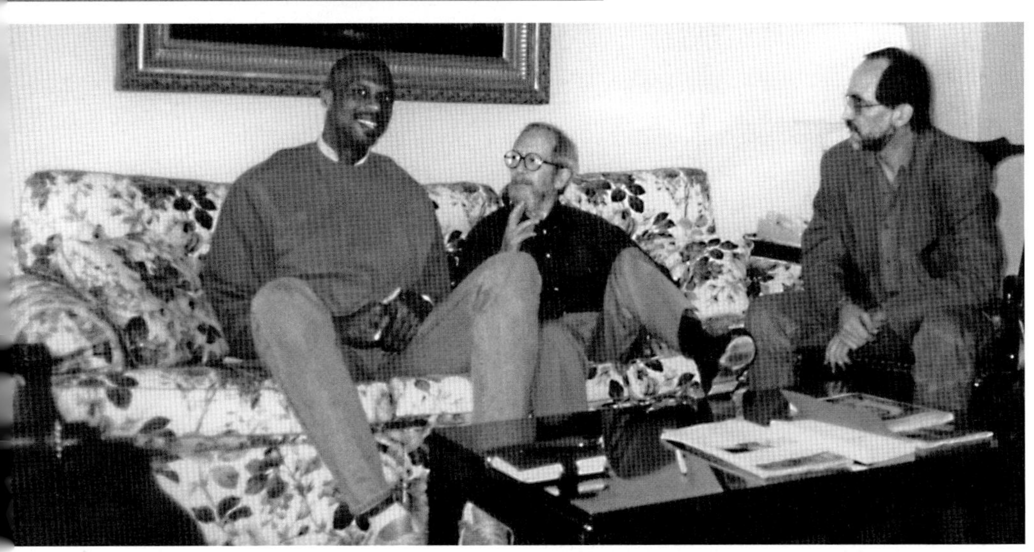

Leonard would make time to meet with high-profile fans with whom he shared a mutual appreciation, an admitted perk of literary recognition. Over the years, his correspondence would deepen with such fellow artists and celebrities as Aerosmith, Sir Elton John, and Steely Dan cofounder Donald Fagen; likewise, literary peers Martin Amis, Margaret Atwood, Jim Harrison, and Mike Lupica could all be counted among his friends. Seen here in April 1991, Leonard taking a few minutes to chat with mutual admirer NBA legend Kareem Abdul-Jabbar.

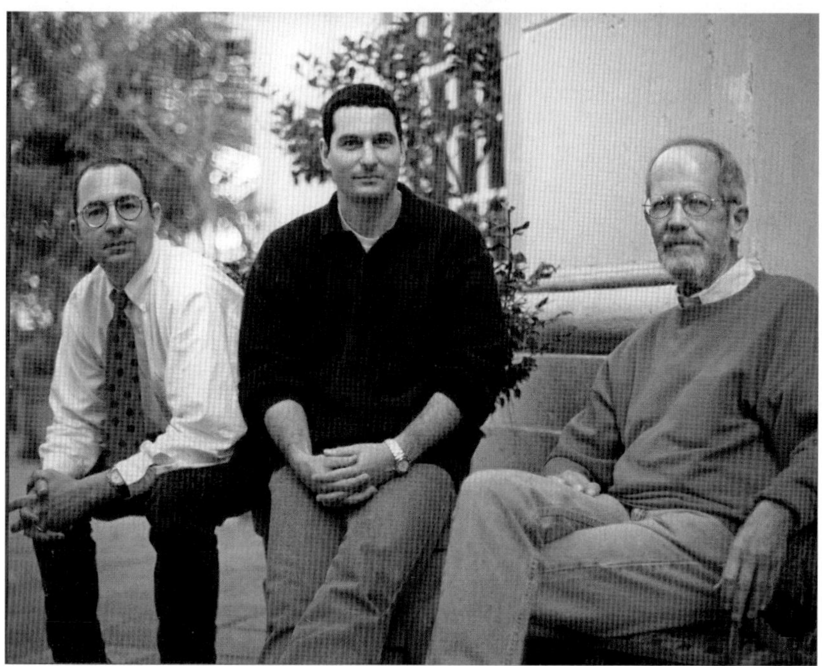

Many fans and critics agree that the success of *Get Shorty*'s 1995 adaptation paved the way for Leonard's broadest readership and popularity to date. Seen here (*left to right*): *Get Shorty* director Barry Sonnenfeld, screenwriter Scott Frank, and Leonard.

Signing an autograph for Rosario Dawson on the set of John Madden's *Killshot* (2008).

Hanging with actor Leonard Robinson, in costume as "Juicy Mouth," on the set of Charles Matthau's *Freaky Deaky* (2012). *Courtesy of the Judd Rubin Collection*

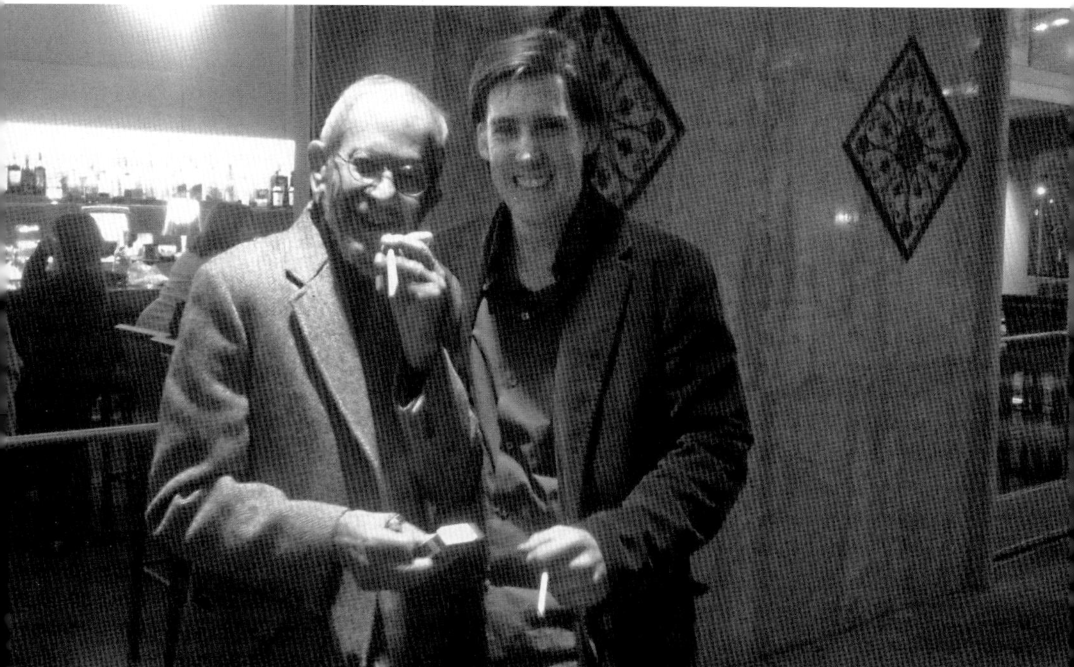

In preproduction with *Freaky Deaky* coproducer Judd Rubin, circa 2011.
Courtesy of the Judd Rubin Collection

Leonard receiving an honorary doctorate from his alma mater, the University of Detroit, in May 1997.

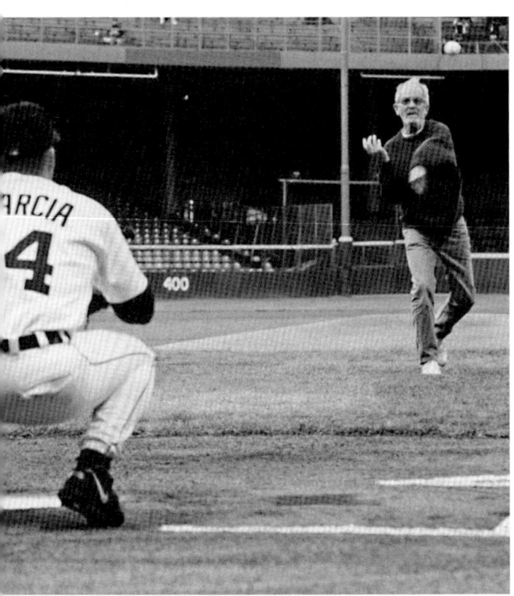

A dream come true for Leonard: throwing out the first pitch at Tiger Stadium, June 15, 1999. He'd asked his oldest son, Peter, to help him warm up his pitching arm a week in advance.

Beginning with his glowing *New York Times* review of 1995's *Riding the Rap*, renowned postmodernist author Martin Amis began a warm friendship with Leonard; seen here bestowing Leonard with his National Book Award for lifetime achievement in 2012.

For over thirty years, Leonard employed professional researcher Gregg Sutter for the various tasks and field work needed for his in-depth detail and historical accuracy. Seen here in Leonard's home office in June 2005 going over research for the ongoing "Carl Webster saga."

Upon the publication of his own debut crime novel, *Quiver*, in 2008, Peter Leonard soon developed a different relationship with his father—that of travel companion on book tours and joint speaking engagements, and creative confidant. *Courtesy of the Katy Dudley Collection*

The hit FX cable series *Justified*—based on Leonard's popular character Deputy US Marshal Raylan Givens—heralded another generation of Leonard fans. Seen here in 2010 on a panel discussion with the series' creator and executive producer, Graham Yost (*far left*), and its star, Timothy Olyphant.

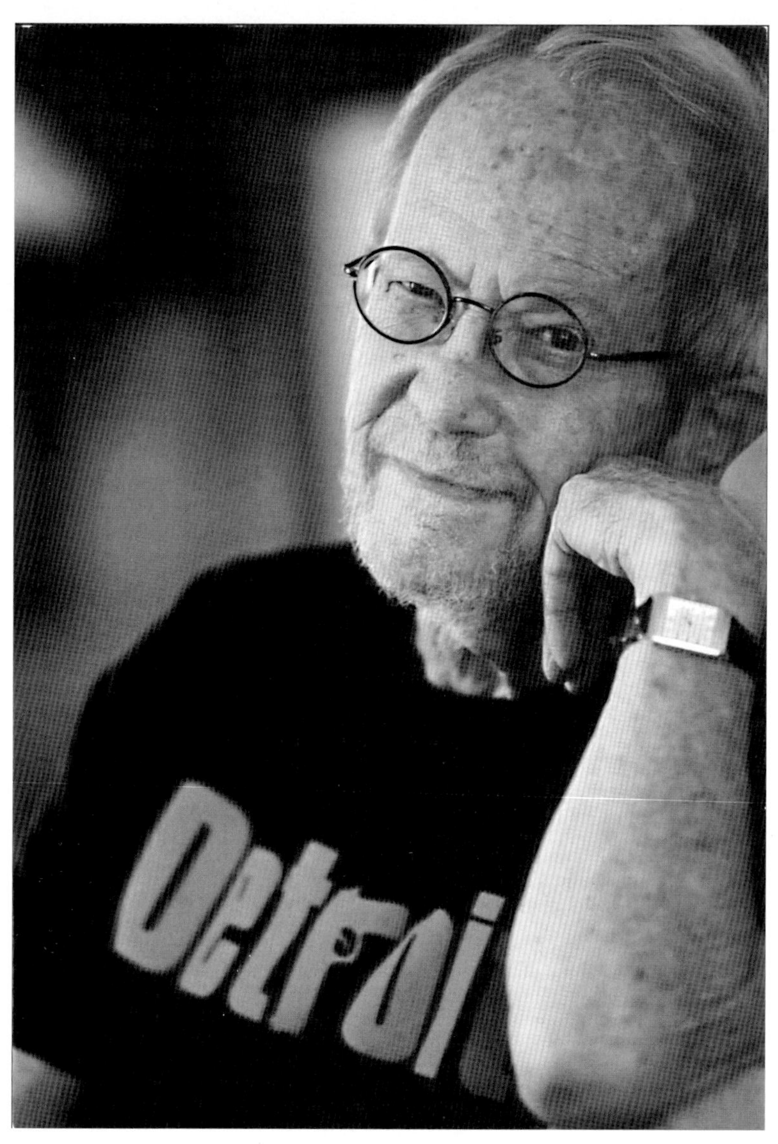

The last official author photo of
"the Dickens of Detroit," circa 2012.

description of a “bad trip” on page 138 of *Woodstock Nation*—and the fact there was “no drug test for LSD”—would be the ideal reference source for one character’s forced psychedelic rabbit-hole journey.)

In his original plot, Leonard opened the novel with Detroit cop Ray Manza getting suspended from the force for misconduct after shooting and “seriously” injuring a suspected rapist. While Manza’s career remains in flux, he is approached by the assistant of a powerful record promoter, Harmon Shane, and offered a high-paying gig to become the personal bodyguard for the promoter’s wife—a beautiful country singer named Milly Shane, who has just recently escaped an attempt on her life via a car bomb. Following the bombing, the promoter is insisting on heightened security—beginning with an experienced bodyguard with previous law enforcement training. It isn’t long before the chemistry between Manza and Milly leads to romance, and the inevitable realization that their tryst had occurred too organically—as if planned. They soon suspect their pairing is a possible setup—Milly’s husband playing them both in a scheme to get rid of his wealthier wife, who has begun to cost him money since retiring from the stage. Ultimately, however, Manza discovers that it is Harmon Shane, not Milly, who was the target of the bomb threat—a “gift” sent by former ’60s radical and old acquaintance Donnie Nix, who’s held a grudge against the promoter over a bad deal for decades.[41]

Leonard used his bomb squad research to consider the ways in which Milly could receive the bomb—first planted within her car, then mailed to her. In the latter, a mysterious phone caller alerts her about the box’s contents and the bomb squad is summoned, bringing the Manza character into play; he would retain the scenario, but change the circumstances and characters later. He also kept a scene in which the protagonist retrieves a bomb planted in the target’s swimming pool. As his research into police bomb squad units deepened, he changed the novel’s working title to *Fireworks*, seemingly inspired at the concept of a bomb squad cop going toe-to-toe with a self-proclaimed “mad bomber.”

Leonard then continued to play with his characters’ names and personalities like Scrabble tiles until all the pieces seemed to fall into logical place: Ray Manza soon became Chris Mankowski, formerly of the Detroit Police Bomb Squad and Leonard’s long-promised “Polish hero”; Milly Shane temporarily became Dawn, before finalizing into Greta Wyatt, an *aspiring* actress and star; and Harmon Shane and his lurid associates were absorbed into a whole new cast of original misfits. Entirely removing a husband from Greta's story, Leonard introduced the wealthy Ricks brothers—yuppie Mark and older brother, drunken Woody, who is the heir to the family fortune. At the story's new beginning, Greta has been raped by Woody Ricks and is in the process of legal retaliation. She now meets the suspended Mankowski while filing a complaint against the elder Ricks. (Prior to making the switch to Chris Mankowski, Leonard envisioned Ray Manza to be the second cousin of *The Hunted*'s Harry Manza—the "dynamite man" who does dirty work for that novel's heavy, Teddy Cass. Leonard had also tied the main plot with a secondary narrative involving Manza's father and his debt to a local loan shark, closely based on friend Bill Marshall's part-time investigator, Ernest "Chili" Palmer. Over the course of his outline, Leonard entwined the two plots, but ultimately abandoned the idea, instead saving Palmer's loan shark character for another book.)[42]

For a full decade, Leonard had been making a conscious effort to emphasize his women protagonists. For the new novel, he'd replaced the Donnie Nix "mad bomber" with a more passive and malleable burn-out named Skip Gibbs, and soon morphed his girlfriend, Patti, into the blackmail scheme's ringleader, the newly named Robin Abbott. For Robin, Leonard faced the challenge of writing a woman character younger than himself, and a true product of her own times: an embittered '60s idealist who, like many of her generation, had seen the silver lining of dollar signs in the Reagan '80s. Following a lengthy jail stint for which she blames the Ricks brothers, Robin has parlayed her former life as a domestic terrorist turned fugitive turned hardened convict into a quiet existence penning Harlequin-esque romance novels. However, she still hungers for revenge against Mark and Woody Ricks, and sees blackmail as her best option. In the story's new, revamped beginning, Robin turns to an old friend who is not only easily seducible—especially under the influence of primo LSD—but a whiz with bomb making: former flame and anarchist, Skip Gibbs, Hollywood pyrotechnic technician. To shape Robin Abbott's background and prime motivations, Leonard used the Weathermen timelines, as well as articles both from the library and then running in the news.[43]

During the final weeks of finishing the first draft in the summer of 1987, Leonard had stayed at the Beverly Hills Hotel in Los Angeles, spying Eddie Van Halen and wife, Valerie Bertinelli, poolside as he studied sketches of a trick explosive known as a "wham bag." He'd noted on the same hotel stationery, "I'm big into my wham bag," and added the device to the book's climax. Once he'd completed the manuscript at the end of the summer, Leonard was also satisfied that he'd found clever ways of including *all* the creative variations he'd hatched for delivering a bomb. However, he still wasn't satisfied with any of the book's working titles. It finally was Joan who suggested the phrase he'd chosen, based on a dance craze around Detroit explained to him while writing "Impressions of Murder" for the *Detroit News* in 1978. One homicide had told Leonard about the fatal "Freaky Deaky"—a funk-inspired grind like a reversed lambada. You did it with the wrong man's girlfriend and it'd get you killed. "We get a feel for that kind of action, huh?" the officer had asked Leonard at the time. "Know when to step outside, so to speak, let them do their own kind of *freaky deaky*. You remember that sexy dance? . . . Man, we had people shooting each other over it." Leonard later told journalist Becky Freligh that he considered Joan to be his best critic, adding, "She can tell when a character is acting out of character."

He dedicated the book to her: "*for giving me the title and a certain look when I write too many words.*"[44]

Freaky Deaky was released in May, earning Leonard his strongest reviews since *Glitz*. "There are so many amusing twists and turns in Elmore Leonard's latest crime thriller, *Freaky Deaky*, that one could almost give the entire plot away without running the risk of spoiling it," wrote Christopher Lehmann-Haupt in the *New York Times Book Review*, comparing Leonard's mature style to that of "free form poetry" and citing Leonard's deliberate use of present-tense energy as a prime example: "*Robin had a hip on the edge of her desk, red sunburst still on the wall behind her, watching him as she fooled with her braid.*"[45] Fred Lutz of the *Toledo Blade* picked up on the author's sly social commentary, writing, "Perhaps most of all, Leonard hates both the idle rich and the crooked rich . . . [He] may not have attempted the major American novel so far, but he has clearly produced a substantial body of work that has major significance. *Freaky Deaky* is just the latest installment."[46] *Newsweek*'s Peter Prescott—long a Leonard fan—was particularly taken with the novel's supporting characters and their historical context, singling out the author's own favorite, ex–Black Panther turned valet Donnell Lewis. "[Lewis] now works as chauffeur, cook, and general keeper of a gross, mentally incompetent drunk worth a hundred million dollars," wrote Prescott. "'Mr. Woody,' Donnell calls him, playing the role of the domesticated black man to the hilt. Rich men with mush for brains are natural targets of opportunity for people as rapacious as Skip and Robin, who are, like Donnell, ex-'60s radicals and ex-convicts . . . Better than anyone, Leonard puts his spin on his third-person narratives, changing his points of view and adapting his prose to fit the style of his characters."[47]

Leonard continued his practice of sitting for a few lengthy, in-depth profiles while on the promotional tour. In May 1988, he spoke with Hilary DeVries from the *Christian Science Monitor*, elaborating on his career and home life with Joan. "From the outside it looks like Ozzie and Harriet," DeVries wrote of the Leonards' Birmingham home. "But the real inside belongs to Elmore Leonard—scribe of the downside of the American dream. 'The greatest crime writer of our time,' somebody somewhere said. 'Oh, don't say that,' says Mr. Leonard, ushering a reporter across all that white carpet, intimidating as a blank page. 'That gets me into trouble with reviewers' . . . Since then it's been seven-figure contracts, movie deals, even that arty Annie Leibovitz photo for the American Express ad campaign—all for Leonard's annual rogue's gallery," the reporter noted.[48] (Only a few months later, *The Guardian*'s Hugh Herbert would offer his own take on the famed photographer's high-profile shoot with Leonard—which was soon used as the new "author photo," starting with *Freaky Deaky*: "*On the back of Elmore Leonard's new novel there's a photo of him, profile, sitting in a pine chair and set against a silhouette scene with one palm tree and a peach-pink sky. His hair and beard are mostly silver now, and he is dressed all in black—beret through sweater to boots—with a black portable typewriter on his knees. Up one edge of the picture, where fancy magazines put their photographers' bylines, it says American Express Travel Related Services, Inc.*"[49])

After revealing to DeVries details about his in-progress novel, Leonard also took a moment to comment on his now-long-standing sobriety from alcohol—including an admission that the AA "12 steps" were still folded in his wallet. ("He'll even give a reading. No. 11, the one about prayer and meditation, is his favorite. He paraphrases: 'Now in the morning, before I get out of bed, I just think about not playing any games or roles—just do the work, just be myself.'")

"How'd you used to feel?" DeVries had asked.

"Hung over," Leonard said.[50]

• • •

It had been nearly twelve years since Leonard had his last drink; he would speak about his former battles with alcohol only when directly prompted by an interviewer. At those times, he remained candid, emphasizing the serenity and contentment that sobriety had brought to his life. In 1984, he had accepted an invitation from Dennis Wholey—the host of *Late Night America*, a talk show out of Detroit, and a recovered alcoholic—to contribute an essay to his anthology on alcoholism, *The Courage to Change*. For the one and only time, Leonard wrote an unbridled, no-punches-pulled chronicle of his youthful addiction, and its effects on his marriage to Beverly and writing career. In April 1988, however, a controversial Supreme Court ruling suggesting that alcoholism was not a documented disease but, rather, an act of "willful misconduct" provoked one of Leonard's rare public political comments. "The justices don't know anything about drinking and its causes if they could come out with such a ruling," he told *USA Today*'s Arlene Vigoda. "Those who wrongly feel it's an act of misconduct will smile smugly and feel reassured; others who feel it's a disease will grumble."[51]

"You know who you look just like?"

"Who?"

"Elmore Leonard—the writer."

"Well," Leonard said, lighting a True green, "I am."

They were sitting in Tiger Stadium at the end of September. Leonard was geared up to watch Jack Morris lead his nineteenth win against the Toronto Blue Jays. Journalist and sportswriter Mike Lupica, who sat beside him, watched the whole thing.

"No kidding?" the usher asked, putting down his bucket of beers, seemingly forgetting the rest of the row beckoning for a cold one.

"No kidding," Leonard said.

As Lupica would write later, Leonard was hard not to recognize, sitting in the stands during a warm Indian Summer night in his usual tweed jacket, round tortoiseshell glasses, corduroy slacks, and ever-present Kangol paperboy cap. Then sixty-two years old and at the top of his game, Leonard could afford to dress any way he wanted—and he drove a Volkswagen bug around Motor City, always to the amusement of his out-of-town guests. For the lengthy *Esquire* profile Lupica was preparing, the two had decided to catch a Tigers game before heading back to the author's Birmingham home. "I'm not all that interested in the way educated people think," he told Lupica. "I mean, my main characters are smart and they've got this attitude, you know . . . I guess I'm still a kid on the corner of Woodward Avenue listening to my friends, who were all blue-collar kids. I was an enlisted man in the Navy. I hung around with enlisted men."

From the kitchen, Joan offered her own take on her husband's success: "Sometimes, the good guys win."[52]

CHAPTER 16

No More Mr. Nice, 1989–1992

> The thing is that there are reviewers who will say, "I like his older stuff better, his paperbacks."
>
> . . . The thing is, those reviewers weren't reading me in the late seventies; they only read me after *Glitz*. Where were they when I needed them?[1]

"It's 10 a.m. and normally crime-fiction master Elmore 'Dutch' Leonard would have sat down at his tidy oak desk half an hour to write," wrote Becky Freligh of Cleveland's *Plain Dealer*. But, Freligh added, "He has just finished writing his twenty-seventh book, *Killshot*, and is content for a while to read others' novels." Leonard admitted to Freligh that he'd once looked at writing "as a chore," but had since changed his outlook: "Since the late '70s, I've gotten to the point where I have fun writing books." He added, "I discovered Hemingway and saw there was another way to do it. That you could leave out a lot and if you were good enough, it was still there."[2]

Leonard had done just that, making his follow-up to *Bandits* a leaner volume. He decided to take his new cast of characters down some decidedly meaner streets—most often within their own psyches. He began in the fall of 1987 and considered titles *Roustabout*, *Up the River*, *Hardhat*, *Contract*, *Hat Trick* (again), *Lock Down,* and *Riprap* (riverboat terminology for a dangerous foundation made of loose bricks) before deciding on the more ominous *Killshot*.

He filled the inner cover of the new green spiral journal with contact information of his primary sources: the Detroit offices for the US Marshals Service and FBI, as well as their main Washington, DC, headquarters; the local law enforcement numbers for Cape Girardeau and contact information for the Missouri Barge Line Company and Century 21's Birmingham real estate office. In the case of any snags with law enforcement, he added old friend Dixie Davies's number at the bottom.

He'd had to relearn much of his previous knowledge on the Witness Protection Program (WITSEC), as much had changed in the way of forensic technology and government protocols since 1977's *The Hunted*.[3] He noted, "Before the witness enters the program, a Witness Security Inspector interviews [the] family to determine their 'vulnerability potential,'" and used it as the basis for much of the story's protagonist couple's nightmarish experience.

Initially, he'd been inspired to create his psychopathic antagonist based on interviews with real-life killer Marion Pruett before quickly splitting the character into a team of two hitmen—a seasoned professional and an arrogant thrill-killer. Leonard already saw the older of the two as a pensive, solemn Ojibway hitman; for his obnoxious pupil, he pruned old character sketches for Skip Gibbs's prototype, Donnie Nix—and briefly considered making him an associate of *City Primeval*'s Clement Mansell.[4] For the killers' prey—a middle-aged couple in the throes of empty-nest syndrome—Leonard had their personalities and occupations set while he toyed with names. He named the novel's heroine Carmen Colson, after his son Bill's soon-to-be-wife; he settled on Wayne Colson after "Matt" refused to talk. Likewise, Leonard's aging hitman went through numerous changes before becoming Armand Degas, while his Ojibway name, "the Crow," was made "the Blackbird."[5]

By September 1, 1987, Leonard had his cast in place. A major device he'd used was creating a parallel between the two killers and the Colsons. Although the personalities of all four primary characters couldn't be more different, their common frustrations with each other as partners supplied both humor and a rare dose of gritty domesticity to the story. Just as Armand Degas cannot force young Richie Nix to have the same coolness and professionalism as his dead brother, Carmen Colson can't seem to make her ironworker husband settle down into a comfortable position alongside her at the Nelson Davies Real Estate office. The characters continued to evolve along with Leonard's research discoveries, via Gregg Sutter, although the primary plot was a constant: the couple witnessing a hit gone wrong, led by Degas and Richie Nix. (He'd also maintained a chilling line from Degas that would also prove the foundational philosophy of his later, most popular character: "The only time you take out your gun and aim it at somebody is when you gonna kill them . . . It's the same as with a hunter, a guy that knows what he's doing . . . one shot, one kill."[6])

For the second major time, Leonard was also able to integrate themes and scenarios from early influence Richard Bissell into his writing. Just as Richard Bissell's *The Pajama Game*'s workers' strike had played a part in Leonard's initial notes on *Picket Line* and, later, Harry Mitchell's union woes in *Fifty-Two Pickup*, Leonard drew inspirations from his early influences *My Life on the Mississippi, or Why I Am Not Mark Twain* and *A Stretch on the River* for Wayne Colson's later work on a commercial barge in Cape Girardeau, Missouri.[7] And although Wayne is a far cry from the chauvinist represented by *The Switch*'s Frank Dawson, Wayne Colson's own passive-aggression and frustration cause the bulk of the couple's problems. He noted, "[Carmen] has energy, ambition (she's a survivor) and she's more intelligent than [Wayne]." He'd also given Carmen the same hobby as wife Joan—handwriting analysis—and incorporated their recent home viewing of Michelangelo Antonioni's 1975 surreal thriller, *The Passenger*, into the fictional couple's ongoing marital cold war.[8]

By the first of January 1988, Leonard had reached the midway point of the novel. Over the following month, he continued to tinker with it, taking only small breaks for a trip to Key West and Miami, as well as conferences in Los Angeles for the proposed *Desperado* series with Walter Mirisch. He and Joan were back on January 21—just in time for daughter Jane's second wedding the following day. He picked up steam at the end of February, and by April 11 completed the first draft. In gratitude for Gregg Sutter's early research excursions to Cape Girardeau, he both based the Colsons' home on his researcher's own house and—as an additional homage—dedicated the book simply, "*For Gregg Sutter.*"[9]

Killshot was released almost exactly one year later—April 21, 1989—and was the subject of another major publicity push by Arbor House. When the publisher rolled out the prospective advertisements for *Killshot*'s release, their tagline read, "How Does 'The Best Writer of Crime Fiction Alive' Top Himself?" Despite Leonard's own vocal modesty, Arbor House ran with the ad—much to the agreement of the author's critics. "Armand Degas, half French Canadian, half Ojibway, was nicknamed the Blackbird when he was a kid on the Walpole Island Indian reservation in Lake St. Clair," wrote fellow crime novelist Richard Lipez in the *Washington Post*. "[Now] in a moment of uncharacteristic midlife confusion (after doing a job for the Toronto Mafia in return for a Cadillac that's the shade of blue of his grandmother's cottage), Armand hooks up with Richie Nix, a man he has no respect for. Nix is a three-time loser whose aim is getting into the *Guinness Book of Records* by robbing banks in every state, except Alaska."[10] The *Tampa Tribune*'s George Meyer added, "The peripheral characters in *Killshot* are very nearly as interesting as the main characters. Consider a convict groupie who wonders: if Elvis had been Jesus, who would he have picked for apostles? And a federal marshal who specializes in seducing wives of participants in the Witness Protection Program . . . If Thomas McGuane were more tight-lipped, he'd aspire to be Elmore Leonard."[11]

What had caught the attention of most critics had been Leonard's effortless placement of Carmen Colson as the true protagonist of the story. Although each of the four principal characters were fully developed, Leonard had constructed a modern heroine who surpassed *The Switch*'s Mickey Dawson in moxie and *LaBrava*'s Jean Shaw in her clandestine strategic abilities; husband Wayne Colson isn't even present for *Killshot*'s final showdown and, in the end, Carmen and world-weary hitman Armand Degas appear as strangely kindred spirits. In the *Sacramento Bee*, Paul Craig concurred, writing, "A woman is the only likable character in Elmore Leonard's new novel, and her good sense and intelligence give energy to a somewhat ordinary plot . . . She is bright and alert to the subtleties of what goes on around her." He added, "Carmen is one of the best of Leonard's protagonists and is quite a change for a writer whose men usually save the day. She's three-dimensional and someone the reader can care about in a story that moves rapidly and entertainingly toward an explosive conclusion . . . It's all Carmen's show."[12]

Leonard spent the rest of 1988 making numerous in-store appearances and taking meetings for film and television projects. In mid-September, he and Joan prepared for their ninth wedding anniversary by shopping for a new, larger home. The size of their combined extended family had steadily grown with the additions of spouses and grandchildren, and with the major successes that had begun with *Stick* and *LaBrava*, the couple could now turn their sights toward a more upscale neighborhood. He and Joan soon found a French Regency–style on an acre of land at 2192 Yarmouth Road in Bloomfield Hills—six bedrooms, nine bathrooms, a three-car garage, large swimming pool and, much to Joan's delight, ample space for a larger garden. Leonard was especially glad to have a spacious living room for his new office. As the final paperwork on Yarmouth was being processed, Leonard and Joan took a trip to Scandinavia—four days in Stockholm, two in Helsinki, two in Copenhagen—with a final stop in London. Only a week later, Leonard was in Hollywood for another round of meetings. He met with CBS regarding a potential television film of *Unknown Man No. 89* on October 18 and was across town the following day discussing a possible *Stick* television series with NBC. Although those projects fell through, he and Swanson closed a deal on the long-gestating film adaptation of *Cat Chaser*—for which Leonard apprehensively accepted the job as screenwriter. (Leonard had also been talking with Bruce Willis for a proposed adaptation of *Killshot*; while in Manhattan for a literacy event hosted by First Lady Barbara Bush, he'd received a call in his room at the Sherry-Netherland hotel from the actor, direct from the set of *Bonfire of the Vanities*. According to Leonard, Willis had been interested in playing Wayne Colson, which puzzled him, as Carmen was the true protagonist of the story. He later told journalist John Milward that he would have been willing to write Wayne into the film adaptation's climax, but "Carmen would still be the one holding the gun." Ultimately, Willis passed.)

Leonard began his script for *Cat Chaser* on October 22 and had it completed in five weeks.

"One habit he developed at the ad agency stays with him," wrote Kevin Gonzalez from the *New Jersey Courier-Post*. "Leonard learned to appreciate unlined, buff-colored paper. He special orders 100-page pads of the stuff, fifty at a time, from PIP [Printing Company]." He added, "During the time an Elmore Leonard original paperback went for 35 cents, he wrote using a 29-cent Scripto, later graduating to a 98-cent Bic. He now uses a designer pen by Yves St. Laurent. It was a gift from his second wife, Joan, 'for which it is nearly impossible to get refills.'"

It was the first major interview held in the new house on Yarmouth, and the journalist focused on Leonard's current work process. To Gonzalez's surprise, not only had Leonard continued to write all of his works in longhand, but had remained steadfast in his aversion to computers. "[Leonard] admits to being a low-tech writer. He [in actuality, daughter Jane] transcribes and edits his handwritten prose with a second-hand, manual Olympia typewriter that he bought 12 years ago. He has put off getting an electric typewriter using the flimsiest of excuses, like, 'What if there's a power outage?'"[13]

Leonard soon revealed to Ian Meyer of the *Toronto Star* that he'd fulfilled his Arbor House contract, putting his untitled new book up for grabs. "I'm a free agent," he said, adding only a hint at the book's subject—his long-promised "Hollywood novel."[14]

As far back as 1983's *Stick*, Leonard had been integrating his own frustrations as a Hollywood screenwriter into the plots of his more humorous recent novels. Journalist Becky Freligh wrote at the time, "There's a character in *Stick*, a Hollywood producer's assistant, who describes the film industry like this: 'The lawyers and the business types answer to the egomaniacs running the conglomerates that own the majors and none of them knows . . . about film or has any kind of feeling for it.' Yes, Leonard says, that's pretty much him talking."[15]

On July 9, 1988, Leonard dated a fresh yellow spiral notebook. His tongue firmly in cheek, he began with the novel's title. It was one that he'd been saving for this very occasion—the two-word directive to finally get a spoiled, pint-sized A-list celebrity to commit to a project: *Get Shorty*.

With only the bare bones of what the Hollywood novel should include, Leonard was already certain that the protagonist should be an industry outsider—someone new to the Hollywood establishment, and instantly unimpressed with how everything is run. The previous year, Leonard had sent Sutter to Florida to meet with private investigator friend Bill Marshall and his part-time associate, Ernest "Chili" Palmer, about the ins and outs of gambling collections and loan sharking—all of which Palmer had done prior to his legitimate job for Marshall. (In 1982, Palmer had taken photographs around Florida for Leonard, including *LaBrava* locations such as the Cardozo Hotel, and, later, had even acted as a form of security-minded tour guide for Leonard and Joan during their research trip to Puerto Rico for *Glitz*.[16]) A stickler for names, Leonard had loved the sound of "Chili Palmer" upon their first meeting, and immediately wanted to use it for one of his characters. As the novel moved along, however, Leonard determined that more than just Palmer's name might be a good fit for his latest protagonist. Sutter interviewed Palmer at Bill Marshall's North Miami home during August 1988. To Sutter, Palmer detailed his entire criminal career, adding the needed details regarding the politics of low-level Brooklyn hoodlums. "When Joe Columbo took over the Brooklyn crew after Joe Profaci died, he borrowed a million dollars from Carlo Gambino," Palmer revealed. "He took that million and gave it to ten different guys, including me, and two partners, to put on the street in Miami. That's how I got into shylocking."[17] Palmer also outlined the methods he had once used to collect on outstanding gambling debts: "Whenever a guy comes to you for shylock money, usually the first thing you tell him up front before you give him a nickel is, 'Do me a favor, *don't* take this fucking money, okay? I'm advising you, don't take this fucking money, because if you take it, you're going to have to fucking pay it back . . . If you can't pay me every week, you're going to feel sorry about it. So if you don't think you can pay, don't take the fucking money.'"

Once Leonard combined those elements with Sutter's research into the underbelly of Las Vegas gaming, the story's pieces quickly fell into place. Leonard envisioned his Chili Palmer as a Miami loan shark frustrated with the incompetence and fiefdom mentality within his mafia organization. Once one of his "borrowers"—a meek dry cleaner named Leo Devoe—uses a false report of his death as an opportunity to escape to Las Vegas with the insurance money, Palmer is dispatched to follow the trail. As a favor to one of the casino bosses, he agrees to stop in Los Angeles to intimidate a B-movie film producer who's holding an outstanding debt to the casino for $150,000. Intrigued at the idea of learning the film trade, Chili, instead, offers to get the producer's investors off his back while the $150,000 is recouped. After all, his quest for the missing Leo Devoe seems to have the makings of a hit film itself. "Immediately after the Florida trip, I flew to Las Vegas," Sutter later wrote. "Elmore had arranged for me to meet Golden Nugget casino manager White Mitchell, for whom Bill and Chili (the real one) had made collections. White gave me details about high rollers . . . Inevitably, I ended in Hollywood. There wasn't much I could tell Elmore about the movie business."[18]

Again, Leonard had considered linking characters from his previous novels—*Glitz*'s Jackie Garbo almost had an appearance, as did *Gold Coast*'s Jimmy Cap—but, ultimately, scrapped the idea. However, *Get Shorty* would include the most real-life anecdotal material than the author had used before. Much of Chili's and Zimm's conversations during their "lessons" about Hollywood came from years of conversations with seasoned professionals Walter Mirisch and H. N. Swanson. He had also assembled the full roster of characters based either on people he had known or as an amalgam of real-life celebrities and Hollywood power players. Soon, producer Bobby Zimm became Harry Zimm, and his ex-wife Diane—a former scream queen tired of the patriarchal politics of the Hollywood establishment—soon became Karen Flores. The novel's central antagonist—a wannabe Los Angeles limousine company owner, dealing hard drugs on the side—named Michael Carter soon morphed into a sly reference to one of Leonard's lesser-known previous characters: Bo Catlett—Chili's nemesis—soon reveals himself to be a distant relative and namesake of a Black Civil War veteran from *Gunsights*. Finally, the titular Shorty—fictional superstar and bona fide diva Michael Weir—was based, quite transparently, on Dustin Hoffman—although Leonard played coy with the direct reference for years. Later, when Hoffman publicly acknowledged his hand in the novel, Leonard was quick to retort: "Does Dustin think he's the only short actor in Hollywood?" (Many years later, Hoffman would even approach Leonard's grandchild and Jane's daughter, Megan Freels Johnston, a movie producer herself, telling her, "Oh, you don't want to work with me, then—I'm Shorty.") For Chili's mentor, Harry Zimm, Leonard seemed to have the most fun jotting his own memories of Hollywood's collective quirks and social norms, putting some of the most biting commentary into the character's mouth—including verbatim quotes from H. N. Swanson and Menahem Golan, respectively. In order to stay current on the film industry's ever-evolving trends—both on-screen and off—Leonard searched through trade magazines and gossip columns, adding bits of dialogue to his manuscript, as well as fragments of character personalities from real-life stars. For Zimm, his random observations included:

> Zimm tells Chili the picture business is conducted in office buildings: "They don't even make the deal standing in the backlot . . . The picture business is full of bottom feeders . . . People in the picture business, so many of them outcasts, attracted to a Hollywood that remains always beyond their grasp . . . People get big names in this business making bad movies. Or an agent or manager becomes a heavyweight and you look at the movies his clients are in and they're all shit . . ."
>
> Harry: Some of those studio assholes, they phone in their work effort.[19]

For a major subplot revolving around Zimm's goal to attain the film rights to a big-budget melodrama entitled *Mr. Lovejoy*, Leonard studied a similar deal struck by director Richard Donner to film the Bill Murray holiday comedy *Scrooged*. For Zimm's backstory as an independent industrial filmmaker turned B-movie schlock auteur, Leonard playfully used experiences working alongside both Bill Deneen and Tom Brank, although he based much of Zimm's experience with special effects projects on Disney executive Bob Rogers. Finally, Zimm's personal reasons for not wanting to play ball with the major studios was based, nearly verbatim, on Oliver Stone's candid interview with *Vanity Fair* in January 1989. "In the thievery category," Stone insisted, studios were using "the vast new millions that came from the videocassette market," in which "only 20 percent of a film's videocassette revenues are allocated back to the film's gross," muddling the ultimate profit distribution to the movie's creators.

Separately, Leonard noted one Stone quote that summed up his book's ultimate thesis: "It's a Mafia—that's what it is. You talk about teamsters, you talk about corruption in this country. The film business is as corrupt as anything there is." The sentiment would later be uttered by drug-runner Bo Catlett. He based much of Karen Flores's career on B-movie scream queen Linnea Quigley (star of *Creepozoids*, *Hollywood Chainsaw Hookers*, and *Attack of the Killer Bimbos*), but her philosophy on Susan Sarandon's interview with the *Hollywood Reporter* earlier that year: "I've never had that kind of shit where my character's name is in the title of the story and the whole story revolves around me . . . It becomes a little upsetting to be overqualified for projects, to be brought in just to make them a bit better," and from Debra Winger on her self-imposed hiatus from acting, "Maybe it was the stiletto heels. I've just never been into fuck-me pumps." Inspired by the women's words, Leonard wrote, "*The Hollywood power game (who's got the biggest dick): when big producers and directors create 'star vehicles' and 'package' the whole film.*" In a section of his notebook entitled "Market Research," he added, "I think all the people involved in market research should be forced to have their wives and girlfriends fill out exit polls when they leave the bedroom. That would be the end of market research."

Although Leonard was widely acknowledged for forgoing traditional outlining and plotting his novels at this point, he knew where his story was headed from the very beginning. He had noted early on in his notebook, "Outcome: They ask Chili if he wants to 'run production' at the studio." But even with all the characters mapped out and a rough idea of the ending predestined, Leonard took special care with *Get Shorty*. Uncharacteristically, the novel proved to be one of the rare instances when he'd started the book over more than once, spending weeks hammering away at the story's opening scenes numerous times before getting them to his standard. He'd sat down to begin the novel on November 21, 1988, only to scrap the first few pages and begin again the following day; he finished his second attempt, amassing thirty full pages, by the first of the new year, but was then forced to shelve it until January 12 while he flew to Los Angeles for a series of more film and television meetings (actor Brian Dennehy had shown an interest in adapting *Swag* as his screenwriting-directorial debut, additionally planning to write the script and take on the role of Frank Ryan). He finished the new, revised version of *Get Shorty*'s opening chapters eight days later. He started again, from the ground up, on February 12.

Although Leonard was settled in the new Bloomfield Hills home during the month of March, most of April was spent on the road: he'd been booked at signings in Atlanta, Washington, DC, New York (for a joint appearance on *Today* with younger author Jay McInerney, then touring with his own third novel, *Story of My Life*, as well as a dinner with publisher Otto Penzler), Philadelphia, Cleveland, Minneapolis, Seattle, San Francisco, Los Angeles (for meetings and dinner with H. N. Swanson), and, finally, Toronto.

Leonard had three hundred pages of *Get Shorty* for Jane to type by August 19 and spent the following week solely working on the novel's ending—the last chapter. He finished the final, revised version on August 24.

He celebrated by attending a Dizzy Gillespie concert.

"He can play it cool like the best of them, then put on the pressure when it counts—and it counts in book contracts," wrote Mary Conroy in the *Capital Times*. "The 64-year-old Leonard, who's been spinning out westerns and crime fiction since the 1950s, just negotiated a contract for three books that's somewhere in the neighborhood of $4.5 million. But that's not all. His contract stipulates what the publisher has to spend on advertising."

Indeed, Leonard had another reason for whipping *Get Shorty* into perfectly lean, salable shape: it was his first novel in a decade to hit the auction block for a high-bidding new publisher. Ultimately, his old stomping ground, Delacorte, successfully won back their prodigal author, marking his return to both the publishing house and his former editor, Jackie Farber.[20] He elaborated to Conroy, "Publishers are owned by conglomerates. It's not like it was in the '50s where you had comfortable old companies with paneled walls, tweed coats, pipes. It's the middle-of-the-road novels that are going to suffer because the companies aren't spending the money to promote them . . . but they'll spend on the books they know are going to sell anyway." And, with his end of the *Cat Chaser* adaptation all but completed, Leonard had no trouble additionally announcing his weariness of the Hollywood game. The journalist had added, "It's no secret that after 15 years of screenwriting, he's leaving the scripts to others from now on."[21]

Upon its release on August 16, 1990, *Get Shorty* not only garnered Leonard the strong reception that both he and Delacorte had hoped for, but its intimate yet humorous take on the Hollywood establishment broadened Leonard's crossover appeal—further establishing his place as, perhaps, the hippest and "coolest" of contemporary authors. Additionally, Leonard's track record as a successful yet notoriously frustrated screenwriter didn't get past the critics. "For Leonard, *Get Shorty* is obviously payback time," wrote the *San Diego Tribune*'s Robert J. Hawkins. "Through the earthy eyes of Chili Palmer, we see a savagely funny Hollywood, populated by people who only know how to make pictures, not conversation. They are greedy, deceitful, inept, brutally indifferent to truth and creative content . . . he probably used his 20-plus years of experience with the movie industry to write this one." He added, "*Get Shorty* (a featured selection of the Book of the Month Club) is so smooth, so clean, so fast. My only complaint is that it needs a hundred more pages. Hey, Leonard? Look at me. You did good."[22] John Krull of the *Indianapolis News* added, "Elmore Leonard must love Hollywood the way a con man loves a gullible widow. He knows an easy mark when he sees one . . . This should come as no surprise."[23] Calling the novel "a crime-caper-cum-comedy-of-American-manner," the *Dayton Daily News*' Terry Lawson made one of Leonard's favorite observations, writing, "[Leonard] is clearly out for a little literary revenge in *Get Shorty*, but the book's obvious message—that in Hollywood, life is little more than movie fodder, and the pitch is more important than the product—never impedes its forward momentum."

Leonard underlined the review's final line: "*Anybody who can turn misfortune into a book as witty and satisfying as* Get Shorty *has obviously long ago learned not to take anything all that seriously—save his craft.*"[24]

As had long been the case, Leonard was most appreciative of the positive notices that came from his literary peers. "Mr. Leonard doesn't know Los Angeles physically in the way he knows Miami and Detroit, but he understands it perfectly," wrote Nora Ephron in the *New York Times*. "He understands that in Hollywood nothing is wasted: every love affair, every divorce, every criminal act has a shot at being, at the very least, a pitch and, at the very most, a major motion picture." Ephron added, "By the time the book ends, Chili's movie has a second and third act, a female lead who used to scream at slime people in Harry Zimm's movies, and Chili is as close to being a good guy as he can possibly be and still be the protagonist of an Elmore Leonard novel. It would be easy to assume that what Mr. Leonard is saying here is that con men are right at home in the movie business; but it seems to me he's making an even wittier point, which is that even tough guys want to be in pictures."[25] (At the time, Ephron had just seen her screenplay *When Harry Met Sally* directed into a breakout hit for its director, her ex-boyfriend, Rob Reiner; the film's director of photography, Barry Sonnenfeld, would soon become an even bigger fan of Leonard's novel and make a major play to bring it to the big screen in only a few years.)

By now a hardened Leonard devotee, novelist Stephen King was asked by the *Detroit Free Press* to act as a guest reviewer. He wrote, "Nobody does it quite the way Leonard does . . . After you've finished one of the moderate-to-powerful cardiac jolts he calls novels, it seems perfectly natural to come away writing like him (or trying to at least)." King added, "What I mean, the man's got his act together. Lotta writers out there probably wish they could say the same thing."[26] Big words from King who, like Leonard, had battled alcohol addiction for years (the fellow author later admitted to having been drunk while delivering his mother's eulogy in 1974—the year Leonard first joined AA—and, throughout the previous decade, found himself binging on cocaine and over-the-counter drugs). King had also dabbled in harsher substances, and had taken longer than Leonard to achieve his own hard-earned sobriety. At the time of his glowing *Get Shorty* review, he was just putting the finishing touches on *Needful Things*—the first novel that he, himself, had attempted since becoming sober.

"References to various Leonard projects and associates are hidden throughout *Get Shorty* [and] the many industry types who are paraded past for the reader's enjoyment all look and sound and act like the awful truth," wrote future Ross Macdonald biographer Tom Nolan in the *Wall Street Journal*. "But for many L.A. readers, the most shocking event in the book will be when a frustrated screenwriter insults a major star during a studio meeting."[27]

Although Leonard had long joked with his closest circle of friends about his intentions to write a Hollywood satire inspired by his years as a professional screenwriter, he remained adamant that the novel was only that—a satire—with no ill will toward the industry that had helped stake his early fiction career. "People see *Get Shorty* as a payback, but I'm not mad at Hollywood," he told Tim Warren from the *Baltimore Sun*. "I know what it's like. I know you take your chances when you go out there with a book. So what? That's the way it's always been . . . Raymond Chandler said you wear your second-best suit that's just been paid for when you go to Hollywood."[28]

The *Milwaukee Journal* soon reported, "Next up from Leonard is *Maximum Bob*, a book about a West Palm Beach judge who likes to give the maximum sentence. Or maybe it's about a 27-year-old probation officer named Kathy Diaz Baker, whom the judge would like to seduce. Or maybe . . . With Leonard, you can expect just about anything."[29]

As he'd done with *Killshot* before it, Leonard had used *Get Shorty* to successfully make relatable protagonists out of antagonists, as well as everyday people not affiliated with either law enforcement or crime. With his next novel, he gave himself yet another offbeat challenge, envisioning a morally dubious lead character whose very status should embody justice; in essence, a self-important—and self-serving—circuit court judge. Leonard had already crafted a memorable corrupt judge in *City Primeval*'s Alvin Guy, although that character's early death kick-started the majority of the novel's action. For *Maximum Bob* (another rare, yet consecutive, instance when Leonard had the book's title decided before putting pen to paper), he aimed, instead, to create a judge who was not corrupt like Guy, yet viewed his courtroom as his own personal fiefdom—in this case, populated with the various hoodlums, hookers, and drug dealers that the streets of Fort Lauderdale could offer. The titular character would also have a patriarchal view of his duties and those civil servants who literally served him, both in and out of the courtroom.

Like *City Primeval*'s fictional Alvin Guy, whom Leonard had based on real-life judge James Del Rio, he based Gibbs on an amalgam of controversial real-life figures from the Florida justice system: judges Marvin Mounts, Carl Harper, "Maximum Marion" Obera, and Robert "Maximum Bob" Potter—the latter of whom had tried disgraced televangelist Jim Bakker, and thus earned his nickname, Leonard noted, "for handing out heavy sentences to defendants who show no remorse or in their own defense."

A new practice in Leonard's research method was color-coding the corresponding articles delivered by Gregg Sutter within his notebook: black ink for primary notes, red ink for the articles and research materials he'd quote or cite from, and blue ink for the actual drafts of manuscripts. He started the notebook off with a brief character sketch of the book's central protagonist—Judge Bob I. Gibbs of the Palm Beach County Circuit Court. "A born cracker," Leonard wrote, whose central goal is "recognition"—"To be somebody." He then combed through hundreds of microfilms and photocopied news articles; Gibbs's cold rejection of one defendant's plea for leniency after he'd personally put him on probation—"I put people in prison when they kill people"—was inspired by one article entitled "Husband's Killing Gets 10 Years," with Leonard noting it to resemble Bob Gibbs's courtroom "wrath." Likewise, Gibbs setting one unlucky defendant's bail bond at a billion dollars had actually occurred in one Florida district court. Across one microfilm scan, entitled "Man Gets 30-Year Sentence: Drug Dealer Given Maximum Jail Term," Leonard scrawled across the top, "How Gibbs got his name."[30] Likewise, Leonard used a piece in *MacLean's* to come up with Gibbs's quote to a wife-beater standing before his bench, "Women—can't live with 'em, can't live without 'em" before handing down the maximum sentence.[31]

But for the vast majority of "Maximum Bob" Gibbs's unorthodox courtroom antics and penchant for attracting some of Florida's stranger criminal offenders, Leonard primarily drew on the exploits of Marvin Mounts. As far back as receiving Mounts's first fan letter in 1985, Leonard had been fascinated with the fire-and-brimstone judge and his draconian take on the law of the land. He'd studied Mounts's career, beginning with the very first press the then-forty-two-year-old neophyte had received in 1974: a lengthy feature profile in the *Miami Herald*. "Materialism is, perhaps, a human trait," Mounts had said at the time. "But I'm content, happy. I'm human enough to want more money—but I ran for this job. I knew what I'd get paid and my family and I have a very good life." It was also noted that the young judge had an original Winslow Homer hanging on the wall of his chambers.[32] A 1984 article in the *Palm Beach Times* clearly demonstrated the type of scenario that would be ripe for a character like Bob Gibbs, outlining Marvin Mounts's strict discipline upon a young woman jogger who had been arrested for jogging topless. Leonard had noted in red ink, "Bob's girlfriend—how they met?"[33] (Another *Palm Beach Times* article from the same year, entitled "Mounts Asked Not to Try Case on Grounds He Hates Defendant" was self-explanatory; Leonard had merely crossed out "Mounts" and wrote in "Gibbs"—then placed the article aside in his notes.)

Unlike his real-life inspiration, the fictional Bob Gibbs had a wandering eye, already weary of his younger second wife and often daydreaming about which of the lovely young attorneys or paralegals who visited his chambers might make the cut as the next Mrs. Gibbs. Thanks to a quirky discovery by Sutter, Leonard became fascinated with the idea of Gibbs being married to a real-life "mermaid"—a professional gymnast who donned carefully constructed wetsuits resembling fins, then put on choreographed underwater shows for eager tourists. True to form, Leonard added another characteristic: it would be revealed that, following a near-death experience, Leanne Gibbs also believed she had attained psychic abilities, and would often be inhabited by the spirit of a young African American girl who'd been killed in the Jim Crow South.

Just as Leonard had positioned female protagonist Carmen Colson as the true hero of *Killshot*'s climax, *Maximum Bob*'s own lead was the author's first female law enforcement officer, West Palm Beach probation officer Kathy Diaz. During the same research trip that had yielded so much information on the Lovely Weeki Wachee Mermaids, Sutter met with both probation officer Karen Trambley and Valerie Rolle, administrator of probation and parole services for Palm Beach County. Leonard was most interested in how these women navigated both the inert patriarchal politics of the justice system, as well as dealt with the dangerous criminals whom they supervised. Rolle had commented, "I've experienced [gender bias] a few times . . . when they come on to you with this 'honey baby' stuff, you kind of have to nip it in the bud. If they get away with it once, they think they can get away with it again." Rolle added, "They're kind of like children—if you don't get them at the beginning, they think they can get away with it. And it's going to be harder." It was just what Leonard needed to put his Kathy Diaz character in front of the lecherous Bob Gibbs's bench.

In his character list, Elmore placed Kathy Diaz at the top, followed by the return of a minor character from 1981's *Split Images*—Officer Gary Hammond, who had formerly assisted Detroit cop Bryan Hurd in his takedown of millionaire killer Robbie Daniels. Now advanced in his own law enforcement career, Hammond returns as Diaz's love interest—a dynamic that would, too, prove a familiar scenario to readers of *Split Images*. (For the first time since he constructed a lengthy background biography for *The Switch*'s Mickey Dawson, Leonard created a separate section within his notebook entitled "Kathy's Motivation"—ultimately taking up five pages of biography—more than any other character. Leonard would later shelve some of the background for another future character he had in mind—an empowered woman US marshal, and the daughter of Marshall Sisco, the literary avatar of close friend Bill Marshall.)

The threat against Gibbs leads to the first—and a particularly memorable—attempt on his life, as an alligator is mysteriously released into his backyard. And for the background for the types of young offenders who would make such a threat against Gibbs, Leonard intended to bring back some fan-favorite characters. From their earliest appearance in the 1978 manuscript for *Gold Coast*—then still titled *Seascape*—and in primitive form in 1969's *The Moonshine War*, the dubious hick Crowe family had provided Leonard with oodles of creative raw material from which to draw. From their mouths had come some of his novels' most memorable moments of dangerous stupidity; likewise, the Crowes had been a perfect villain for equally deadly mayhem. With *Maximum Bob*, Leonard pulled an overtly cinematic trick in "resurrecting" a long-dead fan favorite villain from *Gold Coast*. With little more explanation than finding his deceased brother's hideous powder-blue leisure suit packed away in a trunk and, ultimately, donning it, Elvin Crowe is—in many ways—the return of the older novel's antagonist, and to perfect effect. It would be Elvin's nephew—the moronic and equally stubborn Dale Crowe Jr.—who would be the alligator suspect. (Leonard later told Anthony May, "One of my favorite heavies was Roland Crowe from *Gold Coast* . . . So for *Maximum Bob*, I invented his brother, Elvin. And Elvin has just done ten years for murder. He went after [Cal Maguire] from *Gold Coast*, because he blamed it on the guy and not [Karen DiCilia], who shot Roland . . . and he shot the guy." Leonard added, "He shot the wrong guy and then he did ten years . . . He comes out and he's on five years' probation and the probation officer, Kathy Diaz, she gets him. Of course, he had been sentenced by Bob Gibbs."[34])

Elmore's cinematic structure quickly introduced all the primary characters within the four chapters, as well as the inaugural attempt on Gibbs's life. For this, his next section was simply labeled "Alligators." He wrote: "*A 'nuisance trapper'—licensed to capture gators holed up in residential canals and off golf course ponds . . . The judge's gator man is a licensed 'nuisance' trapper and also 'gigs frogs for a living'—'I hunt frog.'*" In order to save face—and very likely find the perpetrator himself—Gibbs hires his "gator man" to dispose of the deadly reptile with the added incentive that he can keep it for "hide and meat." (Leonard noted that a seven-foot alligator has an approximate $300 value, or $32 a foot for skins and $5 a pound for the meat.)

Leonard got a further handle on the inner workings of the justice system through issues of *Correctional Compass*—the official newsletter of the State of Florida Department of Corrections, and meant to both inform and entertain the correction officers community—edited and vetted by the Office of Information Services and printed by the inmates at the nearby Zephyrhills Correctional Institution. He'd saved the February 1990 issue's "Quiz About the Corrections Biz," which included such stumpers as:

- What utensils do death row inmates get for their last meal?
- What was Cool Hand Luke's crime?
- Who is this man and at which institution did he film a TV segment?

Beside the final question was a glamour shot of a smiling Burt Reynolds.

Leonard began the first draft on January 1, 1990, and had it completed by the first of July. The galley proofs were approved on December 21.

He began his following novel the very next day—right on schedule.[35]

• • •

Whereas some critics had vocally championed his return to the grittier aspects of crime with *Glitz* and *Killshot*, new readers seemed to gravitate toward his recent balance of crime with a somewhat lighter touch, the humor playing a more prominent role in his outlandish characters—and the situations they found themselves in (Bob Gibbs's unsuccessful assassin—the alligator—had even been given its own perspective during its starring scene). The *Houston Post*'s James W. Hall was particularly amused with Leonard's experimentation with bringing an animal's perspective into the narrative, writing, "Early on in *Maximum Bob*, Elmore Leonard's latest, an alligator mysteriously appears in Judge Bob Gibbs' backyard. While the reptile is roaming around in the dark, Leonard gives us a glimpse of things from the gator's point of view . . . It's a very strange interlude, going into the gator's mind like that, an odd and risky moment, even for Leonard, who is used to dipping into some pretty exotic minds."

Hall added, "Yet, I, for one, come away totally convinced that this is how an alligator thinks, the very words it uses. And if it doesn't think this way, then by god, it should. Such is Leonard's magic."[36]

CHAPTER 17

Exits and Entrances, 1992–1995

Richard of Linville Falls, North Carolina writes: "Please quit splitting infinitives. Let's have more Philip Marlow and less *Magnum P.I.* and *Miami Vice.*" I wrote to Richard and told him that I don't feel obligated to religiously keep infinitives intact. And that Abe Lincoln, by his own admission, split a lot more of them than he did logs. A reader in Vancouver says he's not Catholic and never goes to church, but if he ever does, he'll light a candle for me.

A housewife from Charlotte, North Carolina writes: "I have never written anyone a fan letter in my life. This is definitely a first. My husband is getting tired of me spending more time in the sack with a Leonard book than with him. So I told him, 'Get my attention.'"

Now sixty-seven years old, Leonard wore both his age and his status well. But with both age and status came a whole new generation of pupils and detractors—both of which he took in stride. Leonard soon began bringing the various fan letters he received to public appearances, amused by the wide range of diverse readers his writing seemed to transfix. He had begun receiving letters from cops and federal agents complimenting his accuracy—as well as from inmates assuming he'd spent time behind bars; at least one fan thought Leonard was a woman ("Did he even see a picture of me first?") and more than a few African American fans wrote to him assuming he was part of their community. "Well, I've been called anti-Semitic because this guy in one of my books, this Mr. Perez, refers to someone as a 'Jew lawyer,'" he told Mark Marvel from *Interview* magazine. "But look, this character's from New Iberia,

Louisiana, and the lawyer got him sentenced to Angola. I'm not anti-Semitic, but I can't say the same for Mr. Perez. Some readers just don't realize that this is a character's point of view."[1] According to Peter Leonard, there was even one in particular that his father forever treasured among the collection: "Dear Mr. Leonard, I'm currently incarcerated in a federal correctional institution," the letter began. "How I ended up here is a long, unbelievable tale involving dysfunctional women, heroin and pure foolishness. Your books are the first ones I've liked and could share with my beloved, semi-literate fellow criminals and maniacs . . . If it's embarrassing or violates some strange writer's code, please keep your secret to yourself, but if you wouldn't mind terribly we are all wildly curious."[2]

Leonard was additionally amused when scolded not for the content of his books, but his own author photo on the back of the dust jacket. As he later explained, one woman had written that his official Arbor House picture, in which he stood smiling in a dark blue T-shirt with "Detroit" emboldened in a vibrant white, varsity font, had prompted her to write that he looked like one of the characters of his books—"a bum." She had suggested that Leonard take a lead from fellow crime author Gregory McDonald and, in the future, pose in proper shirt and tie. ("He always wore the rattiest clothes and we would tease him about it," recalled daughter Katy Dudley. "He was always in Hawaiian shirts, or this one sweater with a big hole in it. And a lot of rock T-shirts—like his Nine Inch Nails shirt."[3] Christopher Leonard also recalled, "One time, Elmore spoke to a class of students and the teacher ended up writing an article about it. She seemed shocked that he showed up that day wearing Birkenstocks with white socks. She said, 'He could wear anything he wanted, but he's wearing a pair of Birkenstocks.' She just couldn't get over it. Well, after the article ran, my father gave me the Birkenstocks and I sent them to the teacher. I believe she ended up putting them in a 3D frame and mounted it on her wall."[4])

More often than not, however, Leonard's incoming correspondence was positive—and often came from his peers. He'd long established friendships with the likes of the late John D. MacDonald, Donald Westlake, George F. Will, Charles Willeford, Jay McInerney, and Mike Lupica—yet new and established authors continued to, likewise, initiate distant friendships with their favorite crime writer. Following a glowing review of *Killshot* in which he wrote, "Elmore Leonard is not only the best crime writer in the country, but maybe the best writer around, period," newly published hard-boiled author Eugene Izzi followed up with a personal letter of appreciation to Leonard, adding, "You're the teacher—I'm the student." Leonard paid it forward by providing the younger writer with a blurb—just prior to Izzi's death under mysterious circumstances. (In December 1996, the recovered alcoholic and author of more than a dozen books was found hanged outside the window of his fourteenth-floor office in downtown Chicago. It was ruled a suicide, but fans would forever debate Izzi's true cause of death, insisting that his covert investigations into white supremacist organizations for a future novel had led to foul play.) Renowned American short story writer and essayist Raymond Carver had also sent off a handwritten fan letter of his own, claiming that *Glitz* had made him a "rock-hard admirer" of his work. "It's good work, solid," Carver wrote, "[and] your ear is second to none." He added, "I hope that this new book will shake me loose or unfetter me from this minimalist stuff." Carver—another recovered alcoholic—passed away only two months later at the age of fifty. Of his fan letter, Leonard later admitted to Tim Warren of the *Baltimore Sun*, "That meant a great deal."[5]

Although he'd shown only a fleeting interest in poetry during his youth, when he met one of America's best-known living poets at that time—Allen Ginsberg, founding member of the Beat Generation and controversial social justice crusader—Leonard's first instinct was to ask for a poetry lesson. They had met by chance on April 4, 1990, while attending an annual PEN literary dinner banquet in Manhattan. During a joint interview with Martin Amis, a novelist and an ardent fan, he told Charlie Rose that he'd always wanted to write poetry, but didn't know how. "I asked Allen Ginsberg, 'How do you write a poem?' And he said, 'Here, I'll show you.' And he reached down into his canvas sack and he couldn't find a piece of paper . . . Finally, he got something and he was going to write on the back of it. Then he wrote one line that had to do with this candlelight on the table, and just then, [Andrew Wylie] brought over Jamaica Kincaid—and that was the end of my lesson on how to write poetry."

Ginsberg had actually retrieved a photocopy of a recent article on himself from the *New York Times*. On the back, he had written:

You start w/yr thought at

Morgen—

But you might notice the candlelight.
your feet might tap,
silver threads, trumpets . . . past

But my agent tapped my shoulder
"Jamaica Kincad" tall,
a kiss—

Snyder ________

back to primordial syntax

A.G.

for Elmore

4/4/90[6]

Leonard began his next book on December 22, 1990. Again, he'd already picked out his title—*Rum Punch*—and the intention of bringing one or more characters back from both 1978's *The Switch* and 1990's *Get Shorty*. He planned to reintroduce an older, yet no wiser, Ordell Robbie, who'd apparently never abandoned his life of crime after the botched kidnapping of Mickey Dawson, and had since become a high-priced gun-runner. And even after a decade together, Frank Dawson's old mistress, Melanie, would still be loyally by his side. In Leonard's earliest notes, he had Robbie coming into contact with both the fictional bondsman as well as his part-time freelancer for nabbing runaway skips—disillusioned former film producer Chili Palmer. (However, those plans changed with the promise of a proper *Get Shorty* sequel featuring Palmer, again, as the chief protagonist.)

Having started his new project notebook with his regular roll call of important real-life reference contacts, Leonard had started his more than fifty pages of character notes, including the potential return of Chili Palmer. He'd considered a playful in-joke regarding an old review in the *New York Times*, which had branded the author's fictional archetype "the decent man in trouble," adding, "Chili is reading a book entitled *A Nifty Guy at Loose Ends,* [and is] considering it for a movie."[7]

Leonard also envisioned making another key protagonist a Florida bail bondsman—a position the author deemed often misunderstood and inaccurately presented in most fiction. While still working on *Maximum Bob,* Leonard sent Gregg Sutter down to Florida to begin the research that would help reshape *Rum Punch* and lead to a host of new characters. "I interviewed sheriffs, detectives, probation officers, jail guards, coroners, judges, and a few strippers," he later wrote. "In July 1990, [DEA agent] Jim Born introduced me to fellow FDLE [Florida Department of Law Enforcement] agents and his friend, Steve Barborini, an ATF agent, who would be the loose model for Ray Nicolette in *Rum Punch.* I met Steve at a gun show in Fort Pierce where I saw firsthand how easy it was to buy guns in Florida. Gunrunning would be an important component in *Rum Punch.*"[8] (Jim Born recalled, "Dutch wrote the book *Rum Punch* and, just by chance, he has a tall, thin ATF agent, and a shorter, squatter FTL agent, work on the case, which, although I've never specifically asked him, I soon suspected that had something to do with us. Gregg would tell me, 'Oh yeah, he's based it on you two.'"[9])

Although, in Leonard's mind, Ordell's gunrunning operation began with the acquisition of registered firearms stolen from individual houses (a nod to *Swag*), the collective data from Sutter's research and interviews with Born and Barborini would yield far more details into the black market economics of weaponry used by Florida's worst drug kingpins. Leonard noted, "Because the Florida legislature refuses to ban assault rifles and machine pistols, the federal government bans the import, but allows manufacture in the U.S. . . . Still thousands are smuggled out of Florida." Leonard also started a separate section within Ordell's biography for the names and schematics of some of the guns most commonly prone to international smuggling, as well as the ones easily obtainable by Ordell himself.[10] (In the 1997 film adaptation, *Jackie Brown,* Quentin Tarantino kept the line, but gave leading man Samuel L. Jackson an edgier modernization to his AK-47 sales pitch: "When you absolutely, positively got to kill every motherfucker in the room—accept no substitutes!") Leonard's revamped incarnation of an older Ordell Robbie replaced much of the playful naivete and humor displayed in *The Switch* with a hardened career criminal philosophy shaped by years of jailtime and an evolved narcissistic ambition. Drawing from one of the many articles on gunrunning supplied by Sutter, Leonard had given Ordell a pragmatic view on his new career, noting, "[It's] easier to buy a gun in Florida than it is to get a driver's license, marriage license, to join a video rental club, [or obtain] a library card." But, behind closed doors, Ordell has little to no respect for the dedicated "gun collectors" with whom he often associates (referring to them interchangeably as "gun queers" or "barrel-suckers"), yet has no moral trepidations about dealing with the racist and antisemitic dregs within that subculture. Once Leonard had determined to swap Chili Palmer for Louis Gara, the reunited duo's very first exchange included a perfect example of whom Ordell was now willing to do business with. "During that research trip, I learned of a 'Nazi-KKK' rally to be held on Worth Avenue in Palm Beach," Sutter later wrote. "Early on a Saturday morning, I grabbed my cameras and headed over to the bridge to Palm Beach. The *Fort Lauderdale Sun-Sentinel* reported the event under the headline 'Klan Marches in Palm Beach Security Tight as Protesters Heckle Rally.'" He added, "At first, Elmore wasn't going to use this event in the story, but I lobbied hard, and to my great delight, he opened *Rum Punch* with the rally scene."[11]

Sutter's first round of research helped in bringing Ordell Robbie's underground gun operations into greater focus, as well as the real-life figure who would act as a model for Max Cherry—Leonard's noble bail bondsman. Using a newsletter given to him by Judge Mounts, Leonard soon contacted Mike Sandy, who had an office across the street from the West Palm Beach courthouse with a sign on the door that read Private, and soon became the perfect model for Cherry. In his own biographical notes, Leonard had written, "[Max] is always bothered, self-conscious, by the image the bail bondsman seems to have—the reaction of almost anyone connected with criminal law; that he's in a sleazy occupation . . . His wife, Marguerite, reminds him of it." Leonard added, "Marguerite used to tell acquaintances her husband was in Law and let it go at that. She acts ashamed of him and has for 30 years." Leonard noted that Max had initially been a deputy with the Palm Beach County Sheriff's Office, but quickly grew concerned that his wife didn't approve of that career, either . . . "He's good at it, but with mixed feelings, primarily because of the image."

The second primary protagonist Leonard envisioned kept with his recent practice of crafting realistic, empowered female leads. Surrounded by the countless morally dubious characters that populate the world of

Rum Punch, middle-aged flight attendant Jackie Burke seems, at first, the most level-headed and relatable. Her decision to use her frequent business travel as an opportunity to moonlight as transporter for Ordell Robbie's drug finances is more out of desperation than greed. According to Leonard's notes, at the novel's start, Jackie would be working for a significantly smaller Caribbean airline, which, despite her criminal record, had hired her for the years of experience she'd accumulated. However, the pay was also far less and, as a small, blond, white woman, "stands out in the company of the West Indian and Black girls, Bahamians and Hispanics, who make up the majority of the flight attendant roster."

Leonard added, "She's known Ordell for twelve years and can describe the changes in him, from an easy-going guy to an intense, cold-blooded type who plays roles, acts cool, smiles, but is intensely self-serving . . . Against her better judgement, she agreed to carry [thirty thousand dollars] from Freeport to West Palm and she's picked up by a Florida state cop." To accurately depict both the causes of Jackie's dire financial straits, as well as her experiences behind bars, Leonard had combed through Sutter's research on flight attendant training, career trajectories, financial and benefits compensations, and the discrepancies between the men and women of the profession.

Before giving Jackie her proper character name, Leonard had written, "'The Stewardess' would be processed through the booking department of the Palm Beach County jail and held in the women's section of the PBC stockade if bail isn't met." It would be this process that directly leads Jackie into the acquaintance of Max Cherry. However, Jackie's apparent downfall as Ordell's money mule is brought about through the keen eyes of two law enforcement officers, Faron Tyler and Ray Nicolette—inspired by Steve Barborini and Jim Born, respectively. Leonard wrote: "Both Florida boys, though Faron is more of a cracker than Ray. They met in college, University of Miami; Ray is from Miami originally, Faron from upstate . . . [They're] buddies, but competitive, in the way two close friends play one-on-one with a basketball and use their elbows freely."[12]

At the beginning of the novel, Ordell Robbie has just invited old friend Louis Gara—recently released from his own prison stint for armed robbery—to visit him in Palm Beach. Hoping to entice his former partner into his larger-scale gun operations, he makes Louis privy to a scheme he's worked with Melanie to rob a white supremacist gun nut out of his valuable personal arsenal of high-caliber artillery. Ordell also lets Louis in on his ongoing system of using the local "jackboy" gang to do his dirty work—as well as his ongoing fear that, if captured by the police, any one of his dim-witted lackies could put him away for life. Gara's new day job as an office factotum for bail bondsman Max Cherry—the product of a mob-corrupted local parole board—leads Ordell to a solution for all his problems: bailing out any of his incarcerated employees from Cherry's office, then killing them once they're back on the street (brutally demonstrated by his slaying of paroled jackboy Beaumont Livingston). When Jackie Burke is caught with fifty thousand dollars of Ordell's money by Ray Nicolette and Faron Tyler, she becomes his newest target. Aware she's a dead woman as long as Ordell suspects she's made a deal against him, she, instead, makes a deal with Ordell himself: Jackie will bring in a half-million dollars of his hidden stash from the Bahamas in exchange for a percentage—and her life. Unbeknownst to Ordell, she's also made a deal with Nicolette and Tyler to trap Ordell red-handed. And unknown to all—save her lovestruck, reluctant accomplice, Max Cherry—she's got a plan of her own to keep the half-million.

After starting the novel only a single day after sending off the galleys for *Maximum Bob*, Leonard was quickly dissatisfied with his opening and began again the day following Christmas. He was a half dozen pages into his improved second attempt when filming began of an hour-long profile on his career for the BBC (Leonard's sales—particularly of the contemporary crime novels—had only steadily grown in the UK since *Glitz*). Entitled *Elmore Leonard's Criminal Records*, the short-subject documentary was produced and directed by Mike Dibb and Rosana Horsely. Leonard not only agreed to sit for more than a week's worth of interviews beginning on January 7, but helped arrange for sessions with Joan, Gregg Sutter, Walter Mirisch, Judge Marvin Mounts, and numerous Detroit police detectives who had worked with Leonard, including Dixie Davies. The budget even allowed for on-site filming around Detroit's courtrooms and police evidence rooms, and sections of West Palm Beach and Walpole Island.

By May 20, Leonard was two hundred and fifty pages into *Rum Punch*, and had it completed exactly one month later. (He had taken a brief break to accept the first International Association of Crime Writers Hammett Prize for *Maximum Bob* in New York on May 1.) He immediately sent the manuscript off to Delacorte. One day later, he headed to the Santa

Barbara Writers Conference. While sitting at a late dinner at Chasen's in West Hollywood five days after that, Leonard stubbed out his True cigarette and made his first stab at quitting cold turkey.

Rum Punch was released August 3, 1992. To many critics, the novel represented a perfect balance of Leonard's gritty and satirical sides.

"There are few, if any, good guys in the world according to Elmore Leonard," wrote the *Boston Globe*'s John Koch. "Only bad guys and better guys, and the same goes for his females. Few writers get under the skin of shooters and schemers and thugs with Leonard's laconic detachment. His lowlifes, dominated in *Rum Punch* by ruthless gunrunner Ordell Robbie, are disturbingly real. They are not merely shady characters: they are shaded and contoured, flawed flesh and blood so creepily human that we can't rationalize the ugly things they do as fictional set pieces."[13] The *New York Times*' Christopher Lehmann-Haupt wrote of the book's empowered Jackie Burke, "Once again, as in Elmore Leonard's previous novel *Maximum Bob*, the pivotal character in *Rum Punch*, Mr. Leonard's 30th work of fiction, is a woman. This suggests that the author of such crime thrillers as *Stick*, *LaBrava* and *Glitz* is intent on continuing down his path away from stories starring macho men compelled to seduce every woman who falls in their way."[14]

In the *Washington Post Book World*, Michael Dirda wrote, "There are no heroes in *Rum Punch*, only survivors . . . Beneath its fast-moving surface, *Rum Punch* is a novel about growing old, about the way time changes us, about the old dream of starting over again and its cost . . . When Louis blows an important deal, Ordell says to him, with real sorrow, 'What's wrong with you, Louis? . . . You used to be a beautiful guy, you know it?' . . . *The Switch* used to be a satirical and light-hearted caper novel, with a surprising, upbeat ending; but now, knowing what will become of its main characters, it seems bathed in pathos, like the photograph of a smiling wedding couple whose marriage ended in sorrow and bitterness."[15]

The last few years had heralded a new age for Leonard, a time when his personal life appeared to be taking back as much as it had given. With all the success that his books and reenergized Hollywood traction had brought to his work life, he had also suffered a number of personal setbacks. At around the time of his move back to Delacorte with the release of *Get Shorty*, Leonard had received word that his mother, Flora, had died at the age of ninety-five. She had spent her last years living with her oldest child, Margaret, in Little Rock, Arkansas, and Leonard himself had put his writing on hold during the funeral arrangements. Then, in May 1991, H. N. Swanson—Leonard's agent and decades-long mentor in the writing trade—passed away at the age of ninety-one.

Leonard had been emotionally prepared for both, as his sister would often offer updates on Flora's health; likewise, in preparation for his own retirement, Swanson had largely taken a backseat to his clients' career operations beginning in 1990. Leonard had been introduced to one of Swanson's protégés the year before, then-twenty-eight-year-old Michael Siegel, with the intention that he would be taking over Leonard's representation. Leonard later told *Publishers Weekly*: "[Swanson] had Michael [Siegel] working for him. About two years before he died, I said, 'Why don't you let Michael handle me?' . . . Swanie was starting to lose it and Michael was young and sharp. [Now] he's my 'manager,' as far as being technically correct. He's my manager so that he can get into producing films. He's got Andrew Wylie involved primarily for ferreting deals."[16] Wylie later recalled, "I'd known Michael had worked with Swanie as an assistant or something. And then Michael went to CAA and he had a sort of out-of-office alliance with them, doing both literary and film. But then that relationship fell apart and Michael had his own agency. So, in agreement with Michael, I would do nothing without his approval as well as Elmore's and we sort of co-agented the literary work while Michael handled the film properties." He added, "Then Michael sort of moved out of the business and the film side moved to, initially I believe, UTA [United Talent Agency] and then, eventually, [Anonymous Content]. [But] I was doing the front catalog as well."[17]

Although Leonard had already penned a loving chronology of their many years working together for Swanson's memoir, *Sprinkled with Ruby Dust*, upon the agent's passing, he was moved to write an original eulogy for national publication:

> The first time I went out to Hollywood to work, in '69, [Swanson] drove me past his home in Beverly Hills. "The only one on the street," Swanie said, "without a mortgage." He drove me past it again in '72. "There it is, kiddo. Three and a half acres." He took me to lunch a couple of times during that period and to dinner at the Brown Derby on Wilshire when, I think, the only people in the place were Swanie and I and George Raft.

Swanie laughed easily, eyes shining, for a gruff old guy who could scare you to death if you didn't know him. I watched him negotiate with a publisher once. Swanie wanted a new book deal for me. The publisher said, "But that isn't fair, we already have a contract." And Swanie said, "I never said I was fair. Do you want the boy or not?" I must have been twenty years older than the publisher, but to Swanie, I was "the boy."

A framed photograph of Swanie that appeared in *GQ* stands on the bookcase behind my desk, Swanie looking over my shoulder as I work, reminding me, "If it isn't fun, kiddo, it isn't worth doing."

Nine years ago, I dedicated a book to him. "This one's for Swanie—bless his heart."[18]

Less than a month following the publication of *Rum Punch*, Leonard told the *Detroit Free Press*, "I'm writing a movie—my first original screenplay in twenty years, since *Mr. Majestyk* . . . You know, I've [said] many times I never wanted to write another movie, but this one is different. It's an idea Billy Friedkin and I have been talking about for a while. He did [*The*] *French Connection* and *The Exorcist* and gets people's attention."[19]

It had been a decidedly fast courtship between director Friedkin and Leonard. He had heard from the auteur in the middle of June, after Friedkin had already worked out the initial ideas for a Miami-based cop drama he was developing for Paramount called *Improper Conduct*. They had a productive first phone meeting on June 19, during which Friedkin admitted to his own admiration for Leonard's novels and his openness to a fresh take on the material.[20] "Paramount had asked me to rewrite a script they had that was not unlike *Basic Instinct*, which had, that week, made $155 million gross," Leonard later told journalist Anthony May. "They had one kinda like where a cop falls in love with a woman who's involved in crime. And I said, 'No, I don't want to do it.' But Friedkin was involved and he called and said, 'Why don't we do our own?'"[21]

Friedkin's proposal came at just the right time; Leonard had just put the finishing touches on his next book, the story on an aging Miami bookie, tentatively entitled *Pronto*. Within three weeks, he had a list of notes to present to the director and—following two equally productive phone conferences on July 10 and 14—flew to Los Angeles on August 5. They held a meeting together at Paramount the following day.[22]

Once back in Birmingham, Leonard was ready to begin a detailed treatment of the newly renamed *Stinger* on August 15. With the twenty-six-page treatment completed and sent to Friedkin on August 24, Leonard started the screenplay itself the following day. (He had been sidelined earlier that month by the beginning of the East Coast leg of his *Rum Punch* book tour, which had also included an appearance on ABC's *Good Morning America*—and continued to work on the script while on a brief trip to Toronto.) Leonard completed the first draft on September 28 and sent the revised second version to Friedkin on October 2—the month of Paramount's initial preproduction date.[23] Leonard later told Anthony May, "I said, 'Here's the problem, here's this guy who's kind of a wealthy guy, but if he's not laundering money, what's he doing with two or three million bucks sitting there in his house, cash?' And Friedkin said, 'Let's think about it.' I said, 'My least favorite thing to do is to sit with someone and plot. Why don't I call you?'" Leonard went on, "So I left and my agent, Michael Siegel, said, 'Why don't you just forget about it? You've gotten paid up-to-date, you've made enough money on this thing. Go write your book.'" According to Leonard, he returned to the hotel and immediately started brainstorming. The next morning, he woke at five and, instead of reading, sat himself down and tackled the story problem. "It came in five minutes," he later recalled, "[and] then I had to wait three hours to call Friedkin. [Later], I called him up and I said, 'There's a televangelist who uses ESP powers. Open with him' . . . He says, 'I love it! Write it!' It took about three weeks and I sent it to him . . . In the meantime, he started production on *Blue Chips*, a basketball picture—so I haven't heard from him since then."[24]

Just after finishing and submitting *Rum Punch* to Delacorte in the summer of 1991, Leonard began his new story about a Miami-based bookie in the autumnal years of his career. When a stool pigeon saves his own skin by throwing Harry Arno under the bus to both his mob employer (recurring mafia patriarch Jimmy Cap) and the FBI, a cat-and-mouse game leads the bookie and those in pursuit to Rapallo, Italy.

Leonard's initial focus for bookie Harry Arno was, much like *The Hunted*'s Al Rosen, the personal philosophy of a man facing, perhaps, the final season of his life. (Although Leonard himself was, by all accounts, a *youthful* older man, he had opted to make his new protagonist his same age—sixty-six years old, at the time of the writing.) He quickly dispatched now–Florida resident Gregg Sutter to conduct the preliminary research on mob-run sports books and collections, as well as chat with old friends Bill Marshall and Ernest "Chili" Palmer for leads and the needed authenticity. Leonard, however, opted to take Joan on the somewhat more luxurious research trip to Italy—Milan first, then Rapallo; it was also their twelfth wedding anniversary. He later told author Lorenzo Carcaterra, "As soon as I heard the name, I knew I'd found a place for my next book. All I knew about Rapallo was that Ezra Pound spent time there. I researched the town, figured out what Army divisions were there in World War II—that way I could place my main guy there during the war. Once I read up on Pound, there weren't any problems."[25]

Prior to the Italian tour, Leonard had envisioned bookie "Harry Arno" first as "John Nesita," then "Frank Recita," and finally as "Jerry Arno"—a seventy-year-old bookmaker who's been skimming off the top of his mob employers for decades, only now considering a secret retirement exodus to provincial Spain—later Italy. Over the course of four pages, Leonard filled in the needed gaps to flesh out Arno's daily routine as a functioning bookie—including his personal habits, likes, dislikes, and background information. Initially, Harry's Miami stomping ground was to include numerous additional references to previous novels, beginning with Harry's apartment: "Page 70, *LaBrava* . . . [Harry] has Maurice Zola's suite—Maurice has died and his widow, Jean Shaw, has sold the hotel to Jimmy Cap." As part of Leonard's extensive biography on Harry (whose birth name fluctuated between both the author's notes and early outlines), a lengthy section was spent on his time fighting in World War II. Arno had been stationed in Italy, working with the CID (Criminal Investigation Department) Unit, apprehending deserters hiding out among the Italian countryside. During one memorable mission, Arno had been part of a CID team that ventured into Rapallo on a tip that a group of deserters were operating out of that city, selling their stolen goods in Genoa and Milano. "There is a gunfight," Leonard wrote, "[and] the deserters ambush them, and [Harry] shoots and kills one of them. They take the rest of them back to Pisa, the Disciplinary Training Center, where [he] sees Ezra Pound for the first time. Later, he tries reading Pound's poetry."

Having read British biographer Peter Ackroyd's 1981 definitive work on the American poet, *Ezra Pound and His World*, Leonard became fascinated with the Idaho-born expat. Pound had famously forsaken his US existence in order to be on the forefront of the "Lost Generation" literary movement, fostering the early careers of T. S. Eliot and Ernest Hemingway, as well as laboring over a mammoth epic poem of his own, *The Cantos*—written piecemeal over the course of half a century. But Pound's literary reputation was destroyed following the Second World War after his sympathies for Benito Mussolini and Adolf Hitler garnered the writer traitor status in his adopted Italian homeland. He was incarcerated by the Italian resistance in 1945 and extradited to Washington, DC, where he was soon diagnosed by American doctors as a narcissist and psychopath; Pound was ultimately sent back to Italy before his 1972 death.

Like his early research into Confederate general and founding member of the Ku Klux Klan Nathan Bedford Forrest, for 1959's *Last Stand at Saber River*, Leonard had become fascinated at the duality within such a historical icon—revered by some and despised by others—and attempted to examine him through the lens of his fictional protagonist. He noted two quotes, the first from Jean Cocteau to Pound: "The tact of audacity consists in knowing how far you can go without going too far,"[26] and another from Pound's response to Robert Lowell regarding his personal destiny: "To begin with a swelled head and end with swelled feet."[27] Although never implicitly stated, by using *The Cantos* as a motif—as well as Harry's own romanticized memory of his youthful encounter with Pound—Leonard saw those two maxims as mirrors between the poet's life and Harry's own existential crisis.

Although Harry has been operating on the wrong side of the law for the majority of his adult life, his jovial and easygoing style has even earned the (occasional) respect of local law enforcement—particularly one FBI agent named Buck Torres—who's usually happy to turn a blind eye to the bookmaker's source of income. However, that comes crashing down on Harry when Torres sticks his neck out to relay a message picked up on a recent wiretap of Jimmy Cap. Leonard wrote, "Buck Torres tells Arno that the FBI have Jimmy Cap wired. [He] says to Arno, 'I hope you're clean, I hope you haven't been skimming on Jimmy Cap . . . They're gonna get word to Jimmy that you've been skimming—They're making you the bait.'" With girlfriend Joyce's help, Harry escapes to Rapallo, eluding attempts to bring him in from one of Cap's men—an imported Italian hitman, Tommy "the Zip" Bitonti—and a US marshal with whom he dealt a decade earlier during his aborted Chicago testimony. Although Leonard's cast of characters included Italian mafiosi hitmen and a retired stripper who wore glasses and shimmied to Led Zeppelin on stage, it was this latest lawman who would soon take on a life of his own. In later years, Leonard would often cite Raylan Givens as one of his favorite characters to use, admitting that more than once, bringing the modernized cowboy archetype into a story had directly led to a wider narrative playing field and workable plot. A true hybrid of all Leonard's strongest protagonists combined (such as the flawed yet heroic scouts who had populated his earlier Westerns, as well as modern cops like Raymond Cruz, Bryan Hurd, and Chris Mankowski) Raylan soon proved to be an amalgam of all the author's most important character vices and virtues under one hat—quite literally, a Stetson.

In June 1991, Leonard had been a guest speaker at a Western Merchandisers conference in Amarillo, Texas, and, there, met a book distributor named Raylan Davis. At the time, Leonard had only one question for the man: "How would you like to be the star of my next book?"[28] But he merely cribbed Davis's first name and touches of his physical appearance; for Raylan Givens's full characterization, Leonard looked back to his previous lawmen, and—in keeping with certain refined plot symmetries *Pronto* held with 1977's *The Hunted*—carried over a number of important traits from that earlier novel's secondary protagonist, world-weary US marine David Davis. Leonard had long admitted that his one regret over *The Hunted* had been a misplaced emphasis on the story's titular prey, Al Rosen, rather than the stoic-by-trade marine sergeant who reluctantly serves as his protector. With *Pronto*, Leonard was able to tinker with that singular plot device that had irked him for years, now returning to the Rosen-Davis dynamic with Harry Arno and Raylan Givens—only this time organically allowing the marshal to infiltrate the narrative and arise as a fan-favorite protagonist.

Although Leonard began with Raylan's first name before starting the book, the character's surname eluded him. He considered "Raylan Moon" as a reference to the hero of *Gunsights*, then "Raylan Major" before, ultimately, circling back to "Givens"—although he'd briefly toyed with giving the marshal a nickname used internally within the marshal's office, "'Speedy' Givens." Leonard had also considered making Givens a *former* US marshal, now doing skip traces and similar freelance favors for either Marshall Sisco or Max Cherry: early on, Leonard had noted, "Max calls Raylan Moon in Tucson to ask where he thinks Frank Recita might have gone. Moon perks up. He thinks about it [and] calls Max back. Or all of a sudden, stops in to see Max (no longer a marshal) . . . Frank stole Moon's gun and killed a man with it."

Ultimately, however, giving the character an internal conflict regarding his use of violence worked best as a functioning marshal; the questions of a personal code of honor and the justification of brute force had long been among Leonard's recurring themes. Beginning Givens's biography, Leonard noted, "The former U.S. Marshal [is] from Kentucky—Somerset County . . . He's been a federal marshal [for] fifteen years; joined after applying in the fall of 1977 in Detroit. [He] almost quit when his first assignment was to serve striking miners and union leaders of the UMWA [United Mine Workers of America] with a Taft-Harding court order that would force them back to work." Soon, however, Leonard changed Givens's birthplace to Harlan County. He later recalled, "I had to give [Raylan] a background of having been familiar with violence beyond what he might have seen as a marshal. I'd been wanting to use Harlan County anyway, and got hold of a documentary that won an Oscar about twenty years ago called, *Harlan County USA* . . . I got to know [Raylan] then." Leonard added, "I had my researcher look up all kinds of things, not only that movie but he also got me news magazine and newspaper stories about the strike and that time . . . Just little things like that, I think add to it."

Sutter came back with folders of usable background and Leonard pored through it all before beginning his notes.[29] Eventually, he decided that Raylan—like his father before him—would have worked the mines before venturing off to his law enforcement career, but still held sympathy for the career miners who never got out of Dodge. Although much of the dialogue didn't make the cut, Raylan initially explained to Joyce, "Coal companies believe death is something they have to just live with."

Soon, Raylan Givens began to come to life:

> [Raylan] moved from Harlan County to Pike County. He and his dad both worked for a wildcatter when he was twenty-years old, out of Evarts, Kentucky. [He] went to Evarts High School and played football for the Wildcats (in 1973) against their archrivals, the Harlan Green Dragons. They moved to Pike County in the summer of 1974 (he didn't graduate from Evarts High School until he was twenty—was working in between), and from Wildcats football, he became a real wildcatter working wildcat mines with his dad. When his dad was severely injured, Raylan went to work for a stripper [strip-miner]. Shortly after, this man took them all to Detroit.

> Raylan graduated from Wayne State and Oakland University and was a Detroit cop for a few years before joining the U.S. Marshals Service.

Leonard later condensed the biographical material, putting only snippets of background into Raylan's own mouth, as the deputy marshal explains his philosophy on violence to the brutish "Zip," Tommy Bitonti's equally vile henchman, Nicky Testa:

> "I've worked deep mines, wildcat mines, I've worked for strip operators, and I've sat out over a year on strike and seen company gun thugs shoot up the houses of miners that spoke out. They killed an uncle of mine was living with us, my mother's brother, and they killed a friend of mine I played football with in high school. This was in a coal camp town called Evarts in Harlan County, Kentucky, near to twenty years ago. You understand what I'm saying? Even before I entered the Marshals Service and trained to be a dead shot, I'd seen people kill one another and learned to be ready in case I saw a bad situation coming toward me . . . In other words . . . if I see you've come to do me harm, I'll shoot you through the heart before you can clear your weapon. Do we have an understanding here?"[30]

By the novel's second act, Raylan Givens began to take over. Following Harry's escape to Rapallo, Leonard himself had more fun writing Raylan's role larger, devoting the bulk of the second and third acts to the marshal's journey to unofficially extradite the bookie back to US soil. He later recalled, "I thought Harry would take it all the way. Then Harry got to Italy and he changed. I mean, I didn't change him. He changed." Leonard added, "And I thought, 'What am I going to do here? He needs help.' I thought, 'In this frame of mind, he's going to start drinking again and he's going to get deeper into trouble, more disenchanted with the place.'"[31]

Upon his return from Europe with Joan (and following a brief detour to West Palm Beach), Leonard began consolidating his notes with Sutter's, putting together the first outline for *Pronto*. In its final form, *Pronto* took on a pronounced three-act structure, beginning primarily once the main characters had all been properly introduced through Harry's bookmaking operation.

Leonard finally put pen to paper on the second to last day of December. After he had written a day-by-day outline of Harry's story, then the first two pages on December 30, 1991, Leonard added another six and a half pages three days later.[32]

He scrapped it all and began again. He was deep into his reworked first chapter the following day. The second version removed Harry Arno's longtime skimming scheme on Jimmy Cap; Leonard opted to save that revelation for later in the book. Instead, he opened with Harry's signature "senior moment"—bringing up his killing of an Italian deserter during the war and ensuing brief brush with Ezra Pound—in a quiet moment of reflection and sentimentality.

On February 11, he had the first seventy-six pages sent to Siegel and Jackie Farber for their approval; by April 26, he was 217 pages into it, stopping only for an additional Florida trip and one to New York, where he attended the Edgar Awards and, the following day, had coffee with mutual fan Kareem Abdul-Jabbar. The book was completed on June 11. One month later, Leonard was back on the road for the *Rum Punch* book tour.

Pronto was published in October 1993—just prior to Leonard's sixty-eighth birthday.

In the *New York Times*, Teresa Carpenter was taken with the author's evolution toward a more literary approach, writing, "Somewhere along the line, it became fashionable to discuss Elmore Leonard in terms formerly reserved for the likes of Flaubert, an excess of flattery that must certainly cause the man embarrassment."[33]

To many reviewers, however, Leonard's true breakthrough with *Pronto* came not with his use of international intrigue or accuracy within the world of illegal bookmaking; rather, the standout character was Raylan Givens. "It should be noted that Leonard began his career as an author with yarns about cowpokes and villains," observed Dick Lochte in the *Aspen Times*. "His 1981 contemporary police novel, *City Primeval*, was constructed very much like a Western, complete with a shootout in the street . . . when honor and justice were things to be cherished."[34]

Leonard and Joan were just beginning their preparation for the upcoming holiday season when she noticed a shortness of breath.

She had battled the flu throughout November, but her condition only seemed to worsen. As there had been no earlier signs of health issues at any point during their marriage, her rapid deterioration shocked and scared them both. When she was diagnosed with terminal lymphoma almost immediately, there was little time to prepare for what was coming. On December 7, Leonard checked Joan into the Beaumont Hospital Cancer Center in Sterling Heights, only ten miles away. She briefly came home on Christmas Eve for the holidays but, with few other options, began chemotherapy treatment on the last day of the year. The treatment only weakened her further. She returned to the hospital on January 7, and Leonard canceled her upcoming doctors' appointments and visitors.

Joan passed away six days later, on January 13, 1993, a month shy of her sixty-fifth birthday. Her illness had lasted only five weeks. The funeral was three days later, and she was interred at White Chapel Memorial Cemetery, not far from their home in Bloomfield Village.

In a strange twist of fate, only one month later, Beverly's second husband, Bill Decker, passed away unexpectedly from an aneurysm, leading to the rekindling of Leonard and Beverly's close platonic friendship. It would last until his passing years later.[35] She later recalled, "We stayed friends. Years later, at Peter's dinner table after Joan had died, Dutch took my hand and he said, 'You have never said anything bad about me, and I don't understand—why haven't you?' And I said, 'Because you're the father of my children and I loved you.' But it was true—I was never going to say a bad thing about him, because we had our kids and they were wonderful."[36]

Mysterious Press publisher Otto Penzler later recalled, "When Joan died, [wife] Carolyn and I flew out to Michigan, because there was a memorial service. I hadn't told him in advance that I was coming. I really didn't want to disturb him . . . When we came in, he looked up and saw us. And there was this look of utter shock, amazement on his face. And he came over. And again, he hugged me. And then stayed with his head against my shoulder. And he was crying. And I'd never seen him do that before or since."[37]

At the time, Leonard was only a few weeks into his next book but, with Joan's passing, he put all his projects on hold. In March, he opted to speak publicly for the first time about the loss, offering a candid interview to longtime acquaintance Bob Talbert of the *Detroit Free Press*. "My kids and grandkids—and I've got plenty of them around here—have kept me busy," he said. "[But] it's very difficult at times. My attention span is not what it used to be . . . I look around, I get antsy. [Joan's death] came so quickly." Asked about how the recent events had hindered his work life, Leonard offered little. "I'll get an idea soon," he told Talbert. "Start a scene and see what happens. This time, I'm using characters from other books—I've got 'em all sitting around. I want to see what happened to Donnell from *Freaky Deaky*, see if he's still trying to get into some of the wealthy guy, Mr. Woody's, money—and Raylan Givens, a US marshal from East Tennessee in *Pronto*. He started out as a secondary character in the first half of the book and then took over. I have to go back and re-write the first stuff."

Talbert wrote, "Why not bring back some characters? When you lose your best friend, it's smart to gather some old pals around when starting a new project."[38]

Just before *Pronto* went to print, Leonard had been able to add a last-minute dedication to the galleys:

For Joan, always.

In the weeks following Joan's death, Leonard stayed home very little, accepting dinner invitations from family and friends nearly every night of the week. But for all the activity, he wasn't writing.

Although he'd mentioned to Bob Talbert that writing *Stinger* for William Friedkin had been a pleasant experience, it proved a short-term distraction; he had the tweaks completed in a month. On April 23, Leonard looked out his office window to the patch of garden where he'd often watch Joan tending to her flowers and vegetables. The spot was now occupied by the new landscaping gardener he'd hired—forty-four-year-old Michigan native Christine Kent, who also taught French language at the University of Detroit. It took a few weeks, but Leonard soon worked up the nerve to approach her, shyly pretending to feed the squirrels in the backyard. In June, he invited her inside for a glass of wine while he stuck to ginger ale. "I would look out the window, and go out and talk to her about movies and books," he later recalled to *The Guardian*'s Tim Adams. "In June, I called her for a date. I hadn't called anyone for a date in forty-five years."

On June 26, Leonard and Christine went for dinner and a movie, *Sleepless in Seattle*. Much to the surprise of his family, the two left for Florida together three days later. On August 19, they were married in a civil ceremony. Peter, who acted as his father's best man, recalled, "Dad invited Christine into the house, put on Steely Dan, and rolled a joint. I called him that afternoon and I said, 'What are you doing tonight?' And he said, 'I have a *date*.' I said, 'You have a date? Where would you meet anyone? The only place you go is the post office?'"[39] He also noted, "Elmore led a very solitary life. You know, he worked by himself all day and then would want somebody to talk to and have dinner with. He liked *being* married."[40]

"Joan always said, 'If I die before you, you'll get married again right away to a younger woman,'" Leonard told *WHO* magazine soon after. "I said, 'Never.'" Asked about their first encounter, Christine recalled, "I had to tell him, 'Mr. Leonard, I'm on the clock,'" before reminding him that, she too had been married before. He had responded, "That's okay. I don't mind."[41] (Previously, Christine had been married to David L. Regal, the artistic director for the University of Detroit Mercy; together, the two had one grown daughter, twenty-year-old Geraldine.) For her part, Christine didn't mind that Leonard had started smoking again.

The couple used the upcoming *Pronto* book tour as their honeymoon.

Just prior to meeting Christine, Leonard had made his first attempt to write again on May 26, but produced only a single page. He abandoned it immediately and did not return to the story again until November 15—more than half a year later. By then, however, he had a stronger sense of the plot and characters for the novel initially called *Out of Sight*—although he would retain the title, instead, for another book.

Leonard's initial plot moved away from *Pronto*'s chronic malcontent Harry Arno, instead, reintroducing *Freaky Deaky*'s drunken millionaire Woody Ricks, and his personal valet, the former Black Panther Donnell Lewis. In this scenario, Woody and Donnell would be found wintering in Palm Beach when, by chance, the eccentric millionaire insists on attending a psychic reading in nearby Cassadaga. When Donnell returns to retrieve his burned-out employer from the home of dubious "spiritualist" Dawn Navarro, he finds that Ricks has mysteriously up and vanished. Soon, Raylan Givens is brought in to investigate, uncovering a larger plot to kidnap and extort some of the Florida Gold Coast's wealthiest—and most gullible—residents. Although Leonard's notes indicated his excitement at writing various dialogue-driven interactions between two of his all-time favorite characters—Raylan and Donnell—he soon scrapped his initial outline and started again, bringing back Harry Arno into the mix:

NEW PLOT

Harry disappears; Joyce worried about him. Raylan thinks overly worried. "Harry," he says, "is drinking again and maybe had a blackout, or he's gone to Italy." Joyce says, "No"—has reason to believe something—maybe wiseguy-related—has happened to him. Raylan doesn't think so. (KEEP BACKSTORY SIMPLE.)

Leonard cooked up three new antagonists as his primary schemers: Bobby Deo, Louis Lewis, and ringleader Chip Ganz—an ex-flame of Joyce Patton, and hip to the illegal cash fortune Harry Arno claims to have hoarded over the years. (Ganz replaced Leonard's original villain, "Loyall Betts," of whom he had initially noted, "Think of Christopher Walken—Loyall represents pure terror.")[42] With shades of *The Switch*'s Ordell Robbie and Louis Gara, the three plan to keep Harry hostage in a makeshift dungeon, only offering to set him free for a price; in effect, holding the elderly bookie for ransom against himself. Concerned over his apparent disappearance, Joyce coerces her new flame, Raylan, to check out Harry's last-known whereabouts: the home of New Age "spiritualist" Dawn Navarro, where Harry had paid for his own psychic reading.

The scenes depicting both Harry's and Raylan's psychic readings with Dawn Navarro had been mapped out early by Leonard, using actual interview sessions conducted that summer between Gregg Sutter and various real-life Florida hypnotherapists and psychics.[43]

MARIA: I'm just going to do it like you are Raylan. If he came to me for an in-depth reading, I'd use the Celtic cross. If he had a question that was brief and he wanted a fifteen- or twenty-minute reading, I would do a three-card spread.

GREGG: I wonder if Dawn would be apprehensive at this point. She knows that Raylan is coming back. How would that make her feel?

MARIA: Does she have reason to fear him?

GREGG: Absolutely. For one thing, she knows that he's killed a man in the last year because she felt his hand.[44]

Leonard had initially dispatched Sutter to sit with the various New Age specialists after discovering the kitsch appeal of a small town just north of Orlando called Cassadaga, whose miniscule population of approximately 350 people was made up either of psychics or of those who visited them regularly for life guidance.[45]

On May 19, Leonard visited Cassadaga and agreed to a psychic reading for himself. "January of next year, I may take a different tact [*sic*] in writing, a different kind of book—books that involve death and dying," he later noted of the psychic's observations. "That is, to help people understand death and dying and be more comfortable with the idea. This is not to say that I'll give up the kind of writing I've been doing." He added, "After January of next year, Joan will be in touch. Perhaps a scent associated with her."[46] On January 13, 1994, Leonard marked in his day planner, "Joan, a year ago."

On February 5, he'd hit 130 pages of the new book. On April 12, he sent a polished excerpt of the novel—now entitled *Riding the Rap*—to *The New Yorker*, which had agreed to run it in anticipation of the following year's publication. (Although Leonard had previously been excerpted in the *Detroit Free Press, Harper's Bazaar*, and *Playboy, The New Yorker* was the most prestigious slick a younger Elmore Leonard could have ever hoped for.) He continued to work on the full manuscript's ending and revisions throughout the spring and early summer, breaking only for Katy's wedding on July 9. He finished it one week later; after one more revision, he sent the finalized first draft to Michael Siegel and Jackie Farber on August 29.

Delacorte released *Riding the Rap* on June 1, 1995. Although some critics demonstrated greater enthusiasm than others, the general consensus had been a rare lack of focused plotting on Leonard's part. Ruth Coughlin of the *Detroit News* wrote, "That's the problem with *Riding the Rap*—there isn't enough good action. Indeed, there is vintage Leonard throughout: an unparalleled ear for dialogue . . . What's missing is a story." She added, "The good news is that next year is just around the corner."[47]

Perhaps the highest praise came from a longtime admirer, British postmodernist Martin Amis, who acted as guest critic for the *New York Times*. In his review, Amis took the opportunity to write not so much on *Riding the Rap* but on Leonard's full narrative sound and style; in doing so, he would soon be recognized as one of Leonard's greatest literary champions and advocates. "Elmore Leonard is a literary genius who writes re-readable thrillers," Amis wrote. "Mr. Leonard has only *one* plot. All his thrillers are Pardoner's Tales, in which Death roams the land—usually Miami and Detroit—disguised as money . . . And the question is:

How does he allow these gifts play . . . ? . . . My answer may sound reductive, but here goes: The essence of Elmore is to be found in his use of the present participle." Amis continued, "What that means, in effect, is that he has discovered a way of slowing down and suspending the English sentence—or let's say the American sentence, because Mr. Leonard is as American as jazz. Instead of writing 'Warren Ganz III lived up in Manalapan, Palm Beach County,' Mr. Leonard writes, *'Warren Ganz III, living up in Manalapan, Palm Beach County.'* He writes, 'Bobby saying,' and then opens quotes. He writes, 'Dawn saying,' and then opens quotes. We are not in the imperfect tense (Dawn was saying) or the present tense (Dawn says), or the historic present (Dawn said) . . . Such sentences seem to open up a lag in time, through which Mr. Leonard easily slides, gaining entry to his players' hidden minds." He added, "This was post-modern decadence. This was bliss."[48]

Prior to the publication of *Riding the Rap*, Leonard's marriage to Christine suffered an early tragedy of its own. Following a visit to the couple on Sunday, March 13, 1994, Christine's only child, twenty-two-year-old Geraldine Regal, was killed by a drunk driver in Royal Oak. She had been riding alongside her boyfriend, Michael Hostettler, when the passenger side was rammed at high speed while at a stoplight. She had just graduated from the University of Detroit with a degree in psychology the previous year.[49] Although the newspapers kept the culpable driver's name from the press, Leonard and Christine kept a close watch on the court proceedings and attended the responsible party's sentencing on September 14. But by then, a pall had already been cast on their marriage and, as time went on, Christine would—by all accounts—retreat further away from her new husband and his own family. (However, according to many of Leonard's family members, Christine hadn't made the same attempts to get to know the extended family that Joan had previously done. Leonard's granddaughter Shannon Belmont later recalled, "Once [Joan] died and Christine came into the picture, Elmore seemed especially removed from the family as a whole.")

Following the court proceedings, Leonard began attending boxing matches downtown—research for the next book, already underway. He had suffered through a number of tragedies and setbacks at the beginning of the new decade, but its midpoint promised him better days.

CHAPTER 18

Hot, Part Two, 1995–1999

In later years, Leonard would admit the irony that it had taken a cathartic novel like *Get Shorty* for Hollywood to circle back and rediscover his writing.

Upon the book's release, there was immediate interest from studios and major stars, both of which seemed oblivious to the story's commentary on the film industry. Whether or not Dustin Hoffman was fully aware of the role he played in the novel's creation, the star was considering the role of Ernesto "Chili" Palmer for Tri-Star Pictures' proposed adaptation. Likewise, director Jim McBride and fellow A-list actors Al Pacino and Joe Pesci were said to have circled the property for themselves. However, the first set of eyes to immediately envision *Get Shorty*'s cinematic potential was director Barry Sonnenfeld, who had read the book while on vacation. Renowned throughout the industry for his work as cinematographer and director of photography for such filmmakers as Rob Reiner and the Coen brothers, Sonnenfeld had since proven his bankability with comedies *The Addams Family* and the rom-com *For Love or Money*, which finally put him in a position to make a play for *Get Shorty*. "I was going on this cruise with my wife and the only book I had with me was a Tom Clancy novel, which meant I had about eleven hundred pages and wouldn't know until about six hundred pages if it's going to be good or not," Sonnenfeld later recalled. "I panicked and I went over to Hudson News and I saw the paperback of *Get Shorty*. I get on the cruise, love the book, love the dialogue, love the characters, love the world and I immediately felt that the guy who could play Chili Palmer was Danny DeVito." He had worked as DeVito's cinematographer on 1987's *Throw Mama from the Train*, and the two had remained close friends. "I finished the book, I give it to my wife, and I said, 'Read this book and tell me who the lead is,'" Sonnenfeld added. "She finishes it and she immediately says 'Danny.'"

Sonnenfeld immediately rang DeVito with the news that he'd found the "perfect" vehicle for their second collaboration and, in a scene seemingly cut from the source material itself, the actor promised to purchase the rights—sight unseen—for him to star in and produce with Sonnenfeld directing. "Now here's where it gets complicated," Sonnenfeld further explained. "At the time, there had never been an adaptation of any of Elmore's books that had been successful as a movie. I'm not talking about the ones that he wrote—I'm talking about *adaptations* of his books. Part of the problem I think is that the directors didn't understand Dutch's comedy." Sonnenfeld also feared that the subject matter—Hollywood itself—would give almost any film producer pause in funding such a story. Regardless, DeVito took a chance and outbid Joe Pesci, leaving the final greenlight up to Leonard himself. Sonnenfeld recalled, "Michael Siegel calls me back and says, 'Elmore doesn't want to sell us the rights until he talks to you. So you need to call Elmore and me.'"[1]

According to Danny DeVito, he had trusted Sonnenfeld's intuition from the beginning: "Barry wanted me to play Chili Palmer but I said no. I liked Martin Weir . . . With Martin, I tried to be full of myself. It's the closest I've ever come to playing myself in a movie—I'm kidding! I didn't base Martin on anybody, it was just what it was in the script, which was really well written by Scott Frank. It was good fun."[2] Sonnenfeld concurred, adding, "What Scott did was add what the book didn't have—it didn't have a movie structure, and it didn't have an ending . . . So it had no ending or any structure in terms of how Ray Bones gets finished and arrested at the locker. Scott created structure and a fantastic ending . . . [Later], Elmore said, 'I didn't realize that my book was funny.'"[3] (Although Leonard himself wasn't present for much of the shoot—Hollywood also subbing for the early Miami scenes—he did meet with screenwriter Scott Frank when prodded for opinions on the script. He later told journalist Adrian Wootton, "Scott Frank says that he reads the book the first time very quickly, just to find out what it's about and then he reads it again very slowly to find out what the theme is. And then he tells me what the theme is and I say, 'Really? I didn't know that. I thought I was just writing a book.'")

Sonnenfeld later claimed that, initially, Leonard remained apprehensive that the director would understand the nuances of the novel's characters. Sonnenfeld recalled, "I knew why they wanted to speak with me. Up until that point, I had done *The Addams Family* and *Addams Family Values* and Elmore was concerned about that, so I knew what to say to him when I called him—he didn't want me to make this a sort of wacky comedy. And what I said to Elmore was that the reason I loved his book so much—and my whole philosophy as a director—is that if the characters are funny and if the scene is absurd, then you always have the actors play the *reality* of the scene. You don't *play* the comedy. The comedy happens because the scene is funny and that's because the actors aren't trying to be funny—which is what Elmore really needed to hear." He added, "But luckily, Elmore and I shared a very similar sensibility about the comedy, in that you show the audience, but you don't tell them." Sonnenfeld admitted additional relief when, soon after, at a dinner with Leonard, he discovered that one of the author's favorite films was the Coen brothers' *Miller's Crossing*—which Sonnenfeld had shot. "He knew more about that movie than I did—[but] then it took Danny and me over five years to get the movie made because no one wanted to do an Elmore Leonard adaptation."[4] Interviewed soon after, Leonard was candid about the long road in getting *Get Shorty* to the big screen. "It moved from Tri-Star to MGM [and they] wanted to shoot the picture this summer and their first choice for Chili Palmer was Dustin Hoffman. It didn't make sense and yet, in a way, it does." But, as had been one of the many issues with 1985's aborted *LaBrava* adaptation, the actor wanted too much money for the studio to agree.[5]

Ultimately, Sonnenfeld came up with a perfect scenario: DeVito would produce the film, but would additionally *cameo* as the titular "Shorty" himself—the self-absorbed A-list star, Michael Weir (soon changed to "Martin Weir" by screenwriter Scott Frank)—which would require only a few days on set. "It didn't work out with Danny playing Chili," Sonnenfeld recalled. "Thank God he played the role he was born to play, which was Shorty." (Prior to preproduction, Leonard joked, "Danny DeVito wanted to play Chili Palmer [and] I thought, 'My God, everybody's gonna have to be pretty short if he's the normal-size guy in the film.'")[6] DeVito later recalled, "Barry wanted Gene Hackman to play Harry Zimm, [and] it just so happened that his agent was my agent so I called him up. But there was a night scene in the movie and he said he didn't work at night. I said, 'It's only one scene. We'll do it real quick and get you out by midnight.' He said, 'No, I don't work at night.' It was a dealbreaker. Barry insisted it had to be a night scene, and I eventually convinced Gene to do it but he said, 'You only get one night.' During that night shoot I was hanging out with Hackman a lot because I didn't want him to get squirrelly and leave . . . Several weeks later, I went to the editing room with Barry. I said, 'Where's the night scene?' He says, 'Oh, it didn't work so I cut it out.' I said, 'You *motherfucker*.'"[7]

Initially, it wasn't easy for Sonnenfeld to replace DeVito as the lead. He recalled, "Many people passed on the role. I spent time with Dustin Hoffman—who I think actually was 'Shorty'—and I also spent time with Warren Beatty, and no one wanted to do it and we just got lucky to do it with John [Travolta]."[8]

It was also during the time that *Get Shorty* was still being assembled into a salable package that one of the hottest independent films in recent times was making the festival circuit: Quentin Tarantino's second feature, *Pulp Fiction*. Industry buzz surrounded the film, predicting Tarantino was on the way to directorial superstardom and that the film would mark a major comeback for its star, John Travolta. Sonnenfeld later recalled, "Tarantino had dated one of *Get Shorty*'s producers, who gave him the script. He called John and said, 'This is not the movie you pass on.'"[9]

Sonnenfeld also recalled, "We invited [Leonard] to the set while we were shooting and he said, 'I've never been invited to the set of any movie based on any of my books because they never want the writer around.' And I said, 'No, we'd love to have you,' and we had a chair for him that said 'Elmore Leonard' and he never had had a director's chair on the set, so I think he just loved the experience of being on a movie set."[10]

On September 21, 1995, Leonard celebrated the film's completion by attending a Wynton Marsalis concert at the Whitney in downtown Detroit; two days later, he headed to Los Angeles for the press junket.

Ultimately, *Get Shorty* was released by MGM on October 20, 1995, to glowing reviews and strong adult-driven box office numbers, ultimately making $115 million against a $30 million budget. To Leonard's grandchildren, however, the popular culture phenomenon that he became all started with that film's box office success. "When I was really little, I remembered that there was that huge poster for *Joe Kidd* in my parents' closet," Tim Leonard later recalled. "I saw my grandfather's name on it with Clint Eastwood and I knew pretty early that my grandfather wasn't necessarily like other grandfathers. But seeing *Get Shorty* in the theater, seeing his name up there on the big screen, that was the big moment for me when I realized who he was. I saw that and thought, 'Oh my gosh, I'm related to this guy!'"[11] Tim's younger brother, Alex Leonard, concurred, adding, "That year, I even had one friend who went as Chili Palmer for Halloween."[12]

Bill Leonard's son, Max, later remembered, "Maybe when I was like eight or nine years old, I started to understand that he was like very well known—and that was around the time when, like, [Quentin Tarantino's] *Jackie Brown* had come out, and sort of like these big-budget Hollywood films that were based off his work. So, I kind of missed the periods of time when he was struggling and trying to make a name for himself. For me, it was always like he was who he was from the time I was born—this famous big-deal kind of guy . . . But he never had any sort of air about him being some sort of important big deal."[13]

For the first time in more than a decade, there was a scramble for Leonard's properties. Before his next novel was released, the film rights had already sold—further invigorating his search for another great protagonist. "After *Pronto* and *Riding the Rap*, both featuring Deputy United States Marshal Raylan Givens, it was clear that Elmore was having a love affair with the U.S. Marshal Service," researcher Gregg Sutter later recalled. "Inspired by this interest, I sent Elmore a ten-year-old clip from the *Detroit News* showing Deputy U.S. Marshal Anne Garza with a big shotgun resting on her hip, her purse dangling from her other shoulder . . . Elmore took one look at the newspaper photo, called me, and said, 'She's a book!' It was a very satisfying moment for me."[14]

In a new practice for Leonard, he first wanted to "audition" his new character—an empowered, sexy female US Marshal named Karen Sisco (the daughter of recurring private investigator character Marshall Sisco)—and aimed to write a short story featuring the character as her debut. As it happened, old friend publisher Otto Penzler had been vying for Leonard to contribute such a short story to an upcoming anthology of femme fatale–themed tales. Leonard quickly wrote "Karen Makes Out"—a brief vignette about the titular marshal slowly discovering that her new well-to-do boyfriend is actually an elusive bank robber. (As usual, he had tinkered with names, but "Diane Makes Out" and "Denise Gets Her Man" didn't appear to have the same ring to them.[15]) He sent it off to both the new *Mary Higgins Clark Mystery Magazine*—marking the first magazine appearance of an original Leonard short story in more than four decades—and then to Penzler for the *Murder for Love* anthology, published by Mysterious Press at the beginning of 1996. "I knew that he had written Western short stories mostly, but he was such a great writer and I admired him so much, you never know unless you ask," Penzler recalled. "So I asked him if he would write a short story . . . I always figured if a writer is a writer, he'll do it if he can. And some people can't. But Dutch could."[16]

Now assured that Karen Sisco could, in fact, carry a full novel, Leonard soon began expanding upon the scenario from her debut story: a brief May-December romance between her and a charming, older professional bank robber at the twilight of his career. However, he still needed the proper situation and peripheral characters to bring the two together. Sutter later recalled, "A few days after New Year's in 1995, a prison escape in Palm Beach County would provide major background for *Out of Sight*. The Florida Department of Law Enforcement was at the center of the manhunt for the escaped prisoners—all Cuban—and fortunately for us, FDLE agent Jim Born, who had been so helpful on *Rum Punch*, was on the team searching for them."

Leonard and Sutter were soon privy to one of the largest manhunts in Florida history. They met both Born and his fellow FDLE agent Jeff "Hutch" Hutcheon during the hunt, learning the intricate strategies the convicts had used in order to escape; Leonard was most fascinated with the tunnel the convicts had dug—*The Great Escape*–style—from the prison chapel and right to freedom. "When he sat down to write the escape, Elmore brought his own touches to the scene," Sutter said. "[He added] two main characters—bank robber Jack Foley, who would escape with the Cubans, and Deputy U.S. Marshal Karen Sisco, at the prison serving a nuisance warrant, when she is abducted by Foley from the prison parking lot and placed in the trunk of the car—with him."

Although Karen Sisco didn't differ much from Leonard's previous tough and self-reliant heroines such as Kathy Diaz Baker in *Maximum Bob* or *Killshot*'s Carmen Colson, Karen's one vice was her uniquely questionable taste in male suitors. As both a tomboy and a daddy's girl, Karen rattles off baseball statistics and boxing records, while also seeking her father's professional advice when facing a formidable adversary or challenge (shades of Leonard's own advice with his own children)—yet becomes enamored with charismatic bank robbers on two separate occasions, much to her father's ire. (Marshall Sisco is equally disapproving of his daughter's current relationship with *Rum Punch*'s returning ATF agent, the very married Ray Nicolette.) Thanks to her debut appearance in the short story written for Otto Penzler, Karen Sisco was the first character Leonard created for *Out of Sight*—the title itself the leftover alternate for *Riding the Rap*.

Initially, Leonard had named the male lead Ray Brady and would use that name for the majority of his notes and outlines. (He had also considered using Frank Cullen—which would have made the character the older brother of *Bandit*'s Tom Cullen, thus linking the two novels.) But Leonard's chief focus in sculpting the character was diving deep into the chronicles of real-life American bank robberies. His original intention for his protagonist bank robber was for a darker, more vicious figure: "Ray Brady," Leonard wrote, was "a well-known bank robber with different [modus operandi] . . . [who] once blackened his face when he robbed a bank, 'since most of the bank robbers are jigs. Give 'em another one.'" Brady had also killed a man during one robbery, "which got him to Glades for life." Once metamorphosing into "Jack Foley," however, the character became a significantly more pacifistic and relatable protagonist. Although an original character, Foley is presented as an older, somewhat jaded version of the "decent man in trouble" that had led Leonard's earliest successful ventures into contemporary crime. (Had Leonard the contractual right to bring back Jack Ryan or Ernest "Stick" Stickley, not only would the archetype have fit, but either character would have been age-appropriate.) And whereas "Ray Brady" took no issue with killing while on the job, Jack Foley makes his name as a bank robber without so much as carrying a gun.

To get a clearer perspective on how someone like Foley would target his intended banks, Leonard listed the numerous banks located in the Greater Miami–Dade County area, noting which were standalone and which could be found within shopping centers. He also pored through dozens of newspaper scans Sutter had provided, each one reporting on a different—and often bizarre—bank robbery for use as story fodder. He noted real-life career criminal Johnny Madison Williams Jr., who not only pulled off fifty-six bank jobs in eight years, but kept a detailed ledger of each interaction, jotting down the bank's location and amount he got—totaling $870,000 in just under a decade. Williams's signature would be to fire a warning shot into the air at the beginning of each robbery, earning him the FBI's nickname "the Shootist"—much to Leonard's amusement. Sutter soon contacted the FBI offices in both Los Angeles and San Diego, the latter of which provided him and Leonard with a comprehensive list of nicknames granted to previously apprehended bank robbers. Leonard annotated them as he went along: "*The B.O. Bandit; the Bird-legs Bandit (who wore shorts); the Clearasil Bandit (who threatened to sue the FBI for libel); the Chubby-Cheeks Bandits; the Troll Bandit; the Frankenstein Bandit (bags under his eyes); the Harem Bandits (a group of women); the Grampa Bandit; the Mumbles Bandit, the Half-minute Bandit (known for his speed); and the 'Robbing Hood' Bandit (wore a hooded vest).*" (Not to be outdone, one official from Glades wrote to Leonard, "*Dutch, here are a few nicknames of real characters in this prison: Slop Dog, Truck-Head, Mac Marble, Check-In Charlie, Fat Pimp, Trash Car, Food King, Whimp, Bucket head, Fingers Fred, Nubs, Skillet-Head, Rags, Huggie Bear, Keebler Elf.*")[17]

Ultimately, it is Jack Foley's preference for politeness and cordiality *over* intimidation tactics that earns him his robbery track record—and Karen Sisco's fleeting romantic interest.

Among the many unexpected finds pruned from Sutter's research were the FBI's official protocol textbooks on handling and grooming informants and complete guide to field surveillance work; the US Marshals Service's manual for fugitive apprehension; a "Complete Guide to the Auto Theft Game," written by a licensed and bonded forensic locksmith; and—for the unique perspective of Karen Sisco—articles on sexual harassment within the FBI and other law enforcement agencies. On October 10, 1995, Sutter also interviewed Deputy Marshal Patti Clarke of the Marshals Service for additional accuracy. (According to Leonard's notes, Sisco would have already faced gender-infused intimidation at the office. In a section headlined, "FBI Attitude Toward Karen: Condescending," he noted that she would be made to suffer indignities for having been captured by Foley and accomplice Glenn Michaels at all, and would face a reprimanding not necessarily doled out to her male counterparts: "*How did you let yourself be taken to begin with?*" would be the first question posed once safely returned to her Marshals office. Of the relationship between Sisco and Foley, Leonard was sure to read up on both Stockholm syndrome and consult at least one academic paper, "Psychological Observations of Bank Robbery," by Dr. Donald A. Johnston.[18]

Leonard had his first draft completed and sent to Jackie Farber and

Michael Siegel on January 9, 1996—only a few weeks before Karen Sisco would make her first print appearance in the premiere issue of *Mary Higgins Clark Mystery Magazine*. *Out of Sight* was published by Delacorte nine months later to some of the best write-ups Leonard had garnered in years. In the *Detroit News*, Bille Rae Bates praised both the book itself and Leonard's strong female lead, writing, "She's a female with something to prove, and in crafting her, Leonard has shown once again that as an author, he has nothing to prove."[19] David Wiegand of the *San Francisco Chronicle* wrote, "In Elmore Leonard's world, morality is a pretty slippery character. Anyone who spends too much time chasing it down is missing the point of life—that trying to live up to society's notion of right and wrong doesn't count as much as living up to one's code of ethics." He added, "All the Leonard trademarks are in place in *Out of Sight*—unexpected plot twists, violence ironically balanced with offbeat humor, a wonderfully realistic 'chorus' of minor characters—but it's making us like and want to know Jack Foley better that makes the novel so successful."[20]

To Ralph Lombreglia of the *New York Times*, however, the novel's standout element was its romance—regardless of how implausible the reviewer found it to be. "The oldest unsolved mystery on the books, human love, is the case to crack in *Out of Sight*, Elmore Leonard's new novel, in which the cop is a lady with a gift for meeting Mr. Wrong and the robber is a guy who just might have been, in a different life, Mr. Right," Lombreglia wrote. The reviewer, however, had issues with the age discrepancy between the two leads—forgetting that Leonard himself was now married to a younger woman, although with fewer years separating them than those between Karen Sisco and Jack Foley. "And here," he continued, "for this reader at least, *Out of Sight* slides off the road into an Everglades of incredibility. For in order to accept the main action of the rest of the novel, we must now accept that both kidnapped and kidnapper—a female Federal law-enforcement officer and the man who has robbed more banks than anyone in the FBI's computer—experience in the trunk of a moving car a conversational intimacy that leaves them helplessly infatuated with each other, even as Karen Sisco conceals a .38-caliber pistol between her legs."[21]

While many of Leonard's older properties were still yet to be brought to the big screen, newfound interest primarily targeted relatively recent novels within his body of work. However, with the positive word-of-mouth regarding Barry Sonnenfeld's *Get Shorty*, those other properties were soon snatched up by various studios and production companies, as well. And having had a positive experience collaborating on *Get Shorty*, Danny DeVito's Jersey Films remained proactive in bringing more of Leonard's work to both the big screen and to television. Only a month before Delacorte's release of *Out of Sight*, Leonard told Bob Talbert of the *Detroit Free Press*, "The Danny DeVito team starts shooting the movie of it here next March for Universal . . . [It's] the story of a woman federal marshal who falls in love with an old pro bank robber," adding that his first choice cast would include Nicole Kidman as Karen Sisco and Jack Nicholson as Jack Foley, fully playing into the May-December dynamic of the plot. "She's read the manuscript and likes it," he said. "I don't think [Nicholson] has read it yet, but I think they would be great together." (Although Leonard's dream casting wouldn't come to fruition, with up-and-comers Jennifer Lopez and George Clooney taking on the roles, Nicholson would, soon after, score his third Oscar playing opposite the significantly younger Helen Hunt in *As Good As It Gets*.) At the time, only Scott Frank, who had successfully adapted *Get Shorty*, had been hired; soon, however, independent film darling Steven Soderbergh came on board as director.

Leonard had additionally revealed to Talbert that 1977's *Touch*—still considered a relatively recent offering among the author's works, largely due to its 1987 publication—had recently wrapped its own production. Paul Schrader, the *Taxi Driver* screenwriter turned cerebral director of gritty fare, had both adapted the book and directed the film, casting Christopher Walken as Bill Hill and Skeet Ulrich as Fr. Juvenal.[22] (Unknown to Leonard, Schrader had recommended to Columbia Pictures that they pass on Leonard's Steve McQueen vehicle, *American Flag*, in 1972—although Schrader didn't remember doing this.) "I met Dutch at the Telluride Film Festival. I was already a big fan of every one of his books and asked him what was available," Schrader later recalled. "At the time—following the success of *Get Shorty*, in particular—it was a gold rush to acquire his properties. He told me flat-out that there was only one left on the shelf—*Touch*. I had first been offered to adapt it as a script, but I decided to direct it, too." Despite the hot status that Leonard was achieving with big-budget movie adaptations, however, the subject matter of *Touch* remained enigmatic enough to relegate Schrader's adaptation to the film festival circuit and a limited release. He added, "Personally, I thought it was very adaptable. I thought I'd cracked it with the screenplay. But I was wrong [and] people couldn't connect with it. It had difficulty finding an audience. I think it had something to do with the built-in contradiction of the book—if this is a *holy* person, why are they filling it with dirty jokes? It was viewed as 'Three Scumbags in Search of a Book' . . . Dutch was understanding, though, and said to me it had flopped in the cinema for the same reason that it had flopped as a novel—or rather, why he'd had trouble selling it initially. He said to me, inherently, it was a problem he'd faced with the story."

Schrader added, "Years later, I adapted Eddie Bunker's novel, *Dog Eat Dog*. But, to me, that was truly my Elmore Leonard movie, the kind of Elmore Leonard–type story I'd wanted to make."[23]

Leonard had told Bob Talbert that more adaptations were on the way, all for cable television. He had frequently visited the set of director Jim McBride's adaptation of *Pronto*, enjoying the camaraderie with star Peter Falk—who fit the role of Harry Arno like a glove—as well as James LeGros, who became the first actor to portray Deputy US Marshal Raylan Givens on-screen. "Showtime has another one of mine, *Gold Coast*, which I wrote in '78," he told Talbert. "[Turner Network Television] is shooting *Last Stand at Saber River*, a Western I wrote in 1957 and that's got Tom Selleck starring with all those Carradine brothers. [And] *LaBrava*, which I wrote in '83, Buck Henry is [adapting] now."[24]

On the major motion picture front, Leonard joined legions of Quentin Tarantino fans in anticipation of the director's adaptation of *Rum Punch*. Tarantino had long wanted one of Leonard's books to adapt, and had even contacted the author years before hitting the Hollywood stratosphere with *Pulp Fiction*. At the time, Leonard recalled, "He didn't have enough backing, [but] we were willing to go along with him."[25] In fact, the two were fans of each other, as Leonard had admired both Tarantino's 1992 debut, *Reservoir Dogs*, and, later, *Pulp Fiction*. "Tarantino specializes in set pieces," he later told *Playboy*. "In *Pulp Fiction*, these two guys are going to kill somebody and they are talking about what you call a Quarter Pounder with cheese in Paris—a 'Royale' with cheese—and that's what I do. He lets his scenes play, his people talk."

For Tarantino's part, he claimed to owe a big debt to Leonard, stating, "[Leonard] helped me figure out my style. He was the first writer I'd ever read who let mundane conversations inform the characters. And then, all of a sudden—*woof!*—you're into whatever story you're telling."[26] Once Tarantino had completed *Reservoir Dogs* and started his own production company, A Band Apart, agent Michael Siegel presented a plan for the director to have his pick of the litter. Then, following the success of *Pulp Fiction*, Miramax was happy to get their new star director a full bundle of Leonard properties: *Bandits*, *Freaky Deaky*, *Killshot*, and *Rum Punch*. Of the four, the latter two caught Tarantino's eye. As *Pulp Fiction* had also featured ample scenes of hip dialogue between two hitmen, the studio initially pushed for *Killshot*. To Tarantino, however, *Rum Punch* contained a larger, more diverse ensemble of characters, providing a structure more akin to his two previous films. *Rum Punch* also contained intricate subplots woven together into a climax that occurred—of all places—within a suburban shopping mall. The young director also admitted his lifelong love of *Rum Punch*'s returning duo, Ordell Robbie and Louis Gara; at the age of fourteen, Tarantino had been apprehended *at* a shopping mall for shoplifting a paperback copy of the fictional crime partners' first appearance, *The Switch*. Later, Ordell and Louis would provide inspiration for *Pulp Fiction*'s hitmen portrayed by Samuel L. Jackson and John Travolta. Following *Pulp Fiction*'s quick ascent to pop culture phenomenon, studios and fans alike were clamoring to find out what Tarantino's follow-up would be; when he announced *Rum Punch* as his next film, Leonard was introduced to a new generation of fans.

Following the deal with Miramax, however, Leonard didn't hear from Tarantino again for more than a year. When he finally sent Leonard a copy of the completed screenplay for his approval, Tarantino admitted his trepidation in reaching out sooner—largely due to the substantial changes he'd made to the source material. Leonard later recalled, "I questioned him about a couple of things, asked why scenes we both liked were left out . . . That was all I heard from him for about a year and a half, until just before he started shooting, in early June [1996], when he called again. He said, 'I've been afraid to call you for the last year.' I said, 'Why? Because you've changed the title and you're starring a black woman in the lead?' He said, 'Yeah.' I said, 'Do what you want. You're the filmmaker—you're going to do what you want anyway.'" (Leonard later told *The Guardian*, "[Tarantino] says that to pull off the scam that the character does in the book, only a black woman would be ballsy enough to do it.")[27]

Later, Leonard stated his high approval for the finished film. Despite its title change, *Jackie Brown* was, indeed, one of the closest adaptations that had yet been made out of one of his works—its tone, dialogue, and casting were nearly pitch-perfect. In the screenplay, Tarantino had changed the lead character's name from Jackie Burke to Jackie Brown, and opted to cast a legend of the "Blaxploitation" film movement, Pam Grier, in the coveted role. (Tarantino had fought for Grier in the role, as Miramax preferred the more bankable recent Academy Award winner Angela Bassett.) The plot, however, stayed the same, minus the neo-Nazis, jackboys, and Max Cherry's estranged wife. In shifting the location of the story from Leonard's familiar Florida to Los Angeles, Grier's Jackie Brown now worked as a low-level flight attendant for a Mexican airline, assisting Samuel L. Jackson's Ordell Robbie in his money laundering to sources in that country, rather than the Bahamas of the book. None of the changes fazed Leonard, however, who admitted his pleasant surprise at just how much the young director had actually retained from the book. "From the beginning, I was more interested in what Quentin would do *with* the material than how closely he stuck to the book," he later wrote. "The pace is dead-on. Because the characters drive the story, Quentin takes time to show you exactly who they are and what they have to lose, before slipping into the thrust of the plot, the action. And it all works. I couldn't be more pleased."

The film was also a critical and box office hit, leading to further anticipation for Steven Soderbergh's film version of *Out of Sight* the following year. Although he wasn't available to helm the project, *Get Shorty*'s director, Barry Sonnenfeld, again joined Danny DeVito in acting as producers. Sonnenfeld recalled, after *Get Shorty*, "Elmore gave me the rights to *Maximum Bob*, and I directed the television pilot, and then produced it with Alex Gansa. Unfortunately, we saw a different version of the show. He wanted more humor and I wanted it more grounded in reality. Ultimately, in retrospect, even the pilot was a little too funny. Then I wanted to do *Out of Sight*, but I couldn't, and it was my wife's idea to get [Steven] Soderbergh . . . Initially, I was going to do it with Clooney and Nicole Kidman as Karen Sisco and had several meetings with her. But she dropped out when I did. So the project got reignited with Soderbergh, then Clooney and Jennifer Lopez—and both were great."[28]

Bill Leonard recalled, "They filmed some parts in downtown Detroit and we visited the set, which was an old gym. As we approached, there was a table set up outside with a group of young women, all production assistants, signing people in. My dad walked up and said, 'I'm Elmore

Leonard. I wrote the book,' and the girl at the table said, 'Oh my gosh, Mr. Leonard, of course we know who you are! Please come in.' Everyone was so respectful of him. Everyone called him 'Mr. Leonard.'" He added, "Then, when we got inside, George Clooney seemed nervous that Elmore was there watching him. He wanted to make sure he got it right."[29]

Out of Sight, too, proved a hit, although more so with critics than theatergoers. However, it earned *Get Shorty*'s screenwriter, Scott Frank, an Academy Award nomination for his second Leonard adaptation.

Pleased with the finished product, Leonard did take slight issue with the film's coda, which included a new scene not depicted in his novel. In the novel, he had steadfastly stayed true to Karen's literary ancestors—Raymond Cruz and Raylan Givens before her—in demonstrating her code of honor by sending Jack Foley back to prison for his various crimes. In the movie adaptation, however, the final scene depicted Karen using her federal clout to hook Foley up with another inmate—one known for his daring escapes (an uncredited Samuel L. Jackson)—thus promising the audience that the charming bank robber would, indeed, finagle his way to another breakout. Leonard, however, had insisted that such a flip would undermine Karen's core personality as a serious officer of the law. "I didn't agree with the way it ended," he later recalled. "I said, 'It's [Karen's] story. But you end with George Clooney; the focus is on George Clooney as he's being taken away.' And Scott Frank said, 'Well, it's her book, but it's his movie.'"[30]

Clooney also proved popular in Bloomfield Hills upon his visit to Leonard's home for a wrap party with the author's own family and friends. "I walked in the living room and George was standing there by himself," Peter Leonard later recalled. "Everyone was in the dining room, getting something to eat. I introduced myself and we started talking. A few minutes later, the thirty or so women at the party—my wife included—found out George was in the house, and came in the room, circling like vultures. George flashed his megawatt smile and the ladies swooned and I stepped away."[31] Granddaughter Shannon Belmont also recalled, "It was funny because all the older people in my family were trying to relate to him about being Elmore's kids and he's Rosemary Clooney's nephew! I was just laughing and thinking, 'What are you guys doing? It's the star of *ER*!' . . . I just remember we all took turns talking to him at the party and I ended up having to go to work the next day. I could have taken off, since I drank so much at the party, but it was too good an opportunity to tell everyone where I was the night before: 'I drank champagne all night with George Clooney.'"[32]

"This is the fourth recent adaptation of a Leonard novel, after *Get Shorty*, *Touch*, and *Jackie Brown*, and the most faithful to Leonard's style," wrote Roger Ebert in the *Chicago Sun Times*. "What all four movies demonstrate is how useful crime is as a setting for human comedy." He added that the film was the first "to build on the enormously influential *Pulp Fiction* instead of simply mimicking it. It has the games with time, the low-life dialogue, the absurd violent situations—but it also has its own texture. It plays like a string quartet written with words instead of music, performed by sleazeballs instead of musicians."[33] In the *New York Times*, Janet Maslin concurred, writing, "The formerly blond and coltish Karen . . . now looks like a younger sister to Jackie Brown, [and] the casting of George Clooney also departs from the book, since Jack Foley on the page is seasoned and sad-eyed, reminding characters of Harry Dean Stanton. Clooney, who like [Jennifer Lopez] makes the most of a splendid opportunity here, won't be reminding anyone of Stanton at all. Soderbergh plays some graceful time tricks with these two by sometimes letting their daydreams anticipate their long-overdue real romance."[34]

Along with the near half dozen motion pictures Leonard saw adapted from his novels toward the end of the decade, there had also been major interest from television networks for a crack at his source material. As a spinoff to *Out of Sight*, Leonard's original short story, "Karen Makes Out," was used as the pilot episode of an ABC television series that aired in 2003, entitled *Karen Sisco*, starring Carla Gugino in the lead role. Unfortunately, like *Maximum Bob* before it, the series was canceled after a few episodes. Leonard later commented, "They canceled it just when it was starting to calm down."

As a hot property in Hollywood, Leonard soon found himself with a project proposition for which he'd never been asked—writing a sequel to one of his books. Early plans to bring *Get Shorty*'s loan shark antihero Ernesto "Chili" Palmer back for either *Maximum Bob* or *Riding the Rap* had led to little more than false starts; structurally written as ensembles, the stories provided very little for the former star protagonist to do. But with Barry Sonnenfeld's *Get Shorty* a surprise smash for MGM, the idea of a film sequel was inevitable—and something which Leonard hadn't expected. He later recalled, "At the premiere of *Get Shorty*, an MGM executive asked if I thought I could write a sequel. I said, 'I don't know why not.' But I was already thinking of [writing] *Out of Sight* and then wrote *Cuba Libre* as a change of pace, to get out of the 'hip' world for a time."

After considering possible scenarios for Chili Palmer's next appearance, Leonard narrowed it down to two—the cutthroat worlds of high fashion or of the music industry. He attempted to send Chili Palmer into the fashion industry first—meaning, for the first time, using a New York location. He dispatched Gregg Sutter to the swankier areas of Manhattan—America's most influential fashion mecca. "Frankly, fashion was daunting and of little interest to me," Sutter later recalled. "Fortunately, as it turned out, it was of little interest to Elmore, too."

He continued, "Then I got this call from Dutch—'It's getting to be too much like work. We're doing the Spanish-American War.' Meaning, that in one day I'm going from reading fashion-retailing guides and talking to better-dressed guys in the Graybar Building to the [Spanish-American War] and bandits and insurgents and runaway slaves and race riots, and thinking, 'Hey, this is alright.' Thus, I happily began my research for *Cuba Libre*."

Leonard had already eagerly announced his plans for a historical novel based around the 1898 explosion of the USS *Maine* in Havana Harbor and the origins of the Spanish-American War to numerous journalists. For research, Sutter began by combing through old issues of *Harper's Weekly* and consolidating scores of old articles and scans from history books on the time period and, in particular, the culture and lifestyles of turn-of-the-century Cuba. In March 1997, Leonard sent Sutter to Cuba for further digging and location scouting. Sutter, who now lived in Florida, returned with ample photographs of the island's standing historic properties and, ultimately, organized nine thick folders' worth of research material for Leonard's use. (Topics included the US Marines' involvement with the war, a study on the Tampa Riot of June 1898, the Cuban coast and its trading ports, the strategic movements of invading forces, the Cuban blockade, and various newspaper samples from American journalists who had covered the war.)

Leonard also drew heavily from Graham A. Cosmas's *An Army for Empire*, David F. Trask's *The War with Spain in 1898*, Douglas Allen's *Frederic Remington and the Spanish-American War*, and Edwin F. Atkins's memoir of the time period, *Sixty Years in Cuba.* (Ironically, Leonard also found crucial historical details in a vintage Western pulp magazine, not unlike the very periodicals that had launched his career more than forty years earlier.) All helped sculpt the background of lead protagonist Ben Tyler.

With the new novel, Leonard was revisiting the Old West for the first time in nearly two decades. He playfully dubbed the book "a tropical Western"—although the story's Cuban landscape would prove to be new literary terrain. His own status as a recognized popular author also granted the upcoming work a legitimate media buzz that hadn't accompanied his previous period piece *Gunsights* in 1979. Anticipation for the book was further fueled amid industry speculation that the Coen brothers were keen to adapt and film the property as the follow-up to their critical smash *Fargo.*

Rather than a basic start date, Leonard marked Tuesday, April 2, 1996, as his day to "begin thinking about *Cuba Libre.*" Just over a month later on May 7—and with Sutter's newly delivered research materials in hand—Leonard first put pen to paper. He'd also changed his creative process slightly, christening his latest work journal not with a list of contacts and reference materials but, rather, the novel's opening and closing lines: *"Tyler came to Cuba with his horses three days after the Maine exploded. He saw the wreckage and the gulls waiting for bodies to rise to the surface."* For the story's denouement, he added, *"What a girl."*

Unlike his previous decade's regular workflow, *Cuba Libre* would require more reading and study than Leonard had had to perform for any project since *The Moonshine War*. As a first order of business, he marked the first line of his new notebook, "*Maine* exploded February 15, 1898," and proceeded to fill pages with the output of his daily history "lessons." He created a detailed timeline of Cuba's violent past, as well as both the successful and failed attempts at the island's colonization. He noted Cuba's abolition of slavery, foreign investments made by foreign businesses (primarily the same sugar trade in which his own grandfather once worked), and the plight of Cuban freedom fighters who struggled against both poverty and the foreign influence that rallied against their independence from Spain.[35] For additional accuracy, he created biographical sketches of the war's real-life historical players—the Red Cross's Clara Barton, insurgent leader Maximo Gomez, the editors and publishers of the *New York Tribune* and the *New York Herald,* William Randolph Hearst among them. For Cuba's background history, Leonard was largely dependent upon Sutter's literary find, *Our Islands and Their People,* as well as journalist Frank Freidel's illustrated history of the conflict, *The Splendid Little War*. He also sketched his own blueprints for the Cuban harbor where the *Maine* had been destroyed, as well as for Yuma Territorial Prison, although the latter would only be referenced in the book. When studying up on the Caribbean sugar trade, Leonard also took the opportunity to begin a research segue into his own family tree, asking Sutter to find archival information on the death of his grandfather, William Leonard, and the dangerous circumstances that came with working on a functioning plantation year-round.

With his background research complete, Leonard soon typed an eleven-page outline of the chapters and actions—a rarity for his long-form works—and more or less filled in his plot gaps with the details and exposition that the massive research had allowed. As dictated in his project journal, he opened the story with the arrival of protagonist Ben Tyler (who, as a tip of the hat to *Gunsights*, once worked for that book's protagonist, Dana Moon, in the Arizona Territory). After he set foot on Cuban soil only three days following the destruction of the USS *Maine*, his assignment calls for the delivery of thirty horses to a wealthy American sugar magnate named Charlie Burke. Of course, Tyler's suspicion of contraband smuggling is fully warranted, as Burke's true profit comes not from the horses but, rather, the shipment of guns hidden aboard the ship. Within hours of his arrival, Tyler makes the acquaintance of a wide range of eccentric characters that populate Leonard's story: planter Roland "Rollie" Boudreaux and his sultry companion, Amelia Brown; Boudreaux's chief lieutenant, Victor Fuentes; villainous Guardia Civil officer Lionel Tavalera; and Spanish henchman Teo Barbon, whom Tyler reluctantly kills in a gunfight soon after his arrival. Imprisoned in Havana's answer to the Bastille—Morro Castle—he makes the acquaintance of Virgil Webster, one of the *Maine*'s few survivors. Together, the men are transferred to a dilapidated prison, leading to another gunfight—this time between the guards and a small army of Cuban revolutionaries. Amid the hail of bullets, Amelia Brown appears, demonstrating her secret ire at the wealthy oppressors and sympathy for the revolution. And, in a dynamic not unlike that of *For Whom the Bell Tolls*' Robert and Maria, the two find love on the guerilla battlefield. But rather than plan for more bloodshed or exploding bridges, they cook up a scheme for Amelia to fake being kidnapped in order to extort $40,000 in ransom money out of Boudreaux. But as is often the case for Leonard's well-meaning antiheroes, numerous betrayals and twists of fate keep the body count high and the ransom money always just out of reach.

Despite the learning curve required to condense much of the historical research, Leonard completed his first draft on April 7, 1997, and had the final version proofread and returned to Delacorte by July 16—ample time for the publisher's February 1998 release date. (Only two weeks after completing the novel, Michael Siegel successfully sold the property to Universal Pictures, in accordance with the studio's plan of having the Coen brothers adapt and direct the film. Ultimately, however—and with the blessing of Leonard, who'd been unimpressed with their script—the duo opted to film an older screenplay of theirs, *The Big Lebowski*, loosely inspired by the detective fiction of Raymond Chandler.)

In the *New York Times*, longtime admirer Christopher Lehmann-Haupt wrote, "Instead of Mr. Leonard's usual noir-comic, claustrophobic beat of small-time hustlers and con men, the world here opens up to reveal a wide panorama of the Cuban revolution and the Spanish-American War . . . So how does Mr. Leonard thread his way through the chaos of history? Why, by drawing on his considerable skills as a writer of westerns, a genre he perfected in early novels like *The Bounty Hunters, Last Stand at Saber River* and *Hombre*."[36] In the *Detroit News*, critic Tom Long wrote, "*Cuba Libre* is packed with historical detail—in fact, its one weakness is that Leonard delivers a smidgen more history than needed—but it's never dated. The morality is relative, the bottom line is gritty, and there is always wry humor hiding around the bend." He added, "The worst thing about the book, as with all Leonard books, is the ending. It ends, and you don't want it to."[37]

Following the solid sales and critical raves that he had garnered for *Cuba Libre*—with many critics heralding the book as proof that Leonard had fully transcended any specific popular genre—he marked his calendar on August 7, 1997: "Began *Get Shorty II*."

October 30, 1998

Dear Megan,

When you say you are "at a very confusing time" in your life, you really mean your perception of the time is confusing. Right? And as long as that's the case, confusing times can occur all through your life. You can go out to the West Coast and continue to be confused . . .

Be cool. You may not even have discovered yet what you really want to do. That doesn't mean you sit and wait, expecting some kind of revelation. You know the old Zulu proverb: "The future doesn't wait for you; you have to go out and catch it." Hemingway said that if want to be a writer, but you're not writing, then you don't want to be one . . .

Learn your craft or your art.

Dedicate yourself to it.

Starve if you have to.

Don't think as much; do.

Don't be impatient.

Find out if you're any good before you try to sell whatever it is you have.

I'm not saying don't go to L.A. But I know what to expect, that you'll more than likely take your confusion with you, L.A. being the weirdest city in America. On the other hand, you might fit right in. One thing I've noticed, especially in the movie business, the girls are smarter than the guys. But the guys have the power. Really all you have to do is be yourself.

Be cool.

Go with God,

Grandfather Elmore[38]

As far back as his earliest drafts of the screenplay for *Jesus Saves* in 1970, Leonard had attempted to use his own love of music as fodder for fiction. Only with *Glitz*, *Touch*, and, in a minor capacity, *Get Shorty*, did any of his in-depth research into the music industry yield major characters or plots; in the latter instance, his copious amount of work on Michael Weir's younger girlfriend, rock star Nikki, went largely unused, save for bits of dialogue. Once Leonard realized just how far back the relationship between organized crime and the music business went, however, he admitted the ease with which a character like Chili Palmer could assimilate. Having spent the last year and a half immersing himself with the turbulent history of Spain's occupation of Cuba and the events surrounding the Spanish-American War, Leonard opted to accompany Gregg Sutter on much of the new novel's field work. From July 20 through 25 of 1997, the two spent hours around Los Angeles's most well-known rock and roll landmarks in between their meetings with music industry executives. For the trip, he brought along two small reporter's notebooks and heavily detailed the sights and sounds of what would become Chili Palmer's new world.

Their packed itinerary began Sunday meeting with Marilyn Watson, an experienced rock and roll tour manager, and famed producer Rick Rubin. Throughout the week, they continued the momentum, meeting various publicists and representatives for Alanis Morissette, No Doubt, Lisa Loeb, and the Lemonheads; Leonard and Sutter also met with Bon Jovi lead guitarist Richie Sambora and producers the Dust Brothers. Upon meeting legendary rock and roll manager Irving Azoff, Leonard noted that he "knew how to handle difficult performers, ones with emotional problems." He'd also observed that the interior of the Wilshire Community Police Station—where Chili Palmer would be questioned regarding the drive-by shooting death of his close friend in the novel's opening scene—looked identical to the set of *Barney Miller*, while at the trendy Viper Room Club on the Sunset Strip, "They make you wait outside so it looks like there's a line."

Leonard later recalled, "We sat in on Don and Richie Sambora fine-tuning Richie's latest CD, [and] we spoke to artists' managers, the artists themselves, like Aerosmith, and the Red Hot Chili Peppers. We spent a whole day with record promoters. For two hours straight, I listened to a promoter talking on the phone to his guys in the field and radio stations' program directors." (Following his afternoon in the office of Terry Anzaldo, Maverick Records' national promotion manager, Leonard noted to himself, "Consider Chili talking to indie promoter who keeps picking up the phone and saying all this stuff . . . 'Gimme some spins,' 'schmooze,' 'vibes,' 'Miss Thing,' and 'sizzle.'"[39])

According to Leonard, just sitting back and listening to the manner in which so many music executives spoke among themselves was enough to get his imagination spinning. He was taken with how diverse musical genres were marketed and, ultimately, set cultural trends. "Well, I certainly knew about reggae," he said. "I referred to it in a book I wrote in the '70s or early '80s, and Ska I related to reggae—that Jamaican kind of syncopated beat. I heard all kinds of rock-and-roll at home when my five kids were growing up." (All of Leonard's children had memories of Leonard's keen interest in their musical tastes; while Peter Leonard never forgot his father's ability to work through even the loudest demonstration of Jimi Hendrix's latest release in 1968, Christopher—a blues guitarist himself—had always shared his favorite new music with his father. According to Chris, his father had a deep appreciation for lyricists, and cited Warren Zevon's "Excitable Boy" among his favorites—as well as almost all of Steely Dan and Joe Cocker. Bill Leonard later recalled that, in retrospect, it was humorous that he had to be the one to ask his father to lower the volume on the stereo on the soundtrack to *Woodstock*—of which Leonard was a big fan.) Leonard later recalled, "I was fascinated by the music in the film of *Woodstock*. Joe Cocker has been a favorite of mine ever since . . . I've always been aware of Aerosmith and liked their music. I got to meet them in the fall of '97 when they were in Detroit, and I asked them if they would like to be in the book. They said sure, so I made up a scene in which the band in the book opens for them at the Forum."

Following their rock-and-roll-infused itinerary, Leonard and Sutter capped off their trip with a decidedly reserved dinner meeting with Michael Siegel and Scott Frank.

Leonard also immersed himself in the latest musical trends, using his old go-to, *Rolling Stone* magazine—as well as the suggestions of his many grandchildren. According to Alex Leonard—later the drummer for the Detroit-based neo-punk band Protomartyr—his grandfather not only had a deep appreciation for the women of rock and roll, but had distinct favorites, such as a crush on Gwen Stefani—although his personal interests remained firmly rooted in jazz. Leonard himself later elaborated, "I don't have to be inspired to appreciate the power of rock, that force coming at you. And I never wore earplugs. But my vibes are more closely associated with jazz: a structured sound you do variations on, improvising, the artist's personality coming through . . . I can remember watching Dizzy Gillespie on stage and wanting to go home and write." He added, "I don't listen to music when I write, but I think I could play the Modern Jazz Quartet in the background, or Ahmad Jamal—definitely Dave Brubeck's 'Take Five.'"

As reflected in his latest work journal (which, as usual, opened to a veritable "who's who" of important contacts—only this time, major figures within the worlds of A&R, music promotion, radio programming, and rock and roll executives), Leonard's interest in the sordid underbelly of the music world quickly took on a life of its own. One eye-opening volume that greatly piqued his interest in the music scene was Frank Dannen's *Hit Men: Power Brokers and Fast Money Inside the Music Business*—an in-depth chronology of the hoodlums, scoundrels, and bona fide gangsters that had created the popular recording industry. Although much of his earliest interest would play little in the new novel's plot, Leonard's initial focus was fixed on the real-life gangsters who had shaped Black-driven rhythm and blues into the white-washed, radio-friendly pop and rock and roll hits; Roulette Records founder and Genovese crime family shill Morris Levy took top priority, as Leonard meticulously noted the means of using record production for mob fronting, loan-sharking, and utilizing payola to get specific artists on the airwaves. Likewise, he noted the checkered life of influential 1950s disc jockey and promoter Alan Freed and his own career-ending payola scandal, how "cutouts" were used to boost imaginary sales figures, and the unofficial founding of "the Network"—an informal alliance of the "dozen or so top independent promotion men" who truly ran what became "hot" in the public consciousness. In his handwritten chronology, Leonard added the foundations of PolyGram Records, the British Invasion, Phil Spector's "Wall of Sound," and the shift toward funk and disco's long-play records. He noted his amusement that, although Tipper Gore had been a proponent of rating the language and content of record albums, both she and her husband, Vice President Al Gore, were admitted "Deadheads"—the most loyal and dedicated Grateful Dead fanatics.[40]

In accordance with his preference for quick narrative turnaround, Leonard outlined the book's plot to take place over the course of an action-packed six-day period. Unlike previous books, Leonard's approach to writing a commissioned sequel required fewer biographical sketches for his characters than usual; Chili Palmer—a decade older and no longer the hot property he'd been at the end of *Get Shorty*—is still producing films, but has become disenchanted with the Hollywood scene. The studio-mandated sequel to his hit, *Get Leo*, flopped, putting him in the unenviable position of returning to the creative drawing board. He visits the young trophy-wife widow of a murdered friend in the record business, Edie, and offers to take over Athens's business interests representing various LA-based rock and roll bands, transplanting him into the world of record promotion. He soon meets young Linda Moon—a gifted singer doing Spice Girls covers in some of Hollywood's less glamorous nightspots, and sees an opportunity to take her and her band, Odessa, to the top of the charts—while documenting his exploits for his next film.

While on one of his book tours during the early stages of *Be Cool*, Leonard had discovered a young country-rock band called the Stone Coyotes, which seemed to perfectly embody the type of rock and roll his characters would create—a high-energy yet folkish take on hard rock, not unlike his old favorites, Delaney and Bonnie. After catching their set at the Troubadour on Sunset Boulevard, he was determined to put them in the book. He later recalled, "I asked if I could use their music, described how I would do it and have them read a couple of my books. Barbara's husband, Doug Tibbles, the drummer, read one and said to her, 'He's for real.' And that was it." Honored to be asked to take part in Leonard's research, the band even collaborated with the author on lyrics for the fictional Linda Moon to perform. Leonard added, "A critic had described the Coyotes' music as 'AC/DC meets Patsy Cline,' and that, I realized, was exactly what I wanted."

By January 1, 1998, Leonard was nearly halfway through the first draft, taking the book with him on his *Cuba Libre* tour throughout the rest of the month. On January 23 in Los Angeles, Leonard had acted as guest speaker for a Writers Bloc literary event, interviewed by friend and admirer Martin Amis; the following evening—coincidentally the twenty-first anniversary of his sobriety—Leonard gave a signing at Book Soup on the Sunset Strip and an unprecedented reading at the rock and roll club the Viper Room next door.

Delacorte released *Be Cool* in February 1999, only months after publishing Leonard's first collection of his original Western pulp stories, *The Tonto Woman and Other Western Stories*—greenlit after the success of *Cuba Libre*, and displaying Leonard's full versatility to a new generation. "Oscar Wilde was probably the first to fully articulate the importance to mankind of redeeming vices—Oscar would've liked *Be Cool*," wrote novelist Kinky Friedman as guest critic for the *New York Times*. "Like a latter-day Virgil, [Leonard] manages to take the casual reader on a thrill ride through the convoluted, secret, sordid daydreams of a ruthless Russian mobster; a 'Godfather' reject turned Hollywood hit man; a maniacal black pimp named Raji, who longs for more sentient, two-legged fish to fry; and that large gay Samoan bodyguard again, who, like everybody else in this wicked world, wants to be in the movies." He added, "To paraphrase F. Scott Fitzgerald, if you've written one book, you've written one book; if you've written two books, you're an author. I always like to add, if you've written three books, you're a hack. Elmore Leonard has now written 35 novels. He hasn't lost a spiritual step."[41]

Leonard may not have lost a spiritual step, but he hadn't handled a baseball in decades. When he was offered the opportunity of a lifetime, to throw out the opening pitch at Tiger Stadium on June 15, 1999, he immediately agreed. Just as quickly, he asked his son Peter for help. "When Elmore finally got his big chance to throw out the opening pitch, he called me and said, 'Can you come over? I have to practice—I haven't thrown a baseball in years.' It took a while, but he got his rhythm back."[42]

CHAPTER 19

Sundown in Detroit, 2000–2005

"Originally, I was going to tell a story about a missionary Catholic priest in Africa who decides after 25 years that he should get out," Leonard told the *New York Times*. "Then, I read Philip Gourevitch's book, *We Wish to Inform You That Tomorrow We Will Be Killed with Our Families*. That hooked me. I wondered where I could drop my characters into the midst of this genocide, where 800,000 people were killed by their neighbors."[1]

It was rare that Leonard infused his contemporary novels with any form of commentary on global events, especially following the mixed response of 1986's *Bandits*. However, Gourevitch's book on Rwanda had resonated with Leonard, especially as a Catholic (albeit a nonpracticing one) with lifelong ties to the Jesuits. He'd also admitted, "I love Graham Greene: the idea of characters who are Catholic and whose religion meant something to them, as part of the plot."

While fascinated with writing about the seriousness of the African genocide, Leonard opted to use that backdrop against his more-familiar Detroit locations and signature humor. He toyed with the idea of a con artist with a heart of gold, disguised as a missionary priest while evading criminals looking for him in Detroit, and a second character—a woman scorned, who had done jailtime for the attempted murder of her husband, and discovered her knack for stand-up comedy while serving her sentence. "The second book under contract has to do with a woman . . . who uses an alcoholic former Catholic missionary priest, Fr. Ray Dunn—who served in Rwanda during the genocide—to scam a lot of money in the name of charity for her own gain," Leonard wrote to Jackie Farber on December 2, 1998. "The working title is *Pagan Babies*."[2] (Leonard had playfully referenced his own 1981 novel, *Split Images*, naming the new work for a punk band that had appeared in the earlier work.)

Like *Be Cool* before it, Leonard opted to accompany Sutter for much of the field research—including visits to a number of high-security prisons. "These ladies at Broward Correctional in Florida agreed to talk to me about 'humor in prison,'" he wrote to son Chris, who'd recently moved back to Arizona. "I asked them what was funny and they said the guards, because they're so stupid . . . Nine of these ladies are in for murder."[3]

Leonard's visit proved to be a hit with both the prison staff and inmates, as well. Following a note of gratitude to Broward Correctional Institution's administration, its superintendent, John A. Anderson, followed up: "Dear Dutch—Thanks for helping to make our facility better by your visit and upcoming publication regarding one aspect of prison life—'humor.'"[4] Following their interview, one particular inmate had even pulled him aside to ask for a small favor: writing a personal letter of recommendation. Never one to deny a fan, Leonard penned it once he returned home:

May 22, 1999

TO WHOM IT MAY CONCERN:

This is submitted on behalf of a very dear friend of mine, Steve Truedel, a talented young man who is held in high regard by almost anyone who is able to understand where he's coming from. There are those who say he's crass and vulgar. But I can testify to the fact Steve is a perfect gentleman, except those times when he's flying high on blow. Yes, he has been known to shout obscenities in public places; but who doesn't when it's superior goods, and Steve always flies first class . . .

In his role as composer, it was Steve who started the new trend called, "Slam Rap" or, "Tunes for Doing Time." His "White Boy Bitches" and "Yo White Ass Is Mine" are steadily climbing the charts in some of the most infamous correctional facilities. You should discount the word of disgruntled young women who have called Steve such things as a lying lowlife two-faced weasel. This type of appraisal is never entirely true.

Respectfully,

Elmore Leonard[5]

Already acknowledged for his own wry humor, Leonard opened his new work journal, unceremoniously, with a large section of notes on the foundations of stand-up comedy, enumerating the topics that most popular performers commonly tackled in their routines: airplanes and airplane food, shopping malls, recent relationship break-ups, diets and weight loss, and, less frequently, social commentary ("People and Hate") all topped the list. The three key styles, he concluded, were "observational," "political," and "storytelling," but also noted the aura of competition that existed among comedic peers. "Always scheming, wondering what the other comics are doing," he wrote. Cribbing from another comedy legend, George Carlin, Leonard noted, "You want to *kill* and don't want to *die* [onstage]."

A juxtaposition worthy of Leonard, he followed with detailed notes from his readings of the Philip Gourevitch book that had kickstarted his interest, as well as journalist Gérard Prunier's recent compendium, *The Rwanda Crisis: History of a Genocide*, and *Season of Blood: A Rwandan Journey*, by Fergal Keane. Having pored through all three, he began a long section entitled "Rwanda—Its Look and Its People," writing his own chronology of the country's recent tragic events. He noted the country's history of colonialism and current policies regarding the refugee crisis of neighboring nations. And much like the rural Prohibition-era Kentucky town that he'd so accurately described in *The Moonshine War*, most medium-size towns within Rwanda only served "electricity till 10 or 10:30pm," relying instead on diesel generators for the whole community. However, Leonard's protagonist, the newly named Father Terry Dunn, would own a personal generator.[6]

Leonard began *Pagan Babies* in Rwanda, with Dunn—secretly a con artist hiding out in Africa due to his crimes and IRS troubles back home in Detroit, living among the aftermath of the genocide of the Tutsis by the Hutus. Dunn shares his home with girlfriend Chantelle, a beautiful one-armed native survivor of the genocide. During his first Mass, Hutu guerillas had stormed Dunn's church, killing the full congregation but leaving the fake priest alive on the altar to watch. At the novel's beginning, Dunn encounters one of the killers and takes vengeance into his own hands, which forces him to run back to his hometown of Detroit. There, he takes refuge in the suburban home of his brother, an ambulance chaser specializing in special-injury lawsuits, who happens to be working with a particularly unique client—Debbie Dewey, an attractive young woman recently released from prison for attempting to run over her ex-husband, Randy, for his adulterous ways. While incarcerated, Dewey discovered an affinity for stand-up comedy, entertaining her fellow inmates during the prison's frequent talent shows. ("True story," she eventually tells an audience. "I was visiting my mom in Florida and happened to run into my ex-husband . . . with a Buick Riviera. It was a rental, but it did the job."[7]) While performing at a local comedy club, Dewey meets Dunn and they take a quick liking to each other. She reveals that Randy had stolen sixty thousand dollars from her and used it to open an upscale restaurant with the help of the local mafia. The two agree to join forces in an elaborate scheme against her ex: she for the money owed her, and Dunn for "the little orphans in Rwanda," whom he dubs the "pagan babies." Working against both Randy and his chief mob partner, Tony Amilia, the duo aim to scam a total of $250,000, for a fifty-fifty split. Soon, however, Dunn begins to suspect his comedic partner may be an even better con artist than himself.

Leonard worked closely with editor Jackie Farber in what would prove to be their final collaboration together. He began the novel on December 23, 1998, working throughout the early part of the year while still on a book tour for dual releases *Be Cool* and *The Tonto Woman*. Starting in New York, he had dinner with Farber on February 15 and, the following day, signed books at Times Square's Barnes and Noble in between appearances on both *Good Morning America* and *The Charlie Rose Show*—the latter a joint interview with friend and admirer Martin Amis. After another signing at Otto Penzler's Mysterious Book Shop—as well as an after-event dinner with his old friend—Leonard went on to Boston, Seattle, San Francisco, and, finally, Los Angeles, where he appeared onstage at the Viper Room on the Sunset Strip with the Stone Coyotes. Leonard took a hard-earned vacation in West Palm Beach through most of March and, by July, admitted to Jackie Farber that he'd been having difficulties achieving the right tone with the novel's depiction of the Rwandan genocide. He was only fifty full pages into the book by midsummer, but he pushed through and had it completed in time to send to Farber in January 2000. ("One of my favorite stories was with *Pagan Babies*," Mike Lupica later recalled. "[Leonard's] editor had sent along a note saying something like, 'It ends rather abruptly.' And I said to him, 'Well, Dutch, what are you going to do?' And he said, 'I added a page yesterday.'"[8])

Delacorte published the book that September.

"In a move more apt to inspire compassion than readers' confidence, Elmore Leonard begins his latest novel with the grim aftermath of genocidal massacre in Rwanda," wrote Janet Maslin in the *New York Times*. "As he describes Terry's quiet, haunted life in Africa, Mr. Leonard remains noticeably out of his element (though not nearly as far out as when he tried working rock lyrics into *Be Cool*, his shaky 1999 foray into the music business). But then, 50 pages into the story, the happily inevitable begins to happen . . . And the pieces of this crime tale begin falling into place so handily that Mr. Leonard might as well have hung a 'Virtuoso at Work' shingle on his door."[9] Marta Salij of the *Los Angeles Daily News* added her own admiration for Leonard's dip into darker, more serious material. "The opening of Elmore Leonard's *Pagan Babies*, his thirty-sixth novel, is one of his starkest," she wrote. "No, this isn't the dark comedy that fans of Leonard's *Get Shorty* or *Out of Sight* expect, and it isn't Detroit or Miami Beach or Los Angeles . . . We're in Graham Greene territory here, or we would be, except for Leonard's dried-to-its-essence wit, which depends on character, not wordplay. Greene would have his disillusioned priest dither in the African heat, brooding over the failure of faith against evil, but Leonard whips him out of there on the first excuse back to Detroit. Because—but of course—Terry Dunn is not a priest, but a con who ran to Rwanda to beat a cigarette-smuggling rap." Salij added, "Leonard has often written good guys with gray areas, but Dunn is a bad guy with gray areas. He has enough hidden spaces that even why he would join Debbie in her scam is worth reconsidering by the end of the story."[10]

Leonard himself was asked about his shift in both tone and approach to global politics during his interview tour. He told the *Los Angeles Times Book Review*, "I can't think of a novel, or anything in particular for that matter, that prompted a political awakening in me. In that area, I remain half-asleep, never seeing much difference between the candidates. I do recall that longshoreman philosopher saying, when Reagan was running for governor, 'Reagan is a B-actor, and California is not a B-state.' I agreed, but mainly because I never liked the way Reagan wore his cowboy hat."[11]

> Forty-six years ago, Kurt Vonnegut and I appeared in the same issue of the *Saturday Evening Post*—April 21, 1956—with short stories. Vonnegut's was called "Miss Temptation"; mine, "Moment of Vengeance." What's interesting is that you might never know we wrote them. I would

> say we both still had as many as a million words to write on the way to developing our own voices or styles.
>
> Along the way, I've come up with ten rules to keep me out of trouble and on the right track: rules to help me remain invisible and show rather than tell what's going on in the story. If you have a facility for language and imagery and the sound of your voice pleases you, invisibility is not what you're after and you can skip the rules.
>
> Still, it won't hurt to look them over.

As early as the 1950s, Leonard had been inspired by two lists of writing "rules" penned by fellow authors—Wilfred McCormick's "From Idea to Plot (With a Checklist of Questions for All Writers of Fiction)," taken from a July 1955 issue of *Author & Journalist* magazine sent to him by Marguerite Harper; and "The Dirty Dozen: The Basic Elements of the Suspense Novel," by controversial thriller writer Dan J. Marlowe (who'd not only written violent tales of murderous bank robbers but, once widowed in his middle age during the 1960s, shared an apartment with one[12]). Just after the publication of *Freaky Deaky* almost thirty years later, he had told journalist Becky Freligh, "If it looks like *writing*, I rewrite it; I don't want the reader to be aware of me. I don't use anything but 'said.' No '-ly' adverbs; they slow things down too much. 'Quietly' is about the only one I use . . . I was having dinner with George Axelrod, the playwright, and I told him I never used exclamation points. He said, 'You're allowed one.'"

The same month *Pagan Babies* hit store shelves, Leonard had been invited as guest of honor at Bouchercon—the World Mystery Convention—in Denver, and had been asked to prepare a few words. While in his room at the Adam's Mark Hotel, he was still toying with his speech throughout the afternoon. Finally, on two loose pages of unlined yellow paper he'd brought from home, Leonard began to compose a rough list of writing advice that would, eventually, become nearly as famous as his fiction:

1. Never open a book with weather.
2. Avoid prologues.
3. Never use a verb other than "said" to carry dialogue.
4. Never use an adverb to modify the verb "said."
5. Keep your exclamation points under control. You are allowed no more than two or three per 100,000 words of prose.
6. Never use the words "suddenly" or "all hell broke loose."

> 7. Use regional dialect, patois, sparingly.
> 8. Avoid detailed descriptions of characters.
> 9. Don't go into great detail describing places and things.
> 10. Try to leave out the parts that readers skip.
>
> My most important rule is the one that sums up the ten. If it sounds like writing, I rewrite it.

After presenting it to the audience, Leonard was almost immediately swarmed with requests for copies. Inspired by their enthusiasm, he quickly transformed his "rules" into a full-length essay. He initially titled the short piece "Voices," before the *New York Times* ultimately published it as "Easy on the Adverbs, Exclamation Points, and Especially Hooptedoodle" on July 16, 2001. He had used the publication of the list to elaborate on its themes, adding, "If proper usage gets in the way, it may have to go. I can't allow what we learned in English composition to disrupt the sound and rhythm of the narrative . . . It's my attempt to remain invisible, not distract the reader from the story with obvious writing."[13]

Before starting his next book, he signed with a new publisher.

With his Delacorte contract met, he was quickly courted by William Morrow just prior to their absorption into HarperCollins. Another major book was already in the works, and he used it for his next publishing house debut. Jeff Zaleski of *Publishers Weekly* soon reported, "We ask Leonard how he likes being at HarperCollins, which in May of last year announced a reported near-eight-figure deal by which the house gets North American rights to two new Leonard books, as well as the writer's huge backlist. Leonard deems HarperCollins 'great. There's so much energy there.'"[14]

Over the previous decade, he had also warmed to the idea of writing the occasional short story—usually at the behest of Otto Penzler, his friend and publisher of the Mysterious Press. And just as his playful "assignment" for Penzler had led to the creation of Karen Sisco and, ultimately, the entire narrative of *Out of Sight*, so another recent short work would spark the idea for his next novel.[15] With "Chickasaw Charlie Hoke," for the first time, Leonard also leaned into one of his earliest childhood passions—baseball.

In creating the short story's protagonist Charlie Hoke, Leonard assigned himself the fun task of outlining the former Major Leaguer's fictional career. Using his own love and knowledge of the sport, Leonard typed a detailed timeline that followed Hoke from his 1967 drafting to the Baltimore Orioles right out of high school to his 1984 winning season with the Detroit Tigers—the Leonard family's own home team. Before long, and with the character fully fleshed out, Leonard made good use of Gregg Sutter's research into Tunica, Mississippi—the "Las Vegas of the South"—and had the seeds of *Tishomingo Blues*.

The new novel hadn't begun with character "Chickasaw" Charlie Hoke, however. Rather, Leonard had in mind for a professional high diver to be his chief protagonist, as he later told journalist Trudy Wyss. "I think I was still writing *Pagan Babies*, but I was near the end, and I thought of a high diver. I wondered if a high diver might make a good character. Because the guy's eighty feet above the ground, diving into this little tank, he's on the edge every day. He risks his life, or certainly risks injury, every day."[16] He later elaborated to journalist T. V. LoCicero: "I said [to Gregg Sutter], 'See what you can find out about high divers, these divers who go off the top of an eighty-foot ladder.' I said, 'I think that would be an interesting character. Maybe a guy who has been doing it for a while and now, you know, he can't do it forever. What's going to happen to him?' And so he found some high divers."[17]

Sutter had, indeed, delivered on Leonard's obscure request, choosing the Great American High Diving Team—based out of the Miracle Mile Strip Amusement Park in Panama City Beach, Florida—as the focal point of his own research. On the final day of May, Leonard and Sutter flew to Panama City together and met with a team of high-dive experts—Bo, Danny, George, and Randy—as well as their manager and the show's producer, Dean Maxwell. Ultimately, it was Danny "Cosmo" Higgenbottom who proved the perfect template for Leonard's new antihero. "I was born to do this," the daredevil diver claimed. "My dad threw me off the diving board at the age of two."

The visits with real-life high divers proved invaluable in shaping the novel's lead character, Dennis Lenahan, and the dangers that came with the niche profession. "The ladder is put up in eight ten-foot sections, each section secured, stabilized by four wires made of twelve-gauge soft wire from the Birmingham Wire Works . . . Firemen provide the water from a nearby hydrant and [are] given a bottle of whiskey for the favor."

After noting that the team often traveled to such exotic locations as China, Taiwan, Thailand, South Korea, Austria, and Germany—and that two shows a night with three divers performing per show was par for the course—he added, "Divers make up names for themselves. Their ego level is quite high. In fact: 'The better the performer, the least stable the personality.'" He also noted the many different types of daredevil dives that the performers had to master, including the "Spotter Dive"—a back-flip facing forward, back onto the diving board—and the "Flying Reverse Somersault." He added, "Drop a half-dollar on the floor—that's what the tank looks like from eighty-feet up. Others say it looks like a teacup . . . High-diving gives a different (or greater) understanding of time and space. Time slows down . . ."

According to the real-life diving team, teaching interrelated sports such as swimming or gymnastics were frequently used as off-season professions for the divers. With shades of both *Unknown Man No. 89*'s failed baseball hopeful Jack Ryan and *Killshot*'s frustrated Wayne Colson, Leonard noted, "This is where Dennis is in his early 40s, sensing he's at the end of his career as a high diver, but has no other profession or trade outside of work construction. He could go to Ironworkers school and could get into that; high places don't bother him . . . But a job as an ironworker in the winter isn't much fun either."

As was the case with all of Leonard's contemporary crime novels, the research also led to another key element of the novel's plot. He had also become fascinated with the subculture of Civil War reenactments—staged re-creations of actual battles choreographed and performed by history buffs decked out in accurate regalia. Having recently finished Tony Horwitz's *Confederates in the Attic: Dispatches from the Unfinished Civil War*, an investigation of neo-Confederate tendencies in the contemporary South, Leonard decided that these men—philosophical "leftovers" from another century, perhaps the Old West that had been his original forte—would make for a perfect band of social misfits for his new story.

Following a brief aside to visit Leonard's sister, Mickey, in Little Rock, he and Sutter proceeded east to observe various Civil War battlefields. On their itinerary were such historical landmarks as Brices Cross Roads National Battlefield, the site of General Nathan Bedford Forrest's 1864 victory over the Union army; Tupelo, site of the Tupelo National Battlefield (and birthplace of Elvis Presley); and Corinth, Iuka, and Shiloh. "Elmore wrote about all these places in *Tishomingo Blues*," Sutter remembered.

"Back in Michigan, in late August, we attended the Cascades Jackson Civil War Muster, in Jackson. We talked to reenactors and watched realistic battles with cannons and the whole nine yards, until Elmore had had enough and turned to me and said, 'Let's go get something to eat.'"[18]

Of the "reenactors," Leonard himself later told Michael Giltz of the *New York Post*, "Are they serious! It surprises me that the women go along and wear hoop skirts and cook over an open fire and sleep in a tent . . . I can't imagine anyone going out to sleep in a tent for any reason."[19]

Although he would retain a professional high diver as chief protagonist, Leonard began his new work journal with lengthy lists of the book's characters and which side of the Civil War reenactment they would serve. (Now one of America's most popular writers of mainstream fiction, he had also participated in a series of high-profile auctions for charity, incorporating the real names of winning donors to the character roster, thus granting each a literary "cameo" in his latest work. This time around, at least three generous donors had paid thousands of dollars to be included in the novel's climactic Civil War reenactment; Leonard noted their names carefully as he worked out the scene.)

As with each of his books, Leonard utilized core source references for historical context; in the case of understanding the Southern mentality following the Reconstruction era into the modern day, he jotted down quotes from real-life white supremacists and "true believers" in resurrecting the fight of the South's "Lost Cause." Leonard also tasked Sutter with gathering research on the book's dual antagonists—both the groups of white supremacy that would largely show their heads toward the novel's conclusion, and the "Dixie Mafia" (which, Leonard noted, was humorously referred to as "the Cornbread Cosa Nostra" by federal law enforcement agencies). In the case of the white power group "the Dixieland White Knights" (one of over a dozen Leonard listed in existence), there were instances of membership common to both.[20]

Finally, Leonard added a third major theme for the book—early blues music. Although a lifelong music buff, he knew little about the history of early Black music in the United States, and he had initially intended to infuse the novel with his longtime love of jazz. He admitted to journalist Michael Giltz, "I never got into that basic, this-is-where-it-comes-from 'Delta Blues.' I liked Big Band blues . . . When I was in high school, I'd go to the Paradise Theater—which is now the symphony hall. I'd go there to see Black bands, like [Count] Basie and Earl Hines."[21] But, as Sutter later recalled, "As I read over the first act of the novel, I noticed that Robert Taylor, the Black gangster from Detroit, was listening to jazz on his car radio as he drove around Tunica . . . But I felt a major character note for Taylor would be lost if he did not express a profound love for the blues."[22]

Leonard took Sutter's suggestion and began to retool Taylor's musical tastes, intrigued by how much of it had originated near his own birthplace in Louisiana.[23] (Grandson Alex Leonard later recalled, "Elmore had a couple contemporary groups that he liked. But I mean, he really loved Count Basie and kind of jazz people. That was like his big knowledge base. We would tease him, 'You just listen to jazz.' And he'd say, 'No, I like modern stuff. One of my favorite things is—I don't know the name of the song—but it's got the girl with the blue dress.' He goes, 'That's one of my favorite songs.' And the whole family would say, 'What the hell are you talking about?' It took me about twenty minutes to figure out that he's talking about 'Don't Speak' by No Doubt, because in the video, Gwen Stefani's wearing a blue dress."[24])

Beginning with his first Civil War reenactment with Sutter in Flint, Michigan, on June 24, Leonard's first draft of *Tishomingo Blues* followed soon after. But he continued to collect and consolidate notes throughout that summer in between reenactment trips, tinkering with the manuscript draft along the way, and on January 3, 2001, he began a new, revamped draft. By the second week of February, he was able to send the first forty-eight polished pages to Michael Siegel and Jackie Farber (the switch to HarperCollins hadn't yet been confirmed), and he finished the book at 1:45 p.m. on Sunday, June 3. He'd just returned home from his grandson Tim's high school graduation.

Upon its release in February 2002, *Tishomingo Blues* acted as Leonard's debut with HarperCollins's William Morrow imprint. It received decidedly better reviews than *Pagan Babies* and, as Leonard soon told *USA Today*'s Deirdre Donahue, it had replaced *Freaky Deaky* as his "absolute" favorite among his many novels, largely because "he had so much fun writing it."[25]

"We haven't seen *this* Leonard very much since the high points of 1991's *Maximum Bob* (in which a small-time Florida judge tries to off his wife, a former Weeki Wachee mermaid) or 1988's *Freaky Deaky* (in which small-time Detroit '60s radical rejects think one last bombing will be their big score)—but we're sure glad to have him back," wrote Marta Salij in the

Detroit Free Press. "In *Tishomingo Blues*, Leonard has a much better solution in a character like Dennis, who is neither a lawman nor a lowlife, but someone who could plausibly be either one. That makes *Tishomingo Blues* deliciously ambiguous, the characters harder to put your finger on, the plot harder to predict. But one prediction is easy: Leonard's new and old fans will rank this one among his best."[26] Janet Maslin of the *New York Times* likewise praised the work, citing cool and composed drug runner Robert Taylor as among Leonard's best recent characters. "Robert knows a lot about the Civil War, having stolen the complete set of Ken Burns's documentary videos from Blockbuster. And as he tells Dennis, 'History can work for you, you know how to use it.' He demonstrates this by presenting the mobile home mogul, Walter Kirkbride, with a photograph of a lynching. The dead man, Robert says, was his great-grandfather. And it was Walter's great-grandfather who killed him; this story has the desired intimidation effect . . . And there is the reason Robert likes the film *All That Jazz*, which might be the credo of any Leonard hero: 'The man living every minute of his life till the way he's living kills him. Beautiful.'" Maslin added, "The women in this book are especially substantial, to the point where they are as tough and interesting as the men."[27]

For all the solid reviews that *Tishomingo Blues* had garnered, perhaps none was more appreciated by Leonard than fellow author Margaret Atwood's raves in the *New York Review of Books*. "*Tishomingo Blues* is Elmore Leonard's thirty-seventh novel," she had written. "At that number, you would think he'd be flagging, but, no, the maestro is in top form. If, like Graham Greene, he were in the habit of dividing his books into 'novels' and 'entertainments'—with, for instance, *Pagan Babies* and *Cuba Libre* in the former list, and *Glitz*, *Get Shorty*, and *Be Cool* in the latter—this one might fall on the entertainment side; but, as with Greene, those that might be consigned to the 'entertainment' section are not necessarily of poorer quality."[28]

Even before the raves, Hollywood had already come knocking for what would be Leonard's first film adaptation of the new decade—or so it seemed. On August 8, 2001, the *Hollywood Reporter* had announced, "FilmFour, the stand-alone film unit of U.K. broadcaster Channel 4, snapped up worldwide feature film rights" to the book, with Leonard to serve as producer and "full creative partner" on the proposed project. "FilmFour is aiming to fast-track the project's development," the article continued, although, at that point, there had been no cast or director announced.[29] Jeff Zaleski of *Publishers Weekly* soon reported: "Leonard has some ideas for casting the movie. As the novel's magnetic center, drug dealer and ultimate cool cat Robert Taylor, he sees Don Cheadle . . . And for Dennis, the novel's high-diving daredevil hero, Leonard likes Michael Keaton."[30]

Only weeks after the book's publication the following year, Leonard's words rang true with the enthusiastic addition of *Out of Sight*'s scene stealer Cheadle—announced as both the star *and* director by *Variety* on February 21, 2002. But despite the enthusiasm from all involved, the project soon, unceremoniously, was dropped. Gregg Sutter later recalled, "The financing was pulled at the last minute. One of the reasons given at the time was that an American Civil War reenactment story line would not sell in Europe. Elmore was his usual philosophical self about it. Movies were ephemeral; the books were on the shelf forever."[31]

Cheadle, however, was less than philosophical about the collapse of what was to be his directorial debut. When asked about the film's progress by *Comingsoon.net*, the actor had pantomimed a gun with his forefinger and thumb, aiming at the floor. "*Tishomingo* is dead," he said. "Bang! Bang!"[32] Cheadle would, instead, go on to act as both director and star of *Miles Ahead*, a critically acclaimed biopic of jazz legend Miles Davis.

As had been the case with a few other authors in previous years—Martin Amis, Raymond Carver, and Jim Harrison among them—Leonard and Margaret Atwood's was a mutual appreciation. They had originally met at a PEN Canada event in Toronto in March 2000 and kept up a correspondence following Atwood's enthusiastic note of gratitude for his appearance.[33] Upon the release of her 2003 novel, *Oryx and Crake*, Atwood sent along a signed edition to Leonard's Bloomfield Hills home. Leonard was quick to respond:

> *Dear Margaret,*
>
> *You are a master at moving a story, building with flashbacks, telling it in scenes with a lot of white space. I love the book and once I was eighty or so pages into it, got a kick out of what you said in your inscription, "There are some jokes in it." My favorite: "As soon as they start doing art, we're in trouble" . . . You must've had a ball*

writing it, even with all the bioforms and genetic stuff you had to come up with.

It's a wonderful novel; it's so readable.

Take it easy,

Dutch[34]

Jim Harrison had also recently sent his own note of appreciation to Leonard regarding *Pagan Babies*. "[I] have been intending to write for a couple of years to tell you how much I admire your books which, if anything, are getting better," Harrison wrote. "You can cut your fingers and eyes on their lucidity."[35]

But Leonard's long list of fans extended far past his literary peers. While on his numerous research trips with Gregg Sutter for *Be Cool*, Leonard had gotten to know the members of Aerosmith well, even extending to them an invitation to a private pool party at his home in Bloomfield Hills; they accepted on one condition: no alcohol, as all members were, like Leonard, recovered alcoholics. "I wasn't there when Aerosmith came to visit," said Christopher Leonard, "but Peter told me later that all the neighborhood kids lined up outside the fence to get a peek at the band. And my sister Katy had a small child at the time, little Joe. Elmore told me that Steven Tyler picked up baby Joe and Joe screamed—top of his lungs, mouth open—right in Steven's face. Not to be outdone, Steven Tyler screamed right back—his signature high-pitched wail. They got a great photo of it."[36]

Daughter Katy Dudley recalled, "A friend of my husband's was their manager at the time . . . I was with him when he hung out with Aerosmith after their concert in Detroit. I remember after the show, Steven Tyler was in his dressing room sitting at the drums with his shirt off and making up a song about Elmore." She added, "At the pool party, Elmore didn't even put out a spread or anything. I thought that was so weird. I said, 'You've got Aerosmith in your backyard,' and he had, like, a bowl of peanuts or something. And they don't drink so all he had out was bottled water in a cooler. They were all really friendly and didn't complain or anything."[37] (At that time, all of Leonard's children, except for Christopher—running his own restaurant in Tucson, Arizona—lived only miles away: Jane, long his official typist, had also been flipping houses for a number of years. "She renovates homes—she's got a builder's license," Leonard told biographer Paul Challen. "She buys a house for $250,000 and sells it for $400,000." Peter Leonard, at that time, was still running his hugely successful ad agency, Leonard, Mayer & Tocco. However, as his father elaborated, "[Peter] would love to get out of it and write screenplays." Bill Leonard had become the vice president at the J. Walter Thompson agency, working on the Ford account, and Katy was a schoolteacher, often inviting her father to speak to her class.[38])

Likewise, Sir Elton John had enjoyed Leonard's company backstage at one of his performances in Detroit. "Dear Elmore—First I get the privilege of meeting you, and now a signed book," John wrote from his next stop in Atlanta. "I can't thank you enough for the thought, and I can't wait to read the book. Exciting, as [*Be Cool*] is about my business . . . Many thanks and much love, Elton."[39] A huge fan of Steely Dan for over thirty years, Leonard was particularly excited to strike up correspondence with its cofounder, the notoriously reclusive Donald Fagan. "Thank you for your letter," Fagan wrote. "I could hardly believe I was holding a typed letter from you in these hyper-textual times. I'm on tour with Steely Dan (in Houston tonight) . . . Remember the film *One-Eyed Jacks*? It's one of my favorites. Wouldn't it be interesting to see the backstory of the Brando character and the Karl Malden character? They had a kind of father-son Oedipal thing happening, no?"[40]

Excited at the prospect of having Leonard within their esteemed roster of authors, HarperCollins sent him on a multicity *Tishomingo Blues* tour during the spring of 2002, backed by a $250,000 advertising campaign.

HarperCollins had also acquired Leonard's vast back catalogue of over thirty-five novels, soon reissuing his entire body of contemporary crime works with hip, modernized covers by Chip Kidd, the artist who had designed the bold cover of Delacorte's edition of *Cuba Libre*. Andrew Wylie later recalled, "I had first heard about Elmore through Martin Amis and Saul Bellow and they both mentioned him and his work favorably, leading me to begin reading Elmore's work. I had noticed that the books were in different formats and from different publishers, and I thought, 'You know, this looks like a badly organized set of negotiations. What we need is a sort of uniform presentation of Elmore's work' . . . Elmore, in turn, put me in touch with Michael Siegel, whom I also knew. I told Michael that, in my view, Elmore's books were not properly presented and I could work to get things better organized on Elmore's behalf. He agreed and we began working together." Wylie soon arranged a buy-out of the three publishers currently running with Leonard's back catalogue, consolidating the full line under the HarperCollins banner. In an attempt to appeal to a younger audience, the books were redesigned and put into the more-palatable trade paperback format. Wylie recalled, "I remember the deal was made on a Friday, and I told Elmore about it, and there was a sort of penetrating silence on the other end of the phone, and I said, 'Elmore, Elmore?' I thought maybe he died or something from the shock of the figure, and he said finally, 'Clean living pays off.' And I thought that was just great."[41]

By now, Leonard was largely represented for all multimedia deals by Michael Siegel, although it was in agreement that a singular literary agent would be required for the upcoming HarperCollins deal. Ultimately, Leonard began working with Jeff Posternak, who would continue to represent him for the remainder of his career. "Elmore's [publications] were a bit of a mess when we first took him on—his international publications as well—because he had moved from house to house and there wasn't any logic in certain books," Posternak recalled. "In a series of steps, we were able to negotiate to claw back from U.S. publishers the foreign rights back to Elmore so that rather than having a kind of limp, ineffectual reactive association with all these publishers, we were able to do it directly . . . Then we consolidated this back list from, I think, four publishers to one, creating more value for Elmore altogether. The older works became his to control . . . I think there's really no question that it put a kind of reinvigoration into his list."[42]

In addition, HarperCollins planned a publishing blitz, spread out over the first few years. Only nine months after the publication of *Tishomingo Blues*, they released *When the Women Come Out to Dance*, Leonard's first collection of non-Western short stories. Included was a novella he had written for a short-lived online site, Contentville. In January 2001, *The Guardian* reported, "Veteran crime writer Elmore Leonard has become the second high-profile writer to be seduced by the internet, with plans to release his next thriller on the web. His forthcoming book, *Fire in the Hole*, will be available from download specialists Contentville from January 17."[43] While on his promotional tour for *Pagan Babies* in 2000, Leonard had revealed the upcoming short work to the *London Evening Examiner*'s Nick Curtis: "I've just finished a novella for the internet.

It's kind of weird because I won't be able to see it, since I don't have a computer . . . For forty-nine years, I've been writing with a pen, crossing things out and rewriting as I go along. Why change that?"[44]

The contract had stipulated that Leonard provide three pieces of content for the site over the following year: one original novella that had to include a recurring character familiar to readers, and two previously written though never-before-published works. (For the latter two Leonard selected a 1970 novella of *Picket Line* he had initially envisioned as a "scriptment" for producer Howard Jaffe—as well as his 1992 screenplay for director William Friedkin, *Stinger*. However, Contentville would fold before Leonard's second two works were due for online publication.) Although his contract had suggested recurring characters such as those from *Get Shorty* or *Rum Punch*, the recent film adaptations of both books prevented those characters from usage elsewhere. Instead, Leonard brought back old favorite Raylan Givens, last seen in 1995's *Riding the Rap*. Entitled *Fire in the Hole*, the sixty-page novella finally offered Givens's proper backstory, a return to his birthplace in a rural coal-mining town in Eastern Kentucky, and a childhood nemesis who'd grown up to become a white supremacist leader, Boyd Crowder—a true Leonard original, who uses his down-home charm to enlist neo-Nazi hillbillies ("Crowder's Commandos") in blowing up the Cincinnati federal IRS building for coming down on him for back taxes. The story's title came from Crowder's signature holler each time he'd detonate a charge in the coal mines—now his catchphrase when pulling the trigger of his bazooka, which he uses early on in the story to destroy a Black community church, the "Temple of the Cool and Beautiful J.C." After Givens is assigned to the investigation, he first encounters Crowder's sister-in-law, Ava, who'd long carried a torch for the marshal before his law enforcement career, before the showdown with Crowder himself. Heavy on dialogue and unused research materials on white power organizations from *Tishomingo Blues*, Leonard began the story on October 21, 2000, and had it completed in a mere three weeks.

He celebrated by seeing his personal favorite rocker, Joe Cocker, at the Detroit Palace, live in concert with Tina Turner.

Between February 2002 and November 2005, William Morrow–HarperCollins would publish five Leonard books, all to critical and financial success: *Tishomingo Blues*; *When the Women Come Out to Dance*; his first Detroit cop novel in nearly sixteen years, *Mr. Paradise*, in 2004; his first young adult novel, *A Coyote's in the House* (playfully including references to *Get Shorty*'s Harry Zimm and a cameo appearance by Leonard-favorite Harry Dean Stanton) in May; and a full anthology of his pulp magazine works, entitled *The Complete Western Stories of Elmore Leonard*.

For many of the new readers that Leonard had accumulated over the previous decade, *When the Women Come Out to Dance* proved that the author had made his mark on the literary scene as a writer of short stories—and incorporated a few gems that even die-hard fans might have missed. Stories like "The Tonto Woman" and "Sparks" only appeared in older anthologies, while a new novella for the collection, *Tenkiller*, featured the great-grandson of *Cuba Libre*'s Virgil Webster. Not quite the man of action like others in the family (Virgil survived the explosion of the USS *Maine* and the ensuing battles of the Spanish-American War; his son, Carl Webster, was a renowned US marshal and hero of the Second World War), Ben Webster—named, of course, for the legendary jazz saxophonist—is a former rodeo star and Hollywood stuntman who *plays* the role of his forebearers' heroics. Returning home to claim his birthright—Virgil's sprawling acreage in Okmulgee, Oklahoma—Ben finds it overrun by a band of local hoodlums none too impressed with either his city-boy appearance or stoic heritage, and the gang seeks to intimidate him out of his rightful home. Rising to the occasion—and in a scenario reminiscent of Sam Peckinpah's gritty *Straw Dogs*—the younger Webster summons the strength of his grandfather in waging a one-man coup to take the property back.

Leonard began *Tenkiller* on November 27, 2001, and had thirty clean pages completed by the end of the week; on January 16, 2002, he came home from the barber and finished it up that afternoon—just in time for a phone interview with the *Denver Post*. He'd envisioned Bruce Willis in the lead role and immediately sent a copy to the actor who, in turn, announced his interest in developing it as a film; ultimately, however, the duo would go three-for-three in failed projects.

"[Leonard]'s slender and not tall, with thinning gray hair and a goatee that, with his jeans, black turtleneck and leather sandals, convey aging hipster," journalist Jeff Zaleski wrote. "When Leonard settles behind the large antique table at which he works, however, he looks only like a writer. A pen and pad of yellow paper filled with blue script are on the table. Leonard shakes a True Blue out of a pack and lights it."

As Leonard picked up his pen—a recently acquired Pilot Precise V7—he explained to the journalist the importance of his writing tools: "I began writing with a twenty-nine-cent Scripto, and went to a ninety-eight-cent pen in orange. I used a Saint Laurent pen after that." Holding up the new pen, he added, "I started using this two-thirds of the way through *Tishomingo Blues*. Before that, I used a Mont Blanc that I'd been using for several books; it was a table favor at a PEN America function. But this is perfect. I'm trying blue—I like the blue."[45] Leonard had actually been gifted the pens from Pilot itself, the company having sent him a number of models from their enormous line of writing implements, imploring him to try each one until he found a favorite. Once he delivered his feedback on the V7, they'd sent along a complimentary stock for future use. "The Pilot V7 (Fine) has a 'write out' of 1,500 to 1,600 meters," wrote the company's public relations director, Sallie Mitchell. "By averaging the number of pages in your books and the word count per page, we calculate that your next book will be around 84,000 words, or 10,000 meters. With cross-outs and edits, you'll need seven Precise Fine rolling balls. We're pleased to provide you with—your next book!"[46]

When asked by Zaleski about his advancing years, Leonard—in a rare moment—paused for a philosophical answer. "I think it's fascinating to see yourself changing," he responded. "I think I play tennis as well, or run or do anything, but it isn't true. And I find myself being more careful going down stairs . . . I think of it as simply accepting what is. I think I probably get this out of [Alcoholics Anonymous]—twenty-five years next month."[47]

Although Leonard and Christine had been married for more than a decade, he would still receive questions about his previous marriages—particularly how Joan's death had impacted his life and writing. He's revealed to *The Guardian*'s Tim Adams, "I was into a book [at the time], of course, can't remember which one. But death doesn't frighten me at all. My high-school reunion is getting smaller each year, you know. But no one in the books ever really reflects on it, and I don't have too many characters who die of natural causes, I guess."[48]

Having completed what he deemed his favorite among all his novels, Leonard surprised nearly all of his critics and fans with his follow-up to

Tishomingo Blues—by way of a "gift" for his many grandchildren, his first children's book. Before leaving the author's home after their interview, Jeff Zaleski had spied a copy of E. B. White's *Charlotte's Web*—which Leonard admitted reading in preparation for his next work for Harper-Collins Children's. "There's a coyote in the Hollywood Hills," he told the journalist, "an L.A. Street coyote, Antoine, with his own gang, called the 'Howling Diablos.'"[49] Asked why a children's book, Leonard's response was simple: "I have five kids and eleven grandchildren, so I've made up a lot of stories in my time."[50] But as granddaughter Kate Leonard later recalled, as a child, she had specifically asked her grandfather to write a story about a dog for her. "I was so obsessed with dogs," she recalled. "And then he wrote *A Coyote's in the House*. Then I read it when I was twelve and, in it, he calls the female dogs 'bitches.' I was so upset. And I said something to him, and he said, 'Well, that's what they're called.'"[51]

A modernized riff on the classic Mark Twain novel *The Prince and the Pauper*, the book was originally entitled *Richie Makes His Run*. Soon, however, the German shepherd protagonist was renamed the more common Buddy, allowing the more-colorful titular coyote, Antwan, to carry much of the book's humor (even as a talking dog aimed at children, tinges of Samuel L. Jackson's voicing and delivery come to mind). "I wrote a few pages with the dog as the main character," Leonard later recalled. "He was watching the coyotes up on the hill at night, and I thought, 'That's my point of view—the coyote' . . . Once I realized what his attitude would be—that he would just have contempt for dogs, dogs having sold out—I knew I could handle it and that he would be a lot of fun. Then it was just natural, because that's the kind of character who interests me the most."[52] In the story, Antwan, a feral coyote and leader of his own pack, the Howling Diablos, accidentally meets Buddy, a domesticated German shepherd and a retired Hollywood performance dog, used to a life of luxury in his wealthy owner's Los Angeles mansion. The two become fast friends and decide to swap places, giving Antwan a taste of the good life, while Buddy learns to embrace his animalistic roots back in the wild.

Aside from studying *Charlotte's Web*, Leonard assigned Gregg Sutter the task of gathering data on various dog breeds and hunting coyotes native to California, focusing on their behavior and relationships to humans. Among the hodgepodge of various articles Sutter was able to dig up were case studies of police K9 units, hunting bloodhounds—referred to as "cattle cops and dog cowboys"—and studies on the therapeutic abilities that canines had on their human owners.[53]

Leonard began his first draft the first week of 2002 and had it finished in a mere three months, completing it on the final day of March. As it was his first book to require illustrations, he wrote back to HarperCollins on November 19, wholeheartedly approving of artist Lauren Child's playful, comic-book-ish design work for Antwan, Buddy, and friends: "I love it!—Dutch."[54] He dedicated it: *"For my grandchildren: Shannon and Megan; Tim, Alex, Max and Kate; Ben, Hillary and Abby; Joe, Nick and Luke; and for my great-grandson, Jack."*[55]

Despite minor controversies regarding Leonard's use of his signature dialogue and characterizations, now aimed at children between the ages of nine and thirteen, he and Siegel took the unpublished manuscript to Disney prior to its publication. "They said, 'We like it but there isn't a little cuddly animal with a serious problem. It isn't sentimental enough.'" Leonard advised the House of Mouse that he didn't "do" sentimentality.[56]

A Coyote's in the House was published on June 1, 2004—just in time for children's summer reading lists. Brandon Robshaw of *The Independent* wrote, "Leonard captures the rhythms and grammar of Black Urban Vernacular in the speech of Antwan and his friends. They call one another 'man' and greet one another by saying 'wassup'; pronouns and auxiliary verbs, and the word 'if' are systematically omitted. It sounds thoroughly authentic—except for the absence of swearing, but then, this is a children's book. It's a neat trick to make coyotes talk like gangstas, and Leonard pulls it off with style. But is there anything beyond this trick?"[57]

Leonard aimed his next "trick" toward his regular demographic—taking adult readers back to the mean streets of Detroit for the first time in fifteen years.

He'd had a new cop epic in mind even before starting *A Coyote's in the House*, meeting with Detroit homicide inspector Craig Schwartz at 1300 Beaubien the first week of September 2002. The following week, Gregg Sutter flew in from his new home in Los Angeles to accompany Leonard to meetings with Special Investigation Section [SIS] homicide detectives and, on the first anniversary of 9/11, the two rode from the Thirty-Sixth Circuit Court with the squad to meet with witnesses in the shooting deaths of two local civilians. By the end of November, Leonard had the bulk of the research needed for *Mr. Paradise*, and spent the first week of

December on a brief tour in New York. He'd attended a one-act stage adaptation of "When the Women Come Out to Dance," starring Judith Light and Rosie Perez, and presented by Food for Thought Productions. Then he hopped over to Barnes and Noble in Times Square for a signing engagement for *Tishomingo Blues*. After another taping for *Charlie Rose* the following day, he sat with *Newsweek*'s Malcolm Jones on December 5—then flew home in the morning, just in time for a Commodores concert the following night. At the end of the month, he began his first draft.

He'd already outlined the basic premise: a high-priced call girl, paid handsomely by a wealthy sugar daddy (attorney Anthony Paradiso—the titular "Mr. Paradise") to dress in costumes determined by his whim—usually a topless cheerleader, as he watches old University of Michigan football games in the background—and coerces her close friend and roommate, a Victoria's Secret model, to accompany her as backup to one of the weekly trysts. Determined by the old john's coin flip, one girl stays with Paradiso, while the other heads upstairs to please his underpaid valet. During that night's shenanigans, two intruders break into the house, killing the old man and his companion. The homicide investigator, Lieutenant Frank Delsa, soon suspects the dead man's valet, Montez Taylor—revealed to hold a grudge for having been cut from Paradiso's will—as well as a case of mistaken identity when it comes to the murdered girl, Chloe Robinette, and her surviving friend, Kelly Barr.

Of his literary return to Detroit, Leonard told Mike Householder of the Associated Press, "The fact of the matter is that I know where all the streets are now, and I'm too old to learn the streets of another city."[58] But much had changed in the ways of police procedure and forensic analysis since Leonard's last foray to 1300 Beaubien. The old Detroit Police Headquarters had since been condemned and, although the Homicide Division was still there, many other departments had already been relocated to other areas throughout the city. In his notes, Leonard observed: "A captain may be the last to leave a sinking ship, but the . . . Chief Detective of the Police Department was the first to leave the building."

Leonard opted to emphasize that passing of time within the story, even aging his protagonist, Frank Delsa—initially named "Louis Delsa" in earliest notes—to a seasoned and weary investigator at the end of his run. "Sixteen years with the Detroit Police, twelve years or so with the Homicide Section, Squad 7, until early retirement," Leonard wrote in his latest work journal. In a rare instance of series continuity, Leonard emphasized the autumnal tone of *Mr. Paradise* by making Delsa a widower—the husband of now-deceased recurring character Maureen Downey, the noble and witty homicide detective who had appeared in *City Primeval, Split Images* (under the changed name Annie Maguire), and *Freaky Deaky*.[59]

Sitting with a new crop of homicide investigators, Leonard had taken nearly as many notes as his first weeks with Squad 7 back in 1978. Meeting with the Wayne County Medical Examiner, Leonard studied new methods for forensic pathology and the latest crime statistics for the city he'd long called home. "1,200 death calls a year," he wrote, "thirty to forty a day . . . 2,600 autopsies, [and] five-hundred homicides." Leonard noted that discovered bodies always had their hands covered with paper bags, not plastic, in order to retain all microscopic DNA and not to smear fingerprints. Likewise, he listed the "five ways that people die," according to the medical examiners' office: "homicide, suicide, natural causes, accident, [and] indeterminate." He added, "The cause of death may be apparent, but the manner of death may indicate something else."[60]

Sutter also supplied Leonard with a wealth of articles and trade texts to flesh out the details of current police tactics and other elements of the book's evolving plot—including a guidebook published by the National Institute of Bail Enforcement, entitled *101 Useful Tips of Private Investigators* and various glossaries of modern street "gang" slang—which had come a long way since Leonard had created such smooth talkers as Virgil Royal and Ordell Robbie (a "Baby G" stood for "Baby Gangster"—a very young criminal, approximately nine to twelve years old—and "Fry" was a dangerous concoction of marijuana laced with embalming fluid). Leonard also studied *The Rap Dictionary* as well as new laws regulating firearms sales and the history of the Detroit Police Underwater Recovery Teams. As part of Sutter's new data-gathering excursion, a cursory look through Callgirlz.com turned up a full roster of "sexy, elite and discreet professionals" whose chosen stage names included the more exotic Celine ("When she's with you, she is YOURS"), Nina ("Allow me to mesmerize you with my sexy talents—I already have an established clientele from the clubs and now I want to try my wings with you internet-savvy gents"), and—most significantly for Anthony Paradiso's cheerleader fetish—former NBA cheerleader for the Atlanta Hawks turned porn star Kelly Jaye ("a frantic sexual beast who bucks and writhes her way into audiences' dreams," and whose acting credits included *Babewatch, Si-*

ren's Kiss, and *Beaver and Buttface*).[61] On the more serious side of the prostitution racket, Sutter provided Leonard with background on trending "Girl Friend Experience," as well as the modern methodologies used by Detroit's Sex Crimes Unit.[62] For Kelly Barr's profession as a Victoria's Secret model, Leonard reassessed unused material initially gathered for his abandoned, original *Get Shorty* sequel, which would have found Ernesto "Chili" Palmer navigating through the world of the fashion industry.

Leonard completed the novel on June 25.

HarperCollins released *Mr. Paradise* in January 2004. As a show of gratitude for all their help and advocacy for the book, Leonard and Sutter co-organized an official "*Mr. Paradise* Party" for members of the Detroit Police Homicide Section and Major Crimes Unit at the Key Club in downtown Detroit, one week after the book's publication day.[63]

The *New York Times* invited noted novelist and short story master Ann Beattie to act as guest critic for their review. She compared Leonard to one of her own original literary influences—Flannery O'Connor. "[O'Connor] wrote that good fiction comes at you through the senses," Beattie wrote, emphasizing Leonard's use of language as an indicator tool of characterization. "Class figures into it: those in power often benefit by adopting a particular vocabulary; those without power use language to exclude, as well. And everyone knows language can seduce—which can be very enjoyable, but can also be problematic." She added, "But Leonard is no simple moralist . . . In Elmore Leonard's universe, we need to stop laughing. Metaphorically, we are dead and buried if we have learned nothing from history and have fallen so far, we fail to understand that our actions have moral consequences: if we cannot see our ubiquitous disregard for our fellow man as (ironic quotes or not) 'evil.'"[64]

"I've gone on record suggesting that the next time the members of the Swedish Academy think about giving the Nobel Prize for literature to an American, they take a look at Elmore Leonard," wrote Frank Wilson in the *Philadelphia Inquirer*—citing the book as an Editor's Choice for the season. "*Mr. Paradise*, Leonard's first Detroit homicide novel in more than two decades, doesn't give me any reason to change my mind . . . Every page, moreover, sparkles with the angular rhythms and astringent harmonies of the American vernacular."[65]

While promoting both of his recent releases, Leonard already began revealing details about his next novel to interviewers. He'd admitted to

Junior magazine's Sheryl Garratt that his childhood years in Oklahoma had left a lifelong impression on his storytelling sensibilities. "Pretty Boy Floyd, Machine Gun Kelly, Bonnie and Clyde and [John] Dillinger were all committing a lot of robberies in that area," he'd said. "There's a picture of me that was taken in Memphis in the fall of '34 where I'm standing next to a car with my mother and sister. I have one foot on the running board and I'm pointing a cap pistol at the camera. I'm imitating Bonnie Parker . . . There was a picture of her foot on the front of the bumper of a car, holding a pistol with a cigar in her mouth that was probably in every newspaper in the country at that time. That was a great influence on me—in fact, that's probably why I write crime books now."[66]

And to Christopher Heard from *The Gate*, who inquired what he was working on at the moment, Leonard revealed, "I'm about sixty-five pages into my new book . . . haven't got a title for it yet, I've been calling it *A Life of Crime* but that might change. It's set in Oklahoma in the '30s and one of the characters is related to one of the characters from *Cuba Libre*."[67]

CHAPTER 20

A Life of Crime, 2005–2008

In the last decade of his life, Leonard produced six more novels, the first three of which would directly lead to a major reassessment of his importance as a serious American author.

Although he'd long shunned the concept of "legacy" and had never set out to create any one work that could knowingly be deemed his magnum opus, by following his own personal interests and passions, Leonard had inadvertently led himself back to his childhood fascination with Dust Bowl–era bank robbers and post-Western outlaws—his first time since 1970's *The Moonshine War*. Now he sought to create a tapestry of fictional and real-life outlaws and scoundrels, all of whom would be pursued by Carl Webster, the son of *Cuba Libre*'s Virgil Webster—the "hot kid" of the US Marshals Service.

Leonard went to New York for the wedding of Otto Penzler to his third wife in April 2004. Then he accompanied Gregg Sutter to Oklahoma the first week of May. There, the two got the lay of the land and ensured that the areas depicted in the novel still properly fit the book's 1930s narrative. It was during the writing of the book that Leonard changed the title from *Life of Crime* to the more apt *The Hot Kid*, referring to the law enforcement career of its central protagonist, Cuban-American Carl Webster and his evolution into the most renowned lawman of his time. (The title, however, could easily have also referred to Leonard himself: "It doesn't seem that long ago I had hopes of being the hot kid, selling my first story in '51 when I was twenty-five.") He'd also brought back Virgil Webster, Carl's now-fifty-four-year-old retired father, making him a solitary pecan farmer who'd made his postwar fortune by leasing a section of his expansive pecan farm to a corporate oil company. But while the elder Webster was a war hero, his son's claim to fame comes from apprehending the nation's most notorious bank robbers, earning him his nickname and making him, at least, a *spiritual* ancestor to Leonard's more contemporary deputy US marshal, Raylan Givens. "[Webster]'s a showoff, but he's a likable showoff," Leonard told Gene Triplett from *The Oklahoman*. "He was having fun doing it, but he wasn't vicious about it. He never shot anybody in cold blood. He did his job."[1] (In newspaper accounts of his exploits, Webster's catchphrase mirrors Raylan Givens's: "If I have to pull my weapon, I'll shoot to kill."[2])

Leonard's sprawling epic detailed Webster's pursuit of Jack Belmont, the spoiled and sociopathic son of a Tulsa oil millionaire. Belmont's dream is to humiliate his well-to-do oil baron father and dethrone John Dillinger as "Public Enemy No. 1," which quickly brings him into direct conflict with Webster. Ultimately, Webster and Belmont—coincidentally the same age, having both been born in 1906—become skewed mirror images of each other, echoing the psychological kinship of antagonistic "playmates" Raymond Cruz and Clement Mansell from 1980's *City Primeval*. *The Hot Kid* also introduced Louly Brown (her name retained from Leonard's earliest 1970 notes for the unproduced screenplay, *Jesus Saves*)—Pretty Boy Floyd's reluctant moll who soon falls for the more heroic Carl Webster—as well as a who's who of the real-life outlaws that had fascinated Leonard as a child: Bonnie and Clyde, Machine Gun Kelly, John Dillinger, Baby Face Nelson, and, of course, Pretty Boy Floyd. As early as the writing of *Tenkiller* five years earlier, Leonard had begun a notebook with meticulous notes on the Webster family tree, starting with Virgil Webster's birth in 1874 and culminating with the modern-day events of *Tenkiller*—Virgil's great-grandson, Ben, returning to claim the family's home and pecan acreage in Okmulgee, Oklahoma.[3] Even as he worked on his first three books for HarperCollins—*Tishomingo Blues, A Coyote's in the House*, and *Mr. Paradise*—Leonard set Gregg Sutter on the tedious task of assembling a lengthy history of Oklahoma and, ambitiously, a whole series of interlocking twentieth-century historical events. According to Leonard, he had picked Oklahoma as the setting, not so much due to the time he'd spent there as a child but rather because "it's so American. Maybe that might be it, just in a nutshell."[4]

For this, Sutter had his work cut out for him. His data gathering ran the gamut of assembling a full worldview of American daily living following the closure of the Western frontier. Leonard started with a few core texts: two anthologies of essays, *The Culture of Oklahoma* and *Voices from the Oil Fields*, as well as Kenny A. Franks's *The Oklahoma Petroleum Industry* and *An Adventure Called Skelly: A History of Skelly Oil Company Through Fifty Years 1919–1969*, by Roberta Louise Ironside. He pored over histories of western swing bands, Kansas City jazz ensembles, and various radio stars—noting the most popular stations with both white and Black audiences, as well as the cabinet radio models found in the homes of families on both sides of the poverty line. Popular gangster movies—all "pre-code" and loaded with more sex and violence than would be allowed in the coming decades—included many already familiar to Leonard from his years as a movie buff: *Little Caesar, I Am a Fugitive from a Chain Gang, Public Enemy*, and *Scarface*. Musical standards such as "Brother, Can You Spare a Dime," "Puttin' on the Ritz," and "East of the Sun (West of the Moon)" were already tunes he'd heard a thousand times while attending jazz concerts during his teen and young adult years.

While studying a "Midwest Crime Wave Capture/Kill Date" roster, Leonard was astounded to find that nearly all of the most notorious American criminals had found their respective grisly ends the same year he'd posed as Bonnie Parker for his father's camera, and he playfully jotted down that Virgil Webster liked "the look of" Evelyn "Billie" Frechette—one of John Dillinger's many girlfriends.[5] He also read up on the June 17, 1933, bloody shootout between the Verne Miller Gang, which included Pretty Boy Floyd, that left four law enforcement officers dead in the street. Other observations included the fact that by the mid-1930s, there were "twenty outlaws for every doctor," a professional assassin was often referred to as a "torpedo," and "people generally sympathized with bank robbers if no one was shot" during a holdup. In a small section on "Juvenile Crime," Leonard added that in the 1930s, "Half of [the] criminals in [Kansas City] are under twenty-three."[6]

However, not all of Leonard's study of Kansas City's history emphasized its darker underbelly; biographies of musical legends Edward Harry Kelly, Bennie Moten, Charlie "Bird" Parker, "Big Joe" Turner, Mary Lou Williams, and his personal favorite, William "Count" Basie, all made the cut in his biographical research. He was particularly taken with the life and work of L. C. "Speedy" Huggins, a luminary of the Kansas City jazz scene. For good measure his biographical studies also included early Hollywood starlet Jean Harlow; controversial political bosses and brothers James Francis Pendergast and Tom Pendergast, as well as their most outspoken critic, Rabbi Samuel S. Mayerberg; and local businessman turned politician Felix Payne. In addition to his study of nationwide police procedures of the day,[7] Leonard's research extended to the federal level: the early years of the US Marshals Service and their relationship with J. Edgar Hoover's iron-fisted FBI[8]; a brief biography on legendary defense attorney Clarence Darrow also shed light on the judicial system of the time.[9]

Perhaps more so than with any previous book, Leonard's imagination had fleshed out a rich family tree of believable genealogy for their heritage—beginning with the 1874 birth of Virgil Webster and his purchase of the pecan farm for a mere five dollars when he was only fifteen years old. Having missed his chance to meet Geronimo due to the Ndendahe Apache general's participation in Pawnee Bill's traveling "Wild West Circus" (a tip of the hat to the closing chapter of *Gunsights*), Virgil joined the US Marine Corps, leading to his exploits in *Cuba Libre*. Following that novel's events, Virgil married a beautiful and gutsy Cuban girl, brought her to live on his expansive Oklahoma pecan farm, and, in 1906, saw the birth of his only son, Carlos Huntington Webster—his middle name in honor of Virgil's marine colonel. When Virgil's wife, Graciaplena Santos Webster, died during the unsuccessful birth of their second child a year later, he was left to raise the boy alone. At the same age his father had been when he'd purchased the farm, young Carlos—preferring the more Anglo "Carl," encounters notorious outlaw Emmett Long at a local drugstore. (In 1979, Leonard had considered using "Emmett Long" as his pen name for *Gunsights*.) When Long both steals the boy's peach ice cream cone and insults his mixed heritage, Carl stands up to the hardened killer and earns his respect. Soon after, young Carl comes face-to-face with the Mose Miller Gang, who'd long been harassing Virgil and cattle rustling on his property; Carl shoots and kills a member of the gang, setting the fifteen-year-old on a path in law enforcement. Within a decade, he's the "hot kid" of the US Marshals Service.

With the richly detailed Webster family tree completed, Leonard fleshed out the details of Virgil Webster's dual careers—pecan farming and oil drilling. It was only once Virgil's crops became lucrative, however, that he stumbled into the more profitable aspects of his land. Leonard wrote, "A wildcatter asked Virgil [if he] had noticed the rainbow in his creek, the Deep Fork. It meant oil . . . The Texas company struck a gusher at 1,400 feet and Virgil was rich from that day on."[10] Sutter had given Leonard a wealth of information on Oklahoma's long oil history, including a timeline of highlights and the "Historical Tour of Oklahoma's Oil and Gas Industry," provided by the Mid-continent Oil and Gas Association of Oklahoma. Leonard highlighted: "From twenty-two of the years between 1900 and 1935 [Oklahoma] was ranked first among the Mid-Continent Region states in production, and for nine years, it was second."[11]

As he'd long admitted to interviewers, Leonard seemed to have the most fun developing the psyche of chief antagonist Jack Belmont. Although aiming to shame his wealthy father through a prosperous run as the nation's greatest bank robber, Belmont's criminal career begins with numerous false starts and botched attempts at mayhem, unsure if kidnapping or home invasion is the best way to go. (Of note, Leonard deliberately included Belmont's bigoted and nihilistic views on the Tulsa Race Massacre of 1921—one of the worst instances of racial violence in the nation's history—in which mobs of white residents destroyed more than thirty-five square blocks of Black-owned businesses and homes in Tulsa's Greenwood District, known as the "Black Wall Street." Tulsa newspapers of the time had refused to cover the events and many white American historians had notoriously downplayed or outright ignored the tragedy for nearly a century, prompting Leonard to include its reference into the novel.)[12]

For the first time since 1980's *City Primeval*, Leonard already had it in mind that *The Hot Kid* would warrant a sequel. He broke his work journal into two distinct halves, making room for its follow-up, and ended the first section somewhat cryptically: "Advice you don't want comes from more people who give it freely."[13]

By late 2003, he had the seeds of *The Hot Kid* firmly in place. He began the first draft at the beginning of 2004 and, by April, was one-third of the way done. After two trips the following week, one to New York for a PEN America dinner event, then to California for the Los Angeles Times Book Festival, he and Gregg Sutter flew to Tulsa for their field work. On July 31, he reached three hundred pages just before heading to a Prince concert at the Palace at Auburn Hills, and completed the book on October 7—his son Peter's fifty-third birthday. The following week, on his own seventy-ninth birthday, Leonard was due to visit the set of Don Cheadle's *Tishomingo Blues* for its first day of principal photography before the film was squashed.[14]

The Hot Kid was released by William Morrow, an imprint of HarperCollins, in May 2005, earning Leonard raves for his turn into historical drama.

"Elmore Leonard, who will turn eighty this year, continues to amaze," wrote Patrick Anderson in the *Washington Post Book World*. "*The Hot Kid*, Leonard's newest, carries us back to Depression-era Oklahoma, whose residents are far more thrilled by the adventures of bank robbers than by those of presidents or movie stars . . . In one shootout, [Carl] Webster faces down a homicidal strikebreaker and the army of Klansmen he has recruited to burn down a speakeasy . . . [But] will Webster's vanity bring him down, or will his skill with a .38 Colt save the day? Is this finally a comedy or a tragedy?"[15]

The month of *The Hot Kid*'s release, Leonard prepared for the ensuing book tour. Just as he'd kicked off the *Mr. Paradise* tour with a thank-you book launch for the Detroit Police Homicide squad, he now opted to show his appreciation for the community that had helped him the most—the people of Tulsa, Oklahoma. The first stop on the tour, sponsored by the Oklahoma Center for Poets and Writers at Oklahoma State University–Tulsa, took place at the Mayo Hotel, which had figured prominently in multiple scenes throughout the novel. More than five hundred fans swooped in for the free event, and Leonard was presented with proclamations from Mayor Bill LaFortune and Governor Brad Henry. As an homage to Leonard's early roots in the Western pulps, Oklahoma State University–Tulsa president Gary Trennepohl also presented Leonard with a bronze replica of Frederic Remington's *The Bronco Buster*—the famous 1895 statue depicting a cowboy fighting to control a wild stallion, one hand holding a quirt, the other clutching the animal's mane.[16]

Leonard had often joked that if he made it to eighty years old, he'd allow himself to veer from his hard-earned sobriety. "When Dad turned eighty, we threw a big party for him—it was catered and we had a big tent and everything," Christopher Leonard later recalled. "I said to him, only half seriously, 'So, you're eighty now—gonna start drinking and smoking again?' And he said, 'You know, I've done pretty good so far with it, so I think I'll just stay the way I am.' But it was probably the next day that he allowed himself that glass of wine. Then I'd call him up and ask and he'd say, 'Well, sure, I had a glass with dinner'—so it didn't last long."[17]

Peter Leonard recalled, "Elmore had just turned eighty and he came over for dinner one night when Jane was over. He looked at the wineglasses with our red wine in them and said, 'You know, that's what I miss.' He'd told us for years that he'd allow himself to drink, in moderation, if he reached that age—and he did. He hadn't had a drink in thirty years and he took a sip and said, 'This really doesn't taste very good at all.' He'd have a glass at dinner, but I don't think it had the same appeal to him that it once had . . . But he liked smoking weed."

Peter continued, "One time, we were on the way to the Tucson Book Festival and were on the security line at the airport. Elmore had this 'man bag'—like a man's purse. And I said, 'Why are you carrying that thing? What do you keep in it?' And he said, 'I keep everything in here, like my cigarettes.' And then something occurred to me and I said to him, 'Dad, did you bring any joints with you?' And he said, 'Yeah,' and I asked him how many. He goes, 'Seven.' I said, 'Dad, we're only going away for two days,' and he looks at me seriously and says, 'You never know.' We got to the front of the line and Elmore had hidden the joints in his cigarette pack. The security agent looks at the pack, then tosses it back in, no problem. I was incredibly relieved—I thought I was going to have to call the festival organizer to tell him that eighty-four-year-old Elmore Leonard got busted for possession."[18]

Five months earlier, Leonard had flown to New York for an early preview screening of director F. Gary Gray's film adaptation of *Be Cool*. He'd initially lobbied for the film to be made, especially with the participation of *Get Shorty*'s original lead actor, John Travolta. While promoting the original novel in 1999, Leonard had told Fletcher Roberts from the *New York Times*, "I was trying to find out if [Travolta] has read the book, bugging my agent who finally said, 'Why don't you call and ask him?' It took a couple of days to locate him. I called and he was out on a boat and couldn't be reached. But he returned my call a few days later. And I asked him if he had read the book and he said, 'No, I'm not reading anything . . . Oh, by the way, I just bought a 707.' So after I got off the phone, my wife said, 'What were you talking about? All you said to him was "Yeah? Wow."' I said, 'Well, what do you say to a guy who tells you he's just bought an airliner with a bedroom in it, you know?'"[19] Although Leonard had even pictured the *Get Shorty* star reprising his role of Chili Palmer while writing the novel itself, he later admitted, "The studio was frightened of Travolta's new fee, twenty million bucks. I said, 'We get a script written, you get it to Travolta with whatever you want to pay him, and if not, we'll get Benicio del Toro to do it.' Then *he* won an Oscar, so his price went up. And so we are still waiting."[20] They didn't have to wait for long, however; Travolta signed on, joined by Danny DeVito, who also acted as coproducer. However, neither *Get Shorty*'s director, Barry Sonnenfeld, nor its screenwriter, Scott Frank, opted to return. In their place, F. Gary Gray, hot off *The Italian Job*, took the helm, with Peter Steinfeld writing the adaptation. Production for *Be Cool* began in early 2004 and opened in March the following year. It was met with decidedly less critical praise and box office enthusiasm than its predecessor. Gray later admitted to *Deadline*, "With *Be Cool*, I made some assumptions in thinking that movie was going to work. I'd just made a successful PG-13 movie and when I walked in to *Be Cool*, it was rated R and then at the last minute in preproduction I was told, 'Well, you have to make this PG-13.' I should have walked off the film. This was a movie about shylocks and gangsta rappers and if you can't make that world edgy, you probably shouldn't do it."[21] Jeff Posternak later recalled, "I remember seeing a screening with [Leonard] of *Be Cool* and, walking out, he just said, 'Not so good, that one.' But he approached Hollywood with, I think, the correct attitude. It's a different beast and there's only so much control you have over it."[22] Adding insult to injury, the release of the film ended the thirty-year friendship between Leonard and the real-life Ernest "Chili" Palmer. Leonard later admitted that, soon after *Be Cool*'s release, Palmer had doubled back and sued him for additional money to match the life rights of the sequel. Leonard had attempted to avoid Palmer's threat of legal action, writing him a letter a year before the film's release and the ten thousand dollars initially promised for the reuse of his name in the sequel novel. "You know that, originally, when I asked you if I could use your name, we didn't discuss any kind of compensation," he had written Palmer. "When the book sold, I felt I should give you something and picked [ten thousand dollars] out of the air, friend to friend, and then another ten when it was optioned for film . . . Since MGM has no obligations in the matter, but if you want to take legal action, I'm afraid it would have to be against me. I hope you don't choose to do this; we have a good friendship based on trust."[23]

Regardless of Leonard's advice, Palmer took action against him.

Leonard later said, "I brought [character Chili Palmer] back because MGM said, 'Well, you can write a sequel to it, can't you?' 'Yeah.' Well, now Chili Palmer sued me. So I'm not going to write any more Chili Palmer."[24]

Fortunately, Leonard's literary reputation was immune to the rash of unsuccessful film adaptations that had surfaced over the previous year. Where once he'd claimed that the 1969 adaptation of *The Big Bounce* had been "the second worst film" he'd ever seen, George Armitage's 2004 remake starring Owen Wilson as Jack Ryan—which transplanted the action from Michigan's thumb region to sunny Oahu, and eschewed the vast majority of the original novel—prompted him to update his old joke; he'd now seen *the* worst movie ever made. He later remarked, "Every time there was a break in the action, they'd cut away to surfers."[25]

By May 2005, Leonard was already thirty pages into Carl Webster's 1944 pursuit of Nazi POWs, escaped from one of several camps established in Oklahoma during the war. At the time, the book's working title was *Deep Fork*.[26] However, the novel that would soon become *Comfort to the Enemy* was unlike any other creative process that Leonard had ever before dealt with. While working on the book's earliest version that September, he accepted a prestigious and lucrative offer to write a serialized sequel to *The Hot Kid* for the *New York Times Sunday Magazine*, with each installment estimated to run 2,500 to 3,000 words—meaning a rewrite of the existing material.

Although he'd gotten his start as a pulp writer half a century earlier, his youthful bids to place a longer work into a magazine or newspaper for serialization purposes had never come to pass. Had he had success at that age, the growing pains of having to deal with daily print could, most likely, have been avoided. But the *idea* of writing individual installments over the course of three months seemed to fit perfectly into his normal work schedule—and it also held the promise of a completed novel ripe for publication at the end of the story's initial newspaper run. According to the *Times*' editorial guidelines, however, there was one major caveat: "I have to get the whole thing done before the first one is published," he told James D. Watts of the *Tulsa World*. "It could fall through, but I don't know if it's been cleared with their executive board or whatever. In any event, whether it's published in the *Times* or not, it's going to be a book."[27] To John Rebchook of the *Rocky Mountain News*, Leonard was more transparent about the book's plot and the process of working on a serialized novel. Rebchook reported, "The new book takes place ten years in the future [of *The Hot Kid*], and Carl Webster has come home from the war after serving in the 1st Cavalry division in the South Pacific. Leonard was a Navy Seabee on Los Negros during World War II . . . [and] Webster gets shot and returns to serve as a federal agent in the U.S." Leonard elaborated to Rebchook, "I've never written a book that has taken on Los Negros before . . . [and] there were about 35,000 German POWs in more than five hundred different POW camps in the U.S. I didn't know that, or if I did, I had certainly forgotten about it."[28]

As his starting point, Leonard studied two primary texts that Sutter had turned up: Arnold Krammer's *Nazi Prisoners of War in America*—which included full state-by-state rosters of the POW camps throughout the United States—and, more specifically to Leonard's plot, the viewers' guide to the 2004 documentary film *The Enemy in Our Midst: Nazi Prisoner of War Camps in Michigan's Upper Peninsula*. Once certain that the POW camps would form the basis of the book, he tasked Sutter with finding any original wartime articles related to the subject. A May 7, 1945, *Newsweek* article, "Anger at Nazi Atrocities is Rising, but the U.S. Treats Prisoners Fairly," demonstrated the slow revelation of the Holocaust to the American public, and helped shape Leonard's in-camp scenes. It also set him digging deeper into the Holocaust itself, as reflected in the timeline he studied on Nazi Germany's "final solution"—the systematic genocide of the Jewish people—beginning with Hitler's appointment as Germany's chancellor in January 1933 and ending with Adolf Eichmann's trial in August 1961.[29] An article in the *New York Post* from March 17, 1945, by wartime correspondent Ernest O. Hauser entitled "German Prisoners Talk Your Ears Off" provided Leonard with the beginnings of his psychological study into the POW captives' behavior, as did "How War Prisoners Behave," a 1947 piece from *Air Force Times*. With that in mind, he soon began gathering research on such broader topics as Nazi spy rings in America; an organization of German Nazi sympathizers living within the United States calling themselves the "German American Bund"; FBI counterespionage initiatives; daily life in the Afrika Korps; fashion and literary trends during the war (of which Bertolt Brecht's *The Caucasian Chalk Circle* proved particularly fascinating to him); the histories of homosexuality in both Russian and Nazi wartime societies; postwar sedition trials; theoretical alternate World War II history; and even Joseph Stalin's height.[30]

Leonard completed the serialized novel's last installment on September 22, 2005. Although the *New York Times* had initially asked him to submit the entire book prior to the first installment's publication, they'd begrudgingly approved of the work after reading only the first half. His subject matter and dialogue had quickly come under fire; his working title, *Krauts*, did little to help the matter. Likewise, Leonard quickly became frustrated with the language and content mandates that came with writing for the globally circulated newspaper. He later commented, "They rendered my bad guys nearly mute,"[31] later elaborating, "[It] was not a very pleasant experience because I had to pull back . . . my characters couldn't talk as freely as they wanted to . . . The *New York Times* said, 'This is a family newspaper—you can't say that.' And yet, I've got a couple of scenes where they're all sitting around smoking grass and there's nothing wrong with that."[32] (During the story's early run, Leonard sent off a letter to *Times* editor Gerry Marzorati, both expressing his gratitude for the opportunity and conveying his mixed feelings toward the newspaper's editorial hand. "I accepted editorial objections to dialogue references like 'getting laid,'" he wrote. "But still, I'm honored to be in the *Magazine* as your first fiction offerings . . . One last question: when did you ever see an author's name placed below a chapter heading?"[33]

Ultimately, the retitled *Comfort to the Enemy* ran in fourteen total installments from September 18 through December 18. During the serial's publication, Leonard celebrated his eightieth birthday. He marked the date in his day planner: *"E.L. yea!"*[34]

The serialized novel would finally appear in book form as *Comfort to the Enemy, and Other Carl Webster Stories*, first in the UK by Weidenfeld & Nicolson in April 2009, then by HarperCollins for its US edition in October 2010. Despite the excitement surrounding Leonard's first foray into serialized fiction, major reviews only surfaced following the book editions.

"If you seek to capture the essence of law enforcement legend, look no further than Elmore Leonard, the master of the merry and macabre crime scenario with dialogue to die for," wrote Muriel Dobbin of the *Washington Times*. "*Comfort to the Enemy* is a satirical gem about the investigation of a hanging at a German POW camp in Oklahoma, where the marshal meets the captive Nazis and decides they aren't all bad. Carl strikes up a friendship with Jurgen Schrenk, a young captain in the Afrika Korps and a friend of Gen. Erwin Rommel's, who was forced to kill himself after the German defeat in North Africa. Jurgen, once a poster boy for the Hitler Youth, falls into the category of former Nazis who would be happy if Hitler were dead." She added, "Mr. Leonard is on the top of his crime-fiction game, and this collection is even better than usual."[35]

After a brief two-week break, Leonard quickly began writing the third installment of Carl Webster's continuing adventures in January 2006. If the *New York Times* had balked at his original title for *Comfort to the Enemy—Krauts*—it came as little surprise to Leonard when HarperCollins was equally apprehensive at his working title for the follow-up; by April 20, he'd written seventy-five pages of *Hitler's Birthday* and, only two days later, had been told to change it. He'd added four more pages to the manuscript before making the title switch to *Up in Honey's Room*.[36]

Already having decided that Carl Webster would be following in his own real-life footsteps, serving during the war in the South Pacific, Leonard took time to research the very background history of the area that had brought him there with the Seabees in 1944. As more than half a century had passed since his service, he pored over declassified documents and historical analyses that revealed to him US strategic details that had then been kept even from the very servicemen carrying out the tasks. "Beginning with the 1st Cavalry Division's campaign in the Admiralty Islands from February 29 through May, 1944," he wrote, "Carl Webster is wounded early in the campaign and sent home. So by the summer of 1944, he's active in investigating the POW disturbances and has studied the situation, the Admiralties were part of the defenses of Japan's Pacific Empire; it barred [the] Allied advance toward the Philippines."

Because Leonard's full military tenure had been confined to the Pacific Theater, he was forced to educate himself on Nazi Germany and the Third Reich. From the many books and articles Sutter provided, Leonard opted to start at the beginning—the birth of Adolf Hitler and his rise to power. As interested as he was in learning about the dictator's obsession with the occult and astrology, and his insistence that German technological advances would be the key to defeating the Allied forces, he became particularly fascinated with the rumors of Hitler's rumored drug addictions and bizarre sexual fetishes—acts that, ironically, had all been banned under his regime. "Hitler was into methamphetamines, daily injections of Pervitin, in addition to narcotic pills for sleeping and anti-flatulence containing strychnine and belladonna," he noted, adding, "Did he bang Leni Riefenstahl? Maybe. Or his nineteen-year-old niece, Geli Raubal? According to a 1943 report produced by the Office of Strategic Services, in addition to banging her uncle, Geli was obliged to piss on him." He was particularly amused upon learning of "*flusterwitz*"—the "whispered jokes" that circulated among disillusioned German citizens and Nazi officers. Under the heading, "Hitler Jokes," Leonard jotted down a number to save for the mouths of his POW prisoners:

> *"Hitler asks his astrologer, 'Am I going to Die?' 'Of course,' the astrologer says. 'But when?' 'On a Jewish holiday.' 'But which one?' Hitler insists. Astrologer: 'Any day you die on becomes a Jewish holiday.'"*
>
> *"A German who called Hitler a fool is prosecuted on two counts: one, for insulting the German leader; and two, for revealing a state secret."*

Leonard added to his list: "*Werner Finck, [a] cabaret entertainer, would spot Gestapo in the audience and say, 'Am I speaking too fast for you?'*"—then noted that between 1933 and 1945, approximately five thousand death penalties had been handed down by the German courts for treason, a "large number of them for anti-Nazi humor." He soon decided that an exchange of such jokes would act as the icebreakers between Carl Webster and the incarcerated German soldiers who would soon escape the Detroit POW camp.

As a former Sunday school teacher himself, Leonard took note of the Nazi regime's views on the Catholic Church and its practices. "Nazis recognized the Church, but [also] knew they'd have to deal with it sooner or later," he wrote. "They developed Nazi rituals to replace those of the Church, like the Rite of Confirmation. They replaced it with a Nazi version: age fifteen, the boys move from the *Junkvolk* [*sic*] to the Hitler Youth, and girls move from the *Jungmadel* to the League of German Girls."

His notes soon turned toward the Afrika Korps and its military operations, and he jotted down the details of North Africa's geography. As a bit of dialogue Carl Webster would overhear during his time in Los Negros, Leonard jotted down an unattributed quote: "*I haven't met a kraut soldier who didn't act like he was on vacation.*"[37]

With seventy-five pages completed by the end of April, Leonard put the manuscript aside and prepared for two separate summer trips with Christine to Europe: England on May 6, then—following a week's respite at home—France on June 7. He'd taken his notes with him on both trips and returned home once again reinvigorated to return to the book; by July 7, he was one hundred pages into it. Only taking a few afternoons off at the end of July in order to sit for a portrait painted by his grandson Alex (to be used on the banner and promotional materials for a Special Lifetime Achievement Award ceremony given by the Bloomfield Art Association), Leonard finished the book on October 20—a week after his eighty-first birthday.

"I ended up doing Elmore's portrait because I had already done a number of mock-ups for book covers for him," Alex Leonard later recalled. "In the book, there's one character who looks just like Heinrich Himmler, and Elmore asked me to paint Himmler. He said, 'I need, like, three different portraits of Himmler'—which just looked insane. And he showed them to his publisher and, I guess, along with the original title, they were just aghast. But during that period, I also painted Elmore himself, and it was used for the festival in his honor."[38] Leonard celebrated his recent achievements by flying to St. Louis, Missouri, for Game Three of the World Series—his beloved Detroit Tigers versus the Cardinals. (He compensated for the Tigers' 5–0 loss by attending a Bob Dylan concert at the Palace of Auburn Hills on November 2.)[39]

Up in Honey's Room was released May 8, 2007. A first in decades, the novel received decidedly mixed reviews. "One good thing about being a suspense writer of a certain age is that you acquire a lot of incidental knowledge," wrote Jane Smiley, a guest critic for the *Los Angeles Times* and a fellow novelist. "Ever surprising, Leonard has come up with some characteristic methods of adding texture without padding his novels. One involves writing in short paragraphs, with minimal punctuation. Another is leaving out narrative altogether, which he does as a standard technique . . . now in his 80s, and with forty-three books to his credit, Leonard springs eternal."[40] In *USA Today*, Carol Memmott said, "How is it that Elmore Leonard, at eighty-one, can still write a rough, tough sexy novel—as good as *Get Shorty* and *Tishomingo Blues*? . . . New to the cast is Honey Deal, a fearless bottle blonde who helps [Carl] Webster track down two escaped Nazi POWs. Throw in a Ukrainian femme fatale, her cross-dressing manservant and a to-die-for final shootout, and you'll know that you're once again in that heavenly place—aka an Elmore Leonard masterpiece."[41]

The Associated Press's Bruce DeSilva commented on at least one of the novel's most personal in-jokes. "Besides Honey and Walter, Leonard gives himself a lot of material to work with," DeSilva wrote. "There's Jurgen Schrenk, an SS talk commander who wants to become an American cowboy, and his fellow Nazi escapee who falls for a Jewish girl in Detroit and runs away with her to Cleveland. The latter character is named 'Otto Penzler,' Leonard having a little fun with a friend of the same name, whose imprint at Harcourt, Inc., 'Otto Penzler Books,' specializes in crime novels."[42] Touched by the literary shoutout by his friend of more than thirty years, Penzler himself put his gratitude to Leonard in his own review for the *New York Sun*. "More than a quarter century ago, I met America's coolest author and have been blessed with Elmore Leonard's friendship ever since," Penzler wrote. "A couple of years ago, we were chatting about a book he was planning to write about German prisoners of war who were sent to a detention camp in Okmulgee, Oklahoma. His working title was the politically incorrect *Krauts*, so when the talk came around to naming his characters, which is crucial to Mr. Leonard, I humbly (okay, shamelessly) suggested that I had an authentic German-sounding name, so why not use mine? I was kind of going for 'Otto,' but he liked the whole thing, which is how I (or rather my name) came to be a character in his hilarious new novel, *Up in Honey's Room*."[43]

Alex Leonard later recalled, "Elmore used to contribute to the [University of Detroit] fundraiser auction every year and would donate a character. The highest bidder got to have their name in his next novel. Crystal Davidson, who appears in *The Hot Kid* and *Up in Honey's Room*, and Larry Davidson, who appears in *Comfort to the Enemy*, are the mother and father of Scott Davidson, who plays bass in Protomartyr." It was not long after helping his grandfather with his latest book cover that Alex had cofounded the post-punk ensemble—nearly out of financial necessity. "Originally, I had been an art major, mostly because my father and grandfather told me my entire life never to go into advertising," he recalled. "[But] post-college, I worked for five years for the agency that serviced Ford in Dearborn, and having weekly dinners with Peter and Elmore trading advertising war stories was probably the best part of that whole experience . . .[44] Our family's pretty close, and we'd have family dinners once or twice a week. So, Elmore would come over. And Elmore or Peter would say, 'What happened at work today?' And I'd tell him, 'A client came in, ate all of our food, and then pitched us the worst idea I've ever heard.' It really brought them back. Then I couldn't get a job in anything after the Great Recession. Greg, who plays guitar in the band—we went to high school together—and he was already playing constantly. Elmore and Beverly each had given me money for my high school graduation and I used some of it to buy a drum set—because I couldn't get a job. I ended up playing shows on some nights and be out until two or three, then go to work the next day."

Alex continued, "There was a good ten-year stretch where I'd finish an Elmore book and then immediately head over to his house to talk about it. He loved talking about his work. Around 2012 I went to Elmore's with a friend and did a filmed interview where we mostly talk about music. Near the end I played him some Protomartyr. He asked how many members were in the band. I said four and he said, 'That's a lot of noise for only four people.' Classic Elmore."[45]

If the "Carl Webster saga" had proven, once and for all, that Leonard could ride the edge of literary historical fiction—albeit with his own sensibilities and humor thrown into the mix—then the next novel, a return to contemporary crime, would work to tie up a few loose ends.

While doing his regular interview rounds for *Up in Honey's Room*, Leonard had spoken to Neal Rubin of the *Detroit News* about a number of topics—his age, the changing publishing business, and, of course, what was next on his literary slate. Rubin had reported, "[Leonard]'s forty pages into his next book, in which bank robber Jack Foley, the George Clooney character from Leonard's *Out of Sight*, meets Dawn Navarro, the psychic from *Riding the Rap*. Searching his memory bank for a villain, Leonard remembered Cundo Rey, a con man and Cuban refugee from *LaBrava*."[46]

Leonard began his three-way sequel under the working title named for his favorite among the returning characters, *Cundo Rey*, and finally started by the summer of 2007 (he'd also briefly considered naming the book *Foley's Back*[47]). Now in his early eighties, he had no issue admitting to interviewers that, while his age hadn't hindered his imagination or drive to keep writing, his stamina wasn't what it used to be. "I used to do a book in four months," he told journalist Rachel Forrest. "Now it takes eight months, but I think I fool around more."[48] But there were other reminders to Leonard that time moved fast. On January 13 of that year, his beloved sister, Margaret—"Mickey," who had inspired his earliest love of books—passed away at the age of eighty-seven. Notified by her children that Margaret's health had taken a turn for the worse, Leonard had flown to Little Rock, Arkansas, just after the 2006 holiday season in order to spend New Year's Day with her in the hospital; he returned only a few weeks later for the funeral.

As he began his readings of Gregg Sutter's research for the next novel, Leonard also toured for the promotion of *Up in Honey's Room* that May—then accepted an Alumni Achievement Award from the University of Detroit at the end of September. By the time HarperCollins released an illustrated hardcover edition of his famed "rules on writing" the following month, he was finally deep into his first draft.

Leonard had known early on that he would be bringing back three memorable characters for the new novel, ultimately revealing to consistent readers what had occurred after the events of three fan favorites. Of course Jack Foley and Cundo Rey would cross paths while incarcerated together and, likewise, Rey would easily have attracted a "psychic" con artist like Dawn Navarro, whose sex appeal had nearly wooed Deputy US Marshal Raylan Givens over a decade earlier. The only challenge Leonard faced was bringing them all back realistically. Of character Cundo Rey, he later revealed to *Talk of the Nation*'s Neal Conan: "I remember thinking, 'God, I hope he's still alive.' And I looked—I saw his final scene. He was shot three times in the chest, and I thought, '*Oh* . . .' But Cundo Rey was never pronounced dead. So I have a couple of emergency fellows pick him up and say, hey, he's still breathing. And he's in a coma for a while, but then he revives." He added, "Dawn Navarro, I used as a supporting character in another book, and I thought, I've got to use her again. She's good—she has a lot more promise than I was able to bring out in *Riding the Rap*."[49]

Leonard eventually cribbed the novel's eventual title from a list of prison slang common among inmates; while poring through Sutter's first round of research, he noticed the numerous terms used to describe prison buddies, and while "thick as thieves" would have been too cliché and "ace boon coon" too politically incorrect, "road dogs" caught his eye. By the middle of his first draft, Leonard had dropped *Cundo Rey* in favor of the new find.[50]

For the newly named *Road Dogs*, Leonard had tasked Sutter with gathering data on three specific points of the novel's focus: modern jailhouse behavior, with an emphasis on gangs; trends in fake psychic scam artists; and the most expensive real estate throughout the Venice Beach area of Los Angeles. In constructing what Dawn Navarro would have been up to over the previous decade since her part in the kidnapping of Harry Arno,

Leonard looked at various articles on female prisoner behavior, as well as the trauma or poverty that led them to a life of crime.[51]

For Navarro's most recent schemes, Leonard pored through articles on police sting operations into phony psychic operations, as covered by the *Skeptical Inquirer* magazine, as well as the current trend of "big-time" psychics working their game for corporate businesspeople and within the mainstream media; a biography of controversial medium Sylvia Browne supplied Leonard with the career trajectory of the most successful of the bunch. Once Leonard had figured out how to bring Cundo Rey back from the (apparent) dead, he researched the ongoing plight of American fugitives who'd found a safe haven on Cuban soil—protected by the then-ailing Fidel Castro from the long arm of US extradition. Having stashed millions of dollars away while doing his latest prison stint with Jack Foley, Rey owned multiple properties in sunny Los Angeles. For that, Leonard numbered some of the most expensive homes in both Venice Beach and Malibu. Additionally, he looked at the strange discrepancy between Venice's millionaire residents and its large homeless population.[52] A secret millionaire, Rey retains an expensive attorney to get Foley off the charge of kidnapping Karen Sisco during the events of *Out of Sight*—as well as having his bank robbery sentence reduced—but under one condition: he has to housesit Rey's posh Venice Beach home ahead of the smooth criminal's own release the following month. Attempting to do right by his road dog, Foley is immediately suspicious when he meets Rey's longtime girlfriend, Dawn Navarro, who quickly tries to enlist the reformed bank robber into her own psychic schemes—the most ambitious of which would bilk Rey himself out of his ill-gotten fortune.

Writing *Road Dogs* began with a new exercise for Leonard, having to reference three of his own previous novels for both continuity and accurate biographical information of their characters. Double-checking *LaBrava*, Leonard began his latest work journal with bits of background on Cundo Rey's entry into the United States via the 1980 boatlift, which saw more than 125,000 Cuban refugees reaching the Florida shores—of which Rey was one. For Jack Foley, Leonard went page by page through *Out of Sight*, enumerating the fictional bank robber's life story and criminal career. By the time of his latest exploits as depicted in *Road Dogs*, Foley had "three falls: two state times, one federal—plus a half-dozen stays in county lockups," Leonard noted. Working side by side with the original books, Leonard turned the characters' respective backgrounds into chunks of dialogue for the new scenes.

Once the character biographies and corresponding dialogue exchanges had been completed, Leonard, in another creative first, ended his work journal with a full, enumerated outline of what the final 150 pages of the novel's plot would include.[53] As an experiment, Sutter had even taken the pages that Jane had typed up to that point and began a line chart on his computer, calculating the length of each chapter for page-number consistency.[54]

Leonard completed *Road Dogs* on February 17, 2008—approximately the eight months he'd predicted—and HarperCollins released it in May of the following year.

As was their now normal practice, the *New York Times* invited a guest author to pen the review of Leonard's latest work. Stephen King, whose 1985 review of *Glitz* had helped propel Leonard into the literary stratosphere, returned to do the honors. "Elmore Leonard's first novel, *The Bounty Hunters*, was published in 1953," King began. "Fifty-six years later, America's premier literary entertainer is still in business—and business is good. You know from the first sentence that you're in the hands of the original Daddy Cool . . . The fun in the best of his novels—and this is the best in years—stems from the fact that Leonard starts turning the screws on page one and never stops. The dialogue crackles; the supporting characters are crisply drawn; and the story achieves almost instant escape velocity. If you like your crime fiction laced with deadpan wit (Leonard doesn't exactly do humor), then this one'll kill you. Even the worst marchers in Leonard's fools' parade have a certain scabrous charm, and that makes them worth watching. And, appalling or not, rooting for. This is one walk down Crooked Avenue you'll be more than happy to make."[55]

Although now-superstar leading man George Clooney—a status cemented in no small part to his 1998 cinematic turn as Jack Foley—passed on pursuing *Road Dogs* as a film project, *Esquire* magazine strategically held their own review of the novel for their July issue, featuring Clooney on the cover. "The chief pleasure of Leonard is that the line between the good life—money, women, drink, food—and the bad life—prison, poverty, pain—is so clearly and sharply drawn," the review opened. "Nothing in *Road Dogs* is going to make you reexamine your existential underpinnings; Leonard's more interested in sprucing up your conduct." Ironically, the review seemed to succinctly capture the whole of Leonard's own personal philosophy, one that he'd so creatively hoped to convey, at least since achieving sobriety three decades earlier: "Like all good advice, his hook ultimately tells us what we already know. The world may be a cosmic joke, but that doesn't mean it's without meaningful pleasures. A good hot shower, a new white T-shirt, a rib-eye steak, a fifth of Jack Daniels—these are things for which one should be profoundly grateful. And if this seems too easy, just remember that thinking too much can fuck you up."[56]

The release of *Road Dogs* marked another first, not only for Leonard himself, but for the Leonard family: simultaneously, his son Peter's second outing as novelist, *Trust Me,* was published by St. Martin's Press.

Peter Leonard had long had aspirations to also enter the world of fiction. At the age of fifty-two, he allowed his decades-long lucrative career in the advertising world to take a backseat as he finally made a run of his own. "I'd been in advertising for almost thirty years and had just made a new pitch for Volkswagen," Peter recalled. "It didn't go well. I stopped by my father's house on the way home, and I'm wearing gray dress pants and a blue blazer and Elmore's wearing jeans, a Nine Inch Nails T-shirt, and Birkenstocks. He's smoking a cigarette and he has a bounce in his step—really looking like he's having fun. He read me a scene from what he was working on—*The Hot Kid*—while I was standing there. Then, on the way home, I thought, 'All right, if you're going to write, if you're going to really do it, you better do it quick.' It was sort of my epiphany." He continued, "It took about a year to write the novel. When I finally showed it to Elmore and he said, 'When did you learn to write fiction!' and I thought, 'Okay, that's a good review, certainly a lot more positive than the last thing he'd said twenty-seven years ago.' It was so exciting to send the manuscript in and get the approval of the Wylie Agency."[57]

His 2008 debut, *Quiver,* was met with fanfare and solid reviews. However, Peter did note the stylistic differences between him and his father. "The comparisons are inevitable," he admitted. "I chose my father's genre and I tell my stories through the eyes of my characters in shifting points of view, so there are some obvious similarities. But I think there are a lot of differences, too. Elmore Leonard would never write a story like *Quiver*. It's too sentimental."[58]

With two noted novelists in the family, the dual publications of both Elmore's and Peter Leonard's latest works initiated a new phase of their relationship. Beginning with Peter Leonard's first in-store book-signing event in Ann Arbor in May 2008, his father not only made it a point of attending each ensuing stop on the tour to show support, but soon, the two were touring together as dual headliners. "We finished our book tour at the City Opera House in northern Michigan, over five hundred people in attendance," Peter recalled. "Elmore closed out the evening with an anecdote from a ski trip to Aspen years ago. He is in the lodge sitting by the huge fireplace. A beautiful woman was next to him taking off her ski boots. She pulled her right foot out the boot, looked at him and said, 'Ahhh, I think that's better than getting laid.' He said, 'Uh-huh,' in a helpless voice." Later, Leonard admitted to his son, "I've been trying to think of a comeback line for twenty years."

Katy's oldest son, Joe Dudley, remembered both his grandfather and uncle visiting his high school as guest speakers during their book tour—culminating with one of Leonard's classics being added to the curriculum. "My teacher assigned *Hombre* to our class and, of course, my teacher pointed out to everyone that my grandfather wrote it," he recalled.[59] Joe's younger brother, Nick, had a similar experience once he entered class for his sophomore year at Michigan State: "There was a big orientation on everything we were going to cover that semester and about a hundred and fifty students were gathered in the lecture hall . . . During a slide show on this huge screen, the professor clicked to the next slide and it was a picture of Elmore! I freaked out for a second. The professor was a huge fan of Elmore's and talked about how we were going to read *City Primeval* in class. So that ended up being the first of my grandfather's books that I ended up reading."[60]

Peter Leonard soon accompanied his father to Mantua, Italy, where the older Leonard was a featured guest speaker at their annual book festival. "We arrived on schedule but Elmore's luggage didn't," he later recalled. "I loaned him a pair of underwear and a blue dress shirt so he could shower and change . . . After dinner we went back to the hotel. Elmore's bag still hadn't arrived. He called my room the next morning and said, 'I've got to buy some underwear. Will you come with me?' . . . I have to tell you I felt a little strange—I had never gone underwear shopping with my father. We walked in and the shop owner and four female customers all looked at us and grinned. Elmore started opening boxes, taking the underwear out, stretching it. The blonde behind the counter said, 'You can't do that.' Elmore said, 'How am I supposed to know what it looks like?' 'You look on the box,' I said. He bought three pairs." Leonard later claimed they were the most comfortable underwear he'd ever worn—and expressed his frustration that now he'd "have to go to Italy to buy underwear."[61] (A few years later, Peter Leonard wrote of that time, "Whenever we flew economy class I would approach the gate agent and say I was travelling with an elderly gentleman who needed assistance, so we could board first. The agent would say, 'Where is he?' I'd point to Elmore a few feet away, a vacant look on his face. In a feeble voice he'd say, 'Are we in the airport?'"[62])

An extension of their playful banter before audiences, Leonard soon conducted an interview with his son for publication, in which the two discussed their respective careers and individual views on the writing process:

> ELMORE: John D. MacDonald said you have to write a million words before you know what you're doing, have real control over your sound that you're consistent with what you want your prose to sound like.
>
> PETER: Well I've got a few years to go then.
>
> ELMORE: Do you like to write?
>
> PETER: I do. I'm surprised how much I like it. It's very satisfying.
>
> ELMORE: I would say you are definitely on your way.
>
> PETER: Thanks, Pops.[63]

CHAPTER 21

Justified, 2008–2013

By 2008, Leonard had been singing the praises of Ernest Hemingway for more than half a century; in all that time, however, he'd never fully explored the works of Hemingway's contemporary—equal parts friend and literary adversary—F. Scott Fitzgerald. That changed just after his eighty-third birthday, in October 2008, when Leonard was honored with the F. Scott Fitzgerald Award for Literary Excellence by Montgomery College in Rockville, Maryland—not far from Scott and Zelda Fitzgerald's final resting places.

Leonard's acceptance speech drew largely upon his conversations with the late H. N. Swanson, who'd once represented Fitzgerald himself. "'Scott asked me to read a novel he'd just completed called *Trimalchio of West Egg*,'" Leonard recalled Swanson relaying to him of their 1924 conversation. "And Swanie says, 'I thought it was the best thing of his that I had ever read. But I told him, 'That's a horrible title.'" To this, Swanson claimed, he had suggested *Gatsby*—or, *The Great Gatsby*. In a room of Fitzgerald scholars and Elmore Leonard enthusiasts, the anecdote killed.

Once he'd returned home to Bloomfield Hills the following day, the experience had ignited in Leonard a newfound interest in Fitzgerald's life and works. Leonard's discussions with Swanson regarding Fitzgerald mostly had to do with the agent's time trying to sell the author's works to the screen. When he'd been introduced to Leonard through Marguerite Harper a decade and a half later, their first sales together had been the television and movie rights to early pulp stories "The Captives" and "Three-Ten to Yuma"—the latter of which had since gone on to become a Western cinema classic. And fittingly it was now just before Leonard's

Fitzgerald Award that the film garnered its own big-budget Hollywood remake. Directed by James Mangold—hot off the smash-hit Johnny Cash biopic *Walk the Line*—the new *3:10 to Yuma* starred A-listers Russell Crowe and Christian Bale, replacing Glenn Ford and Van Heflin, respectively. With a new rash of Westerns then trending throughout the movie industry, the film opened at number one at the box office and earned nearly unanimous, solid reviews. Leonard, however, didn't get a dime for the film, as it was a studio-helmed remake based on their own original film, although he did approve of the finished product—save for the largely reworked climax. He later admitted, "It was a dumb ending."[1]

Jeff Posternak later recalled, "*3:10 to Yuma* was one of his classic Westerns that got remade, and with a huge budget—a major studio production. And I remember him laughing because, historically, in Hollywood you get about a third of the initial purchase price for the remake rights. It makes sense in the moment, but in Elmore's case, he had a long career . . . Then, he got something like a $15,000 check [for *3:10 to Yuma*] and I think that he was a little chagrined that that's how it worked."[2]

But what the new *3:10 to Yuma* had accomplished for Leonard, however, was a refreshed interest in his older Western fare. When that film went on to become his first cinematic Western since 1972's *Joe Kidd*, it was soon apparent that a new generation could be more receptive to his darker, earlier stories. With that in mind, Canadian television producer Graham Yost admitted later that Leonard's novella *Fire in the Hole* was more than enough proof that the character of Raylan Givens could carry his own show. "Well, the first thing is, you know, I've been reading Elmore's fiction since *LaBrava*, which was the early '80s, and then I went back and read a bunch from before that," Yost later told the online trade magazine *Act Four Screenplays*. "But what got me about *Fire in the Hole* initially was that it was set in a part of the country that television shows usually aren't set. So that appealed to me, that it was something new. But the big thing, the reason I wanted to do this show . . . was I thought it'd be great to have a hero. Raylan, who has his dark side. He's got his anger issues and all that. But the guy is a hero."[3] As far back as 1995's *Riding the Rap*, fellow novelist Martin Amis had praised Leonard's US marshal for a multitude of the same reasons. "Raylan is perhaps the cleanest character, dead straight and 'all business,'" he had written in his review for the *New York Times*. "Raylan isn't postmodern—he is an anachronism from out of town. And he is fascinating, because he shows you what Mr. Leonard actually holds dear—the values he can summon in a different kind of prose, in different American rhythms, those of Robert Frost, or even Mark Twain."[4]

Yost called Leonard on March 31 to discuss his ideas for the project, all of which sounded promising to the author. It was initially entitled *Lawman*, but the producer soon devised an even better title for the prospective series—one keeping in line with Raylan Givens's philosophy to never pull his gun unless intending to shoot: *Justified.*

On July 28, the show was given a thirteen-episode order by the basic cable network FX, allowing the showrunners and writers to push the boundaries of the series' more adult-oriented content.[5] The pilot, directed by co–executive producer Michael Dinner, was filmed throughout Pennsylvania—Pittsburgh, and suburban Kittanning and Washington—and used as its initial storyline a proper adaptation of *Fire in the Hole*.[6] Leonard and Yost, along with Carl Beverly and Sarah Timberman, also shared executive producer credit. Cast as Raylan Givens, actor Timothy Olyphant won almost instant acclaim for his tough and sympathetic portrayal; as his nemesis Boyd Crowder, actor Walton Goggins proved so popular among the showrunners, his character was spared the death sentence of the original source material and made the series' ongoing co-lead. Janice Rhoshalle from *Emmy* magazine wrote, "Not surprisingly, the show's writers often have Leonard on their minds—but also on their wrists, where they wear plastic royal-blue wristbands ordered by Yost and embossed: W.W.E.D. [What Would Elmore Do?]"[7]

Mike Lupica later recalled, "*Justified* affirmed his faith that Hollywood could get it right. What a joy *Justified* was for him—that they got it right . . . [But] Graham and Tim [Olyphant] and the *Justified* people really viewed their job as being caretakers of a public trust. They understood completely what a giant this man was and they treated him like royalty."[8]

At the time, Leonard had just completed his latest novel and hoped to contribute to the show even more (he claimed, having been given an honorary status as executive producer, he felt obliged "to do something"[9]). "I would love to give them enough for an hour," he later claimed. "Maybe something that they can start the next season with. I want to help them in every way I can."[10]

On the night of *Justified*'s premiere, March 16, 2010, Leonard was visited by NPR's Noah Adams, and agreed to give the younger reporter a personal tour of "his" Detroit while the interview took place. "In November, I started reading about pirates in the Gulf of Aden off of West Africa—Somali pirates," he told Adams. "I have a woman who is shooting her film about pirates. She makes documentary films, and she's in a little boat out in the gulf, and she's meeting pirates and shooting them and getting along pretty well. So, by page 152 or 153, where I am right now, it's about to switch over into something else. We're about to bring al-Qaida into the story."[11]

Since his HarperCollins debut a half decade earlier, Leonard had been given free rein on almost all his editorial decisions. But more so, he was granted an additional freedom to have a hand in all his books' promotional materials—something rare for most authors. Before completing the first draft manuscript, Leonard wrote to HarperCollins with a summary of the work in progress, later to be used in *Djibouti*'s press notices:

> *Dara Barr, documentary filmmaker, is at the top of her game. She's covered the rape of Bosnian women, Neo-Nazi white supremacists, post-Katrina New Orleans, and has won awards for all three. Looking for a bigger challenge, Dara and her right-hand man, Xavier LeBo, a six-foot-six, seventy-two-year-old African American seafarer, head to Djibouti, on the Horn of Africa, to film modern-day pirates hijacking merchant ships . . . The most successful pirate, driving his Mercedes around Djibouti, seems to be a good guy; but his pal, a cultured diplomat, has dubious connections. Billy Wynn, a Texas billionaire, plays mysterious roles as the mood strikes him. He's promised his girlfriend, Helene, a nifty fashion model, he'll marry her if she doesn't become seasick or bored while circling the world on his yacht. And there's Jama Raisuli, a Black al-Qaeda terrorist from Miami, who's vowed to blow up something big. What Dara and Xavier have to decide—besides the best way to stay alive—should they shoot the action as documentary, or turn it into a Hollywood feature film?*[12]

For the first time since the writing of *Bandits* in 1985, Leonard was heavily inspired by daily news reports of international affairs and US foreign policy. Like nearly all Americans, he'd followed interrelated terrorist connections to al-Qaeda in ongoing world news briefs and reports, and was soon linking together the plot of the next book. With an emphasis on George W. Bush's War on Terror, Leonard combed through articles on the occupation of Iraq, as well as that country's own retaliation and treatment of international news correspondents; the Bosnian War and ensuing claims of atrocities against the Bosnian people by Serbian soldiers; various cases of international piracy, and both a history of Djibouti and its modern reputation as "Sodom-by-the-Red Sea." (Leonard noted, "Djibouti means 'my casserole' in the Afar language . . . ninety-four percent of the country's inhabitants are Muslim.") Finally, Gregg Sutter provided Leonard with notes and advertisements for both the mobile film equipment that a documentary filmmaker like Dara Barr would use on a regular basis, and the type of thirty-foot trawler yacht that Barr would commission for her project.

Working in chronological order, Leonard annotated an article Sutter turned up from 1956, "The One-shot Killer," a profile on American hunting armorer Roy Weatherby and his latest invention: a high-velocity rifle, able to down an elephant in a single shot. Skipping ahead nearly half a century, a piece in the *New York Times* by Chris Hedges, entitled "Djibouti Journal," provided Leonard with his early working knowledge of the growing pirate phenomenon; he underlined the details of one ship, the *Gift of the Most Merciful*, owned by fifty-four-year-old Somali pirate Captain Mohammad Haj Farah. A 2008 article by Reuters' Ganesh Sahathevan gave Leonard a clearer look at the close ties that modern Somali pirates had to al-Qaeda and other terrorist organizations. Leonard also studied the US Department of State's official profile on Djibouti—noting, "sixty percent of all shipping in the world passes through [the] Gulf of Aden"—as well as a report on "Black America, Prisons and Radical Islam" by the Center for Islamic Pluralism, and the Navy Department Library's "Statements and Evolving Ideology" of al-Qaeda.

Rather than start a new notebook this time, Leonard wrote his notes on a large sheaf of his yellow typewriting paper. For the first time in years, he detailed the novel's outline down to the page numbers, breaking the story's arc into a three-act structure.[13] Combining his biographical notes with the early drafts of a speech for the upcoming PEN Awards dinner in Beverly Hills, Leonard wrote, "I had a good time developing [the characters], fitting them into the story . . . The idea is to have a good time when I'm writing and surprise myself with unexpected scenes. *Djibouti* took me a year and a ton of research material . . . I think it works."[14]

Mike Lupica later recalled, "When *Djibouti* came out, one of the galleys arrived and Gregg would call every one or two days asking if they'd arrived. 'Did it get there yet, did it get there yet?' And I said, 'No, but let me walk down to the mailbox and check.' For days. Well the reason if you wanted to know was that was the book he dedicated to me. I still have that galley: 'To Mike, my friend who keeps me in T-shirts.' I was always either buying him T-shirts or variations of his white Reebok sneakers."[15]

By the end of September 2009, Leonard was nearly three hundred pages into the book; he had the final draft completed on January 14, 2012. He'd taken only a few brief breaks in his workflow: one for a series of four career-spanning interviews with Boston University English professor Charles J. Rzepka during late 2009 and—on October 31, November 20, and December 19—for maintenance calls on his well-worn electric typewriter.[16]

The rush to finish the latest book had come at the cost of at least a few missed accolades. In August, Leonard had to decline an induction into the Hall of Honor at University of Detroit Mercy, due to the novel's pending deadline. He'd written to the dean, Charles E. Marske, "Would it be possible to hold my induction into the Hall of Honor until another time? . . . Right now I'm putting all of my effort into completing my next novel that deals with Somali pirates hijacking ships off the coast of East Africa. I need to finish the book and get it published before the hell-raising Somalis are subsequently finished and have to return to fishing."

He added, "I lost time touring my latest, *Road Dogs*, in June and July, the reason I'm now under the gun to finish this one."[17]

Lupica wasn't the only person Leonard had in mind with the book; pleased with his grandson Alex's initial mock-ups for the cover of *Up in Honey's Room*, he again asked for similar assistance with the latest book's design. "He saw his beautiful photo of a woman in Djibouti with all kinds of fancy jewelry in her face," Alex Leonard later recalled. "[He asked] 'Can you do something like that?' And HarperCollins ended up using the mock-up for the eventual hardcover design idea . . . I was honored and pretty excited that he'd asked for my help."[18]

Upon *Djibouti*'s publication by William Morrow–HarperCollins on October 12, 2010—one day after Leonard's eighty-fifth birthday—critics and reviewers agreed that the novel "worked." In the *New York Journal of Books*, A. J. Kirby wrote, "Pirates. Fast cars. Billionaire playboys. Boats. Guns and gun-smugglers. Explosions 'fifty-times more powerful than the bomb . . . dropped on Hiroshima.' Sex. Helicopters. Terrorists. An exotic location. Champagne—lots and lots of champagne. *Djibouti*, Elmore Leonard's new novel (and his forty-fifth in a prolific career) provides everything you'd expect from a Leonard novel . . . Leonard doesn't just make his characters talk; he makes them sing."[19] The *San Francisco Chronicle*'s Alan Cheuse added, "Now that with the power of various pocket-size handheld devices you can virtually hold a movie in your hand and watch it flash past, here comes the master of the movie on the page, the indomitable Elmore Leonard. With his latest publication (getting up toward his fiftieth publication!), he gives you every advantage of an action film and some of the best dialogue anyone has written since Hemingway. I know that's a mouthful, but he's worth every word of our praise."[20]

In the *New York Times*, David Kamp wrote, "Once *Djibouti* finally kicks into gear, it becomes a propulsive, bracingly brisk read, almost a different book . . . It takes some hanging in there, but *Djibouti* winds up being a first-rate Leonard offering, one that will find you pawing your touch-screen reading device in untoward ways to find out what happens next."[21]

Now a standing member of the Academy of Motion Picture Arts and Sciences, Leonard was finally in a position to have "screener copies" of the year's most acclaimed films sent directly to his home. Having already cast his votes for that year's Oscars, Leonard soon sent a few fan letters of his own. To director Rob Marshall, he wrote, "I saw *Nine*, then had to see it again. It's one of my two favorites up for awards this year. The other is *The Hurt Locker*."[22] However, Leonard hadn't mentioned to Marshall that the director of *The Hurt Locker*, Kathryn Bigelow, had been an early inspiration for *Djibouti*'s lead protagonist, Dara Barr; to her, he sent a signed copy—and his blessing to direct its adaptation.

HarperCollins marked the occasion of Leonard's forty-fourth novel with some of the most creative promotion the author had received since signing with Don Fine's Arbor House more than three decades earlier. Along with gratis copies of *Djibouti* for participating booksellers, reader sweepstakes, and a number of cross-promotional campaigns with FX in conjunction with *Justified*—now declared a runaway smash for the network—the publisher created a playful faux US passport, credited to the "United States of Elmore Leonard," complete with an insert of Leonard's current author photo, life stats, and a synopsis of *Djibouti*'s globe-trotting plot. They'd also sent along a CD of choice excerpts from Leonard's many audiobooks—titled *44 in 85*, declaring the number of books he'd written in as many years.[23]

By the time *Justified* had premiered and was declared a bona fide television hit, Leonard had been granted more recognition than at any other time period in his life. (May 12, 2006, had been proclaimed as "Elmore Leonard Day" by the State of Oklahoma and the city of Tulsa; he'd received the Cartier Diamond Dagger Award from the UK's Crime Writers Association; the 2006 Louisiana Writer of the Year; the Raymond Chandler Award at the Noir Festival in Courmayeur, Italy; the Owen Wister Award from the Western Writers of America in 2008; and, the following year, the Lifetime Achievement Award from PEN USA.) However, he'd traveled to almost all the ceremonies accompanied not by his wife, but by his son Peter.

Christine Leonard's trips to their North Palm Beach condominium had become more frequent and lengthier—four total in two years. Having returned from her sixth in March 2011 she announced that, after eighteen years of marriage, she wanted a divorce.

As he had done upon the passing of Joan in 1993, Leonard sought the company and solace of his family and friends. Grandson Alex Leonard later recalled, "Peter called him one night after his divorce and said, 'Dad, you want to come over for dinner? What are you eating?' And Elmore said, 'I'm having a Chunky soup.' And Peter said, 'You can't eat that garbage.' So Elmore goes, 'It's actually pretty good.' After that, used to come over all the time."[24]

Peter Leonard remembered, "He would come over to our house for dinner three or four nights a week. I would hear his Volkswagen pull up in the driveway behind the house and he'd come in with a bottle of wine. He'd do a little tap dance on the wood floor in the kitchen and he'd hand me the bottle of wine. Then he would light a Virginia Slims 100 and start talking about what he did that day—writing."[25]

Despite the emotional toll that the divorce proceedings were having on Leonard, his newfound availability seemed to benefit one major group—his grandchildren, who had all yearned for more time with him while growing up. "There was a time during the last few years of his life when he sort of put the pen down and just started hanging out with us, and that was the best," Tim Leonard recalled. "We really got to know him even more. I felt like I didn't know him like this, you know. He got more interested in us and less about the characters."[26] Alex Leonard recalled, "My cousin Megan told me, 'You should just go over to Goppa's house if you want to see him. He loves sweets, so just bring him some chocolates and go hang out with him.' About that time, I'd been reading a lot of his books for the first time and would visit him and ask all sorts of questions . . . Later, a friend of mine, who's in the Army, came over for dinner while he was on leave. During dinner, Elmore turned to John and said, 'All right, soldier—you have the sniper rifle up and the target is in sight. But a little girl with a balloon walks in front of your sniper scope. Do you take the shot?' "[27]

Tim Leonard added, "I remember I called him one day to ask if some friends and I could go swimming at his place . . . Elmore came out to smoke a cigarette and just started talking to the group of us. He said he saw us swimming outside his window and felt like a Haitian prisoner, locked up on the other side of the fence and just wanted to say 'Hi' because he wanted to get across the fence to the beautiful girls on the Dominican side of the fence." He added, "[But] I felt like there was another layer to it, like he was an older man looking back at his youth passed and he couldn't cross back into it. But like everything about him, it would just stay with you—at least for a little while after. That's just how he was."[28]

While Leonard himself couldn't enjoy the swimming pool or tennis court with the same energy as he used to, he was happy that his place had become a refuge for his grandchildren and their friends, and was now always open to hosting them. Peter Leonard's daughter, Kate, later recalled, "Elmore went through his divorce from Christine and became single at the same time that my one-year relationship in college ended. So, he'd talk to me about being single like we were the same age, going through the same thing. Coming from him, it was so funny."[29] Leonard had similar humorous conversations with Bill's oldest daughter, Hillary, during her periodic visits from Colorado. "I remember that when I was living in Boulder, I was single and just 'dating around,'" Hillary recalled, "and I remember talking about girls with him. He never made me feel weird, it was never uncomfortable—it just felt so normal to be able to talk about that stuff with him. He was so cool and so accepting of everyone, and I felt very in that moment. And for us to be sitting around talking about women together—it was really funny."[30]

Leonard was soon invited by the publisher of *The Paris Review*, actress and arts patron Drue Heinz, to a Scottish writers convention called The

Edinburgh Conversations, slated for August 2012; unfortunately, his ongoing divorce proceedings took precedence. "I have serious misgivings about my frame of mind were I to attend," he wrote to Heinz. "My coming divorce is crowding out of my mind all thoughts of talking about humor in my books. At this point, I'm not even sure any of my scenes are funny." Leonard went on: "Sometime later this month, the opposing attorneys will meet with the judge assigned to the case and see if we can come to an agreement on how much I will have to offer Christine to assure that her life of leisure continues . . . . I know I would not be able to give it my best shot were I to appear following these negotiations, and I am truly sorry."[31]

Otto Penzler later recalled that the last few times Leonard was able to travel to New York, he didn't seem to be the youthful and energetic author he long remembered. "Dutch didn't speak a whole lot," Penzler admitted. "He was much quieter, he showed his age, which he hadn't done until those last couple of times. It was a little depressing, in fact, because he was so much less engaged than he had been in all the years that I knew him . . . One night—I'm going to say that was five years before he died—we finished dinner kind of early. And I said, 'Would you like to go and hear some music?' It was a place called Arthur's and we got there at about 10 o'clock or so, and the sets were about forty-five minutes long. We sat down and he got his 'near beer' and I got a beer and listened to the set. And before we left he said, 'I can't stay too late because the car is getting me at 6 a.m. because I'm on *Good Morning America* tomorrow.' And that's the Elmore Leonard that I remember. But the last couple of times were not like that at all."[32]

Leonard made an exception to his social hiatus. On November 14, he traveled to Cipriani, New York, as the recipient of the prestigious National Book Award—a recognition for his contribution to American literature. Rather than a contemporary compatriot, they had selected one of Leonard's friends and greatest champions—British postmodernist Martin Amis—to present the honor. For his opening remarks, Amis praised his favorite of all American authors, emphasizing Leonard's use of the present participle. "What this means, in effect," Amis said, "is [Leonard] has discovered a way of slowing down and suspending the English sentence—or, let's say, the American sentence. Because Mr. Leonard is as American as jazz."

"This is a nice act to follow," Leonard said once taking the podium. His playful retort—"What I do is describe Martin Amis as a complete literary star, at the top of his game, and then I might mention that I've appeared as a category on *Jeopardy!*"—brought the room to thunderous laughter. Later on during a quiet moment, however, when asked why he thought it had taken so long to be recognized for such a renowned achievement as a National Book Award, Leonard offered, "Perhaps because I've written so much."[33]

A month earlier, Leonard had revealed to *Publishers Weekly*'s Jonathan Segura he was already deep into his *Djibouti* follow-up—the first full-length Raylan Givens novel in fifteen years. He'd been urged to write new Givens material by both the producer of *Justified*, Graham Yost, and its star, Timothy Olyphant. "They need real storylines to go with [the show], so I'm writing three. What they don't use I'm going to sell as a book," he told Segura, adding that he'd already found two of the three plot motifs: organ trafficking, the controversial mining method known as mountaintop removal, but "the third one he's not sure yet." Within weeks, however, Leonard had figured out the plot of the third story: women bank robbers and high-stakes poker.[34]

As he'd done with *Djibouti*, Leonard wrote the bulk of his notes for his next novel—already simply entitled *Raylan*—on a sheaf of his unlined yellow paper, rather than a larger, comprehensive notebook. While with the previous novel, the workflow had been largely dictated by ongoing typewriter malfunctions, this time, the interconnected nature of the three separated tales worked best on individual piles of sheets. He tasked Gregg Sutter with gathering the research material for each of the three. For the novel's consistency, Sutter gathered lists of "Mountain Dialect" and "Redneck Boy Names," then a full Rolodex of real-life Kentuckians with the last name "Crowe," so as not to accidentally infringe on the privacy of living persons (there turned out to be hundreds).

Much had changed in the rural areas of Harlan County since Leonard first researched the area on his own for *The Moonshine War* back in 1968. No longer were bathtub gin and various homebrew concoctions the most illicit among black-listed contraband; by 2010, methamphetamines and OxyContin had, unfortunately, become the drugs of choice among the state's youth. Atop one article from the *Lexington Herald-Leader* entitled "6 of 16 in Drug Bust Arrested Last Time Most Are Involved with OxyContin, As in February Roundup," Leonard noted, "[OxyContin is a] miracle drug for chronic pain suffers—traded for marijuana in East Kentucky."[35] Leonard coupled that with a history of marijuana growers and sellers in Kentucky from 1986 through modern day. Sutter also provided Leonard with numerous articles on the organ black market and the technical specifications for organ transplants and hemodialysis options. From the Environmental Protection Agency, Leonard read firsthand accounts and testimonials of real-life members of "Coal-Fed Families"—an organization made up of those dependent upon the coal-mining industry for their livelihood, and the political and lobbyist groups working against them. Local newspapers, as well as the *Washington Post*, carried stories regarding the opposition, namely the environmental impact on strip-mining and other recent trends in the industry.[36]

Leonard consolidated his stacks of notes and, for the first time, handed them to Sutter to type up on the computer for a page-by-page, chapter-by-chapter breakdown. Ultimately, each of the three Raylan tales amount to the length of a novella—each just over the length of *Fire in the Hole*, as well as the original length of Leonard's first publication, "Trail of the Apache" in *Argosy*, fifty-nine years before.

Leonard completed *Raylan* on April 19, 2011. It was his forty-fifth novel, and the last one he would finish in his lifetime. It was published by William Morrow–HarperCollins the day after Christmas, 2012.

In his write-up for the *New York Times*, guest critic and novelist Olen Steinhauer praised Leonard's economy of language, wit, and themes—and added a final line that could have described the book's author himself: "The three primary antagonists are female. This might be what *Raylan* is really about. Not gambling, mining or organ trafficking: It's about women, and one marshal's relationship to them . . . the women are often the smartest characters in the room, despite the fact that each of Raylan Givens's three antagonists is more than a little hung up on him. But who wouldn't be? A morally astute sharpshooter with nice Southern manners, a sense of humor and a clean cowboy hat—you don't find men like him every day."[37]

Leonard had long hoped to see one of his personal favorites among his novels, *Freaky Deaky*, adapted by Hollywood. At one time, director Quentin Tarantino had considered making it himself, ultimately opting to turn *Rum Punch* into 1997's *Jackie Brown*. Finally, in July 2011, he met with director Charles Matthau—son of acting legend Walter Matthau—to discuss a possible film version of the hit 1988 novel. Producer Judd Rubin later recalled, "It's not just one of Elmore's best books—I think it's one of *the* best books, it's a masterpiece." He added, "[Matthau has] always been an independent producer and didn't have a studio. I think he made a very significant offer from his own pocket, which is rare. You know, you don't see that a lot. So, I really credit Charlie for making it happen."[38]

During dinner at his son Peter's home, Leonard listened as Matthau expressed his own passion for the story as well as ideas regarding possible casting and retroactively moving the novel's action to 1970s-era Detroit, so as to attract a younger crop of stars for the primary roles. "For eighteen years, I've wondered why *Freaky Deaky* hasn't made it to the screen," Leonard later recalled. "I think the problem was seen as the time period. *Freaky Deaky* takes place after the hippies, the counterculture 'Revolution for the hell of it' period; but what year does the movie represent? Charlie Matthau said, 'We'll make it look like '74, the cars, the music, the characters will say 'ball' instead of using the F word.' And he did it."[39] Of the controversial changes to the original novel's time period, Rubin added, "The time [of the story] was changed. But the reason why Elmore's stuff resonates is that he's much more focused on character than on plot . . . I think a lot of the magic in Elmore is, as a reader, realizing what some of these characters may or may not do."[40] Ultimately, Matthau's plan worked, with Billy Burke, Christian Slater, Crispin Glover, and Michael Jai White joining not long after the state of Michigan granted generous tax incentives to keep the production in the accurate locations depicted in the original book. Leonard visited the set on July 22, wishing the cast and crew good luck and posing with some of the cast members clad in their period-accurate costumes. (He was particularly fond of White's turn as Donnell Lewis, and Leonard Robinson as Juicy Mouth.) The film, however, had only been given a limited release in April the following year and earned dismal reviews from critics. (Likewise, Daniel Schechter's adaptation of *The Switch*—newly entitled *Life of Crime*—eventually opened in a limited run the next year. Starring Jennifer Aniston as Mickey and Yasiin Bey and John Hawkes as Ordell Robbie and Louis Gara, respectively, the film fared better than *Freaky Deaky*, but did little to change Leonard's old opinions regarding his film adaptations.)

Leonard's granddaughter Hillary vividly recalled attending the premiere of the film while still a student at Colorado University. "We had a whole screening room to ourselves, which felt special—and a bunch of people who'd worked on the movie were there, including Charlie Matthau. Afterwards, we all went to dinner and Charlie Matthau sat right across from us. I could literally feel him working up the courage to ask Elmore what he thought of the movie—like you could cut the tension with a knife. He finally worked up the nerve and asked Elmore. And Elmore didn't even look up; he just said, 'I didn't like it.' And I think I left, I felt so awkward. But that was very Elmore. He didn't miss a beat. He was just honest."

However, Hillary continued, the trip also led to one of the most memorable times she'd ever experienced with her grandfather. As the Colorado governor, John Hickenlooper, was a great fan of Leonard's work, he'd offered his own mansion to the family for their Denver stay. "That night at the mansion when we were all together, Elmore asked me, 'Did you bring any weed?' And I did!" Hillary recalled. "I had hoped to smoke with him, so I'd stopped and bought his favorite strain, 'Blue Dream,' and packed a bowl for us . . . At one point, Elmore started tap-dancing. He always ended it with like a one-two-three move, then with one leg out, sticking out his little tongue. It was so funny." (According to Hillary, it was that night that eventually inspired all the Leonard grandchildren to band together and get a "Dutch" tattoo—replicas of his famed Naval ink—on their own bodies as a sign of family solidarity. "Of course, I'm a super-lesbian so, at first, all my girlfriends thought it said, 'Butch' until I explained that it was for my grandfather!"[41])

On the small screen, however, *Justified* continued to soar. Soon entering production of its third hit season on FX, the series had been the recipient of numerous accolades and awards—and finally earned Leonard his first for his contributions to television. On May 22, he flew to New York for dinner with its producer, Graham Yost, as well as Mike Lupica and Michael Siegel. The following afternoon, Leonard won his first and only Peabody Award for his role as the show's executive producer—a job, he continued to insist, required "very little work" other than providing the source material. He celebrated over dinner with Siegel, Jeff Posternak, and Andrew Wylie before flying home the following morning.

With the popularity of *Justified* far outweighing the box office misfire of *Freaky Deaky*, and *Raylan* being another literary bestseller, it could have been a given for Leonard to immediately start yet another adventure featuring the fictional lawman. However, the novel that would prove to be the last he would work on during his lifetime began, rather, as a series of fascinating false starts—the first of which was a surprise potential sequel to 1979's *Gunsights*. It would have marked Leonard's first true Western since that earlier book, and his first time reentering the genre's sepia-toned terrain since *Cuba Libre*.

For this first incarnation—tentatively entitled *Sweetmary*, then *The Sweetmary War*—Leonard had pulled *Gunsights* off his shelf and dug in, refreshing the details of its protagonists, Brendan Early and Dana Moon. For the follow-up, however, equal emphasis would have been paid to Maurice Dubus, the journalist who'd immortalized the pair and their ongoing battles against Phil Sundeen during the events of "the Rincon Mountain War," as well as ex-soldier Bo Catlett.

Leonard began with a small sheaf of notes, detailing the final showdown of *Gunsights* and where the characters would have been following their time as traveling entertainers. Satisfied with his self-imposed crash course into the earlier book—and with solid references made to his classic *Hombre*—Leonard began:

> The newsmen who came to Sweetmary this time thought at first it must be the land war still going on: the mine company running off the reservation people, the Apaches and a mix of other souls living in the high country . . . this is where Dana Moon, the Indian agent, was still living. They'd ask Dana: didn't that war end when you shot Phil Sundeen?
>
> Kate Moon, Dana's good-looking young wife, was sitting on the porch of their home reading, of all things, *The Rincon Mountain War* by Maurice Dumas, the *Chicago Times* reporter, who'd stayed close to Dana Moon and Brendan Early to learn what there was to know about the war.

Scrawled below the typed paragraph, Leonard noted his choice as one of the three primary leads, should the story be turned into a film or series: Christian Slater, who had impressed him during the making of *Freaky Deaky*. He also added notes on a new character soon to be introduced: "*Black character investigating claim for land court—Lt. Henry Ossian Flipper, 'first negro to graduate from West Point.' Bo Catlett knows him—'smarter than most whites.'*"

Dissatisfied with his opening, Leonard quickly started from scratch:

> Maurice Dumas, the *Chicago Times* reporter, rode the horse he rented in Sweetmary seventeen miles to see Dana Moon, the Indian agent at White Tanks. Maurice wanted to give Moon the first copy of his book, *Gunsights: The Rincon Mountain War* . . .
>
> "It's my first book," Maurice Dumas said, "hot off the press. You'll see inside it's dedicated to you and Bren Early, heroes of the Rincon Mountain War."
>
> Moon said, "Nothing about Kate?"
>
> "I had to hold her," Dumas said, "from kicking over Mr. Fly's camera. You think she wants to see that picture again, standing there in raggedy clothes? Couldn't comb her hair?
>
> "It's a moment of history," Maurice said.

As a bit of self-referential humor, Leonard had Dumas recount how he'd had to "fight my publisher to use *Gunsights* as the main title." Aside from his disapproval that Kate's place as the true hero of the original Rincon showdown, Moon is additionally disgusted that photographs of Bo Catlett had been cut from the book, insinuating it's due to the color of his skin. To this, Dumas retorts: "I sent my publisher photos of Bo and the 10th Cavalry colored fellas living up there. I sent photos of the Mexican families and the reservation people, but the publisher didn't include any of them, saying they didn't want an historical account to become a picture book."

Leonard soon abandoned the *Sweetmary* project, instead using his research from Gregg Sutter to tell a new story set in the modern era. What would remain the same, however, were the themes of bigotry and valor—all wrapped up in the similar archetypes of modern-day cowboys and strong women protagonists. And while the new novel wouldn't be set in the Old West, it would still feature a corrupt lawman and a disapproving progressive warden (shades of *Forty Lashes Less One*). What was already certain, however, was that the antagonist—a racist immigration agent who uses his status primarily to abuse the people of color who crossed his path—would be known by a certain ominous moniker: the "*Ice Man*." He revealed to the *Wall Street Journal*: "Right now I'm writing a story called *Sweetmary*. 'Sweetmary' is a private prison in Arizona. The immigration and customs enforcement use that prison. They'll arrest people and just throw them in prison and let them wait." He added, "The main character is a guy who had been a champion bull rider. His girlfriend is an actress who makes vampire movies. He was spending so much time with bulls that she had to leave."[42]

Leonard tasked Sutter with conducting research into three primary areas: bull riding, drug smuggling across the Mexican border into the United States, and the federal agency known as ICE—Immigration and Customs Enforcement. Along with recent reports on immigrant fugitives wanted by the US Marshals Service and various real-life accounts of escaped drug runners, Sutter had also given him various cases where ICE agents had abused their authority out of spite for the immigrant communities targeted within their jurisdictions.[43]

Although unclear where it would fit into the novel, Leonard began his latest—and final—work journal with notes on "Slab City"—a real-life unincorporated city in the Sonoran Desert, in Imperial County, California. Referred to by *Smithsonian Magazine* as a "squatters paradise," the man-made community had fallen through the cracks of civic construction following the end of World War II and was founded by "off-the-grid" residents not long after. Eventually made up of more than two thousand trailers and RVs of members opting for a hedonistic, alternative lifestyle, the surreal landscape later offered a free lending library and internet café—but no law enforcement jurisdiction. In effect, it had become a strange hybrid of the Old West and *Mad Max*—making it an ideal hideout for illegal immigrants coming through the nearby Mexican border, and a perfect backdrop for an Elmore Leonard tale.[44]

By then, Leonard already had his characters, if not the full plot or final title, worked out. The new novel told the story of three primary characters—Kyle McCoy, a champion bull rider who'd retired from competition and used his career winnings to set up shop breeding bulls. Now very wealthy, he hired Mexicans and young men of Apache descent to care for his herds. An unbiased man, he was protective of his employees, and when three of them are thrown into the Sweetmary private prison for mouthing off to a bigoted ICE agent one night at a local bar—the infamous "Ice Man," Darryl Harris—McCoy swoops into action to use his community clout to have them released. Harris, however, has already put in the machinations to stage a fake escape of the three young men—Victor (McCoy's bull-riding protégé), Nachee, and Billy Cosa—giving him an alibi to justifiably gun them down. Harris's corrupt ways have already come to the attention of Sweetmary's new warden, a retired US marshal of the old school named Jerry Kearns, and an internal investigation of the

Ice Man's practice of locking up immigrants on a whim is already underway. In an effort to kill all four birds with one stone, Harris tricks Kearns into being present during the escape, using the opportunity to shoot the warden in the back, rendering him a quadriplegic—and, unintentionally, a living witness to the agent's scheme. However, Kearns isn't the only witness to Harris's plot: straight-arrow and tough-as-nails corrections officer Alexandria "Aly" Sarafa (cut from a similar cloth as a young Karen Sisco) runs to assist in preventing the escape. She sees Harris shoot the warden and kill Billy Cosa. Knowing that she's now a marked woman, Sarafa leaves Harris entangled in the barbed wire fence and hops into her car with both Victor and Nachee, and the three take the disabled Kearns for medical attention. With Kearns safely delivered to a hospital specializing in spinal care, the three then vanish as fugitives, initiating a manhunt to find them. Additionally, the entire episode had been witnessed from the prison window by another witness—newly hired office clerk Celeste Delong.

For Leonard, Celeste had initially been the strongest and most complex character. Once he began putting pen to paper, her background and ulterior motives drove the plot. Originally named Carole (although Leonard soon changed it as he went along) Celeste was more than a mere office clerk: years before the events of the novel, she'd been a dedicated "Buckly Bunny" of the Bull Rider Groupies, dressing in the tacky attire known to draw the attention of star rodeo champions. After a weekend-long tryst with Kyle McCoy, Celeste pulled herself together and got a makeover, reinventing herself as a highly paid cocktail waitress, then as a live-in nursing assistant reading crime novels to an elderly man (an early draft named him as Ed McBain). When the old man dies, she finagled her way into trading nude photos of herself to his grown sons in exchange for one of his homes in Palm Springs. As she later tells Darryl Harris, she'd wanted to live closer to her estranged mother, adding that her stepfather had insisted on being called "Mr. Earl" in homage to the 1955 song "Speedoo" by the Cadillacs—one of Leonard's personal favorites—but the track is unfamiliar to Harris. (Leonard had playfully referenced the song "Speedoo" in the book for multiple reasons. Although he'd been a fan of the song during his youth, years earlier, he'd also considered it as his unofficial "grandfather name" upon the birth of his first grandchild, Jane's daughter, Shannon. Eventually, however, "Goppa" won out. Peter Leonard recalled, "All the little ones in the pool would chant, 'Goppa, Goppa! Do another dive!' Then, Elmore would come over for dinner and say, 'God, if I hear that one more time . . .'"[45])

At that point, Leonard found himself at a creative standstill. He'd mapped out the further chapters—including the manhunt for the missing fugitives—but realized he needed one more character to work alongside Celeste in her search. After a few days of consideration, he brought out the big guns; enter Raylan Givens—invited to join the party by none other than warden Jerry Kearns. In a complete rewrite of the interrogation scene, Givens and Julie Reyes hit it off, with the promise of further sexual tension and a possible romantic fling.[46]

"With the book he was working on when he died, I can remember one of the last conversations we had," Mike Lupica recalled. "He was so excited because once he put Raylan into that book, he was flying. In the last conversation we had—about five hours before Gregg called that night to tell me that he had the stroke—was him reading aloud and Raylan showing up in this book. He was just completely happy. It's like he came out of this forest and he could see blue sky again . . . He was as excited as I'd ever heard him."[47]

But that was as far as Leonard got.

He'd retitled the work in progress *Blue Dreams*—both for the type of marijuana that, presumably, Darryl Harris would be illegally involved in bringing across the border as his side hustle, and for his own personal favorite strain of cannabis.

On July 29, 2013, however, he suffered a massive stroke while writing, forcing him to put the book aside.

The previous year, Leonard had been asked by *The Guardian* to complete a "Proust Questionnaire"—a list of psychological inquiries used interchangeably as a revelatory litmus test of its recipient and as a parlor game attributed to the twentieth-century French novelist. Leonard's responses were his usual blend of humor and serious autobiography:

> *What is your idea of perfect happiness?* Having the time to practice my craft without interruption.
>
> *What is your greatest fear?* Not able to find ribbons for my typewriter.

> *What would your motto be?* "Good as his word."
>
> *How would you like to die?* Saying absurd last words to my family at my bedside and watching them smile.
>
> *Do you believe in life after death?* Yes. I'm dying to see what it offers.
>
> *How would you like to be remembered?* As funny—easy to live with.
>
> *What is the most important lesson life has taught you?* Don't talk about what you want to do in life. Do it.

But when *Vanity Fair* asked Leonard to submit an identical "Proust Questionnaire" just prior to the National Book Awards, the author was in a decidedly different mood. Admittedly feeling his age, having difficulty getting *Blue Dreams* finished and in the throes of his divorce from Christine, Leonard took the duplicate set of questions less seriously. Laden with sarcasm, his patience for redundancy seemed to seep through:

> *What is the trait you most deplore in others?* Guys who use the word "snot."
>
> *What is your greatest regret?* Selling a book to a film producer who doesn't get it.
>
> *What or who is the greatest love of your life?* I'll let you know when I'm 90.
>
> *If you could choose what to come back as, what would it be?* Charlie Sheen.
>
> *What is your most treasured possession?* I don't have any.
>
> *What is the quality you most like in a woman?* Long legs, good taste, and not a big ass.
>
> *Who are your favorite writers?* Hemingway and my son Peter Leonard.
>
> *How would you like to die?* Does it make a difference? You're dead.
>
> *What do you most value in your friends?* That they get it.[48]

To most readers, Leonard's answer to the stock question, "Which historical figure do you most identify with?" raised the most eyebrows. Provocatively, he'd answered "*Nathan Bedford Forrest*"—the founder of the Ku Klux Klan and the unseen chief antagonist of his early Western,

Last Stand at Saber River, even going so far as to dramatize the Confederate general's 1864 atrocities at Fort Pillow within the novel; Forrest had also been the dubious hero to the vile Dixie mafia chieftain Walter Kirkbride in *Tishomingo Blues*.

After the questionnaire ran on November 9, 2012, without the editors batting an eye, Leonard told his son Peter, "I'm retiring from sarcasm."[49]

At the time, he was still in the slow-going process of completing *Blue Dreams*. He'd been satisfied enough with the first few chapters to accept an offer from *The Atlantic* to submit a teaser of the book for their June issue. He selected the second chapter from the manuscript—the unjust arrest of Victor, Nachee, and Billy Cosa by Darryl Harris—to adapt into a short, standalone piece. He titled it "Ice Man" and completed it for Jane to type and submit to the magazine on February 23. It would be the last short story of his to run in his lifetime. (The previous year, in its thirty-ninth issue, *McSweeney's* ran his "Chick Killer," the final appearance by Karen Sisco, now on the hunt for a serial murderer of women.) In February 2013, Leonard completed what would be his last appearance in a major periodical, a humorous essay on the selection of Pope Benedict XVI's replacement as head of the Catholic Church. He had titled it, "The Old Boys Club," but the *New York Times* ran it as "For Pope: A Dude Like Dad."

Although he insisted that completing *Blue Dreams* remained his top priority, in January 2013, Leonard accepted an invitation from the University of South Carolina to accept the Thomas Cooper Award, complete with a gala dinner and honorarium. In his personal letter to Leonard, university dean Thomas McNally had extended the invitation to Peter Leonard, in the hope that a future tour of the campus's prestigious Irvin Department of Rare Books and Special Collections could sway the author and his son to place his volumes of letters and manuscripts within their esteemed archive library.[50] (Leonard had been approached to establish such a literary archive by various institutions as far back as 1967, but had always declined, insisting such a move would be premature in his career.) During a return visit to the campus on May 1, 2013, however, Leonard was finally convinced that it was time to place the accumulation of his life's work in a proper archive. According to associate dean for special collections and director of the Irvin Department of Rare Books and Special Collections Elizabeth Sudduth, Leonard was particularly excited to see the library's large collection of rare Fitzgerald manuscripts and correspondence, as well as the earliest drafts of Higgins's *The Friends of Eddie Coyle* (Higgins and James Ellroy had already established their own archives within the same walls). In addition, the archive included one of the largest Hemingway collections in the nation.[51] During a dinner hosted by the department heads, Leonard went outside to smoke a Virginia Slims 100, where Peter soon found him. "This is where I want my stuff to go," he told his son.[52]

Upon returning from his second trip to Columbia, South Carolina, Leonard received a letter from Dan Alpert, senior vice president of Detroit Public Television. He had included a review praising the network's recent documentary on the life and career of Johnny Carson. "Dear Elmore—you know that I feel you belong on PBS's *American Masters*. I thought that you would enjoy this article and reconsider sitting for [our] interview to let us capture you on film. Please call me."[53]

Again, Leonard insisted that he was busy writing his forty-sixth novel. He had long made it a practice to mark important dates within his day planner far in advance. For the year 2013, he'd marked August 11 as his oldest child, Jane's, sixty-third birthday. It was his last entry.

On July 29, he received a call from Sutter that he'd been offered the Scripter Award from the University of California. Again, Leonard told Sutter to respectfully decline, stating, "I have to write my book."[54]

After hanging up the phone, Leonard went back to his writing. Just after nine that evening, he suffered a massive stroke. He spent three weeks in the Intensive Care Unit and Hospital hospice at William Beaumont Hospital before returning home.

Bill Leonard later recalled, "I wasn't present when he died. I was living in Colorado and came home soon after his stroke. I visited him in the ICU where he lay unconscious. I stroked his head, kissed him and told him I loved him. He seemed to react, though it's impossible to say if he knew it was me . . . I went back to Denver knowing that that was the last time I'd ever see him."[55] While in his hospital bed, Leonard had the unexpected occasion to play catch with his grandchildren—Katy's sons—one last time. Grandson Joe Dudley later remembered, "While we were sitting there, talking to him and making him smile, he reached over and picked up his little stress ball they'd given him for his muscles—a soft little ball that you would squeeze for strength training—and he tossed it to me. So we all sat there and began playing catch with him one more time while he was in the bed."[56] Nick Dudley added, "I was about thirteen then . . . He couldn't really speak or move too much. They gave him a stress ball to squeeze and we all played catch again. I'll always remember that—it was great to have that moment with him."[57] The youngest sibling, Luke Dudley, recalled, "We played back and forth, catching to him in his hospital bed . . . That's the last memory that I have of him, and it was a special one."[58]

Leonard's family had placed a hospital bed in the middle of his office—always his favorite room in the house—and he was surrounded by many of his children and grandchildren.

At 7:15 a.m. the following morning, August 20, he passed away peacefully in his sleep. Christopher Leonard called his brother Bill in Denver to break the news. When Bill looked at that day's *USA Today* only hours later, the newspaper had already run one of the first obituaries on the top corner of the front page. He later recalled, "Any man would be lucky to live so long."[59]

"I remember when he died, we were all there in his office—his writing room—and everyone had set him up on a bed there, and nobody touched any of the things on his writing desk," Hillary Leonard later recalled. "Later, I walked over and looked down at his yellow pad and I noticed that the last word he had written was '*Time*'—and I got kind of a chill. That was the last word he wrote."[60]

Elmore John Leonard Jr. was eighty-seven years old.

CHAPTER 22

"The Great American Writer"

It's interesting watching yourself grow old.

My first experience with death was when my father passed away. He was fifty-six at the time and I was only twenty-three. My mother lived until she was ninety-two. Everyone said I took after my dad, but I think I'm more my mother's son.

As for my own death, I think I would like to be in bed and be aware enough—maybe under a little morphine—to make it somewhat absurd. And I'd like to have some funny lines to keep my family smiling and laughing.

I believe in an afterlife. Heaven, I'm sure, is great. I don't like to think about hell—who does? I think it might be a place of overwhelming remorse. Cremation is fine with me. I don't know where I'd like to be scattered, though. A lot of people don't realize it, but there isn't that much dust to scatter—there's far more bone matter.

If I end up being laid out in a funeral home, I'd like people to be happy about it and regard that time as a celebration of my life. I'd want them to play certain songs on a loop: Frank Sinatra's "Fly Me to the Moon" and "With a Little Help from My Friends" by Joe Cocker. I might have a couple of others, maybe Count Basie.

There would be a ceremony at the funeral hall but no long procession to the ceremony. Heck, I'm gone, I don't care. I used to tell my five children stories when they were little, just making it up as I went along, pretty much like my novels. It would be great to be remembered for them when I'm gone.

Perhaps my epitaph could read, "He wasn't a bad writer."

That would be nice.

A military funeral was held for Elmore Leonard on August 24, 2013, at Holy Name Catholic Church at 630 Harmon Street in Birmingham, the community where he had lived nearly all of his life. Numerous friends and collaborators from over the years came to attend, including Beverly, Mike Lupica, Graham Yost, and Timothy Olyphant. Navy officers later conducted a "farewell to arms" flag presentation and played "Taps" for their fallen brethren. The flag was handed to oldest daughter Jane following the presentation.

In accordance with what had always been Leonard's top priority, the occasion was truly a family affair. Grandsons Tim, Alex, Max, Ben, Joe, Nick, Luke, and great-grandson Jack acted as pallbearers, one of their grandfather's signature Kangol hats laid across the casket; his granddaughters Shannon, Megan, Hillary, Kate, and Abby recited the Mass's "Prayers of the Faithful," while his great-granddaughters Eliza and Jane greeted the more than three hundred visitors who'd come to pay their respects. Leonard's grandsons-in-law acted as ushers, and his daughters-in-law presented the gifts to the altar; Katy's husband, Jim Dudley, led the procession, bearing the cross. Leonard's second son, Christopher, welcomed the congregation. For the occasion, he'd worn a pair of his father's notorious Italian dress loafers, which didn't quite fit.[1] "When I hug my brothers and sisters," Christopher told the crowd, "I'll be hugging my father. When I see them, I'll see my dad."[2]

Longtime friends Gregg Sutter and Mike Lupica presented the first and second readings. And although Monsignor John Zenz and Reverend Father Joe Grimaldi presented the Gospel and Homily respectively, it was Leonard's two sons, Peter and Bill, who offered heartfelt—and humorous—eulogies for their father.[3]

A moment of meditation was held before the consecration of the bread and wine. The family had insisted its soundtrack include Joe Cocker's "With a Little Help from My Friends."

"Elmore was truly gifted with creativity, skill, and talent," Fr. Grimaldi said during his homily. "The twinkle in his eye showed he also enjoyed having fun."[4] Not to be outdone, Mike Lupica had opened the buttons of his dress shirt to reveal a replica of the black T-shirt he'd gifted to Leonard years earlier; in bold white letters, it read: "*Not now. I'm writing.*"

"We lost a good one," Peter Leonard said, later echoing the sentiments for a special essay he prepared for *The Guardian*. "Elmore was the coolest guy I knew. Unlike most dads, Elmore didn't preach or give a lot of advice.

'You can be whatever you want,' he would say. 'Just do it well.' When my brother Chris couldn't figure out what to do after college, Elmore sent him a postcard that showed a photograph of hunters standing next to a pile of dead seals. On the back my father wrote: 'Chris, have you considered a career in killing baby seals? I hear there's good money in it.'"[5]

Leonard's youngest son, Bill, had prepared a special eulogy—one for which his father would surely have approved: "Elmore Leonard's 10 Rules of Parenting" but, playfully, with an eleventh that seemed to sum up his father's philosophy:

1. Always be fun. When your kids are little let them ride on you like a horse.
2. Let them work the stick shift in your car when you run errands.
3. Buy them gum. Every time you take them to the grocery store, let them have gum.
4. Never read your kids bedtime stories. Instead, make up your own stories. They'll be more memorable.
5. Teach by example. If you want to instill a good work ethic, then get up at five in the morning and do your work, before you go to your job. If you want your kids to be neat, then hang up your pants as soon as you take them off. And put shoe trees in your good shoes.
6. Eat the food your kids leave behind, right off their plate. Don't let them leave those little pieces of fat or gristle. Fat is flavor.
7. Be encouraging. Tell your kids they can be whatever they want to be. My dad told Katy, "You can do whatever you set your mind to. Why don't you drive a taxicab? Think of the people you'll meet."
8. Make your own traditions. My dad turned Saturday lunch into a weekly burger party where all of our friends were welcome and every week was a different combination of friends and family and neighbors. He turned ordinary lunch into something memorable.
9. Be available. For advice. For talking. For just being together. And always at a moment's notice.

10. Throw great parties. Often. With plenty of champagne and dancing.
11. Above all else, stay young. Walk (although he hated walking), play tennis, read, see movies. Hold on to your sense of wonder and never stop being curious.

Following the funeral, while Leonard's friends and adult children broke off into little groups to share their own personal "Dutch stories," his grandchildren got together and celebrated the life of their "Goppa." The older grandchildren, at least, got to celebrate the best way that they knew how: by smoking their grandfather's favorite strain of cannabis—Blue Dream. Ben Leonard later recalled, "I'm a lawyer in the cannabis industry in Colorado, and when I last visited Michigan, marijuana hadn't been legalized in as many places as now, and I knew I would have to find a way to get it on the trip. And for a long time, Elmore was my weed dealer in Michigan. Whenever I would visit, I would get weed from him. So, the last time I saw him was probably one of the greatest times we ever had together. I had never had the opportunity to just sit and talk with him for long conversations. But this time, I was going to go up north to our family's cottage, which is Beverly's. And I stopped at his house to get some weed. When I got there, he opened the door and said, 'Well, are you busy?' and I said, 'No,' so we ended up smoking weed together. We just sat on the couch and watched baseball and had beer and weed and cigarettes. It was great—and up until then, I'd never gotten to have that type of moment with him. I just didn't know that it would be the last time I'd see him."

According to Ben, it was only during his grandfather's funeral that he remembered where he'd hidden that final stash—at Beverly's house. He added, "After the funeral, all of us hung out at Peter's house and one of my cousins said, 'You know what would be really nice right now? Some of Goppa's weed.' I don't know how it popped into my mind, but I was like, 'I have the last stash!' So, we drove over to Beverly's house and secretly got it from the armoire."[6] Ben's sister, Abby, added, "We closed the door and it was a cute moment—a special moment. The whole party, we felt his presence. And now, being in that room together, smoking his weed out of his pipe, we just said, 'Thanks, Goppa.' And kind of giggled."[7]

Tim Leonard later recalled of his grandfather, "He had this very childlike outlook, like he was always looking at the world with curiosity and wonder, like he was still a young boy in a way. I think that he must have funneled that into his writing and it fueled all his ideas. But his attitude would come through in his characters and just in the rhythm of his writing . . . He sort of had that, too—that attitude about life."[8]

For Leonard's younger grandchildren, the last decade of his life proved to be an invaluable time period, when many of them finally had the opportunity to spend the quality time with him that, previously, his writing had almost exclusively dominated. "I remember him coming around a lot in the later years of his life for all our family dinners," recalled Joe Dudley. "I would watch him and he was just really cool—listening to everyone else, then lighting a cigarette when someone would ask him his opinion. I'm pretty sure he was the only person allowed to smoke cigarettes at the table. Everyone would just be glued to what he'd say and would just stop what they were talking about to listen . . . But he just felt like a normal grandpa to me, to be honest—he was just cool."[9] Joe and Nick's brother, Luke, added, "When I think of Grandfather, I think of his determination—how he got published and stuck with it. To me, his life story shows that he never quit."[10] Granddaughter Abby Leonard shared similar sentiments: "I think about him a lot more in my older age, especially when I consider the age he was when he started writing. He's one of the most inspirational people in my life, pushing my creativity. When I think of what inspires me, it really is my grandpa. I think of how cool he was and how grateful I am that I'm related to him."[11]

Within days of Leonard's death, obituaries praising his life and work ran nationwide and abroad. "What made Mr. Leonard stand out among other chroniclers of crime and punishment was his voice—laconic, funny, unsentimental—and his ruthlessly coherent vision of life in the lower depths," wrote Louis Bayard in the *Washington Post*. "Mr. Leonard, in marked contrast, was a quiet, reserved, owlishly bespectacled man who lived in the Detroit suburbs and sported Kangol caps and tweed jackets. He had no rap sheet; he never owned a gun . . . When a professor rhapsodized about his 'patterns of imagery,' Mr. Leonard's initial response was, 'What's he talking about?' Mr. Leonard liked to quote the review from a librarian at a Connecticut prison: 'While you ain't caught on with the crack and cocaine heads, you have got a following amongst the heroin crowd.'"[12]

In *The New Yorker*, Joan Acocella offered her own final thoughts on Leonard's career, writing, "Leonard is most famous for the quality of the prose. He could do a vernacular speech as wonderfully as the greatest masters in that specialty (e.g., Philip Roth), yet it never sounds like dialect . . . The narration itself sounds like a voice." She added, "The highbrows may read him, but on the subway. That will change. In 2012, PEN America gave him a Lifetime Achievement Award, as the author of some of the best writing of the last half century . . . I bet we'll soon see a Library of America volume devoted to him."[13]

Of course, many of the newspaper and magazine eulogies had been written by critics who'd doubled as fans of Leonard themselves. It wasn't long before they began inquiring about his unfinished manuscript of *Blue Dreams*—then believed to be the very last of the author's unpublished works. By then, Peter Leonard had authored seven successful novels of his own, many touching upon the same crime themes and dark societal underbelly beloved by his father's fans—making him the most logical choice to complete the book. Ultimately, however, Peter Leonard opted to forgo *Blue Dreams* and, instead, pen his own Raylan Givens adventure. He told Kurt Anthony Krug of *The Voice*, "I felt it was sacred—it was Elmore's last work of fiction. Around the same time, my brother Christopher said, 'Why don't you write a Raylan novel?' I liked that idea because the *Justified* writers had kept Raylan going for six seasons [and] to me, a precedent was established." He added, "Elmore created [Raylan Givens]—I just borrowed him . . . I feel like I knew him pretty well." He added, "I did this book as a tribute to my father."[14]

Although Peter decided not to continue with further Raylan Givens novels, following the solid release of his *Raylan Goes to Detroit* in September of 2018, it did provide fodder for FX's highly anticipated *Justified* revival. By then, the hit series had taken its final bow on April 14, 2015, to rave reviews and audiences clamoring for more. It wasn't until March 2021 that the series' original producers found a fun creative loophole to bring back the television incarnation of Raylan Givens, while retaining the spirit of Elmore Leonard. By taking his 1980 classic *City Primeval* and swapping original protagonist Raymond Cruz for an older, wiser Raylan, they'd presented a hybrid project that acted as both an adaptation of the book and a proper sequel to the hit show. With Timothy Olyphant back in the hat and wearing the US marshals star, *Justified: City Primeval* premiered as a limited series July 18, 2023, to rave reviews and the promise of even more Raylan to come.

For his legions of fans, there was also more Elmore Leonard to come. While preparing their father's manuscripts for the University of South Carolina's archive, Leonard's children came across scores of his unpublished short stories—his earliest attempts at fiction and the literary experiments that agent Marguerite Harper had implored him to write but failed to sell. But to their amazement, the stories were significantly better than Leonard had ever let on, and demonstrated many of the themes and scenarios that would populate his later bestsellers. "These stories remind me of growing up with my father," Peter Leonard wrote in the eventual collection's foreword. "They remind me of playing hide and seek with guns. They remind me of the bullfight poster that hung in our family room, a dramatic shot of Manolete holding his sword and cape ready to finish off a charging bull—and they remind me that my father was always writing." He continued, "In these stories you'll see Elmore experimenting with style, trying to find his voice, his sound. You'll see him start a story with weather. You'll see him use adverbs to modify the verb 'said.' You'll see him describe characters in detail, breaking several of the famous '10 Rules of Writing' he developed almost fifty years later. And you'll also see glimpses of Elmore's greatness to come."[15]

Over the following few years, *The New Yorker*'s Joan Acocella's 2013 prediction came true, as the Library of America published their own deluxe four-volume hardcover set of major, curated works from Leonard's bibliography. For the first three volumes—released between 2014 and 2017 and which covered Leonard's literary output throughout the 1970s and early 2000s—Gregg Sutter acted as editor and curator. He had also compiled a comprehensive chronology of the author's life and career milestones, along with an academic series of notes revealing much of Leonard's real-life references and in-book inspirations. The final volume, retroactively covering Leonard's Western era and edited by Terrence Rafferty, included four of his best known novels of the genre—*Last Stand at Saber River*, *Hombre*, *Valdez Is Coming*, and *Forty Lashes Less One*—along with a handful of his best-known short stories, "Three-Ten to Yuma" and "The Captives" among them.

Although in 2013 Leonard had insisted to Detroit Public Television's

VP Dan Alpert that his schedule was too busy to sit for an *American Masters* documentary, the network's desire for a show dedicated in his honor remained strong as ever. With the full participation of family and friends, filmmaker John Mulholland's *Elmore Leonard: But Don't Try to Write* eventually aired in July 2022. Narrated by Campbell Scott—who had performed a number of Leonard's bestselling audiobook adaptations—the Leonard family, Gregg Sutter, and a host of writers and collaborators from *Justified* offered their own anecdotes and insights into Leonard's legacy.

In 2021, Hollywood powerhouse Quentin Tarantino offered his own unique homage to Leonard and his influence on the director's career. With his debut novel—an adaptation of his own 2019 film, *Once Upon a Time in Hollywood*—the visionary lover of all things retro kitsch insisted that the paperback include faux advertisements for his own favorite paperback "pulp fiction" novels of literature's past. Of course, a classic ad for Leonard's *The Switch*—the very novel that Tarantino had shoplifted as a teenager—featured prominently within the roster.

But the loss was deepest for those who knew Leonard personally and often worked alongside him. "He was a wonderful guy, very nice, very unpretentious," recalled Andrew Wylie. "But to me, what was particularly interesting about Elmore's work was that he put the language of angels into the criminal class . . . This is especially true if you look at Elmore's work in the context, say, of Martin Amis and Saul Bellow, as both Martin and Saul were interested in the criminal class, as it were, and understood that everyone had a sense of humor and an interesting perspective. So, [Elmore] is quite egalitarian and had a kind of wonderful embrace of what many people consider degenerate and thoughtless, which actually is *not* degenerate and not thoughtless, [but] *is* comical and sophisticated."[16]

Jeff Posternak, Leonard's friend and literary agent, offered his own take on the author's legacy: "We represent Nobel Prize winners and Pulitzer Prize winners and National Book Award winners and writers that are doing the most complicated, innovative things with language that you can imagine, and biographers and historians that are doing incredible research—and Elmore is right in here because he was just so good. I think his sort of language and his use of dialogue absolutely transcends genre . . . His books are still strongly and widely read and it'll continue."[17]

Likewise, close friend Mike Lupica recalled his own years with Leonard: "It was a deep friendship and I guess I'd convinced myself that he was going to live forever. Dutch was always the coolest guy in the room. The only thing better than reading Elmore Leonard is *rereading* him. But really, I guess the only thing better than even that was knowing him . . . He was a great writer. He was a great friend, and he was a great role model. He taught me the value of putting in the time . . . He dismissed the idea of writer's block. He always said, 'Writer's block just means you got up from your desk.'"[18]

But for those of us who grew up with the other Elmore Leonard—the invisible narrator who put only the most hip, smooth, and *coolest* lines into the mouths of his characters, keeping us turning pages for more than half a century—the closing words of *Hombre*, his most famous Western novel, perhaps ring just as true:

> Maybe he let us think a lot of things about him that weren't true. But as Russell would say, that was up to us. He let people do or think what they wanted while he smoked a cigarette and thought it out calmly, without his feelings getting mixed up in it . . . He did what he felt had to be done . . . So maybe you don't have to understand him. You just know him . . .
>
> You will never see another one like him as long as you live.

When the plot he'd long ago chosen finally became available, Leonard was interred in Greenwood Cemetery in Birmingham on October 11, 2016—what would have been his ninety-first birthday.

The headstone reads, "*The Dickens of Detroit.*"

POSTSCRIPT

Even as a child, I was aware that I wanted to be a writer. However, it wasn't until I was eleven that my mother handed me a copy of *Get Shorty* and I discovered the first narrative voice that excited me. At such a formidable age, I couldn't possibly understand the intricate nuances of Elmore Leonard's style and humor, yet soon enough, I was trading in Encyclopedia Brown and Spider-Man for Chili Palmer and Juicy Mouth.

I went on to read everything of Elmore's that I could get my hands on. By fifteen, I was writing my own crime and mystery stories, and although I was aware that he didn't often write first-person narratives or tap into the "gumshoe" fiction that my own stories were pathetically trying to emulate, Elmore's opinion seemed the only one that would matter to me. Later that year, I wrote an awful short story about a private detective who aspires to write for the pulps. When it was curtly returned to me by *Alfred Hitchcock's Mystery Magazine*, I was heartbroken.

I hadn't even been rejected by a girl yet; a magazine editor had gotten to me first.

Instead of approaching the teachers at school who didn't take me seriously (and often reprimanded me for reading Elmore's novels during class), or my parents who wouldn't have approved of my juvenile literary attempt at sexual tension, I sent it to him—the one person I *needed* to take me seriously. I packed up my story with a letter to Elmore begging for help and sent it care of his publisher at the time, William Morrow. My mother showed me how to properly address it.

Three weeks later, I received a thick manila envelope in the mail that changed the course of my life. It was postmarked "Bloomfield Hills,

Michigan," and I immediately knew who it was from. I'll never forget retrieving it from the mailbox that day, feeling like Moses descending from Mount Sinai clutching two stone tablets. After all, those contained ten rules, too.

Elmore Leonard had, indeed, taken me seriously; he even said so at the bottom of his letter to me—carefully typed on his official letterhead. Beneath it was my story, proofread in his unmistakable blue penmanship that I'd read about in so many interviews. My hands shook while I read his suggestions; it was like we'd collaborated together.

In addition, Elmore had gifted me a brand-new short story of his own—"Sparks"—typed on his legendary yellow paper. Elmore wrote that it hadn't even yet been published and, as proof, the lean manuscript still contained his own handwritten edits and last-minute changes for his daughter Jane to typeset. I was one of the first set of eyes to read it, and he urged me to study the dynamic between the two lead characters, which, he wrote, was somewhat similar to the one in my own story. I couldn't read it fast enough.

He wrote that his response to me was something he'd "never done before." (It wasn't until I had the honor of delving into his copious banker boxes of fan mail at the University of South Carolina years later that I found he'd been telling me the unexaggerated truth. And it wasn't until flipping through his daily planner for the year 1998 that I found he'd taken a busy afternoon off from writing in order to respond to me; decades after changing my life, with this realization of his generosity and kindness, he had done it again.) "The main reason I'm doing this is because you're 15 years old and seem very serious about learning how to write," his letter continued. "It takes time, maybe a million words before you have confidence in what you're doing—but it's worth it. I sold my first story when I was 25, in 1951. Good luck."

When I met Elmore six months later at his New York dual book signing for *Be Cool* and *The Tonto Woman*, he remembered me. Elmore Leonard actually knew who I was! I could hardly speak when we shook hands for the one and only time. He signed my copy of *The Tonto Woman*, "Chad—Write every day, whether you feel like it or not." I never forgot those words, and I went home vowing to live by them. Years later, I saw an interview with Neil deGrasse Tyson who spoke of his single teenage encounter with his own hero, Carl Sagan: "I already knew I wanted to be a scientist. But after meeting Carl, I knew what kind of *person* I wanted to be."

For me, my brief childhood encounter with Elmore was something like that.

Six years later, I finally had a short story accepted by a magazine for the first time. It was about a heavyweight champion boxer who'd lost only a single bout in his entire career. It forever haunted him and, every night, he would relive that loss in his sleep. I sent it to Elmore and he responded with a letter of congratulations. "I like the story, I like the writing," he wrote, "but I think you should settle down a little more, try not to be so loud in your writing. Look at the look of a page in the story; it explodes." He reminded me to keep my exclamation points under control. Ever the natural editor, he'd counted mine and playfully scolded me that I was only allowed three per one hundred thousand words; my story contained thirty-nine.

The summer following Elmore's first correspondence, I coupled it with a letter of recommendation from my English teacher and attained an internship at a local community newspaper. Indeed, only six months after Elmore wrote his letter of encouragement to me, I saw my name in print for the first time. (The first article I was ever assigned had been about an armed robbery at Blockbuster Video. I couldn't help but feel the excitement that my first published article would be somewhat reminiscent of *Swag*.) A staff position followed and, from there, I was eventually able to get articles and feature stories into magazines. Eventually, I had the accreditation to have my first book, *Nothing's Bad Luck: The Lives of Warren Zevon*, published in the spring of 2019. It had taken approximately one million words—the precise amount Elmore had predicted to me twenty-one years earlier.

My second book, *Beast: John Bonham and the Rise of Led Zeppelin*, followed three years later. I was given a generous blurb from Peter Leonard, along with the blessing from the Leonard family to take on Elmore's story as my next project—truly, the single greatest honor of my professional life. I was granted that permission in Peter's home in Michigan, where all of Elmore's children (except Bill, whom I was honored to meet soon after) gathered to meet me for a two-day period of sharing Elmore stories. As one of the most memorable experiences of my life, I'd only wished that my mother had still been alive for me to call and share all the details.

For the record, even twenty-seven years later, I have made a habit of rereading Elmore's first letter to me a few times a year. How could I not? Although I eventually made my way into journalism and nonfiction, his invaluable advice remains in the back of my mind every time I sit and write—and rewrite, and rewrite—until I'm satisfied that my narrative voice has been made sufficiently invisible—or as close as I can shield it within nonfiction.

Biographer Richard Holmes has often compared the relationship between a biographer and their subject as akin to "a handshake across time." With that in mind, it has been the honor of my lifetime shaking Elmore Leonard's hand once more and, this time, properly making his acquaintance—a journey that started with his unexpected patience for an impatient kid who revered him. I only hope that he would have approved of this book, and its readers will view it as the loving portrait it was intended to be. As a teenager, I could barely speak when he stood in front of me; as an adult, I don't get the opportunity to tell him what a difference he made in my life. I suppose this book is my simple way of thanking him and letting him know.

Dear Mr. Leonard: as you had advised, I've written every day—whether I felt like it or not. For twenty-seven years.

And you were right again.

It was worth it.

—C. M. Kushins

ACKNOWLEDGMENTS

Although it may not be all that fair to play favorites, writing the life and work of Elmore Leonard is a personal and career high point that is going to be difficult to top. Knowing this, I owe a tremendous debt of gratitude to every individual who assisted in both my attaining this opportunity and the research that produced the book.

First, and most important, my wife—Diana Serhal—who has made my life during and after this book the happiest and most joyful it has ever been. Her patience, enthusiasm, counsel, and enduring love are experiences new to me; I'm not only forever grateful to be her husband and partner, but am unabashed in admitting that this book is wholly dedicated to her.

My agent and one of the best friends I have ever had, William Clark, not only ensured that this book went into the correct hands at every step, but was as much a muse and inspiration as Elmore Leonard was to me during my childhood. Not only did William suggest Elmore as my subject, but he assured me of his faith that it was the book I was born to write.

I am not only grateful to be signed to HarperCollins—Elmore's own publisher, a dream in itself—but am so fortunate to have been paired with the wonderful and patient editor Nicole Angeloro. We are not only of like minds when it comes to preferences in books and authors, but in our respective processes and work ethic, only making this project ever more enjoyable.

For the first time in my career, I was honored to have worked alongside a research assistant, Lindsay "Red" Swarat, whose own passion for writing and research rivals only my own. A wonderful student with, no doubt, a tremendous literary future of her own, I am heavily indebted to

Red for her diligence and for reassuring my faith in the next generation of biographers.

Finally, it cannot be overstated that this book would not exist without the incredible and unprecedented blessing and trust of the Leonard family—Beverly Decker, Jane Jones, Peter and Julie, Chris and Suzie, Bill and Carmen, Katy and Jim Dudley; also, Shannon Belmont, Megan Friels, Tim, Max, Alex, Kate, Ben, Hillary, Abby, and Luke, Nick, and Joe . . . They're an amazing group, and I'm blessed to have gotten to know all of them through the process of writing Elmore's story. Never before have I been granted the help and guidance of a subject's family, and I am humbled that it all came from Elmore's—which he treasured above all else during his lifetime. Their memories and anecdotes, editorial assistance and suggestions and, more than anything, friendship, only led further to prove my suspicion: kindness and generosity are, indeed, hereditary.

From my own family, I thank my brothers Brandon and Sean, nieces Sera and Kylah, and my new additions, Emilia Juni, Judit Rybar, Petra Rybar, and Jamal Sadek. Knowing them now, it is no wonder that my Diana is as wonderful as she is.

Although the many interviews conducted for his book are cited accordingly, I would like to thank the following individuals for their time and efforts in helping bring Elmore's full story and creative life to the page: Eddie B. Allen Jr., Charles Ardai, Jim O. Born, Scott Burnstein, Emily Deinert, Jackie Farber, Mike Lupica, Jeff Posternak, Lee Purcell, Judd Rubin, Charles Rzepka, Betty Kelly Sargent, Paul Schrader, Michael Siegel, Barry Sonnenfeld, Gregg Sutter, and Andrew Wylie. Alvaro Brechner, the incredible Nikki Grosso, Peter Hale, Bubba Lemann, Art Luzak, Bill Morgan, Simon Pettet, and Howie Sanders each provided their own encouragement and friendship during the process, and I am indebted to all.

During my time at the University of South Carolina, I was blessed not only to spend my days submerged in the manuscripts and personal notes of Elmore Leonard (another dream in itself), but to have been assisted and befriended by a number of wonderful scholars and experts in their respective fields. I am additionally indebted for the aid and generosity of Mike Berry, Katie Hoskyns, Richard Layman, Tom McNally, Kate Moore, Anthony Morgan, Celia Nesbitt, Patrick Scott, Elizabeth Sudduth, Skip Webb, and Michael Weisenberg—the latter of whom taught me how to read *into* the details of manuscripts left behind. Likewise, the student volunteers of the Thomas Cooper Library at USC were inspiring and encouraging in their own enthusiasm and interest in my project. A great debt of thanks to Manuela Cano, A. D. Foster, Lexi Gastelu, Mary Jones, Anna Vo Nguyen, Luka Schwartz, Abby Scott, Jacob Stewart, Sara Tuttle, V.B., Reham Al Yah Yaai, and Jonathan Yi.

Although the University of South Carolina is home to the definitive Elmore Leonard archive collection, I was greatly assisted by the diligent librarians Patricia Higo at the University of Detroit, Louise Hilton at the Margaret Herrick Library in Beverly Hills, and Cassidy Polack at the Lilly Library at Indiana University. Their patience for me was insurmountable.

A huge thank-you to my friends at the Anne Frank Center at USC and the University itself: Christian Anderson, Amy Austermiller, Morgan and Trey Bailey, Chris Beyers, Jan Erik Dubbelman and Dienke Hondius in Amsterdam, Coy Gibson, Mario Hayes, Gabrielle Johansson, Sam Livoti, Claire Mattes, Devin and Kisha Randolph, Doyle Stevick and Kara Brown, Donna Tarney, Aidan Thomason, and Cara Wilson-Granat.

Through my wife, Diana, I am additionally blessed to have made a wealth of friends around the world, all of whom shared their own encouragement and interest in my book. Thank you so much to Juan Cruz Acevedo Acuna, Tessa Groen and Soufiane Dargaoui, Katinka Halapi, Katinka Hasprai and Endre Juhasz, Fanni Hedi and Ivan Milovanov, Emese Kristof and Bence Horvath, Monika Meszaros, Imola Nagy and Adam Hilbert, Chantel Stam and Leon van Amsterdam, Eszter Sukosd and Szabolcs Feher, Szandra Toth, and Theila Tziampiri and Benjamin Sadler. Additionally, my enduring gratitude to James Abbate, Ben Adams, Daniel Adler, Greg Andersson, Logan Ard, Kevin Avery, Raechel Blakeney, Lisa Blue, Allen and Kristie Boulos, Kieran Brooks, Chris Burreta, Ric Chavez, Rich Clark, Robert and Brittany Currie, Rod and Mary Lu Dalton, Teresa "Teta" De Cata, Chibuike Dialaekwe, the late Sal DiPeri Sr., Sal DiPeri Jr., Einar Einarsson, Fiona, Peter Galasso, the wonderful Anita Gevinson, Max Greenspan, Dave Grohl, George Gruel, Laurence Harrap, James Heinz (my brother for life), Matt Hodge, Latrell Jamison, Joe Kay, Gwendal Lebaubenchen, Albert and Michelle Lee, Tom Lehmann, Dan Leo, Liam, Wynton Marsalis (my first celebrity interview when I was seventeen, who not only instructed me to "develop my ear," but set me on a life path to interview my heroes—of which he was the first), Cathy Masrour (the first teacher and librarian who believed in my writing and requested Elmore Leonard books for the high school library at my suggestion), Jay McInerney, Andrews Mensah, Jerred Metz, Sam Milgrom,

Zarah Muller, Derek Muro, Carrie Napolitano, Neil Nathan, Maxime Nouraoui, Sarah Ortiz, Ben and Kerri Owens, Russell Papia, D. J. Pocket, Laurie Poma, Ryan Rayston, Tom Rizzuto, Ben Schafer, Phil Sciarillo, Kristin Ryan Shea, Lauren Sidel, Lindsey Strickland, Sunny, Selma Turac, Miriam "Miri" Alberti Vall, and Frieda Alessa von Borzyskowski.

I remain eternally grateful to all.

NOTES

1. Childhood, 1925–1943

1. United States Census, 1860, Michael Leonard.
2. Louisiana Parish Marriages, 1837–1957; William Leonard and Margaret Connelly, June 23, 1891; citing Orleans, Louisiana, United States, various parish courthouses, FHL microfilm 907,786.
3. Ireland Births and Baptisms, 1620–1881; Mary Ryan in entry for William Leonard, 1871.
4. United States Census, 1900, William Leonard, First Precinct New Orleans, City Ward 1.
5. "Well-Known Engineer Killed," *Times* (Shreveport, LA), January 6, 1909, p. 1.
6. *Harper's Monthly*, vol. 73, 1886.
7. Lemann family papers, Manuscript Collection 168, Louisiana Research Collection, Howard-Tilton Memorial Library, Tulane University, Louisiana.
8. "Well-Known Engineer Killed."
9. "William M. Leonard," obituary, *Times Democrat*, January 6, 1909, p. 2.
10. "Plantation Tragedy," *Daily Picayune*, January 6, 1909, University of South Carolina Special Collections Department (hereinafter USC).
11. "Well-Known Engineer Killed."
12. "William M. Leonard," obituary.
13. Rzepka, Charles, "The Elmore Leonard Interviews," crimeculture.com/?page_id=3435.
14. Walters, Katherine Kuehler, "World War I," *Texas State Historical Association Handbook of Texas*, 1952, Military Service Records at the National Archives; United States World War I Draft Registration Cards, 1917–1918; United States Census, 1910; United States Veterans Administration Master Index, 1917–1940.
15. Texas, County Marriage Index, 1837–1977.
16. United States Census, 1920, Adolph Rive.
17. Rzepka, "The Elmore Leonard Interviews."
18. "Chronology," in Gregg Sutter, ed., *Elmore Leonard: Four Novels of the 1970s* (New York: Library of America, 2014).

19. Challen, Paul, *Get Dutch! A Biography of Elmore Leonard* (Toronto: ECW Press, 2000).
20. "Certificate of Baptism," Elmore John Leonard, Church of the Incarnate Word, New Orleans, Louisiana, USC.
21. Pelfrey, William, *Billy, Alfred, and General Motors: The Story of Two Unique Men, a Legendary Company, and a Remarkable Time in American History* (New York: AMACOM Books, 2006).
22. "Chronology."
23. Rzepka, "The Elmore Leonard Interviews."
24. United States Census, 1930.
25. "Chronology."
26. Rzepka, "The Elmore Leonard Interviews."
27. Zachel, Frederick, "Leonard's Big Score," *January Magazine*, December 2000.
28. Challen, *Get Dutch!*
29. Zachel, "Leonard's Big Score."
30. "Chronology."
31. Leonard, Elmore, "Homework," April 4, 1933, USC.
32. Rzepka, "The Elmore Leonard Interviews."
33. "Chronology."
34. *First Edition*, WNET TV, 1984.
35. *First Edition.*
36. Rzepka, "The Elmore Leonard Interviews."
37. *First Edition.*
38. Rzepka, "The Elmore Leonard Interviews"; Challen, *Get Dutch!*
39. Challen, *Get Dutch!*
40. Roberts, Fletcher, "Novels Are Nice, but Oh, to Be a Rock Star," *New York Times*, March 14, 1999.
41. Leonard, Alex, interview, April 6, 2023.
42. "Chronology."
43. Grissom, C. Edgar, *Ernest Hemingway: A Descriptive Bibliography* (New Castle, DE: Oak Knoll Press, 2010).
44. Shah, Diane, "For Elmore Leonard, Crime Pays," *Rolling Stone*, February 28, 1985.
45. Hall, James W., "'Maximum Bob' Stirs Up Gators, Guns, and Muck," *Houston Post*, July 14, 1991.
46. United States World War II Draft Registration cards, "Elmore John Leonard," 1942.
47. "Margaret Leonard Madey," obituary, *Arkansas Democrat-Gazette*, January 16, 2007.
48. Rzepka, "The Elmore Leonard Interviews."
49. Challen, *Get Dutch!*
50. Capeci, Dominic J., Jr., and Martha Wilkerson, "The Detroit Rioters of 1943: A Reinterpretation," *Michigan Historical Review* 16, no. 1 (January 1990).
51. Capeci and Wilkerson, "Detroit Rioters of 1943."
52. "Chronology."
53. "Seabee History: Formation of the Seabees and World War II," US Navy, Navy Department Library, Naval History and Heritage Command, July 1, 2014, https://www.history.navy.mil/library/online-reading-room/title-list-alphabetically/h/history-of-seabees/ww2.html.

2. Seabees and the Pacific Theater, 1944–1946

1. US Navy, "Ancient Order of the Deep," membership card, October 1944, Elmore Leonard Collection, USC.
2. "Chronology," in Gregg Sutter, ed., *Elmore Leonard: Four Novels of the 1970s* (New York: Library of America, 2014).
3. Leonard, Elmore, letter to Ruthann Finneran, November 4, 1944, Elmore Leonard Collection, USC.
4. Leonard, Elmore, letter to Ruthann Finneran, November 4, 1944, Elmore Leonard Collection, USC.
5. Leonard, Alex, interview, April 6, 2023.
6. Leonard, Elmore, letter to Ruthann Finneran, May 24, 1944, USC.
7. Leonard, Elmore, letter to Ruthann Finneran, August 3, 1944, USC.
8. Leonard, Elmore, letter to Ruthann Finneran, August 10, 1944, USC.
9. Leonard, Elmore, letter to Ruthann Finneran, November 23, 1944, USC.
10. "Chronology."
11. "Seabee History: Formation of the Seabees and World War II," US Navy, Navy Department Library, Naval History and Heritage Command, July 1, 2014, https://www.history.navy.mil/library/online-reading-room/title-list-alphabetically/h/history-of-seabees/ww2.html.
12. Leonard, Elmore, letter to Ruthann Finneran, December 11, 1944, USC.
13. Leonard, Elmore, letter to Ruthann Finneran, January 5, 1945, USC.
14. Leonard, Elmore, letter to Ruthann Finneran, January 12, 1945, USC.
15. Leonard, Elmore, letter to Ruthann Finneran, February 24, 1945, USC.
16. Leonard, Elmore, letter to Ruthann Finneran, February 7, 1945, USC.
17. Leonard, Elmore, letter to Ruthann Finneran, March 19, 1945, USC.
18. Leonard, Elmore, letter to Ruthann Finneran, May 11, 1945, USC.
19. Leonard, Elmore, letter to Ruthann Finneran, April 24, 1945, USC.
20. Leonard, Elmore, letter to Ruthann Finneran, May 27, 1945, USC.
21. Leonard, Elmore, letter to Ruthann Finneran, September 10, 1945, USC.
22. Rzepka, Charles, "The Elmore Leonard Interviews," crimeculture.com/?page_id=3435.
23. Leonard, Elmore, letter to Ruthann Finneran, September 25, 1945, USC.
24. Leonard, Elmore, letter to Ruthann Finneran, October 13, 1945, USC.
25. Leonard, Elmore, letter to Ruthann Finneran, November 9, 1945, USC.
26. Vosbein, Terry, "Stan Kenton's Progressive Jazz," *All Things Kenton*, 2018; Steve Voce, "Pete Rugolo: Arranger Crucial to Both Miles Davis and Stan Kenton," *The Independent*, October 23, 2011.
27. Leonard, Elmore, letter to Ruthann Finneran, March 3, 1946, USC.

3. Aspirations and Traffic, 1946–1950

1. "Obituary—Joseph Anthony 'Joe' Madey," *Arkansas Democrat-Gazette*, January 14, 2003.
2. Leonard, Elmore, "University of Detroit, Report card, 1946–1949," USC.
3. "University History," University of Detroit Mercy, https://www.udmercy.edu/about/history.php.

4. "University of Detroit: A History: Timeline 1940–1949," University of Detroit Mercy, https://www.udmercy.libguides.com/c.php?g=751277&p=5381265.
5. Rzepka, Charles, "The Elmore Leonard Interviews," crimeculture.com/?page_id=3435.
6. Leonard, Elmore, "University of Detroit, Report card, 1946–1949," USC.
7. University of Detroit, Yearbook, 1949, USC.
8. Challen, *Get Dutch!*
9. Rzepka, "The Elmore Leonard Interviews."
10. Rzepka, "The Elmore Leonard Interviews."
11. Rzepka, "The Elmore Leonard Interviews."
12. Leonard, Elmore, "The Kitchen Inquisition," *Varsity News*, November 19, 1947, University of Detroit Collection.
13. Rzepka, "The Elmore Leonard Interviews."
14. Decker, Beverly, interview, September 7, 2022.
15. Decker, Beverly, interview, September 7, 2022.
16. Leonard, Elmore, "University of Detroit, Report card, 1946–1949," USC.
17. Rzepka, "The Elmore Leonard Interviews."
18. "Chronology," in Gregg Sutter, ed., *Elmore Leonard: Four Novels of the 1970s* (New York: Library of America, 2014).
19. Rzepka, "The Elmore Leonard Interviews."
20. Challen, *Get Dutch!*
21. Decker, Beverly, interview, September 7, 2022.
22. Rzepka, "The Elmore Leonard Interviews."
23. Challen, *Get Dutch!*
24. Rzepka, "The Elmore Leonard Interviews."
25. "Obituary—Joseph Anthony 'Joe' Madey," *Arkansas Democrat-Gazette*, January 14, 2003.
26. Challen, *Get Dutch!*
27. Leonard, Elmore, "University of Detroit, Report card, 1946–1949," USC.
28. "Chronology."
29. Decker, Beverly, interview, September 7, 2022.
30. Decker, Beverly, interview, September 7, 2022.
31. Devlin, James E., *Elmore Leonard*. Twayne's United States Author Series (New York: Twayne Publishers, 1999).
32. Rzepka, "The Elmore Leonard Interviews."
33. Decker, Beverly, interview, September 7, 2022.
34. Rzepka, "The Elmore Leonard Interviews."
35. "Elmore Leonard: An Interview," in Matthew J. Bruccoli and Richard Layman, eds., *The New Black Mask Quarterly* no. 2 (New York: Harvest/HBJ, 1985).
36. Rose, Peter, "Forgettable Films Make Career of a Writer Who's Almost Made It," *Arizona Republic*, June 20, 1982.
37. Prial, Frank J., "Elmore Leonard: It's No Crime to Talk Softly," *New York Times*, February 15, 1996.
38. Geherin, David, *Elmore Leonard*, Literature and Life (New York: Continuum, 1989).
39. Rzepka, "The Elmore Leonard Interviews."

4. Ad Men and the Arizona Territory, 1950–1952

1. Geherin, *Elmore Leonard.*
2. "A Detroiter Tells: How to Be an Author," *Detroit Free Press Roto Magazine*, January 24, 1954.
3. Whitehead, Jean, "Author's Wife Sees Movies as Research," *Detroit Times*, ca. January 1954.
4. Dudley, Katy, interview via email, August 14, 2023.
5. Sutter, Gregg, "A Conversation with Elmore Leonard," in *The Complete Western Stories of Elmore Leonard* (New York: Mariner Books, 2004).
6. "Elmore Leonard: An Interview," in Matthew J. Bruccoli and Richard Layman, eds., *The New Black Mask Quarterly* no. 2 (New York: Harvest/HBJ, 1985).
7. Bruccoli and Layman, "Elmore Leonard: An Interview."
8. Geherin, *Elmore Leonard.*
9. Shah, Diane, "For Elmore Leonard, Crime Pays," *Rolling Stone*, February 28, 1985; Devlin, James E., *Elmore Leonard.* Twayne's United States Author Series (New York: Twayne Publishers, 1999).
10. Leonard, Peter, foreword to Elmore Leonard, *Charlie Martz and Other Stories: The Unpublished Stories* (New York: William Morrow, 2015).
11. Whitehead, "Author's Wife Sees Movies as Research."
12. "A Conversation with Elmore Leonard."
13. Geherin, *Elmore Leonard.*
14. "A Conversation with Elmore Leonard."
15. Leonard, Elmore, "Red Hell Hits Canyon Diablo," *10 Story Western Magazine*, October 1952.
16. Bender, John, letter to Elmore Leonard, April 23, 1951, USC.
17. Rzepka, Charles, *Being Cool: The Work of Elmore Leonard* (Baltimore: Johns Hopkins University Press, 2013).
18. Ellsworth, Fanny, letter to Elmore Leonard, May 21, 1951, USC.
19. Rzepka, *Being Cool.*
20. Bender, John, "Copy of letter from *Argosy*," August 2, 1951, Elmore Leonard Collection, USC.
21. Bender, John, "Copy of letter from *Argosy*," August 17, 1951, Elmore Leonard Collection, USC.
22. Bender, John, letter to Elmore Leonard, October 16, 1951, USC.
23. Bender, John, letter to Elmore Leonard, December 27, 1951, USC.
24. O'Connell, James B., letter to Joseph Madey, December 14, 1951.
25. O'Connell, James B., letter to Joseph Madey, December 14, 1951.
26. Harper, Marguerite, letter to Elmore Leonard, November 20, 1951.
27. United States Census, 1910.
28. Cranwell-Deinert, Emily, interview, June 14, 2023.
29. United States Census, 1930.
30. Harper, Marguerite, letter to Elmore Leonard, November 29, 1951.
31. Harper, Marguerite, letter to Elmore Leonard, November 29, 1951.
32. Harper, Marguerite, letter to Elmore Leonard, December 12, 1951.
33. Challen, *Get Dutch!*

34. Sutter, Gregg, "A Conversation."
35. Leonard, Peter, interview, April 25, 2023.
36. Leonard, Bill, interview, February 15, 2023.
37. Dunn, Bill, "Dutch Treat," *Writer's Digest*, August 1982.

5. Advances and Advancement, 1952–1955

1. Harper, Marguerite, letter to Elmore Leonard, February 25, 1952.
2. Harper, Marguerite, letter to Elmore Leonard, May 14, 1952.
3. Harper, Marguerite, letter to Elmore Leonard, May 20, 1952.
4. Leonard, Elmore, "Ledger," USC.
5. Harper, Marguerite, letter to Elmore Leonard, August 28, 1952.
6. Harper, Marguerite, letter to Elmore Leonard, September 18, 1952.
7. Leonard, Elmore, "Three-Ten to Yuma," typescript with annotations, 1952, USC.
8. McGilligan, Patrick, "Interview with Elmore Leonard," *Film Comment*, March–April 1998.
9. Leonard, Elmore, "Three-Ten to Yuma," typescript, September 20, 1952, USC.
10. McGilligan, "Interview with Elmore Leonard."
11. Harper, Marguerite, letter to Elmore Leonard, April 11, 1952.
12. Harper, Marguerite, letter to Elmore Leonard, October 6, 1952.
13. Harper, Marguerite, letter to Elmore Leonard, October 30, 1952.
14. Roberts, Richard E., letter to Marguerite Harper, November 5, 1952.
15. Harper, Marguerite, letter to Elmore Leonard, October 30, 1952.
16. "A Detroiter Tells: How to Be an Author," *Detroit Free Press Roto Magazine*, January 24, 1954.
17. "A Detroiter Tells: How to Be an Author."
18. Harper, Marguerite, letter to Elmore Leonard, May 7, 1953.
19. Harper, Marguerite, letter to Elmore Leonard, May 15, 1953.
20. Harper, Marguerite, letter to Elmore Leonard, September 10, 1953.
21. "A Detroiter Tells: How to Be an Author."
22. Decker Rogers, Constance, letter to Elmore Leonard, October 1, 1953, USC.
23. Olney, Austin, letter to Elmore Leonard, October 30, 1953, USC.
24. Olney, Austin, letter to Elmore Leonard, November 2, 1953, USC.
25. Decker Rogers, Constance, letter to Elmore Leonard, November 2, 1953, USC.
26. Harper, Marguerite, letter to Elmore Leonard, November 5, 1953.
27. Harper, Marguerite, letter to Elmore Leonard, December 29, 1953.
28. Olney, Austin, letter to Elmore Leonard, December 16, 1953, USC.
29. Olney, Austin, letter to Elmore Leonard, January 8, 1954, USC.
30. Olney, Austin, letter to Elmore Leonard, January 15, 1954, USC.
31. Review of *The Bounty Hunters*, *Boston Globe*, January 24, 1954.
32. "Something Extra-special in Adventure," *Montgomery Advertiser*, January 31, 1954.
33. "Leonard's Western Is Lively Reading," *Hutchinson News-Herald*, February 21, 1954.
34. Birney, Hoffman, "Roundup on the Western Range," *New York Times*, April 11, 1954.
35. Challen, *Get Dutch!*
36. Sutter, Gregg, "Dutch," *Monthly Detroit*, August 1980.
37. Challen, *Get Dutch!*

38. Whitehead, Jean, "Author's Wife Sees Movies as Research," *Detroit Times*, ca. January 1954.
39. "A Detroiter Tells: How to Be an Author."
40. Olney, Austin, letter to Elmore Leonard, May 10, 1954, USC.
41. Olney, Austin, letter to Elmore Leonard, August 5, 1954, USC.
42. Olney, Austin, letter to Elmore Leonard, September 14, 1954, USC.
43. Olney, Austin, letter to Elmore Leonard, September 24, 1954, USC.
44. Devlin, James E., *Elmore Leonard*. Twayne's United States Author Series (New York: Twayne Publishers, 1999).
45. Leonard, Elmore, *The Law at Randado* (New York: Houghton Mifflin, 1955).
46. Sutter, Gregg, "A Conversation with Elmore Leonard," in *The Complete Western Stories of Elmore Leonard* (New York: Mariner Books, 2004).
47. McGilligan, Patrick, "Interview with Elmore Leonard," *Film Comment*, March–April 1998.
48. Leonard, Elmore, "Ledger," USC.
49. Harper, Marguerite, letter to Elmore Leonard, January 22, 1954.
50. Leonard, Elmore, *Malaya*, unproduced screenplay, 1954, USC.
51. Harper, Marguerite, letter to Elmore Leonard, November 5, 1954.
52. Harper, Marguerite, letter to Elmore Leonard, February 9, 1955.
53. Sanford, Nolan, "Leonard Comes Through in Another Top Western," *Houston Chronicle*, January 9, 1955.
54. Review of *The Law at Randado*, *Oakland Tribune*, February 13, 1955.
55. "Novelist, 29, Uses West as Set for Second Book," *Detroit Free Press*, ca. January–February 1955.
56. Olney, Austin, letter to Elmore Leonard, April 27, 1955, USC.
57. Harper, Marguerite, letter to Elmore Leonard, June 5, 1955.
58. Campbell-Ewald advertisement, *The New Yorker*, June 1955, USC.

6. Chevys and Hollywood, 1955–1961

1. Harper, Marguerite, letter to Elmore Leonard, June 17, 1955, USC.
2. Harper, Marguerite, letter to Elmore Leonard, August 22, 1955, USC.
3. Harper, Marguerite, letter to Elmore Leonard, August 29, 1955, USC.
4. Harper, Marguerite, letter to Elmore Leonard, October 26, 1955, USC.
5. Herbert, Hugh, "Detroit Spinner," *The Guardian*, October 1, 1988.
6. Steinbeck, John, *Sweet Thursday* (New York: Viking Press, 1954).
7. McCormick, Wilfred, "From Idea to Plot (With a Check List of Questions for All Writers of Fiction)," *Author & Journalist*, July 1955.
8. Geherin, *Elmore Leonard*.
9. Olney, Austin, letter to Elmore Leonard, September 14, 1955.
10. Jones, Malcolm, "For Elmore Leonard, Writing Is Hard, But It's Not Work," *St. Petersburg Times*, April 16, 1989.
11. "Elmore Leonard," in Dennis Wholey, *The Courage to Change: Personal Conversations About Alcoholism with Dennis Wholey* (New York: Houghton Mifflin, 1984).
12. Wootton, Adrian, "Elmore Leonard: 'I'm Glad I'm Not a Screenwriter. It Would Be So Frustrating,'" *British Film Institute* [*BFI*], 2006.

13. "*The Tall T* (1957)," American Film Institute, https://catalog.afi.com/Catalog/moviedetails/52387.
14. Harper, Marguerite, letter to Elmore Leonard, February 14, 1956, USC.
15. "Chronology," in Gregg Sutter, ed., *Elmore Leonard: Four Novels of the 1970s* (New York: Library of America, 2014).
16. Harper, Marguerite, letter to Elmore Leonard, May 17, 1956, USC.
17. Buerge, Hal, "Critics Okay Lathrup Author's Third Novel," *Birmingham Eccentric*, April 26, 1956.
18. "New Center Author Is Post First-Timer," *New Center News*, April 30, 1956.
19. Leonard, Elmore, *Last Stand at Saber River* (New York: Dell, 1959).
20. Harper, Marguerite, letter to Elmore Leonard, June 4, 1956, USC.
21. Challen, *Get Dutch!*
22. "Story of the Week: When Elmore Leonard, a 'Rising Young Writer of Western Novels,' Debuted (Sort Of) in *The New Yorker*," Library of America, May 3, 2018, https://www.loa.org/news-and-views/1410-flashback-when-elmore-leonard-a-rising-young-writer-of-western-novels-debuted-sort-of-in-the-new-yorker/.
23. Harper, Marguerite, letter to Elmore Leonard, October 30, 1956, USC.
24. Challen, *Get Dutch!*
25. Barrington, Lowell, "Moment of Vengeance," Prod. 817, *Schlitz Playhouse of the Stars*, 1956, USC.
26. Harper, Marguerite, letter to Elmore Leonard, November 8, 1956, USC.
27. "New Center Author Sells Rights to Movies," *New Center News*, April 29, 1957.
28. McGilligan, Patrick, "Interview with Elmore Leonard," *Film Comment*, March–April 1998.
29. Decker, Beverly, interview, September 7, 2022.
30. Leonard, Elmore, letter to Julien McKee, June 13, 1957.
31. McKee, Julien, letter to Elmore Leonard, June 19, 1957, USC.
32. Fine, Donald, letter to Elmore Leonard, July 8, 1957.
33. Harper, Marguerite, letter to Elmore Leonard, July 23, 1957, USC.
34. Beck, Henry Cabot, "3:10 to Yuma, on Track?" *True West*, October 1, 2007.
35. Harper, Marguerite, letter to Elmore Leonard, November 17, 1957, USC.
36. Leonard, Elmore, "The Bull Ring at Blisston," *Short Stories for Men Magazine*, August 1959.
37. Harper, Marguerite, letter to Elmore Leonard, November 17, 1957, USC.
38. Leonard, Elmore, letter to H. N. Swanson, December 16, 1957, courtesy of the Margaret Herrick Library.
39. Fine, Donald, letter to Elmore Leonard, January 2, 1958, USC.
40. Fine, Donald, letter to Elmore Leonard, January 16, 1958, USC.
41. Harper, Marguerite, letter to Elmore Leonard, January 24, 1958, USC.
42. Yagoda, Ben, "Elmore Leonard's Rogue's Gallery," *New York Times*, December 30, 1984.
43. Harper, Marguerite, letter to Elmore Leonard, March 17, 1958, USC.
44. Shah, Diane, "For Elmore Leonard, Crime Pays," *Rolling Stone*, February 28, 1985.
45. Geherin, *Elmore Leonard.*
46. Harper, Marguerite, letter to Elmore Leonard, April 30, 1958, USC.
47. Harper, Marguerite, letter to Elmore Leonard, June 30, 1958, USC.

48. "Leonard anticipated certain [cultural] shifts," said future crime fiction scholar Charles Rzepka. "He was on the ground floor as things moved towards the era of *The Searchers*, and giving the American Indian a voice in their own through representation—really turning a jaundiced eye on the history of extermination basically of the Aboriginal population in the United States especially from the 1870s throughout Andrew Jackson's policies right up to the present day. Leonard's right there, certainly with *Hombre*."
49. Harper, Marguerite, letter to Elmore Leonard, September 22, 1958, USC.
50. Fine, Donald, letter to Elmore Leonard, September 19, 1958, USC.
51. Fine, Donald, letter to Elmore Leonard, July 23, 1957, USC.
52. Leonard, Elmore, letter to H. N. Swanson, September 16, 1959, courtesy of the Margaret Herrick Library.
53. Swanson, H. N., letter to Elmore Leonard, October 2, 1959.
54. Harper, Marguerite, letter to Elmore Leonard, October 20, 1959, USC.
55. Goldstein, Richard, "W. C. Heinz, Writing Craftsman, Dies," *New York Times*, February 28, 2008.
56. Heinz, W. C., letter to Elmore Leonard, October 11, 1958, USC.
57. Harper, Marguerite, letter to Elmore Leonard, March 3, 1958, USC.
58. Leonard, Elmore, letter to Christopher Leonard, February 23, 1978, courtesy of the Christopher Leonard Collection.
59. Fine, Donald, letter to Marguerite Harper, October 26, 1959, USC.
60. Harper, Marguerite, letter to Elmore Leonard, December 8, 1959, USC.
61. Harper, Marguerite, letter to Elmore Leonard, May 27, 1960, USC.
62. Harper, Marguerite, letter to Elmore Leonard, March 17, 1961, USC.
63. Jones, Malcolm, "For Elmore Leonard, Writing Is Hard, But It's Not Work," *St. Petersburg Times*, April 16, 1989.

7. Bouncing, 1961–1970

1. Leonard, Peter, interview, April 25, 2023.
2. Leonard, Christopher, interview, September 2022.
3. Harper, Marguerite, letter to Elmore Leonard, April 1, 1961, USC.
4. Alexander, Geoff, "Elmore Leonard and Bill Deneen," Academic Film Archive of North America, https://afana.org/elmoreleonard.htm, December 2012.
5. Alexander, "Elmore Leonard and Bill Deneen."
6. Leonard, Peter, interview, May 26, 2023.
7. Leonard, Bill, interview, February 15, 2023.
8. Jones, Jane, interview, September 7, 2022.
9. LoCicero, T., ed., *Dutch on Dutch: One of the Last In-Depth Interviews with the Incomparable Elmore Leonard* (TLC Media, 2014).
10. Leonard, Christopher, interview, September 7, 2022.
11. Leonard, Elmore, advertisements, Hurst, ca. 1961–1962, USC.
12. Leonard, Elmore, letter to Marguerite Harper, May 31, 1966, USC.
13. Harper, Marguerite, letter to Elmore Leonard, October 31, 1961, USC.
14. Harper, Marguerite, letter to Elmore Leonard, January 26, 1962, USC.
15. Lupica, Mike, "St. Elmore's Fire," *Esquire*, April 1987.

16. Leonard, Elmore, and Jean W. Ross, "Elmore Leonard: An Interview," *Contemporary Authors New Revision Series*, vol. 28 (Gale, 1989).
17. Harper, Marguerite, letter to Elmore Leonard, November 30, 1963, USC.
18. Leonard, Elmore, "The Only Good Syrian Foot Soldier Is a Dead One," in *Charlie Martz and Other Stories: The Unpublished Stories* (New York: William Morrow, 2015).
19. Rose, Peter, "Forgettable Films Make Career of a Writer Who's Almost Made It," *Arizona Republic*, June 20, 1982; Wootton, Andrew, "Elmore Leonard: 'I'm Glad I'm Not a Screenwriter. It Would Be So Frustrating,'" British Film Institute [BFI], 2006.
20. Stevens, Dale, "The Suburbanite Who Writes Westerns," *Detroit News*, April 20, 1967.
21. Leonard, Elmore, letter to Marguerite Harper, May 31, 1966, USC.
22. Harper, Marguerite, letter to Elmore Leonard, June 9, 1966, USC.
23. Leonard, William, email to C. M. Kushins, May 29, 2023.
24. Leonard, Elmore, letter to Betty Ballantine, December 7, 1965.
25. Leonard, Elmore, letter to Donald Fine, August 2, 1966, USC.
26. Rzepka, Charles, "The Elmore Leonard Interviews," crimeculture.com/?page_id=3435.
27. Rzepka, "The Elmore Leonard Interviews."
28. Leonard, Elmore, *The Big Bounce* (Greenwich, CT: Fawcett Gold Medal, 1969).
29. Lupica, "St. Elmore's Fire."
30. Swanson, H. N., letter to Elmore Leonard, May 31, 1966.
31. Swanson, H. N., letter to Elmore Leonard, September 28, 1966.
32. Roberts, Richard E., letter to H. N. Swanson, November 4, 1966.
33. Swanson, H. N., letter to Elmore Leonard, January 3, 1967.
34. Swanson, H. N., letter to Elmore Leonard, January 23, 1967.
35. Stevens, Dale, "The Suburbanite Who Writes Westerns," *Detroit News*, April 20, 1967.
36. Swanson, H. N., letter to Elmore Leonard, July 25, 1966.
37. Hatch, Phyllis, Western Union telegram to Elmore Leonard, April 20, 1967, USC.
38. Harper, Marguerite, letter to Elmore Leonard, August 5, 1966.
39. Swanson, H. N., letter to Elmore Leonard, May 5, 1967, USC.
40. Swanson, H. N., letter to Elmore Leonard, May 9, 1967, USC.
41. Swanson, H. N., letter to Elmore Leonard, May 9, 1967, USC.
42. Lupica, "St. Elmore's Fire."
43. Krasny, Jill, "Elmore Leonard's Son on His Father's Work Ethic," *Esquire*, June 24, 2015.
44. Leonard, Christopher, interview, September 7, 2022.
45. Leonard, Christopher, interview, September 7, 2022.
46. Wootton, "Elmore Leonard: 'I'm Glad I'm Not a Screenwriter. It Would Be So Frustrating.'"
47. Swanson, H. N., letter to Elmore Leonard, September 12, 1967, USC.
48. Swanson, H. N., letter to Elmore Leonard, November 24, 1967, USC.
49. Wootton, "Elmore Leonard: 'I'm Glad I'm Not a Screenwriter. It Would Be So Frustrating.'"

50. Rhashalle, Janice, "Leonard's Law: An Interview with Elmore Leonard," *Emmy*, August 20, 2013 (originally published 2009).
51. Alexander, "Elmore Leonard and Bill Deneen."
52. "Chronology," in Gregg Sutter, ed., *Elmore Leonard: Four Novels of the 1970s* (New York: Library of America, 2014).
53. Devlin, James E., *Elmore Leonard*. Twayne's United States Author Series (New York: Twayne Publishers, 1999).
54. Leonard, Elmore, "The Broke-Leg War," outline, 1967, USC.
55. Leonard, "The Broke-Leg War."
56. Leonard, "The Broke-Leg War."
57. Swanson, H. N., letter to Elmore Leonard, January 29, 1968, USC.
58. Leonard, Elmore, "The Moonshine War"—research, ca. 1968–69, USC.
59. Swanson, H. N., letter to Elmore Leonard, September 25, 1968, USC.
60. Devlin, *Elmore Leonard*.
61. Herbert, Hugh, "Detroit Spinner," *The Guardian*, October 1, 1988.
62. Thomas, Kevin, "Patrick McGoohan—TV Spy Who Came Over for the Gold," *Los Angeles Times*, November 14, 1969.
63. Wootton, "Elmore Leonard: 'I'm Glad I'm Not a Screenwriter. It Would Be So Frustrating.'"
64. Swanson, H. N., letter to Elmore Leonard, March 18, 1968, USC.
65. Swanson, H. N., letter to Elmore Leonard, July 2, 1968, USC.
66. Swanson, H. N., letter to Elmore Leonard, August 22, 1968, USC.
67. Decker, Beverly, interview, September 7, 2022.
68. Leonard, Bill, interview, February 15, 2023.
69. Weiler, A. H., "Big Bounce Arrives," *New York Times*, March 6, 1969.
70. Swanson, H. N., letter to Elmore Leonard, February 14, 1969, USC.
71. Rose, Peter, "Forgettable Films Make Career of a Writer Who's Almost Made It," *Arizona Republic*, June 20, 1982.
72. Espen, Hal, "Rules of the Road, His Hard-Earned Lessons," *Los Angeles Times*, May 17, 2009.
73. Leonard, Elmore, "The Moonshine War"—research, ca. 1968–69, USC.
74. Kuebler, Harold, letter to Elmore Leonard, December 3, 1968, USC.
75. Swanson, H. N., letter to Elmore Leonard, January 22, 1970, USC.
76. May, Carl, "Characters Colorful in Moonshine Novel," *Nashville Tennessean*, July 13, 1969.
77. Fusco, Andrew G., review of *The Moonshine War*, *Dominion Post*, August 3, 1969.
78. Oates, Vivian, "A String of Successes for Leonard," *Birmingham Eccentric*, undated, ca. August 1969, USC.

8. On the Line in Hollywood, 1970–1971

1. "Elmore Leonard," in Dennis Wholey, *The Courage to Change: Personal Conversations About Alcoholism with Dennis Wholey* (New York: Houghton Mifflin, 1984).
2. Leonard, Elmore, letter to H. N. Swanson, January 15, 1970, courtesy of the Lilly Library, Indiana University.
3. Swanson, H. N., letter to Elmore Leonard, February 19, 1970, USC.

4. Swanson, H. N., letter to Elmore Leonard, March 5, 1970, USC.
5. Jaffe, Howard B., letter to Elmore Leonard, April 14, 1970, USC.
6. Leonard, Elmore, "*Picket Line*—Notes ('*See How They Run*')," undated, ca. 1969–70, USC.
7. Leonard, Elmore, "*Picket Line*—Notes," undated, ca. 1970, USC.
8. Leonard, Elmore, letter to H. N. Swanson, May 1, 1970, courtesy of the Lilly Library, Indiana University.
9. Leonard, William, interview, February 15, 2023.
10. Roberts, Oral, letter to Elmore Leonard, June 14, 1970, USC.
11. Leonard, Elmore, "*Jesus Saves*, treatment, typescript," June 1970, USC.
12. Rzepka, Charles, interview, February 26, 2022.
13. According to Leonard family interviews, for the name of Hill's amour, Leonard had, again, been cheeky in choosing as his inspiration an unlikely close family friend. "Louly was a friend of ours for many years," Beverly Decker later recalled. "I'd known her since she was a little girl—my very first date had been with her older brother when we were in the eighth grade. His mother drove us to the movies and Louly—whose real name was Louise—was three years old and rode with us in the backseat of the car. And she became a nun—Sister Louly—although then, she preferred 'Sister Louise.' And we stayed close friends for life." Daughter Jane Jones added, "We knew Sister Louly since we were children, and Dad helped sponsor her missions for the Maryknoll Sisters. She lived in Cambodia for years and did her missionary work there. I remember there were times when their money would run out and Dad would cut a check and she'd say, 'We wouldn't have our Order in Cambodia if it weren't for you.' Later on, he used her name as a gun moll in *The Hot Kid*—and she loved that." According to Christopher Leonard, his father's unpublicized philanthropy was something that reached back as far as his friendship with Franciscan brother Juvenal Carlson. He recalled, "Juvenal had taken a vow of poverty and I remember one time, he needed a car to drive all the way from Detroit to South America—so, Elmore just gave him a car. I remember asking him, 'Wait, you gave him the car?' And my dad said, 'Here's the thing—he needs a car. What am I going to do, give him half a car? No. Someone needs a car, you give him a car.' Dad would give anyone anything if they needed it . . . Later on, he sponsored a number of African children. He'd show us letters with their photos and names. He'd say, 'This is your new brother in Africa,' and just send something like twenty-five dollars a month to them for years."
14. Leonard, "*Jesus Saves*, treatment, typescript."
15. Leonard, Elmore, "Travel Journal and Itinerary," 1970, USC.
16. Swanson, H. N., letter to Elmore Leonard, June 8, 1970, USC.
17. Leonard, Elmore, "*Jesus Saves*, treatment, typescript."
18. MacLeod, Robert, letter to Elmore Leonard, May 20, 1970, USC.
19. Leonard, Elmore, letter to Howard Jaffe, July 12, 1970, USC.
20. Leonard, Elmore, "*Picket Line*—Treatment, corrected typescript," 1970, USC.
21. Leonard, Elmore, letter to Howard Jaffe, July 22, 1970, USC.
22. Leonard, Elmore, "*Picket Line*—screenplay, typescript," 1970, USC.
23. Leonard, Elmore, "*Picket Line*—screenplay, corrected typescript with manuscript notes and additions," 1970, USC.

24. Review of *The Moonshine War*, *San Francisco Examiner*, August 14, 1969.
25. Cuskelly, Richard, review of *The Moonshine War*, *Los Angeles Herald-Express*, undated, ca. June 1970.
26. "Mix in 'Moonshine War' Fails at B.O.," *Hollywood Reporter*, June 25, 1970.
27. Swanson, H. N., letter to Elmore Leonard, June 25, 1970, USC.
28. McGilligan, Patrick, "Elmore Leonard Interviewed," *Film Comment*, March–April 1998.
29. Swanson, H. N., letter to Elmore Leonard, August 11, 1970, USC.
30. Jaffe, Howard B., letter to Elmore Leonard, September 15, 1970, USC.
31. Leonard, Elmore, letter to H. N. Swanson, August 28, 1970, courtesy of the Lilly Library, Indiana University.
32. Swanson, H. N., letter to Elmore Leonard, September 4, 1970, USC.
33. Swanson, H. N., letter to Elmore Leonard, September 11, 1970, USC.

9. A Nifty Guy at Loose Ends, 1971–1972

1. "Elmore Leonard," in Dennis Wholey, *The Courage to Change: Personal Conversations About Alcoholism with Dennis Wholey* (New York: Houghton Mifflin, 1984).
2. Swanson, H. N., letter to Elmore Leonard, October 5, 1971, courtesy of the Lilly Library, Indiana University.
3. "Elmore Leonard," in Wholey, *The Courage to Change*.
4. Swanson, H. N., letter to Elmore Leonard, January 18, 1971, courtesy of the Lilly Library, Indiana University.
5. Leonard, Elmore, letter to H. N. Swanson, January 29, 1971, courtesy of the Lilly Library, Indiana University.
6. Leonard, Peter, interview, May 26, 2023.
7. DeLorean, John, interview with Gerry Kelly, UTV, 1996.
8. Kibbee, Roland, letter to H. N. Swanson, February 3, 1971.
9. Cannon, Bettie, "Our Resident Writer of Violent Films Is a Quiet Guy Who Likes to Hear Guns Go Off . . . On the Screen," *Detroit Free Press*, February 7, 1971.
10. Leonard, Elmore, "*Joe Kidd*—Treatment (as *Sinola*), typescript," 1971, USC.
11. Eliot, Marc, *American Rebel: The Life of Clint Eastwood* (New York: Harmony Books, 2009).
12. *Joe Kidd* (as *Sinola*), purchase agreement, March 8, 1971, USC.
13. "*Joe Kidd*—Announcement," *Variety*, April 7, 1971.
14. Barnard, Ken, review of *Valdez Is Coming*, *Detroit News*, undated, ca. April 1971.
15. Kanfer, Stefan, "Burt Force," *Time*, April 26, 1971.
16. Eichelbaum, Stanley, review of *Valdez Is Coming*, *San Francisco Examiner*, undated, ca. April 1971.
17. McGilligan, Patrick, "Elmore Leonard Interviewed," *Film Comment*, March–April 1998.
18. McGilligan, "Elmore Leonard Interviewed."
19. Beckerman, Sidney, letter to Elmore Leonard, undated, ca. 1971, USC.
20. "*Joe Kidd*—Update," *Hollywood Reporter*, October 29, 1971.
21. Leonard, Elmore, "*Joe Kidd*—Final screenplay, revised typescript," September 15, 1971, USC.

22. McGilligan, "Elmore Leonard Interviewed."
23. Leonard, Elmore, letter to H. N. Swanson, August 31, 1971, courtesy of the Lilly Library, Indiana University.
24. Leonard, Elmore, "*American Flag*—Screenplay, summary, corrected typescript," undated, ca. 1970, USC.
25. Leonard, Elmore, letter to H. N. Swanson, October 1, 1971, courtesy of the Lilly Library, Indiana University.
26. Terrill, Marshall, *Steve McQueen: Portrait of an American Rebel* (New York: Donald I. Fine, 1994).
27. Leonard, Elmore, letter to Patrick Kelly, October 26, 1971, USC.
28. "Elmore Leonard," in Wholey, *The Courage to Change*.
29. Leonard, Elmore, letter to Patrick Kelly, October 26, 1971, USC.
30. Leonard, Elmore, letter to H. N. Swanson, October 6, 1971, courtesy of the Lilly Library, Indiana University.
31. "*Joe Kidd*—Update," *Hollywood Reporter*, December 17, 1971.
32. Leonard, Peter, "Elmore Leonard Remembered by Peter Leonard," *The Guardian*, December 13, 2013.
33. McGilligan, "Elmore Leonard Interviewed."
34. Leonard, Elmore, "*Joe Doran Is a Dead Man*—typescript," February 4, 1972, USC.
35. Leonard, Elmore, letter to Clint Eastwood, March 7, 1972, courtesy of the Lilly Library, Indiana University.
36. McGilligan, "Elmore Leonard Interviewed."

10. Birth of the Cool, 1972–1974

1. Leonard, Elmore, Introduction to *The Friends of Eddie Coyle*, by George V. Higgins (Henry Holt and Company, 2000).
2. Mirisch, Walter, *I Thought We Were Making Movies, Not History* (Madison, WI: University of Wisconsin Press, 2008).
3. Leonard, Elmore, letter to H. N. Swanson, February 25, 1972, courtesy of the Lilly Library, Indiana University.
4. Sutter, Gregg, "Dutch," *Monthly Detroit*, August 1980.
5. Leonard, Elmore, letter to H. N. Swanson, March 10, 1972, courtesy of the Lilly Library, Indiana University.
6. Leonard, Elmore, letter to H. N. Swanson, April 14, 1972, courtesy of the Lilly Library, Indiana University.
7. Purcell, Lee, interview, April 15, 2023.
8. Schrader, Paul, "Memorandum: 'Synopsis' of *American Flag* for Columbia Pictures," July 26, 1972, USC.
9. Leonard, Elmore, letter to H. N. Swanson, November 25, 1972, courtesy of the Lilly Library, Indiana University.
10. May, Anthony, "Interview with Elmore Leonard," *Contrappasso Magazine*, December 2012.
11. "Elmore Leonard: An Interview," in Matthew J. Bruccoli and Richard Layman, eds., *The New Black Mask Quarterly* no. 2 (New York: Harvest/HBJ, 1985).

12. Leonard, Elmore, letter to H. N. Swanson, February 12, 1973, courtesy of the Lilly Library, Indiana University.
13. Leonard, Elmore, letter to H. N. Swanson, April 13, 1973, courtesy of the Lilly Library, Indiana University.
14. Farber, Jackie, interview, November 25, 2023.
15. Farber, Jackie, letter to Elmore Leonard, June 28, 1973.
16. Barry, Philip, letter to Elmore Leonard, September 11, 1973, USC.
17. Mirisch, *I Thought We Were Making Movies, Not History*.
18. Callendar, Newgate, "Criminals at Large," *New York Times*, June 23, 1974.
19. Dunn, Bill, "Dutch Treat," *Writer's Digest*, August 1982.
20. Shah, Diane, "For Elmore Leonard, Crime Pays," *Rolling Stone*, February 28, 1985.
21. Leonard, Elmore, *Notebooks* (Northridge, CA: Lord John Press, 1991).
22. Leonard, William, email to C. M. Kushins, September 28, 2023.
23. Goodman, Ellen, letter to Elmore Leonard, *Detroit Free Press*, undated, ca. 1971–72, USC.
24. "Elmore Leonard," in Dennis Wholey, *The Courage to Change: Personal Conversations About Alcoholism with Dennis Wholey* (New York: Houghton Mifflin, 1984).
25. "Chronology," in Gregg Sutter, ed., *Elmore Leonard: Four Novels of the 1970s* (New York: Library of America, 2014).
26. Alcoholics Anonymous, *Twenty-Four Hours a Day*, March 1974.
27. Leonard, Peter, "Traveling with Elmore," Peter Leonard Books, 2009, http://www.peterleonardbooks.com/traveling-with-elmore.
28. Mirisch, *I Thought We Were Making Movies, Not History*.
29. Eliot, Marc, *Steve McQueen: A Biography* (New York: Crown Archetype, 2011); Marshall Terrill, *Steve McQueen: Portrait of an American Rebel* (New York: Donald I. Fine, 1993).
30. Douglas, Kirk, letter to Elmore Leonard, November 1, 1973, USC.
31. Leonard, Elmore, letter to Kirk Douglas, November 29, 1973, courtesy of the Lilly Library, Indiana University.
32. Leonard, Elmore, letter to H. N. Swanson, November 29, 1973, courtesy of the Lilly Library, Indiana University.

11. Nourishing the Lord of Life, 1975–1977

1. Leonard, Elmore, letter to Christopher Leonard, January 28, 1974, courtesy of the Christopher Leonard Collection.
2. Kelly [Sargent], Betty, letter to Elmore Leonard, November 8, 1974, USC.
3. Sargent, Betty, interview, January 20, 2023.
4. Leonard, Elmore, "*Swag*—outline," undated, ca. 1974, USC.
5. Leonard, "*Swag*—outline."
6. Griffith, John, "Police Hired by Hudson's," *Detroit Free Press*, December 3, 1966; John Griffith, "Ex-Convict Held in Knife Slaying of Hudson Clerk," *Detroit Free Press*, December 9, 1966.
7. Leonard, Elmore, *Swag* (New York: Delacorte Press, 1976).
8. "Chronology," in Gregg Sutter, ed., *Elmore Leonard: Four Novels of the 1970s* (New York: Library of America, 2014).

9. Kelly [Sargent], Betty, letter to Elmore Leonard, July 1, 1975, USC.
10. Sargent, Betty, interview, January 20, 2023.
11. "Notes," in Sutter, ed., *Elmore Leonard: Four Novels of the 1970s*.
12. Kelly [Sargent], Betty, letter to Elmore Leonard, September 21, 1976, USC.
13. Talbert, Bob, review of *Swag*, *Detroit Free Press*, March 12, 1976, USC.
14. Review of *Swag*, *The New Yorker*, May 31, 1976.
15. Willeford, Charles, review of *Swag*, *Miami Herald*, April 18, 1976, USC.
16. "Notes."
17. Decker, Beverly, interview, September 8, 2022.
18. Leonard, Peter, interview, May 26, 2023.
19. Leonard, Bill, interview, February 15, 2023.
20. Leonard family, roundtable interview, September 8, 2022.
21. Leonard, Bill, interview, February 15, 2023.
22. "Elmore Leonard," in Dennis Wholey, *The Courage to Change: Personal Conversations About Alcoholism with Dennis Wholey* (New York: Houghton Mifflin, 1984).
23. Leonard, Elmore, "*Fifty-Two Pickup*—Israeli notebook," 1975, USC.
24. Leonard, Elmore, "*Fifty-Two Pickup*—'Israeli Version,'" 1975, USC.
25. "Notes."
26. Leonard, Elmore, letter to H. N. Swanson, August 5, 1976, courtesy of the Lilly Library, Indiana University.
27. Leonard, Elmore, letter to H. N. Swanson, May 10, 1977, courtesy of the Lilly Library, Indiana University.
28. Sutter, Gregg, "*The Hawkbill Gang*—Notes," undated, USC.
29. "Elmore Leonard," in Wholey, *The Courage to Change*.
30. Leonard, Elmore, "*Unknown Man No. 89*—Research materials," ca. 1975–76, USC.
31. Leonard, Elmore, "*Unknown Man No. 89*—early draft," ca. 1976, USC.
32. Leonard, Elmore, *Unknown Man No. 89* (New York: Delacorte Press, 1977).
33. Leonard, Tim, interview, April 7, 2023.
34. Leonard, Elmore, letter to Christopher Leonard, October 17, 1976, courtesy of the Christopher Leonard Collection. In his excellent academic study of Leonard's life and career, *Being Cool: The Work of Elmore Leonard* (Baltimore: Johns Hopkins University Press, 2013), Professor Charles J. Rzepka makes a strong case for Leonard having inadvertently tapped into a positive psychological state referred to as "Flow." In laymen's terms, this concept, developed by psychologist Mihaly Csikszentmihalyi in 1970, can be described as being "in the zone"—a state of intense and natural focus set upon a given task, almost to the point of exhalation or a form of spiritual transcendence. Coincidentally, the practice of "Flow" is also an ancient Chinese concept within the framework of Taoist philosophy, Wu Wei—which translates to "effortless action" or "not trying," both accurate descriptions of Leonard's postsober approaches to his fiction and personal beliefs. The concept is typified in the Zhuangzi Taoist text from which this chapter takes its name.
35. Callendar, Newgate, "Decent Men in Trouble," *New York Times*, May 22, 1977.
36. Rose, Peter, "Forgettable Films Make Career of a Writer Who's Almost Made It," *Arizona Republic*, June 20, 1982.
37. Leonard, Elmore, letter to H. N. Swanson, April 29, 1977, courtesy of the Lilly Library, Indiana University.

38. Krasny, Jill, "Elmore Leonard's Son on His Father's Work Ethic," *Esquire*, June 24, 2015.
39. Leonard, Elmore, "*The Hunted*—Research," ca. 1976, USC.
40. Leonard, "*The Hunted*—Research."
41. Graham, Fred, "The Alias Program: The Incredible Rise and Downfall of a Mafia Witness," *New York*, January 19, 1976.
42. Leonard, Elmore, *The Hunted* (New York: Dell, 1977).
43. Wootton, Andrew, "Elmore Leonard: 'I'm Glad I'm Not a Screenwriter. It Would Be So Frustrating,'" British Film Institute [BFI], 2006.
44. "Chronology."
45. Ogorek, Michael, "Elmore Leonard: Fast Fiction," *Birmingham Patriot*, September 22, 1976.
46. Leonard, Peter, interview, April 25, 2023.
47. Leonard, Elmore, letter to H. N. Swanson, November 20, 1976, courtesy of the Lilly Library, Indiana University.
48. Bar Am, Zohar, letter to Elmore Leonard, August 23, 1976, USC.
49. Leonard, Elmore, letter to H. N. Swanson, August 18, 1977, courtesy of the Lilly Library, Indiana University.
50. Swanson, H. N., letter to Elmore Leonard, "draft," undated, ca. 1976, courtesy of the Lilly Library, Indiana University.
51. Leonard and Ross, "Interview with Elmore Leonard," *Contemporary Authors*.
52. McGilligan, Patrick, "Elmore Leonard Interviewed," *Film Comment*, March–April 1998.
53. Leonard, Elmore, letter to H. N. Swanson, December 27, 1976, courtesy of the Lilly Library, Indiana University.
54. Swanson, H. N., letter to Elmore Leonard, January 11, 1977, courtesy of the Lilly Library, Indiana University.
55. "Elmore Leonard," in Wholey, *The Courage to Change*.
56. Lukas, J. Anthony, "Elmore Leonard: Under the Boardwalk," *GQ*, December 1984.
57. Lupica, Mike, "St. Elmore's Fire," *Esquire*, April 1987.

12. Dutch Free, 1977–1979

1. "Elmore Leonard," in Dennis Wholey, *The Courage to Change: Personal Conversations About Alcoholism with Dennis Wholey* (New York: Houghton Mifflin, 1984).
2. Leonard, Elmore, letter to H. N. Swanson, June 2, 1977, courtesy of the Lilly Library, Indiana University.
3. Leonard, Elmore, letter to H. N. Swanson, June 2, 1977, courtesy of the Lilly Library, Indiana University.
4. Sargent, Betty, letter to Elmore Leonard, June 24, 1977, USC.
5. Sargent, Betty, interview, January 20, 2023.
6. Fisher, Emily, "Tennis Mom: Overseeing Child's Game Becomes Her Career," *Detroit Free Press*, August 29, 1976.
7. "The Nation: Neo-Nazi Groups: Artifacts of Hate," *Time*, February 28, 1977.
8. Drew, Lisa, letter to H. N. Swanson, July 6, 1977, USC.
9. Dienstfrey, Harris, letter to H. N. Swanson, September 27, 1977, USC.

10. Applebaum, Stuart, letter to Elmore Leonard, February 28, 1978, USC.
11. "Chronology," in Gregg Sutter, ed., *Elmore Leonard: Four Novels of the 1970s* (New York: Library of America, 2014).
12. Leonard, Elmore, letter to Marc Jaffe, July 20, 1978, USC.
13. Leonard, Elmore, letter to H. N. Swanson, undated, ca. 1977–78, USC.
14. Lupica, Mike, "St. Elmore's Fire," *Esquire*, April 1987.
15. Trost, Cathy, "Behind Every Hit Record in Motor City, There's a Nick Stream," *Detroit Free Press*, May 29, 1977.
16. Leonard, Elmore, letter to H. N. Swanson, July 7, 1977, courtesy of the Lilly Library, Indiana University.
17. Archdiocese of Detroit, Tribunal, letter to Elmore Leonard, September 13, 1977.
18. Koltz, Tony, letter to Elmore Leonard, February 1, 1978, USC.
19. Rosenthal, T. G., letter to Elmore Leonard, February 2, 1978, USC.
20. Leonard, Elmore, letter to Christopher Leonard, February 23, 1978, courtesy of the Christopher Leonard Collection.
21. "Chronology."
22. Carlson, Fr. Juvenal, letter to Elmore Leonard, August 4, 1978, USC.
23. Florence, Heather Grant, letter to Elmore Leonard, September 28, 1982, USC.
24. "Chronology."
25. Leonard, Elmore, letter to H. N. Swanson, October 21, 1977, courtesy of the Lilly Library, Indiana University.
26. Wootton, Andrew, "Elmore Leonard: 'I'm Glad I'm Not a Screenwriter. It Would Be So Frustrating,'" British Film Institute [BFI], 2006.
27. Mortimer, Lee, "Underworld Confidential: Virginia Hill's Success Secrets," *American Mercury*, June 1951.
28. Marshall, William, letter to Elmore Leonard, January 23, 1978, USC.
29. Leonard, Elmore, letter to Christopher Leonard, March 8, 1978, courtesy of the Christopher Leonard Collection.
30. Leonard, Elmore, letter to Christopher Leonard, April 1, 1978, courtesy of the Christopher Leonard Collection.
31. Leonard, Elmore, letter to Christopher Leonard, April 1, 1978, courtesy of the Christopher Leonard Collection.
32. "Elmore Leonard: An Interview," in Matthew J. Bruccoli and Richard Layman, eds., *The New Black Mask Quarterly* no. 2 (New York: Harvest/HBJ, 1985).
33. Leonard, Elmore, letter to Marc Jaffe, July 20, 1978, USC.
34. Leonard, Elmore, letter to Christopher Leonard, April 6, 1978, courtesy of the Christopher Leonard Collection.
35. Leonard, Elmore, letter to Christopher Leonard, May 22, 1978, courtesy of the Christopher Leonard Collection.
36. Devlin, James E., *Elmore Leonard*. Twayne's United States Author Series (New York: Twayne Publishers, 1999).
37. Leonard, Elmore, letter to H. N. Swanson, December 30, 1978, courtesy of the Lilly Library, Indiana University
38. Leonard, Elmore, letter to Marc Jaffe, July 20, 1978, USC.
39. Leonard, Elmore, letter to Marc Jaffe, July 20, 1978, USC.
40. "Chronology."

41. Leonard, Elmore, letter to Christopher Leonard, August 9, 1978, courtesy of the Christopher Leonard Collection.
42. Sutter, Gregg, "Dutch," *Monthly Detroit*, August 1980.
43. "Elmore Leonard: An Interview."
44. Rhashalle, Janice, "Leonard's Law: An Interview with Elmore Leonard," *Emmy*, August 20, 2013.
45. Leonard, Elmore, letter to H. N. Swanson, December 30, 1978.
46. Leonard, Elmore, "No More Mr. Nice" press release, undated, ca. 1979, courtesy of the Lilly Library, Indiana University.
47. Nadel, Gerry, "Who Owns Prime Time? The Threat of the 'Occasional' Networks," *New York*, May 30, 1977.
48. Leonard, Elmore, letter to Christopher Leonard, November 23, 1978, courtesy of the Christopher Leonard Collection.
49. Leonard, Elmore, letter to Christopher Leonard, February 22, 1979, courtesy of the Christopher Leonard Collection.
50. Leonard, Elmore, letter to Christopher Leonard, March 23, 1979, courtesy of the Christopher Leonard Collection.
51. Leonard, Peter, interview, May 26, 2023.
52. Shah, Diane, "For Elmore Leonard, Crime Pays," *Rolling Stone*, February 28, 1985.

13. High Noon in Detroit, 1980–1982

1. Jones, Jane, interview, September 7, 2022.
2. Belmont, Shannon, interview, March 4, 2024.
3. Jones, Jane, interview, September 7, 2022.
4. Dudley, Katy, interview, September 7, 2022.
5. Leonard, Peter, interview, April 25, 2023.
6. Leonard, Christopher, interview, September 7, 2022. Decades later, Peter's daughter, Kate, would be initiated into the unofficial "club," not only brandishing a fake ID much like her grandfather's, but suffering a similar fate due to its use. "I guess troublemaking is in my blood—but I only got in real trouble one time," she recalled. "I was nineteen and going to Michigan State, and I had a fake ID that said my name was Jamie Murray-Langer, I was from Colorado, and I was five foot eleven. So, I'd purposely wear tall shoes when I'd go out to bars and use it. Well, I was out with my friend and, as we're waiting in line to get inside, a cop came right up to me and asked to see my ID. I was so confident when I handed it to him and was proud that I could name the zip code and my astrological sign and all the tricky questions I knew he could ask. But I got arrested anyway and he took me to the East Lansing Police Department. They asked if I wanted to call anyone and I said, 'No,' and they sent me to sit on a mat in the cell. I slept the whole time while there were all these women around me crying, some freaking out. In the morning, they made me breathe into the Breathalyzer because I had refused the night before, but I still blew numbers and was still in trouble. I bailed myself out and my neighbor gave me a lift home. And my mom was so pissed at me. She said, 'You have to call your dad right now and tell him what happened.' So I did—I called Peter and told him I'd spent the night in jail. And he said, 'Welcome to the club.'" Kate added, "We went out to dinner that

night and as soon as we sat down, I'm immediately served wine. And Elmore just keeps asking me questions, like just loving that I'd gotten arrested. Then he, my dad, and I all ordered the same thing, but my mom ordered something else. And Elmore said to her, 'Well, you didn't get arrested,' like we were in this *actual* little club."

7. Leonard, Peter, interview, May 26, 2023.
8. Leonard, Elmore, letter to H. N. Swanson, January 24, 1980, courtesy of the Lilly Library, Indiana University.
9. Applebaum, Irwyn, letter to Elmore Leonard, August 24, 1979, USC.
10. Smith, Dinitia, "Donald Fine, 75, Publisher of Suspenseful Best Sellers," *New York Times*, August 16, 1997.
11. "Elmore Leonard: An Interview," in Matthew J. Bruccoli and Richard Layman, eds., *The New Black Mask Quarterly* no. 2 (New York: Harvest/HBJ, 1985).
12. Leonard, Elmore, letter to Christopher Leonard, January 31, 1980, courtesy of the Christopher Leonard Collection.
13. Wilkinson, Alec, "Elmore's Legs," *The New Yorker*, September 30, 1996; "An Interview with Gregg Sutter on Elmore Leonard's 'Dialogue-Driven Crime Novels with an Emphasis on Character,'" Library of America, *Reader's Almanac* (blog), August 25, 2014, https://blog.loa.org/2014/08/an-interview-with-gregg-sutter-on.html.
14. "*City Primeval*—Notes," in Gregg Sutter, ed., *Elmore Leonard: Four Novels of the 1980s* (New York: Library of America, 2014).
15. Leonard, Elmore, letter to Christopher Leonard, May 14, 1980, courtesy of the Christopher Leonard Collection.
16. Grant, Hank, "Rambling Reporter," *Hollywood Reporter*, May 22, 1980.
17. Grant, Hank, "Rambling Reporter," *Hollywood Reporter*, June 3, 1980.
18. Leonard, Elmore, letter to Christopher Leonard, March 31, 1981, courtesy of the Christopher Leonard Collection.
19. Leonard, Elmore, "*City Primeval*—Meeting notes," March 11, 1981, USC.
20. Leonard, Elmore, letter to Christopher Leonard, May 14, 1981, courtesy of the Christopher Leonard Collection.
21. Leonard, Elmore, letter to Christopher Leonard, April 20, 1981, courtesy of the Christopher Leonard Collection.
22. "*City Primeval*—Notes."
23. Cook, Bruce, review of *City Primeval*, *Detroit News*, undated, ca. 1980.
24. "*City Primeval*—ad, via Arbor House," undated, ca. 1980, USC.
25. Leonard, Elmore, letter to Christopher Leonard, April 20, 1981, courtesy of the Christopher Leonard Collection.
26. Leonard, Elmore, letter to H. N. Swanson, April 10, 1981, courtesy of the Lilly Library, Indiana University.
27. Leonard, Elmore, letter to Christopher Leonard, July 7, 1981, courtesy of the Christopher Leonard Collection.
28. Leonard, Elmore, letter to Christopher Leonard, July 14, 1981, courtesy of the Christopher Leonard Collection.
29. Dunn, Bill, "Dutch Treat," *Writer's Digest*, August 1982.
30. Leonard, Elmore, letter to Shane O'Neil, November 21, 1979, USC.
31. Leonard, Elmore, letter to C. Robert Manby, undated, ca. 1981, USC.

32. Leonard, Elmore, letter to Christopher Leonard, November 8, 1980, courtesy of the Christopher Leonard Collection.
33. Leonard, Elmore, letter to Christopher Leonard, January 29, 1981, courtesy of the Christopher Leonard Collection.
34. Leonard, Elmore, *Appearances: A Proposal on Domestic Violence*, script, March 10, 1980.
35. Obstfeld, Raymond, "Paper Crimes," *Armchair Detective*, Summer 1983.
36. Leonard, Elmore, letter to Christopher Leonard, November 19, 1981, courtesy of the Christopher Leonard Collection.
37. Rose, Peter, "Forgettable Films Make Career of a Writer Who's Almost Made It," *Arizona Republic*, June 20, 1982.
38. Mills, Bart, "This Star Hates What They've Done to Travis McGee," *Philadelphia Inquirer*, May 18, 1983.
39. Leonard, Elmore, letter to H. N. Swanson, September 31, 1981, courtesy of the Lilly Library, Indiana University.
40. Leonard, Elmore, "Dope: George Moran," typescript, undated, ca. summer 1980, USC.
41. Leonard, Elmore, letter to Christopher Leonard, August 7, 1981, courtesy of the Christopher Leonard Collection.
42. Leonard, Elmore, letter to Christopher Leonard, January 3, 1981, courtesy of the Christopher Leonard Collection.
43. Wilkinson, Alec, "Elmore's Legs," *The New Yorker*, September 30, 1996.
44. Leonard, Elmore, letter to Christopher Leonard, November 2, 1981, courtesy of the Christopher Leonard Collection.
45. Leonard, Elmore, "*Cat Chaser*—Research," ca. 1981–82, USC.
46. Leonard, Elmore, letter to Christopher Leonard, November 2, 1981, courtesy of the Christopher Leonard Collection.
47. "U.S. Steps into the Dominican Crossfire," *Life*, May 7, 1965.
48. For background, Sutter had provided Leonard with articles including: "Caribbean Crusade" (*Christianity Today*); "Border Strife in Hispaniola" (*The Nation*, November 27, 1976); "Dominican Republic, Inc." (by Fr. Joseph Mulligan, *National Geographic*, October 1977); and "The Dominican Republic—An Undiscovered Land" (*Black Enterprise*, January 1980).
49. Leonard, Elmore, "*Cat Chaser*—Research."
50. Leonard, Elmore, letter to Christopher Leonard, December 28, 1981, courtesy of the Christopher Leonard Collection.
51. Leonard, Elmore, letter to H. N. Swanson, August 26, 1981, courtesy of the Lilly Library, Indiana University.
52. MacDonald, John D., letter to Donald Fine, April 25, 1982, USC.
53. MacDonald, John D., letter to Elmore Leonard, May 10, 1982, USC.
54. "*Cat Chaser*—advertisement," *New York Times*, June 13, 1982, USC.
55. Leonard, John, "Books of the Times," *New York Times*, June 11, 1982.
56. "Mystery and Crime," *The New Yorker*, July 12, 1982.
57. Willeford, Charles, "Book Reviews," *Miami Herald*, August 29, 1982.
58. Rose, Peter, "Forgettable Films Make Career of a Writer Who's Almost Made It," *Arizona Republic*, June 20, 1982.

59. Cybulski, Tom, "'You Got to Read a Lot,' to Learn to Write Like an Author," *Detroit Free Press*, October 28, 1982.

14. Dickens Rising, 1982–1985

1. Rose, Peter, "Forgettable Films Make Career of a Writer Who's Almost Made It," *Arizona Republic*, June 20, 1982.
2. Yagoda, Ben, "Elmore Leonard's Rogue's Gallery," *New York Times*, December 30, 1984.
3. Leonard, Elmore, letter to Christopher Leonard, March 20, 1982, courtesy of the Christopher Leonard Collection.
4. "The War over Corporate Fraud," *Dun's Review*, November 1974.
5. Leonard, Elmore, "*Stick*—Research, cons & frauds, clippings, 1972–1982," USC.
6. "Women and the Executive Suite," *Newsweek*, September 14, 1981; "Women: The New Venture Capitalists," *Business Week*, November 2, 1981.
7. Sachs, Lloyd, "Elmore Leonard: Big Noise from a New 'Stick'?" *Chicago-Sun Times*, December 26, 1982.
8. Leonard, Elmore, letter to Christopher Leonard, July 21, 1982, courtesy of the Christopher Leonard Collection.
9. Fine, Donald, letter to H. N. Swanson, August 25, 1982, USC.
10. Yagoda, "Elmore Leonard's Rogue's Gallery."
11. *The Washington Post*'s Jonathan Yardley would prominently make this connection in his own review, stating, "Stick, as he re-enters [civilian life] . . . is a man adjusting; Leonard has Jack Henry Abbott firmly in mind as he depicts Stick's attempts to relearn the rules of the world outside" [*Washington Book World*, February 20, 1983].
12. Grant, Hank, "Rambling Reporter," *Hollywood Reporter*, March 31, 1983; Hank Grant, "Rambling Reporter," *Hollywood Reporter*, February 8, 1983.
13. Leonard, Elmore, letter to Christopher Leonard, January 22, 1983, courtesy of the Christopher Leonard Collection.
14. Yardley, Jonathan, "Elmore Leonard: Making Crime Pay in Miami," *Washington Post Book World*, February 20, 1983.
15. "A Plot Just Right for a Burt Reynolds Romp," *Daytona Beach News-Journal*, February 6, 1983.
16. Leonard, Elmore, letter to Christopher Leonard, March 25, 1983, courtesy of the Christopher Leonard Collection.
17. McDowell, Edwin, "Donald Fine Is Dismissed as Arbor House Publisher," *New York Times*, October 26, 1983.
18. Kelley, Bill, "Burt Reynolds to Shoot Film in South Florida," *South Florida Sun-Sentinel*, August 11, 1983.
19. Leonard, Christopher, interview, September 7, 2022.
20. Leonard, Bill, interview, February 15, 2023.
21. Shah, Diane, "For Elmore Leonard, Crime Pays," *Rolling Stone*, February 28, 1985.
22. Leonard, Elmore, letter to Burt Reynolds, June 12, 1984, courtesy of the Lilly Library, Indiana University.

23. Leonard, Elmore, letter to H. N. Swanson, June 22, 1984, courtesy of the Lilly Library, Indiana University.
24. Lupica, Mike, "St. Elmore's Fire," *Esquire*, April 1987.
25. Mitchell, Sean, "Stick Wars in Hollywood," *Los Angeles Herald Examiner*, April 26, 1985.
26. Leonard, Bill, interview, February 15, 2023.
27. Maslin, Janet, "The Screen: *Stick*, with Burt Reynolds," *New York Times*, April 26, 1985.
28. Byrge, Duane, review of *Stick, Hollywood Reporter*, April 26, 1985.
29. "Yeah, but Weren't the Costumes Great?" *Daily News*, December 5, 1984.
30. Nathan, Paul S., "Rights and Permissions: Elmore Leonard Auction," *Publishers Weekly*, September 2, 1983.
31. Leonard, Elmore, letter to H. N. Swanson, November 25, 1983, courtesy of the Lilly Library, Indiana University.
32. Mirisch, Walter, *I Thought We Were Making Movies, Not History* (Madison, WI: University of Wisconsin Press, 2008).
33. Sachs, "Elmore Leonard: Big Noise from a New 'Stick'?"
34. Cook, Bruce, "'Stick' May Make a Star of Little-Known Leonard," *USA Today*, February 25, 1983.
35. Leonard, Elmore, letter to Christopher Leonard, September 16, 1982, courtesy of the Christopher Leonard Collection.
36. Leonard, Elmore, letter to Christopher Leonard, November 15, 1982, courtesy of the Christopher Leonard Collection.
37. Leonard, Elmore, letter to Christopher Leonard, January 22, 1983, courtesy of the Christopher Leonard Collection.
38. Marshall, Bill, letter to Elmore Leonard, January 3, 1983, USC.
39. Lyon, Danny, "Pictures from the New World," Aperture, New York, 1981.
40. Leonard, Elmore, "*LaBrava*—notebook," ca. 1982, USC.
41. Blakemore, Erin, "This Tinseltown Tyrant Used Sexual Exploitation to Build a Hollywood Empire," History.com, October 17, 2017.
42. Bar Am, Zohar, letter to Elmore Leonard, August 23, 1976, USC.
43. "Elmore Leonard: An Interview," in Matthew J. Bruccoli and Richard Layman, eds., *The New Black Mask Quarterly* no. 2 (New York: Harvest/HBJ, 1985).
44. Wilson, Robert, "*LaBrava*: A Bravura Work of Suspense," *USA Today*, October 28, 1983.
45. Prescott, Peter S., review of *LaBrava, Newsweek*, November 14, 1983.
46. Fuller, Richard, "Hot Slanguage, Cool Caper," *Houston Post*, December 25, 1983.
47. Schultz, Randy, "Author Who Walks on the Underside of Florida," *West Palm Beach Post*, February 26, 1984.
48. Leonard, Elmore, letter to H. N. Swanson, October 17, 1983, courtesy of the Lilly Library, Indiana University.
49. Leonard, Elmore, letter to Walter Mirisch, October 17, 1983, courtesy of the Lilly Library, Indiana University.
50. "*Glitz*—Notes," in Gregg Sutter, ed., *Elmore Leonard: Four Novels of the 1980s* (New York: Library of America, 2014).

51. "*Glitz*—Notes."
52. "Elmore Leonard: An Interview."
53. "*Glitz*—Notes."
54. Leonard, Elmore, letter to H. N. Swanson, October 5, 1984, courtesy of the Lilly Library, Indiana University.
55. Leonard, Elmore, letter to H. N. Swanson, March 16, 1984, courtesy of the Lilly Library, Indiana University.
56. Articles Leonard used most prominently included: H. G. Bissinger, "A Thief and a Gambler," *Detroit Free Press*, January 15, 1984; Daniel Heneghan, "Former Casino Manager Fined for Accepting Use of Car," *The Press* (Atlantic City), August 18, 1983; Mike Marlowe, "Out of Control!: Leaderless and Trigger-Happy, the Philadelphia Mob Is on a Killing Spree That Has Left the Whole Underworld Shaking," *Philadelphia*, November 1982; David J. Spate, "Cheats Catch Casinos' 'Eye,'" *The Press* (Atlantic City), April 4, 1982; and Stephen Warren, "Former Tropicana Cashier Held on Larceny Indictment," *The Press* (Atlantic City), April 1, 1982.
57. Pileggi, Nicholas, "Money Laundering: How Crooks Recycle $80 Billion a Year in Dirty Money," *New York*, October 31, 1983.
58. Macnow, Glen, "Portrait of a Rapist," *Detroit Free Press*, August 14, 1983.
59. Schram, Bradley, letter to Elmore Leonard, March 16, 1984, USC.
60. Lukas, J. Anthony, "Elmore Leonard: Under the Boardwalk," *GQ*, December 1984.
61. "*Glitz*—Notes."
62. Leonard, Elmore, "*Glitz*—Notebook No. 2," ca. 1984, USC.
63. "Elmore Leonard: An Interview."
64. "Short Subjects," *Publishers Weekly*, August 17, 1984.
65. Carter, Michael, "*Glitz*—Arbor House Letter," November 27, 1984.
66. King, Stephen, "What Went Down When Magyk Went Up," *New York Times*, February 10, 1985.

15. Hot, Part One, 1985–1989

1. Yagoda, Ben, "Elmore Leonard's Rogue's Gallery," *New York Times*, December 30, 1984.
2. Reed, J. D., "A Dickens from Detroit," *Time*, May 28, 1984.
3. Yagoda, "Elmore Leonard's Rogue's Gallery."
4. Mirisch, Walter, *I Thought We Were Making Movies, Not History* (Madison, WI: University of Wisconsin Press, 2008).
5. Howe, Sean, "How Martin Scorsese's Elmore Leonard Movie *LaBrava* Is One That Got Away," *Vulture*, August 23, 2013.
6. Leonard, Elmore, "*LaBrava*—screenplay," synopsis, typescript, July 28, 1983; first revision, typescript with notes, November 22, 1983; second revision, typescript, August 1984; screenplay summary and scene outline, edited typescript, no date; revised screenplay outline, edited typescript, May 18, 1985; screenplay outline, fourth draft, July 10, 1985; screenplay outline, fifth draft, edited typescript, July 30, 1985; final revision, typescript, November 13, 1986, USC.
7. Mirisch, *I Thought We Were Making Movies, Not History*.

8. Friendly, David. "Dustin Hoffman Signs Rich Deal with Cannon," *Los Angeles Times*, January 29, 1986.
9. "Chronology," in Gregg Sutter, ed., *Elmore Leonard: Four Novels of the 1970s* (New York: Library of America, 2014).
10. Mirisch, *I Thought We Were Making Movies, Not History*.
11. Harmetz, Aljean, "*Cotton Club* Investor Sues Partners in Film," *New York Times*, June 10, 1984.
12. Mirisch, *I Thought We Were Making Movies, Not History*.
13. Dawson, Nick, *Being Hal Ashby: Life of a Hollywood Rebel* (Lexington, KY: University of Kentucky Press, 2011).
14. Dawson, *Being Hal Ashby*.
15. Gold, Richard, "Hoffman Reps Reject Cannon Optimism," *Variety*, April 1, 1985.
16. Dawson, *Being Hal Ashby*.
17. "Chronology."
18. Lupica, Mike, "St. Elmore's Fire," *Esquire*, April 1987.
19. "Arbor Pays $1.1 Mil for 'Bandits' Book," *Hollywood Reporter*, September 20, 1985.
20. Leonard's research into the Sandinista-Contra conflict was extensive. Primary articles used as source material included, but were not limited to: Joel Brinkley, "C.I.A. Primer Tells Nicaraguan Rebels How to Kill," *New York Times*, October 17, 1984; Richard Cohen, "If the Facts Fail You, Just Tell a 'Nicaragua,'" *Washington Post*, undated, ca. 1984; Francisco Goldman, "The Children's Hour: Sandinista Kids Fight Contras and Boredom," *Harper's*, October 1984; "Why Are We in Central America?" *Harper's*, June 1984; "Should the C.I.A. Fight Secret Wars?" *Harper's*, September 1984; Michael Kramer, "What to Do About Nicaragua," *New York*, undated, ca. 1984; "Nicaragua's Rebel Jesuits," *Newsweek*, September 3, 1984; "The Secret Warriors: The C.I.A. Is Back in Business," *Newsweek*, October 10, 1983; "El Salvador: The Death Squads: Can They Be Stopped?" *Newsweek*, January 1984; Don Oderdorfer, "Nicaragua Asks World Court to Halt U.S.-Backing Mining," *Washington Post*, April 10, 1984.
21. Ruhlman, Michael, "Letting the Characters Do It," *New York Times*, January 4, 1987.
22. Broun, Heywood Hale, "Elmore Leonard's Contra Caper," *Washington Post*, January 4, 1987.
23. Schwab, Nikki, "Ronald Reagan Responsible for Tom Clancy's Rise," *U.S. News and World Report*, October 2, 2013.
24. Tyre, Peg, "*Moonlight*er Buying *Bandits* Rights?" *Intelligencer*, undated, ca. 1987.
25. Conroy, Mary, "Author Knows How, When to Play It Cool," *Capital Times*, August 3, 1990.
26. Lupica, "St. Elmore's Fire."
27. Robertson, William, "Two Different Approaches to Crime Fiction," *Miami Herald*, September 6, 1987.
28. Rule, Philip C., review of *Touch*, *Los Angeles Times*, August 30, 1987.
29. Greeley, Andrew, "Elmore Leonard's Miracle in Detroit," *Washington Post Book World*, August 23, 1987.
30. Leonard, Elmore, letter to H.N. Swanson, September 3, 1986. Courtesy of the Lilly Library, Indiana University.

31. Mills, Bart, "Novel 'Glitz' May Become a TV Movie," *Los Angeles Times*, April 4, 1986.
32. Leonard and Ross, "Elmore Leonard," *Contemporary Authors.*
33. Leonard, Elmore, "Duell McCall—Original first draft, corrected typescript," August 8, 1985, USC.
34. Hill, Michael E., "Leonard Saddled Up for TV Western," *Washington Post*, April 7, 1987.
35. "*The Rosary Murders*—Update," *Daily Variety*, June 6, 1986.
36. Swanson, H. N., letter to Elmore Leonard, January 5, 1981, courtesy of the Margaret Herrick Library.
37. Leonard, Elmore, letter to Christopher Leonard, May 21, 1982, courtesy of the Christopher Leonard Collection.
38. Grigg, Mona, "Is It Fun Being Dutch Leonard, or What?" *O&E Magazine*, September 10, 1987.
39. Greiner, Virginia, "How Elmore Leonard Gets in 'Touch,'" *Washington Times*, October 22, 1987.
40. "Chronology."
41. Leonard, Elmore, "*Freaky Deaky*—Notebook," undated, ca. 1987, USC.
42. Leonard, "*Freaky Deaky*—Notebook."
43. The research gathered by Gregg Sutter for Leonard's *Freaky Deaky* was among the most extensive he'd conducted yet; the far-reaching background and historical context needed to properly dramatize the residue of the 1960s hippies counterculture required hundreds of articles. They included, but were not limited to: John M. Carlisle, "U.S. Indicts 13 in Weatherman Plot," unknown, July 1970; Peter Collier and David Horowitz, "Doing It: The Inside Story of the Rise and Fall of the Weather Underground," *Rolling Stone*, September 30, 1982; "Panthers Acquitted of Assault," *Detroit Free Press*, June 11, 1970; "Detroiters Get Jail in Draft Raid," *Detroit Free Press*, June 11, 1970; "On Your Knees, Men: The Gals Attack," *Detroit Free Press*, August 11, 1970; Ann Getz and Robert M. Pavich, "Bullets End a Father's Dilemma," *Detroit News*, May 9, 1970; Mike Gormley, "New Political Rock Group: The Up Begins Where the MC-5 Left Off," *Detroit Free Press*, July 3, 1970; Jennifer Holmes, "Women's Prison," *Detroit Free Press*, July 3, 1983; J. F. terHorst, "Nixon Meets with Students on Their Own Grounds," *Sunday News—Detroit*, May 10, 1970; Tom Ricke, "Generation Gap Ends in Death," *Detroit Free Press*, May 9, 1970; Carol Teegardin, "John Sinclair: A Long, Strange Trip It's Been," *Detroit Free Press*, undated, ca. early 1970s; "10 Convicted in Invasion of Draft Office," United Press International, June 6, 1970; and "Rock-Rest Ban Upheld by Court," United Press International, August 1, 1970.
44. Freligh, Becky, "Writer Shoots from the Hip," *Plain Dealer*, May 15, 1988.
45. Lehmann-Haupt, Christopher, "Elmore Leonard's New Thriller, *Freaky Deaky*," *New York Times*, May 2, 1988.
46. Lutz, Fred, "A Witty Shakedown in Motown," *Toledo Blade*, May 8, 1988.
47. Prescott, Peter S., "The Cop Story as Comedy," *Newsweek*, May 16, 1988.
48. DeVries, Hilary, "Tales of Low-Lifes Bring Fame and Fortune," *Christian Science Monitor*, May 18, 1988.
49. Herbert, Hugh, "Detroit Spinner," *The Guardian*, October 1, 1988.
50. DeVries, "Tales of Low-Lifes Bring Fame and Fortune."

51. Vigoda, Arlene, "The Alcoholics' Side," *USA Today*, April 21, 1988.
52. Lupica, "St. Elmore's Fire."

16. No More Mr. Nice, 1989–1992

1. Leonard and Ross, "Elmore Leonard," *Contemporary Authors.*
2. Freligh, Becky, "Writer Shoots from the Hip," *Plain Dealer*, May 15, 1988.
3. Leonard, Elmore, "*Killshot*—Notebook," undated, ca. 1988, USC.
4. Leonard, "*Killshot*—Notebook."
5. Leonard, Elmore, "*Killshot*—Chapter breakdown," undated, ca. 1988, USC.
6. Leonard, "*Killshot*—Notebook."
7. Leonard, "*Killshot*—Notebook."
8. Leonard, Elmore, "*Killshot*—Early draft section," edited typescript, undated, ca. 1988, USC.
9. Leonard, Elmore, *Killshot* (New York: Arbor House, 1989).
10. Lipez, Richard, "Bang, Bang, Blackbird," *Washington Post*, March 26, 1989.
11. Meyer, George, "Elmore Leonard—His Aim Is Still True," *Tampa Tribune*, March 26, 1989.
12. Craig, Paul, "A Woman Saves the Macho Crowd's Day," *Sacramento Bee*, April 30, 1989.
13. Gonzalez, Kevin, "'Dutch' Leonard Has Ear for Writing," *New Jersey Courier-Post*, April 26, 1989.
14. Meyer, Ian, "Leonard Sets His 27th in Seamy Side of Toronto," *Toronto Star*, April 15, 1989.
15. Freligh, "Writer Shoots from the Hip."
16. "Chronology," in Gregg Sutter, ed., *Elmore Leonard: Four Later Novels* (New York: Library of America, 2016).
17. Leonard, Elmore, "*Get Shorty*—notebook," July 9, 1988, USC.
18. Leonard, Elmore, "*Get Shorty*—Notes," in Sutter, ed., *Elmore Leonard: Four Later Novels*.
19. Gross, Michael, "Table Envy," *New York*, November 7, 1988; Cathryn Jakobson, "Buzzwords: Ignore Them at Your Peril," *Premiere*, August 1989.
20. May, Anthony, "'Doing What I Do': An Interview with Elmore Leonard," *Contrappasso Magazine*, 2012.
21. Conroy, Mary, "Author Knows How, When to Play It Cool," *Capital Times*, August 3, 1990.
22. Hawkins, Robert J., "Loan-Shark Attack in Hollywood Hot Tubs," *San Diego Tribune*, August 17, 1990.
23. Krull, John, "A Trick Pulled on Hollywood," *Indianapolis News*, August 18, 1990.
24. Lawson, Terry, "Criminally Funny," *Dayton Daily News*, August 5, 1990.
25. Ephron, Nora, "The Shylock Is the Good Guy," *New York Times*, July 29, 1990.
26. King, Stephen, "This Leonard Cat Belts Out a Winner," *Detroit Free Press*, July 29, 1990.
27. Nolan, Tom, "Hollywood Hustlers," *Wall Street Journal*, August 9, 1990.
28. Warren, Tim, "Telling on the Movies," *Baltimore Sun*, August 21, 1990.
29. "Elmore Leonard: He's Learned the Hollywood Lesson," *Milwaukee Journal*, September 9, 1990.

30. Pristin, Terry, "On-Time Justice Is Judge's Policy," *Los Angeles Times*, December 26, 1986.
31. "Disorder in the Court: More and More Judges Behave Erratically," *MacLean's*, April 24, 1989.
32. Van Howe, Tom, "His Friends Now Call Him 'Judge,'" *Miami Herald*, March 11, 1974.
33. Carnevale, Carol, "Her Topless Jogging Conviction Upheld," *Palm Beach Times*, February 28, 1984.
34. May, "'Doing What I Do.'"
35. Leonard, Elmore, "Day-planner—1990," USC.
36. Hall, James W., "'Maximum Bob' Stirs Up Gators, Guns, and Muck," *Houston Post*, July 14, 1991.

17. Exits and Entrances, 1992–1995

1. Marvel, Mark, "Elmore Leonard Gets Large," *Interview*, June 1991.
2. Leonard, Peter, interview, September 7, 2022.
3. Dudley, Katy, interview, September 7, 2022.
4. Leonard, Christopher, interview, September 7, 2022.
5. Warren, Tim, "Telling on the Movies," *Baltimore Sun*, August 21, 1990.
6. Ginsberg, Allen, "Poem for Elmore Leonard"/correspondence, April 4, 1990, USC. When talking about this poem in later years, Leonard had insinuated that either Ginsberg hadn't completed it, or the copy no longer existed; it was later found by the author on the back of a piece of paper attributed to correspondence with Ginsberg. With sincere gratitude, the author wishes to thank the Estate of Allen Ginsberg for permission to print this poem in its entirety, as well as Peter Hale, Bill Morgan, and Simon Pettet for their incredible efforts to transcribe the text as close as possible to Mr. Ginsberg's original intentions.
7. Leonard, Elmore, "*Rum Punch*—Notebook," ca. 1990–91, USC.
8. "*Rum Punch*—Notes," in Gregg Sutter, ed., *Elmore Leonard: Four Later Novels* (New York: Library of America, 2016).
9. Born, Jim O., interview, March 30, 2023.
10. Leonard, "*Rum Punch*—Notebook."
11. "*Rum Punch*—Notes."
12. Leonard, "*Rum Punch*—Notebook."
13. Koch, John, "Leonard's 'Rum Punch': A Story of Stings," *Boston Globe*, July 30, 1992.
14. Lehmann-Haupt, Christopher, "How to Make a Fast Buck Without Really Dying," *New York Times*, July 23, 1992.
15. Dirda, Michael, "Dreams Die Hard," *Washington Post Book World*, July 19, 1992.
16. Zaleski, Jeff, "Dutch in Detroit," *Publishers Weekly*, January 21, 2002.
17. Wylie, Andrew, interview, September 29, 2023.
18. Leonard, Elmore, "For Swanie, Bless His Heart"—notes and first draft, ca. 1991, USC.
19. "Screenplay from Elmore Leonard Is on the Way," *Detroit Free Press*, August 23, 1992.
20. Leonard, Elmore, "Day planner[s]—1991, 1992," USC.
21. May, Anthony, "In Australia: An Interview with Elmore Leonard," *Contrappasso Magazine*, 2012.

22. Leonard, "Day planner[s]—1991, 1992."
23. Leonard, "Day planner[s]—1991, 1992."
24. Romano, Lois, "Elmore Leonard: The Mystery and the Man," *Washington Post*, September 8, 1992.
25. Carcaterra, Lorenzo, "Talk with Elmore Leonard: The Art of Writing *Pronto*," *People*, October 25, 1993.
26. Terrell, Carroll F., *A Companion to* The Cantos *of Ezra Pound* (Berkeley, CA: University of California Press, 1980).
27. Ackroyd, Peter, *Ezra Pound and His World* (New York: Scribner, 1980).
28. "Chronology," in Gregg Sutter, ed., *Elmore Leonard: Four Later Novels* (New York: Library of America, 2016).
29. Franklin, Ben A., "The Scandal of Death and Injury in the Mines; Nobody Knows What the Cost of a Century of Neglect Has Been," *New York Times*, March 30, 1969; William K. Stevens, "New Coal Dispute Recalls 'Bloody Harlan,'" *New York Times*, August 29, 1974.
30. Leonard, Elmore, *Pronto* (New York: Delacorte Press, 1993).
31. May, "In Australia."
32. Leonard, "Day planner[s]—1991, 1992."
33. Carpenter, Teresa, "On the Lam in Rapallo," *New York Times*, October 17, 1993.
34. Lochte, Dick, "Leonard: A Contemporary Spaghetti Western," *Aspen Times*, December 11–12, 1993.
35. Leonard, Peter, interview, April 25, 2023.
36. Decker, Beverly, interview, September 7, 2022.
37. Penzler, Otto, interview, July 10, 2022.
38. Talbert, Bob, "Work, Grandchildren Help Elmore Leonard Cope," *Detroit Free Press*, March 28, 1993.
39. Leonard, Peter, interview, September 8, 2022.
40. Leonard, Peter, interview, September 7, 2022.
41. "Partners in Crime," *WHO*, February 21, 1994.
42. Leonard, Elmore, "*Riding the Rap*—Notebook," 1993, USC.
43. Leonard, Elmore, "*Riding the Rap*—Research, psychic readings," 1993–1994, USC.
44. "Raylan/Dawn Tarot Card Reading with Maria Cernuto, August 28, 1993," in Leonard, "*Riding the Rap*—Research, psychic readings."
45. May, "In Australia."
46. Leonard, Elmore, "*Riding the Rap*—Notebook," 1993, USC.
47. Coughlin, Ruth, "A Dutch Treat," *Detroit News*, May 6, 1995.
48. Amis, Martin, "Junk Souls," *New York Times*, May 14, 1995.
49. DeVine, Lawrence, "Childhood on Stage and in the Wings Led to Visual Arts," *Detroit Free Press*, March 14, 1995.

18. Hot, Part Two, 1995–1999

1. Sonnenfeld, Barry, interview, January 21, 2021.
2. Bland, Simon, "Danny DeVito and Barry Sonnenfeld: How We Made *Get Shorty*," *The Guardian*, February 22, 2021.
3. Sonnenfeld, Barry, interview, January 21, 2021.

4. Sonnenfeld, Barry, interview, January 21, 2021.
5. May, Anthony, "In Australia: An Interview with Elmore Leonard," *Contrappasso Magazine*, 2012.
6. Bland, Simon, "Danny DeVito and Barry Sonnenfeld: How We Made *Get Shorty*," *The Guardian*, February 22, 2021.
7. Bland, "Danny DeVito and Barry Sonnenfeld: How We Made *Get Shorty*."
8. Sonnenfeld, Barry, interview, January 21, 2021.
9. Bland, "Danny DeVito and Barry Sonnenfeld: How We Made *Get Shorty*."
10. Sonnenfeld, Barry, interview, January 21, 2021.
11. Leonard, Tim, interview, April 7, 2023.
12. Leonard, Alex, interview, April 6, 2023.
13. Leonard, Max, interview, September 7, 2022.
14. "Chronology," in Gregg Sutter, ed., *Elmore Leonard: Four Later Novels* (New York: Library of America, 2016).
15. Leonard, Elmore, "*Out of Sight*—Notebooks," undated, ca. 1995–96, USC.
16. Penzler, Otto, interview, July 10, 2022.
17. Leonard's research for *Out of Sight* was copious. Among others, the primary sources of his plotting and characterizations were: Scott Hiaasen and Meg James, "1 Escapee Killed, 1 Caught," *Palm Beach Post*, January 11, 1995; Gary Kane, "Near-Home Prison Policy Fills GCI with Killers," *Palm Beach Post*, January 22, 1995; E. A. Torriero, "Hunt Narrows to 2 Killers," *Fort Lauderdale Sun-Sentinel*, January 12, 1995; Dennis B. Levine, "The Inside Story of an Inside Trader," *Fortune*, May 21, 1990; Robert Blau, "Rectory Routine Changes After Knock in the Night," *Chicago Tribune*, November 15, 1990; Bill Montgomery, "Home-Invasion Thefts Show Similar, Frightening Pattern," *Atlanta Journal*, June 1, 1995; Cherokee Paul McDonald, "The Robber Who Painted His Face," *Fort Lauderdale Sun-Sentinel*, undated, ca. 1990–95; "Man's Confession Ends Robbery Career: 56 Banks in 8 Years," *New York Times*, July 14, 1994; "South California, the Bank Robbery Capital, Says Holdup Cop," *Miami Herald*, March 4, 1994; Julie Tamaki, "God Told Him to Rob Banks, Man Testifies," *Los Angeles Times*, undated, ca. 1990–95; Ron Russell, "5 Bank of America Branches Robbed in One Hour: 'Just Another Day in L.A.,'" *Los Angeles Times*, July 29, 1992; Donald A. Johnston, MD, "Psychological Observations of Bank Robbery," *American Journal of Psychiatry*, November 1978.
18. Leonard's additional plotting and characterization came from the following research, all available in the USC collection: "*Out of Sight*—Research, Federal Law Enforcement Training Center student text, informants, no date"; "Research, Federal Law Enforcement Training Center student text, surveillance, no date"; "Research, interview notes, multiple persons, no date"; "Research, interview notes, multiple persons, talking about the Cajuns, no date"; "Research, Marshals, articles, February 4, 1993"; "Research, Marshals, interviews, Jim Born, 2 December 1991"; "Research, Marshals, interviews, Deputy Marshal Patti Clarke, October 5, 1995."
19. Bates, Bille Rae, "'Sight' Lines," *Detroit News*, September 19, 1996.
20. Wiegand, David, "Get Foley," *San Francisco Chronicle: Northern California's Complete Literary Guide*, August 11–17, 1996.
21. Lombreglia, Ralph, "Mr. Wrong," *New York Times*, September 8, 1996.

22. Talbert, Bob, "Movie Deals Piling Up for Local Author," *Detroit Free Press*, July 14, 1996.
23. Schrader, Paul, interview, January 30, 2021.
24. Talbert, "Movie Deals Piling Up for Local Author."
25. May, Anthony, "In Australia: An Interview with Elmore Leonard," *Contrappasso Magazine*, 2012.
26. Grobel, Lawrence, "Pulp Fiction," *Playboy*, May 1995.
27. Leonard, Elmore, "Pulp Fictions: Tarantino and Me," *The Guardian*, April 18, 1997.
28. Sonnenfeld, Barry, interview, January 21, 2021.
29. Leonard, Bill, interview, February 15, 2023.
30. Wyss, Trudy, "Crime Fiction's Big Daddy: Elmore Leonard Writes His Favorite Novel," *Borders*, February 2002.
31. Leonard, Peter, "Traveling with Elmore," Peter Leonard Books, 2009, http://www.peterleonardbooks.com/traveling-with-elmore.
32. Belmont, Shannon, interview, March 6, 2023.
33. Ebert, Roger, review of *Out of Sight*, *Chicago Sun Times*, June 19, 1998.
34. Maslin, Janet, "'Out of Sight'—A Thief, a Marshal, an Item," *New York Times*, June 26, 1998.
35. Leonard, Elmore, "*Cuba Libre*—notebook," undated, ca. 1996–97, USC.
36. Lehmann-Haupt, Christopher, "Viva la Genre! Elmore Leonard Visits Old Havana," *New York Times*, January 22, 1998.
37. Long, Tom, "It's Another 'Dutch' Treat," *Detroit News*, January 17, 1998.
38. Leonard, Elmore, letter to Megan Freels Johnston, October 30, 1998, courtesy of the Megan Freels Johnston collection.
39. Leonard, Elmore, "*Be Cool*—notebooks," ca. 1997, USC.
40. Leonard, "*Be Cool*—notebooks."
41. Friedman, Kinky, "The Palmer Method," *New York Times*, February 21, 1999.
42. Leonard, Peter, interview, September 7, 2022.

19. Sundown in Detroit, 2000–2005

1. Weiner, Jon, "Elmore Leonard's Secret: 'Clean Living and a Fast Outfield,'" *Los Angeles Review of Books*, October 11, 2000.
2. Leonard, Elmore, letter to Jackie Farber, December 2, 1998, USC.
3. Leonard, Elmore, letter to Christoper Leonard, undated, ca. 1999, courtesy of the Christopher Leonard Collection.
4. Anderson, John A., letter to Elmore Leonard, January 19, 1999, USC.
5. Leonard, Elmore, letter of recommendation, May 22, 1999, USC.
6. Leonard, Elmore, "*Pagan Babies*—notebook," ca. 1999, USC.
7. Leonard, Elmore, *Pagan Babies* (New York: Delacorte Press, 2000).
8. Lupica, Mike, interview, June 20, 2023.
9. Maslin, Janet, "'New Elmore Leonard?' 'Yeah. You Know. Punks,'" *New York Times*, September 7, 2000.
10. Salij, Marta, "Leonard Brings Readers into New Territory," *Los Angeles Daily News*, September 3, 2000.

11. "A Politerary Convention," *Los Angeles Times Book Review*, August 13, 2000.
12. Kelly, Charles, "The Wrong Marlowe," *Los Angeles Review of Books*, March 10, 2012.
13. Leonard, Elmore, "Easy on the Adverbs, Exclamation Points, and Especially Hooptedoodle," *New York Times*, July 16, 2001.
14. Zaleski, Jeff, "Dutch in Detroit," *Publishers Weekly*, January 21, 2002.
15. "*Tishomingo Blues*—Notes," in Gregg Sutter, ed., *Elmore Leonard: Four Later Novels* (New York: Library of America, 2016).
16. Wyss, Trudy, "Crime Fiction's Big Daddy: Elmore Leonard Writes His Favorite Novel," *Borders*, February 2002.
17. LoCicero, T. V., ed., *Dutch on Dutch: One of the Last In-Depth Interviews with the Incomparable Elmore Leonard* (n.p.: TLC Media, 2014).
18. "*Tishomingo Blues*—Notes."
19. Giltz, Michael, "*Blues* Traveler," *New York Post*, February 3, 2002.
20. Leonard, Elmore, "*Tishomingo Blues*—notebook," ca. 2001.
21. Giltz, "*Blues* Traveler."
22. "*Tishomingo Blues*—Notes."
23. "*Tishomingo Blues*—Notes."
24. Leonard, Alex, interview, April 6, 2023.
25. Donahue, Deirdre, "37 Books Later, Words Still Inspire Leonard," *USA Today*, January 29, 2002.
26. Salij, Marta, "Perfect Form: Diving Tale *Tishomingo Blues* Is Pure Elmore Leonard," *Detroit Free Press*, January 27, 2002.
27. Maslin, Janet, "Leaving Out the Parts Readers Skip," *New York Times*, January 28, 2002.
28. Atwood, Margaret, "Cops and Robbers," *New York Review of Books*, May 23, 2002.
29. "FilmFour Gets Case of 'Blues,'" *Hollywood Reporter*, August 8, 2001.
30. Zaleski, Jeff, "Dutch in Detroit," *Publishers Weekly*, January 21, 2002.
31. "*Tishomingo Blues*—Notes."
32. "Don Cheadle: *Tishomingo Blues* Is Dead," *Comingsoon.net*, July 6, 2007.
33. Atwood, Margaret, letter to Elmore Leonard, March 30, 2000, USC.
34. Leonard, Elmore, letter to Margaret Atwood, undated, ca. 2003, USC.
35. Harrison, Jim, letter to Elmore Leonard, "late October" 2001, USC.
36. Leonard, Christopher, interview, September 7, 2022.
37. Dudley, Katy, interview, September 7, 2022.
38. Challen, *Get Dutch!*
39. John, Elton, letter to Elmore Leonard, February 1, 1999, USC.
40. Fagan, Donald, letter to Elmore Leonard, July 14, 2006, USC.
41. Wylie, Andrew, interview, September 29, 2023.
42. Posternak, Jeff, interview, September 22, 2023.
43. Azeez, Wale, "Elmore Leonard to Publish E-novel," *The Guardian*, January 12, 2001.
44. Curtis, Nick, "On-line with the Dickens of Detroit," *London Evening Standard*, undated, ca. September 2000.
45. Zaleski, "Dutch in Detroit."
46. Mitchell, Sallie, letter to Elmore Leonard, April 23, 2002, USC; Sallie Mitchell, letter to Elmore Leonard, May 21, 2002, USC.
47. Zaleski, "Dutch in Detroit."

48. Adams, Tim, "The High Priest of Low-Life America," *The Guardian*, January 25, 2003.
49. Zaleski, "Dutch in Detroit."
50. Householder, Mike, "Author, 76, Releases 37th Novel, *Tishomingo Blues*," Associated Press, February 15, 2002.
51. Leonard, Kate, interview, September 7, 2023.
52. Garratt, Sheryl, "Elmore Leonard Profile," *Junior*, September 2004.
53. Leonard, Elmore, "*A Coyote's in the House*—Notes," ca. 2002, USC.
54. Leonard, Elmore, letter to Marjorie Braman, November 19, 2003, USC.
55. Leonard, Elmore, *A Coyote's in the House* (New York: HarperCollins Children, 2004).
56. Garratt, "Elmore Leonard Profile."
57. Robshaw, Brandon, review of *A Coyote's in the House*, *The Independent*, August 27, 2004.
58. Householder, Mike, "Elmore Leonard Returns with the 37th Novel, '*Tishomingo Blues*,'" Associated Press, January 29, 2002.
59. Leonard, Elmore, "*Mr. Paradise*—notebook," ca. 2003, USC.
60. Leonard, "*Mr. Paradise*—notebook."
61. Leonard, Elmore, "*Mr. Paradise*—Research," ca. 2003, USC.
62. Goodell, Jeff, "Explanation of the Girlfriend Experience," *New York Times*, April 8, 2001.
63. Leonard, Elmore, and Gregg Sutter, "Invitation—*Mr. Paradise Party*," January 8, 2004, USC.
64. Beattie, Ann, "First, Let's Kill the Lawyer," *New York Times*, January 1, 2004.
65. Wilson, Frank, "Pleasure with 'Paradise': Leonard's Latest Has the Incisiveness of Poetry," *Philadelphia Inquirer*, January 18, 2004.
66. Garratt, "Elmore Leonard Profile."
67. Heard, Christopher, "An Interview with Elmore Leonard," *The Gate*, March 15, 2004.

20. A Life of Crime, 2005–2008

1. Triplett, Gene, "Elmore Leonard Takes a Page from Oklahoma History," *The Oklahoman*, May 13, 2005.
2. Leonard, Elmore, *The Hot Kid* (New York: HarperCollins, 2005).
3. Leonard, Elmore, "*The Hot Kid*—notebook," ca. 2003, USC.
4. Triplett, "Elmore Leonard Takes a Page from Oklahoma History."
5. Leonard, "*The Hot Kid*—notebook."
6. Leonard, "*The Hot Kid*—notebook."
7. Houston, Noel, "Kimes On City 'Goodwill' Tour Seeks Parole, Meets Rebuff from Bankers," *Oklahoma News*, October 30, 1934; "*True Detective* Mysteries: The Line-Up: Watch for These Fugitives," *True Detective*, December 1934.
8. "Ex-deputy U.S. Marshal Killed in Restaurant," *Daily Ardmoreite, Morning Edition*, January 31, 1919.
9. Leonard, "*The Hot Kid*—notebook."
10. Leonard, "*The Hot Kid*—notebook."

11. Mid-continent Oil and Gas Association of Oklahoma, "Historical Tour of Oklahoma's Oil and Gas Industry," ca. 2003.
12. Leonard, "*The Hot Kid*—notebook."
13. Leonard, "*The Hot Kid*—notebook."
14. Leonard, Elmore, "Day planner," 2004, USC.
15. Anderson, Patrick, "The Marshal and the Millionaire's Son," *Washington Post Book World*, May 15, 2005.
16. Walker, Danna Sue, "Tulsans Celebrated New Leonard Novel with Author," *Tulsa World*, May 26, 2005.
17. Leonard, Christopher, interview, September 8, 2022.
18. Leonard, Peter, interview, September 7, 2022.
19. Roberts, Fletcher, "Novels Are Nice, But Oh, to Be a Rock Star," *New York Times*, March 14, 1999.
20. Adams, Tim, "High Priest of Low-Life America," *The Observer*, January 26, 2003.
21. Fleming, Mike, "F. Gary Gray Q&A: The Hard Life Lessons That Led to 'Straight Outta Compton,'" *Deadline*, August 14, 2015.
22. Posternak, Jeff, interview, September 22, 2023.
23. Leonard, Elmore, letter to Ernest Palmer, March 12, 2004, USC.
24. Wootton, Andrew, "Elmore Leonard: 'I'm Glad I'm Not a Screenwriter. It Would Be So Frustrating,'" British Film Institute [BFI], 2006.
25. Wootton, "Elmore Leonard: 'I'm Glad I'm Not a Screenwriter. It Would Be So Frustrating.'"
26. Triplett, "Elmore Leonard Takes a Page from Oklahoma History."
27. Watts, James D., Jr., "Pulp Diction," *Tulsa World*, May 8, 2005.
28. Rebchook, John, "*The Hot Kid*: Leonard Calls Hemingway His Prime Example," *Rocky Mountain News*, undated, ca. May 2005.
29. "Holocaust Timeline," The History Place, https://www.historyplace.com/worldwar2/holocaust/.
30. Leonard, Elmore, "*Comfort to the Enemy*—Research," undated, ca. 2005–06, USC. Leonard's research for *Comfort to the Enemy* soon bled into what would become its sequel, *Up in Honey's Room*. Articles that inspired the plots and characterizations included, but were not limited to: Jonathan Alter, "Just a Matter of Inches," *USA Weekend*, April 28–30, 2006; "German American Bund," *Holocaust Encyclopedia*, https://holocaustencyclopedia.com; Daniel Engber, "Where Do Mob Nicknames Come From?", *Wired*, undated, ca. 2005; Michael Pollan, "Power Steer," *New York Times*, March 31, 2002; Bob Nelson and Nola Smith, "Study Guide for Bertolt Brecht's *The Caucasian Chalk Circle*," The BYU Pardoe Theatre, February–March 2000; Wayne R. Dynes, ed., *The Encyclopedia of Homosexuality* (New York: Garland Press, 1990); "The Munich Trial," *Time*, March 3, 1924; "Plate Glass Riots," *Time*, October 27, 1930; "Nazi Probe," *Time*, June 18, 1934; "Protocols of Zion," *Time*, November 12, 1934; "Catholic Fighters," *Time*, June 19, 1939; "Eleven Minutes," *Time*, November 20, 1939; "The New Ludecke," *Time*, January 1, 1940; "Hypnotized Men," *Time*, January 29, 1940; "Beautiful but Subversive," *Time*, December 16, 1940; "Detroit Housecleaning," *Time*, May 6, 1940; "Something Burning," *Time*, January 20, 1941; "Secret Agent," *Time*, June 23, 1941; "The Onrush," *Time*, June 30, 1941; "Battle of Detroit," *Time*, March 23, 1942; "Milquetoast Gets Muscles," *Time*,

April 13, 1942; "Crackdown on Coughlin," *Time*, April 27, 1942; "7 Generals v. 8 Saboteurs," *Time*, July 20, 1942; "Sordid Story," *Time*, November 9, 1942; "Story Book Reading," *Time*, September 6, 1943; "The Curtain Rises," *Time*, May 1, 1944; and U.S. Department of Justice and Federal Bureau of Investigation, "German Espionage and Sabotage Against the U.S. in World War II: George Dasch and the Nazi Saboteurs" (FBI handout), March 1984.

31. "Chronology," in Gregg Sutter, ed., *Elmore Leonard: Four Novels of the 1970s* (New York: Library of America, 2014).
32. Wootton, "Elmore Leonard: 'I'm Glad I'm Not a Screenwriter. It Would Be So Frustrating.'"
33. Leonard, Elmore, letter to Gerry Marzorati, September 26, 2005, USC.
34. Leonard, Elmore, "Day planner, 2005," USC.
35. Dobbin, Muriel, "Comfort to the Enemy," review of *Comfort to the Enemy, and Other Carl Webster Stories*, by Elmore Leonard, *Washington Times*, November 12, 2010.
36. Leonard, Elmore, "Day planner, 2006," USC.
37. Leonard, Elmore, "*Up in Honey's Room*—notebook," 2006, USC.
38. Leonard, Alex, email interview, April 2, 2023.
39. Leonard, Elmore, "Day planner, 2006," USC.
40. Smiley, Jane, "Just Say Noir?" *Los Angeles Times*, May 6, 2007.
41. Memmott, Carol, "Mysteries Roundup: Leonard Leads the Hard-Boiled Pack," *USA Today*, May 17, 2007.
42. DeSilva, Bruce, "Elmore Leonard Creates New, Great Woman," Associated Press, April 30, 2007.
43. Penzler, Otto, "One Hell of a Novel," *New York Sun*, May 16, 2007.
44. Leonard, Alex, email interview, April 2, 2023.
45. Leonard, Alex, interview, April 6, 2023.
46. Rubin, Neal, "Leonard Still Gets His Kicks Writing Novels," *Detroit News*, April 17, 2007.
47. Leonard, Elmore, "*Road Dogs*—notebook," ca. 2007–08, USC.
48. Forrest, Rachel, "Smooth Like Honey," Seacoastonline, May 6, 2007, https://www.seacoastonline.com/story/news/local/portsmouth-herald/2007/05/06/smooth-like-honey/52906986007/.
49. "Interview—Elmore Leonard," *Talk of the Nation*, June 11, 2009.
50. Leonard, Elmore, "*Road Dogs*—Early revised draft, edited typescript," undated, ca. 2007, USC.
51. Ramsland, Katherine, "Female Offenders: Bad Girls," Crime Library, undated, https://mail.crimelibrary.org/criminal_mind/psychology/female_offenders/1.html.
52. Leonard, Elmore, "*Road Dogs*—Research," ca. 2007–08, USC. Articles supplied by Gregg Sutter for Leonard's novel included but were not limited to: Pamela Chilton and Dr. Hugh Harmon, PhD, "Seven Simple Steps for Discovering Your Past Lives," Odyssey of the Soul, https://odysseyofthesoul.org/press/pastlives.htm; *Distinctive Homes: Malibu*, vol. 8, no. 6; Michelle Hamer, "Bad Girls," *The Herald Sun—Australia*, March 22, 2008; *Homes & Land: Malibu to Beverly Hills*, June 1998; Kyra Kyles, "Is It in the Cards? Facing More and More Skeptics, Psychics Turn to Corporate Gigs for Money," *Chicago Tribune*, September 18, 2006; Lacy, Marc, "U.S. Fugitives Worry About a Cuba Without Castro," *The New York Times*, May 12, 2007;

and Musella, David Park, "'Psychic' Con Artist Caught in Police Sting," *The Skeptical Inquirer*, May 1, 2005.

53. Leonard, "*Road Dogs*—notebook."
54. Leonard, "*Road Dogs*—Research."
55. King, Stephen, "Cold, Blue Steel Smile," *New York Times*, May 17, 2009.
56. Review of *Road Dogs*, *Esquire*, July 2009.
57. Leonard, Peter, interview, May 26, 2023.
58. Slotter, Mike, "Peter Leonard in the *Spotlight*," *Shots: Crime & Thriller Ezine*, March 2009.
59. Dudley, Joe, interview, March 14, 2023.
60. Dudley, Nick, interview, March 27, 2023.
61. Leonard, Peter, "Traveling with Elmore," Peter Leonard Books, 2009, http://www.peterleonardbooks.com/traveling-with-elmore.
62. Leonard, Peter, "Elmore Leonard Remembered by Peter Leonard," *The Guardian*, December 13, 2013.
63. Leonard, Peter, "Interview by Elmore Leonard," Peter Leonard Books, 2009, http://www.peterleonardbooks.com/elmore-interview.

21. Justified, 2008–2013

1. "Chronology," in Gregg Sutter, ed., *Elmore Leonard: Four Novels of the 1970s* (New York: Library of America, 2014).
2. Posternak, Jeff, interview, September 22, 2023.
3. "Elmore Leonard and Graham Yost—Interview," *Act Four Screenplays*, August 20, 2013.
4. Amis, Martin, "Junk Souls," *New York Times*, May 14, 1995.
5. "FX Calls '*Lawman*,'" FX, press release, July 28, 2009.
6. Owen, Rob, "'Justified' Another Worthy FX Offering," *Pittsburgh Post-Gazette*, March 15, 2010.
7. Rhoshalle, Janice, "Leonard's Law: An Interview with Elmore Leonard," *Emmy*, August 20, 2013 (originally published 2010).
8. Lupica, Mike, interview, June 20, 2023.
9. "Chronology."
10. Rhoshalle, "Leonard's Law: An Interview with Elmore Leonard."
11. Adams, Noah, "Elmore Leonard, at Home in Detroit," *All Things Considered*, NPR, March 16, 2010.
12. Leonard, Elmore, "*Djibouti*—Notes," ca. 2009, USC.
13. Leonard, Elmore, "*Djibouti*—Research," ca. 2008–9, USC. Research materials and articles provided to Leonard by Gregg Sutter included but were not limited to: Milton Allimadi, "Somalia's Pirates: The Laws of Supply and Demand," *Media Watch*, November 25, 2008; "Somali Islamists 'Hunt Pirates,'" *BBC News*, November 22, 2008; Steve Bloomfield, "British Company Claims Ownership of Kenya's Colourful Nation," *The Independent*, March 6, 2007; "Ship of Dreams," *Centralian Advocate (Australia)*, July 18, 2008; Andrew England, "U.S. Military Grows in Djibouti," Associated Press, September 30, 2002; Chris Hedges, "Djibouti Journal; By Ancient,

Languorous Boat to a Frightening City," *New York Times*, June 3, 1994; "Piracy Boom Spurs Fear, Two More Slips Hijacked," *Hobart Mercury (Australia)*, November 20, 2008; Martin Kane, "The One-Shot Killer," uncited, October 8, 1956; Geoffrey Macnab, "'A Bible Salesman or the Rolling Stones. They're All Just People,'" *The Guardian*, August 19, 2005; Eamon Martin, ed., "United States Declares Occupation of Iraq," ACLU, Associated Press, *WIRED News*, undated; Stephanie McCrummen, "Somalia's Godfathers: Ransom-Rich Pirates," *Washington Post*, April 20, 2009; Kitty McKinsey, "Mass Rape in Bosnia: 20,000 Women, Mostly Muslims, Have Been Abused by Serb Soldiers," *Southam News*, January 23, 1993; Randall Mikkelsen, "Somali Piracy May Get Worse—U.S. Experts," Reuters, November 24, 2008; Krittivas Mukherjee, "India Says Trawler May Have Delivered Attackers," Reuters, November 28, 2008; "Don't Miss; Tuesday, July 22," *National Post/Financial Post (Toronto Edition)*, July 19, 2008; Al Pessin, "Admiral Skeptical as U.S. Seeks to Pursue Pirates onto Land," *Voice of America News*, December 13, 2008; Steve Russell, "Africa's Aging Harlot Keeps Red Light Glowing in a Desert Wasteland," *Toronto Star*, August 5, 2000; Mary Ellen Schultz, "Excuse Me, But Did You Say, 'Djibouti' . . . or 'Dji-beauty?'" *Travel World News*, February 2001; Kang Siew Li, "Efforts to Combat Piracy in Malacca Strait Pay Off," *Business Times (Malaysia)*, July 14, 2008; Maj. W. Thomas Smith Jr., "High-Seas Pirates Increasingly Working with Jihadis," *Middle East Times*, November 27, 2008; Bret Stephens, "Why Don't We Hang Pirates Anymore?" *Wall Street Journal*, November 26, 2008; Mark Stratton, "The Heat Is On: Djibouti, On the Horn of Africa, Is Truly a Holiday Destination for Adventurers; Mark Stratton Finds Its Lunar Landscape and Sensuous Waters Strangely Seductive," *The Independent*, November 3, 2002; and Robert Tait, "Iran Arrests American Journalist 'Over Wine Purchase,'" *The Guardian*, March 2, 2009.

14. Leonard, "*Djibouti*—Notes."
15. Lupica, Mike, interview, June 20, 2023.
16. Leonard, Elmore, "Day planners—2009, 2010," USC.
17. Leonard, Elmore, letter to Charles E. Marske, August 13, 2009, USC.
18. Leonard, Alex, email interview, April 2, 2023.
19. Kirby, A. J., review of *Djibouti*, *New York Journal of Books*, October 11, 2010.
20. Cheuse, Alan, review of *Djibouti*, *San Francisco Chronicle*, October 17, 2010.
21. Kamp, David, "Pirate Latitudes," *New York Times*, October 22, 2010.
22. Leonard, Elmore, letter to Rob Marshall, January 16, 2010, USC.
23. Leonard, Elmore, "*Djibouti*—notes," ca. 2008–09, USC.
24. Leonard, Alex, interview, April 6, 2023.
25. Leonard, Peter, interview, April 25, 2023.
26. Leonard, Tim, interview, April 7, 2023.
27. Leonard, Alex, interview, April 6, 2023.
28. Leonard, Tim, interview, April 7, 2023.
29. Leonard, Kate, interview, September 7, 2023.
30. Leonard, Hillary, interview, March 21, 2023.
31. Leonard, Elmore, letter to Drue Heinz, July 10, 2012, USC.
32. Penzler, Otto, interview, July 10, 2022.
33. Leonard, Peter, interview, May 26, 2023.

34. Segura, Jonathan, "The Hit Man," *Publishers Weekly*, November 15, 2010.
35. Estep, Bill, "6 of 16 in Drug Bust Arrested Last Time Most Are Involved with OxyContin, As in February Roundup," *Lexington Herald-Leader*, September 26, 2001.
36. Leonard, Elmore, "*Raylan*—Research," ca. 2009–10, USC. Research materials and articles provided to Leonard by Gregg Sutter included but were not limited to: Sue Armstrong, "He Knows Where the Bodies Are Buried; Got a Question About Corpses? Prof. Bill Bass Is Your Man, Says Sue Armstrong," *Daily Telegraph*, October 28, 2008; "Pot Growers Retaliate Against Stepped-Up Enforcement," Associated Press, June 16, 1986; Jim Gilchrist, "The New Body Snatchers," *The Scotsman*, February 5, 2008; Amy Goldstein, "5 Killed in Kentucky Mine Explosion; One Miner Survives; Accident Brings 2006 Coal-Mining Deaths to 31," *Washington Post*, May 21, 2006; "Modern-Day Body Snatcher Pleads Guilty: Former Dentist Michael Mastromarino Illegally Sold Parts from More Than 1,000 Corpses to Transplant Companies," *New Scientist*, March 29, 2009; Valerie Honeycutt Spears, "Marijuana Operation Kept Under Wraps for a Decade; Drug Ring Discovery," *Lexington Herald-Leader*, November 20, 2005; and William Sherman, "Chief Ghoul Gets 54 Years; Harvested 1,600 Bodies for Parts," *Daily News*, March 19, 2008.
37. Steinhauer, Olen, "Back on the Case," *New York Times*, February 2, 2012.
38. Rubin, Judd, interviews, May 10 and May 16, 2023.
39. Rhoshalle, "Leonard's Law: An Interview with Elmore Leonard."
40. Rubin, Judd, interviews, May 10 and May 16, 2023.
41. Leonard, Hillary, interview, March 21, 2023.
42. Alter, Alexandra, "Why He Writes, at 86: 'I Might as Well,'" *Wall Street Journal*, January 13, 2012.
43. Leonard, Elmore, "*Blue Dreams*—Research," ca. 2012, USC. Research materials and articles provided to Leonard by Gregg Sutter included but were not limited to: "Suspect Thought to Be Bank Robber," *Ann Arbor News (Michigan)*, January 24, 2006; Maira Ansari, "Metro Drug Ring Tied to Mexican Cartel," uncited, November 21, 2012; David Ashenfelter, "Immigration Official Indicted; Charges Tie Bribes to Sex Crimes, Murder," *Detroit Free Press*, October 3, 2007; Susy Buchanan, "Three Charged in Beating of American-Indian in Arizona," uncited and undated; "ICE Officer Arrested for Pot Smuggling," *CBS News*, October 19, 2011; "Bank Robber Jokes in Court," *Cincinnati Inquirer*, February 2, 2008; "The White Robber Who Carried Out Six Raids Disguised as a Black Man (and Very Nearly Got Away With It)," *Daily Mail Reporter*, December 1, 2010; Chris Garcia, "Director Takes Culture of Bull Riding for a Ride," *Austin American-Statesman (Texas)*, March 2, 2010; Miriam Garcia, "Inmate Conditions at Immigration Centers in Pinal County, AZ, Are 'Inhumane,' ACLU Says," KSAZ, June 24, 2011; Ed Godfrey, "PBR: 6:50 Tonight, 2PM Sunday at Oklahoma City Arena; Breeding Bad Bulls," *The Oklahoman*, February 12, 2011; David Holthouse, "Revenge of the Verdes: Natives Finally Glean a Few Reparations for a Legacy of Genocide," *Phoenix New Times*, August 5, 1999; Dahr Jamail, "Razing Arizona: War on the Migrant Worker," *Pacific Free Press*, May 16, 2010; Victoria Kim and Andrew Blankstein, "Victim in ICE Shooting Was a High-Ranking Manager," *L.A. Now*, *Los Angeles Times*, February 17, 2012; Melissa MacBride, "SoCal Gamblers Targeted by Robbers," KABC, December 8, 2008; Richard Marosi, "Unraveling Mexico's Sinaloa Drug Cartel," *Los Angeles Times*, July 24, 2011; Darsha Philips,

Subha Ravindhran, and Eileen Frere, "ICE Shooting Erupted Amid Job Counseling Talk," KABC, undated; Gregory Pratt, "Immigrants Who Fight Deportation Are Packed into Federal Gulags for Months or Years Before Their Cases Are Heard," *Phoenix New Times*, June 23, 2011; Jacqueline Stevens, "America's Secret ICE Castles: Immigration Agents Are Holding U.S. Residents in Unlisted and Unmarked Subfield Offices," *The Nation*, December 16, 2009; and Jeff Wolf, "Animals are Athletes, Too," *Las Vegas Review-Journal*, December 5, 2007.

44. Leonard, Elmore, "*Blue Dreams*—notebook," ca. 2011–13, USC.
45. Leonard, Peter, interview, September 7, 2023.
46. Leonard, Elmore, "*Blue Dreams*—Draft, incomplete, edited typescript," undated, ca. 2011–13, USC; Elmore Leonard, "*Blue Dreams*—Partial typescript," undated, ca. 2011–13, USC.
47. Lupica, Mike, interview, June 20, 2023.
48. "The Proust Questionnaire—Elmore Leonard," *Vanity Fair*, November 9, 2012.
49. Leonard, Peter, interview, May 26, 2023.
50. McNally, Thomas F., letter to Elmore Leonard, January 17, 2013, USC.
51. Sudduth, Elizabeth, interview, September 25, 2023.
52. Leonard, Peter, interview, May 26, 2023.
53. Alpert, Dan, letter to Elmore Leonard, May 22, 2013, USC.
54. "Chronology."
55. Leonard, Bill, interview, February 15, 2023.
56. Dudley, Joe, interview, March 14, 2023.
57. Dudley, Nick, interview, March 27, 2023.
58. Dudley, Luke, interview, March 25, 2023.
59. Leonard, Bill, interview, February 15, 2023.
60. Leonard, Hillary, interview, March 21, 2023.

22. "The Great American Writer"

1. Leonard, Bill, interview, February 15, 2023.
2. Schaefer, Jim, "Hundreds Attend Elmore Leonard Funeral in Michigan," *USA Today*, August 24, 2013.
3. Leonard family, "Elmore Leonard, Funeral Mass program," August 24, 2013, USC.
4. Schaefer, "Hundreds Attend Elmore Leonard Funeral in Michigan."
5. Leonard, Peter, "Elmore Leonard Remembered by Peter Leonard," *The Guardian*, December 13, 2013.
6. Leonard, Ben, interview, March 5, 2023.
7. Leonard, Abigail, interview, March 18, 2023.
8. Leonard, Tim, interview, April 7, 2023.
9. Dudley, Joe, interview, March 14, 2023.
10. Dudley, Luke, interview, March 25, 2023.
11. Leonard, Abigail, interview, March 18, 2023.
12. Bayard, Louis, "Elmore Leonard Dies: 'Get Shorty' Author Was 87," *Washington Post*, August 20, 2013.
13. Acocella, Joan, "Postscript: Elmore Leonard (1925–2013)," *The New Yorker*, August 21, 2013.

14. Krug, Kurt Anthony, "Peter Leonard's Latest Book Returns to Father Elmore's Raylan Givens," *The Voice*, March 11, 2019.
15. Leonard, Peter, foreword to Elmore Leonard, *Charlie Martz and Other Stories: The Unpublished Stories* (New York: William Morrow, 2015).
16. Wylie, Andrew, interview, September 29, 2023.
17. Posternak, Jeff, interview, September 22, 2023.
18. Lupica, Mike, interview, June 20, 2023.

INDEX